A SHADOW ON THE WING

History, destiny, conspiracy...

In 1927, Charles Lindbergh was the first lone pilot to cross the Atlantic. Soon after he landed, however, the flight log was stolen from the cockpit of the Spirit of St Louis. It was never recovered. That much is fact...

Hella Köll first meets Lindbergh in 1923, and falls in love with him. She is determined to acquire the flight log as the ultimate souvenir of her hero, so when it becomes available on the Black Market she makes her bid, only to find she is not the only person willing to go to great, even murderous, lengths to obtain it...

A SHADOW ON THE WING

A SHADOW ON THE WING

by

Kerry Jamieson

Magna Large Print Books
Long Preston, North Yorkshire,
BD23 4ND, England.

British Library Cataloguing in Publication Data.

Jamieson, Kerry
    A shadow on the wing.

    A catalogue record of this book is
    available from the British Library

    ISBN 0-7505-2626-2
    ISBN 978-0-7505-2626-5

First published in Great Britain in 2005 by Hodder & Stoughton
A division of Hodder Headline

Copyright © 2005 by Kerry Jamieson

Cover illustration by arrangement with Hodder & Stoughton Ltd.

The right of Kerry Jamieson to be identified as the author of this work has been asserted by her in accordance with the Copyright, Designs and Patents Act, 1988

Published in Large Print 2006 by arrangement with
Hodder & Stoughton Ltd.

Magna Large Print is an imprint of Library Magna Books Ltd.

Printed and bound in Great Britain by
T.J. (International) Ltd., Cornwall, PL28 8RW

'[The next morning], while touring the hangar where the *Spirit of St Louis* had been parked, Lindbergh was shocked to see that the crowd had ripped off pieces of the actual plane as souvenirs; a lubrication fitting and the clipboard with his log of the flight were gone...'

A. Scott Berg
Lindbergh

Dedication

For Hamish Scott –

My husband, my friend, my partner – all wrapped up in the world's biggest smile! Thank you for finding me. Thank you for waiting for me.

1

Minnesota, 1923

Ari Köll was looking for buttons again. Sent out by his mother from the farmhouse as soon as he had arrived home from lessons. She had been washing dishes when he came in. Hella was always washing dishes; she loved the hot immersion of hands, the slip of suds along the tender skin of her inner arms. Sometimes she would wash the same plate over and over again because there was nothing else in the house that needed cleaning. There weren't enough chores to keep her busy and never enough dishes to wash because they ate simple meals here – enormous boiled potatoes and slabs of meat with everything – which she hated. Hella liked clean, solid chunks of white fish and sour cider. Whenever she had to cook the thick rashers of bacon Magnus loved so much, she tried to think of St Lucia's night: the young women in their crisp white dresses, the long beech tables covered with snowy cloths like skate-polished ice rinks and the silver platters of rollmops, the crystal dishes of soured cream, the pewter steins of dark red beer.

'You'll go out now and find that missing button at once,' his mother had said.

She had noticed, without looking at him, that his collar was hanging loose.

13

'It's not normal to send a little kid out looking for things all the time,' said Ari.

'Well, you don't want to be a normal little kid,' said his mother. 'Do you?'

'You're not normal either,' sniped Ari, thinking she had meant her comment as an insult and returning the slight.

'You should pity the sons of ordinary mothers,' Hella said. That was what she always told him when he complained about her inconsistencies. 'They will have small lives inside their skins. Their petty hearts will drum like little dark fists inside their chests, trying to get out.'

As she said it, she pounded quite hard against her own left breast. The beating made a dull, hollow sound there like a marble in a stone bowl but, at the same time, bubbles flew from her fingertips and navigated the kitchen, carrying with them the souls of rainbows.

'You can expect more because of me,' Hella said. 'Because I am your mother, you can anticipate stars.'

That was how his mother spoke – convoluted sentences like the scrolls on a baroque carving – because English was her second language, learned from her mother Eleanor, and its poetry had been hard earned. Hella had an excellent vocabulary and astonishing beauty, though her mother's friends had sometimes commented that her chin was too stiff. Her hair was thick and gold, the colour of butter, and her smile was rare but worth the wait.

She turned away from her son after her decree and Ari pushed his bottom lip out at the back of her head. He didn't pity the sons of ordinary mothers. He envied them. They ate eggs, not fish, for their breakfast and their buttons were allowed to fall off. Ari's were not. Whenever he lost a button, he had to trudge back along the path to school to look for it. His mother double stitched all the buttons she sewed. When one pulled loose, a second secret loop was there to catch it, so it hung like an eyeball on a nerve down the front of his shirt. To lose a double-stitched button must be intentional, his mother said, and that kind of carelessness was a sin.

Hella talked a lot about sin. It was a convenient explanation, Ari thought, for her general dissatisfaction with him. His mother didn't even believe in God. Ari had never understood this safety catch for buttons either – his mother was a woman who had once walked out of a circus tent when she saw the high-flyers were performing above a net.

'Anybody can do that!' she had exclaimed as she dragged him away. 'That's not daring; it's practice only.'

Hella rated daring highly. She saw herself, Ari suspected, as something of a desperado, coming to America all alone and finding work, leaving behind her elderly parents and their money and their big yellow house on Strandvägen with its polished red door.

Ari was too little to remember the train from Stockholm to Malmö, the steamer to Copenhagen, the ship to New York, the train to Duluth or the bus to St Cloud. His mother recounted the journey regularly, making it a little more dire with

15

each telling, but Ari had just turned six when they first arrived on the farm and he only recalled the look of disgust on his mother's face when she had first seen their new home. Now that he was eight, Ari knew that she had expected better but that pride had made a return impossible. He understood that. He would have hated seeing her knock once more on her parents' polished red door; he would have hated seeing her bow her head beneath Eleanor Köll's heavy, forgiving hand. So perhaps he and his mother were more the same than they were different.

Hella Köll was the daughter of a genteel physician from Ystad and an English adventuress. Ari didn't remember his grandfather very well. The man was just a tall tower, which ended with a snow-capped roof of white hair. His genius, according to Hella, had been subjugated by the poppy. Whoever Poppy was, Ari had never met her. He imagined she was a fiery, dragon-coloured woman with henna-dyed hair and, for some reason, she was associated in his mind with sulphurous smoke.

He remembered his grandmother quite clearly, though. She was the daughter of a British high commissioner and she told tales about India and the Indies. Sometimes Ari mixed the two places up. In one of his dreams, a tiger ran off along an endless stretch of white beach with a cricket ball in its mouth, chased by a gang of ebony-skinned boys. In another, a flaming babaloo cake was presented to a turbaned maharajah. Ari loved his grandmother's stories – always told in her beautiful English, never her acquired Swedish tongue –

16

but he remembered how he had needed to follow her from room to room through the house as she talked or she would just walk away like a ghost lost halfway through a haunting. She seldom left their home, preferring to talk about how much she missed the tropics rather than going outside to find the weather sunny. Ari also knew, somehow, that there was an unbridgeable gulf between his grandmother and his mother but he had not discovered the cause of it.

One day, when the maid must have burned something on the stove because the house on Strandvägen was filled with its own peculiar purple haze, Hella had bundled Ari out the polished red door and they had left their lives behind them.

For months beforehand, Hella had planned this departure but her son had known nothing about it. As the cold train slid like a steel eel along its midnight rail, Hella explained that she had arranged a position as a housekeeper in the United States through the personal ads in an agricultural magazine and then via letters. She had shown him the letters he couldn't yet read and had pointed out how refined the handwriting was, how much store she put in the good, thick paper. Ari thought the letters looked short, shorter even than his first primer, but he didn't say so. Instead, he said the writing looked very proper and very neat.

'America's heartland!' Hella had said over and over again during the journey. 'A land for the heart.'

They had rocked in syncopated rhythm in their compartment bunk that night. Ari had felt her body's electricity, blue and glowing like St Elmo's fire, prickle along his skin. He loved her most when she was like this, burning up with a new idea and a new place to go. Before, there had been boat trips between the islands and weekends away in Mariefred but this was the furthest they had ever dared to go and they were daring it together. Ari pretended he had been asked what he thought about the move and had decided to go along with her; he pretended he was unafraid.

'America's heartland,' Ari had repeated in his mind right up until they arrived at the gate of the brown homestead. They had greeted the silent farmer with the nice handwriting. Ari thought the man looked old enough to be his grandfather, though he wasn't nearly as straight up and down; there were no long creases in his trousers. On their first night in the farmhouse, Hella had whispered to Ari as she held him close once more (and he was never sure afterwards if she had spoken it in a dream): '...and a flat brown heart it is.'

The disappointment in her voice had unnerved Ari though he didn't fully understand why. He only knew that the heartland was profoundly, but inexpressibly, wrong for her.

Hella called the ageing farmer Magnus but told Ari he was Far Glassen. Far meant father, so Ari chose not to address the man and tried to pretend that he was transparent – the way his name sounded in English, insubstantial as glass.

His mother looked at him now as though she could read his thoughts about the bad-tempered old man.

'Go on out this minute,' Hella scolded him. 'I'll

have to steal some time to sew it on after dinner.'

Ari knew it was no use arguing with her. She was a woman who always got her own way. Ari tried to slam the screen door as he went out onto the porch but it was on a spring and would only close at its own pace. His mother had even conspired to rob him of the satisfaction of his petulance.

Ari took the exact route he had just walked. The button would be far off. A lost thing was never close to the place you were when you first realized it was missing. As he went, Ari imagined his father, his real father, walking towards the house, a duffel bag slung over his shoulder, his cap at a rakish angle. It was all just a terrible mistake that he had died in the war; he had really been searching for them for all these years.

'Your father had bad yellow hair,' was all his mother had told him about the man. 'Thick and matted like the cheap summer straw we use to thatch the rabbit hutches.'

Ari didn't discern that she said it fondly. In his mind, it was just one more item on the list of things she had said to upset him.

'Was my father a hero?' Ari had asked one day when they were banging the dust from the carpets with fireplace pokers.

'No,' said his mother. 'He was just a man.'

And she had whacked the carpet again.

Ari had come to realize during their first terrible year in America's heartland that, for a woman with so many opinions, his mother used few words when she was uneasy or angry. She spoke in her dreams, though; she dreamed frequently. To Hella, gestures were everything. She beat the carpet. She smashed drawers shut. She plopped her hands into her lap and left them looking up at her face like a pair of frozen claws, imploring for something valuable to hold.

Instead of a soldier, Ari met Magnus Glassen coming up the road. They passed without speaking. At the last minute, Ari stepped off the path to let the man go by, then wished he hadn't. Why didn't Glassen ever make way for anybody else? And why was he coming home for lunch when Hella had made them both a cold meat stew and bread to take with them that morning?

The missing button was particularly unwilling to be found and it was hot. The sky was the washed-out blue of an old dishcloth, not a committed colour but an indolent, petulant pastel that couldn't be bothered. There was no sea to reflect here, not even a lake nearby. They were reliant on rain for water in this corner of Minnesota, and rain was fickle. Ari used the toe of his boot to nudge the crabgrass from the fringe of the path. This raw edging was just the kind of place a rogue button would seek out for a den. Ari kicked at the dust half-heartedly. His neck was burning.

Often, Ari was sent on a hunt when he was sure none of his own buttons was missing. He was looking instead on behalf of the fat, old oaf. It was Glassen who had lost a button and wouldn't take responsibility for it. Ari had spent so many hours searching for buttons that he had once found one that didn't belong to any of them – a bone button his mother said was very fine and she had used it to close the throat of a blouse she was sewing. Whenever she wore that blouse afterwards, she would sit with one finger touching the button and Ari knew then that it must be one of the things that reminded her of home: a bone button, a silver bowl with two goldfish swimming along the bottom of it, a whalebone corset, a winter goose. A Swedish goose, Hella had informed him, was much whiter than an American one – whiter even than a washed swan.

Suddenly, a noise like a tractor engine came from the sky. Ari looked up at once and saw something he could scarcely believe: a red airplane – a real one, with a man in it – was passing overhead. His mouth fell open in amazement and a whirlwind of dust swizzled in. It went right down into his lungs in a gritty rush and Ari bent over in a coughing spasm. When he could open his eyes again, the airplane was gone but he saw something on the ground – a coin-sized circle of white. It was right there in the middle of the path where he had already looked: his misplaced button.

Ari held it up as if to show it to somebody but nobody was around. There was just the wheat, tall and dry, a filthy yellow the Yankee banjo songs call 'gold' but which his mother called 'stoft' – dust.

Ari was too far away from the farmhouse to see his mother flying out the door and pushing her way through the fields. Hella moved through the wheat along the furrows the tractor had made the previous Fall. Her feet stumbled in the ruts. Their uncertainty surprised her. Hella had imagined herself accustomed to monotony and straight lines. The earth was arid. It cracked beneath her

21

boots and crumbled into clods. Her soles left imprints, which gave the impression of weightiness though she was as slight as an early birch. The air between the stalks was tangible and coarse, worse than the clouds she had beaten from the carpets when she had first arrived with Ari.

The wheat was disorientating, too – the way it swooned and supplicated in the mildest breeze. It pressed its parched ears against her face; its awns scratched her. Hella remembered the rasp of Magnus's stubble along her cheek, the thick, cold wetness of his tongue forced into her mouth a few moments before and she stopped for a second to lean over and retch. There was nothing in her stomach – an empty yawp of bile-flavoured air came up instead and she despised herself for bowing over because dignity was really all she had left.

Up ahead, Hella saw the green umbrella of the Swedish oak. It was her landmark, an anchor that rose incongruously upward from the sea of wheat. She made her way towards it. It was the terminus of a pointless journey, merely a touchstone she could keep in mind until she reached it. Then she would try to find another destination and move on towards that. If only she could move from tree to tree until she found her way back to Sweden. She hated that she could never leave one tree behind without having the next one in sight. It was because of Ari. He had to have some kind of stability and an education. If she had been alone, she would have left this place years before.

She touched the bark of the oak. She had watched this foreign tree over foaming dishes from the kitchen window every day. It was not at home on a farm in Minnesota. It did not move in wind as other trees did. It was stalwart. Like her, it longed for a hillside near Skåne.

Hella heard the plane a few seconds after her son. She couldn't see the boy from where she stood but she looked about for him, nonetheless. She knew Ari would be desolate if he missed it. He had the fascination all young boys held for airplanes. She hoped the pilot might land somewhere nearby then they could walk over and visit him. Ari would love that but Magnus didn't allow unscheduled departures from the farm.

The plane swooped back into view and waggled its red wings in the sunlight. Hella's hands went involuntarily to her cheeks. The machine was as joyful as a ruby butterfly. She could hardly believe it when the airplane dropped lower and lower and then swept in to land in the fallow cow pasture beside her oak.

Without thinking, Hella ran towards it. It slowed and swung round at the far end of the field, invisible from the farmhouse. Had Magnus heard it? God bless the only hill in Minnesota which might shield it from him.

When she reached its tail, Hella staggered to a stop. The pilot might have been disconcerted by a farm girl racing towards him, but he wasn't. He tugged off his goggles and pulled himself lightly from the cockpit, hopping down off the wing. He had that tall, unchallenged grace Hella associated with Scandinavian men. He was blond and fine featured with the slightest cleft in his chin.

'Hello,' he said. 'No cows, that was lucky!'

'Hello,' she said, and then, just to see, *'God dag.'*

'God dag!' he said and smiled.

'You're Swedish!' she said and she laughed without covering her mouth.

The young man shook his head. He was about her age – twenty-three or twenty-four, no older – and kind. Hella could tell that already.

'No, I'm an American,' said the pilot. 'Swedish grandfather, though. We had a farm round here but I can't find it now. I hoped you wouldn't mind me using yours for a pit stop.'

'I don't mind at all,' she said. 'It's not mine, though. I'm the help only. The farmer's up at the house.'

'A long walk?' he asked.

'Not if we're to walk it together,' Hella said boldly. 'It's over the hill only. I can take you there quite quickly.'

'I might have to find some lodging,' said the young man. 'The engine's overheating a little. If I can borrow some water and let her cool over-night, I'll make it to Duluth in the morning.'

'However we can help,' Hella said.

The pilot was very beautiful, she saw now. He looked at his boots a lot. He had that slight discomfiture at his own attractiveness which meant a shy disposition. Hella wanted to talk. She desperately wanted to hear about the world outside but he hauled an empty gasoline can from the front seat and started off across the field. Hella skipped for a few strides until she caught up with him.

'How long have you been here?' he asked.

'Two years,' she said.

'That bad?' he asked, hearing the despair.

Hella stopped dead at that remark and the pilot stopped beside her.

'Yes,' she said. 'That bad.'

Then she started walking again so that he wouldn't feel obliged to say anything more or offer to help her. She knew he would have, though, given the chance; he was that sort of man.

They reached the porch at the same time as Ari. The boy had run all the way to tell his mother about the plane only to find her talking with the pilot.

'An airplane!' he exclaimed.

'And the pilot,' said his mother.

'Hello,' said the man to Ari.

'This is Ari,' said Hella, directing the introduction to nobody in particular. She said it hurriedly and didn't explain that the boy was her son. 'And I'm Miss Köll.'

They shook hands.

'Go in to your Far,' Hella said to Ari.

Ari's face darkened.

'Go in!' she said again.

'And you are Mr...' she paused, waiting for the man to insert his name.

'Mr Lindbergh but call me Charles,' he said. 'Please.'

Hella felt she couldn't repeat that – not a first name from a stranger – but she liked it. It was formal and upright like the man himself. He was tall enough to stoop through the door as they went in. She liked that, too.

Magnus was nowhere about. Hella smiled happily and offered Charles some iced coffee – an

25

indulgence she made with fresh cream skimmed from the top of the dairy pails before they were carted to town. She was the only person in the household who drank it but she made sure her jug stood in prize place in the cold box, right on top of the ice brick.

The young man kept standing as he drank from the glass she handed him.

'Please sit,' she said.

'Is the man of the house not in?' Charles asked.

'No,' Hella said. 'He must have made off to the fields once more.'

Charles looked about the pristine kitchen, awkward now and unsure.

'But our water is free,' said Hella light-heartedly. She leaned towards Charles to take the empty gasoline can from his hand. 'And so is our hospitality,' she added.

Her butter-gold hair brushed the shoulder of his flying suit. Hella went to the basin where she kept an enormous jug of well water under a fly net. She looked back over her shoulder at Charles as she filled his can.

Ari watched his mother with fascination. She had become in the last five minutes a different woman – shinier. The grey dust had fallen away and revealed the gilded person inside. It had only taken a vigorous emotional shaking.

'We could use a housekeeper like you at the flight school,' Charles said, taking in the ironed tablecloth and curtains, the regimented rows of plates in the drying rack.

'Could you?' said Hella and she swung around so quickly that water from the jug splashed the pinafore of her apron and spread a dark mark across her heart.

'Yes,' he said. 'We live in a sty over there. The guys are so keen to learn now, they have to cram us into barracks.'

He was only making polite talk, Hella realized. The cold spill from the jug reached her skin and chilled her.

The man finished his coffee and smiled. His lashes were bleached by the sun, soft pale feathers around his eyes which made him look even younger than he probably was and somehow exotic.

'What kind of airplane is it?' asked Ari.

'She's my Jenny – a Curtis JN4-D,' said Charles and he bent his long form over in the chair to bring himself closer to Ari's level. 'She's an old rust bucket but I love her. We're barnstorming all over the Midwest this summer at agricultural shows, weddings and what have you, giving people rides.'

Ari looked up at his mother. Her face reminded him they were penniless.

'I could take you up for free, I expect,' Charles said, as if he had read Ari's mind. 'For rescuing me.'

Hella turned round again.

'You would do that for me?' she said. 'You would take me up?'

Charles looked momentarily disconcerted.

'Sure I would,' he said. 'I need to get a mechanic to her tomorrow but she'll have cooled off enough overnight to take you up for a quick flip in the morning.'

'How much?' said Magnus Glassen from the door.

He had loomed in like a storm cloud.

Charles stood up immediately and reached out his hand.

'Sorry for the invasion, Sir. The young lady here was good enough to offer me a drink...'

'How much a trip?' asked Magnus again.

'Usually it's three dollars for fifteen minutes but I wouldn't dream of charging Miss Köll here...'

'That's exactly what we charge for a night's accommodation,' said Magnus. 'Three dollars ... and it's in the kitchen on the floor.'

'That'd be just fine, Sir. Thank you,' said Charles.

'I have a quilt for you,' interjected Hella. 'And there's dinner, too, of course.'

'That'll be another fifty cents,' said Magnus. 'Our hospitality isn't free, you know.'

Hella flushed red at that direct contradiction of the impression she had been trying to cultivate. Her skin suffused with angry blood right up to her throat.

2

Ari stood above the sleeping figure of the pilot, hoping the man would wake of his own accord. It must be midnight by now, he reckoned, and the kitchen floor was cold on his toes. The lamp he had taken from the chest beside his mother's bed (and lit in the passageway so that she would not be disturbed) threw long, reptilian shadows from familiar objects. The shadows slinked and pounced at one another in the corners of the kitchen and in the dark square hole beneath the wash sink.

Ari looked down at the sleeping man's form. It was curled up against the side of the coal stove, which had still been warm when he had fallen asleep. Ari didn't want to touch the man. His shoulder rose and fell on the waves of dream-lessness. He seemed deeply contented beneath their best quilt. Hella had taken this handmade treasure from her own bed and she and Ari had made do with a sheet that was almost ragged. It was partly the cold in the early hours that had woken Ari and decided him on this visit.

Suddenly, the pilot sat bolt upright and cracked his head on the protruding handle of the oven door. He winced but didn't curse. He looked Ari straight in the eye and then they both looked towards the closed kitchen door to hear if they had unsettled the house. As co-conspirators, they both breathed again after a few seconds. Ari didn't speak. He felt foolish and tongue-tied now that he had the pilot's attention. He simply thrust out his hand and revealed his most precious possession – a small tin airplane his mother had found for him in a thrift store in St Cloud. It wasn't any particular make, just a simple airplane shape which had once been painted pale blue but most of the paint had chipped off now and the toy was scuffed.

Charles took the toy with reverence. He held it

on the palm of his hand like a man holding a dazed bird up for gentle inspection before placing it safely under a bush to recover.

'That's grand,' he whispered. 'We could use a plane like this in the mail service. It looks reliable and fast.'

He saw the boy's smile and that he was shivering.

'Come here,' said Charles. 'I'll show you a favourite game of mine when I was a kid.'

Hella had cleaned the kitchen table completely after dinner. She had scrubbed it with a capful of the sheep's disinfectant diluted in an enormous bucket of water – the result was a not disagreeable smell like clothes just washed with astringent soap. Charles took one end of the quilt and gestured for Ari to take the other. Together they draped it over the table like a cloth. It was too large and bunched onto the floor on all four sides but this seemed to be the idea. Charles urged Ari underneath and soon they were both sitting knee-to-knee, safe from the stray breezes that stole into the house through gaps in the wallboards.

Ari sat quite comfortably, cross-legged, but Charles had to stoop and eventually he lay on his side with his legs curled up to his chest. He took the lantern from Ari's hand and rested it on the curve of his hip, holding it steady with one hand while he manoeuvred the small toy airplane with the other. Ari saw the shadow it projected against the quilt wall and grinned.

'During the war, the pilots flew reconnaissance … scouting missions out over the sea.'

Ari was transfixed. The floor below them melted

away and became an ocean that had no limits. The patterns on the quilted squares became paisley clouds and floral ones. The aircraft flicked across this varied tapestry of sky.

'What were they looking for?' Ari asked.

'Munitions factories, bunkers, enemy airports on land. At sea, they were trying to spot U-boats and ships that might be spying on us.'

'And if they saw them?'

'By the end of the war, they were dropping bombs right out of the cockpits, raining them down from the sky. Kaboom!'

Ari put a fist into his mouth to stop his giggle of excitement.

'He's not my father, you know,' he was determined to get this out. 'Mr Glassen's my mother's boss. My real father's dead in the war probably.'

Charles seemed uncomfortable at that. He didn't say anything so Ari bumbled on to put him at his ease, to let him know that it was something he had known about almost his whole life and that it didn't make him nearly as sad as it used to.

'Were you in the war?' he asked Charles.

'No,' said the pilot. 'I was a bit too young.'

'Well, my father was,' said Ari boldly again. Then he added, so as not to sound prideful, 'He wasn't a hero on anything, though.'

'Who was he fighting for?' asked Charles.

'Us, I think,' said Ari.

He had never really considered that his father might have been anything other than an ally. Then he saw that he was being teased.

Charles rumpled his hair. 'Of course he was. And they were all heroes, you know, every last man of them. There just weren't enough medals for everybody to have one.'

'I think that too!' said Ari. 'About him being a hero, I mean. Only my mother doesn't.'

'She probably just misses him,' said Charles. 'Sometimes the people who get left behind are angry and lonely. Think about that next time she seems sore at you.'

'I will,' said Ari and he felt happier than he had in a long time. 'Could you not stay and visit a while?' he asked.

It was an audacious thing to ask, Ari knew. He felt sure it was very bold and what his mother called unseemly but he didn't care.

'I have to earn a living,' said Charles. 'Summer's the best time of the year for taking people up and you can feel that Fall's already on its way.'

'I'd like to be a pilot one day,' said Ari.

'You will be, then,' said Charles matter-of-factly. 'I think there'll be more jobs in flying than anybody dreams of. I think it'll be bigger than trains and ships put together.'

He handed Ari the toy airplane and held the lantern for him so that he could make it swirl and loop against the quilted sky and the dark black storm clouds of the table's legs.

The quilt was rudely flapped up and Ari saw the skirt of his mother's white nightgown and her bare feet with their painted nails. She always had painted nails. It was a habit she got from her mother. Hella kept her polish hidden at the back of the stove and Ari knew that sometimes they went without soap because she needed a new bottle.

'Ari Köll!' she hissed. 'What are you doing here? I'm so sorry,' she exclaimed to Charles. 'He snuck out and I didn't hear him go.'

They both crawled sheepishly from their hiding place beneath the table. Ari saw that his mother had left her woollen gown on its hook behind the bedroom door. Perhaps she had been so startled by his absence that she had forgotten how sheer her nightgown was.

'He was no bother, Miss Köll. We were talking about airplanes. I wasn't even properly asleep yet when Ari here came visiting.'

Hella knew that was a lie. The night was well underway, hours old already, and she was acutely aware that her son must have roused the man.

'You're very kind to say so but you're a paying lodger here. I don't expect entertaining a child to be a part of any guest's obligations.'

She grabbed Ari by the top of his arm, the tender spot just under the armpit where her nails hurt most, and dragged him towards the door.

'It really wasn't that way at all. I was just telling Ari he ought to be a pilot.'

'If he doesn't get enough sleep to concentrate on his work tomorrow he won't have the schooling to be a pig farmer,' she said. 'And even Mr Glassen has managed that feat. Please get some rest,' she said and she pushed Ari out into the passage. 'Unless, of course, you'd like some coffee?' she added suddenly.

'No, Ma'am,' Charles answered courteously. 'I wouldn't put you out by asking it.'

'It wouldn't be any trouble,' Hella said. 'I'm up now, after all.'

'Still, sleep does sound like a good idea.'

Hella smiled and closed the door very quietly behind her. As soon as she did, Ari saw the fear return to her face. It came as a shadow, black as a crow, and settled in the lines around her mouth, which were invisible by daylight. Together, they crept along the passage past Glassen's open door. Ari saw his mother pause at the floorboard that groaned. He thought he was the only one who had worked out exactly where it was. He looked at his mother as they stepped carefully over it together. Hella smiled at her son and for a second he smiled back at her. They were both prisoners but they had each coveted small, vital pieces of knowledge that might assist in their escape one day.

They didn't speak again. Ari lay down beside his mother on their lean bed and felt her settle. For hours, they dozed and pretended to sleep. Several times in the night, Ari felt his mother stir and move tentatively as if to slip from the bed. Each time, he pretended to wake and cling to her so that she had to lie still again. Each time, he felt the tension in her relax as she rocked to soothe him back to sleep but he would not allow himself to drop off. He had a sudden terror that she might sneak out with the pilot in the night and fly away. That she would use some mysterious womanly power she possessed to encourage Charles – who was Ari's friend, not hers – to help her escape from Glassen ... and also from him.

When Ari woke the next morning, without ever feeling himself drift away, his mother was gone.

34

He leaped from his bed and ran through the house, searching for her in every room. The quilt Charles had borrowed was back at the foot of their bed and the kitchen table was set for breakfast. Ari ran out onto the porch in his bare feet. His pyjama pants dragged in the dust but he didn't care. He ran for the far field and when he reached it he saw his mother and Charles climbing into the Jenny.

Charles secured Hella in the front seat and pulled himself in behind her.

'You might need the blanket,' he said to her over the roar of the engine.

Hella looked down and saw the oily crocheted bundle at her feet. She thought about the deep blue night of winter back home, the way the afternoons roared in, wearing the black clouds as a cloak, and jumped the iron-frosted lakes in a single bound. She laughed delightedly.

'No,' she said. 'I don't feel the cold.'

They trundled down to the far end of the field and accelerated. The wheels left the ground, bounced back into gravity's clasp once more then wrenched free and soared. Hella looked down and noticed Ari's figure below them. He was standing beneath her tree, still in his pyjamas. As they gained height, he seemed to retreat, pulled away from her by a force she could not see.

'It's wonderful!' she screamed.

From up here, the fields had the expensive textures of mohair and pure wool; the fence posts were delicate stitches, each reservoir a gleaming mirror. Glassen's farmhouse was a carved wooden toy, freshly painted with nothing hidden behind the window sashes and no sweaty desperation inside. The trees resembled puffs of green cotton candy and when she looked carefully, Hella could see where the horizon curved – a promise that the world was indeed round and that if she could stay aloft long enough, she would end up back where she had started.

The wind had blown her cheeks red by the time they landed.

'I have to be going!' yelled Charles. He hadn't switched the engine off. 'Jump down carefully. Mind the propellers.'

Hella nodded and climbed out onto the wing.

The engine blast sucked her dress against her lean curves. Charles thought she was extraordinarily beautiful. As she passed him to hop down, he took hold of her arm and stopped her. The drum of the engine met with the beating of his heart. He pulled her down very gently and their lips touched. She was a cool kisser at first, controlled and detached, then instantly ardent. Charles felt his blood leap in his veins for one glorious second. He wasn't a man who did such things but this girl was so contained yet enticing, he could not resist her.

'I'll be at the Little Falls Fair next Saturday. See if you can come,' he said. 'Bring Ari. I'd like to take him up, too.'

'I couldn't wake him this morning,' Hella said. 'After the excitement of last night ... I just let him sleep.'

'Next week, then,' said Charles.

Hella nodded once.

'We'll come to the fair,' she said. 'I'll ask for you

when we get there.'

She realised she still hadn't told Charles Lindbergh her first name. He had politely called her Miss Köll throughout their brief acquaintance. She leaned in close to his ear and whispered damply:

'You should know my name. It's Hella. Hella Köll.'

Her lips and her tongue were so close to the whorls of his ear that Charles imagined he could feel their wetness delving in there. His skin shivered in delight.

Hella didn't even look at Ari as the plane taxied away. He stood like a small chain gang escapee in the shade of the Swedish oak. Hella bit her lip and wondered if she should tell him about the fair. Better not, in case it didn't happen. She didn't want to disappoint the boy. Ari eventually skulked off towards the house but Hella remained watching the speck of red until it was long invisible then she watched the place where she imagined it might be.

In the distance, the postman's truck rattled along Rural Route 71. Hella couldn't hear it through the thunder of blood in her ears but she saw the dust it dredged up in its wake – a cloud that was a portent of the turbulence to come.

That night, Hella clutched Ari close once more, afraid that Magnus would want a visit from her. She knew the old man wouldn't dare haul her away from the boy. The small shield of his body protected her. Hella lay awake for as long as possible and dreamed of the pilot's long elegant fingers, his powerful jawbone and the even, tanned texture of his skin. And when the exhaustion and excitement of the day demanded that she close her eyes at last, she intoned his name until she fell asleep: 'Lindbergh ... Lindbergh...'

3

They were sitting silently at the breakfast table when the deer crashed in. It came at full tilt right through the screen of the kitchen door, shattering the brittle wooden frame to shards. As it smashed through, splinters rained down into Ari's oats and, absurdly, the first gesture he made was to push his plate away as if he was suddenly full. For a few seconds, they were all as bewildered as the soft brown animal. It must be blind or mad to behave so erratically. Usually, the gentle herds kept to the deep green shadows of the pine forests, seldom venturing out among the pasture grass or the sweating wheat.

This deer was a doe with melted chocolate eyes. A stake of sharpened wood from the jamb had torn its flank and blood ran down from the wound and dripped onto the kitchen floor. The deer's pelt shivered like a miniature velvet ocean. It tried to spring away on its small hooves but only managed to thrash in its own spilled blood, slip and panic. Its eyes rolled white like boiled eggs peeled from their shells.

Hella didn't even let out a shriek at the unexpected invasion. She went very still and stood up quietly with a dishcloth spread open in front of her. She intended to shoo the animal out but Magnus sidled past her into the parlour to retrieve his shotgun from where he had left it leaning against the wall of the entrance hall.

The deer must have smelled the cordite as Magnus moved the rifle and it suddenly found its footing and leapt. It landed right on top of the breakfast table this time, upturning dishes and clattering spoons to the floor. Blood splashed across Ari's face and he screamed a short sharp yelp. The pieces of plate on the floor looked like Easter egg shells dipped in cranberry sauce. The curtains were splattered.

The deer jumped again, ungainly and destructive, and travelled relentlessly through the house – through the front room and through the room Ari shared with his mother. Cornered at last, it made a final bound. It smashed through the glass of the small bedroom window, dragging net curtains behind it like a dishevelled bride fleeing the church.

It rested on the grass outside for a few moments. Stunned, it knelt on its front legs like it was praying and Ari felt certain it would lie down on its side and die. But it found some secret reserve of strength and rose to run. It even leapt once like a gazelle to test its power then it made a straight sprint along the far fence. One final bound to clear the barbed wire and it was free.

Magnus came into the room behind Ari and Hella with the gun balanced over the crook of his elbow. The three of them stood silently together.

The ferocity of the reluctant intruder had wrecked their morning.

'I'll get some struts to shore up the windows until I can get new panes,' said Magnus.

Hella said she would sort through the damage in the kitchen.

'Water, Ari,' she said.

Ari heard her but he kept watching the spot where the deer had last been visible. If it ran that fast, he thought, and never stopped, sometime next year when they were sitting at their breakfast table it would stampede through the house again, having traversed the world. The idea depressed him. Not because they would be interrupted again but because they would still be here.

Magnus came back in from the chicken coops with a few boards slung under his armpit and a hammer and nail jar clasped in his hand.

'Hold the boards,' he said to Ari.

Ari spent the next ten minutes helping Magnus hammer boards across the kitchen door. The water in Hella's sink ran pink when she rinsed the floor rags. They all remained quiet about the strangely unnerving incident. A hundred miles of open space all round them and a wild animal had torn a direct path through their house.

Hella thought of the superstitious country folk back home who left their front and back doors unlatched at night for fear that their house had been built on a faerie path. If the little people were allowed a way through, they were content and closed the doors behind them but if they were locked out and prevented passage, their fury would curdle milk and bring in dry rot.

'Deer don't do that,' was all Magnus said. He seemed unsettled.

'That was a deer,' said Hella in an even tone. 'So apparently deer must do that, at least from time to time.'

Ari smiled to himself. He loved his mother when she was like this – just a little bit disrespect-ful but not so blatantly that her cheekiness could be easily discerned. She looked up and saw her son smiling and winked a quick wink. He felt completely happy for the first time since Charles had told him his father ought to have received a medal for his bravery in the war. It was the way he had felt as a very little boy in the house on Strandvägen when his grandparents were away and his mother used to pretend it was her home. They would play that just the two of them lived there and there was nobody in the world who could kick them out onto the street on into the dusty wheat.

Ari and Hella stared at each other for just a second longer. The joyful chaos of the deer's pass-age was between them and something else was, too. Something that was large and indefinable, something between mothers and sons.

They all smelled the smoke at the same time. It rushed into their nostrils on a single waft of air and they stopped what they were doing and looked together in one direction. The fire was coming up from Brand Johansson's north field. It was rippling the sky with an enormous bubbling heat that consumed even the normal warmth of the day. They could not hear it yet but there was a glow of orange along the cusp of the horizon

41

that stretched for miles.

'It won't reach us,' said Magnus just as Ari came to the realization that it would.

Ari knew in an instant that this would be their salvation. Fire was a thing that purified, a biblical element of purging and refinement. Fire would set them free. He saw in his mother's eyes that she knew it, too. He saw something like glee there and terror. The deer had been a herald.

When Magnus gave her orders, though, Hella took them.

'Water down the roof. I'll get the cows in.'

Magnus trudged off to the dairy pasture in the unhurried manner of a man who is suppressing deep fear.

'Quickly!' Hella said to Ari. 'My things.'

They raced inside and Hella threw her suitcase on their bed. It had been placed at the front of the cupboard months before to be easily accessible.

'Get from the kitchen drawer my white linen.'

Ari knew where to go. The linen had been unpacked into the server in a gesture of goodwill and solidarity during the first week of their stay but Hella had never brought it out or let Magnus's lips touch it. Ari felt a surge of bitter pride at his mother's vicious brand of stoicism. He was hers – just like her – and proud. They were going to run for it now. Why hadn't they dared before? Not having anywhere to go was an irrelevance now. The fire made flight imperative.

Back in their bedroom, Ari thought about gathering his possessions together and realized in a moment of startling clarity that he had none. He had his clothes, the button he had found the

42

evening before – his mother had not had the chance to sew it back onto his shirt because Charles's visit had distracted her – and his toy airplane. That was all.

Hella's suitcase was almost full – her silver bowl with two goldfish swimming along the bottom of it, her whalebone corset – she squeezed it shut and took Ari's hand. As they approached the front door, Ari saw Magnus coming back from the dairy paddock. Hella saw him too and with a deft movement she dropped her case and kicked it hard so that it slid across her polished floor and skidded behind the door just as Magnus came through it.

'The roof's still dry!' he roared. 'Don't you see a fire's coming?'

'The well bucket's gone down,' said Hella. 'It's stuck.'

Magnus cursed and pushed past Hella, shoving her so hard that her shoulder slammed into the wall. They looked out and saw that the fire was only a field away.

The heat was enormous – a sticky, woven net that came down over their heads. Hella's face went instantly red but whether the flush was because of the sudden change in temperature on anger, Ari couldn't tell. He only knew that when he looked at her, her eyes had become underground coal pits with flames licking out of them.

'Once it's over the drive, we'll never get out,' Hella said to herself and looked towards where Magnus had gone out. She ran after him and screamed, 'Once it's over the drive, there's no way out!'

'We're not running,' said Magnus. 'It'll pass over us.'

'It'll pass right through us!' screamed Hella. Ari thought his mother's voice was high – like a real woman's – for the first time and she kept shrilling, 'Like the deer, straight through and no stopping.'

Ari watched Magnus stride back into the house and catch his mother by the throat with one huge brown fist. His fingers sank deeply into her white skin.

'We're not running,' he said.

Ari stood transfixed as Hella went calm under the power of Magnus's hold.

'We're not running,' she repeated calmly.

It was her iciest voice. It meant she had decided on something.

'I'm sorry,' Magnus said. 'You have to help. The farm...'

He swept his hand round as if to indicate the three generations' worth of gravemarkers in the cemetery, the buried babies and old-timers whose bodies fortified the soil of a family farm.

'I understand,' said Hella. 'We'll stay.'

She touched Magnus's cheek with the back of her hand. Ari had never seen her display the slightest tenderness towards this bloat of a man before and he could scarcely believe it now. Magnus took a second to gently press his cheek against the pressure of her knuckles before he turned away. As soon as he did, Hella picked up a sturdy porch chair and crashed it down on the back of the man's head. He crumpled like a paper puppet.

'Help me,' she said.

Ari saw what she meant to do and he grabbed Magnus's immobile arm and pulled. Between them, they got his enormous bulk into the kitchen. Through the slats of the boarded-up window, Ari could see the flickering yellow of the fire's body as it moved round the back of the house, looking for a way in.

'Get my things and go out,' said Hella. 'Head for the oak. I'll meet you.'

Ari picked up the suitcase and carried it. It cracked smartly against his ankles but the thick smoke made breathing so difficult that he hardly noticed. He was running through the pain of thudding purple bruises. He looked back. Hella was behind him. She was almost beside him when she suddenly stopped and turned around. She ran back towards the house and in through the front door. What had she forgotten there? They had everything she owned.

Through the snick and crinkle of burning wheat, Ari heard a rhythmic thudding. Magnus was pounding on the kitchen door. How had he come round so soon from the blow? The banging went on for several precious minutes before Hella came flying out through the door again. The fire lunged across the porch and tried to grab her skirt but missed. She wrenched Ari by the arm and attempted to force him away from the drive and towards the wheat. She was heading for the oak.

'We can't lose the drive!' shouted Ari.

It was obvious to him but his mother stopped and looked around desperately. A black tentacle of smoke smudged her face from his view. She

45

breathed it in and coughed violently. Then Ari saw his mother do an astonishing thing: she looked up. Hella shielded her eyes from the heat of the fine and looked into the sky. At first, Ari thought she was imploring God but then he understood she was waiting for the plane to rescue them. She wouldn't save them; Ari would have to do it himself.

He pulled her back to the drive. It was not where it had been; it was moving around in the blinding smoke. For a second, Ari was sure Magnus was going to lurch from the house in a ball of fire and drag them back inside like some hellish trapdoor spider, then he saw something that was more substantial than an elusive ball of smog. It was a cloud of dust coming up from the dirt surface of Rural Route 71. Just ahead of the disturbance was the rumble and rust of the postman's truck.

Ari roared an incoherent scream that never gave up strength. He waved his arms; he dragged his mother. They were almost at the mailbox but the truck was going to pass them by with its huddled group of blackened passengers in the back. Somebody saw their figures and rapped on the cab window behind the driver's head. The truck skidded to a halt for a few seconds. Hella scrambled aboard and dragged her suitcase after her. One of the men pulled Ari in.

'Magnus?' one of the men asked.

'We can't find him,' said Hella. 'One minute he was beside us and then he was gone!' She touched her mouth with one filthy hand and blew gently to indicate a genie disappearing from a bottle. The lie left a black mark on her lips.

'It ain't your fault, Ma'am,' said the man and he put a consoling arm around her shoulder.

Hella shuddered sweetly against him. Her face was streaked with black soot; her eyes were red from grit mixed in with crying.

Ari watched her and started an uncontrollable shivering. He thought of all the nights during the preceding week when she had kept him awake with her muttering. He had strained to make out what she was saying and now he knew that it had been a premonition not a dream she was having.

He thought about the thudding he had heard when his mother had raced back into the house. It had not been Magnus's fists pounding on the door; it had been the sound of his mother hammering nails into a board to secure that door shut. Magnus could not have come streaking from the house like a human torch, as Ari had imagined in his fright – his mother had confined that particular human conflagration to a single room.

Ari thought about the words his mother had whispered over and over again in her sleep. Now he knew for certain what she had been saying to herself all those nights, willing it into being: 'Let him burn... Let him burn...'

4

The waiting room of the Midwestern United Farmers' Bank in Little Falls was crowded. The patrons trying to make their way to the tellers' windows had to shuffle past the rows of burned-out families. The men stood with their hats in their hands while their wives tried to slap the smoke from their sons' shirtfronts.

Eventually, Mr McGill – the harassed-looking manager – came out from the glass cube of his office wearing the too-tight spectacles he donned when he wanted to look official. Without any air of real authority, he weakly requested that the women and children move out onto the pavement where ice cream would be provided – as impractical a sop as Hella could imagine.

The manager gave Hella a fierce stare. She didn't budge from her place on the bench when the other wives drifted outside.

'Ma'am?' he asked.

'I'm not moving,' she said and Ari's small, exhausted body went stiff with anxiety beside her. 'I'm here on my own accord. No husband,' she said.

'That's Magnus Glassen's help,' whispered someone.

Feet shuffled in the crowd. Throats were cleared. Hella sat very still. Silence and immobility frightened Americans, she had discovered. They were

48

ill-equipped to deal with any display of patience or inaction. Mr McGill turned his back on the rock of her non-compliance and scurried away.

By noon, everybody was restless. Most had slept under charity at neighbours' farms or on credit in the cheapest rooms in town. Some families had spent the night on park benches or, as Hella and Ari had, on the sidewalk outside the bank. They were dirty, hungry, tired and shocked. The fire had swept across eighteen holdings and blackened over a thousand hectares of grain to char.

Thanks to a campaign five years earlier, all eighteen families were miraculously insured through the same cut-rate company who had sent a slick-talking young Jew round door-to-door to sell them policies covering every eventuality. The premiums had been low enough that most of the farmers had managed to keep them up. If times had been tough over the preceding years, they would have let them lapse – good intentions were prey for hungry mouths – but the last few years had been prosperous. The return to full-focus agriculture after the war partnered by generous government incentives had made farming a good business again. Still, fire was a plague nobody could predict and now all eighteen families, along with sundry domestic hands and itinerant labourers, had arrived at the same bank, looking to make their claims.

It was early afternoon before Mr McGill left to join his chauffeur in his new black Buick and head out towards the town's airstrip to collect a Mr Benjamin Gold – the owner and underwriter of the Minnesota Workmen's Insurance Foundation – and drive him to the bank to face the claimants.

A man carrying a camera stepped from the car when it returned and Mr Gold got out behind him wearing a neat suit. Its pinstripes seemed to hold him erect so that he walked as a perfect vertical. He was not a large man but be had a tall presence and an enormous smile. He might have been mistaken for a jaunty visiting jockey if the racecourse had been open that day. He stepped into the bank with genuine concern on his face but whether that emotion was evoked by the sight of the destitute or whether the abacus in his brain had begun to tally his losses, Hella couldn't tell. She looked over at him from her position on the bench as he passed and they were almost at eye level. Hella admired tall men like Charles Lindbergh. This one looked more like a merry troll from *The Wonderful Adventures of Nils*, which she used to read to Ari in the original Swedish.

The first thing Gold saw among the charcoal and ash was the yellow of her hair and the disdain on her perfect face. Grimy and sweat-stained as she was, he saw her in a jewelled dress – emerald-coloured – with scarlet lipstick and he took in a deep breath.

Which one was her husband? He wondered as Mr McGill led him into his office.

The two men negotiated for less than an hour. Gold was a man of enormous wealth, involved in the funding of the mass production of radiators for the automobile industry in Detroit. His family had always been in banking but he fancied himself as a freer spirit and had decided on automobiles almost from the beginning. The claims in this current case were not arduous in light of the premiums being paid to his enterprise from thirty-five states and Gold was feeling magnanimous, buoyed up by blonde hair. Of course, there had been no real need for him to personally inspect the site of this humdrum disaster but he had heard that the trout fishing near St Cloud was excellent and he had always fancied himself a fly-man.

Gold settled every account generously. Mr McGill was in the euphoria of delight at how easily the whole matter had been handled. He practically burst the arms off his spectacles – such was the rush of blood to his temples.

'And set them all up tonight in a good hotel. They can come in and collect their wired funds in the morning.'

Mr McGill made the extraordinary offer to the men in the lobby and the seventeen caps of the seventeen family heads (Glassen's was conspicuously absent) were doffed towards the glass room where Benjamin Gold still sat. Most of them hadn't stayed in a hotel room before.

Gold held his breath. He wanted to see who went with the honey-haired woman and her boy. The pair did not move. Slowly, after all the questions had been answered, appointments had been made for the next morning and a telephone call had been placed to the hotel to book out nearly two floors of their accommodation, the bank finally cleared of the smell of smoke.

Still, the woman remained, quiet and dirty on the bench but without any sag to her shoulders.

51

The boy slept against her. He was as handsome a boy as Benjamin Gold had ever seen. Long and lean, the way he had yearned to be as a boy. This lad could probably slam a baseball over the neighbourhood fence to the cheer of his friends. Gold had never played baseball himself. He had been forced by his mother to learn the violin but he had quit that as soon as he was allowed to. He had never been an athletic boy; had never even seen a real game of Brooklyn stickball in his life. The woman needed a bath; a tub of sweet-smelling, rose-coloured water and lilac bubbles, and jasmine blooming from a basket on the bathroom window sill. It was the one thing almost every woman fell for – an expensive bath. Gold saw McGill talking softly to her and stood up to go out into the business of the bank.

'Shouldn't you be at the police station, then, Ma'am?' McGill was asking her.

'Why hasn't this young woman been helped, McGill?' Gold interrupted. 'It was my understanding that all the holdings were insured and I've just approved all the claims.'

'Miss Köll isn't a policy holder, Mr Gold,' explained the bank manager. 'She's Mr Glassen's help-maid. He was one of your clients.'

'And where is he?' asked Gold.

The woman named Miss Köll – and the 'Miss' had been clearly enunciated by McGill – looked up at him. She had the purple-blue eyes of a van Gogh iris. Astonishing.

'Is he not here himself?' Gold queried.

'He's dead,' said the woman and her son woke up at the word and pulled away from her – some

52

nightmare had suddenly roused him.

'I was just saying that if she feels he's died in this tragedy,' said McGill, 'she ought to be at the police station.'

'I wondered if there might be any money?' said the woman named Miss Köll but her voice was dull with doubt. There was a suitcase beside her and the boy – these represented the extent of her worldly possessions, Gold imagined – but she had those eyes and who knew what worth might be placed on them? Benjamin Gold valued them rather highly indeed.

'They will find his body on the farm,' said the woman.

'I'll take Miss Köll in your car,' announced Gold. 'If she'll allow. We'll stop at the police station and collect a man on our way out to her farm. I planned to see the wreckage for myself anyway. I've brought a photographer with me to document some of the damage for the firm, too.'

Ari watched his mother offer her pliant hand to the man. Gold reminded Ari of a pair of black patent brogues he had once seen his grandfather wearing – all gloss and shine – like a starling wing.

'You're very kind,' said Hella and she sighed prettily. It was a sound that managed, at the same time, to convey a needy weariness and to deflate her stature and bring it more in line with Mr Gold's own.

'I'll be here in the morning,' said Gold to McGill. 'To supervise the distribution of the funds. Call the hotel again and see if there's a room still spare for Miss Köll and her boy...'

'Ari,' said Hella. 'That's his name.'

'A good Jewish name,' said Benjamin Gold and he rumpled Ari's hair.

'It's Scandinavian,' said Hella coldly. 'It means an eagle in Norse.'

'It means a lion in Yiddish. Both good totems,' said Mr Gold. He was always the conciliator, the oil poured on turbulent water.

'It means an eagle,' said Hella again.

'She's not a policy holder,' inserted a frustrated Mr McGill once more.

Benjamin Gold's smile twinkled.

McGill was almost sure he could see the white paste a dentist had adhered to the man's teeth to cover the stains of age and overindulgence. Nonetheless, they sparkled.

'But she may well be a beneficiary, Mr McGill,' said Gold. 'I'm sure if you look at Mr Glassen's policy again, and more carefully, you'll discover I'm right.'

Ari sat beside his mother on the leather seat of the bank manager's Buick. The photographer sat opposite them with his wooden tripod folded between his knees. Gold had swept into the police station a few minutes before and the chauffeur sat with the engine off but his gloves on the wheel, ready to depart at a moment's notice – such was the pace of business in New York, he imagined.

Ari moved his weight up and down, bouncing on the silent sprung seats.

'Better than a bank bench?' asked his mother.

Ari nodded.

'Well, I suppose if one has to wait anyway then

54

leather is better than wood,' she said.

Gold appeared at the top of the stairs to the station house with two uniformed officers. One of them looked important yet he still walked a step behind the diminutive Jew. Gold hopped into the back of the car and the photographer squashed up to make room for him as if he were a much larger man.

'The good sergeant and his man will follow us,' Gold said and he gave the driver directions to the farm. 'Do you know the place?' he asked, implying that he himself was practically a local. 'Out on 71?'

The driver nodded.

'Yes, Sir,' he said as he pulled the car into the street.

The country road was deserted. Ari watched the vehicle flash past the charred remains of forests as splintered as blast sites.

'Looks like the war,' said Gold.

'You were in the war, Mr Gold?' asked Hella with sudden interest.

'No,' said Gold. 'I'm imagining.'

Hella looked out the window then, too.

'I don't think it's something you can imagine,' she said quietly.

Ari accidentally bumped against her. Why couldn't she sometimes shut up?

'You're right,' said Gold and it was very awkward for the next five minutes.

'It was my heart,' he said suddenly as they came in view of Glassen's postbox. 'They wouldn't have me.'

Now she'll say that was convenient for him,

55

thought Ari. She'll ruin our chance of the hotel with hot water that runs from taps. But Hella didn't say anything; she only nodded. It looked to Ari as if she was belatedly trying to appear sympathetic.

The postbox was a charred twist of tin on a burned wooden spindle; it no longer looked able to support the weight of letters. Hella gazed towards the farmhouse. Its roof was almost gone. The rooms stood open to the sky, still hazy with retained heat.

'You were in the house when you finally decided to run, Ma'am?' asked the older of the two policemen when their car arrived a few seconds later.

'Yes,' said Hella. She looked tired and harassed.

'And Mr Glassen wasn't with you. Then he must have been caught in the barn on the milking sheds. We'll start there.'

'No,' said Hella.

'You weren't in the house?' asked the policeman.

'We were...' Hella held her head in her hand. 'I'm sorry,' she said. 'It's just that it's all so black and different now.'

'I should have taken you straight to the hotel,' said Gold and Ari's heart leapt in his chest. The bath ... store-bought soap that smelled like a herb pot ... white towels he didn't have to fold himself.

'She's really too exhausted, Sergeant,' said Gold.

'Quite alright,' said the senior officer. He had put in a claim a few weeks before on a policy held by the Minnesota Workmen's Insurance Foundation and payment was pending. He was planning on buying a new icebox for his wife with the proceeds... 'We'll just start at the far end and work our way back to the house.'

Doing it this way, it took them almost half an hour to find the body. The remains of the buildings were still smoking and hot to the touch. Pulling away debris in search of a body was dirty work and there was the cooked smell of beef where the cows had been trapped in their stalls. It was not the rich smell of barbecued steak, more like the stench of a blood stew.

Ari watched his mother and pretended to admire the Buick from all angles while they waited. The photographer snapped off a few images with his camera. Hella didn't glance towards the searchers or the house. She didn't wring her hands or scratch or witter away unnecessarily. She coolly answered Mr Gold's endless questions and her blood pumped evenly through her body in time with the metronome ticking of her heart.

The officers' clothes were singed and their hands were swollen with heat by the time they kicked in the front door and entered the farmhouse.

Ari went in after them. Hella followed with Gold holding her arm to help her through the doorway. The photographer was right behind them. Ari saw immediately that the kitchen door had burned through to its jamb. Hella saw him notice it. The extra planks from the pile Magnus had used to shore up the kitchen window were a burned bundle in the hall. There was an exploded jar on the floor. Its lid lay buckled beside a spray of molten glass. The nails it had contained had been transformed into a gnarled tangle of points and heads like a ball of savage string. Ari picked it up. It was still warm with the residual heat of the fire. He put the lump in his pocket; it smouldered there.

The remains of Magnus Glassen were stuck to the kitchen floor like a lump of steaming tallow poured out of a bucket. He lay face down. His hands curved into fists like a fretful infant's. Hella turned away and buried her face in the starched discomfort of Gold's shirtfront. Ari kept looking; he was determined to see it all.

'Dead,' said the sergeant. It was the most ludicrous of expositions.

'He's holding something!' said the junior officer, desperate for intrigue of any kind.

With the sergeant's permission, he pried the death grasp open. In the silence of the kitchen, one of the rigour-stiff fingers snapped with the dry click of a winter twig and the sergeant flinched. Hella clutched Gold closer.

'It's nothing,' said the junior officer, disappointedly. 'Must have been just a reflex.'

He dumped the hand back down; it landed at an obscene angle.

'There's a blanket in the Maria,' he said and his sergeant nodded.

As the man went out, the small cluster of people left in the kitchen tried to look suitably subdued. The sergeant assumed that Glassen must have succumbed to smoke in the final minutes of his life and dropped to the floor, leaving the fire to rage over him, just as he had suggested it would do in the last frantic moments before Hella and

Ari had made their escape. Magnus's arm, singed free of its chambray work shirt, was very white compared to the rest of his body. It was quite unspoiled by fire. The broken index finger pointed straight at Hella where she stood with her back turned. Ari wondered how they could neglect to see that every finger on that hand was bloodied, half the nails were torn out at the quick where Magnus had desperately scrabbled against the door to free himself in his final minutes.

The photographer stepped forward and prepared to raise his flashbulb. Hella swatted his arm and said, 'How could you?'

'For the local rag?' the man implored Gold.

Gold shook his head in irritation and the man stepped back – so there never was a shot of Magnus Glassen's head looking like a hock of boiled ham and no image preserved of the accusing finger, except the one that pointed perpetually in black and white on the front page of Ari Köll's mind.

'I wonder why he ended up here. Why didn't he run with you?' said the sergeant.

To allay any further speculation, Hella suddenly pulled away from Gold and said, 'It was this farm. He was quite incapable of leaving it. He was trapped here by family history and all the old ghosts from the graveyard.'

Nobody could match the drama of that and they stayed quiet until the officer returned with the blanket and the two policemen fashioned a hammock from it with Magnus Glassen's body swinging inside. The dead man's hand was carefully tucked into the shroud and they carried him

59

between them down to the Maria.

Hella and Ari were transported back to town in style in Mr Gold's borrowed car.

They pulled up alongside the Washington Hotel. Mr Gold went in to see if a room had been secured and Hella sat docilely staring at her reflection in the car window. Ari tried to rub the ash trapped in the stitching of his right boot along his left sock. He wondered if there was any of Mr Glassen on him – on his sock or his skin or his sole.

'It's quite funny really...' said Hella. Ari looked up at her. 'You'll be Ari Gold, a golden eagle now ... isn't that supposed to be the symbol of America?'

Ari wasn't quite sure what she meant.

'That's the bald eagle,' he said.

Hella shrugged then suddenly she looked past herself and saw something in the street that made her slap both palms against the car window. She strained to see for a few seconds then yanked the door open. A tall, slim man was crossing the street a block away. He was wearing a cream summer suit and he had light hair.

'It's our pilot, Ari! It's Charles, Charles Lindbergh... Run and catch him. Tell him it's me. Go quickly.'

Her eyes were as large as quartz-stone moons. Ari saw the man's back and wondered if his mother had seen his face; he seemed a long way off to instantly recognize.

'I can't chase after him,' said Hella. 'Not down the street. You have to go!'

Ari leapt from the car; he saw his mother clap

her hands delightedly as he went. She seemed to be trapped. Even with the door open, she would not get out. She preferred to send him on these awkward errands. Ari ran fast. His target was only just stepping up onto the far sidewalk by the time he reached him.

'Sir!' he shouted and then brazenly, 'Charles!'

The man turned round and revealed himself to be a stranger. A nice-looking, handsome man – as tall, as fair, as slim, but not the equal of the man Hella had decided he was.

'Wrong fellow, my young lad,' said the man kindly.

Ari wanted to be sure the man turned enough for his mother to see that it was not the pilot. Otherwise she would forever accuse him of allowing her chancc to slip away.

Ari started back towards the car at a slow walk. There was no need to hurry now. His mother's dream would not be caught today, no matter how fast either of them ran.

Ari examined her face as he got within easy sight of the car. It was a mask of regret and sorrow. A sad contrast to Benjamin Gold's; he came out from the hotel with his smile on high beam.

'They've only got the presidential suite left but never mind. It's the company's pleasure to pay for it after your taxing ordeal this afternoon.'

The photographer, for reasons of his own, snapped the three of them going up the stairs to the reception. Always afterwards, when the images had been developed and delivered, it was this particular photo of that day which Ari remembered.

In the picture, Gold is forging his way through

the hotel doors. He is caught in the precise instant of taking Hella's suitcase from her hand. Ari and Hella had turned as they sensed the photographer lifting his flashbulb and they are both staring directly at the lens. Ari was tired from his run, stooped and dirty, but it was Hella who was most revealed in that celluloid second. Ari thought, whenever he looked at the photograph, that it was the first moment in her life when his mother, at twenty-four, appeared old.

5

New York, 1927

Benjamin Gold, like Solomon Grundy in the nursery rhyme, died on a Saturday. Hella found him in his bed with the sheet stretched tightly across his chest and tucked neatly under each armpit as it always was. Benjamin had slept like this every night of the four years she had known him. He had never, in all that time, disturbed the smooth sweep of linen; such was the tranquillity of his conscience.

Benjamin had been good to Hella and she conjured up memories of him for a few minutes as a kind of regretful consolation – the first fur coat he had given her, black as a wet seal, the Harry Winston brooch in the shape of a ballet shoe – each ribbon lace a thread of pink diamonds – and the mongrel puppy she had chosen from the basket of a street-corner hawker and which the doorman had adopted when it kept piddling on the Turkish rug.

Hella rested her cool cheek against Benjamin's colder one and lay beside his body as she had seldom done during their marriage. There was no swish of heartbeat from inside him, no sound like water moving through an underground cave, only silence and the unremarkable remains of an untroubled soul, which had departed from its body in the night. Hella stroked Benjamin's hands, smiling a little at the ostentatious wedding band he had chosen for himself. The slim, modest ring she had selected clicked against it with a small sound of remorse like the hard carapaces of mated beetles upon parting.

After a few minutes, Hella stood up and swept back the thick blue curtains from the picture window – velvet was vulgar in a bedroom, she had always thought – and took in the extraordinary vista of the Washington Bridge swinging high above the East River. It was a bruised purple March; winter had skulked about the street corners later than usual that year, pulling hats from the heads of unsuspecting pedestrians and heaping meddlesome snow in the doorways. Wan sunlight filtered through the glass without warmth and shone upon the corpse as it had done every morning upon the living man.

It was the last moment of peace Hella was to experience for the next two months and, sensing the turmoil to come, she opened the window and took in a deep, icy breath of taxi smog to sustain her. She thought about the chill mornings of home when the ice had knocked on the door with its skeletal knuckles. She shivered but would not admit to feeling cold, not even to herself.

Hella had come to Benjamin's room on most weekend mornings. Careful not to wake Ari in his bed a few doors away, Hella preferred to visit her husband in the early hours. Often, she sat at his feet among the morning papers and coffee cups to tell him about her plans for the day. Benjamin would listen to her ideas for improving the building's small front garden then tell her she could make a start the following week. He would send her with their driver to an upstate nursery he knew, if she would only remind him. She could make a day of it, he said – take a friend, stop for lunch at a farm, perhaps. The event never materialized, however.

She would tell him she intended to join the stitching circle run by the Swedish Women's League and he would laugh: 'Aren't those the rather sturdy farming sort? Not your type I would have thought, my love.'

And always he would ask her to leave her hair down that day, claiming he could see from his office window when she was coming up the street. That was nonsense, of course – besides hats were very much in fashion that year and the hairstyles were all swept up.

Hella got up and went in her bare feet down the passage of their Sutton Place apartment. She came to where Ari slept at the far end of the house. The boy's room was so remote that the servants' stairs twisted past its furthest wall but Ari had selected it for himself when they had first arrived and there had been no cause to object. Hella was not the kind of mother, she believed, who denied without reason.

Hella knocked softly on her son's door and went in. Ari was instantly wide awake. Like her, he was a morning person, alert and ready to converse sensibly as soon as he had opened his eyes.

'He's died in the night, Ari,' Hella said.

At first, Ari thought she was talking her way through some kind of somnambulant dream – that the ghost of Magnus Glassen had finally walked all the way from St Cloud to Manhattan and found their door. Did ghosts find you out because of scent? Like wolves, could they follow a trail over miles and months? His mother exuded a perfumed vapour behind her wherever she went these days, so that her real mother smell was all but hidden. How had Magnus Glassen's ghost known her?

'Mr Gold's died in his sleep. I don't know how but he's quite still and cold.'

Ari just blinked at her. He thought of poison.

'Should we plan to go now, do you think?' she asked him.

She seemed a little bewildered for all her calm.

'Go where?' he asked her.

'Oh, I don't know. Back home somewhere.'

'You're his wife,' said Ari.

He didn't know what else to say.

'Oh, but not really...' she said.

'Yes, really,' said Ari. 'You renounced your faith and everything!'

'I never had a faith to renounce,' she said.

'But you're always going on about God,' he accused.

'I always had God,' Hella said belligerently and Ari went silent. 'That's not the same thing as faith at all!'

It was impossible to understand her when she was like this. Ari was splashed with momentary guilt when he wondered if he would be allowed to miss school that week. He was almost twelve and had just entered a prestigious preparatory on Long Island which abounded with real Jews, not reluctant blond converts like himself.

Ari wanted their dark eyes and sallow faces, their grasp of Hebrew and all the secrets that set them apart. Ari was the outsider. They called him Harry Cole or Harry Gold and he hated the name – so dull and somehow sleazy like a comic book gumshoe. They had names as bright as burning bushes, holy as tongues of fire: Ezekiel, Elijah, Gabriel. They owned ancient mysteries and laid claim to magic scrolls dug up by goatherd boys like buried treasure. Ari was just the adopted bastard son of one of the more eccentric members of their clan. He was what his mother had made him: the constant outsider. He blamed her.

'I'll call a doctor, I suppose then,' said Hella.

'He'll have to be buried today,' said Ari. 'That's the law.'

'What law?' asked his mother.

'The Jewish law,' said Ari.

'Isn't it Sabbath?' she asked.

Hella had asked this question weekly since meeting Benjamin Gold. She was not stupid; she simply refused to grasp the notion of a day that

66

ran from sundown to sundown when it was obvious that things began at the start of new light, at the moment of rising.

'I'm sure the brothers will help me with that sort of worry,' she said.

Hella had been an instant favourite with Benjamin's three older brothers when she had unexpectedly arrived back with him from his trip to Minnesota. The four Gold boys were all, in their own ways, collectors and Hella was viewed as something of a quaint acquisition – a rare and fragile find to be cared for and pandered to. The brothers doted on Hella; it was their wives who detested her and prevented them from getting to know her better.

'Am I coming to the funeral?' Ari asked her with mock sorrow.

'Were you ever properly fond?' she asked.

'Not really,' said Ari. 'He was kind to us, I suppose.'

His mother looked at him darkly and he knew she thought him ungrateful.

'Yes, he was kind and kindness ought not to be discarded so,' she said. 'It's more enormous than love even, I sometimes think, and that's reason enough to mourn the loss of it from this world. Get on your dark suit.'

Hella went down to the kitchen where she startled the junior maid and the one she called the Friday boy having toast in the scullery. She had asked this pair several times to make use of the rough, casual table that ran along the middle of the kitchen like an enormous butcher's block but they would insist on using the two old upright chairs with missing slats. They wedged them in behind the pantry door which seemed to Hella such an unnecessary discomfort. It struck her suddenly that it was the privacy they were after and then, recognizing the deep blush across the young man's cheeks, that these two were in love.

It was this irrelevant revelation that made her cry. In four years, neither the boy nor the girl had witnessed a tear from Mrs Gold and they both leapt up. They took one of her arms apiece and helped her to sit.

'I believe Mr Gold has passed on in the night,' she explained.

Just then, the housekeeper came in and ascertained the situation in a few short seconds. She made Hella a cup of thick, scalding coffee and placed a call to the brothers who arrived less than fifteen minutes later. Hella was still in her padded argent silk gown and bare feet but she made a fetching sight, curled up like a silver cat on the kitchen chair. The brothers came dressed in black as if they were, as representatives of their nation, perpetually prepared for tragedy.

They tipped their hats to Ari who had come down to see what was happening. He stood in the doorway, as tall as any of the grown men, and Hella thought how beautiful his light was against their darkness – his tousled hair and his perfect boy's face. The eldest of the brothers, Isaac Gold, was a physician and he went up and officially declared his own brother's death.

'He went so peacefully, Mrs Gold. I know you'd appreciate knowing that.'

'I think I would have preferred something of a

fight,' she said.

Ari bumped his hip purposefully against the doorframe. The hinge squealed. He had been waiting for his mother to say something inappropriate and she never failed him.

His three uncles, each in succession like the wise men bestowing gifts, passed him and kissed his golden hair – as if he were a real son. Ari wanted a real father then more intensely than ever before. Even a dead father to mourn would be better than the vacuum he had inherited. He wanted his own real grief to nurture. His mother and the three brothers went into the front room to talk about arrangements.

Ari estimated that Hella was, at that moment, worth about one and a half million dollars. He doubted she would get a cent. Then again, perhaps she knew something of which he was unaware. He thought of poison again.

Ari's main memory of the rest of that day was of pinched feet. The doorman (who had adopted the puppy) had been sent over to Bergdorf Goodman's to bring back a pair of boys' dress shoes since the ones Ari wore to school were considered unsuitable. The man had returned with a stiff, uncompromising pair of Johnston & Murphy brogues and they had rubbed Ari's heels to blisters.

After the service, Hella went up to her room and locked herself in. She stayed there for hours. Ari saw the light from under her door when he went for milk in the night. It left a slash of yellow along the carpet. He paused in the passage and watched the strip of gold. Cold wind blew against his slippers; he could feel it even through their fur lining. His mother had her window open in there. She always flagellated herself with cold. It was a uniquely Swedish form of torture. He would, for years afterwards, associate his mother with those two aspects of that night – a cold, piercing wind and a slice of light.

By the next morning, Hella had abandoned her silent vigil for one of the odd, futile exhibitions of principle she sometimes embraced: she threw her hats out the window.

Hella scoured the house for hatboxes, opening disused closets and the cobwebbed crawlspace under the stairs to find them. Benjamin – who had met her every prodigal whim with the indulgence of a father for a beloved, blameless child – had always objected to expenditure on hats. He had first fallen in love with Hella's hair and hated it to be covered, so she had shopped for hats secretly during her first giddy years of wealth.

Most of the headwear was preposterously unsuitable for any occasion to which the Golds might be invited. There was an enormous yellow ornamentation punctured by silk sunflowers, and a black and white picture hat with a razor ring of porcupine quills piercing its brim, and a raspberry ostrich feather concoction with a gaudy rhinestone buckle.

There must have been three dozen hats in total and Hella threw them all out.

The small garden she had so seriously intended to cultivate each summer was covered in a white swaddling of snow that morning. The bushes were sugar-frosted lollipops and the hedges were long, low walls of shiny icing. The hats landed softly – some upturned, some the right way up. Ari peered down at them. Hella's hats looked like a handful of cheap confectioner's baubles scattered onto the dirty icing of some cake that had sat too long in a wedding baker's window.

There was no sense in trying to stop his mother before she was through. Ari waited patiently. When all the hats were gone – even the ones she had worn publicly several times and of which Benjamin had taciturnly approved – Hella sat down in the middle of the floor like a bony blue Buddha. Her feet were chilblained and had a greyish hue like the pictures of the North Sea in his boys' adventure books.

Ari went over to her. He kicked off his slippers and sat down so that their knees were almost touching. Hella reached out at once and took his right foot in her hands, rubbing it gently to warm it up.

'Sore feet?' she asked, seeing his blisters.

'They're okay.'

'Don't say "okay". Say "perfectly fine" or "very well, thank you".'

'Okay,' he said. She smiled.

'You look cold,' he told her.

'We don't feel the cold. We're Swedish.'

'You don't like hats any more?' he asked.

'I liked best the ones I used to buy myself from the mercantile in St Cloud.'

'You hated St Cloud,' he said, missing the point.

It seemed to Ari that his mother was always

hankering simultaneously after the future and the past. Only the present was neglected – the very place where she had to live was always unbearable.

'I brought you a peace offering,' Ari said.

'Aren't we at peace already?' she asked. 'I thought the war was over years ago.'

It had not been his intention to upset her but she looked wounded.

'It's something for you, not for us,' he said. 'I think you'll like it.'

Ari handed his mother the morning newspaper. He had folded it so that only the story he meant to show her was visible.

The headline read: *Orteig Prize Draws Flying Daredevils.*

Hella began to read it aloud in her well-pronounced English.

The much-hyped prize of $25,000 offered by million-aire hotelier Raymond Orteig to the first man to fly single-handedly across the Atlantic is attracting daring flyers from all four corners of the United States.
Although a transatlantic crossing was completed years ago, several stops were made en route during that flight. Orteig, an aviation enthusiast, is convinced a non-stop flight between North America and Europe will be the next great human achievement and will connect those two continents as never before in the hearts and minds of men. A passenger commute between New York and Paris in less than two days is barely a decade away, Orteig claims.
Although Orteig first offered his generous incentive in 1919, it has never been claimed. This latest attempt by

a handful of brave explorers is scheduled to commence at Roosevelt Field, Long Island on May 18. Spectators eager to see the men safely off are expected to number into the thousands. Among the confirmed entries are Commander Richard E. Byrd, a hero flying ace of the war, Andrew Chamberlin, a barnstormer working for Dixie's Flying Circus in Alabama and the young mail-carrier pilot, Charles Lindbergh from Minnesota...

Hella's voice trailed off.

Ari grinned.

'Do you think it's him?' he asked.

Hella's face was awash with light. She pinched her blue lips together in excitement and the faintest flush of blood, the colour of ash roses, came back into them.

'Of course it's him!' she exclaimed.

'I thought we could go to the start,' said Ari. 'If you see him, he might even remember how we helped him that day.'

'He will remember,' said Hella with finality.

'It's something to look forward to anyway,' Ari said and he took back the paper.

'Don't you scrunch that up!' said Hella.

She snatched the sheets from his hands and smoothed them out with the heel of her palm.

'So, come May, we'll be at Roosevelt Field?' he asked.

Ari was happy again. His mother had undergone some sort of resurrection of the spirit. She seemed to suddenly notice how her hair had straggled down from its comb. She pushed it back behind her ears with embarrassment. She rubbed

73

her palm across the bare skin of her cheeks and realized she wasn't wearing any make-up.

'I need to ask the brothers if we can go,' she said. 'I'll put in a call and see if they'll come round to discuss it.'

Ari wondered at her. Hadn't she just bought her freedom for a second time at great cost?

Hella perused the newspaper once more, flicking it open and scouring the surrounding pages.

'No picture,' she said.

She sounded disappointed.

'Maybe when the time gets closer,' said Ari.

'Yes,' she said. 'Ari, it's your job to check the newspapers every day for these stories. It's a project for us to do together. It's history, is what it is!'

She read the article aloud again from the place where she had paused.

The flyers will make the three-and-a-half-thousand-mile trip between the continental United States and Paris, France in less than forty-eight hours. They will be travelling solo to reduce weight and face imminent danger and possible death at every moment.

That was apparently the end of the article and Hella rested the paper on her knees.

'"The day of a man's death is greater than the day of his being born,"' she quoted quietly to herself.

Ari thought she meant that Lindbergh would die in the attempt but she looked up with wet, sparkling eyes and said to him, 'Wouldn't it be grander, Ari, to see him land?'

6

Paris, 1927

That morning, the headlines of the broadsheets seemed to be printed in ink of a darker black. Ari read them aloud to his mother as they sat in a patisserie enjoying chocolate croissants. When they headed home along the Rue de Rivoli that night, the newspapers seemed to crackle more sharply in the roadside fires of the itinerant fruit pickers. In the makeshift pressroom of the hotel, the journalists smoked up a fog bank as the Reuters wires vibrated with the insistent energy of imminent occurrence.

Charles Lindbergh had braved the sodden dawn of Roosevelt Field, Long Island, the previous morning and gone for glory. In a brief, bright window between storms and mist, his plane – the *Spirit of St Louis* – had trundled onto the runway from the wet grass verge of the airfield and just kept going. After a thousand feet of powering forward, Lindbergh had passed the point of no return. An accumulation of human will had urged the plane on and up – sheer desire providing the first lift beneath the wings.

Lindbergh's *Spirit* had whooshed through puddles, splashing up a hundred tiny rainbows as it went, before its wheels finally left the earth. The plane cleared neighbourhood power lines by only twenty feet then sailed out over the Atlantic. Lindbergh was Columbus with the last of Spain behind him and a blank parchment ahead that would one day be a map of the world.

Perhaps Raymond Orteig's prize, that phenomenal $25,000, had fuelled his daring though several pilots had been lost in the bid to claim it since the hotelier had first made his extraordinary offer in 1919. The French were the latest nation to sacrifice men in the attempt. They were still grieving for Nungesser and Coli who had disappeared without a trace somewhere among the cold Atlantic swells.

Lindbergh had been the only flyer that day to risk the inclement weather and America had another chance at achieving the feat. Their man was the stuff of heroes – all the newspapers acknowledged it. Charles Lindbergh was a pressman's idol. He was a tall, appealing character who photographed well and whose quotes – spoken in modest, Midwestern fashion – transferred easily onto the page and into the hearts of common men.

Hella had kept every clipping she could find about the man. She looked closely at the photographs until the images of Lindbergh's face disassembled into a series of incoherent dots. She cut out, glued and pressed each item in a scrapbook. Like a girl, she coveted the very shape of his name on a page. Then the time had come for Paris...

For a day and a night, as ordinary people shopped in the markets and had their shoes shined and rocked cantankerous babies in the small morning hours, at the back of their dull brains was Charles Lindbergh – all alone on a maiden voyage that would link two continents, once and irrevocably. Ari and Hella had made the trip in the conventional way – by liner. It had taken them nine days but they were ready to greet him.

In the foreign city, Ari had hunted down any hint of the story. It had become a hobby over the preceding months and it made his mother happy. He had never seen her so joyful as when she shopped for clothes for their trip. When they reached Paris, she declared her fashion provincial and shopped for several more days. Ari suspected it was her way of coping with nerves. He twiddled his hair.

Ari asked the concierge of the George V for news every time he passed through the lobby. Was there any word of Charles Lindbergh? Had the wireless mentioned anything?

At last, it was reported that a steamer had spotted the plane a few hundred miles off the Irish coast and the French government ordered all airfields from Cherbourg to Le Bourget to be lit through the night.

After an early dinner, Ari stood at the window of his hotel room and looked out over the higgledy-piggledy chimney pots. His mother's excitement was contagious; several unsuspecting guests in the hotel had caught it. Ari felt a trilling in his blood. He assumed the casual confidence of a matinee idol and practised his swagger in the bathroom mirror.

Lindbergh was above him and Ari's hopes were

attached by invisible strings to the rudder of his plane. Ari raised his hand quietly and touched the smooth pane of the window. Now and again, the glass trembled tenuously against his fingertips and he knew the *Spirit of St Louis* was still aloft; felt deep inside that Lindbergh was alive.

For almost half an hour he stood there, not daring to move. It was a vigil now; he was holding inside his heart a chalice that he dared not spill. Ari watched the slow lava flow of late evening light drain from the rooftops of the opposite buildings. As it seeped away, tiny rays caught the glossy feathers of one distinct, settling pigeon – anointing it alone among all the others with plumage of fire.

It was almost nine o'clock when his mother tapped once on their interconnecting door and crept into his room. She had a rosy glow across both cheeks.

'He's been spotted,' she whispered. 'I think he'll try to reach Le Bourget. Get dressed, we're going.'

She giggled behind her hand – suddenly a child at twenty-eight – and she shone with some fleeting, internal illumination.

When Ari got to her room, an unshaven man in a charcoal sweater was hanging on the doorframe. He had the crimson jacket of the hotel waiters folded over his arm and he checked the corridor nervously and often.

'I've got someone with a stolen car to take us... Hurry,' Hella said and she laughed.

This seemed to upset the man.

'Elle n'est pas volée, Madame Gold!' he said, hurt.

78

'*La voiture appartient à mon oncle de Nice.*'

'Oh, I know,' Hella chided him. 'But let's pretend.'

'*Nous devons partir maintenant.*'

'We're coming,' she said to the waiter. And then to her son, 'You're going to see it, Ari. We're actually going to see it.'

The slowing traffic told them they were near the site. Their driver didn't hesitate, though. He ramped his rusty Citroën up the side of a break-water mound and onto its level summit. They raced along this way for almost a mile, passing a tailback of stalled motorists.

Above them, disoriented by the crazed trail of lights and unable to locate the runway, Lindbergh flew five miles past Le Bourget before turning back.

The Citroën's engine roared as they approached the fan end of the field, down a narrow lane over-grown with grass and grooved by the hooves of a century of cows. They shot through the two rotted planks of a disused gate and right out onto the airfield itself.

There were angry arguments going on beyond the fence. Several cars were bogged down in mud and a crying woman was flailing at a policeman, but they were in.

The *Spirit*'s silver wings caught the glow of ten thousand headlights as they dipped down towards the runway. The waiter from the George V – imagining Le Mans now – gunned along beside the slowing plane. All the way to the end, they raced it. The tailskid bumped the ground a

79

few times before the plane slowed and finally swung round to stop.

There was a moment of silent astonishment before one hundred and fifty thousand people broke through the barrier of gendarmes, flattened the fences and began to run across the field towards the plane.

Ari and Hella leapt out of the car and began to run, too. They had less ground to cover than any of the others and Ari was a good runner. He had his mother by the hand but she couldn't keep up; her heels sank in the mud. After a few seconds, she stopped, breathless, and bent over with a muscle cramp in her side. It was all happening at half-speed like a March of Time newsreel melted in the projector. Ari had a second to see his mother's devastated face – she had never expected a public response like this; she had imagined some kind of intimate reunion. A single strand of her yellow hair had fallen loose and tangled across her right eye.

'Go! Go!' she shouted at him.

Ari wasn't sure if she meant it, then he saw she did. She was smiling. Their hands slipped apart and he saw her wink at him before he had to turn away from her to sprint on.

An exhausted Charles Lindbergh got out of the cockpit to see a swell of cameras and people and shouting all bearing down on him, but a young American boy reached him first. The boy looked oddly familiar in the few seconds they were alone together. He had that indefinable American polish and he was so well nourished and hearty and beaming that the flyer had to grin.

80

To Ari, Lindbergh looked infinitely older than he had before. For a moment, the pilot reached out and supported himself on the boy's shoulder as he hopped down off the wing, knees buckling slightly against the leaden weight of the earth.

'Well flown,' is all Ari could think to say.

Charles Lindbergh took Ari's hand – not shaking it formally but grasping it in both of his own as if only this human connection could convince him that he was alive again.

Ari felt the gravity of those thirty-three and a half hours Lindbergh had spent in solitary hope and something that must have been greatness suddenly rocketed through him – a transfusion of courage. A cold, crackling fire seemed to frost and spark across his palms. The sensation came in a most distinct fashion through the very tips of his fingers where they touched the palm of the other man's hand. Not from the pads of the fingers where the fingerprints are embedded but from the very tops of the fingers themselves – that tender skin, seldom touched, right before the nail hardens away feeling.

Lindbergh wasn't doing it intentionally. The powerful knowing wasn't flowing in the opposite direction either; Ari was certain of that. It was an instantaneous coincidence of chemistry that had imbued the boy with the knowledge and memories of this other, greater man. Yet only the memories of the three thousand miles Lindbergh had been without any other interfering contact.

Suddenly, Lindbergh was pulled away from him once more, lifted onto the shoulders of the crowd who carried him aloft on their hysterical, triumphant tide.

Ari panicked. He didn't think he would find his mother but he knew if he made it back to the Citroën, she would do the same. They had a connection with things like this. His mother called it practicality – their brains just both came up with the simplest and most rational plan – but Ari had always thought of it as a kind of sixth sense, something almost magical they shared.

Behind him, he could hear a ripping sound. The crowd was actually tearing away small pieces of the fabrication from the plane as souvenirs. Ari could see the raised truncheon of a gendarme and then a group of the men were fighting to surround the *Spirit of St Louis* and beat back the masses. As soon as they could, they trundled the aircraft towards a distant hangar that was more like a draughty barn. They would post guards that night, Ari thought, and he was almost sad that he had not managed to grab a piece of history for his mother. Ari could barely see past all the bumping shoulders now. Women's hefty hips and men's bony elbows bashed against him. He caught one more glimpse of Lindbergh being carried away. The man looked distinctly ill at ease like a wreck survivor bobbing on an unreliable raft.

In the darkness, Ari came across a woman's shoe stuck in the mud. He squelched it free. It was crusted with rhinestones of the palest coral – an evening shoe for a lady's left foot. It looked brand new and Ari wondered which socialite had decided to wear it to such a manic event, as if she were attending a premier. He took the shoe with

him to show his mother; they would laugh about
it.

Already, Ari's heart was sinking. He knew it was
not his own heart but his mother's he could sense
inside him. He knew this slowing of excitement,
this dulling, was her pulse superimposed over his
own. He dreaded finding her now; the purpose of
their lives for the past few months was over. She
would come crashing down like a torn kite. Perhaps he could find out about Lindbergh's press
conference. If they were selling tickets, she would
be able to buy their way in with no problem but
they seldom sold tickets to those kind of events
which was precisely what made them so
tantalizing to the rich, Ari knew.

Ari found Hella sitting in the grass surrounded
by the headlights of the Citroën. She had asked
the waiter to switch them on and they scoured a
path for him along the darkened runway. As he
approached, she raised her arm to signal him and
it ripped through the light like a shard of black
lightning. She had not stood up, it seemed, from
the place where she had first stumbled, having
sensed the futility of running after her son. Ari
sat down next to her and put the shoe in her lap.
For a second, she smiled.

'If I ever lose a leg, I will wear it to the opera,'
she said.

They sat like that for a while. The wind came
up and the ragged tatters of their souls flapped
like parachute silk from their chests.

'Did you see him?' she asked.

Ari nodded.

Suddenly, he had an idea.

'You won't believe what he said,' Ari told her.
'He spoke to you?'

Ari grinned and he inflated with happiness at the scheme he had just stumbled upon.

'I was the first one there,' Ari told her. 'He used my shoulder as a rest when he climbed down from the cockpit.'

Hella's hand flew to her mouth, covering a smile.

'No!' she said.

'He shook my hand and said hello. It felt like electricity.'

'No!' said Hella again, even more delighted.

There was no stopping Ari now. His reckless heart controlled him.

'He said, "From the farm near St Cloud!" and he looked just as astonished as you can imagine.'

'He remembered you!' she squealed.

Her voice was hardly even like this. It floated like birdsong through the warm night.

'He remembered us... He said, "How is your mother?"'

'After all those hours near death and so polite,' Hella said.

She clapped her hands the way the Norsemen had done to invoke their thunder god: two loud cracks to Thor that reverberated through the darkness.

'Then he got pulled away,' Ari said.

He was unsure how much more he could realistically make up. Hella looked disappointed and Ari wished he had embroidered further for her sake, but then her face gladdened.

'It's only because it's so busy and crowded,' she

said. 'Next time we'll have coffee. He doesn't even know about the fire...' Hella stood up and tried to brush the grass stains from her skirt.

'Or about Mr Glassen,' said Ari.

His mother's eyes looked coldly at him. She always seemed surprised when he mentioned the man's name as if she expected her son to have forgotten it by now.

'What does that mean, Ari?' she said. Her tone held a warning.

'Nothing,' he said.

'You're so odd about that man,' she said and then she went down on her knees in front of him. She was tall but her eyes were well below the level of his own.

'Do you still think about his body? Is that why you always talk about him and use his name to me?'

These questions were more like building blocks to construct a lie.

'No,' said Ari.

'Good,' said Hella. 'Because if you find yourself worrying about it often, there are places we can send you where a doctor will listen.'

Ari shook his head. He knew the kind of doctors she meant.

'We'll tell Mr Lindbergh everything when things calm down. Now is not the time.'

'Are we going back to the hotel?' Ari asked.

'No; there's a little farm just across the field. Our driver's gone to see if we can take a room.'

7

It took Hella a few moments to wake Ari the next day. It was unlike him to be so sluggish. She shook him softly, rocking his small form back and forward so that it rolled on the coarse sheets like a small boat at sea. When his eyes opened into hers, they looked fearful.

She sat back, suddenly afraid, too – terrified by her son's naked unhappiness. They had shared a bed in the small cottage, something they had not done since their days on Glassen's farm, and the smell of Ari's body – his hair like warm grass and the dusty boy-smell of his shoulders – had made Hella happy. Whenever he slept, he was little again; only when be woke did he retrieve all the animosities and accusations of a full-grown man.

'What's wrong?' Hella asked. 'Are you sick?'

Ari's expression softened.

'Bad dream,' he said.

'I thought you had left that nonsense in the cradle,' said Hella.

She got up quickly and went over to the wash-stand. The eaves of the farmhouse sloped so alarmingly that she had to crouch to reach the bowl. She had rinsed out Ari's shirt the night before and hung it under the window sill to dry, ready for the morning.

'This house has a mad roof like the farms in Dalarna,' she said. 'They're built right into the hills so the goats can jump onto the shingles and eat the winter moss. When you see it, Ari, you'll think it's a scene from a children's picture book. Goats eating the tops off little cottages like ginger houses.'

'Gingerbread houses,' said Ari.

'Gingerbread houses,' said Hella, contritely.

Ari liked it when she let him correct her just as she corrected him. It implied they were equals.

'Gingerbread houses,' Hella said again.

It was an act of contrition, this generosity, or a sign of gratitude that Ari's nightmare had not been about Glassen. In truth, it hadn't been. It had been about a man with small round spectacles and a mouth as wide as an oven, wide enough to swallow a small boy – just like in the Grimm Brothers' fairy-tale. His mother had been speaking about gingerbread houses and Ari had been imagining a man with a mouth like an oven who swallowed up children like Hansel and Gretel's witch – how had they both been imagining the same story at the same time?

'I washed your shirt. It's a bit cleaner than yesterday,' Hella said. 'I didn't really want to wash out all the grass marks. It's a historic stain this. Perhaps you'd like to keep it like this as a souvenir of Le Bourget?'

Ari's hand stole to his chest; his sternum bone ached. There was a brown bruise the size of a man's fist right in the centre of his ribcage. He put his palm over it to hide it from his mother and sat up.

He watched Hella go about her morning tasks. She had slept in her petticoat but Ari could hardly tell. Her underwear was nicer than most women's dresses, he often thought. Hella pulled her yellow hair back and tied it into a knot. Despite her brutal treatment of it, it shone on stubbornly; it always grew strong and thick, no matter how poorly she treated it. Hella splashed some cold water onto her face. A drizzle of it ran down her back and darkened the light blue lace near the strap. She was beautiful. Without knowing a man's desire, Ari knew that. Whenever there was a book where the heroine was strong and virtuous, she was always drawn in this way – that was based on looks alone, of course. It did not take into account the capriciousness of Viking blood.

'Will he be on the radio, do you think?' Hella asked. 'Will they say where he slept last night?'

'With the American ambassador,' said Ari, without thinking, 'in Paris.'

'How would you know that?' Hella said, turning around.

Ari shrugged, buying time to establish a lie that might work.

'You've been down in the night and seen the morning paper!' Hella accused with a grin.

Ari shook his head.

'I'm only guessing,' he said. 'I don't really know.'

'An odd guess for a little boy,' said Hella then she went back to inspecting her teeth in the speckled shaving mirror.

Ari thought his mother looked more at home in this tiny room than in the New York apartment of the late Benjamin Gold. There, she was constantly fretting about things that didn't seem to matter. She studied menu cards from the cook when there were only ever two of them at the table. She bought three different garnishing sets from Bloomingdale's department store, then said the tomato roses cook made using them didn't look real. She constantly rearranged the tiny ornamental soaps in the crystal bowl of the guest bathroom. Here, she had a shirt to wash and no space to move in and she stepped over the clutter like a dancer practising steps from a ballet.

Ari missed her so desperately he thought he was going to cry. Not her, the mother he had always known, but the girl he knew she must have once been, the light which must have flashed from her hair when the sun was out.

The waiter who had driven them out to Le Bourget had spent the night in the barn. He looked cold and his chin was stubbled with a coarse growth of beard. He waited for them beside his car. Ari saw his mother press franc bills into the farmer's hand and into the hand of the farmer's wife who spoke no English. The woman bobbed a curtsey as if they were royalty.

Ari had seen, as they were presented with plates of eggs and rashers of bacon as thick as toasted crumpets, that the house only had one room downstairs. The farmer and his wife had slept on the kitchen floor while he and his mother had taken their bed. They imagined his mother finer than themselves because of her hair and the fox fur she had slung across her shoulders and round her neck like a flaming noose.

They had eaten in silence. Hella had managed an egg but scooped the bacon onto Ari's plate. Ari hadn't eaten bacon for years. It tasted stronger and saltier than he remembered. Ever since their time on Glassen's farm, Hella had despised bacon. Perhaps it was because Glassen had reminded them both so much of a hog with his fat pink belly and his thick hair like fibrous roots growing from every stretch of skin. Benjamin Gold had thought of Hella's disdain for bacon as a commitment to her conversion; he hadn't known her very well. Ari looked about the modest kitchen. It was not so long ago, he reflected, that they had been working in a farmhouse like this.

They squashed into the car and the waiter, eager to get back to Paris and enjoy some proper sleep before his shift, began to reverse. As they backed slowly out of the narrow area behind the house, the bumper hitched on something. The car was hung up for a moment; its near wheel rotated in the soft earth. Mud flew out from the spinning tyres and sprayed across a neatly tended area of lawn beyond the fence.

The farmer came roaring from the house, waving his arms and yelling. The waiter stuck his head out the window and there was a heated exchange. After a few minutes of angry shouting, fuelled by the waiter's exhaustion and some incoherent rage on the part of the farmer, they managed to change down a gear and pull gently free.

The waiter crossed himself and looked close to tears as they drove off.

'What's happened?' asked Hella.

The waiter tried to explain in his broken English, 'It is the grave of his son, a boy lost on the Somme. No body inside it but a place where they pretend he is having his rest.'

Hella turned round and watched the scene as it faded behind them. Their tyre had uprooted some vivid flower, a wild poppy perhaps, from the edge of the burial mound and the farmer was holding it in his hand.

'Why doesn't he plant it again?' Ari asked. His voice was quite shrill. 'Why doesn't he plant it again? It'll grow if he puts it back.'

Hella faced forward again, determinedly.

'Sometimes they don't,' she said. 'I expect the farmer knows his plants well enough.'

Later, unexpectedly, she touched the driver's arm with her glove.

'Ari's father died in the war. I'm sorry about the grave.'

The waiter took his eyes off the country road and its tangles of untended hedges.

'He was for France?'

'Yes, he was for France. He was for England, mainly, I suppose. He believed very much in the ideals of freedom.'

The waiter nodded.

'I have the bear feet,' he said regretfully.

'Bare feet?' said Hella.

'L'ours...' he said and he made claws from his hands and roared with uncanny realism.

'Oh, bear feet.'

'Yes, you know, very straight.'

'You have flat feet?' said Hella and he nodded.

'You could hardly have been old enough any-way,' she said. 'All you men regret the fact that you missed out on mud and blood and pain. Honestly, it's the ultimate masochism. Besides, there'll be another war along shortly. There always is.'

'Never more. Germany is over,' he said. 'No army, no navy. Thank Versailles!'

'Eventually that will have to change,' said Hella. 'They'll have to be allowed a navy. They have ports.'

'I lost my brother,' admitted the driver. 'He was a sailor, looking after the convoys, you know? They were torpedoed out of the water. He drowned or burned on the sea. Germany will never sail again if France can still speak.'

Later, as they got out of the car and went up to the grand doors of the George V, Ari stopped his mother by clasping her arm. He had been waiting for the right moment to ask and the right moment was usually when his mother was caught off guard and so undefended.

'Was that true about my father... He believed in the ideals of freedom?'

'No,' Hella said, as if he were calling her to task over an irrelevance. 'But it gave the man comfort, didn't you see that? Why do you always begrudge other people their small comforts, Ari?'

One last incident passed in Paris before they left. It happened on the last morning just as one of the chambermaids was packing Hella's new dresses in tissue. They were called down to the lobby and asked to accompany a policeman round to the side alley of the hotel. The arrival of the policeman had caused quite a stir and the hotel manager was full of apologies and scrapings which

Hella swished aside with her hand. She was a practical woman, she said, and only needed to be told what had caused all the concern.

Somebody had thrown a brick through the window of the waiter's car – or the car of his uncle from Nice, as he had claimed. There was a small stack of cobbles abandoned by a road repair crew in the doorway of the hotel's utility entrance and it was easy to see that this was the source of the projectile, which lay on the back seat of the car amid a shower of glass.

Nothing had been taken from the car (nothing of value had been stored inside it) and there had been no attempt made to damage the interior or make away with the vehicle itself. The crime was recorded in the notebook of the attending gendarme as an act of senseless vandalism, spurned on, he believed, by the hysteria over Lindbergh's arrival. He tut-tutted in a peculiarly blasé French manner and spat on the pavement.

Hella gave Ari a suspicious look and he stared back at her unflinchingly. They were staying in a proper hotel where people came and went and the lobby was never free of several members of staff. Here, if Ari had snuck out of bed somebody would surely have seen him.

'Did you see anything happen with this car?' she asked.

'No,' said Ari.

He kept his secret cradled to his chest like a match flame in a breeze.

'We know nothing whatsoever,' said Hella but Ari noticed that she had brought her purse down with her. To secure it from the maid's curiosity or because of her belief that cash solved most dilemmas?

'This man was kind enough to drive us all the way to Le Bourget yesterday,' said Hella. 'To see Mr Lindbergh land.'

'*L'Américain!*' exclaimed the policeman.

He understood English well enough, it seemed.

'And I feel oddly responsible for this unexpected damage to his vehicle by some manner of hooligan boy, no doubt.'

Hella opened her purse and angled it towards the policeman so he could see the neat edges of the bills. Surely she wouldn't try to bribe a policeman, Ari thought. Not when she knew she was innocent of any crime...

Hella handed the waiter a month's wages – more than enough to repair his car – and then she blithely handed the same amount to the policeman who touched the visor of his cap with his baton and turned away without a word, wishing all transgressions could be tidied away so neatly.

Even the hotel manager stood expectantly by but Hella snapped her purse shut under his nose.

'Are you coming up to carry my bag?' she asked him.

'Of course, Madam. Are you leaving us today for New York?' he enquired as they walked.

'No, we're going to Sweden before we make our way home. My father has passed away.'

8

Stockholm, 1927

The news of his grandfather's death hit Ari hard. He followed his mother onto the various trains and ferries they took to Stockholm in a kind of daze. He hardly ever thought about his grandparents but the idea of losing them saddened him somehow. His mother had stressed their solitary partnership so strongly and so often that Ari had always felt alone in the world except for her. He resented Hella for isolating him from his only remaining family until it was too late to know them properly. He had always held a small desire that through his grandfather he might learn something of his father. The old man might have some stories to tell him of how Hella had met her lover.

He was also disconcerted by how the news had slipped past him. He must be less adroit at judging his mother's moods than he imagined. Either he was unobservant or the telegram telling Hella of her father's passing must have been greeted with subdued emotion. Ari had not even noticed the day it had arrived. Thinking back, he could not pinpoint any one date when his mother had appeared sorrowful or distressed. Apart from her rather elaborate but brief mourning period for Benjamin Gold, she had entertained surprisingly few emotional outbursts. There had been only the excitement of seeing Charles Lindbergh again and talk about their trip to Paris.

Ari ruminated over all this as their ferry moved across the water from Copenhagen to Malmö. As the Swedish coastline came into view, Ari had hoped he might feel an overwhelming sense of belonging, or homecoming, that would be so strong he would decide to stay on with his grandmother. This would be the ultimate slight against his mother. He tried to remember his grandmother properly but could not. Perhaps she would be small and round and comforting. She would bake biscuits and do his sums with him in the kitchen while she cooked dinner. He couldn't imagine her that way, though. If she had produced his fierce, formidable mother, she must be another kind of woman entirely.

Ari left the shelter of the cabin and stood against the ferry railings in the wind. He watched the dark landmass approach, growing greener and rockier as it came. He felt nothing. No connection to the place. It scared him. If this was his home, the source of his true nature, it was forbidding. On a summer's day, his mother had assured him, Malmö was a popular coastal retreat for Swedish families. There would be donkeys on the beach selling baskets full of *polkagris* – a kind of peppermint candy cane Ari vaguely remembered from his childhood. But it was a low grey day, too early in the season for many visitors and those who had arrived early had kept to their hotel rooms. Ari wondered if he would ever find his own place, his home. The cold gripped him. The salty air stung his face and splashes from the bow-wave dampened his shoes.

'We'll get you boots,' said Hella, as she came up beside him. 'You need boots here to feel comfortable.'

She was wrapped in a fur coat and looked like a Russian princess with her bunches of honey-blonde hair propped up on her sable collar.

'One more train and we'll be there.'

'Does my grandmother know we're coming?' asked Ari.

He deliberately called the stranger 'my grandmother', implying an intimacy with the woman he had obviously never experienced. He was trying to exclude his mother.

'She knows I'll come,' said Hella enigmatically. 'His death is the only thing I would come back for. Besides, we were so close by, in Paris; it seems cruel to ignore his going without even the excuse of distance. I'd like to say goodbye to the old man.'

'Did you love him?' asked Ari.

'You ask the strangest questions for a boy,' said Hella and she smiled. 'You're really quite odd in a way, Ari. Some bohemian girl who likes over-wrought emotion will have to take you on, I expect.'

'Having feelings isn't the same as being over-wrought,' said Ari.

'No, you're right and I quite like it in you. Don't think I don't.'

'Then answer my questions,' said Ari.

He meant all the questions he had asked her over the years about his father, all the desperate pleas his mother had ignored when he had so needed to know more, to feel as if he were the result of something that had been meaningful and that he wasn't just a lost soul in some foreign city with no lodging booked for the night and the streetlights being switched off slowly, one by one.

'I did love him. Of course I did!'

Ari's heart lunched. Then he realized she was speaking about her father, not his.

'My father was gentle and kind and contented. It was my mother who browbeat him and nagged him for happiness. He tried so hard to give it to her. He never realized she couldn't be happy. She was incapable of it. She's that sort of woman. He retreated into his own vices as a way of dealing with his disappointment, I think. It's so terrible never to be able to live up to someone's expectations, to be constantly disappointing them.'

'I know,' said Ari.

It was his chance to tell his mother that she made him feel that way. He tried to form the words but a large wave splashed the deck and they had to jump back to avoid being soaked. The moment of opportunity had passed.

'We've missed his funeral, of course. That was over a month ago now. I'm just coming to pay my respects and then we're leaving again.'

'Why didn't you tell me he had died, if you've known for a month?'

'I didn't want to ruin your trip. You seemed so excited about the possibility of seeing Mr Lindbergh again and I try not to hurt you unnecessarily,' said Hella. 'It's a kindness not to always ruin things for people.'

'I don't mean to ruin things,' said Ari but his mother wasn't listening.

She was looking over the water towards her home country and reminiscing.

'I think I loved my father best in the summer,' said Hella. 'So many Swedes have summer homes, Ari. It's not an unusual thing like it is in America. Not just for the very rich. We had a summer cottage on the shores of Lake Mälaren, just twenty minutes' walk from Mariefred but completely isolated on its own little bay. In those days, you had to take the coal steamer out to the skerries, there was no train, and you passed all the medieval castles looking down at you as though they were going to swallow you up. Then the town would come into view around a bend – all the red wood cottages with their yellow doors and the flocks of blue bicycles floating along the lakefront paths like low-flying cranes. We had a herb garden there and we used to stuff the fish we caught with lemon slices and handfuls of wild dill. You wrap it in a tin package and poach it over a wood fire. My mother never cooked, only my father, and often we would go to the Mariefred cottage alone when mother said she felt too ill to travel. We had bicycles there and a boat. My father loved boats. That's the one thing the Americans don't know about the Swedes – we're boating people, still Vikings at heart, and we'd rather be in a hammock swaying than in a stagnant bed.

'When I was a child, my favourite thing to do was to make candles as gifts for my father. We had an old-fashioned mould at the cottage in Marie-fred and I would ask Mr Karlsson from the neigh-

99

bouring farm for a few drops of creosote to add to the wax. That way as it burns down it smells like a freshly varnished boat hull. We used to sleep by the fire and burn the candles and imagine we were in a boat, lost at sea, and heading together who knows where. That's when I remember loving him most.'

'Could we go?' asked Ari.

'To the cottage?'

'Yes, just for a day.'

'I suppose we could, if it's still there. I don't know if my father kept it up after I left,' said Hella. Her voice sounded regretful. It was a tone Ari was not familiar with.

'Did I ever tell you your father wanted to build boats?' she said, as if they spoke of her lover often and this might just be one fact she had neglected to mention.

'You've never told me anything about him,' said Ari.

'Nonsense,' said Hella and she made a small clicking sound of pique with her tongue. 'Yes, he came to Sweden to learn about boats because he was a very good carpenter or wood turner or something. He had a fancy to make these beautiful handcrafted boats with totally new shapes for the Henley set. That's what he wanted to do – design and build boats by hand. I should have known what a dreamer he was when he said that. Every man in Sweden imagines a career surrounded by boats but unless you fish with a whole modern fleet, you just can't do it.' She sighed. 'You have to have a real job these days.'

Ari wanted to ask his mother what her job was

but she was a woman. It seemed obvious to him that she had always made a living out of being beautiful and cold to men.

Hella stopped talking abruptly.

'No doubt your grandmother will tell you all about your father,' said Hella resignedly and Ari began to wonder if this was the real reason for their visit to Stockholm: to absolve his mother of having to tell him the dreadful story of his paternity for herself.

'I need a hot cup of coffee,' she said. 'Come inside and stir ten spoonfuls of sugar into some black molasses,' she said.

Hella drifted away from the rail. Ari remained. Ahead, Sweden and the past came more clearly into view. He could see now the small red fishing shacks dotting the harbour entrance. They looked very resilient and hopeful against their dark green forests full of trolls.

They arrived at the house on Strandvägen just as it was getting dark. The riders were heading back to their stables after a Sunday afternoon out in the parks. Their steaming horses trotted along the middle of the car lanes and the taxi they were travelling in slowed to accommodate their passing.

Hella clapped her hands together. The suede gloves she wore muffled the sound.

'I had forgotten about the horses!' she cried. 'Oh, Ari, how could I have forgotten this is a city of horses?'

Ari could only see the steaming flanks of the mounts and the legs of the long, sleek men in

101

their shining black boots as the thoroughbreds passed their taxi window and mingled with the regular traffic. The Stockholm riding schools weren't going to give up their right of way to the buses and the automobiles.

'Do you recognize the sign?' asked Hella, pointing at a road marker in Swedish.

'No,' said Ari. 'I don't remember any of it.'

'Just as well,' said Hella. 'It's not home any more.'

'Where is home?' asked Ari. 'Mr Gold's apartment?'

'No, I'm still looking for it,' said Hella. 'For both of us.'

They passed the rows of formally planted trees that were juicy with lime-coloured buds. They passed the facades of the posh embassy buildings with their flags fluttering into the street.

'My father always wanted to live in the old town, in Gamla Stan, where the houses are like little crippled men all leaning up against one another,' said Hella.

She looked out the back window of the taxi but her view of the island of which she spoke was blocked by the masts of boats and the hump of Skeppsholmen rising up out of the green waterway. Up ahead was the bridge over to another of Stockholm's fourteen composite islands – Djurgården – which was made up of dozens of parks, both manicured and wild. This was the island from which the migrating deer sometimes swam over to Östermalm and got their hooves tangled in the lines from the boats. Sometimes their frantic kicking alerted the quaymaster and he did his best to free them. More often they drowned in the small hours of the night from exhaustion and their bloated bodies had to be fished out of the drink and buried in some remote corner of a public cemetery. Because of this habit, every now and then the city gravediggers would hit antlers with their spades. The deer corpses would be pulled from the ground and burned on a fire. It was lucky to have a deer in your grave before your coffin was interred, Hella explained to Ari, and usually the news was passed on to the deceased's family.

The street seemed to run forever along the waterfront but eventually their taxi pulled up outside a building and Hella asked the driver to carry their trunks inside. They had been followed from the train station by a luggage truck and the driver of that vehicle would need assistance. Ari stood on the sidewalk while his mother organized the bags. The houses here, like the people, seemed taller and thinner than in New York. They were all capped with verdigris spires or turrets which made them appear even grander and somehow wiser than American buildings. Ari thought it was probably their age but even the newer ones had a fairy-tale appearance.

Just across the road from where they had stopped, the park ran along the waterfront as far as the eye could see. The riverside lights were coming on up and down the road. Ari noted how elaborate they were – just like deer antlers with glowing, golden orbs atop each spike. They were painted green and looked quite magical compared to the wooden – or more recently, concrete

– posts of Manhattan. The park was broken every now and then by flights of white stairs which ran down to the dozens of marinas that serviced the citizens of Östermalm. The lights caught the sails of the evening pleasure craft as they prepared to go out. It was cold and clean and Ari felt happily tired and more than ready for the haven of a bed.

The front door of the house opened quietly and an elegant lady came through the front door and to the gate.

Hella hissed something at Ari before the woman could reach them. It sounded like: 'Remember, she's poison!' but Ari couldn't be sure of the words. The woman was clearly old enough to be his grandmother. She wore navy blue so that she seemed like a harbinger of the impending night. There was a small stretch of lace at her wizened throat that broke the colour of the dress and emphasized her pallor. Her skin was fine and smooth like ricepaper, almost transparent, and Ari imagined he could see blue blood pumping through the veins in her forehead and hands. Once, she must have had the natural strawberries and cream complexion of the Englishwoman but now she used a rouge that stained her cheeks into two startling apples, giving her the appearance of a clownish cadaver.

'Mama,' said Hella.

The woman did not acknowledge the greeting on the arrival.

'Is this my grandson?' she asked in a tremulous English voice.

'It is. He's twelve now.'

'He looks just like me,' said the woman.

'He's got a bit of all of us,' said Hella and she passed her mother and went into the house. In Sweden business was never conducted in the street; even fond farewells were completed in the front room before the door was opened to the passing traffic.

The dinner that night was an unexpectedly formal affair. Ari would have preferred cheese and bread or an apple in the kitchen but he was made to dress in a suit and brilliantine his hair, which he hated. The three of them sat squashed up around one end of an enormous table in a long hall. There were four courses served by an old family retainer who seemed older than his grandmother by a generation and who doddered in and out with an annoying dragging of his soft slippered feet. The table was set with silver and a pewter urn. Ari recognized the goldfish swimming along the side of the enormous salver and caught his grandmother's eye.

'Does your mother still have the caviar bowl?' said the old lady.

She smiled and her teeth, which must be dentures, were white as snow – not suitably aged for a woman of her years but as uniform and slippery as tiger teeth.

'She took it when she left us. I haven't had a complete set since.'

The old woman laughed a high girlish giggle. Ari felt uncomfortable at the way most of the conversation was being directed at him as if his mother wasn't present.

'She knows how an incomplete set drives me

crazy,' Eleanor Köll continued. 'I think that's why she did it. Even with the cupboard closed, that empty place where the caviar bowl should be calls out to me so that I can't sleep at night. You knew that, didn't you Hella?'

'I took the bowl because it was the only thing I thought beautiful in the whole house and because father used to like it so. It was a reminder. I didn't think he'd mind.'

'A reminder of what, my dear?' said the old woman.

'Of father.'

'You'll need it now more than ever, then. There's no chance of seeing him again. I got him a lovely patch in the cemetery on Kungsholmen. Will you visit your grandfather's grave?' she asked Ari.

He looked over at his mother but she was busy with a plate of *kotbullar*, dipping each meatball generously into loganberry jam before eating it.

'I think we aim to,' said Ari.

'My word!' exclaimed his grandmother. 'You've raised him as a real little Yank.' Then, to return the conversation immediately back to herself, 'Promise me when I go you'll inter me in Barbados, Hella. There's a cemetery there at the top of a hill right in the middle of a mango grove. The fruits plop down onto the graves and when they sell them in the market they always tell you they're cemetery fruit. It makes them more expensive and you feel quite guilty eating them but they do taste more delicious.'

'Don't you think next to father would be more appropriate?'

'I always dreamed of being buried in that mango orchard. Ari, promise me you'll try.'

'I'll try, Grandma,' said Ari, though the notion of manoeuvring the old woman's body across the ocean and up a hill to a mango orchard was fraught with complications.

'You'd better arrange it with your lawyer, Mama,' said Hella. 'It's not practical to ask Ari and me to take care of that. We're on the other side of the world.'

'But I had my heart set on Barbados and the mangoes,' said the old woman.

Ari was still struggling with the logistics of the hillside cemetery. How would he get the body up there? He might have to borrow a handcart or a wheelbarrow and push her ... it was almost comical to contemplate and he tried to suppress a smile.

'You're so ridiculous even a twelve-year-old boy can see it!' said Hella and she slammed her glass onto the tabletop.

'Can't we just have one nice dinner?' said her mother. 'When I can reminisce and you'll allow it?'

Hella sat back in her chair and Ari could see that she was trying. Her mother leaned over and touched her hand.

'He forgave you right away for leaving,' she said, 'I want you to believe that, Hella. He knew you had to go and when I explained that you needed your freedom, that you felt smothered here with such an old man for a father, he did try to understand. He would have preferred more frequent letters, of course, but...'

So his mother had written to her parents after they had left Sweden. Ari would have given anything to read that correspondence. He wanted to see how she had described their life, Glassen, the drudgery of the farm, their salvation through Mr Gold.

'He understood that you were young and impetuous and that America with its more modern ways would have made life easier on Ari. Society would perhaps even have acknowledged him fully...'

'That's enough, Mama,' said Hella. 'Nobody ever had a problem acknowledging Ari except you.'

'I don't mean anything by it. I always loved you, Ari,' said his grandmother. 'But your mother was so wilful and headstrong even as a child. She was flighty. She never settled to anything. She always wanted to be off at the cottage or running wild and her father indulged her. He took her on these crazed flights of fancy. Off on boats to who knows where, into the wilderness of the countryside where there wasn't so much as a light bulb or a wireless.'

'He did it to get away from you,' said Hella, finally standing up. 'And now he's succeeded.'

She tossed her napkin on top of a puddle of gravy on her plate and went out.

'I'm going up to wash,' she shouted. 'Didn't you think we might be exhausted and wanting to rest rather than enduring a fancy dinner on the first night?'

Ari thought he could see tears in his mother's eyes – but whether of regret or exhausted fury, he couldn't say. Hella went up the stairs and Ari thought he had never seen her look so tired. Bitterness stooped the shoulders, he reckoned. It stooped the shoulders and it stunted the heart.

'I never could do anything right when it came to her, Ari.'

'She says the same about you,' he answered bravely.

He didn't know if he should follow his mother or take the opportunity to speak about his father.

'We always thought you a blessing,' said his grandmother. 'We never minded, once you were born, that some dreadful cad had taken advantage of your mother.'

She suddenly seemed to realize that she was speaking to a young boy.

'Well, never mind that. He was a very nice boy at first. We all thought so and your mother was very taken with him but he wasn't her sort... A dreamer and a bit of a charlatan but not in a nasty, malicious way. Just wayward and wild and not set on a good career the way we would have wanted for her. So, we discouraged it and he left to return to England and, of course, the war claimed him as it did so many. Your mother must have told you the telegram came here.'

Ari shook his head. His fork was halfway to his mouth and he didn't want to move it further in case the gesture stopped her talking. She was quite like his mother in this regard. Hella would get a faraway look in her eyes and she would talk for hours unless something slight, a movement or a gust of wind ruffling the curtain, brought her to a stop.

'Your grandfather and I said you and Hella could both stay with us for as long as you needed. You'd be provided for and I knew you'd be a comfort to us in our old age. We were glad to know we'd be cared for and Hella would have you as a companion and all the benefits of this house as long as she was willing to have us here and care for us. Marriage was out of the question, of course, but she could have made a life for herself with the church and the city charities. It was all worked out for the best but then she just went off. So irresponsible, Ari. I hope you can see that in her. She's not to be trusted. Not where reliability is concerned, she's not.'

Just then Hella came stalking back through the door. She was in a gown without slippers and her wet hair was tangled down her back. She came round the table in a whirlwind and put both hands possessively on Ari's shoulders. He was halfway through a spoonful of burnt custard and it fell onto the white tablecloth as she pulled him up.

'Come, Ari,' said Hella.

She had realized her mistake in leaving him in her mother's care for any length of time and had pulled him away the way she might have snatched his hand from a hot stove when he was a toddler.

'Was my father wild?' asked Ari as they went up the stairs at a run.

'Did she say that?' asked Hella.

Ari nodded.

'Well, she got that right, at least. He was wild ... and beautiful. So be proud,' she said.

9

The next morning, they woke early and went downstairs to the kitchen. There was a young maid in the scullery and she was sharing a pot of coffee with the ancient manservant. Unlike the flaxen Swedes, this girl was small and dark with a square jaw and the kind of thick glowering brows that almost met in the centre of her forehead.

Hella addressed her in Swedish but she answered in English.

'I am Birgit,' she said.

Her voice was very loud in the echoing kitchen and she didn't lower her eyes as she spoke. She obviously felt she was in the right on some issue concerning the house.

'My mother took you on?' asked Hella.

'Yes,' said Birgit. 'She has been lonely since her husband died. She wanted a woman about the place.'

'Then you're new and you don't know me,' said Hella. 'I'm the new owner of this house and my mother is staying here under my grace. I'm not even sure she requires the help of a maid but I'm here to assess her needs and see what's fair and comfortable.'

Birgit's eyes flashed. She bobbed a reluctant curtsey and Hella said to her, 'We'll just take sandwiches this morning and some roast chicken if there is any. We're going to go out to Mariefred.

Is the cottage still there, do you know?'

There was some shuffling of feet and a bit of confusion. Birgit spoke to the old gentleman in Swedish and Hella chimed in occasionally. The three of them conversed for several minutes. Ari couldn't understand what was being said but he gauged that the cottage was still theirs and available to visit.

'Is there *fruktsoppa?*' asked Hella casually swinging the door of the icebox open and looking for the sweet, chilled fruit soup.

'The cherries aren't good yet,' said Birgit. 'And the apricots are too expensive now.'

Hella left the door of the icebox open as she drifted away. Birgit came up behind her and slammed it shut to keep the cold in. Ari saw his mother's lips curl up at the side in a smirk.

'Just a few pancakes, then, and butter and preserve. Wrap everything for me and put it all in a basket. We'll take it with us.'

'Madam is in the dining room with the breakfast. We came in early specially to cook for you,' said Birgit quite petulantly.

'You've wasted your trip, then,' said Hella, 'and a lot of food. Just what I asked for please in a basket small enough to carry.'

Just then, the milkman came to the area gate and whistled for Birgit. Ari looked out through the kitchen garden to the service alley. There was a huge dog beside the man; it was so large Ari had thought at first it was a pony. It was harnessed to a cart and was delivering the milk and cream from Stockholm's nearest farms.

'They still use the dog?' said Hella. 'How quaint.'

'What kind of dog is that,' said Ari. 'Can I pet him?'

'No,' said Hella. 'He's working. I didn't think you'd still see them these days.'

The milkman took his cap off his head and called out respectfully to Hella in Swedish. They exchanged a few terse sentences. Birgit went down the path and took the small wooden crate from the man. Hella shut the door behind her as soon as she was inside the kitchen.

'What did he want?' asked Ari.

Hella didn't answer him. She crossed the kitchen and went into the dining room.

'He asked if you wanted to pet the dog,' said Birgit. 'He said it was friendly and liked to be fussed by boys. Your mother said no. She said that you were afraid of dogs.'

Birgit gave Ari a withering stare and Ari wondered how long she would keep her job if she had any more altercations with his mother.

'I like dogs,' said Ari.

'Shame on you both to break an old woman's heart,' hissed Birgit. 'A shame on your mother for it!'

She barged past him in a temper, still carrying the crate. The milk bottles clunked so loudly against one another that Ari thought she had broken one of them.

'We're getting out of this house,' said Hella, coming back into the kitchen. 'We're taking a boat over to Mariefred. The cottage is still ours. Apparently my father spent a great deal of time there, escaping my mother, these past few years. It's in decent shape. We might stay the night, so

113

pack a small bundle and I'll put it in a rucksack.'

'Only if I can carry it,' said Ari.

He was afraid that she might snoop through his things if they were mingled with hers.

'Bring what you need,' she said. 'We'll travel light. It'll be such a relief.'

It took them a little over three hours to reach Mariefred on a southern inlet of Lake Mälaren. Hella was quiet and angry-looking throughout the journey and Ari stayed away from her, leaning over the steamer's railings and ordering endless mugs of hot chocolate in the vessel's small restaurant. He picked up a book somebody had left on a shelf and tried to remember the language but it was quite gone from his mind. Every now and then, he caught a word that whispered to his memory but he couldn't quite grasp its meaning. It was like trying to remember a dream upon waking. The ferry tied up at a mooring right in the middle of the town. They disembarked outside a fishing shop and went through it to reach the short quay that led onto the main street.

'It's quite a walk to the cottage,' said Hella. 'Can you manage?'

Ari nodded and changed the rucksack to his other shoulder. Hella had their food basket and she glanced around them looking quite baffled for a few moments. The place must have changed greatly in the six years since she had last seen it.

'You came here as a little boy,' said Hella. 'Don't you remember any of it?'

Ari shook his head. The wooden fences and the

greenness of the grass looked odd to him after his years in New York. There were the spring flowers – small and spiky and as hardy as heather – on the banks bordering the path. There were insects, small misty clouds of them, but no butterflies.

'Will we walk it?'

Ari nodded and they started off down the road that led to the west. His mother stopped in at a shop and bought some milk, promising to return the glass bottle in the morning, and small bags of coffee and sugar.

'We might go back tonight, if it's not as I remembered,' she said. 'There's a late ferry in the evening.'

'Are we going to see Grandpa's grave tomorrow?' asked Ari.

'We can, if you like. I don't care to see it myself. This is where he would have liked to have retired. This is where his heart was.'

They had planned to walk the narrow track all the way to the outcropping of rock Hella had pointed to in the distance. At its base was a clutch of pine trees growing from a steep descent to the water.

'The house is just hidden by that little bluff,' she said. 'You don't remember this?'

But when they were barely out of town, a woodman's cart stopped for them and they hopped up onto the jumbled logs.

'We'll pay for some kindling when we stop,' she said and they jounced along for a further five minutes. Hella whistled loudly just as the road forked. Ari didn't think he had even heard his mother whistle like that, piercing and harsh and uncouth. He wished he could ask her to show him how but that was something a father would have taught him to do.

'Just down the hill,' she said.

Something in her voice sounded frightened and Ari knew she was unsure about how she would feel to see the place again. He wondered if it had been a good idea to suggest they visit here.

Up ahead, past a bend in the overgrown path, the cottage appeared like a compact schoolhouse nestled against a coppice of pines. It was painted the traditional red and seemed in excellent repair. The grass grew right up to the wooden steps and in front was the drop down to the shingle beach and the water.

Hella opened the door. There was no lock. Ari could see a single expanse of space separated into a living area and a kitchen. There was an internal door into what he supposed was a bedroom. He had already spotted the outhouse among the pines.

'Somebody cleans,' said Hella. 'My father must have arranged that. I wonder if the town knows he's dead.'

The cabin was tidy. The table was scrubbed clean and Ari could still smell some kind of carbolic soap in the air. There were blankets rolled at the feet of the two bunks and fresh pillowcases stuffed with mothballs and folded into a cotton bag in the kitchen cupboard. A small lantern stood in the middle of the table. Hella removed the hurricane shutter to reveal the candle inside. There was just a sliver of wax left around the wick but she leaned over and smelled it. Her eyes

116

snapped shut as if the scent was sharp but it was only the pungency of memory.

'It's one of my candles,' she said. 'He must have saved it all these years.'

Hella left the room suddenly and Ari unpacked their meagre provisions. He didn't want to interfere with his mother's brooding, so after he was finished he left the house and went down the shale path that led to the boathouse on the shoreline. It was out of view of the cottage windows. He could feel the stiff breeze coming in from the lake. There were gulls, thin white arrowheads against the grey clouds and he could see small minnows in the warmer water where it licked the stones of the shore. He had never seen water this clean and this cold. It glinted like a sword blade and cut just as sharply on the hand when Ari dipped his fingers in.

He went over to the boathouse and tried to open the door. It was stuck fast.

'There's a trick to it,' said Hella. She had come up behind him. 'You have to lift it and then pull. Strange how I remember that,' she added and she touched her fingers to her lips as if to keep emotion inside.

They stepped together into a gloomy space. Water lapped in under the far doors that opened onto the lake. Slats of bright light dissected the room.

'There's not a boat any more,' she said wistfully. 'There used to be one filled with rugs which we could take out onto the water, even at night. We used to terrify each other that we might not find the boathouse again if a gust of wind snuffed the lantern out but we always did.'

'Who's we?' asked Ari.

'Your father and I. That summer we had together we spent a week here with my father. It was the last time my mother came with us. It was very warm that year and we were here in the middle of summer – July 1914. My father used to make me put straw here on the siding so nobody would slip when they got into or out of the boat. Even when I was little, it was my job to sweep the straw into the lake every morning and go up the road to buy fresh from the Karlsson farm. My father gave me all sorts of outdoor chores when we were here. I used to love it. And your father used to draw his magical boats here, too. He scratched them for me in the sand up under the pines, he scribbled them on the blank pages of old books. I don't think they ever would have sailed, they were so fantastical, but I used to tell him I was sure they would.'

'What was his name?' asked Ari.

Hella looked surprised that he didn't know.

'His name was Phillip,' she said.

She did not relinquish the last name. Ari had not expected she would. She had to keep some things; they might come out later.

'He was in the navy and his ship was torpedoed. A U-boat got them and they went under in flames. Very few survived. Your father didn't...'

Hella stopped talking. The story was over. Ari saw a square of concrete in one corner. It was the size of a shoebox. He picked it up.

'What's this?' he asked.

'Oh, that's one of our candle moulds,' said Hella.

She took the object from him and struggled to separate the rubber seal that held the two halves together.

'You put a wick down the middle and close it tight then you pour the wax in the hole here at the top and leave it to cool. When you break it open, you get a perfect candle shape...'

Ari took the mould from her once more. He closed it and examined the hole where the hot wax was poured in. It was just the right size to be stopped with a cork.

They decided not to rush for the last ferry and stayed the night cuddled up together under the hand-stitched quilt and the woollen blanket. They lit a fire in the stove. Ari was a bit afraid that his mother might go crazy out here and that she would refuse to let him take her away from this place. They had eaten all their food early in the evening.

'Will you starve before morning?' Hella asked, as if reading his thoughts.

Ari shook his head.

'I have a plan. We could go over to the farm tomorrow. The Karlssons' son, Henk, probably still works it. He'll remember me and they'll give us a good breakfast like you've never had before. Can you wait for that?'

Ari nodded again. He enjoyed the way she held his head cradled in her lap. She was stroking his hair and if he sat up to speak with her, she might stop.

'Can we light the candle?' he asked.

'Of course,' said his mother. 'It might only burn

for a few minutes. It's very low already.'

'I'd like to smell the boats,' he said.

'Unless you've been on a proper handcrafted boat, you might not know the smell. It's only recognized by true sailors.'

She struck a match and lifted the glass from the lamp. The wick took a few seconds to take then the flame stood tall and thin, a trail of blue smoke sprang in a tortured curve from its tip like a ghost released.

'Now imagine you're on a boat.'

The wind had come up and the house creaked rhythmically. Every now and then a breeze squeezed in through the corking between the planks and the flame guttered. Hella sat down next to Ari and started to rock him again.

'I sometimes think I was meant to be a Viking,' she said quietly. Her slow movement sent his body swaying back and forward on the bed. It felt like sea swell. 'I think I would have liked that, having lots of children and a house on a hill so I could see the Norse boats coming back in. And at night you could help me light great pyres along the rocky cliffs to guide them home. We'd stand on the hills with the wind freezing us and the fires scorching us and wait patiently.'

'There aren't any Vikings left,' said Ari pragmatically.

'I know,' said Hella. 'These days the Vikings are the explorers like Mr Amundsen and Mr Lindbergh.'

'Maybe my father would have been an explorer.'

'No,' said Hella sadly. 'Your father did what he

120

was told. He was very polite. He didn't like to fight.'

'You like to fight,' said Ari and he turned his head to look up at her.

The candle flame made her cheekbones very slanted and somehow sly. Her forehead was long and white and her eyes were a frightening shade of preternatural blue like a wolf's.

'I do,' she said. 'I'm afraid I do.'

'You don't have to all the time,' said Ari.

'But you do, Ari. If you're to get what you want you have to fight all the time.'

'What if you never get it?' he asked. 'The thing you keep fighting for?'

'I'm disappointed by life anyway,' said Hella. 'It's not as if I'm risking much.'

'Maybe you should aim for things you can get,' he said. He was very careful not to mention specific people but she knew what he meant.

'I can get him,' said Hella. 'You'll see. We'll have him back.'

'I can smell the boat,' said Ari, as his eyes grew heavy.

'Can you?' she asked. 'Yes, I can smell it now, too. Just a trace of it.'

Then the candle went out and the smoke from it was lost in the absolute darkness of the night.

Ari woke to the sound of the zipper on his rucksack. He sat upright in bed and jumped out from under the covers, snatching the rucksack from his mother's hands. She still had one of the blankets round her shoulders and he wondered if she had slept.

121

'I'll do it,' he shouted.

'Ari!' she shouted back.

He saw that he had startled her and any loss of composure always made her angry. 'Don't grab so. What have you got in there I can't see?'

'I said I would carry it,' said Ari desperately.

'There's no food left in it. I said we'd go up to the farm to eat.'

'I'm going down to the water to wash.'

He took the rucksack with him and backed towards the door.

'Have you liked the camping?' she asked.

'It was cold,' said Ari. 'I felt cold all night. I prefer a house with a fire and no draughts.'

'I packed you an extra jersey.'

'I'm not so cold now,' he said and he skittered down the shale path, slipping a few times as he went. He checked the side zipper when he reached the far side of the boathouse where his mother couldn't see him. Everything he'd packed was still there. He brushed his teeth in the cold clean water. It was a novelty. On the distant waters of the lake, a boat suddenly spooled out an enormous white canvas sail and Ari watched it pass against the black-green wall of the pines. Then he went into the boathouse for one final look at the place where he imagined his mother and father had first kissed.

The Karlssons were still working their family farm but, contrary to Hella's prediction, the old man was in charge, not his son. They recognized her and welcomed her in. They spoke no English but Ari could tell they were consoling her on the news of her father's passing. They graciously gestured for Ari and Hella to sit at their table and then settled in around them. Two of the little girls, twins, made makeshift places for themselves at the sink. Mrs Karlsson dished up a bowl of porridge for Ari but when he went to pour the milk out, he surreptitiously sniffed the jug. The creamy white froth was curdled; he could smell it. He looked over at his mother and tried to catch her eye without announcing the fact to the whole kindly family.

'It's supposed to be like that,' Hella smiled. 'It's sour milk for good taste in the cereal. Try it.'

The little girls giggled behind their hands and Ari poured the milk sparingly onto the steaming oats and stirred it in.

His mother kept chatting away happily in Swedish, no doubt informing the Karlssons of her mother's reluctance to visit the cottage. Ari concentrated on trying to taste the sour milk in the porridge but he could not. There was just a rich round taste with a fullness to it like fermented apples. Suddenly, his mother stopped eating. Ari had heard one name he recognized amid the cacophony of conversation.

'Lindbergh?' he heard his mother repeat to Mrs Karlsson.

'*Ja,*' said the woman, nodding.

'What is it?' asked Ari of his mother.

'You won't believe this,' she said. 'They say the neighbouring farm used to be rented in the summer by a dentist from Ystad and his family. The Lindberghs, she remembers their name was.'

'It's not the same family,' said Ari. 'It's not

123

necessarily him.'

'Of course it's him. Every summer we were here and he was spending his holidays boating on the same stretch of the lake, walking through the same woodland paths.'

'It's not the same family,' said Ari. 'Didn't our Mr Lindbergh say he'd never been to Sweden?'

'It's his father, then, for certain,' said Hella. 'We're connected, don't you see? Even that summer when I was with Phillip, Charles was just a heartbeat away, waiting for me to find him.'

'He said he'd never been here!' Ari reiterated but she wouldn't listen. She was talking earnestly with Mrs Karlsson again.

Ari didn't see how it could be true. As far as he knew, Lindbergh might be a fairly common Swedish name. There might be hundreds of families who shared it.

'We need to go,' said Ari. 'We'll miss the ferry.'

The whole Karlsson family had gathered around them to watch them eat. Ari thought of the farm where they had spent the night in Le Bourget. He thought of the man with the small round spectacles and the spittle flying from his mouth. Ari hated being watched while he ate and he suspected their hosts were being polite and neglecting chores to keep them company. As soon as they left and began the walk back down to their cottage, he noticed the little girls scurrying off to the henhouses and he heard Mrs Karlsson slosh a bucket from the hearth into a stone basin to wash their breakfast dishes.

Rather than heading all the way down the shale path to the cottage, Hella veered off onto the path to town.

'Aren't we going to say goodbye?' Ari asked.

'Best not to look back,' said Hella. 'I cleaned and closed up. Mrs Karlsson will go down now that she knows we've visited, and tidy up properly. She's the one who my father had looking after the place. I'll get mother to send some money and we'll have to decide what to do with the cottage. I'm sure the Karlssons will want to take it on as their own. It's a good base for a boat.'

'But it's ours,' said Ari. 'I don't want you to give it away. Promise me you won't and don't let Grandmother do it either.'

'Don't be sentimental about it, Ari. We've both got to look forward now.'

'I'm not sentimental. I want to come back one day.'

'I didn't think you liked the wild life,' said Hella.

'I do,' said Ari. 'I get it from my father.'

Hella looked at him oddly then. 'Don't start imagining you know him now just because I've given you a name.'

'How else will I know him?' asked Ari and he kicked a stone.

'Stop that! You'll scuff your new boots.'

They never did get to Ari's grandfather's grave. Hella and Eleanor met with the lawyers and discussed the house. They were like two strangers thrown together by a mutual acquaintance who was now departed. They were distant and overly polite. Hella's father had left her a great deal of money and the house on Strandvägen when her

125

mother died.

'You can have it now,' said Eleanor. 'I'm not long for this world.'

'Of course you are,' said Hella. 'Unless you decide not to be but that doesn't seem to have worked for you in the past.'

'What do you mean?'

'Deciding to be unhappy hasn't worked to kill you off,' her daughter answered.

'Being unhappy hasn't worked for you either,' spat back her mother. 'Besides, I'm not unhappy. I'm just disappointed with the way things worked out for me... Then you were born and I had such high hopes. You had such natural beauty and such a way with thinking and words. I knew you'd make a brilliant match – a Nobel laureate or a doctor or a scientist. Something grand and worthy.'

'Not a boat maker,' said Hella.

'No,' said Eleanor. 'Never a boat maker. It's absurd, a profession for men who can only work with their hands.'

'What about a boat designer?' asked Ari.

'That's the same thing, my love,' she said kindly to her grandson.

'And a banker?'

'Wonderful, only you're not speaking of that Israelite, are you, my love? He wasn't suitable at all. They're not our kind ... just look at their dark colouring. Hella, you standing beside that man must have looked absurd, a travesty.'

'How about a pilot?' asked Ari.

'Too gauche for words,' said Eleanor.

'What about a famous aviator and explorer,'

said Ari. 'A hero.'

'Now that would have been very glamorous, wouldn't it, Hella?'

'It will be,' said Hella. 'It will be.'

10

New York, 1929

Contrary to the myths that would sprout up later, there were no suicides on Wall Street that last Tuesday in October. Nobody believed it was real for one thing and nobody anticipated the devastation the bubble-burst would bring. There was panic and there were worried phone calls and grave concern in the offices of the enormous mansions on the park but nobody jumped from their windows or threw themselves in front of subway trains because nobody had grasped that this was it. They were still playing jazz in the speakeasies on 110th Street. You could still buy a hotdog and a pennant with a picture of Babe Ruth on it at Yankee Stadium for fifty cents. The girls at Radio City were still putting on their high-kicking shows. The realization that their golden age had come to an end would sink in more slowly and with less fanfare. It would come when the headlines had quietened down and the grinding months of exploring every option to no avail had creaked by.

Ari's most substantive memory of that day was

of his mother coming in and throwing her fur-lined gloves down on the front table. It was Tuesday evening – later they would come to call it Black Tuesday – but on the day itself it was just the beginning of another week and Hella had been out shopping at Macy's and had come in to the apartment having collected the newspaper from the doorman on her way up. In the elevator, she had ignored the thick black headlines shriek-ing 'CRASH!' and had focused instead on a small story on the bottom of page two.

'Can you believe this?' Hella said, calling out to Ari as she left hatpins on every table from the entrance hall to the living room where he was sitting listening to the wireless.

'Have you seen this?' she asked again.

Ari had the maid and the window washer clus-tered around the set with him. The traditional manners of the house had been forgotten when they had started to appreciate the deep concern in the newsreader's voice as the day had progressed.

'That dreadful Mr Hearst has offered Charles a million dollars to star in a motion picture with that even more dreadful mistress of his, Marion Davies. Charles has turned it down, of course, but how vulgar! It's all over the papers...'

Hella's voiced trailed off as it finally sank in that the situation she had walked in on was most incongruous.

'Why are the staff in with us?' she asked.

She was not angry, only surprised.

Ari looked up at her with a white face.

'How much of our money is in the market?' he asked.

128

'What market?' she asked.

It was not a suitable conversation to be having with the help present but somehow, without understanding exactly how the system worked, Ari had managed to comprehend that the market crash would have dire consequences for their lives.

'The stock market, Mother. How much of Mr Gold's money is tied up in bonds?'

'I don't hold with those things,' said Hella. 'I told the Gold brothers to take everything out of paper and put it into steel and railways.'

'But it's in shares?' said Ari. The maid's feather duster drooped. 'Shares in railway and steel companies.'

'No,' said Hella. 'It's in government projects. I'm a Swede, we know that a government's the safest business in the world.'

'We may be alright,' said Ari. 'I think we ought to call the Golds and see if they'll come over.'

'As long as they don't bring their tedious wives... I can't stop thinking about that Marion Davies with her pouting mouth and her phoney curls. I don't think that woman looks at all well on the screen.'

Ari wondered if his mother would ever like another woman and then he wondered, and at fourteen it was the first time he had ever wondered this, if anybody had ever really liked his mother. She had no friends, the men who clamoured for her attention seemed enthralled by her harshness and her beauty but had anyone really liked her or wanted to talk with her and hear what she had to say? Did she have anything to say? Seeing her standing there with her fur which was too warm for this early in the winter and her focus on the most insignificant articles on this momentous day, Ari felt he had experienced a kind of epiphany that was an essential part of growing up.

The Gold brothers could not be reached by telephone. The lines throughout the city were jammed and the exchanges could not cope. Eventually, Ari sent the kitchen boy across town on his bicycle to take a message by hand. There was more paper on the street than usual, as if people in offices everywhere had been riffling through filing cabinets and back rooms looking for answers. The useless discarded bits of paper they had unearthed had made their way into the street to clog the gutters and blow about in the damp alleys. The boy came back an hour later. One of the Gold brothers had not answered his door. The maid had said the family was not at home to visitors. The second, Isaac Gold, the doctor who had declared his brother dead, had left the city suddenly for a country house near Montauk. The third, the accountant named Jacob, was not yet home from his office. He had called to say he was working late. It was three days before he came over, looking gaunter than ever in his funereal black suit, and held a solemn meeting with Hella in Benjamin Gold's study.

They were together for several hours and when he left he scurried off so hurriedly that Ari feared the worst but perhaps he was hurrying back to try and save his own family from ruin somehow.

'Half at least is gone,' said Hella to her son.

'Will we lose the house?'

'That's the odd thing,' she said. 'We probably

won't. We have half left and we should be grateful for that apparently. Most people, people Jacob knows, have nothing left. They don't quite realize it yet, of course, but they are broke. They won't be able to make payments on their homes and they will have to sell their cars and their furs and their jewellery to keep up appearances for a while but Jacob thinks that in six months' time what we have left will be enough to buy this building.'

Ari's hands went to his lips. He was trying not to cry.

'Are the Gold brothers going to be okay?'

'Jacob is and he thinks Isaac will be fine. Together they're going to try and float Ruben until the storm is over. He has nothing left. He owes money, in fact. Speculating was a pastime of his apparently.'

Ari felt he was understanding life as an adult very clearly now. All the freedoms he envied came with so many responsibilities he had never considered.

'Will you have a cup of coffee with me, Ari?' Hella asked him.

It was a considered request, not nearly as casual as it sounded. 'I would like you to have a cup of coffee with me and we'll devise a plan – for the two of us – to get through this.'

Ari had never drunk coffee with his mother. He had a Coca-Cola or a fruit juice but he was never allowed coffee. It was for grown-ups.

'I'll get the maid to bring it in.'

The maid was subdued but she knew to serve the coffee in their best silver service with milk and cream and demerara sugar. The atmosphere was one of tense concern and worry.

'Will we help Ruben?' asked Ari.

'Yes,' said his mother, 'of course we will but there are three whole families there and just two of us. The money would go quickly.'

'Will we stay here?'

'Jacob thinks those who can should try and hold out. We have to keep the staff for as long as we can. They'll need the jobs now with so many of their family members out of work.'

'Can this be true?' said Ari. 'Can it all fall apart so easily?'

'Jacob took my hand,' she said. 'He took my hand and looked into my eyes and told me that it could. That it will.'

'What do we do?'

'I haven't told him about the Swedish money, the money from my father. We have quite a lot, more than a lot, but my mother has to be kept, too.'

'Let's keep the staff,' said Ari. 'All of them.'

'Yes,' said Hella. 'I agree. Over my dead body will a single one of them leave or take a pay cut.'

She had said it and it would be so. Ari knew that for sure. She had set her chin in just the way she chose when there was no room for negotiation. This was the real Hella – not the slightly vacuous beauty who alternated between frivolous senselessness and acidic sniping but a woman of such strength that she had escaped a destructive mother, stood up to Mr Glassen and made Mr Gold save them. They both took their first sip of coffee together. Of course, Ari had tasted coffee before. It was not entirely new to him but he had never drunk it like this: never in front of his mother with her full consent. They drank quietly together, sharing the slightly bitter adult taste of it and Ari realized that despite everything, he had always, in a very odd way, liked his mother.

A grey haze settled on the city that winter. Partly it was the general shock and dreariness that had descended on its populace and partly the number of outdoor fires that had begun to burn under the bridges and on the river islands and in the parks and ancient cemeteries. Between the graves of the men who had made America great, the itinerant families camped. They boiled water in billycans inside the vaults of the Rockefellers and they pissed against the wall of Andrew Carnegie's tombstone. They slept on top of the dead and counted themselves lucky that the cemetery walls created a bulwark against the wind and snow.

The cars with their 'For Sale' signs lined the sidewalks of Museum Row and rails of furs stood out in the rain in the Garment District because the storerooms were overflowing. The auctioneers threw Chippendale furniture in with plywood lots. Priceless antiques were sold as jumble and ended up in fireplaces as kindling. These were the things the newspapers didn't mention. Obsessed with numbers and the human plight, there was no mention made of the dogs that roamed the streets, their leather collars in tatters, eating from garbage cans. At night, those who could still afford to dine out would hear the chefs fighting their way through the packs of dogs that haunted the back alleys to reach their kitchens. There were poodles and dachshunds and little pampered terriers now mange-riddled and fearsome, reckless with starvation.

The papers did not deign to mention the museum curators with no budget who searched the auction houses to rescue the furniture that would end up as firewood. Once, on his way home, Ari had seen a man in his stocking feet smiling with a lamp under his arm coming out of the front door of Christie's. They caught each other's eye and the man said:

'Tiffany,' as he held the lamp out. 'I got it for a pair of old shoes.'

Those with money bought up the niches in the same way the loathed carpetbaggers had raped the South. Others spent what they had on keeping their staff and even hiring the family members of their existing help to do menial jobs. For the first time in years, front doorsteps were scrubbed by hand and exterior windowframes were repainted. Private gardens became more elaborate and more beautifully tended while the parks grew tangled and wild. The pathways were overgrown with dandelions and knee-high grass; duckweed took over the lakes and ponds. The city workers weren't being paid or were being laid off by the hundred and sometimes the garbage stood on the sidewalks for days waiting to be collected. It drew the dogs and the people hungry enough to scavenge.

Hella never thought she would see the likes of it in America. It was something she imagined might happen in Mexico after a drought or perhaps in India. Ari kept his eyes turned down when he

134

walked. He tried not to meet the desperation in the faces of men his senior. The fresh fruit in the markets grew meagre. The stalls of ripe apples and pears and oranges that used to colour every corner were moved inside the stores to eliminate pilfering. Then the supply dried up altogether. It was tinned peaches or nothing. The farmers had been hard hit by inclement weather and the rock-bottom prices offered from buyers who could not afford to pay a fair rate. The Midwestern dust bowl grew ever larger. Poor farming conditions had finally taken their toll and without the cash to buy fertilizer, the land wheezed its last dying breath and refused to sprout a single grain. Ari often wondered what the Glassen farm must look like now. Had it survived, bought up by a success-ful neighbour, or was it derelict with its burned-out shell of a farmhouse still a charcoal wreck against the sky?

Hella became more involved in charity work. She helped organize food collections for soup kitchens and she begged time from doctors to hold weekend clinics on the sidewalks outside the hospitals. She never served personally but only Ari knew how much she did with what they had.

The Depression had one most surprising side effect. It threw people like Charles Lindbergh into the limelight. A normally modest and retiring man, Hella knew, it seemed the press would not leave him alone. He was interviewed constantly on the radio; his wry comments made the front pages along with those of the likes of Will Rogers. When they had tired of the deprivation and the same monotonous tales of loss and suffering, the

135

Hollywood news teams turned to the remaining heroes for a boost to their message. The last item on every cinema newsreel was about Charles Lindbergh. He had joined the Pan American team to develop aircraft and promote the aviation industry. Since his transatlantic feat, airline ticket sales had risen from 5,000 in 1927 to over 500,000 by 1930. He was almost solely credited for this injection into the American economy and his status as an icon grew by the week.

Ari was permitted an astonishing amount of freedom while Hella was coping with the results of the Depression and often he merely placed a call to the doorman and left a message telling his mother when he would be home. More often than not, he would reach home before her and retrieve the note he had left from the doorman without his mother ever knowing he had not been in doing his homework since four o'clock.

He would wander the streets, trying on the Dodgers baseball jackets in the Macy's boys' department and wandering through the Frick Collection in his school uniform because admission was free to students. The building was heated and many people had taken to wandering its corridors for hours a day in the winter. Mostly, they congregated in the library of the great house. The room had been left as the steel magnate had enjoyed it in his heyday. The enormous leather-bound ledgers still lay open on the desk, the silver-capped inkwells and the transport time-tables and antiquated telephone still sat on the desk. The unemployed men, who had once been bankers or railway conductors or shopkeepers, stood forlornly round the room in grey clumps and looked at this citadel of power. This was how America had been run, with the steel fist of industry at the helm. Now it was all demeaning lines and chits of paper that expired before you had the chance to use them on the incorrect form, already completed in triplicate, to get milk powder for the baby.

The lines around the construction sites grew longer by the day. Casual labourers waited for an accident so they could get a place. The Catholics crossed themselves for forgiveness at wishing another's misfortune; their wives lit candles by the dozen in St Patrick's Cathedral. It was not unusual to find pathetic posies of wilted violets or small candles burning as tokens in front of the statues of the great men of the city. Having given up on God, some turned to these fallible heroes in acts of faith.

Ari's classes dwindled in size and the head-master sent out an emergency flyer claiming that he might have to close the school and combine its pupils with the boys of St Ignatius but the parents gathered their resources and funded the place privately. Ari suspected the father of Hymie Bath-shevis, a boy in his class, of raising most of the funds personally. He was a brash, vulgar man who had made his money in bakeries and he'd been heard to exclaim loudly at one of the parents' meetings: 'Seems us yids are the only ones getting a first-rate WASP education these days!'

Hella had gone up to him afterwards and shaken his hand. 'From WASP to Yid, thank you,' she had said and she had smiled. He had smiled too and Ari's heart had sunk, though he needn't have worried. Mrs Bathshevis, a small, ferocious woman with a streak of white hair through her black mane that reminded Ari of a badger pelt, had snuffled protectively over to her husband and interrupted his intimate conversation. Then she had, quite literally, taken him away from Hella.

The first two years of the Depression were the worst. That was when the greatest changes in circumstances were felt. After that, everybody knew they were in the same boat. The number of suicides lessened, people got used to their new lives and they survived. The rich began to have parties again. Everybody had more help than they needed and it was not unusual for a family with money to employ two nannies per child and two chauffeurs – one to drive the car and one to clean it. It might have been seen as conspicuous consumption but in many cases it was charity. Often, a man would ask to split his job and his wage with his brother, so that the money might be shared among the extended family and the brother have the dignity of work.

Hella's house was dense with servants. She paid a living wage and Mr Bathshevis sent bread every morning to the Gold house. It was intended for distribution to Hella's various soup kitchens but a few loaves were always taken and given to each of the servants. It was the butchers and the grocers with suppliers close by in Long Island who did well. People had to eat and Hella courted these contacts fiercely. She included these men in lavish dinner parties and gazed upon them with the intense attention of her extraordinary eyes, making every donation worth those thirty seconds when she made each of them feel like the most desirable man in the world.

One Friday, Ari decided to stop by the Odeon off Broadway before heading home from school in the afternoon. He didn't stay to see the cowboy picture that was playing because an item in the opening newsreel distressed him so badly he had to leave the theatre. There was footage of Charles Lindbergh getting out of his car and going into work with a secretive smile on his face and a snapshot taken by a reporter of him and a young woman leaving a church in New Jersey. Charles Lindbergh had married the girl he had been courting for many years. The soundtrack of laughter and ringing bells followed Ari all the way home. He wondered if his mother had heard.

11

New Jersey, 1932

To the guests who visited the apartment on Sutton Place, Hella Gold was the epitome of confidence. She was a gracious, competent hostess and a sharp wit. She appeared contented with her life. She seemed like any other vivacious young widow, steeped in charity work and not at all eager to hitch herself and her new-found freedom to just any man who might come her way. To the public eye, Hella appeared happy and even carefree in her own frosty Scandinavian way. Only Ari knew that she fostered an impossible fire, which burned so darkly inside her that it consumed all other pleasures. She would say things to him that were so outlandish he could do nothing with them except pretend they had never been said. Often, they implied an intimacy with Charles Lindbergh which Ari wanted desperately to dispel. But without her illusions where would his mother be? Free, or just floating lost on a vast nothingness?

Being sent away to high school was a great relief. Ari had spent so many hours in New York's museums that he was drawn to the art classes and the thick tomes of classical literature, the odd convolutions and mysteries of Latin. To his mother's disdain, he did abominably in science and mathematics. He just didn't have a mind for figures and he began to wonder where his future career would lie. He seemed unprepared for any kind of professional work and it concerned him. If they had stayed in Sweden, Ari thought he might have followed in his grandfather's footsteps and become a doctor. Perhaps the old man's love for biology and anatomy would have rubbed off on him. if they had stayed in Minnesota, he felt sure he would have become a farmer. With no family of his own, Glassen might have left Hella and Ari the farm and Ari might have grown old there with a wife and children of his own. All the possibilities crowded in on him, and all the might-have-beens confused his thinking, so that he felt as if his life could twist and turn at any moment; planning was futile. He blamed his mother for causing this sense of insecurity. She was as unpredictable as ever.

When Ari came home to the New York apartment on weekends and holidays, Hella threw loud, glittering parties for flocks of people Ari was sure were not her real friends. She took on work for the Margaret Sanger society in addition to her other chosen charities. She attended lectures on psychology at New York University. She functioned as an elegant and often photographed member of high society – and became something of an eccentric pet for the gossip columnists who adored her outlandish remarks and, with that capricious tenderness understood only by the professionally malicious, treated her kindly.

Ari understood, though, the parties were for him, not the guests. Hella's numerous charity benefits and functions were mere busywork so that Ari would not worry about her. The truth was that, for his mother, there was only Charles Lindbergh. Hella listened to the man's press conferences on the radio – snatched sound bites which were inadequate to nourish her needs. She showed up at science fairs and the inaugurations of airport terminals – anywhere he might be in attendance – but despite her careful machinations, she never met the man again. Ari was drawn along in his mother's wake to these events but for him it was all about the planes, the weighty miracle of flight, that gentle peeling away from the earth.

The announcement of Charles Lindbergh's

marriage to Anne Morrow had been a terrible blow. Hella had followed the young couple's romance with cultivated detachment. She thought Anne too tall for a woman. As the daughter of an ambassador, Anne was too highly strung to be a suitable match for the aviator; all the warmth and passion had been bred out of her like some snorting, neurotic mare.

After the wedding photos' appearance in the press made the event an actuality, Hella wandered round the house for days with quaking hands she had to clasp together to quiet. She touched the leaves of the potted palms and they fluttered. She seemed a fragile, trembling bowstring that would not be stilled.

After Will Rogers interviewed the couple on his radio show, the cook called Ari at school and begged him to come home; the doctor was called, then sent away, then called again. Then, on the evening of the third day of her self-imposed mourning, Hella had come down to dinner in full evening dress – a floor-length gown with a slit up to the hip just like Mary Pickford had been seen to wear. His mother had decided how to play it – Ari saw that at once. The marriage would be a mere complication in her relationship with Lindbergh, the second act where an unexpected event comes between the lovers and they are parted for a while. This was better than a smooth road; this was just the sort of turbulence any human journey required to make it valuable. Hella would wait. The outcome was now more distant but still inevitable. It gave her drama; it gave her a tragedy to overcome. It was the role of a lifetime and she starred in it – an exquisite figure on a stage of her own making, with nobody else suspecting the play at all, and her son the only member of the audience.

Ari was beginning to hope that the marriage and then the announcement of the Lindbergh's first child might still the waters. Sometimes, for months, Hella would not even mention Charles Lindbergh's name and Ari would start to hope that the fad had passed but then something would happen to show him that his mother's calm was only a surface tranquillity, that the rip of the current was still spooling wildly underneath...

On a night in late winter, at one of her gilded soirées, the conversation turned to Hollywood idols and Hella made a little joke about being a secret fan of a certain celebrity.

'Who is it?' asked the lady to her right.

'It's not a film star,' said Hella. 'It's a real person.'

'Who?' asked the woman again.

'It was quite a big crush for a while really!' teased Hella.

The assembly was silent and then she spilled out the name in a champagne-flavoured gush, 'Charles Lindbergh!'

All the men in the room groaned.

'Enough of that man already!' one of them said.

The women only hummed their agreement deep in their throats and smiled slyly. The conversation moved on to other things: German rearmament, French hysteria over it. Ari was enjoying the heated exchange between a retired admiral and a journalist.

'They've been ruined by Versailles,' said the journalist. 'You have to leave the vanquished with some dignity or you'll have to fight your battles all over again.'

'Provided we keep them down, they'll have nothing to fight those battles with,' said the admiral smugly, 'no matter how big an upstart their Mr Hitler insists on being.'

'It was their navy that nearly swayed things in their favour,' said the journalist, 'and Scapa Flow really saw the end of that. German naval supremacy is lying in a wreck on the ocean floor.'

'And I would have loved to watch their end, I can tell you!' exclaimed the admiral. 'Over fifty ships and every bloody sub they owned...'

Ari was fascinated by the talk of scuttling the German fleet, the last U-boat commandeered by an ally nation or blasted apart so that it went down, down, down like a great dying whale ... then he saw his mother watching him. Her eyes were two blue chips of glacier heart.

He went quite cold.

'See how I pass for completely normal?' she seemed to be saying. *'See how they'd never even suspect?'*

She had been testing her guests to see how well she could maintain her charade of a harmless, slightly girlish interest in a famous man and she had succeeded beautifully.

Bored with the men's arguments, the woman to Hella's right leaned in towards her. She covered Hella's hand with her own as if to imply a Masonic connection. She whispered secretively, 'I also think Mr Lindbergh's a real dream!'

Hella pulled her hand away so swiftly in pique

144

that the cutlery rattled and the water sloshed in the bowl of roses. She didn't like it when people used the word 'dream' in association with Charles Lindbergh. She did not like that at all.

The next day, when the shells from the crayfish were still in the garbage can and the house was imbued with a subtle, unoffensive, scent of the sea, Hella announced to the servants that she had rented a house in Hopewell, New Jersey for the remainder of the winter. It was mid-February. Hella's party of the night before had been the first after the social lull following the Christmas celebrations and it was still very cold in the city. The guests had come in shaking the snow from their hair in silver sparkles so that it was indistinguishable from their diamonds. It was not a popular time of year to rent a holiday house. Ari knew there was something more to this scheme. Hella resented his guessing the truth and this resentment was the only thorn in the side of her joy as she packed up three cars with essential luxuries and headed them in convoy across the Hudson.

The house was old and small and shellacked with a coating of cold gritty dust. It was shabby with the wear of a hundred creaking Decembers. At night, it complained constantly as it moved uncomfortably about on its foundation bones. It grew dust on its window ledges and sprouted cobwebs in its corners. Ari had never seen such an inhospitable place, wrecked as it was upon the rocky outcrop of a dishevelled wood. The nearest general store was a nerve-wracking drive away because the car slithered on the unsalted roads and the wind seemed to come in through cracks in the paint. Hella took to it. She was giddy with the discomfort of it, of having to make do and struggle and overcome, even now that discomfort was completely unnecessary.

When Ari came in late from school on Friday nights, having been collected by a taxi at the train station, he would find his mother sitting in the living room with the back of her chair to the fire and her bare heels propped up on the window sill. She kept a cashmere rug on the seat but she would only ever sit on it; she refused to pull it up around her shoulders. Ari noticed that his mother watched intently for a light that came to them from a few miles across the fields. It was like the receiver light of a transistor radio, turned on and off by the interference of trees. Hella gazed at it and it warmed her more than the real fire she had eschewed. Ari had worked it out after only a few days – that distant, uncertain illumination was the light from the Lindberghs' home.

On the first of March, Charles Lindbergh ran into Hella and Ari. It was completely unexpected and it happened in just that way: he ran into them and not the other way round.

They had left the house in a hurry, trying to make it to the grocery store before it closed for the day. A dark stain smeared across the horizon suggested that late evening storms were on their way. Hella had tied her hair back in a braid for expedience; she hardly ever wore it that way any more but she had been rushing. She had thrown an expensive coat over her velvet palazzo pants and her shoes were unsuited to snow.

Ari was almost as tall as her now and Hella was gripping him as her heels slipped on the last of the season's ice which still clung to the sidewalk. They were laughing together as they negotiated their path when a tall young man stepped out of the drugstore and bumped into them. The door tinkled shut behind him and the pharmacist immediately pulled the blind down to indicate he was closed. Mr Lindbergh had been a special customer but he didn't intend to stay open late for just anyone.

Charles Lindbergh was holding a brown paper bag with the red sword-and-serpent logo of the medical profession on it. Hella saw this image quite clearly before she looked up and saw the man's face. After all the grainy photographs and artist's impressions of the preceding years, here now was the real person. Lindbergh reached out to clutch at her elbow when he thought she was about to fall. Ari stood still and let his mother's arm drop from his hold.

'I'm terribly sorry,' said Charles. 'That was almost an accident!'

Hella said nothing. It wasn't that she was too shocked to speak. She had known all along this moment would come but she wanted the man to recognize her and, to Ari's amazement, he did.

'I'm sorry,' he said again and then grinned boyishly at his constant unnecessary apologies. 'But I think we've met before, haven't we?'

'We have, Mr Lindbergh,' said Hella. 'We came to your rescue when you had some sort of radiator trouble in Minnesota. It was years ago now. Nineteen twenty-three, I think. We were living on a farm near St Cloud.'

'Hella Köll!' he said, remembering the illicit whisper of that name, the tongue so nearly creeping into the deep crevice of his ear. Charles went a little red at the memory and felt an uncomfortable stir of guilt when he thought about Anne waiting for the baby's medicine at home.

'And Ari,' he said, turning his attention to Ari.

Lindbergh's glance passed from the woman's beautiful face to that of the boy – he was a young man now really. Lindbergh thought he had seen this boy before. Not all those years ago on the remote farm but more recently. Despite his acute powers of observation, Lindbergh couldn't quite place the face. For Ari's part, the proximity of the man sent his fingers tingling, the way they had when Lindbergh had clasped his hand at Le Bourget. Ari thought he anticipated an immense and impending sadness; he shoved his hands deep into his pockets. His mother would have said that was rude in the presence of company but the cold made it excusable. Hella herself had a bemused look on her face. She hadn't expected Lindbergh to recall her son. She wasn't to know that this affinity for remembering names was a particular trick of Charles Lindbergh's – an uncanny knack which meant nothing; it was just one of the ways in which he exercised his powers of observation and recollection.

'Yes,' said Hella. 'You're quite right, of course.'

The cold from the icy sidewalk was drifting up her ankles but she didn't feel it. Ari kept looking

148

at the snake on the drugstore bag. Why do they use a serpent? he wondered. Didn't it mean poison? He thought about Mr Glassen. He hadn't thought about the man for years.

'My former employer died in a fire,' Hella said, as if she had read Ari's thoughts. 'We've been in New York for almost ten years now.'

'It's just so odd running into you here like this. Once I placed you it all came back to me in a rush – that day...'

Charles was thinking of that soft torrent of panting air in his ear again. He looked around for a coffee shop. He was glad, if he did have to ask them for coffee (and it seemed as if he might because they were not showing any signs of moving on) that the boy was there. It was more seemly that way.

'We've followed your exploits quite closely actually,' said Hella.

'You're very kind,' said Charles. 'It's all been a bit of a burden sometimes what with trying to manage a marriage and a baby, too.'

Hella's face clouded over at the mention of the child.

'I'd suggest coffee,' he said. 'But the baby's not very well... It's only a cold but you know how it is.'

He held up the brown bag as proof of his word. The snake was suspended on its sword like a venomous oracle.

'Another time, then,' said Hella. 'For nostalgia's sake.'

Her grace was effortless and chilling. This episode was only a beginning for her, one of the milestones along the road of her predetermined fate. She had no need to rush.

'We're staying in a strange old house near the wood this winter...'

'Then you're a stone's throw away from us!' said Charles happily. 'Will you come to the house one day and get that coffee I promised? Anne would love to show off Po.'

'Po?' asked Hella quizzically.

'It's the silly thing I call him,' explained Charles. 'He's Charles Junior really.'

'We will come by and talk about Sweden,' said Hella.

'Oh,' said Charles, slightly embarrassed. 'In all honesty, I've never been there. I did tell you that, I think.' And then he added, afraid that his words may have been a little rude, 'My grandfather told me stories about the country, though, and I'd like to hear more from a real native.'

'I'll call and introduce myself to Anne, then.'

'Yes.'

Charles was backing away. The baby's temperature was once again foremost on his mind. Hella waved goodbye and herded Ari into the grocery store across the road with barely five minutes to spare before closing. She didn't say a word about the encounter – not then – she kept silent and packed it away on ice in her heart to defrost and devour privately later on. She had always been secretive about her sorrows but she was selfish with her joys most of all.

The exhilaration Hella felt was real, though; she couldn't sleep that night. She sat by the window watching the lights from the Lindbergh home, so she was perhaps the first person outside the household and the New Jersey police department who knew something was terribly wrong. The white and blue flashes of the police cruisers semaphored their message through the trees in the small hours. Hella almost sent Ari running across the ice-crusted fields to see what had happened but she assumed it was just some intruder – an unwelcome interloper who had trespassed on the Lindberghs' lives and had to be dragged away from their property like a common criminal.

They gathered what had happened from the newspapers. For months there was little else to read about. Though Hella tried to visit the Lindberghs during those first few desperate weeks of distress, claiming to be an invited friend, nobody was allowed near the property. Everything that Hella and Ari learned, they learned from the press reports so it was difficult to decipher the truth from the fabrications.

Each morning, Ari added the next dreadful instalment to their repertoire. He sat at their modest kitchen table with its scratched top and he held the newspaper in exactly the same way Charles Lindbergh held his paper, though neither man knew it. All the accounts accumulated into one coherent vision. So much detail had been supplied that it was possible to imagine the events in their entirety like a moving picture in black and white. It was almost possible to scent the smells of a quiet living room at the front of the Lindbergh homestead...

It was after nine o'clock in the evening. Charles

151

Lindbergh had arrived home late from his quick outing to the drugstore but the medicine he had purchased sat on the mantelpiece, the package unopened because baby Po's health had improved dramatically during the day and Anne was reluctant to dose him unnecessarily. Charles was relieved. He sat by a fire near the window. Through the woods he could make out the distant lights of another house. Was it Hella's place? What a dreadful dump to be stuck in for the winter. Lindbergh liked the boy. It crossed his mind that he owed Ari a flight. He vaguely remembered how the mother had taken up his offer instead of letting her son enjoy the treat.

Ari imagined he could smell the sap of the damp wood snapping in the fireplace. He could feel the pleasant searing of good cognac being slowly sipped. He even heard the small sound outside, like a box being dropped – something wooden at any rate – and a small scuffling sound but, like Lindbergh, he would have ignored it.

Lindbergh's day had been constructive but he was glad to be home. A biting wind had dropped the temperature into the low thirties. The shutters were rattling and perhaps that had masked the sound of a crude ladder being placed against the outside wall of the house a few feet from where he sat reading. Lindbergh was drowsy and contented, warmed by a soak in a bath and a good meal. He was planning the next day's schedule – unaware that his life would be shattered by the events of that very night. Betty, the nursemaid, passed the living room door as she went upstairs to check on the baby. Lindbergh could not know that he was about to experience the last thirty seconds of peace left in his life. He had conquered the world in 1927 but March 1st, 1932 would conquer him. His plane was coming down. There were flames.

Unknown to Lindbergh, during the last twenty seconds of peace in his life, Betty had found the baby's crib empty. As he turned the page of the newspaper in which he was engrossed, imagining the next two lines were the most important thing, Betty had knocked on the bathroom door behind which Anne was bathing.

'Do you have the baby, Mrs Lindbergh?' she asked, already feeling that something was flying out of her control.

Anne's bewildered voice said, 'No.'

'Perhaps the colonel has him, then.'

Anne got out of the bath, went into Po's room and scoured the bedclothes for the child. He was gone. The sheets were cold.

Betty ran back down the stairs. Lindbergh looked up at her. He marked his place in the article with a finger, as if he would go back to it again.

'Do you have the baby?' Betty asked him frantically.

'Isn't he in his crib?' Lindbergh asked.

Her face told him the awful truth. Her hands went up to cover her mouth. Lindbergh pushed past her, raced up the stairs and found Anne. He looked straight at her, at the way she was holding the baby's rumpled blue sheet in one clenched fist and he said, 'Anne, they have stolen our baby.'

153

The police were called. A call from the Lindbergh house was like a summons from the president. The family searched the house while the police forces of two states began to arrive. At some point, the unlatched window in the southeast corner of the nursery was discovered. Anne flung it open and the wind howled in.

'A baby!' she cried out as a wail reached them from the woodpile stacked against the house but the wind whipped even that small hope away before she could lay her hands on it.

'That was the cat, Mrs Lindbergh,' said Betty as she wrestled the window closed.

A ransom note had been left at the scene, propped on a radiator. It demanded $50,000 in cash. The ladder – a roughly hewn thing – was broken in three places and lay like discarded bones on the Lindbergh's front lawn.

The baby eagle, as the press touted him, was lost. He would not be found alive. His little body had been rotting in the woods less than two miles from the house since the night of the kidnapping. The investigation was relentless, though. Cars were searched; people carrying blond infants were questioned savagely. Nearby orphanages and mental asylums were inspected. Fantastic tales surfaced of intricate conspiracies and guilty family members.

The police showed up at Hella's door and questioned her about odd occurrences in the night. She told them she had seen nothing, and that nothingness she had seen devastated her because she had been watching so diligently. She did not tell the police this. If she had, the eyebrow of suspicion would have been raised in her direction. They took her name, though, and her New York address and moved on to the next home, the next possibility, with hope dwindling beneath the crunch of so many official boots.

It was the twenty-second day of the widest police search ever initiated in American history, when two men travelling along a remote road in New Jersey stopped for one of their party to relieve himself in the woods. Sixty feet from the road, the man looked down and saw a small skull and a baby's foot peeping up out of the leaf-muddy soil.

The officers he called followed him back to the site and agreed it was a baby, badly decomposed and lying face down in the dirt. The size of the body and the still-golden hair suggested it was baby Po. A wild animal had eaten his left leg but the eyes were blue and the dimpled cleft in the chin told them they had found him.

An autopsy performed in Trenton showed the cause of death to be a fractured skull due to external violence. It was suggested that the ladder had broken as the kidnapper attempted to climb down it. He had lost his balance for a second, smashing the baby's head against a rung or the side of the house. Po had been dead only seconds after he was taken.

Lindbergh viewed the baby himself. This first son of his had been created with the woman who he loved still but who he had loved most passionately at the moment of conception. He'd had wishes for his son and dreams for him that his baby head had been too small to hold for itself.

When the skull had cracked open in that deadly instant, even the smallest desires it might have held had drained away.

A man on a ladder had extinguished the lights of Paris from Charles Lindbergh's mind as surely as a council lamplighter would have extinguished them a hundred years before.

12

New York, 1935

They followed Charles Lindbergh's life as spectators follow the ball at a tennis match, fixated on it and patently ludicrous to any who might have been looking on – but there was nobody looking on. Benjamin Gold's three brothers were coping in their own way with the effects of the economic slide on their private lives and fortunes. One of them, Jacob the accountant, had caused a major scandal in the city by divorcing his wife and remarrying a much older woman. Hella was full of scorn for the decision but Ari thought her derision was due to the fact that the news had unsettled her. She relied so heavily on her beauty and considered it so powerful that any man leaving his wife for someone she considered less attractive threw the laws of her universe into question.

Benjamin Gold's money had seen them through the worst times in comfort. Conditions had stabilized somewhat and the WPA programmes were starting to give people hope again. Bridges and dams were being built out west. They were sending those with medical training out to the farms to prevent diseases spreading. There were vaccination programmes and literacy programmes and skills training programmes, everything designed to give work to the tutors and the possibility of a job to the learners. Hella liked Franklin Roosevelt and listened to him on the radio. Some of the extra staff they had taken on in kindness came with embarrassed looks and said they had found better-paying work elsewhere. Hella was happy for them and told them to take it. The crisis, it seemed, was easing. This worried Ari. His mother was good in a crisis when she was being kept busy. Now, she had time on her hands again and no plan for her life.

One night, Ari got up for water in the night and sensed that the house was not as quiet as it should be. Hella's light was on; Ari could see it under her door. He stood on the threshold and waited to hear if she was moving about in there. Sometimes, his mother just had a bad night and, unable to sleep, she would get up and rearrange her cupboards or change the linen on her bed in the small hours. There were no furtive sounds tonight, though. That was bad. It meant she was sitting still in there and thinking.

For months after their return from Hopewell, she had been lost in despair. Every year in Sweden (she had once told him) there were tales of women who went out in blizzards to get firewood from a shed which stood no more than a few feet from their back doors and were disoriented by the wilderness of white. Often, they were found frozen the next morning within sight of the lamp-lit windows, their hands inches away from the edge of the porch or the landmark of a well wall which might have directed them, but they had been so utterly blinded by the swirling snow that they had missed their chance at salvation.

That was how Ari saw his mother, though there was never any swirling chaos around her. Hella pulled through the days like a ship's prow pulls through thick, dark water, barely rippling its surface. The bitter snow, the tumultuous waves – she carried these inside her, so that if a mortician ever opened her up on the autopsy table it would all come slopping out as polluted snowy slush.

Ari decided to knock. He had always been forced to seek tentative admission when he felt sure other boys were granted the same without ever having to ask. Hella was sitting on the bed wearing the silver padded gown she favoured. The sheets were a stone grey and the hangings draped from the four posters were the colour of charcoal, so that she looked the image of Hans Christian Andersen's Ice Queen in her alpine lair. In her hand, Hella held a shoe. Ari was perturbed to see that it was the single shoe he had found stuck in the mud on Le Bourget field: the peach-coloured evening heel he had thought so inappropriate for such an adventurous outing. Hella had kept it all these years; she clutched it now as an amulet – a single shoe that would never have a partner, poignant and pointless, the quintessence of abandoned possibilities in that greatest of fairy-tales.

'I knew, of course, that the baby would have to die,' Hella said; it was a non sequitur, even to silence. She turned the shoe over and over in her hand.

Ari was fixated on her. He could not prevent himself from waiting for what might come next. Her moments of madness held a fantastical allure with their breathtaking unpredictability.

'For everything to work out between us, I knew it had to happen but when I think of holding you at that age and what Anne must have felt – something inside me breaks.'

'You could talk to somebody about it,' said Ari. 'Like a doctor...'

'I don't need a doctor. I'm perfectly well, thank you.'

'You sound sad,' Ari said. He didn't know how else to express his care.

'It's because I used to think that man who took the baby was part of the plan,' she said. Her voice was a dull monotone. 'I used to think he was a part of what was meant to be. I would say to myself, "Hella, now events are afoot; the future is in motion." But lately I've taken to thinking I ought to have done something like that myself.'

'What are you saying?' said Ari.

The room was very cold.

'It's all stagnant now, Ari, and I have to do something. But surely not the new baby?' She seemed to be asking this nonsensical question of an invisible presence. They had both read an article about the Lindberghs' newborn only the

159

day before... 'I'm surely not to think about their new baby...?'

Ari had to stop her before she said any more. He had learned where to start if he wanted Hella's attention. 'I've been meaning to tell you something about the plane,' he said. 'All these years and it suddenly came to me that I might never have told you about it...'

Hella's blue eyes flicked up to meet his own, sharp and suspicious but at least focused. The shoe stopped moving in her hand.

'That night at Le Bourget, did you hear the ripping?' he asked.

Hella readjusted her frozen position, lifting her body up then settling it back down more comfortably.

'No,' she said, 'I was quite far away, you recall. What was the ripping?'

'It was people pulling at the plane,' Ari told her. 'Tearing it apart.'

He lowered his buttock until it rested on the very edge of the mattress. He didn't sit fully, not yet. His mother did not object, though. He was winning.

'They were actually grabbing pieces of it to keep.'

'Were they really?' Hella asked. 'How strange.'

'When the French soldiers saw what was happening, they cleared a path to get the plane into that barn so it would be easier to guard but before they did, there was already a hole torn out of the wing...'

In Ari's mind, the shape of the remembered tear was long and thin. It sloped down to the right so that it resembled a woman swimming with her arms stretched out ahead of her in mid-stroke and her legs trailing behind. That shadow on the wing had formed a woman swimming or perhaps falling through air. The place where the fabrication was most tattered became her hair, splayed out in a torrent around her.

'As they rolled it away, the shadow of that tear was the last thing I could see because it was so dark, a deeper blackness against the blackness of the wing.'

'Do you think they kept the pieces they took?' asked Hella. 'Those thieves... Do you think they know what those scraps mean?'

Ari thought his mother would have made a wonderful Catholic. The Lutheran faith of her father had been too austere for her but Catholics kept little bits of their God all around them like the spoils of spiritual hunters. They surrounded themselves with rosary beads and votive candles and incense sticks and memorial cards.

'I don't know,' said Ari. 'I wonder where those souvenirs are now?'

He sat down properly and swung his legs up under him. His mother did the same and they were knee-to-knee again.

'Maybe we should hunt it down?' she said and her lips turned up a little at the corners. 'Chase around the world after a fragment of material.'

'They took the log, too,' Ari added.

'What?' said his mother.

Ari smiled because his mother had always been the world's greatest advocate of 'pardon'.

'The flight log he wrote on the way over,' said

161

Ari. 'It was missing the next day. Don't you remember?'

'They never found it?' she said. Then she realized it, 'You're right. They never did!'

'It was just a bit of scribbling to while away the time, I suppose,' said Ari. 'But I bet the Smithsonian would pay a million for it.'

'I would pay a million!' said Hella. 'My name might even be in it,' she speculated, then amended her speculation, 'my name *will* be in it! He'll have been thinking of us surely with all those hours on his hands...'

Sometimes the things his mother said really frightened Ari.

'We should hire someone to look for it for us. Offer the thief money. It was probably an idiot farm boy from one of those nearby onion scratchpatches who has no idea what it's worth...'

Ari had only been planning this conversation as an opening, a preamble to a revelation that might distract her for several more months but now he began to see how it all might work out in another way entirely.

'There'll be a fire one day and some halfwit will have buried it in a barn. It'll just go up in smoke if we don't rescue it.'

Glassen's burned body came back to Ari and he realized that that had been the moment when he had first known his mother to be capable of anything. He tried not to think of the man these days. As he got older – and he was almost twenty now – Ari found it more and more difficult to believe in his childhood terrors: moths, deep water, darkness, the fact that his mother had

162

killed someone.

Hella's hands were twisting and bunching her robe. They left creases in the silk like fingers swirled through whipped cream. At least she had put the shoe down on the sheet. Ari surreptitiously moved the shoe away from Hella's grasp; she did not seem to notice it now. Somehow, Ari felt as if he had prised a loaded weapon from the hand of a would-be suicide.

'Or one day, somebody will just throw that precious thing out with the garbage. It ought to be found, Ari.'

'A hundred years from now, it'll come to light,' Ari said. He was formulating a plan; his insides swelled with compassion and magnanimity. 'You'll see.'

'I will speak to someone,' Hella said. 'I'll get someone to see to it tomorrow.'

She leaned forward and took her son's face in her hands and kissed his forehead. He could never remember her doing that before. He felt oddly befuddled and warm in his stomach; little coals glowed there beneath the skin like a tiny stove to warm his blood.

'It'll be alright now, my love. I'll get myself together, you'll see. We have a new project,' she said. 'You always need a project, Ari. Once I thought I would study medicine and be a women's doctor...' she stopped. 'But never mind that now. Tomorrow we'll meet a real detective!'

Hella conducted interviews for weeks, asking each potential applicant how he proposed to tackle the task. She ran through the legitimate

163

agencies in a matter of months. Her infuriating relentlessness and constant phone calls put them off. Her retainer cheques were returned. These agencies had used the official paths open to them: they had placed notices in all the French newspapers – cryptic messages offering rewards – and had even made surreptitious approaches to the remoter members of the Lindbergh family. They had received no intelligence in this way but the advertisements had resulted in an unexpected side effect that Hella Gold had not anticipated. She was swamped with offers of Lindbergh memorabilia.

Lindbergh's goggles, a map he had used and autographed copies of his book (she had seventeen) all made their way, at great cost, to Benjamin Gold's study. Once, Hella and Ari had taken a train to Chicago to bid in an auction for his flight suit. The suit had been a gentleman's size thirty-four inches and Hella had announced to the entire assembled room that she was a friend of Mr Lindbergh's and that the suit was at least six inches too short for the man.

'Do you imagine he flew halfway around the world with that crotch cutting up into him?' she had demanded.

There had been a communal gasp of indrawn breath.

'This item is a fake and the seller the worst kind of charlatan.'

She had stormed out and Ari had scurried after her.

That debacle had further determined her to seek assistance in her search from other sources.

164

She called first the cook, then the chauffeur, then the kitchen boy, into Benjamin's study. Several of the maids were also summoned for private interviews. The window washer was a last resort. He stayed with her for almost half an hour and left with a white envelope in his hand...

Oddman and Brown called on a Sunday morning, confirming their status as an unconventional duo. Hella had asked Ari to sit in on the meeting. He was unsettled to note that she seemed a little nervous about the arrival of the two men but they proved fascinating to Ari.

He loved their names at once. They had got them mixed up somehow. Julian Oddman was a straight-laced university student of about thirty who wore a drab, mottled suit that matched his tortoiseshell spectacle frames. He had neat side-whiskers but was clean shaven about the face. He was neat as a pin, tall and serious. His hat sat atop his head like a stack of plates balanced by a conjurer and he held his neck stiffly as if it might come crashing down.

Kit Brown was enormous, almost completely bald and husky-voiced. He wore a pink and burgundy striped shirt, no jacket and burgundy shoes so garish they might have been called red. He looked like a boxer squashed into the gaudy get-up of a dancehall dandy. Unlike most pairs of this sort in popular fiction or comic cinema, both of them were brains.

Brown had started his career as a shop steward in a Belfast brewery and he had some tales to tell, he assured Hella. He had left as a young man of

165

twenty and made his way to America with an uncle who had served with the Black and Tans...

'Making me none too popular among that rowdy republican lot back home,' he roared. 'My uncle taught me all there was to know about finding what prefers to stay lost. Not much gets past me and if my uncle hadn't got that bottle in the throat he'd be sitting here beside me now. I met Oddman here at the night university where I was studying history in the evenings ... actually, we met in an art class I took as an extra.'

Hella was so delighted by this absurd revelation that she clapped her hands.

'What kind of art class was it, Mr Brown?'

'Just Brown, please, Ma'am,' said Brown. 'It was a survey on the works and theory of the Pre-Raphaelites. Oddman's audited it three times.'

'There's been a different lecturer each time,' interjected Oddman. 'There are different things to learn.'

Ari looked at Oddman carefully while Brown spoke. The monotone of his brownness gave him a sleek, uniformed glamour. He looked like an otter and his eyes were a startling shade of light brown that was almost russet. Ari thought he was perhaps the most handsome man he had ever seen.

'We like to offer a unique service to our clients, Ma'am,' Brown was saying. 'I'm the fox, so to speak, and Oddman's the owl. I sniff it out and he authenticates it.'

'Furniture, silver, Chinese porcelain, Egyptian antiquary and documents,' said Oddman. 'I specialize in documents,' he added.

166

'You'll never be caught out again,' said Brown. 'I heard about that business in Chicago. That flight suit went for almost a thousand dollars. Apparently they didn't take your outburst too seriously. Two buyers left the salesroom after you but the rest stayed – the house was convinced you were a plant smuggled in to bring the price down.'

'Would somebody do such a thing?' said Hella, aghast.

She was more shocked by this announcement than by the revelation that Oddman and Brown knew about the escapade which she and Ari had imagined to be clandestine.

Ari could see that his mother was acting and that she was delighted to be hearing about criminal cleverness she secretly admired or which at least thrilled her.

'Ah, Ma'am. You'll be learning a lot from us, I can see that.'

She leaned forward and said quite breathily, 'I'm a keen student!'

'Now on to the nature of the acquisition,' said Brown.

He was leading the meeting now and Hella was ready to follow.

'You may think it strange,' said Hella.

'Not too long ago, I spent the better part of the year hunting down medieval chastity belts for a German fellow!' roared Brown.

Hella giggled and it was a giggle of genuine happiness. It sparkled round the room like an un-expected dragonfly. Ari liked Brown enormously already. The man was not intimidated by the

167

opulence of the room or the woman who had most men sweating into their collars.

'It's a book,' said Hella.

'Rare books,' said Oddman. 'A speciality of mine.'

'Not a rare book exactly. More of a one-of-a-kind.'

'Illuminated scripts ... another speciality,' said Oddman.

'It's a journal actually. A very brief one, I imagine. I don't know what it looks like or who has it but I will pay almost anything...'

Ari wondered if she should have shown her hand that early in the game but decided she had set her mind on forthrightness with these men and perhaps she was right. Ari thought they would know a faker.

'A challenge,' said Brown. 'What is it? Or should I say whose is it?'

'It belonged to Charles Lindbergh. The notes he wrote during that first transatlantic flight. The pages were taken from the cockpit some time between his landing and the next morning when Lindbergh visited the plane along with the American ambassador to collect it.'

'Fascinating,' said Brown.

'It has no value in itself,' said Hella. 'I'm just a collector of items of interest related to Charles Lindbergh, as you apparently know.'

'The nabbing of that baby doubled prices,' said Brown.

'Did it?' said Hella, shocked.

'Oh, they went up something scandalous,' Brown said, implying that Lindbergh's history was part of his area of expertise, too.

Ari knew what had happened. Prior to their arrival at the Golds' residence that day, Oddman and Brown had undertaken a period of reconnaissance on Hella and Ari to anticipate what they might be asked to do. If they had come prepared for Lindbergh collectibles then somebody beside Ari knew of his mother's obsession. Rather than easing his mind of the fear that he bore the weight of her obsession alone, the realization unsteadied him. He had somehow failed to protect her.

'People offered Anne Lindbergh their babies. Did you know that? Wrote her letters offering to give her one of their brood to replace the little chap. Well meant, I suppose, but still... Prices rocketed after that. His signature was worth more than the president's for a while there. He's the most sought-after spokesman for consumer products in America. Pan Am have nabbed him now but even Foxy Nolan doesn't get more to say he brushes with Gleam toothpaste or whatever.'

'I didn't know any of this,' said Hella.

Ari thought the news that other men and women were as fixated as she was might disturb her – Hella had always imagined her doting to be a private thing – but instead it steeled her resolve. She loved competition.

'I'll be up against other bidders?' asked Hella.

'Shouldn't think so,' said Brown. 'If the seller knew what he had, he'd have put it up on the market during the hype of thirty-two. That would have made financial sense.'

'How could he have done that? It's certainly stolen property, isn't it?'

'Oh, I don't mean on the legitimate market, Ma'am. There's a black market for all manner of merchandise. Art stolen from museums, dubious pictures of well-known people – film stars and the like – if you'll excuse me for even mentioning it. And, of course, whenever one of these celebrity types is in the news for something or other there's a price hike. Thirty-two would have been the time to put out feelers for discreet buyers for anything to do with Lindbergh but now is a good time, too, with the trial on. Prices are bound to soar again so we'll be watching.'

'Before you go, Mr Brown. Could I ask a small favour? It's not a test, you understand, only a personal matter with which you may be able to assist me.'

'Go ahead, Ma'am. If it's within our power...'

Hella took a blue airmail envelope from the desk drawer and removed a sheet of paper from it. She passed the sheet to Brown who, without looking at it, handed it over to Oddman.

'If it's written, it's Mr Oddman's department,' he explained.

Oddman turned the paper over and examined the back first; he was leaving the excitement of the actual writing for later. He looked at the way the ink had blotted through in places. He moved the paper back and forward against the light from the window. Then he turned it over and examined the letterhead. He leaned forward and gently plucked the envelope from Hella's hand. He looked at the stamps and the franking mark. He smelled the glue which had adhered it.

'Swedish lawyer's letter. Typed on a good new

machine by an excellent typist. She applies an extraordinary evenness of pressure to all the keys. The ink's no more than a month old. Quite expensive, though – in keeping with the type of supplies an affluent lawyer's office might use. He's employed a very pricey nib for the signature – Mont Blanc or Cartier, almost certainly. The detail on the seal is quite extraordinary and its use a little arcane these days, implying an established, well-to-do enterprise that doesn't feel the need to be a slave to fashion, I'd say. This letterhead is not new, though. They ordered their stationery from last year's budget and this has sat at the bottom of a box, giving the letter an impression of age it doesn't really possess. The envelope has the usual rippling of damp. It's been transported in one of the lower mailbags of a transatlantic liner; it absorbed some moisture from the deck boards. There's slight smudge to the franking which affirms that. It was sorted right here in Manhattan – see the crunch on this bottom right-hand corner? – they have a newfangled sorter at Central Mail that sometimes jams up and it always leaves this crinkle. Completely authentic, I'd say. Did you have reason to doubt it?'

'Not really. It's a notice of my mother's death actually. I didn't really expect she would have gone as far as faking that. Though she might have done anything to have me home, I suppose.'

Ari's eyes opened wide. They had not spoken about his grandmother since that day years and years before when his mother had described her girlhood but he thought he would have been told about the old woman's death.

'Condolences on your loss,' said Brown.

'I passed, I hope,' said Oddman quietly, embarrassed now by his flamboyant display over so private a letter.

'I said it wasn't a test,' said Hella. 'But thank you for bringing your experience to bear.'

She looked sad. Perhaps some buried part of her had hoped the letter was a hoax. Now that her mother's death had been authenticated she was unprepared for her reaction. There was a moment of uncomfortable silence. Oddman broke it by leaning forward and tapping the newspaper that lay in front of Hella on the desk.

Bruno Hauptmann's face stared back at them from the courthouse steps. Ari had already read the article. It was headed: *'Lindbergh Baby Killer Still Cries Innocence.'* As he had read it, he had run his fingertips along the formulation of nine random letters that spell the magical incantation: L-IN-D-B-E-R-G-H. The tips of his fingers had warmed as he touched the name.

Bruno Hauptmann, German carpenter from Queens, New York, was today granted permission to speak with journalists from his cell in Flemington, New Jersey. He is awaiting an appeal scheduled for October 9th of this year to see whether his conviction of January 13th will be upheld. Hauptmann was sentenced to death by electric chair and experts in the legislature anticipate the order will be upheld. Hauptmann still maintains his innocence despite overwhelming evidence to suggest he is guilty of the kidnapping and subsequent murder of famed aviator Charles Lindbergh's baby son. 'A crime this heinous in nature cannot go unpunished. It demands the ultimate sentence,' said Judge Trenchard. The Lindbergh family were unable to comment on Hauptmann's impassioned plea for clemency this morning. They are visiting family in Little Falls, Minnesota.

'We'll start this afternoon,' said Brown.

'On a Sunday?' asked Hella.

'Does that bother you, Ma'am? It's not *midsommardagen* is it?' asked Brown, naming a favourite Swedish holiday.

Hella opened her mouth in surprise and joy. Such little things could delight her.

'We'll do some preliminaries on the potential for success,' he added.

Oddman had not spoken for some time now. The four of them stood up and filed out the room in an awkward line. At the front door there was another slight shuffle caused by too many people in a confined space. Even though the foyer was large, Brown took up a great deal of the available room.

It had all been amicable and exciting. For once, Ari was eager to speak to his mother about her expectations of the men. Then he realized that on such a mission, their failure was inevitable and he felt ashamed. As the men donned their hats, Brown tapped the newspaper Ari was still holding.

'That man's going to see hell before too long,' he said. 'Just about right for a baby-killer.'

'There's a lot of speculation that he's been set up,' said Ari. 'That he isn't the real kidnapper after all or at least not the only one.'

'Hauptmann? A patsy? Well, if he was stupid

173

enough to let himself get stitched up...' Brown let Ari complete the rest of the sentence in his head.

'You'll be hearing from us soon, Ma'am,' said Brown.

Oddman simply lifted his fragile hat and put it back down on his head with care.

They were all smiles until Brown leaned forward to open the door. As he did so, he spoke quietly to Ari for a few seconds and slipped a business card into his hand. The boy pulled away at his words and though Hella waved courteously as the two men started off towards the elevator, Ari's face was frozen.

'What did he ask you just then?' she said.

'He only said goodbye,' said Ari.

'Nonsense!' said Hella.

She said it in the same way another person might shout: 'Liar!'

'It was something about Hauptmann, wasn't it?'

'He asked me to let him know if I wanted a lock of Hauptmann's hair,' said Ari.

13

Stockholm, 1935

If the Depression had hit New York City hard, Sweden had not escaped the misery. Ari remembered Stockholm as a kind of storybook city filled in with primary colours and tall thin houses all squashed together like a row of emaciated giants seen in a dream. He remembered the place in bits and pieces. Waiting to cross the streets between men on horseback, looking over the Norjbro to Gamla Stan and seeing the small stone houses of the old city coming up out of the water.

The house on Strandvägen was closed up and the front lawn was overgrown but Birgit, the surly maid, was still on retainer and she greeted them at the door. The old Swedish gentleman who wore slippers instead of shoes because of his bunions had endured a heart attack the week after Eleanor Köll's death and had lingered for a few days in a private infirmary at the estate's expense until he had passed away quietly in the small dark hours one night. Birgit was the only member of the household left. She looked at Ari suspiciously and he thought for a second that she had mistaken him for his mother's much younger lover until he drew closer and she seemed to recognize him.

'Do you remember me?' he asked quite fondly. She looked so severe, he felt he ought to break the tension. 'I'm the little boy who's afraid of dogs.'

He was mocking himself to appease her. He was almost six foot two now and slim and handsome, nearly twenty, and he didn't hide behind his mother so much or fear strangers so greatly.

'You look well, Birgit.'

Her face changed dramatically at his compliment.

'I'm married,' she said happily and she blushed prettily along the neck of her uniform.

'Have you been running the house yourself?' asked Hella as they went through into the front hall.

'Yes, Ma'am,' said Birgit.

She was almost light with happiness as if the burden of Eleanor had been lifted from her, and had revealed a more sprightly, fun-loving girl.

'We were not sure how to handle the house. The lawyers asked me to simply cover everything over and I purchased some cheap sheeting from the haberdasher to stop the dust.'

The grand house with its artefacts from four continents was just a barren landscape covered over with snowy cotton. Lumps and bumps were unrecognizable as fine tables and lamps and statues and tribal masks. Even the gilded mirrors and the enormous oil paintings – one of which Ari was sure was a Vermeer – were covered. Only the deep olive-green walls remained as they had been, lit by the crystal chandelier that hung above the staircase to the upper floors.

'I'm living just off Lutzeng now. It's only a ten-minute walk. I will cook for you and clean and wash what needs washing while you're here.'

'Can you find another post?' asked Hella.

Ari remembered how keen his mother had been to have the girl fired when last they visited. The Depression, it seemed, had developed in Hella a preoccupation with people's jobs and welfare. Birgit's hands went down to her stomach and she smiled a lovely broad smile that lit up her features. Even the joining eyebrows didn't appear so intense.

'Ah,' said Hella. She smiled, too. 'I see.'

'The baby will come in the winter and Joop doesn't really want me slithering about on the icy streets in case I fall. He has a very good job with the city council. He campaigned on behalf of the Social Democrats for parliament and Per Albin Hansson himself offered him the post in local government. He organizes need-based assistance for the unemployed. We do very well and I've only stayed on here to see to Mrs Köll and then to watch the house until you came.'

Ari was astonished by how happiness could transform a life. He could hardly recognize the girl. He saw Hella watching her with something like awe. Would his mother be cruel? Ari could never tell. He could see she was jealous of this girl's modest little life, her new-found light.

But Hella took Birgit's hand and said, 'You look so well, Birgit, and you mustn't work if there's a baby coming. Let your Joop take care of you and enjoy being spoiled a little. After working for my mother, you've earned it.'

Birgit bit her lip, unsure of whether to say something or not. 'She was difficult in the last few years. She kept asking forgiveness from somebody called Phillip.'

Hella went quite still.

'I don't know anybody by that name and she wouldn't allow herself to be comforted.'

'We don't know any Phillips either,' said Hella. 'I'm sure you were a consolation to her. I simply must have a bath. Is the water still on?'

Birgit bobbed a curtsey.

'Yes, Ma'am. And there's ice in the icebox and the electric's running. We didn't want to cancel anything until we knew what you wished.'

'When I was last here, you thought me cruel for leaving...'

Birgit's eyes went down to the wooden floor-boards.

'I had no right...'

Ari tried to step back and appear to look through the net curtains out into the street. This stilted conversation was about two women trying rather ineptly to apologize. Both had grown up in the preceding few years, as the world had grown up, but words did not seem to flow.

'She was not easy. I know that now,' said Birgit.

'She deserved a better daughter,' said Hella.

They had both said their piece and there would be tranquillity in the house for the next few days.

Ari tossed a dust cover from his mother's bed as she drew herself a bath. She took her hair down from its pins at the dressing table and coiled it loosely in a headscarf to prevent it getting wet.

'Choose anything you want from the house. I'm getting an estate auctioneer in tomorrow and the whole lot is going.'

'Can I have something of Grandpa's?'

'Anything we can carry or ship home with us.'

'You promise me anything,' said Ari.

'Why do I feel as if I'm being made to make a promise I won't be able to get out of?'

'It's important,' said Ari.

'Anything, then. You just name the thing.'

'It's in the cottage at Mariefred,' said Ari.

'I'm not going back to Mariefred, Ari!' said Hella annoyed. 'Why didn't you take it last time?'

'I didn't know I'd want it.'

'What is it?' she asked.

'The mould for the candles that you and Grandfather used to make.'

'That's not worth anything!' said Hella.

She was confused by the choice but because he had chosen something with sentimental meaning for her, she softened a little.

'It's broken by now, or taken by the Karlssons. It won't be there.'

'It might.'

'We probably don't own the cottage any more.'

'Did you sell it?' Ari asked in terror.

'No, you asked me not to but I must now. You have to see that. I don't want any holdings here. I can't care for them across an ocean; it's too difficult. I want everything in America.'

Ari was relieved. She seemed to be relenting.

'I'll ask Birgit if she knows anything about it,' he said.

'I'm not going to Mariefred,' Hella said again. 'I've told you that.'

'But I want to go. I'll be there and back in a day. I'll go tomorrow while you're dealing with the house and the lawyers. I'll say goodbye for us.'

'I've already said goodbye,' said Hella. 'Years ago. It's you who must hanker after the past.'

'Thank you,' said Ari and he kissed her on her silky hair. He could tell she was pleased but she swatted him away as if annoyed.

Ari skidded down the stairs to catch Birgit before she left for the night.

'I want to go out to Mariefred in the morning,' he said. 'Do you know if we still have the cottage?'

'I think Miss Eleanor kept it on,' she said.

She was peeling turnips and sweet potatoes and cutting them into small cubes for a soup. She was very precise in her work and Ari found he liked the way she moved.

'I could go out there myself tomorrow,' said Birgit. 'Miss Eleanor made me promise to visit the Karlssons and I haven't found the time to do it yet. She left an envelope for them. I expect it's money for looking after the cottage. Perhaps in the letter she gives them use of it, I don't know.'

'We can go together if you like,' said Ari. 'As I said, I need to make the trip. If you don't feel like it, I can go alone and take the envelope for you.'

'How's your Swedish these days?' asked Birgit.

'I don't speak it at all any more.'

'I'd better go with you, then,' said Birgit. 'There might be some explanation required for the letter.'

Birgit looked quite different dressed in her street clothes. In the house, she wore a plain blue shift with an enormous beige apron swathed across the front of it. Now she had on a new green coat with pewter toggles and a red scarf. She was quite pretty and Ari was aware of her as a woman. He didn't yet have a girlfriend of his own. He wanted somebody special and all the girls he'd met in New York were posh and glossy and seemed so much older than he was and so much more knowing. He was hopeless with girls, though everybody teased him about his looks. Ari sensed that Birgit was flirting with him a little but maybe she was only teasing him the way older women sometimes did with boys.

Birgit smiled across her cocoa at him in the ferry. It was a cool day and rain snakes slithered down the ferry windows. Birgit had brought along an umbrella but Ari only had his overcoat and hoped they wouldn't have to walk the miles to the cottage in a downpour. That would make the trip back very uncomfortable.

'You look as if you belong,' she said. 'Just like a Swede.'

'I don't belong,' said Ari. 'Not anywhere.'

'Oh, stop!' said Birgit, and then she looked down nervously into her cocoa, remembering he was something like her boss.

'Stop what?' said Ari.

He was genuinely surprised.

'You have a wonderful apartment in New York, yes? A mother who cares for you but lets you be, money, a future in America. What's there to be so sorry about?'

'I worry about my mother,' said Ari.

It was the plain truth. No embellishment was necessary. He wondered if Birgit would under-stand him. She did.

'Your mother is like her mother,' said Birgit. 'Very difficult and...' she struggled for the word for a few moments, wanting to get it just right. 'Dissatisfied,' she said emphatically.

Ari wondered how she knew.

'Miss Eleanor would walk the house complain-ing about how everywhere else she'd lived was better. Old admirers had been better than her hus-band; the weather was better in India or Jamaica. She never found the now. Do I make sense?'

Ari nodded. He was almost too choked up to speak. Somebody, not a friend or a confidant but a stranger, could understand.

'Miss Eleanor always wanted to be somewhere else with somebody else but if it had happened, she would have missed Sweden and her home and her husband. It was a terrible way to live,' she said finally. And then she said the word again, 'Terrible.'

'I don't want to be that way,' said Ari.

Birgit reached across and rested her hand on his. He was overwhelmed by the small gesture. He felt tingles in his stomach and tears pricked the corner of his eyes, so that he had to swallow a few times to keep them down.

'At the end, do you know what Miss Eleanor said to me?' said Birgit. 'She said how happy Hella would have been if she had been allowed to marry her young man at sixteen. She even started to imagine that the world would have worked out perfectly if she had not sent the boy back to England. Can you imagine? Something she would never have dreamed of considering at that time, something unspeakable to her, but now it had become the perfect answer... If only...'

'My grandmother sent my father away?'

'Oh, yes. She sent him with a scolding back to England and he had to join the army. Your mother blames her unhappiness on that decision by her parents, no? She blames his death on them.'

'I don't know,' said Ari.

'I think that is what happened,' said Birgit. 'That was the cut that never healed.'

The Karlsson family welcomed Birgit warmly and Ari could see that she had been out here many times, probably on errands from Eleanor or because she liked the farm and the little twin girls straight out of a picture book on Sweden. Ari just tried to smile at them all and be courteous though he was uncomfortable not being able to understand the language. Every now and then Birgit threw a translation his way.

'They can't believe you're the same boy from eight years ago,' she said. 'You're a young man now. They think you're very handsome.'

She winked at the twins and they giggled behind their hands just as they had done when he had been concerned about putting sour milk in his porridge.

'If you're going to visit a while,' said Ari, 'I'll walk down to the cottage.'

They refreshed the directions for him and he started off. It was the tail end of summer here and soon they would be planning for the harvest. Some of the trees had started their long, slow turn to orange and there were dried pods all along the rutted paths. The cottage looked just the same; perhaps it appeared smaller. It needed a fresh coat of paint – a job usually undertaken in the summer – but the Karlssons had felt the Depression and there was no money to spare on paint. The little cottage looked dull under the dull sky; it peeled red flakes like the back of a farmer's sunburned neck. The trees across Lake Mälaren cast their flaming reflections into the grey water like a silver mirror and there were skeins of birds in the sky flying south.

Ari looked in on the cottage but didn't enter. There were more objects inside – a few extra chairs around the table and new quilts on the beds. It looked as if a few of the older Karlsson children had been given permission to bunk down here for the summer. Ari was glad it was being used. He headed for the boathouse. It was also looking dilapidated and unloved. The door was hanging a bit off its hinge but there was a boat inside now, bobbing on the building's gentle internal tide. It was a small rowing boat which looked second- or even third-hand. Ari supposed the children fished from it in summer. He wondered if the older boys took their girls out in it to the middle of the lake, the way he imagined his father must have taken his mother. There was no straw on the decking that formed the boarding platform. All the straw was going to animal feed for the upcoming winter, there was none to spare.

He hardly dared to look for the item he sought. Part of him was certain it would have been removed in the preceding years but when he looked into the gloom, it was there, a concrete block lying in the middle of a coil of rope just as he remembered leaving it.

'Ari!' He heard Birgit's voice. It was still far off. She must be coming down the path from the farm. He picked up the keepsake and put it under his coat. He didn't want Birgit to think he was sentimental. This would help his mother, he was sure. This might even end her obsession. Events like his grandmother's timely death had all slotted into place for him to come back to this decrepit little cottage in the middle of a distant country. It would work out.

'I'm down here,' he shouted out to Birgit as he emerged from the boathouse. His voice sounded strong and carefree; it rang right up the hill and into the woods. She heard him clearly. She waved.

14

New York, 1935

On their first day back in New York, Ari made his way north on the D-train into the heart of the Bronx. His mother was still giving orders about the unpacking to the servants when he slipped out on an imaginary errand. Oddman & Brown's card showed they had offices off the Grand Concourse. Ari was unfamiliar with the subway station and the street onto which it exited. He asked directions but when he reached the place where he thought the offices should be, he could not find them. His heart began to sink. Oddman & Brown were frauds; the card was a fraud. Ari searched in vain for a further ten minutes and was almost in despair when he decided to ask one last time for help.

A young woman was walking slowly up the street with a small dog on a leash. Ari thought the dog was an Irish setter and he saw at once why she had settled on that particular breed. The girl's hair and the dog's fur were almost exactly the same colour. Although it was midsummer, her hair was a Fall maple – deep shining red curls bounced on her shoulders and she wore a plain fudge-coloured dress that accentuated her pale skin and narrow waist. She looked like a delicious Halloween candy and Ari thought she was beautiful. He ignored the other people passing him on the sidewalk and waited for the girl to reach him. He felt suddenly confident in this foreign neighbourhood. He knew if he stammered and made a fool of himself he was unlikely to run into her again.

'I'm sorry, Miss...' Ari said. 'I'm looking for a place of business and I'm lost.'

'Oh, let me see,' she said and pulled his hand closer so she could examine the card he was holding out.

'You're practically on top of it,' she said. 'I guess the entrance is down there.' She pointed to a narrow side street between two buildings. 'They often say Grand Concourse when they mean a side street. It sounds, well, grander, I guess.'

The girl smiled and Ari smiled, too. He had no idea how to keep her longer. The dog strained at its leash. She allowed the tug to get her moving again and she passed him, her eyes lowered to the pavement. As she went, she reached up and pulled her hair behind her ear so he could see that her smile still lingered.

'I'll scout it out,' he said after her. 'Thank you.'

'Good luck,' she said.

The encounter had pleased Ari. His mother was always going on about his looks but that was his mother. This time, a beautiful girl had liked him. He was sure of it.

He found the office easily after that. It was located behind a glass-panelled door with a gold embossed nameplate. The sign read 'Oddman & Brown' and beneath that 'Professional Procurement & Evaluation – Services Offered to Commercial and Private Clients'. Ari was a little surprised to have found the door. He had begun to doubt its existence. He felt relieved.

He went into a room that was crammed from floor to ceiling with objects and artefacts. Something jangled above his head and he spun round but it was just a bell above the door. He almost knocked a pile of books off a corner table as he moved. There was the smell of wood oil and varnish. Drop cloths covered some of the larger pieces and Ari imagined they must be armoires or dressers. There was barely a square foot of floor space free of expensive clutter. From the ceiling a magnificent chandelier lit the gloom. It threw a golden light over the hundreds of glittering objects. There were paintings all packed against each other along one wall, lamps and crystal bowls and silver samovars and bits of jewellery in glass cases and an enormous desk just like the one in the Frick Collection behind which Henry Clay had plotted the growth of his empire.

Nobody was around – the dazzling bits of finery and the furniture were the sole occupants of the office. Ari ran his hands along the bevelled edge of a Venetian mirror. It came away dusty but the mirror itself looked aged and beautiful. It softened his reflection so that he looked like a photograph of a star from the pages of *Silver*

Screen. It was one of the magical mirrors that reflected any face in the way it most wished to be seen.

'Genuine or not?' said a voice.

Ari turned to see Oddman at the top of a flight of stairs that was almost hidden by an enormous armoire.

'What does your gut say?' he added.

'Genuine,' said Ari and then, to give his gut added credibility. 'Definitely.'

'Well done!' said Oddman. 'That's what I say, though Sotheby's disagrees. I think it's genuine eighteenth-century Venetian. I told them if they were so sure it was a fake I'd take it off their hands, and bought it for a song. It's hung in the house of a banker on the Upper East Side for generations but last week...' He made a long slow whistle and formed his hand into an arch that fell and fell. 'Swan dive,' he added. Ari thought about the tear on the wing of the *Spirit of St Louis*, the woman falling.

'Anyway, it's an Oddman & Brown acquisition now. It'll be gracing our new offices just down the road from the Museum of Modern Art. Sorry about the disarray, Mr Gold. As you can see, we've just received the items we bid for from the banker gent's estate...'

'My name's Ari,' said Ari. 'Or Mr Köll. I was never actually adopted by Mr Gold.'

'Come upstairs,' said Oddman. 'Brown's got a nip on offer.'

Brown was wearing a teal-blue suit with gold stitching around its cuffs and collar. It was a colour his mother called peacock – a name which suited Brown exactly. His shirt was yellow. Ari was suddenly glad that he was no longer forced to wear his school blazer. He felt young and insubstantial beside this man – a human willow, too pliant to withstand the slightest wind.

The strange thing was that neither Oddman nor Brown seemed surprised to see him. They had both acted as if it was perfectly natural for Ari to show up like this without an appointment.

Ari accepted the offer of a whiskey and it came as half a glassful of burnished bronze in a singing crystal tumbler. He was not a great drinker. The boys from school would meet in the taverns on Friday evenings but Ari never went along. He had even missed the celebrations at end of the school year. Ari had been accepted at Princeton and Yale (between them, Benjamin Gold's three brothers were alumni of almost every Ivy League institution in the Tri-State area). He hoped he had passed his courses; he was not academic.

'It's been less than a month, Mr Köll,' said Brown. 'I admire high expectations, they keep us sharp in our business but...'

'I'm not here to check up on progress or anything,' Ari jumped in. 'I have to explain the situation.'

'Your mother?' said Brown.

'She has a thing ... it's a real problem, I think ... only other people don't see it.'

'Bit of an obsessive personality type,' said Oddman, so casually that it washed away any stigma from the layman diagnosis.

'Yes,' said Ari with relief. 'I've tried so many times to talk to her about that night and Mr

189

Lindbergh and all of it and to give her...'

'So the question is, do we fuel the fantasy or do we let it be?' said Brown. 'I see your predicament, Mr Köll, but appreciate ours. We've been employed by your mother and we are in the business of doing business ... for profit, you understand.'

'Oh, I do. I do. You're not getting my meaning. I want you to find it for her. I want you to give it to her. It's going to work out just as well this way.'

'Good. I'm glad you're so positive about it. Often, women just want a bit of adventure, you know. Women with means and women with intellect that isn't too often challenged, like your mother, need a bit of excitement, see?'

'I do know that,' said Ari. 'But she's been like this for as long as I can remember her.'

'You're her son,' said Brown. 'You don't see her as the rest of us do.'

He winked lasciviously at Oddman and the man smiled for the first time in response. Oddman's smile turned his face into a furrow of laughter lines and changed it utterly. He was like two people, one unaware of the other.

'I need to ask you to arrange something for me...' said Ari.

'It's all arranged, Mr Köll. The seller wants us on his patch, though.'

'What?' said Ari. *Pardon! Say pardon!* said his mother's voice in his head. 'Which seller?'

'Your mother wanted a specific item,' said Brown. 'That flight log. We've located it but the seller's a way off. He seems legitimate. We've looked into the provenance, at least, and it's plausible. Oddman will have to get his eyes on it

190

properly before any money changes hands. We'll go down and meet the seller, if your mother is willing to assume the expense. Negotiate a price that's fair to both parties.'

'Someone's selling the flight log from Lindbergh's crossing?'

'That's right,' said Brown. 'That is what she's after, isn't it?'

'And you've found it in less than a month?'

'It's rather easier when the seller wants so badly for it to be found,' said Brown.

'Where is he, this seller?' said Ari sceptically.

'Key West,' said Brown.

'Key West, Florida?' asked Ari, incredulous.

'That's right... Have you heard good things?'

'No,' said Ari emphatically.

Small-town corruption, bankruptcy, drinking – these things he had heard.

'Good marlin fishing,' said Oddman.

'Fish a speciality of yours?' asked Ari quite violently.

The room went very silent. The two men froze in place. The rudeness hung in the air like a bad smell.

'I'm sorry,' said Ari. 'I'm just shocked. I didn't think you'd ever find it.'

Motion returned to the space. Oddman resumed his circular pacing, passing behind the back of Ari's chair every few minutes and sending chills along his spine.

'They have marlin bigger than whales down there,' said Oddman. 'You can fight one for a whole day and it'll still beat you.'

'We'll pop by and see your mother on Sunday,'

said Brown.

'Fine, thank you,' said Ari.

He was about to stand up and go, sensing they were dismissing him, when he said, 'I'd like to know a bit more, actually.'

'Can't hurt,' said Brown. 'Through a hundred convoluted connections you can't imagine, we got wind of a collector in Havana. Well, not so much a collector as a man through whose hands rare items of value sometimes pass. We've been sending telegrams back and forth for a few months on another matter as it so happens but when we mentioned the log, he suggested that such an item might have been in his possession not too long ago. It came in from France and, so he claims, it ended up less than a hundred miles away from his base – in Key West. Some eccentric recluse took it off his hands for a small fortune. We sent out a few feelers and I've just received a telegram informing us that this current owner's ready to talk. Oddman and I can go down in our professional capacity as your mother's represent- atives but I sense she'd prefer to accompany us.'

'I know she would,' said Ari.

'There you have it, then. It might be a hoax but Oddman will get to the bottom of that quick enough. I'd regret it if it turns out to be a wasted journey, of course, but my nose says it's not.'

'What's the man's name?' asked Ari.

'Taft,' said Brown. 'Silas Taft.'

'Sometimes, you find your whole life is a dis- appointment to you, Ari,' said Hella that night.

She was packing her leather bag for the train.

192

She folded a white linen dress into it and a pair of sandals. Ever since their trip to Europe, she packed lightly. 'I packed an evening gown for every night we were in Paris,' she had once explained. 'He was right there and we never saw him. Then I run out to get chicken stock for the soup with my hair in braids and ridiculous shoes on my toes and he walks into us. Whatever you're wearing will be unsuitable when Fate shows up, you might as well be comfortable.'

Now, she faced the window and looked down at the low sluggish slip of the river beneath their window.

'You're disappointed by love and cheated by death. For those few months when I was sixteen, your father was so much my reason for living, I didn't have another stored by in case he went away. Later, there was the war and bodies listed like ingredients in a complicated cake recipe – rows and rows of names that meant nothing, just constituent parts mixed up in the war. Then one day, there is a name there that means everything though you don't take the meaning in at once. Your heart leaps up inside you because it is his name there on the page – this name you love so much and which fills you with the pride of recognition and the memory of all the perfect secret lovemaking you have shared. Then you see that the name is not a symbol of that at all. It is the demarcation that all that is over.'

Ari was breathless. She had never told him any of this.

'It's none of it for a boy's ears, especially not a son's.'

It is! He wanted to shout. I'm twenty now and I need it so much. If he spoke, though, the spell would be broken. He tried to carve the words in their correct order in his mind so that they could never be lost. Already they were running away like sand through an hourglass, already he was losing the sequence and the exact way she had said 'perfect secret lovemaking'.

'As a schoolgirl, you imagine there will be guilt but there is not. The guilt only came later, came over me like a flock of ravens. He was visiting Sweden, probably hoping to avoid the war, and my mother took to him in the market. He helped her with some menial difficulty to do with carrying groceries and she brought him home. He was staying in a room on Soderleden between the cemetery and the railway line; he hadn't heard English in weeks and then he heard my mother in the market. He got to know my parents and they liked him. They invited him to join us in Mariefred for a week's holiday.

'One day, after we had been together in the boathouse, he walked back to the cottage ahead of me and I saw there was still a piece of straw in his hair from where we had been lying together on the landing. It was the same colour as his hair and I wondered if my parents would notice it; if they would take its meaning. It was a dare to myself, you see? I could have called after him. I could have run after him and shaken it from his hair before anyone saw or guessed but I chose not to. It was a conscious choice, a game I decided to play. I never forgave myself for that, for toying with Fate.

'My mother saw that straw, of course, and she knew at once. She asked Phillip to leave right away, to take the ferry to Copenhagen at once and then go home to England. She forced him to go. She implied he owed himself to the war. Maybe he had felt that way all along, too, because he left without a fight; I didn't think he would last long after that and he didn't. Barely six months had passed when I heard that he had died. He had asked that the war office inform me. He had no other family. So, the two of you never shared the planet, never slept under the same moon. He had a sky of burial dirt before you were ever born.'

Hella turned away from the window. She had been saying all this to her own cold reflection.

'After those wonderful days – with the straw smelling of sunlight and the feel of a lover's warm skin – it's only disappointment and duty.'

Ari wanted to tell her to try and be happy. The story of his father had buoyed him up and he felt glad. He understood the animosity she had held for her mother. She had opened up to him.

Hella's tone suddenly changed. She sounded lighter, 'And then sometimes life is so full of unexpected joy again, you could laugh out loud. Every now and then there is an airplane over-head. It's too high to grasp, but the possibility of it, the excitement of where it might be going and the man it just might be carrying ... that can carry you along for years.'

15

Geographically, it missed being a tropical paradise by about a hundred miles. Situated at twenty-four degrees north, Key West was the last of an archipelago of islands scattered from the tip of Florida. The place's original Spanish name was foreboding: *Cayo Hueso* – Island of Bones. The first settlers to arrive on its beaches had found them strewn with skeletons – the victims of an ancient Indian massacre – but over the centuries the island's name had been anglicized to Key West – sanitary, innocent sounding.

By the late 1800s, the small island was home to the most affluent city per capita in the United States, the vast wealth of its natives the result of their dubious expertise as wreckers. Ships that were lost on the rag-tag reefs that surrounded the Keys were plundered for their cargo. Sometimes, survivors' skulls were smashed against the rocks to prevent them reporting the strange pyres lit on the coast which they had mistaken for lighthouses and which had led their vessels astray.

The prosperous merchant captains of the town built grand houses with many doors; they strung them round with wide balconies and decorated them with gingerbread – the ornate, wooden carvings which took a ship's carpenter months,

196

even years, to create. On the tops of their sumptuous houses, they built widow's walks where their lonely wives, and then their ghosts, would prowl and pine. From the most impressive to the more modest, Key West houses had one distinct feature in common – steep roofs that funnelled the run-off rain into cisterns for there was only one freshwater well on the island. It was a place owned by the sea. The smell of the ocean reached its most inland parts; gulls squabbled and snatched on its street corners. The salt in the cracked boards of the unpainted houses served as a reminder that this island would always be – through necessity and choice – isolated, self-sufficient and reticent.

It seemed incongruous that a town with so many open windows and verandas should also be so secretive. The narrow plots made for shallow frontages but allowed for deep backyards that joined the deep backyards of houses a street away. Conches, the title given to those born on the island, always stuck together. They didn't snoop. If their neighbours could hear them plotting or beating their wives or rutting through their open shutters then they could hear the same thing, too, on nights when the wind was blowing the other way. It was a town that worked on a system of stranglehold secrets. It worked well and local ventures prospered.

It was a man's sort of place. The few women who lived in town did little more than compete to design the most lush and elaborate ornamental gardens on their large properties; their husbands built the seven-storey Colonial Hotel that dominated the skyline of the business district. Conches owned fleets of ships and cigar factories in Cuba. They had contracts with Macy's to supply natural sponges to the women of New York and with Kroger's markets to provide tinned turtle soup to the entire western seaboard.

Then came the Crash. The island's population dwindled from 26,000 to 10,000 in less than ten years and Key West was suddenly the poorest town in the Union. The people who moved in then were those who had minimal requirements when it came to cuisine and culture. The lavish entertainments of the high days disappeared. A simple breakfast at the Electric Kitchen set diners back twenty-five cents. The town was left with fifty bars to drink in and fifty churches to repent in afterwards. There was a boxing match every second Friday, cockfights and dogfights proliferated. Key West, by bizarre reversal (and divine retribution, the godly types insisted) became a mosquito-meddled backwater, forgotten and forlorn, with one railway in and no road that went all the way out.

At Key West's only station, the afternoon locomotive's engine sighed out steam. Its work was done; this was the last stop on the line. Anyone wishing to travel further had to board one of the Peninsula and Occidental steamships that pushed down to Havana, ninety miles away.

Ari gathered up his suitcase and helped his mother step down into the heat. Key West had a small overgrown airstrip but Hella insisted that they travel by train or car. She did not wish to blur the memory of her first flight with the subsequent monotony of others. That flight remained in her mind a kind of supernatural experience and she would not taint it by acknowledging that hundreds of people travelled that way every day.

The island air hung as rich and thick as Turkish coffee above the town; it moved heavily in and out of their throats. The few remaining passengers dispersed. The days when ladies and their spat-shoed suitors teemed off the train in colourful shoals were over. Practical work boots, repaired often, had replaced pretty pink heels.

Several dispossessed travellers waited listlessly for the next train out. Always, the most desperate were the women. Ari watched them. A spindly green stem of a girl bounced a baby on her hip. A blow from a hand hardened with a wedding ring had torn her lip; her eye was as shiny as a black opal. Another much-older woman languished against the waiting-room wall. Thick mascara made tarantulas of her lashes; the tops of her stockings showed. She stroked her cleavage invitingly, pretending to dab at it with a grey handkerchief. Ari looked away; he did not want to appear shocked. He hurried along the platform and went down the stairs at the far end to look for a taxi. As he glanced over his shoulder, he saw that Hella had approached the garish woman and started up a genial conversation with her.

So this was America's Eden. The place creaked like a deserted gold-rush town. It was like an abandoned traveller in the sun with all his battered luggage at his feet. The air hummed with heat and prickled with the constant high-pitched wheeze of insects. Overflowing garbage

199

cans were rotting beneath the tattered palms. Pyramids of flaking lobster traps and torn fishing nets scaled the walls of the clapboard houses. A three-legged dog peed against a lattice of strangler fig. The pedantry of a government sign was ignored – the words 'NO PARKING' were half obscured by two cars up on blocks.

Ari sat on his suitcase and waited for a taxi to pass. There was nobody about.

After a few minutes, the stationmaster meandered out from his office. He walked over to Ari who stood up; he wasn't eager to be mistaken for a loiterer.

'Sit yourself down,' said the man. 'Whoever you're waiting for, they'll likely show themselves sometime.'

Ari was relieved. The man seemed keen to stay and chat. 'I'll give you the nickel tour,' he said. 'That there's Duval Street. Some eating establishments and such down that way. There's a dime store and a barbershop with the dentist up above it. Just opposite's a sandwich place and further down is Chica's. You want some music of a night, they got a mechanical piano that plays for you. Over to your right you got the fishing boat dock where what's left of our fleet ties up. That there's the Coca-Cola factory. Closed now. They say there's no water for bottling but truth is we had a torrent two weeks back. They just done gone and closed it. No good reason. I'm still drinking Coca-Cola. Ain't you still drinking it?'

'Yes, Sir,' said Ari. 'I'm still drinking it.'

'Only when I can afford it mind,' the man added, daring Ari with his expensive shoes and smart luggage to make the same claim. 'Ain't never gonna open her up again neither. That's for sure. So that's the tour.'

He held out his hand and Ari grinned for a few seconds until he realized the man was entirely serious.

'They don't pay me to give you folks the tour, you know. They don't pay me at all no more, it seems. No damned pay packet for two months running.'

Ari fumbled in his pocket and gave the station-master fifty cents. The man snorted and stuffed the coin in his pocket then he went back into the fermenting vat of the waiting room. A few seconds later, he opened his door and yelled, 'Who are you waiting for anyhow?'

'Taxi cab,' said Ari.

'There ain't no taxi cabs here, son. You gotta arrange it ahead of time if you want a car any-where.'

The door slammed shut again. Ari watched the shadows singe away from the edges of the heat-stroked buildings. The three-legged dog watched him inexorably. Flies flickered round its eyes. The sun pressed him down as he waited.

Ari studied the railway timetable which was chalked onto a blackboard. The next train in from New York didn't arrive until Saturday after-noon. Ari had the queasy, uneasy feeling that he had started to fall, that the ground beneath him was far less substantial than it appeared to be. It was probably the unnatural temperature.

Somewhere far away, Ari heard the purring roar of an airplane engine. His heartbeat caught the rhythm like a pianist picking up a ragtime refrain. It started to soar again. The sound swooped in and out of audible range then became louder. Ari sought its source in the blue of the sky and found it. It was a Lockheed Sirius, an amphibious aircraft with an overwing, and it was painted red like a boy's first toy wagon. It seemed as delighted as a kingfisher set free from a cage. It shook its wings and rolled in delight, then it was gone.

Ari was still hoping to catch one more glimpse of it when his mother breezed past him.

'Mrs Alvarez says we can walk to the hotel from here. It's barely a block away.'

'Mrs Alvarez?'

'That unfortunate woman on the platform,' Hella explained.

'She knows our hotel?'

It was a sinister omen which turned out to be groundless. The Colonial Hotel was comfortable and clean. The concierge at the front desk looked surprised to see them. A name badge pinned to his chest read 'Antonio Bolivar' and he had the impressive moustache of a Santa Anna revolutionary, the perpetual tan of a Mexican gaucho.

'Mrs Gold!' he exclaimed. 'We would have sent a man to collect you and show you over, and a porter for the bags. We were expecting you on Saturday, though.'

'Our business couldn't wait. Can you accommodate us now?'

'But of course!'

Señor Bolivar clicked his fingers and a stooped young man loped over to take their bags. Usually, a waistcoated clerk met guests at the railway station and walked them across the street and into the reception but that day there was only the boy from the supply boat who did odd jobs around the hotel while his father was off running goods to the outlying Keys. The boy was a hunchback and Señor Bolivar could never remember his name. The manager tried to keep him out in the garden, weeding or tending the lawn which stretched down to the swimming pool but the boy liked to mingle with the guests and make them uncomfortable. Señor Bolivar imagined they tipped generously to ease their disquiet at his deformity.

'I can manage,' said Ari, trying to retrieve his case from the hump of a boy.

'Nonsense,' said Hella. 'Let the man do his job; he's obviously quite able.'

The boy made his way through the whirring fans and potted palms of the lobby to an elevator. They rode to the top floor where Hella had taken a suite for herself and a room for her son.

After the boy had laid her case out, Hella looked into her change purse.

'Thomas Cook says a nickel a bag,' she said. 'Does that seem fair?'

She was holding her slim travel guide to Florida in her hand. The boy looked at her quite sharply but then he smiled.

'If that's what your Thomas Cook fellow told you,' he answered, 'I guess it's alright.'

'I can show you right here,' Hella continued, pushing the appropriate page under the boy's nose.

'I'm just learning to read,' said the boy. 'That's

too much for me. I'm learning by crossword puzzles.'

Hella pulled the book away as if it was about to be soiled.

'But if you want to know anything about this island, you ask for me. The name's Quozzie.'

'Who calls you that?' snapped Hella. This cruelty had upset her.

'The whole town... I'm named after a famous fellow in a book. I never read it for myself, of course, but the hero is called Quozzie.'

'Quasimodo,' said Hella quietly.

'That's the fellow!' said Quozzie delightedly. 'You got it in one. You'll remember it now.'

'I will remember it,' said Hella.

The boy left in a loping run.

'I believe I will remember it forever,' Hella said and she turned to face Ari. She smiled at him and said, 'Some things benefit from comparison. I don't believe I've ever thought you more handsome than I do at this moment.'

'It's only luck,' said Ari. 'Being beautiful.'

'Funny, it never brought me any.'

Ari wanted to remind her of Benjamin Gold. That it was her hair which had saved them from a life of service or slavery on a dustbowl farm – a random selection of colour in the womb.

'Are Oddman and Brown here?'

'They'll be down on Saturday. They've organized their own accommodation. I think they're staying in a lodging house.'

Hella looked out the window and found the vivid blue of the Atlantic below her instead of the slurry of the East River.

'I want to go down into the streets and get a sense of the place,' she said. 'It's not quite Paris, is it?'

'I didn't like Paris,' said Ari. He had never told her that before.

'I didn't like it either. This will suit us both better, I think.'

Hella laughed and grabbed her straw hat. It was almost evening but the sun was still fierce.

As they passed Señor Bolivar at his desk, he held up a small bottle of green liquid.

'Juice of the cactus,' he said. 'For the mosquitoes.'

Hella brushed away his concern with a breezy quip. 'I'll bite back,' she laughed.

The streets were rich with smells. In the roadside cafes, pineapple slices and bubbling raw molasses sizzled in battered saucepans. Sticky balls of fresh fish were wrapped in banana leaves and deep fried. Each piece was a dumpling to be eaten with the fingers along with rice and lentils, boiled soft and stuffed into the mouth by the wooden spoonful.

Often, Ari and Hella had eaten in the Oak Room of the Waldorf Astoria. Meals of prosciutto wrapped around melon slivers the colour of peach mousse followed by rare rack of lamb drizzled over with raspberry coulis. Here, the seamen had set up makeshift canteens for themselves. Hella offered one of the cooks a dollar and was given a choice: conch meat and breadfruit, buttered and baked together, or crawfish – shellfish which come up out of the mud looking as red as if they'd already been boiled – steamed between two dustbin lids.

Ari chose the latter. As they walked home, he plucked off the crustaceans' heads and sucked out the rich juice inside just as he had seen the other men do. The meal was as salty as a mouthful of seawater; the titbits of white meat he squeezed from the shells as scrumptious as any three-course meal.

16

It was barely dawn, still dark in the bedrooms of the Colonial Hotel, but Ari never slept well in strange beds. Since childhood, he had been restless whenever they were away from home and it was his late-night wanderings that had brought him the greatest trouble. He got up, dressed, and went down to the pool. The water moved relentlessly even though the morning was perfectly still. It was not yet five o'clock. There was nobody about. Dew prickled the palm leaves and made the small stretch of grass very green, gauzed with spiderwebs. There were no throaty booms of river barges, just the soft slapping of water against the hulls of the pleasure boats. The fishing fleet was already out.

Ari saw Quozzie come out of the gardener's shack with a net. Ari waved at the hunchbacked boy and he waved back jovially. Quozzie began to fish the few leaves from the pool's surface, dragging the net back and forward in hypnotic rhythm.

Distantly, Ari heard the sound of an engine. It rumbled louder and he looked up to see the red Sirius streak past again. It was flying lower this time and its shadow passed right over the pool. Ari got to his feet but the plane was lost from his view. It flashed across the island gardens on the far side of town. It mottled the stagnant pools of rainwater in the potholed streets, then the unruly hedges of the abandoned naval station, then the beach, with its bird-shaped shadow.

Two boys chased its form along the shore. Their nimble feet were hardened against the rough remains of the ancient coral. They were vagabonds, the sons of a seaman from the naval yard who had taken work as a dishwasher at the Electric Kitchen and a dubious Haitian holy man. Their skins were the tones of two continents; they contrasted against each other like sapodilla bark: one pale delft Dutch and one the ebony black of Hispaniola – both were generations from home.

These two had been best friends for a whole month; their friendship a summer triumph over the temptations of other boys whose dogs had given birth to pups or whose fathers had bought new wirelesses. The pair had declared the southern beach their own. They had protected it from within a sand fortress stocked with clods and stones. For three weeks they had defended it against older boys and even the sailors who brought their Cuban dancehall girls down there for sex when the last bars closed.

The two boys inspected the swags of seaweed along the tideline and collected snails for the fish tank they planned to buy one day. They examined a dead crab caught up in fishing line and discovered what they thought would be the find of the day – a red and white float attached to a brand new sinker. They agreed to steal some bamboo from the convent garden that afternoon and make a hook from a paper clip and fish for salties off the pylons like Sad Sam. The dark boy spotted a shape on the curve of sand ahead.

'Treasure!' he hollered.

They scampered towards it.

'Pirate treasure!' echoed the other as they raced along.

The first boy skidded to his knees in front of the pile; his partner landed beside him a second later. They looked expectantly down at a rumpled tweed suit. There was a man inside it. Two sets of eyeballs bulged. Both boys looked at one another and turned their backs to vomit up their breakfasts in unison: peppered mackerel omelette and honeyed grits respectively.

Ari gave up hope that the airplane would make another pass and walked over to where Quozzie was working. There were lemon trees in pots lining this end of the pool. Their leaves were crusted with salt. Ari could smell the tart fruit, too, and the combination reminded him of a tropical cocktail. Before he could reach Quozzie, however, Ari was nearly bowled over by two ragged boys. Both were without shirts and one had a rope fashioned into braces to hold up his britches. They were certainly not hotel guests. They almost knocked Quozzie down with their eagerness. The young man listened to their garbled message and smiled.

'Okay, okay,' said Quozzie and he dropped his leaf net onto the deck.

'What's happening?' asked Ari. 'What's going on?'

Quozzie winked at him.

'They say they've found a body on the beach,' he said.

'What?' said Ari with shock.

'It's a drunk most likely,' said Quozzie. 'They don't usually lie, those two. It's bound to be something or other if you feel like tagging along for the trip.'

Ari picked up his hat and followed the cripple's rolling stride. The beach was some distance away.

'They always come to you?' asked Ari as they half walked, half shambled along.

'They say de la Croix shouts,' said Quozzie. 'And he does some, I'll give them that.'

'Who's de la Croix?' asked Ari.

'Local keeper of the peace,' explained Quozzie. 'We got ourselves a regular sheriff named Willis French but he's got a family in Key Largo, too, so he's not often about.'

Ari didn't want to ask what the 'too' meant.

They made the south shore of the island and Ari followed Quozzie from the safety of the dune grass out into the desert of the beach. He crunched along the crushed coral sand; it slipped inside his shoes and grated against his socks. They arrived at the soggy shape, half buried in the sand. The two boys stood a way off, scratching their knees and biting their lips behind a gossamer shield of sea oats. Ari glanced casually down over Quozzie's stunted shoulder.

He saw a profound deadness. The man was verdant with sea moss. A crab crouched where the soft centre of his throat should have been. The raw tubes of his trachea goggled up at them just like the eyes of the crustacean did. He was eaten away in places, one arm skeletonized. One eye was gone, replaced by a slimy-skinned sea worm in a cosy coil.

Ari's voice came out small and screechy, 'Oh, my God!'

He knew he would never be able to un-see that sight. For years to come – in nightmares and on lonely streets – what he had just seen would jump down from the shadows and terrorize him. Ari stumbled a few steps across the sand, scuttling away from the sea-drenched stink of the body. Quozzie grabbed him by the shirt collar. It required quite a stretch for him to do it and Ari thought that if the boys were judging them by their stature, he should be the calm, mature, capable one and not the other way round.

'Mr Gold, calm the damn down!' Quozzie's voice cracked out above the tumble of the tide.

'I'm okay,' said Ari but he felt his gorge rise.

Quozzie shouted out to the boys, 'You go on and get Mr de la Croix now like you should've done right off.'

They ran.

'How long will it take him to get here?' asked Ari, recovering a little.

'He won't get here at this rate. They've gone and tore off in the wrong direction. I told you they didn't like him much.'

'What do we do?'

'You gotta go,' said Quozzie.

'I'm a guest!' shouted Ari and then immediately repented of the snobbery.

'Alright then, you stay with the body and I'll go.'

'No, I'll do it,' said Ari. 'Tell me the way. Will he be in this early?'

'Somebody ought to be.'

The courthouse on Whitehead Street was a peach-coloured, coral building with the fossils of seashells still visible through the skin of its sides. Ari tried the impressive glass doors that formed the entrance. They were locked. He traced the exterior wall until he came to a small side gate. This was open. He entered a courtyard where a single lemon tree grew out of what looked like builders' rubble that had never been cleared away. The lemons were ripe; their smell pungent and sweet-sour. Ari reached out and touched one as he passed. The smell came away on his fingers. He put his hand to his nose unconsciously and took in the sharp slap of citrus. There was a smaller, older annex on the other side of the ruined courtyard. Ari found a door almost hidden behind creeping lilac and went in.

Inside, a middle-aged woman sat behind a desk in a box of a room painted grey on all six sides. She was reading a tawdry romance novel with a lurid cover and she slipped it into a drawer as soon as she saw him. She'd kept her bob despite the fact that a softer style would have suited her better. She could not seem to give it up. Part of Alice still lived in the 1920s. Having missed out on all the champagne and shrimp cocktails when they were actually around, she now lived in a mirage of them ... her dreams smelled of oyster shells and Chanel No. 5.

'I need the police,' said Ari.

'Did you just walk in through the back?' asked Alice.

'I did. I need a policeman,' he repeated.

'That door is for employees only,' she insisted. 'Everybody knows that.'

'I didn't know that. I'm a visitor here. We've found somebody on the beach. A body of somebody.'

A small man came into the room from a back passageway at that.

Deputy Oscar de la Croix was short and podgy, soft around the middle where a belt divided his two hemispheres into twin swells. His uniform was strained at the buttons but perfectly pressed; neat creases ran down the short legs of his trousers. He was balding with dark tufts of hair jutting out above each ear.

De la Croix eyed Ari appraisingly. Then he took out a long, slim, silver lighter. He displayed it grandly like the woman who shows you the jewellery at Tiffany's before you decide to buy. He lit a cigar which shared his shape – bulbous in the middle and stubby, tapering too quickly at both ends. The man took a few indulgent puffs.

He said to Ari, 'You from up north?'

Ari nodded.

'My name's Ari Köll,' he said. 'I'm visiting from New York. Are you Deputy de la Croix?'

'I'm Acting Sheriff de la Croix,' said de La Croix.

'Are you?'

'You been drinking, boy?'

'No, Sir. Quozzie from the hotel ... the one with the...' Ari trailed hopelessly off.

'I know Quozzie,' said de la Croix.

'He's waiting with the body. On the beach.'

'Well, alright then,' said de la Croix.

He took his hat down from a coat peg.

'And you say you found this body?'

'Sort of ... two boys found it.'

'Not that duet again!' said Oscar and he put his hat back on the peg again.

Ari lost his temper.

'There's a man dead and if you're the law you better get down there!'

Green guilt slopped around in Ari's stomach like pea soup in a bowl. He seldom raised his voice.

'I better go take a gander, Alice. Can you hold the fort?'

'Sure can,' said Alice and she took her novel from the drawer.

The deputy swaggered out of the annex and Ari walked beside him.

'It'll be a drunk...' he said in a casual sing-song voice.

'It's not a drunk,' said Ari. 'His eye is gone. His arm's down to the bone.'

De la Croix started walking faster. He reached up and lassoed in his unruly chin with his tie.

Oscar didn't ever let on that he was nervous. He was quite good at concealment. Even though his

213

size suggested clumsiness, he was not. People saw his girth and thought he was slow and lazy but he was a fourth generation law-keeper. His great-granddaddy had been a sheriff when lynching was the way to see things settled. He had worked in Kansas and Oklahoma and the westernmost territories before they even had their names on a map.

Then the de la Croixs had worked their way south – often under a cloud of disgrace. Oscar sometimes fancied they had once been tall, up-standing gentlemen with fine, chiselled features and the length of bone good nutrition brings. As error had crept in, as misjudgement and the hundred small corruptions men are prone to had invaded their make-up, the de la Croixs had shrunk. Their backs had bent. Their noses had pugged up on their fattening faces. Their eyes had travelled closer together. Their hairlines had receded and their mistakes had brought them closer to the humble soil. Oscar was the last of the lowly, self-inflicted, stunted de la Croixs and these days there wasn't that much to live up to. His granddaddy had worked in Atlanta, his father in New Orleans and then Mobile. Each move earned them a little less respect and brought them to a town slightly less respectable. Oscar had wound up in Key West. You couldn't go further south than that and still consider yourself an American.

When they reached the beach, de la Croix strode out to where Quozzie was waiting. Ari stopped behind the sea oats where the two boys had been joined by a sailor. When de la Croix noticed that Ari wasn't alongside him, he stopped and beckoned with his hand. Ari didn't want to see the body again but he obeyed.

De la Croix wanted Ari beside him. Ari saw the situation from the other man's point of view. Oscar was a subordinate, used to orders and here was Ari: his suit was tailored, his shoes were costly. It was calming for Oscar, on this brief desolation of beach, to have Ari beside him.

'Help me out here,' the deputy whispered. 'Help me out a bit.'

It was almost a plea and Ari responded to it immediately.

'Sure,' he said.

Ari sensed the public pack gathering around the two boys like taut-eyed wolves in the tall grass, pacing and waiting, watching every move they made. Together, Quozzie, Ari and de la Croix looked at the body for a second time. So this was death. Not glossed over with silk pillows and cloying perfume and coroner's lipstick but death as open as a wound.

'Anybody know him?' de la Croix asked the two men.

They both shook their heads.

'Dressed nice,' said de la Croix. 'Not a local.'

Ari looked closer. Because he had been asked, he made a more detailed examination of the man's features. In his mind, he tried to close the gaping jaw, restore the colour of life to the skin, replace the one eye.

'Wait,' said Ari.

He reached down and touched the man's one closed eyelid. The skin felt like rubber, no more repugnant than leather. He gently pulled the lid up and was confronted with an iris the colour of

215

tiger skin. It was the amazing brownish-red eye of Julian Oddman.

'I do know him,' said Ari.

'Suddenly you know him?'

'It's a man from New York who's working for my mother.'

'You didn't recognize him before?' asked de la Croix.

'I've only met him twice. He's supposed to be arriving here on Saturday.'

'He's early, then,' said Quozzie – one of those stupid things people say under stress.

'And late!' said de la Croix.

He walked over to the gathering crowd. He needed to get a message to Doc Saul.

'You stay put!' he called back to Ari.

The medical examiner – just a local general prac-titioner who had been elevated to the rank by virtue of having lived on the island the longest – came across the sand half an hour later with two assistants. The police force (which had dwindled since the town's bankruptcy a few months earlier) could only supply one half-uniformed officer for crowd control. The haunches of the eager on-lookers rose up on the fringes of the crime scene. They had sniffed out the scent of carrion.

Key West was a town where bodies did crop up occasionally. Sailors stabbed other sailors with bottles. Men crushed the skulls of their wives against doorposts in fits of temper. Children died of malaria and yellow fever. But this body held a certain mystique because of its location. The pub-lic swam off this beach; if the body had not washed ashore, his ghost might have reached up with fingers like tug-weed and pulled them under.

Dr Howard Saul claimed the man was about thirty-five and in good health at the time of his death.

'Drowned?' asked de la Croix.

'He wasn't out swimming,' said Ari. 'He's fully clothed.'

'They drink and fall off piers and boats all the time,' said de la Croix.

'Oh,' said Ari and decided to keep his mouth shut.

The activity on the beach slowed to a tableau: Oscar and Ari staring into the pit of Oddman's missing eye from one side and Quozzie and the Doc looking down from the other – as if they had agreed upon a moment of silence to grieve. It was the Doc who had the sense to look away first.

'Guess I'm gonna take him to my surgery,' he said. 'I called by the morgue on my way over and they're out of ice. I can look him over at my rooms, though.'

Oscar and Ari watched as the forlorn, funereal procession gathered up the body in a sheet and crossed the beach to the parking lot where an even bigger crowd waited for them. People parted to let the contagion through. They loaded the body into the back of the doctor's Ford.

Oscar kicked the sand about a little with the toe of his shoe then he abandoned the scene, too. Ari was about to follow him when he saw something lying among the curious confusion of their footprints. It was a soggy slip of paper with a few letters scrawled on it, just some torn sliver from a purple-paged notebook. The letters *'ves airp'* and below that *'ikes re'* were all he could decipher on it. Ari slipped the damp scrap into his coat pocket.

When he looked up again, de la Croix was already some distance along the boardwalk. The beach was just a stretch of dead coral blown through with wind again. The brief hours of human intervention swept clean from its surface.

Ari followed de la Croix forlornly. He felt tired and confused. His brain was a bee that refused to settle in his head.

Oscar saw him. 'You gonna come by and tell me what you know?' he called over his shoulder as he marched along the pier.

'I ought to tell my mother I'm okay. She's at the Colonial,' said Ari.

'How old are you?' asked de la Croix. 'You gotta tell your mama everything?'

Ari reddened and hid his face by bending over to empty the sand from his shoes. The salt was already crusting where the leather sole met the instep.

This was the new pier built by the navy, concrete and correct in maritime fashion. The remnants of the old one stood twenty feet to its starboard side. There were only wooden pylons left like the ribcage of a dead elephant that had lain down in the sea and couldn't get up again. Out ahead of them, Ari saw a shape on one of the disused ribs – the figure of a person sitting all alone at his post. Oscar leaned on the pier rails near to the man. Ari could only see the man's back; his face was cast in the direction of his line.

'How's things, Sam?' the deputy called.

The man called Sam just nodded slowly without looking at them.

'You doing so-so, then?'

The man nodded again.

'Good. Good,' Oscar said, self-conscious about this bizarre shouted conversation.

'You see all that commotion some ways along the beach earlier?'

Another nod.

'Tell me one last thing, Sam...'

The wind stopped for a moment and the sun shimmied on the water.

'Where was the tide pushing in from last night?'

Sam hooked his rod under his armpit. Awkwardly, he reached out his hand like an Ancient Greek oracle and pointed west over the water. Ari and Oscar followed the trajectory of his finger. Their eyes skipped like stones over the water then came to rest on a slim bulge on the horizon. Sometimes, it was a discernable shape then it was as if it wasn't really there at all.

'Yup,' said Oscar. 'That's what I was afraid of.'

In the brilliant light, Ari saw that where Sam's left arm should be there was only a stump cut away right beneath the shoulder. That was why he held the rod and pointed with the same arm – it was the only one he had. On the waves below, his uneven shadow bounced up and down on the swells like a cork bobbing in the sea.

Oscar walked back towards Ari and right past him.

'How does he get out there?' Ari asked.

'Nobody knows,' said Oscar.

219

Back in the parking lot, Doc Saul was wiping his hands on a pristine towel. Instead of the blood that would usually stain it, there was the green slime of things that live in rock pools. He went into a huddle with de la Croix but Ari could hear them.

'I need to take a closer look at him. Might have been an accident but...'

'Let me know,' said Oscar.

The man nodded and got into the cab of his Ford.

'You're gonna tell me everything you know about this man,' de la Croix said to Ari.

'Should I meet you at the courthouse?'

'No,' said de La Croix. 'I'm killing two birds with one stone...'

Oscar motioned with his hand towards the half-real Key that Sam had indicated. He looked into Ari's sickly face, then clapped a hand on the boy's shoulder.

'You like boats?' he asked gleefully.

17

The sheriff's department had an understanding with the local fishermen. The deputies didn't enforce any restrictions too fiercely and when the authorities needed a boat from time to time the fishermen didn't complain too loudly. They received a government chit saying they'd be reimbursed for the fuel they used assisting law enforcement and these slips of promising pink paper were stapled by the hundred in the local bars as wallpaper to cover the spots where the damp was getting in.

A fisherman who smelled of some powerful, astringent soap that was almost as bad as the odour of fish he was trying to conceal allowed them to board. He was in his forties. The sun had stripped his hair of colour, leaving it as white as a wave-crest. He had a crooked brown grin and around his neck was a leather thong crowded with the snaggled teeth of sharks.

'This here is Lucian, Quozzie's father,' said Oscar by way of introduction. 'Lucian, this here's a witness on a death we got this morning.'

'My name's Ari Köll,' said Ari.

'Welcome aboard, Harry Cole,' said Lucian.

He didn't shake Ari's hand; he made a casual salute instead. Ari felt relieved. He imagined fish guts dripping from the man's fingers. His empty stomach rolled over inside him.

Once, Ari had taken a ferry tour across the Hudson River to visit the Statue of Liberty and that was the full extent of his nautical expertise. It made him sad when he considered how much his father had loved boats. He thought he might take a sailing course out on Long Island when they got back to New York. He wobbled like a tightrope walker on the unpredictable deck of the *Alexa Lee*. Oscar chatted happily to Lucian who was pleased that this trip coincided with a run he had planned – delivering supplies to the very Key they needed to visit.

As the boat powered out of the harbour, Ari

saw several tea crates loaded with goods. He prodded the tarpaulin covering one of them with the toe of his shoe and it fell away. Inside, there were fresh vegetables – onions, potatoes and celery all jiggling together.

De la Croix scooted over closer to him.

'Tell me everything you know about that body,' he said emphatically. 'He got family?'

'I don't know,' said Ari. 'Aren't you going to write anything down?'

Oscar tapped his skull enigmatically. 'Shoot,' he said.

'The man's name is Julian Oddman. He has a partner named Kit Brown – Christopher, I guess it is. Christopher Brown. They're both from New York City. We have their calling card back at the hotel...'

'Who's the "we"?'

'Myself and my mother, Mrs Hella Gold.'

Oscar nodded.

'Go on,' he said.

'We were meeting them – Mr Oddman and Mr Brown – here on Monday for business.'

'What sort of business?'

Suddenly Ari looked around him and saw water everywhere – blue as a Navajo necklace. He was at sea in more ways than one. What should he say? Wasn't their proposed purchase of the flight log totally illegal? What had happened to Oddman? Why had he arrived in Key West two days early? Had it been a kind of scouting trip to surprise his mother with information as soon as she arrived? Ari thought it was best to say nothing for the time being.

'It's my mother's business,' he said. 'You'll have to ask her. I'm here for the fishing.'

Ari remembered what Oddman had said about the big game fishing in the Keys, how enthusiastic he had been about the marlin, and he was swept with a sudden sadness.

'The marlin are as big as whales down here, they say,' Ari added.

Oscar de la Croix took in the boy's lichen-coloured face; his pale, smooth hands with their pianist's fingers and smiled.

'If you say so,' he said.

Ari had the feeling that the short interview hadn't gone well.

'So now I'll tell you something,' said Oscar. 'This man we're gonna meet is one of our last rich ones. We did seem to gather them in at one time ... years past.' Oscar seemed wistful. 'He comes into town a few weeks in a row then he don't come for months on end. Folks say he travels all over the world but they hardly ever see him on the train. He has more fancy forms of transport, I guess. Boats and such. He's a war hero, decorated and all. Enjoys his sport fishing and so on. He'll radio Lucian here to bring his supplies out. Newspapers, books, food. Only the very best mind. What best you can still get in town. The rest comes down from New York City or Washington, DC or Chicago – all rushed in before it gets stale.'

Ari felt he'd been given permission to snoop a little. He pulled another of the tea crates closer and examined its contents. There were tinned peaches and pears, evaporated milk and powdered custard, bottle after bottle of foreign wine and one of Irish whiskey. Astonished, Ari picked up a bag that bore the label of a deli in midtown Manhattan not far from where he lived. He had eaten Reuben sandwiches there for lunch several times. The bag contained speciality mustards and relish and a tinned ham from Germany the size of a boar's head. There were even flowers, fresh, lying in their plastic box and awash with chilled water that had started out as ice in Savannah the night before.

'Where did he come from?' Ari asked.

'Don't know. His accent is English. Some say he was a German spy. That's the women talking, of course. If you ask me, he's just one of those regular eccentrics. I reckon he made his money bringing booze in from Cuba during Prohibition. Now that drink is flowing again, his source of money's dried up, of course, but if you had a successful little sideline in rum back then you could live on the profits for the rest of your days.'

There were newspapers in the boxes, too. The *New York Times* Ari picked up was three days old already. Ari had read this very issue the day before he left home. The feeling that he was living in three days snatched away from regular chronology came over him. He was out on the water; the place he was heading towards might not be connected to the rest of the world at all. It might appear there only when he arrived, it might cease to be the moment it slipped from his view.

It took them just under half an hour to reach Long Dead Key. They followed the curve of its coastline to a wooden jetty that stretched out eighty feet from the leeward side of the island. Each pylon, sunk deep into the coral bed, had a steel hook on its outer side – a hurricane lantern hung from every single one. They were clean and filled with kerosene in anticipation of bad weather. Perhaps this place was always the first to see storm clouds stampeding in from the south like dark mustangs.

Lucian looped a rope around a bollard and began to unload his cargo onto the pier. He hauled each crate up a ladder that reached down to where the *Alexa Lee* was moored. Ari slapped his hat against the side of his leg. After only a day, it looked droopy, limp with humidity. Oscar and Ari walked along the pier towards the shore. The hurricane lanterns chinked against their hooks in the ceaseless wind. There was the constant swish and crack of the sea and the dazing noise, drifting in and out of earshot, of mosquito squadrons hunting.

'It's more welcoming at night,' de la Croix volunteered. 'When they're all lit, it's quite something.'

Where the pier joined the land itself, there was no path. They tackled their way through the bush for a few hundred yards. It was well stocked with things that bit and stung. The fallen mangrove leaves created a mulchy base to the floor and Ari's shoes slid along it. Like the hat, the shoes had been in the islands for about a day and were virtually ruined.

Up ahead of them, the foliage ended abruptly and they spilled out onto an impressive length of manicured lawn. They walked up towards the

225

house through a formal garden of exotic flowers and stone sundials and naked gravel. There were vine trellises and roses that should not have been able to grow in this native soil.

The house was a two-storey Spanish mansion, softened with creeping plumeria that shawled it in a misty mauve. The shutters were green and looked freshly painted. There were balconies circling out from every window and the house curved about a central courtyard where an apple tree shaded plushly upholstered furniture and a brilliant blue fountain.

'They say a pirate built it eighty years ago. It was a ruin until he got hold of it. He does keep appearances nice, though, don't he?'

'It's like he's living in the Boom,' said Ari.

As they entered the courtyard, the cool that pooled in the shaded places absorbed them. This was the freshest Ari had felt since he had stepped off the train. The place was relaxed and still. The water washed against the side of the fountain. A bird's wing shuddered among the leaves of the apple tree but it didn't sing. There was no cacophony or commotion. The ant traffic along the red-tiled veranda moved silently.

Then Ari saw the man. He sat like a white sable in one of the straight-backed chains – a slight, handsome man with unruly hair in a cream linen suit and brocade waistcoat. He was harlequinned by shadows from the tree, half his face entirely in darkness.

'Sir,' said de la Croix reverently. It was half a statement of awe, half an apology.

'Oscar,' said the man.

His greeting was imbued with resignation and something that suggested tedium or tiresomeness.

'This here is Mr Ari Köll.'

'Ah-ha,' the man said, as if they had heard of one another.

'Ari, this is Mr Silas Taft.'

Ari baulked. He thought he might have flinched visibly at the mention of the name Oddman and Brown had announced as their contact in Key West. Oscar didn't appear to have noticed. Taft leaned forward into the light. Ari saw immediately that one of his eyes was crinkled round with scar tissue and quite milky.

'Köll. Is that German?' The slight was fleet and intentional.

'It's Swedish,' said Ari. 'It means the keel of a boat.'

'It just sounds German, then?' Taft asked.

He indicated his useless eye.

'The Germans did this to me. In a stable near Reims.'

De la Croix broke in, 'Sorry for the intrusion...'

'Not at all. You just barge on in any time, Oscar.'

An awkward silence followed. Ari believed he could hear the ants marching across the tiles now. Taft took a patch made of a rich, textured fabric – ivory-coloured – from a table and put it over his bad eye.

'So what is it I can do for you, Oscar? Last time, your boss was following up on the rantings of some hysterical children's group. This isn't a continuation of that fiasco, is it?'

'Oh no, Sir.' Oscar was red-faced with embarrassment. 'Willis and I are through with that.'

Ari wondered what they were talking about.

'It's just that we've developed a situation over in town and I was wondering what your thoughts might be as regards it.'

'You need my advice on something?'

Oscar's hat pinwheeled so fast in his hands that it created its own breeze.

'Not exactly. It's about a body...'

Oscar mumbled through things unassisted by Ari who looked around him and discovered that he could see right through the house...

The doors behind Taft were open, their ectoplasmic curtains pulled back. Inside was an elegant room decorated with stuffed cushions and polished mahogany with brass fittings – brass by the sea was an act of defiance. Straight through that room and out the open doors at the other end and there was more grass and then what looked like stone steps leading right down into the sea. It was quite far away and distorted by the strange perspective of looking through two sets of windows but he was almost certain that a figure – a girl entirely naked – was coming up out of the Gulf of Mexico.

She shook her head like a dog, throwing out a corona of bright water. Ari had never seen a bare woman. He had seen thighs fleetingly on Long Island beaches, breasts through the thin fabric of screen stars' dresses, necks and shoulders and calves in daring evening gowns but they had never connected to create the whole, fabulous, fluid animal. Where the parts met had always been a mystery. The movement of her muscles as she dried herself on a red towel pulled her tanned skin in luscious, languid directions he never dreamed of. She was completely careless of her nudity, of the hair between her legs, of her lack of suntan lines. She was simply the long reach of womanhood men hardly ever get to see by sunlight.

Oscar's voice intruded rudely on his sudden desire. 'So, taking into account the tide and all, we were wondering if you'd had a visit from this fellow last night, or the night before even. Perhaps you thought he'd made his way safely home but he lost control of a boat...'

The girl slipped into the house and disappeared completely from sight at the top of a spiral staircase.

'No,' Taft snapped. 'Do you know who he is?'

'Ari here thinks it's someone he knows from New York ... a Mr Oddman.'

Taft eyed Ari with his one terrifying eye.

'Never heard of the man, I'm afraid. We've had no guests here, Oscar.'

'You and your daughter?' said Ari.

Oscar looked at him curiously.

'Mr Taft doesn't have a daughter,' said Oscar.

'Sorry, you and your wife, then...' said Ari.

'He doesn't have a wife. Damn boy!'

'Then who is the young lady of the house?' Ari asked.

'That young woman is under my protection. She is my ward.'

'Your ward?' Ari's eyebrows flew up his forehead.

'That's right,' answered Taft.

'I have heard of such things. They tend to come up in romantic fiction.'

'Was there anything else you wanted to snoop about?' Taft asked Oscar, ignoring Ari's expression of disbelief.

'Nope,' said Oscar, really meaning it. 'We are all done here.'

Silas walked them to the dock. The pace was swift. Ari made sure that he remained a few steps behind the other two, so that when he swung around and trotted back up the lawn it would have seemed awkward and unnatural for Taft to follow. He'd nearly reached the house before he shouted across the garden to them, 'Forgot my hat. I'll be right back. Go ahead.'

The girl leaned against the frame of the French doors wearing a man's long-sleeved shirt – opened low. On her head was Ari's hat; her hair was tucked up under it with twists that fell loose. When he had looked back at his mother on Le Bourget field all those years ago, the very same kind of strand had fallen across her cheek before she had told him to run on.

'It's yours?' she said.

She touched the hat and stepped forward, closer. The way she moved suggested malaise and suppressed energy at the same time.

'Yes, it is, Ma'am.'

The girl shook her head. Another lock tumbled free.

'I'm no Ma'am. My name's Cleo.'

She removed the hat from her head. She didn't hand it to him, though.

'I'm Ari Köll. I'm visiting from up north.'

'New York City!'

'Yes, but I'm not from there originally. My family's Swedish really.'

He felt odd calling what he had a family – it was just his mother and himself now.

She laughed like a balloon bursting in the quiet.

'I never met anybody from Sweden before,' she added. 'Then again, I never meet anyone.'

They had started a very slow dance around the courtyard, their bodies several feet apart. Ari watched every knot of the apple tree she touched as she wandered round it, every chair back she dragged her fingers across. They became, at her touch, isolated sacred places – the world's smallest churches. Ari followed her, keeping the distance between them constant. At times, her back was turned to him as she talked; at times, her eyes were up against his. She plumped a cushion, sat down for just a second in Taft's chair then rose again. Ari followed her in a complete circle around the fountain. His footsteps landed in the spaces hers had vacated just a second before; he imagined the spots were still warm through the soles of his shoes because her toes had touched them.

Cleo was about to hand him his hat at last when she thought better of it and suddenly raised it to her nose. She sniffed a short, sharp intake of air like the scenting of a sly animal.

'You smell strange,' she stated.

'It's the heat,' he began to apologize.

'Not bad at all. You smell of old books.'

231

'Oh,' he said, charmed by her and feeling inept.

He was thinking of some distant June. He was eating a sundae in a glamorous café in midtown. The long spoon he held had bulged with pipless papaya and the skinned segments of oranges. They were all juicy fruits but none were as strange and wonderful as this girl. None of them were as delicious as Cleo-fruit.

'You working with Oscar?' she asked.

'No, I'm involved in something that's happened back in town.'

Cleo slid behind the French doors again. Half her slim leg showed and one tail of her shirt and the curve of one buttock, a shy cheek.

'I think you're nice, Harry Cole,' she said.

'Ari,' he said, 'not Harry. My name's Ari Köll.'

Her hand curled around the jamb. He saw skeletal bones instead of fingers. He thought of a missing eye and a frilly-lipped sea slug bulging from a cavity.

'Did a man visit here last night?' he asked.

'Didn't Si tell you that?' Her voice was wary.

'He said nobody came.'

'Then nobody it is,' she answered flatly.

'I need to speak to you some more. Another time, though.'

'Okay,' she said simply.

'Thank you,' said Ari.

Then she threw back her head and laughed with outrageous abandon – mouth open, rude as a belch.

'You're an easy man to please,' she said.

'Where can we meet?' Ari asked.

'If you get a boat tomorrow, I'll swim out to

you. Just don't come in too close.'

All the way back to the dock, Ari looked behind bushes for Silas Taft's single eye. It would come glinting out at him, yellow as a bee sting, he was sure. But when he reached the pier, Taft and Oscar were standing at the end of it, fanning themselves with their hats. Ari was a little breathless.

'It took a while to find it,' he said. 'The breeze blew it into the garden.'

It was always easy to blame things on the wind.

'Ahhh, the many convenient functions of a hat,' said Taft. 'That must be why I always wear one, I suppose.'

He put his white straw panama back onto his head.

Oscar and Ari climbed down to the *Alexa Lee* and Taft had the height advantage at last.

'Oscar, you won't be out here again in this regard, will you? Because I'm assuming you won't be.'

'No. A return won't be necessary,' Oscar assured him.

The boat engine revved and they slipped their moorings.

Suddenly, Taft called out after them, 'Mr Köll!'

Ari looked back.

Silas pointed to his eye patch. 'It's just the one eye. Remember that.'

18

Ari found his mother in the sun lounge of the Colonial Hotel. She was sitting in front of a dense palm tree; he saw her blonde hair first against the plant's green foliage. She was speaking with someone who was facing away from Ari, hidden from his view by the tall fan back of one of the chairs. The weaving round the legs of the chair had unravelled and curls of wicker like wood shavings lay around each foot. A small calico cat was playing with these springy coils as Ari crossed the floor towards his mother. A man's arm reached down suddenly from the chair and caught the cat by the scruff of its neck and tossed it across the polished floor. It scooted along on its hind legs, yowling with surprise and indignation. Ari saw his mother giggle. She was sitting on the edge of her chair and for a second he thought the man she was speaking with must be, by some bizarre coincidence, Charles Lindbergh. She looked so utterly happy.

'Ari!' she said when she saw him. 'You must meet Mr Underwood.'

Ari didn't even look at the man.

'I have to speak to you,' he said.

He needed to tell her about Mr Oddman and Mr Taft and explain that he had withheld information from the police... He could hardly remember why. He had to see de la Croix that evening with Oddman and Brown's calling card. His mother ought to go along with him.

'Don't be rude,' said Hella and she seemed disproportionately irritated with him.

Ari turned to where the man had stood up from the chair and saw a tall, handsome, nondescript figure with very short brown hair and a pleasant smile. Ari wouldn't have noticed him in a crowd. He was unassuming, pleasant natured – one of a hundred similar men who visit Florida hotels in search of lonely widows. Ari had heard about them from the boys at school. One of his acquaintances, Ruben, now had one for a stepfather. Generally, they had polish, some education and a lot of reading but not a penny from a stable job. They were as unreliable as church roofs.

'Good day,' said Ari.

The man bowed a little when he took Ari's hand and his grip was just right, firm but not crushing.

'We have to speak...' Ari repeated to his mother. 'Do you know where I've been all day?' he almost hissed.

'Quozzie said something about a drunk drowning at the beach. Was it terrible? I'm sorry, Mr Underwood,' she said to her new admirer. 'He's a highly strung boy,'

Ari resented that. He was no longer a boy and he thought he had proved himself surprisingly controlled throughout the day considering what had happened.

'I'm not a boy!' he said and it sounded like something a boy would say. 'I apologize Mr Underwood, I do need my mother's attention for just a minute.'

'Not at all,' said the man.

There was the slightest accent there; Ari couldn't place it. Perhaps he was Nordic and that's why his mother was so charmed. People were always pleased to meet fellow homelanders when they were on holiday. It was almost ridiculous how grateful they were to have it confirmed that home was still where they had left it.

Hella was annoyed by her son's insistence but she shook hands with Mr Underwood and said, 'I will try the Casa Marina one night on your recommendation.'

'We'll try it together. Meet me there at seven o'clock. I'll send a car.'

Hella blushed and looked down coyly; Ari was sure she could redden sweetly at will. Mr Underwood, satisfied that he had succeeded in arranging to see her again, sat back down in his chair. He clicked his fingers twice, the sound was very loud, and the small calico cat came trotting back across the room. He stroked it fiercely with his smooth tanned hand and it purred.

Freed from propriety at last, Ari clasped his mother by the top of the arm and pulled her outside through the doors onto the deck. Two men were throwing a football in the swimming pool and several women were shrieking at their splashy horseplay. Ari took his mother round the back of the shed where Quozzie kept his equipment. Here, a pump chugged and gurgled. The concrete slab floor was damp with surprisingly cold water. Ari could smell oil. Hella tried not to get her shoes wet.

'What is all this nonsense, Ari? I'm going to dinner with Mr Underwood tonight. Did you hear?'

'The dead man was Julian Oddman ... your so-called drunk who drowned.'

It took a second for Hella to take it in. To her credit, she was not a woman who questioned and dithered and demanded to be told everything several times before she chose to believe it. She had never asked Ari if he was sure of a thing. As her son, she took it for granted that he would always be sure; he tried not to disappoint her.

'He must have come here early for some reason, maybe just to meet Mr Taft and set up the viewing. I don't know. He's dead, though. He's drowned accidentally or something. The doctor will tell the sheriff this afternoon. The truth could be worse, though. The point is we have to reach Brown and get him down here to meet this sheriff and answer some questions. I didn't mention we knew about Taft.'

'How does Mr Taft come into this?'

'I met him today. I'm not certain he knew who I was but the sheriff took me out to his house on a remote Key because that's where they think the body might have drifted in from. It's all speculation. Oddman might have knocked his head on a dock railing when he was drunk and fallen into the water. I just didn't say anything about the flight log on the black market. I said we were here on business but nothing else.'

'I shouldn't think they'd care,' said Hella. 'It's not guns or drugs or government secrets, after all.'

'They will care if somebody's dead because of it.'

'We'll ask Mr Brown what to do,' said Hella.

She touched Ari's face.

'The sun's kissed you,' she said and she smiled. 'It looks good on your nose.'

'Taft has a daughter,' said Ari. The truth was bubbling up inside. As much as he wanted to, he couldn't keep Cleo to himself. 'Not really a daughter but a ward.'

Hella made a snorting sound.

'Convenient,' she said.

'No, really!' Ari insisted.

'Is she beautiful?'

'She's very beautiful.'

Hella snorted again.

'I'm glad we made the trip. You need to see something of the world beside its art. You ought to know more about its artifice.'

'What do you mean?'

'Wealthy men never have beautiful daughters,' said Hella enigmatically. 'That's one of nature's rules.'

'Why do you have to ruin everything?' he asked.

He said it quietly for maximum cruelty but she just looked into him with her violet eyes.

'Because that's what everything comes to eventually – a ruin – and I'm impatient.'

'I won't let you spoil it,' he said.

'We need to call Mr Brown,' she said. 'Though he's probably left already.'

Hella slipped past him and back out into the light. Ari skulked for a few moments more. He was trying to quell his anger at his mother's carelessness. As he paced behind the pump house, he delved his hands into his pockets in frustration and felt a small piece of paper there. It was the fragment he had found under Oddman's body and it was almost dry now. He wished he had a sample of Oddman's writing so he could decipher whether or not the man had written it himself. He placed the scrap against the pump-house wall and it stuck there like a wet sliver of papier mâché, He glanced at the letters again: *'ves airp'* and then *'ikes re'*, but his brain didn't seem able to puzzle out what the letters might mean. He left the fragment clinging to the wall with its weeping indecipherable message. He was tired of the thudding of the pump and the oily smell. He followed Hella out. Two of the women by the pool had seen both of them emerge, one a few minutes after the other. They smiled knowingly. They sipped from their tall blue glasses and followed Ari with their eyes.

Kit Brown wasn't at his office. The phone line buzzed and buzzed in Hella's ear and she shook her head at Ari to let him know that nobody was answering. Perhaps the man was already on his way to meet them. The next train arrived on Saturday, Ari remembered. Hella thanked the clerk behind the reception desk and returned his telephone to him across the counter.

'Would you place a call to that number again at six o'clock this evening and send a message for me if you get through to anyone?'

'Yes, Ma'am,' said the clerk.

'What should I say to the sheriff?' Ari asked Hella.

She didn't answer him at once.

'Let's go and find Mr Brown's calling card,' she said.

Back in their room, Hella found the card at once. She was using it as a bookmark in the volume of poems she was reading. Ari looked at the small rectangle.

The card read 'Oddman & Brown: Procurement & Acquisitions'. There was the Grand Concourse address and an exchange number below that.

'It doesn't actually mention investigations,' Ari said.

'Won't they ask what he was procuring for us?'

'I suppose they will. What can we say? What could possibly be of any real value down here?'

Before Ari could say anything more, Hella took the card from his hand and tore it across.

'Tell him you couldn't find it,' she said. 'The death was a terrible accident. Tell your sheriff that we've notified Mr Oddman's partner and he's coming down to meet us and collect the body on Monday.'

'Okay,' said Ari.

'Don't say "okay",' said Hella, distractedly.

'What are we going to do? Are you still going to meet Taft?'

'We'll wait to hear what Mr Brown suggests,' said Hella. 'If Mr Oddman's met with an accident then I don't see why we shouldn't go ahead with our plans. It's terribly unfortunate but he must have been very drunk or stupid to fall off a quay and drown like that.'

'He didn't seem very stupid when we met him,' said Ari.

'Will they tell you their findings ... about the

body, I mean?'

'Dr Saul might,' said Ari. 'If I can find his rooms.'

'We haven't done anything illegal, Ari,' said Hella and she leaned over and kissed his hair. One of the unexpected heart-wrenching gestures he never knew what to do with.

'I'm going to take my dinner with Mr Under-wood. You need a shower, Ari. You're all rumpled.'

Ari thought of Cleo in the rumpled shirt; almost everything his mother said had managed to conjure up some element of her.

Ari nodded. He was resigned to being alone in this as in everything else.

'I'll go to my room and then try and see if I can find the doctor's place.'

He couldn't fathom his mother's detachment, her astonishing self-involvement.

'A slug was eating his eye,' he said from the door.

That at least made her pause and look at him before he went out.

Dr Saul's surgery was in a prominent, brick build-ing in the heart of the commercial part of town. Built in the height of the Twenties, it had hand-carved, wooden balconies and every embellish-ment of stonemasonry. Curlicues and vines grew petrified about the doorframe. There were even gargoyles on its roof – one munched on a human soul as it glared down at the passing traffic; another had a drainpipe extending from between its lips to vomit out muddy water from the gutters when it rained. It seldom did and the creature's grooves were silted up with weeks of desiccated sea salt. Along the facade, living creepers grew untended, too. They created scarves for the gargoyles and intertwined with their own stone replicas. The surgery reeked (even from outside) of stale human tissue.

Ari went in through the patients' door and discovered himself alone. There were no consultations on Friday afternoons, it seemed. Doctor Saul didn't help the poor for free any more. Now that he had joined their ranks, he neglected them. Ari looked around for a place to hang his coat. Somebody else's coat dangled from the antlers of a stuffed Key deer mounted on the wall. The creature's face was moth-eaten, its eyes fearful. A tongue protruded slightly from between its grey lips in a grimace of humiliation. There was an umbrella stand made from an elephant's foot; it held several walking sticks. Everything here had once been alive and was now preserved, inanimate, for study. Ari experienced the sensation of insects crawling over his skin.

The doctor appeared, having heard the door, and led Ari into his private room. Though much of the apparatus was gleaming and the sheets on the bed, like the doctor's coat, were shockingly white, the room seemed dark. Thick lace curtains obscured the windowpanes and threw creeping lace patterns, like leprosy, over the doctor's face. The place was preternaturally quiet and sterile. Nothing shifted its weight or moved.

'Deputy de la Croix said the man was your friend,' said the doctor.

'No,' said Ari. 'He was a business associate. I'd

only met him a few times.'

'I'd like to know what manner of business you are in,' said the doctor.

'I've just left school really,' said Ari, feeling young and foolish, a fake.

'I only ask because his throat's been slit.'

'What?' blurted Ari.

'A sharp knife across the throat and no hesitation. It's a vicious theft or some kind of personal vendetta if you ask me, though I never am asked to offer opinions of that kind. I'm supposed to leave that to the officers of the law.'

'I can't believe it. I thought the crabs had...'

'He's been in the water less than two days, I think.'

Suddenly the doctor forced out, as if under terrible pressure, 'Would you like to see him... Not squeamish, are you?'

'I hardly knew him,' Ari said again. He sounded bewildered, even to himself.

Dr Saul opened a side door and they went into a vestibule room. The steel table dominated but the place was the same cold, dark white as the office. Oddman's body was neatly arranged on blocks of ice on the table. As the ice bricks melted, the water ran along channels in the steel and dripped through a drain in the floor that sounded as deep as a canyon. The trickling was the only sound. Freed of his seaweed restraints, the man's skin was pale and marbled with reddish-black veins.

Ari touched the bones of one of Oddman's fingers with one of his own.

'Barracuda probably,' said Saul. 'A shark would

243

have done worse.'

'How does something like this happen?' asked Ari. It was a question for God really.

'It's a depression, son,' said Dr Saul knowingly. 'People are drinking too much, getting into fights.'

'It couldn't have been an accident?' Ari asked again.

'Not unless he fell against a knife. This one had a razor-sharp blade; there's no tugging against the skin – the cut's as clean as a whistle. Decay's been accelerated by his being in the water but he's only been adrift for a short time else the fish would have finished him off.'

'Murder,' Ari said.

It was a statement of fact ... and Oddman's body had floated in, they initially thought, from Taft's island. It had to have something to do with the deal, the flight log. Ari thought he was going to be sick. He hadn't eaten all day and the acid-rich juices swam about in his stomach.

'What the hell!' Oscar's voice burst through the door. His bulk followed it. He pressed his chest into Ari's heaving stomach. His eyes glared up at the boy from their inferior height.

'Is this your body?' he demanded of Ari. The phrasing seemed somewhat bizarre. 'IS THIS YOUR BODY?' he yelled again.

'No,' Ari stammered.

'What are you trying to do to me, Doc?'

'I thought he was part of it all...' said the doctor, befuddled. 'He's got a right to see his friend, doesn't he?'

'He's not my friend,' said Ari.

'This is NOT your body!' de la Croix repeated.

The doctor felt he better get the worst news out now.

'It's a murder, Oscar,' he said. 'The man had his throat slit for him.'

'Jesus!' shrieked the little man. 'And he knows all about it now, does he? What if he's a suspect, Dr Saul?'

'Is he?' asked the doctor.

'I don't know yet,' said Oscar.

'But you dragged me out to the Key. You suggested the connection between Mr Oddman and Mr Taft!'

The doctor's eyes swished back and forward between the man-high boy and the boy-high man.

'That was when I thought Taft might be in all this.'

'How do you know he isn't?'

'He never even met the man,' said Oscar. 'He doesn't even know him.'

'I happen to know he does,' said Ari.

He immediately wished he hadn't admitted that.

'You better spill what you know right now, boy,' said Oscar.

'My mother wants to buy his house.' It came to him in an explosion of genius. 'Mr Oddman and his partner Mr Brown contacted Mr Taft about viewing the property and that's why we're here.'

'He was an estate agent?' asked Oscar.

The explanation had deflated him.

'He's more like a consultant. He sourced relevant properties, valued them, brought buyers and sellers together.'

'And you say his partner's here on Monday?'

'That's right. But I know Ms Taft must know of Mr Oddman because they've been in communication about this meeting for a week at least. I don't know why Taft would deny knowing him.'

'Why didn't you speak up on the island when he said it?'

'Mr Taft doesn't know I'm the son of his potential buyer. If all this is a misunderstanding and a barfly killed Mr Oddman, I don't want to sour my mother's deal.'

'You're a ruthless kid, you know that?'

Ari felt sick again. Nobody had ever called him vicious or ruthless before yet in his heart he knew it to be true.

'Is your incinerator fired up, Doc?' Oscar asked.

'Haven't used it for weeks,' says the doctor, looking over his shoulder through the net curtains to where a large kiln stood at the end of his backyard.

'You gonna burn him?'

'You can't do that!' said Ari. 'Not until his partner's had a chance to see him, surely.'

'You've identified him already.'

'I'd prefer you didn't. Can't you ... keep him somewhere?'

Ari looked at Dr Saul.

'I can keep him another day or so on ice, I guess,' he said.

'Do it,' said de la Croix, and to Ari he added, 'I hope your Mr Brown has some substantiation to offer,' he said.

'And Mr Taft?'

'Mr Taft isn't going anywhere. He's a respected member of our community and no killer. I'm gonna have to start in the bars tonight,' he sighed deeply. 'That's where the culprit will turn up.'

Oscar and Ari went out together then peeled off in separate directions. The gargoyle on the roof levelled its clawed finger at Ari. It pointed him out to passers-by on the busy street, as if he were the guilty party.

Ari was exhausted when he returned to the hotel.

'Señor!' Señor Bolivar called out to him across the lobby.

Ari went over to the man who looked as crisp as a lettuce leaf despite the heat. Ari resented him a little.

'I placed that call to New York your mother requested at six o'clock precisely. No answer. I took it upon myself to try again just a half hour ago but there is still no response to the ring. I hope it is not urgent?'

'No, the gentleman we're trying to reach will soon be arriving personally.'

'The police were asking for you this afternoon...'

'Which police?' asked Ari.

'Our sheriff, Mr de la Croix. He wanted your home address in New York City.'

So Oscar had been suspicious enough to ensure he would be able to find them should they decide to run off in the night.

'He called your building and had the doorman confirm your residence there...'

'It's fine,' said Ari. 'I think you probably know

247

that Quozzie and I were involved in finding a body this morning. They need our address as a matter of formality only.'

'But the dead man was your friend, no?' asked Señor Bolivar.

'No, he wasn't,' said Ari.

This was a small town, he reminded himself, and the encounter with Señor Bolivar had been a lesson in the need for discretion. He reassured the manager once more then went up to his room. He saw how burned his face was in the mirror above the basin. He looked like somebody else; his skin was unfamiliar to him. Could a life's accumulated goodness be swept away by a stray wave, a single inclination towards pettiness and spite? He felt desperate, lonely. He thought about Cleo. He thought about their arrangement to meet; he wondered if she would honour it. At least the next day was Saturday and he would have a reprieve from Oscar de la Croix's questions – presumably a small-town sheriff wouldn't work on a Saturday. Was a murder investigation the exception? They had to wait for Brown to arrive; he would have to take some responsibility for working the whole matter out. There must still be a way, surely, to remedy the whole mix-up... But Oddman was dead. If that was an accident, a bar fight as de la Croix had suggested, it might still be okay. Ari might be able to go on. If not, how could he possibly approach Brown with his dilemma?

He lay in a hot bath until he reddened in the water; his whole body became a scarlet letter that marked him. Later, he went down to the pool and watched Quozzie plough up and down the surface of the water with his net. This was the hunchbacked boy's favourite task; Ari could see that now. He liked the peaceful monotony of it. He caught nothing; he merely unsettled the quiet stillness of the water's surface as the darkness came in.

Ari had a small supper in the empty dining room – the tourists had abandoned Key West as surely as the turtles had. He had seen the cannery on their way to the fishing dock that morning. Its gate was chained shut. The deep turtle pools were empty. Every now and then a dark blue shape would surface then it would dive down again and disappear. The cannery had closed.

Ari knew his mother might stay out half the night if there was dancing, and men to admire her, but it was barely nine o'clock – Ari was about to go up to his room – when Hella came flying through the lobby and shouted out his name.

Señor Bolivar looked up from behind his desk. His moustache froze in shock; he hadn't imagined this refined lady could roar so.

'Ari!' Hella shouted it again as she nipped off her gloves. She slapped them down on the coffee table, terrifying the sleeping calico cat.

'You won't believe this!' she shouted.

Ari hurried over and made his mother sit down. She took a deep breath and lowered her voice. Ari presumed that her enchanting Mr Underwood had made an unsavoury suggestion but that was something his mother usually took in her stride.

'That Mr Underwood,' she said furiously. 'He's

here to buy our log!'

'What?' said Ari.

'He came right out and told me that he's here to purchase a rare document...'

'It might not be the same thing at all.'

'He mentioned Mr Taft as the seller,' she hissed.

19

Ari woke to the screech of green parrots from the jacaranda tree outside his window. It was a sound he had never heard before, like tin pots crashing onto a steel counter. As soon as he opened his eyes and oriented himself, he felt calmer. The heat was an early riser. It was up before him and had already settled in for the day. Unemployed, and with nothing much to do, it sat heavily on the slats of the public benches and baked the sandy sidewalks to stone.

Ari passed the traffic of people on weekend errands – the long-suffering wives leading their contrite, stooped husbands. The women were dressed in their best and, as they marched along, they fanned themselves against the heat with limp shopping lists. The blooms on their cheap floral dresses were wilting; the silk buds on their hats were singed; their fainting gloves were held erect only by the framework of their fingers. Unaccommodating collars choked the men and braces were cinched up tight to keep their trousers on.

Ari had left his mother in bed and ordered room service for her. She was scheming and furious. She had refused to receive messages or calls from Mr Underwood. Señor Bolivar was under strict instructions to rebuff any attempts to contact her, so it was impossible to tell if any such efforts had been made. Ari and Hella had both agreed that Taft would have to be approached about the matter of inviting another buyer but they would wait for Brown's arrival before doing anything. There was only one more day of uncertainty to endure. The evening train would bring the clear head and imposing bulk of a skilled player in this sort of game.

Ari reached the charter boat quay and found a sailor stitching floats to the edge of a net. The man was leaning up against a pile of old tractor tyres and he held the net stretched taut between his toes and his fingers as he worked.

'I'd like to rent a boat,' Ari said. 'For fishing. I want to go fishing.'

The man looked Ari over. He took in the hat and the linen suit and the new pair of brown brogues.

'Do you, now?' he said.

His tone seemed to suggest that there hadn't been a fool of Ari's stature on this quay for many a year. In the high days, they had probably humoured the odd eccentric – the odd writer – who would show up from time to time and hire a proper boat with a captain to seek out the big game fish but this city slicker was stupid and solo. Ari knew he looked more like a boy who planned to tie a piece of string to his big toe and fish for minnows like Huckleberry Finn than a marlin fisherman.

'I just need a small boat I can manage,' said Ari.

'Motor or manpower?' asked the fisherman.

'Motor,' said Ari.

'I got just the thing for you.'

The vessel had started its maritime career as a lifeboat for the *Casandra*, a British cutter wrecked near Sandy Key in 1910. It was salvaged by a Conch captain and lovingly restored as an outsized rowboat for his sons. The three boys had named it *Calamity Jane* and had run it aground on numerous occasions during their sailing adventures. It had suffered under a further five owners since then. One had added a rickety engine and renamed it *Bravado*.

The fisherman recounted its history as he gave Ari a rudimentary lesson on the outboard. Ari seemed to remember that it was bad luck to rename a boat. It took him a while to get the hang of the engine. The *Bravado* battled the swells in the harbour entrance but on open water, it fared better. Ari dropped the anchor – a concrete brick with a chain that had been linked through one of its holes then padlocked closed – and bobbed half a mile off the coast of Long Dead Key for almost an hour. The sink and swell of the bow made him sick. The sun was as fierce as a ginger tomcat; it reminded Ari of the fire that had devoured Glassen's farm. He thought of his mother and the sound of hammering. He wondered now if any of the events he recalled had actually happened or if the active imagination of a boy had dreamed them up. The other big adventure in his life had been real enough, of course. He knew that because he had tangible proof of it. Ari turned the pages over in his mind as he watched for signs of movement among the juts and coves of Cleo's Key.

Cleo popped up out of the water unexpectedly and, before Ari knew it, she had tugged herself into the boat, buoyant as oil and just as slippery. Her swimsuit was white, cut daringly high on the thigh and low in the front.

'You're still got your shoes on!' was the first thing Cleo said as she squeezed the sea from her red hair. She leaned forward immediately – careless of the instability she brought to the boat – and started unlacing his shoes. 'I never wear them here. They get full of sand. They're pure nuisance.'

'I learned that yesterday,' said Ari.

His feet were revealed – albinos at the ends of his legs.

Cleo giggled.

'I've never seen feet that white,' she said. 'Let the sun get at them.'

She rested his ankles on the edge of the boat; he left them exactly where she had placed them.

'Thank you,' he said.

He felt stupid and very young beside her.

'It's a good swim out,' she added casually.

'This won't land you in trouble, will it?'

'Oh, yes, it will!' she exclaimed.

'He doesn't let you off the island?'

Ari felt a frisson of anger. She had become, for him, the fair woman Douglas Fairbanks always spotted at the window of the burning tower.

'I visit town all the time.'

253

As she talked, Cleo took Ari by the shoulders and eased him forward, pulling his jacket off one arm at a time. He had never met a stranger as comfortable with touching people as this girl who was bronzed brown on all her exposed bits. She was the only redhead he had ever seen who tanned like a South Pacific islander.

'Who are you?' he asked.

'I'm just me,' she said, surprised.

'No. I mean where do you come from? I know you're not Mr Taft's daughter.'

'Definitely not!' she exclaimed.

'So who are you?' It sounded impertinent, even to Ari who was always getting tongue-tied and saying the wrong thing.

'I'm a girl from a big family who gave me up on account of too many mouths to feed and the State took me on. I lived in a home for lost kids. It wasn't too bad, I guess. Always real crowded, though, and with this smell of burned cabbage, and at night the railway cars passing rattled your teeth if you were in a top bunk. Si took me over for a donation to the home mother.'

Ari was appalled.

'He bought you?'

Cleo shrugged.

'Maybe,' she said, as if the commercial aspect of it had never offended her, as if she understood that people with money could simply have the things belonging to the people with none.

Cleo rolled up Ari's sleeves next until his arms were exposed. They were thin and ridged by hungry veins.

'When was all this?'

'A few, years ago now, I suppose,' she said.

'Is that why there was a protest from some children's welfare organization or something? I heard de la Croix mention it.'

'Children's welfare!' laughed Cleo. 'I'm sixteen.'

'But you weren't at the time,' said Ari.

'That wasn't about me,' said Cleo. 'That was about a girl Si used to know called Cherry. And that childcare bunch – so-called – consisted of several old biddies in town causing a rumpus when a few of their husbands took a shine to her at the dogfights. They couldn't decide whether they were mad at Silas for having brought her here or their men for flirting with her or the dogfights for being dogfights! It all blew over eventually but a couple of them felt burned by the whole affair – that old librarian, Mrs Jasper, plus a few other dried-up spinsters. Sheriff Willis and Oscar got caught right in the middle of it because their secretary, Alice, also had her feathers ruffled somehow but there wasn't anything illegal about what Silas was doing...'

'Where is she now?' asked Ari. 'This girl Cherry?'

Cleo shrugged. 'She left before I got here.'

Ari didn't want to ask her if Silas and she had ever been lovers – that would surely have been illegal. He almost didn't want to know.

'Will you ever leave? When will you leave?' Ari struggled with the words.

Could Cleo come back to New York with him and his mother? Ari wanted the two women to meet; he wondered if his mother would like the girl. Would Hella ever really like another woman?

'I might ... I'm waiting to see,' Cleo said and she smiled softly at Ari in the shy manner he liked.

'And Mr Taft. What does he actually do?'

'He's an importer ... or an exporter, I can never remember which. I used to hear whispers, though,' Cleo said. 'That he ran rum up from Cuba and cane spirit from the islands. I guess that could be true. He knows some powerful men in Havana, that's for sure. It's a trading business he runs. He's always surrounded by books and documents of all kinds, ancient piles of paper...'

'And people visit him to buy them?'

Cleo frowned.

'Not often. There's hardly ever anyone on the island but Si and me and the maid service.'

'And a man never visited on Wednesday or Thursday night last? A bookish-looking man wearing a brown suit?'

'Nobody like that,' she said.

Cleo began rolling up Ari's pant-legs. It seemed outrageous but Ari didn't want to stop her. Her fingers brushed his skin beautifully. When she was finished, Cleo stood up, put her hands into the back of her swimsuit, and produced a waxy-skinned mango.

'Mango?' she asked lightly.

It had been held against her during the swim; her skin had been pressed all along it. Ari watched her pierce the skin of the fruit with her thumbs and delve into the flesh. She split the fruit open, dividing it in half. Ari looked at this lush, dripping, damp-haired girl with her tanned legs curled under her, crouched over half a mango. She was the one thing he hadn't counted on when

256

this journey had begun. He had never imagined anything good coming out of it. Perhaps he had inherited his mother's pessimism – and she was a pessimist despite her claims of pragmatism.

'Are you even real?' Ari said suddenly.

Cleo snorted a little; mango juice trickled down her chin.

'As real as anything you'll find around here, I suppose,' she said.

She sounded a bit sad all of a sudden. Her face had unexpectedly lost its animation.

'I'm sorry,' Ari said. 'Have I said something wrong?'

'It's okay,' Cleo replied. 'So you're here to buy the book?' she added quickly.

Ari was completely floored by the statement.

'You know about that?' he said.

'Yup,' she said casually.

If Cleo knew who he was then Silas Taft must know, too.

'He knew who I was when I came out to his house?' asked Ari.

'Sure he did,' said Cleo. 'He preferred not to say so in front of Mr de la Croix. It doesn't mean he knows anything about Mr Oddman's death because he doesn't. He's just eager to get on with the deal.'

'Well, we know about the other buyer. You can tell him that. My mother met Mr Underwood last night by chance and she isn't at all pleased. How many more are there?'

'Only the two of you. It wasn't planned this way...'

'Sure it wasn't,' said Ari.

257

'But now the item goes to the highest bidder. That's just good business practice.'

'Do you know what the item is exactly?'

'A rare book,' said Cleo.

'Why does Mr Underwood want it?'

Cleo shrugged. 'Why does your mother want it?' she countered.

'She's obsessed with the author.'

'Mr Underwood's obsessed with the content, I think,' said Cleo, enigmatically.

'What does he think is in it?' Ari asked.

He couldn't imagine anybody wanting the stray jottings of a pilot, rambling and incoherent on a long flight – only his mother chased down the wind in that way.

Cleo was losing patience, Ari saw.

'I don't know anything about that! Si is sorry about you losing your friend here but he needs to know if your mother wants the book or not.'

'She does,' said Ari. 'But...'

Cleo looked into his eyes and suddenly he tingled all over. It was the way she looked, the way she pressed her wet swimsuit against his arm.

'Do you want it or not,' she whispered harshly.

Her breath was just slightly ragged. Ari tried to keep the shudder he felt still inside his skin.

'We want it,' he said.

Cleo looked back at her island and said in an exuberant non sequitur, 'Ari, do you like flying? I could take you up one day if you do.'

Ari connected her with the plane he had seen above the island.

'The plane, the red Sirius – it's yours?'

Cleo nodded. 'Si gave me lessons, too, for turning sixteen last year. I only needed five – I'm what they call a natural.'

'You fly it?'

'I certainly do,' Cleo said.

She smiled and the inside of her mouth was orange with the memory of mango. It made Ari do an audacious thing. He borrowed courage from Charles Lindbergh, his hero, and leaned forward. He thought the leaning might take forever; it seemed to take at least an hour just to reach her mouth and then his lips were there. Ari devoured her slowly – the delicious, wet mystery of her tongue and her slick teeth and the plump flesh of her ripe lower lip. She began to pull away from him after a while, backing towards the end of the boat.

As Cleo's body slipped so slowly from his hands, Ari's mouth stayed connected to it. His tongue trailed down her chin and her neck, the tops of her breasts above the costume neckline, the thin fabric itself stained through with the taste of mangoes. His mouth scored her stomach and then, as she slipped over the edge into the sea, her thigh and knee and calves in rapid succession. To the very end of her feet, his mouth tasted her but was not satisfied.

The experience left him bereft of breath and thought. Ari simply watched as she swam away from the *Bravado* with steady strokes.

In that one moment, all things had been irrevocably altered. Cleo's body on his mouth had obliterated all memory of his life before. The path ahead seemed clear and straight. He would rescue her. Cleo would be his deliverance from mediocrity; he would be her relentless saviour.

The afternoon was long and lush and all blued through. The gardens crazed with bees. The magnolias hung lank and paralysed against the broken trellises. Only the trees offered relief from the heat among their shadows. Ari stood taller now; the taste of mango was as loud as orchestra brass in his mouth. The pool deck of the hotel smelled of coral dust and lemon-tree fumes as Ari walked across it, barefoot and hatless, his hair ruffled by sea spray.

He saw his mother sipping an iced tea from a long, convoluted glass. Mr Underwood sat beside her. They were talking to Oscar de la Croix. Hella's eyes seemed to burn through Ari as he approached, as if he had placed her in an untenable situation. She didn't give his appearance away, however, so he stood back quietly and listened as they kept speaking.

'Mrs Gold is going out to look the place over tomorrow,' said Mr Underwood. 'It wasn't seemly to conduct business on a weekend,' he added. 'By then her agent will be here to assist her.'

'And to enlighten me as to his friend's unfortunate demise,' said Oscar.

'Well, I doubt that,' said Mr Underwood. 'He's unlikely to know much about it, is he? He's been travelling for the past few days. Surely you've got some more obvious suspects in mind. There must be known cutpurses operating locally...?'

Mr Underwood let his sentence rise as a question. In the midst of his mental turmoil, Ari's mind

260

fixed on the one irrelevance in the conversation: Mr Underwood's use of the word 'cutpurse'. It was so quaintly archaic – surely 'mugger' or 'pickpocket' would have been more appropriate?

'I spent last evening in the bars,' de la Croix explained. 'Friday's the perfect night to catch all the vermin out and about but there weren't any stories circulating.'

'Would there be?' asked Underwood. 'If there's been a murder, wouldn't the perpetrator be wiser to keep silent?'

'They all end up mouthing off to someone and this is a small town, Mr Underwood.'

Ari walked up to announce his presence.

'And where have you been?' said Hella coldly.

Ari wasn't sure if he was more surprised that the sheriff had tracked his mother down or that she had allowed Mr Underwood to come to her aid.

'Sheriff de la Croix is just asking about my purchase of Mr Taft's house. He didn't even know it was on the market.'

'Everything's on the market to the right buyer, isn't that right Mr Underwood?' said Ari.

'It's the cornerstone of capitalism,' said Mr Underwood lightly and he laughed.

Hella swatted the air near her nose with an angry hand. She was trying to kill a mosquito that was bothering her but she missed it.

'Are you any closer to finding Mr Oddman's killer?' Ari asked Oscar.

'No, and it's troubling me some,' said Oscar. 'See, this town's less gracious element have got two ways of getting into hot water. One, they get into a scuffle at some heated event like the dogs or the boxing and they go at it. Sometimes, I have to say, there's a bit of stabbing or slicing goes on ... but it's high blood, that. Two fellows get hot and have it out there and then and usually there are a dozen witnesses. The other way, they're after money and they see some out-of-towner looking rich and plump and they cosh him over the head and take what they want – wallet, watch, and so forth – but they hardly ever kill the fellow. There's no need to. They can get what they want without too much violence and if they do get caught it's not a hanging offence. They ain't gonna slit the fellow's throat. See my conundrum?'

'That's clever,' said Mr Underwood. 'Very deductive of you.'

He sounded as if he was holding down a fit of pique. Underwood's bitter tone surprised Ari, then he realized that Underwood was the kind of man who never imagined anybody could match him for intellect or cunning – that some Southern hick might be able to evoke his surprise, galled him.

'I'll keep on it,' said Oscar. 'I'll get in touch with your Mr Brown as soon as he arrives and I might share a boat out to Mr Taft's place with you when you go out to look it over tomorrow. It makes for good economy with fuel short as it is.' Then he added – and it seemed to Ari it was included purely to unsettle them – 'I got nothing much else to do this week.'

Oscar placed his floppy hat on his head, tipped the brim towards Hella and left them alone together. They all had the sense to wait until he was long gone before they began to speak.

'Where have you been?' Hella repeated to Ari.

'Are we all friends again?' said Ari, looking at Mr Underwood.

'Mr Underwood arrived just before that little man showed up with his infernal questions. We've agreed to a healthy truce.'

Never, thought Ari. She will never let him have the flight log. She will die for it. Then he thought, chillingly: she'd probably kill for it, too. He thought of Oddman and shook his head to clear it. He was being hysterical. His mother wouldn't slit throats. It was preposterous.

'We're both going to look the article over to-morrow,' said Mr Underwood. 'If that ridiculous little sheriff isn't breathing down our throats...'

Again the idiom was a little off. Mr Underwood was foreign. He was passing for English-speaking but Ari didn't think he was. Where had he come from?

'...Perhaps it's not worth anything, after all this,' Underwood continued. 'Your mother and I have agreed that it'll go to the highest bidder – if it's authentic.'

'Our authenticator is dead,' said Ari. 'That puts us at a disadvantage, don't you think?'

'I'm an expert myself,' said Underwood. 'I'll know at once if it's not real.'

'I'm not sure that helps us,' said Ari.

'You'll have your Mr Brown by then,' said Underwood.

'What is it that you do exactly, Mr Under-wood?'

263

'I'm a civil servant. An attaché.'

'For whom?' asked Hella – so she had also picked up on a slight accent and the troubling vocabulary, too.

'The government of Belgium,' said Mr Underwood.

'And you're here on behalf of your employers?' Underwood shook his head.

'What would the Belgian government want with Charles Lindbergh's flight log? I'm off the clock on this one. It's a personal matter,' he said. 'I have extensive experience with rare documents and I've been trained to spot a hoax.'

Ari wasn't happy with the way things were working out. He didn't know how he was going to salvage their lives from the mess. To intensify his guilt, he felt solely responsible for creating the whole predicament. Hella smiled, though, and Ari saw in that strained smile that his mother didn't trust Underwood either. He was glad of that.

'We'll just have to take your word as a gentleman,' she said.

20

A note came to the hotel from Brown that evening. He had arrived on the 2:30 p.m. train and was settled in at a boarding house off Olivia Street. Ari wondered if de la Croix had made good on his promise to meet the man off the train – if he had, they were sunk. Ari ran all the way to

Brown's lodgings. He took a left turn on Angela Street. Then crossed over Duval where a cigar store Indian was peeling his war paint outside a mercantile. Ari turned right on Elizabeth and finally made a left into Olivia... So many of these tired roads were named after women, he noted.

Ari went down an alley past the side of a dreary building to where the path unexpectedly widened out into a yard. The hidden house was a beauty: a wooden cottage with a wraparound balcony draped with hanging baskets of peonies and frangipani. The evening sun sat mottled and lazy on the front mat.

A woman came out of the house; she had flour on the side of her face where she had accidentally brushed it while baking. Ari thought he recognized her, then placed her as the woman he had been introduced to in Oscar de La Croix's office. Her name was Alice, he remembered.

'Oh, it's you,' she said. 'Hope all that trouble got itself sorted out. Mr de la Croix's like a cat on a hot tin roof over that body. He wants to get it sorted before Willis gets back from Marathon.'

'I'm sure he'll work it out,' said Ari glumly. 'I didn't know you ran a boarding house, too.'

'How could you know that?' she said in a friendly manner. 'You being a visitor and all. Are you visiting my Mr Brown?' she asked.

'Yes,' said Ari. 'Is he here?'

'Sure is, I'll take you up.'

At the back of the cottage was an empty garage with a flight of steps on its side that led to a narrow landing and a door on the second storey. Ari followed Alice up. Alice lit a lantern outside

265

the door – the palm shadows were dense here – then stopped. Ari remained on the step below her; she talked down to him.

'There's no electric out here,' Alice explained. 'It was my husband's room after the war.'

She knocked on the door.

'Visitor for you, Mr Brown!' she sang out sweetly then she pushed past Ari and went back down the stairs.

When Brown opened the door and smiled a greeting, Ari's relief was palpable. Brown stood like a cartoon hero in the frame – he wore no shirt and his tanned muscles rippled beneath his pink braces.

'I'm just going down for a shower,' he said. 'Glad you popped over to say hello.'

It all sounded so mundane that Ari didn't know where to begin. He knew he wanted to cry and couldn't. Brown went back into the room and slung a towel around his neck; he picked up a leather shaving bag from his suitcase. Ari saw that the room was small and quaint with low attic windows and exposed roof beams. There was a neat bed covered in a patchwork comforter and hanging from every beam by invisible wires were dozens of balsawood airplane models. Some had military colours, others were painted with the tails of Pan American, still others were pure imagination. A warm breeze sifted through the insect screen that covered the window and the planes circled on their limited strings.

'Her husband made those himself,' Brown explained. 'He must've gone soft after the war. The facilities are out back and there's a shower down below in the garden. It's just cistern water but it should be cool, she assures me.'

'She's the sheriff's secretary,' said Ari.

'She said she had another job during the week,' said Brown carelessly. 'I've got to take my breakfast before seven o'clock.'

He was completely unaware of the terror sheriffs held for Ari at the moment.

Brown started down the stairs in his bare feet. Ari followed him.

'I have to talk to you,' Ari said.

'You talk and I'll wash,' said Brown and he went behind a grove of elephant ears. It was still hot even though the sun was hissing below the horizon. Birds Ari couldn't see nestled down among the twigs and twittered. The iron cistern tank was attached to the top of a wooden platform with four legs. Brown went in under its belly and stepped onto the damp concrete base of the structure.

'Quite an adventure, this!' Brown exclaimed happily and he reached up and pulled on a chain, soaking himself with a downpour of chill water.

Ari looked about them. They were completely hidden from Alice's house by tropical vegetation; from across the garden came the scratchy sound of a record playing some sticky-fingered blues or jazz tune. Brown washed the sweat from his body in warm rivers; Ari turned away and waited for the man to finish.

'I have to tell you something...' said Ari. 'A few things really and you have to hear me out before you say anything. I have to tell you how it happened...'

Then Brown said an extraordinary thing.

'Tell both of us. Oddman is settling into his room a few blocks away. Why don't we meet you at your hotel in an hour?'

'What do you mean, he's settling in?' asked Ari.

The sun tipped below the fence and it was instantly cold in the garden. Had he made a terrible mistake and misidentified the body? Relief surged through Ari's veins, then was sucked away just as quickly.

'Oddman's probably having a quick wash and unpacking his things,' said Brown. 'He travelled down with me on the train and he's also a bit the worse for wear.'

Why was Brown saying this? It struck Ari that he didn't know these men at all. His mother had discovered their dubious exploits via a window washer from the Bronx. Nobody back home knew the real nature of their mission, they were essentially alone and – Ari felt sure – in certain peril, though he couldn't quite decide on the source of it. Oddman and Brown had been in their home, they had known about Benjamin Gold's money, Hella's vast inherited wealth...

Ari started to back away through the elephant ear grove, stumbling in the muddy slush Brown's shower had made of the grass, but Brown already had the towel wrapped around his waist and was walking his way.

'What's wrong?' he asked when he saw Ari's startled retreat.

'You're saying Oddman came down with you today?'

'You knew that was our plan, didn't you?' asked Brown.

Ari could see the man's eyes scrabbling for understanding.

'Why would you lie?' Ari was surprised that he had uttered his thoughts out loud.

'Lie about what?'

'About Oddman arriving with you. He got here days ago...' said Ari.

Instead of going for his throat, as Ari had imagined he might – a vicious attack that would end his life – Brown put his wet forehead in both hands and said, 'Shit! You ran into him, didn't you? I told him you might. Look, Ari...' Brown's voice was supplicating, seductive, 'It's not been as easy as we suggested. I'm not one hundred per cent sure about this Taft fellow. He's let another buyer in on the deal like a fool...'

'I know!' said Ari. 'A Mr Underwood. We've met him, too.'

'Oddman called me on Thursday and told me the news. He wasn't sure of Taft and he especially didn't like this other buyer. Plus,' continued Brown, 'some initial research suggests, only suggests mind you, that Taft may not be on the up-and-up. I didn't want your mother to buy a dud item, honest I didn't. I had my suspicions about Taft quite early on, so I asked Oddman to come down here and get a jump on things, try to get a gander at the book before your mother got all excited. Just in case it wasn't the genuine article. Oddman only needed a few minutes and he'd have let me know. The good news is there hasn't been a peep from him since his call about Underwood, so I guess he's happy it's alright...'

The explanation soothed Ari somewhat but

Brown had trotted it out by rote, as if he'd had it prepared for some time. Ari wanted to believe him. It sounded feasible, plausible. It was a relief to be able to trust the man again.

'Run into him in the library, did you?' Brown continued.

'On the beach,' said Ari.

'He took to the beach, did he? Daring fellow. Burned red as a cock's comb, I'll wager.'

'He's dead,' said Ari.

It came out small and insubstantial; it did not convey the weight of Oddman's body.

'How'd you mean?' said Brown dumbly.

'Somebody's killed him. He was found with his throat slit. Tell me it's got nothing to do with this, with us, Mr Brown. Please tell me it's a stranger killing for profit...'

Ari's demands to be appeased in the face of the other man's obvious shock and grief, made him remorseful.

'I'll kill him!' said Brown. His voice went down at the end as when one describes a casual statement of fact.

'Who?' asked Ari.

'The man who did this,' said Brown.

'The local sheriff's sniffing about. His name is Oscar de la Croix and he's half stupid, half sharp. He might cotton on to the whole mess. That's why I don't think you staying here with his secretary is a good idea.'

'I didn't know what you meant by that. You seemed so edgy.'

'Let's go up to your room,' said Ari.

They sat together on the bed quilt – there was

270

no other space in the room – and Brown towelled his hair dry and dressed in a daze.

'Tell me everything about that phone call,' said Ari. 'When exactly did you last speak to Oddman?'

'He called on Thursday morning like I said. He'd been out to look at the book as soon as he got in on Wednesday night...'

'So Taft lied to us about not having a visit from him!' said Ari. Cleo had lied, too, but Ari didn't dwell on that. It was quite possible that Taft had met with him in secret. Cleo might easily not have seen Oddman, never known he was there.

'Oddman told me not to worry about the flight log. It was the real McCoy. Then he broke the news that Taft had told him another buyer had showed up out of the blue, uninvited – a man called Underwood. What had Oddman baffled was how this Underwood fellow knew the log was for sale and then he asked to be in on a fair auction. Taft insisted he didn't know the answer. Oddman said he didn't believe a word of that. How could Underwood have found out about the flight log being for sale? It wasn't exactly common knowledge and we had to actively seek it out, didn't we? Underwood couldn't have known about it unless Taft had put the word out discreetly to drum up additional interested parties.'

Ari told him about the story they had concocted about buying Taft's house.

'That's quite good, that is,' said Brown. 'Did you come up with that yourself?'

Ari felt proud and disgusted with himself at the same time.

271

'My mother and I have been desperate for you to arrive and tell us what to do.'

'I was hoping you'd tell me,' said Brown, and Ari's heart sank.

21

Lucian was waiting for them on the *Alexa Lee* early the next morning. It was a full house with five passengers aboard. Hella was squeezed in between de la Croix and Brown. Underwood and Ari, the two slimmest men on board, sat beside each other on the narrower of the two benches. It was an uneasy trip. Lucian revved the engines at full power and it took less than twenty minutes to reach the mooring on Long Dead Key but during that time little was said. Underwood seemed most uncomfortable of all. Ari presumed it was because de la Croix was patently dissatisfied with the man's explanation that he was only looking out for Hella Gold's interests; the reasoning seemed lame now that the enormous Mr Brown was in her corner. The deputy was also piqued that Ari had managed to find time with Brown before he had; Brown had adopted their fabrications easily and slipped into the persona of an eccentric realtor.

'You often broker land in the tropics?' de la Croix asked him.

'Hardly ever,' said Brown. 'It's my first time actually but I know the place will be ideal for Mrs

Gold's needs. She wants solitude, privacy, a large garden she can nurture. The Taft place sounded ideal.'

Oscar mumbled, 'Malaria, hurricanes, heat,' then added, 'but you haven't seen it for yourself?'

Brown shook his head. 'I've just heard good things.'

'I saw it with you on Friday,' said Ari to de la Croix. 'I think it's perfect.'

'It floods,' said de la Croix.

Silas Taft was less than pleased when the delegation trekked up to his house across his lawn. Brown fed him the line about viewing the house and Taft, without any choice in the matter, fell in with the ruse. He called Cleo down and said they were showing the house. He looked most disgusted at de la Croix's presence.

'In the market for a mansion, Oscar?' he asked sarcastically.

'I'm still puzzling over that body of mine,' said Oscar. 'I thought a boat trip escorting potential townsfolk out to their new home might be just the thing to clear my head some.'

The group was too large to move about together, so Taft took half the party consisting of the sheriff and the two potential buyers from room to room upstairs while Cleo led Brown and Ari around below.

Cleo took them through the large kitchen where bunches of dried herbs and copper pots hung from a ceiling grid of heavy steel. There was a butcher's block in the middle of the floor. Marble counters. An immense porcelain basin stood in

273

the corner near a gas-fuelled cooking range which looked like it sported a black lead grin. Two maids were cleaning and Cleo greeted them in Spanish. She twittered away as she poured Ari and Brown a Coca-Cola. She seemed to be enjoying the play-acting and pointed out features of the house as they went.

She showed them a small room tucked away beneath a narrow staircase that ran upwards from one corner of an immense pantry. The stairs rose into darkness; Ari couldn't make out where they ended. On a table tucked beneath the stairs stood a radio and a headset. Cleo twiddled the dials on the set.

'This is our only contact with town. We can call Lucian through the harbourmaster's office. Send for supplies.'

Ari took a lantern from the wall and lit it while she talked. He took two steps up the staircase and held the lantern above his head trying to see what was up there.

'Attic,' said Cleo. 'It runs the whole length of the house. It's where we store things. It's a big junk room really.'

Ari began his ascent. The stairs creaked damply and were unnervingly pliant.

'Careful,' said Brown but he didn't follow.

As Ari climbed, he felt the heat grow sharper. The attic room acted as a kind of cooling system for the house; the dust and heat seemed to collect up there. Ari passed the top storey of the house, he was sure, but there was no outlet to it from this staircase. He kept twisting upwards until he stumbled out into a low dark room that stretched forever. There were shelves on sturdy stilts which contained racks of wine, and trunks and boxes. Ari looked into the box nearest to him and saw old clothes, assorted china. The windows were low and illuminated his feet as long as he stayed near the perimeter of the room but when he ventured towards the middle, his lantern emitted the only light.

At the far end of the attic, he found a chest. Ari looked back in the direction of the stairway. It seemed distant. The light coming up from the kitchen far below was barely visible from here. Ari wanted so desperately to be back in the house with its maids cleaning quietly and everything freshened and dried by twelve hours of sunshine a day. He tried the lid of the box with one hand. It was not locked. He fumbled about in the back waistband of his trousers and removed the object he'd concealed there in a leather chamois. He placed it inside and closed the lid once more, noting the box's size and shape so that he could find it again.

Suddenly, the fear of dark, cramped places took hold of his chest. Ari thought he might never make it back to the light and the fresh air. He rushed, scrambled and tripped his way back towards the staircase; he slipped as he descended.

'You okay?' Cleo asked casually as he emerged hurriedly into the vestibule as if something had been pursuing him. 'It's hot and dusty up there.'

She crinkled her nose. Her innocent words took all the fear from the place. Still, Ari imagined navigating the attic at night with just a match for light – a tiny flame that would gutter and gutter

275

before going out.

'I'd like to see the office where your father works,' said Brown.

'Nobody goes in there without him. And he's my guardian,' said Cleo sweetly. 'Not my father.'

'Whatever you say, sugar-puff,' said Brown and he gave her such a knowing look that Ari was offended by his attitude.

'You should keep your hair like that, by the way,' said Brown snidely. 'I like it.'

Cleo pulled her red locks back at once and tugged them into a knot at the base of her neck so that they didn't hang free the way Ari liked.

'Cleo, is it?' said Brown and Cleo nodded sharply. 'Cleo, I'm going to need a private word with Mr Taft at some point. Would you let him know that?'

Ari knew he wanted to cross-question the man about Oddman's visit and subsequent death. Ari wanted himself and his mother to be long gone before that happened. He was considering coercing his mother to move when they got home to the city so that they could not be found at their given New York address in the future – either by Mr Brown or the State of Florida Police Department.

'Silas bought the house in the late nineteen twenties,' said Cleo. She was determined to keep the topic away from Silas's study and prevent them from entering that particular room. 'It has quite a history. Nobody had lived out here for years. A buccaneer had built it in the late eighteen hundreds. It was rumoured that he had diverted ships carrying the red bricks out to build Fort Jefferson and paid their tolerant captains a tidy sum to be allowed to skim off every load. Using these purloined supplies, he built the house and the piazza. He planted the apple tree and had the fountain built. Apples were his favourite fruit, so the story goes. Apparently he had seen enough scurvy in his life to decide him upon eating fresh fruit every single day.'

'Fascinating,' said Brown sarcastically.

'It was abandoned for many years at the turn of the century. It was Silas who returned the property to its former glory. He ordered railcar after railcar from Miami filled with exotic plants and shipped men out here by the dozen to rebuild the gardens. He imported the chandelier from Salzburg and an Italian father-and-son team are contracted twice yearly to care for the roof of terracotta tiles. They come out here with kneepads and brushes and do a tile at a time until the roof gleams. Stephanopoulis Brothers of Tarpon Springs visited for a weekend last winter, all expenses paid, and refitted the courtyard fountain with two thousand mosaic tiles the colour of the sea; they also got the water pumping up from the natural well again. The whole place has been refitted from top to bottom with a style that combines high-society London with the best of siesta living.'

'Is that what Taft told you?' smirked Brown.

He was looking at a painting on the wall – several girls in tutus struck by a green stage light.

'That is by Monsieur Edgar Degas,' said Cleo.

'That is by a man called Monsieur Lenny Trout who's in prison in Birmingham for forgery,' said Brown.

Cleo went quiet. She had always loved the picture. She had loved the sound of the artist's name when Si had told it to her. She had memorized it.

The party consisting of Taft, Hella, Underwood and de la Croix eventually converged in the living room. Once again, it was awkward.

'We'll both have to look it over again, I suppose,' said Underwood.

He looked knowingly at Taft and Ari knew they were talking about seeing the flight log at last.

'Are you also thinking of putting in a bid, Mr Underwood?' asked de la Croix. 'That don't seem fair since you only know about the place because Mrs Gold told you about it in friendship.'

'I'll take any buyer,' said Taft. 'You can both come again when you've got more time and less people in tow.' He looked at de la Croix. 'That way you'll get a real sense of what a valuable piece of a property it really is.'

Hella nodded at that. She and Underwood would have to make another trip. This one had been a mere pretence to give credence to their lies to the sheriff. It was becoming a farce.

Cleo walked them down to the boat and Ari hung back so he could speak with the girl.

'Where will you be tonight? I need to speak with Silas alone.'

'Everybody seems determined to get their piece of Si tonight,' she said.

Ari had decided on a plan and nothing would sway his resolve now. He was going to broker his deal with Silas, let his mother buy the log – she could easily outbid Underwood, he felt sure –

pay Brown his finder's fee and get them out of the Keys as soon as possible. As far as Ari was concerned, if he never encountered Taft, Underwood or Brown again that would suit him perfectly well. Oscar would have to let Oddman's death go as a misadventure. Everything might still work out. And Cleo... He had to help her, too.

'You're in luck!' said Cleo. 'We're coming into town for the fights tonight. At eight o'clock on Emma Street ... somebody will show you the way.'

22

Ari left the Colonial Hotel at seven o'clock with directions from Señor Bolivar. By the time he saw Oscar de La Croix waiting for him outside an ice cream shop on Truman Avenue, it was too late to avoid the man. The shop was painted with pictures of long-forgotten sundaes – faded strawberry, mocha and coconut – and Oscar blended into the picture. He had changed his attire and was now dressed in a light blue suit with too-wide lapels and a fresh blue shirt. Oscar had a laden ice cream cone in his hand and when he saw Ari coming down the street towards him, he abandoned the wall against which he had been leaning and fell in step with the boy. They did not speak. Ari couldn't believe his bad luck. They just walked along – an odd pairing of height and shape on an uncertain heading.

'You know how Taft lost his eye?' asked de la Croix.

Ari shook his head. How had de la Croix guessed he was going to meet Taft? The little sheriff knew something wasn't right and he didn't seem willing to let anybody get on with their business as long as that business might be suspicious.

'Well, I'm gonna tell you the story the way I heard it so you can understand a little something about Mr Silas Taft... He was with British special ops in the war, they tell me. He had a degree in languages from some fancy English university and they mostly kept him busy reading papers they'd snatched from German bunkers and that sort of thing. But, when the war was almost done, he found himself in France on a standard transport trip from the coast to Paris when the truck he's travelling in goes off the road. Taft and another fellow have to hump it over to the next village where there's supposed to be a British garrison stationed. Like I said, the war was practically over by then but the odd pocket of German diehards were still sniping out of spite, so Silas and this other fellow hunker down in a stable for the night.

'Inside, they come across a few German bodies and a boy, a Jerry soldier, who ain't wounded but who's hiding away in there out of terror, sort of cowered down like the stable rat. This kid lets off a round and it clips old Silas in the eye, chips the bone from his socket but don't enter his head or nothing. His partner puts a bullet into the kid's head and that's the end of him but Silas is lying there in a stable – blinded by blood, exhausted – and he knows he's a goner if he can't come up with a plan. Silas figures the Germans will be back for the bodies of their missing, so he lets the other fellow fall asleep, tells him they'll make a plan in the morning and while he's lights-out, Silas puts on the dead Jerry boy's jacket and helmet and he gets the boy's weapon ready and he waits.

'It's just after dawn when they come. Silas hears two voices speaking in German but he doesn't wake his friend who's still sound asleep. Oh no, Silas just points his gun at the sleeping man and waits. The Germans knew there had been losses around this stable and they have been sent to collect and identify bodies just like Silas thought.

'They come through the doors casually, expecting only their own dead and what they see is just what Silas had manufactured for them to see: one of their own, badly wounded in the head. Although the man must be near to death, he appears to be holding a gun on a British soldier. By now, the noise has woken the fellow Taft is with and he's totally confused, especially since Taft is yelling in German: "Help me! Please, help me!"

'The Germans are still confused, see? Maybe Taft's accent isn't that great so he tries one last phrase, one these men have heard so many times over the years as they've gathered up their wounded. "I can't feel my legs!" Taft shouts, and he points at his legs stretched out in front of him.

281

'That did it, I guess. Both Germans drag their rifles off their shoulders and shoot a round each into Taft's mate's body. And as they turn to do it, Silas puts a bullet into each of them. That's Mr Taft's great war story as far as I can decipher it from the whispers I've heard. He made it back to his own lines after that. Made it home and then came out here to the middle of nowhere to disappear in style.'

That was the end of Oscar's tale. It had almost stopped Ari in his tracks with its audacity and horror. De la Croix seemed unfazed by the treachery it illustrated. He just shrugged complacently and said, 'Might be lies, of course.'

'What if it isn't?' said Ari but Oscar seemed to have forgotten the purpose of his cautionary tale. He was running his ice-cream-tacky fingers along the sides of a few sleek cars parked on Emma Street. They were so new that it looked as if they were only driven out of their garages for special occasions.

'They park here and walk down,' said Oscar. The ice cream had stained his tongue purple. 'Looks better that way,' he added.

They had reached the southwest corner of the island populated mostly by blacks and Cubans. An abandoned lot was illuminated so that it shone among the unlit houses. The plot was large and vacant, shot through with weeds and scrappy grass. Once, a chain-link fence had been strung across the entrance to the roadway but it lay crinkled on the asphalt now and pedestrians stepped easily over it. Two banks of tatty bleachers rose on either end of a fenced-in circle strewn with beach sand. Dozens of paper lanterns flickered haphazardly from the overhanging trees, throwing crooked shadows from upright men. The noisy mob was dressed in its Sunday best: loud ties, panama hats and intricately tooled leather belts with silver buckles jostled for Ari's attention.

They passed vendors selling homemade brew. A makeshift table created from crawfish traps offered frozen popsicles and spicy salsa tacos. Several men carried large, embroidered bags – inside them living things scrabbled and twisted. One man opened his bag and pulled out a feisty cockerel by its craw. He bowed with a flourish to the assembled crowd and they cheered.

A lank Cuban did a listless, liquid rumba towards them, rolling his hips to the music from a wind-up phonograph. He removed the cigar from his chops before embracing Oscar fiercely.

'Deputy de la Croix,' he said with a concerned tone. 'You here tonight officially?'

'No. Don't worry about it.'

'Ahhh, that's good,' sang the Cuban. 'I was just checking, you know, because the money's decided to show.'

He pointed across the arena to where Silas Taft stood looking directly at them. His feet were slightly apart, his arms were crossed; his face was even. He seemed, at that moment, a formidable adversary.

'That man can give me the creeps,' said the Cuban quietly. 'He comes into town a few times each month and pretends he's a local. He greets me by name though we've never been intro-duced. The boys at the oyster yard, the shuckers, they say he's got skill with a blade and he knows when somebody's coming up behind him. Don't come up behind him, is all I'm saying.'

'Well, you wanted him, boy,' said Oscar to Ari. 'Go get him!' He laughed and gave Ari an undignified shove.

Ari took in a deep gulp of air which filled his lungs with the taste of chilli beef and sour cream. As he made his way over to Taft, Cleo stepped into sight. She was wearing a long, gold slip of a dress like a pagan idol. Behind her right ear, the moon bloomed – a yellow hibiscus flower with a red, forked tongue. She was barefoot, both soles to the earth.

Taft bought her a Coca-Cola and placed his hand on the small of her back as he ushered her behind the bleachers. She was being sent away to wait out the bloodshed. Ari knew how her skin would feel against his palm; it would be cooler than expected. The silk would slither along his lifeline, filling that crucial groove with fire. The dress would cling, ever so slightly, to the sheen of perspiration and musky warmth that filmed the small of a woman's spine.

Ari approached Taft through the grey dust of the descending evening. Taft was handling a chunky roll of newly minted twenties. All around him, cash was changing hands.

'Ari,' he greeted. 'Where's your lovely mother?'

'I wanted to come alone,' said Ari. 'I'd like to speak with you. I think I may have a mutually beneficial proposition.'

'Mutually beneficial,' said Taft. 'I like that. Go ahead and make your play.'

Before them, two handlers faced off in the centre of the ring. Both were holding the necks of their sacks and eyeballing each other like prize-fighters.

'I'm trying to salvage a situation that began some time ago... I believe it's in everyone's best interests if this fiasco concludes in the way I suggest,' Ari said.

'Lay your plan on the table, Ari,' said Taft. 'But I'm obliged to tell you – in my experience things never end up the way you expect no matter how hard you try and manipulate them. There's always this awkward unexpected thorn you just can't plan for. Still, I'm open to hearing your thoughts.'

Taft seemed amenable.

Then Underwood came over and Ari's spirits sank.

'It's all above board, I take it,' said Taft. 'This plan you're proposing. Mr Underwood can hear about it, I presume?'

'It's about Cleo,' said Ari, suddenly changing his intentions. 'And I'd prefer some privacy.'

Underwood had complicated everything from the start. Ari was furious about his inclusion in the whole mess.

'How do you come to be here anyway, Mr Underwood? All the way from Belgium but trying so hard to sound American. This was a simple transaction between my mother and Mr Taft before you got wind of it somehow. How did that happen, by the way?'

'Am I being interrogated?' said Underwood. He had assumed a wounded voice.

'I'm just surprised how incurious everyone is about your interest. Everyone knows my mother has an unhealthy obsession with Charles Lindbergh...' There, he had said it. 'But nobody has offered an acceptable explanation as to why you might want the flight log.'

Ari felt he was speaking plainly for the first time since events to buy the log had been set in motion. It felt clean and honest.

'I must say, I'd like some answers in that regard,' said Taft. Then he added to Ari, 'To be square with you, Ari, it was Mr Underwood who sought me out when he heard I had the log in my possession. Just like Mr Brown did on your mother's behalf. I didn't exactly go looking for buyers.'

'And how did Mr Brown and Mr Underwood come to know you had the log?' said Ari. It was a question that had always puzzled him.

'Men of my sort, and by that I mean resourceful men, have a wealth of connections.'

He expected that answer to suffice, Ari could see. It was the same explanation Brown had given him and it had unsettled him at the time, especially considering how quickly they had located the possessor of the log.

In the ring, the handlers loosed their animals. They went at each other, hissing. Their steel spurs slashed amid a blur of emerald wings. Ari watched the fight through a veil of cigar smoke. In the ring, the birds were weakening. The action fizzled out when one of them simply lay down and refused to get up again. It allowed the other to peck at its head without caring.

286

'That was mine,' said Underwood disconsolately.

Underwood yelled at the losing bird's minder in Spanish, no doubt chastising him for the amount of money he had lost on his useless bird. The minder allowed Underwood into the ring. He made a gesture with his hand to indicate the bird was at Underwood's mercy. Underwood placed the heel of his boot above the cockerel's slumped head and crushed it into the blood-stricken sand.

'I can't discuss it while he's here,' said Ari.

'Tomorrow, then,' said Taft. 'I just want the money. I don't care where it comes from.'

While the men stayed to watch the rest of the fights, Ari went to find Cleo. He saw her blowing away from him like a jewelled tumbleweed at the end of the street. He watched her gold dress moving off the way a castaway might watch the swell of a sail on the horizon. She was walking west through the area they called Bahama Village where sad harmonicas wailed and old men smoked slow pipes, muting the street-lights with silver haze. Cheers and groans came from the front rooms of the bolito houses where poker games would go on into the small hours.

Cleo stopped outside a building which must have been a store. It was too gloomy here to make out any signage. There was a Coca-Cola icebox out on the porch and she leaned into it and took out a bottle. A man who blended into the night stepped forward and snapped the lid off for her with his teeth. She had no money, nowhere to keep any, but the dark man seemed to know her. They spoke for a few moments and

Cleo went up the porch stairs and disappeared into the house with him. Ari was about to go in after her, afraid for her, when she reappeared. She was carrying something else now, a small object that almost fitted into the palm of her hand. She laughed with the black shape of a man for a few moments before gliding on.

She alone had safe passage in this quarter. He was unknown. When he passed a junkyard dog on a chain, it eyed him suspiciously and the engine of its throat revved. Its lip slipped up over its incisors and Ari could see a red tongue and yellow plaque along its gumline.

The gardens here were planted with perennial shadows. Some of the Cubans had hung old sails in the trees and they billowed open – unexpected and white – above the tin roofs to scare the crows from their bedraggled corn. Oleander blooms were open to the midnight bats. Their aroma was opium to mosquitoes and small nocturnal animals whose eyes were bigger than silver quarters. Crickets scraped their legs in ghostly violin solos – the sound like dry grass heads blown together in a people-less country.

Cleo had reached a black and white lighthouse painted like a candy cane by the time Ari caught up with her. The lighthouse was spiralled by an exterior staircase and Cleo stood on the third step from the bottom on the other side of a chain from which a sign saying 'DO NOT ENTER' hung lopsidedly.

'You still chasing after me?' she asked.

She sat down on the crooked staircase and sipped her Coke. When Ari got close enough,

Cleo handed him the bottle. He wanted to taste her lips on it more than he wanted the sweet drink. Glass didn't hold smell and taste as well as the fabric of her swimsuit had but Ari imagined her lipstick smelled like peaches. Its blush clung to the lip of the bottle, tenuous and soon to melt away.

'Do you feel safe out on your own at night?' he asked.

'They know me here,' Cleo said simply. 'I always walk up to Front Street on my own after the fights. I'll meet Si at the boat at ten.'

'Will you be home tomorrow?'

'I'm nearly always home,' she said, then added, 'when I'm not out or up.'

She indicated the sky with the neck of the bottle.

'You promised to take me flying,' Ari reminded her.

'Well, I'm someone who keeps her promises,' she said. 'I promise you.'

Cleo took Ari's hand and they walked around the lighthouse and down onto the beach. They walked slowly because Ari was unsure of his footing where Cleo was concerned. After a while, she sank down into the cold, damp sand. The moon was tangled in her hair.

'Would you like to see New York?' he asked her. 'Maybe you could visit with us for a while?'

Cleo turned to him.

'You'd take me to New York?' she said. Her voice was different when she said it, no longer low and purring but genuinely surprised. 'I've always wanted to go ice skating in Central Park.

I've never seen snow let alone ice. Does it come down slowly like they say?'

Ari nodded.

'We could go skating this winter. My mother's an expert. She grew up in Sweden. They skate there all the time, months and months of the year. She could teach you. If you'd like to come with us,' he said. 'I'd ask my mother...'

She cut him off before he could finish. 'I keep forgetting you're so young... You can't take me anywhere of your own accord.'

'You're only sixteen,' he said.

She turned to him and touched his cheek.

'And old enough to be your mother,' she said enigmatically.

Ari tried to press his cheek against her fingers so that she would know how much he welcomed the touch.

'You're a really nice boy, Ari. I really like you. I hope you remember me saying that when you go.'

'I'm serious about you coming with us.'

'I'm sure you are,' she said.

'Well I am,' he reiterated.

'I feel like a swim tonight,' she said, breaking the moment.

She got up and dusted the sand from her skirt. She left the object she had been carrying in the sand. It was a small glass bottle, large enough to hold a tot or two of spirit, with a cork in its neck. It was empty as far as Ari could make out.

He looked up and saw Cleo at the shoreline. Most people pause at the edge of water. They stop to see if it will be cold or too deep. Cleo didn't. She walked straight into the sea as if the element was as natural to her as land. She had all her clothes on and as she got deeper, the skirt billowed up around her like a giant anemone.

Ari went in after her. First, he removed his shoes and placed his socks neatly inside them; he took off his tie and braces and jacket. He loaded them all on top of the bowl of his upturned hat. He took off his watch and his money clip – the baggage he always seemed to carry with him.

All the while, Cleo watched him with a kind of sad fascination, watched all the small expensive bits of him being peeled away before he himself was at last exposed to her like the soft, pale meat inside an oyster shell, delicious and unprotected. The water was not cold or rough but warm like a twilight swimming pool at seven o'clock in the summer.

Ari took the bloom from her hair and dropped it beside them in the water. He wanted the perfect symmetry of her, unmarred by flowers. She pulled the top of her dress down off her shoulders and down, down all the way to her waist, revealing breasts as brown as the rest of her with nipples dark and cool to the fingertips. Ari bent his head over and let his tongue find them, hard and cold as ice chips. He pulled her closer.

He wanted to be inside this girl's body more than he had ever wanted anything before in his life. The desperation disappeared as soon as he entered her. He saw the bloom and the moon as two twin gold circles on the surface of the dark water before they shattered apart in the turbulent waves and sank in pieces to the bottom of the sea.

23

Ari woke up as a castaway. It was Monday morning, Labor Day, and he was lying on the cold grit of the beach with waves sloshing against the soles of his feet. At first, his aspect was so skewed that he felt as if he was adrift on a distant planet and the blue stretching out ahead of him was the beginning of space. Then, as he woke more fully, he realized it was the sea he was watching – that cool, accommodating bed of the night before. He smiled without thinking and his lips grated on the sand. He pushed himself up onto his elbows and yawned indulgently. He refused to worry about what his mother would think.

Some time in the night, he and Cleo had come ashore, pulling out of the gravity of the water together and emerging onto dry land where they had lain entwined. He had slept. She must have left soon afterwards to keep her rendezvous with Taft. What would the man make of Cleo's soaking clothes? Ari sought traces of her passage in the sand but her footprints had already been blown from the beach. She had taken her little glass bottle with its cork stopper away with her, too.

Ari looked out over the water to the east but he could not see Long Dead Key. His clothes clung to him with a salty sting he barely noticed. He rubbed the grains from his face and stood up.

The beach was abandoned this early. There was not a soul to tut-tut at him waking up there.

Everything had changed, Ari thought. There was a luminosity to the sky. It was shot through with a weird light like yellow neon. It augured good things – tranquillity and resolution. Ari had been raised in places that slipped under snow every year. His ocean was one which displayed its twee, disciplined ripples on Long Island beaches. This sea was different; these beaches were as wild as those that had greeted shipwrecked sailors in the tropics.

Ari couldn't know that his perfect morning-after sky was anything but peaceful. Already, at the charter docks and fishing boat keys, the sailors were looking in exactly the same direction as he was – their eyebrows knitted in concern, their gnarled hands knotting ropes.

Beyond the horizon, a force was growing, lifting warm salt water into its heart and spinning it with the power of a thousand thunderstorms. Throughout the preceding days, ever since Hella and Ari had stepped from the train, a vast stretch of ocean in the mid-Atlantic had been super-heated by the equatorial sun. The warm vapour had evaporated into the atmosphere, cooling as it ascended until a vast cushion of cloud hundreds of miles in diameter had formed. As the cooling clouds sank, they generated power under which the entire system began to spin – a vortex of heated vapour, wind, lightning and ice particles all spiralling westwards towards Florida.

A naval weather station in Miami picked it up early. They had a fleet from Virginia on man-oeuvres in the Gulf of Mexico and they needed to get the vessels out of the storm's path. The system was upgraded to a hurricane on Monday morning as Ari approached the Colonial Hotel.

Hella and Underwood were standing on the front steps. Hella was putting on her lacy day gloves and she was wearing the white linen sundress she had packed for best. A large-brimmed hat flopped atop her blonde hair.

'I thought you had given up on hats,' said Ari as he came within earshot.

'Mr Underwood likes them,' Hella said.

She didn't ask him where he had been. By her expression, she was too mortified to bring up the fact that he had clearly spent the whole night away from the hotel. She didn't comment on the state of his suit or his rumpled hair and tie. She just half turned her back on him and said, 'We've managed to avoid that dreadful little sheriff this morning, so we're going straight out to Long Dead Key to see Mr Taft to sort this business out once and for all. I can see you're not going to be of any help to me, so perhaps you'd care to wash up and be presentable enough for dinner? We may have something to celebrate.'

'One of us will,' said Underwood.

Hella laughed. They seemed to be enjoying their rivalry now. Ari knew Hella could afford to be flippant since there was no limit to what she was willing to spend on the log and she doubted Underwood had the guts to match her into the tens of thousands. With limitless resources, magnanimity came easily.

'I'm bringing a girl home with us,' said Ari.

'To dinner?' said Hella. 'Not that little jade of Mr Taft's?'

'Not to dinner,' said Ari. 'I've asked her to come home with us to New York. Her name's Cleo... I've told her she can leave with us when we go.'

'Really, Ari!' said Hella and Underwood laughed out loud. 'Some little trollop from the tropics, honestly! And where will she live? With us, in a city she doesn't know. She has no training, I suspect, no prospect of a job. She's actually done rather well for herself here if you think about her limited opportunities.'

Hella was growing more and more heated as she spoke.

'And when she tires of you, what then? Do we kick her out? Think it through.'

'We're not leaving her here with that man. He's a crook, I'm sure of it.'

'Here's to business with crooks,' said Underwood, raising an imaginary glass. Hella glared at him and he walked a few feet away in the direction of the fishing boat quay.

'We'll talk about it properly later,' said Hella fiercely as soon as Underwood was far enough away. 'It's untenable, Ari, you must see that. Now tidy up. You're a disgrace!'

She went after Mr Underwood, who offered her his arm. She took it gratefully. At that moment she felt she needed somebody strong to lean on.

'She's not a souvenir!' was Hella's parting shot.

His mother's diatribe had made Ari self-conscious about his appearance. He decided not to face the immaculate Señor Bolivar who seemed

295

never to leave his post at the front desk. He felt ashamed now that Cleo had left him to sleep alone in the sand as if he had been just another man who entertained his sordid dalliances on public beaches. Underwood's knowing smirk had embarrassed him, too.

Instead of going in through the front doors, Ari snuck down the side of the hotel and through the gate that led to the front lawn and the swimming pool. He saw Quozzie cleaning the pool and he decided he didn't want to run into the boy either. To give himself time to formulate a way to avoid the meeting, he slipped behind the pool pump house where he had first conducted that breathless conversation with his mother, telling her that Oddman was dead. Oddman seemed to have been lost in all the subsequent intrigue. Had his murder been nothing more than an unfortunate coincidence or were Underwood and his mother at that moment heading into danger? Quozzie looked over in his direction. Ari ducked deeper along the narrow alley to avoid being seen. He felt ridiculous.

Then Ari saw it. The scrap of damp paper he had found under Oddman's body and stuck carelessly to the casing of the pump. It had dried there and clung like a skin to the surface. The letters were easier to read now. Somebody who liked puzzles, and Ari thought immediately it was probably Quozzie because of the childish handwriting, had completed the words using nothing more than imagination.

The 'kes' of 'kes airp' had becomes 'likes' and the 'ves' had become 'loves'. The other two word fragments had been too much of a challenge and Quozzie had left them. Perhaps he ruminated over their meaning as he swept the pool, back and forward with the net, back and forward. Ari now found something profoundly disturbing about the scrap of paper. He had a free afternoon and he felt as if time was running out for him and his mother. He was nervous about her being alone with Underwood, but Quozzie's father would be with them on the boat trip over to Long Dead Key and then Silas and Cleo would presumably be on the island once they reached it. It was unlikely she would ever be completely alone with the man. Ari knew he had to find out what he could about the note. Where was the rest of it? It had been tucked into one of Oddman's jacket pockets, he was sure, but why was only a scrap of it left? The answer came to him in a flash: because somebody, unwilling to touch the body too extensively, or physically unable to turn it over, had tugged at a corner of the paper and got most of it but left a torn scrap behind. Ari could only imagine who that might have been. One of the two boys, eager for a reminder of the escapade but frightened to meddle too much with the corpse, had snatched it away before running to get help from Quozzie.

Ari came out from behind the pump house but Quozzie was nowhere in sight. He found Señor Bolivar in his office and asked if he knew where Quozzie was.

'To whom are you referring, young Mr Gold?'

Ari was loath to describe the boy simply as a hunchback.

297

'The boy who cleans the pool,' he said.

'Ahhh, yes,' he said. 'I have sent him to the laundry for the sheets not two minutes ago.'

'How do I get there?' asked Ari.

Laundry was an aspect of the hospitality trade with which guests seldom concerned themselves. They didn't want to see dirty sheets and towels. They wanted clean bathrooms and fresh linen and discreet, unobtrusive maids. The laundry contracted by the Colonial Hotel was situated in a sparsely populated section of the island. The lot it occupied had been zoned for a new hotel just before the Depression hit. The foundations had already been poured and the shell of an entrance lobby had been constructed but the building had progressed no further when financing from the north had dried up. The result was an enormous square cement box of a room which led out onto an unscreeded concrete slab that would have been the ground floor for the three storeys of rooms. The ingenious proprietor of the Sunshine Laundry had hung row upon row of wire lines across the ugly, lumpy patch and they flapped with white linen from the hotels, grey towels from the barbershops and a few uniforms from the practically deserted naval station which only housed a few military weathermen these days.

When there was no answer at the front door – a sheet of corrugated tin attached to the wall with bent wire hinges – Ari went through the vacant lot at the side of the building and round the back. Here, a doorway was open to the ocean breeze. Quozzie was sitting with his back against the cool wall. This was the shaded side of the building in the early morning. Somebody had given him a sandwich and he nibbled at it. He smiled at Ari as a cloud of steam billowed out past his head through the open door.

Ari looked in. A dozen young Cuban women were hard at work inside. The three nearest the door, and the only ones he could see clearly in the general interior gloom, were young and very lovely with their silky black hair up in headscarves and their eyes the colour of golden syrup. One of them saw Ari watching her and raised a haughty chin at him. She stood up straight, pushing her breasts out, and wiped the perspiration from her face with a rumpled pillowcase. There were no windows for ventilation in the room and concrete sinks steamed with dirty scum-coloured bubbles and roiled with towels.

'I'm waiting on the fresh sheets,' explained Quozzic.

'I need to speak with the boys from the other day. The two who found Mr Oddman's body. They obviously know you. Do you know where they live?'

Quozzie scratched his chin and left a streak of sauce from the sandwich there.

'I only know their daddies. I ain't sure where they live or nothing. One of their daddies is a Pieter Laken. He used to wash the bottles at the Coca-Cola factory...'

He was painfully slow in his consideration.

'But that closed down, didn't it?' prompted Ari.

'Yup,' said Quozzie ponderously. 'I guess I did hear that. I think he might work at the Electric

Kitchen now, washing dishes after lunch and dinner. I don't know if he does the breakfast things, too. The other boy... Well, you don't wanna be messing with his daddy.'

'Who's the other boy?' asked Ari. He was determined to see them both this morning and have some answers before his mother got any deeper into trouble.

'He's some kind of preacher for a church I don't want nothing to do with. He calls himself Judas Jones.'

There was a sudden sharp movement in the laundry room. Ari looked in to see that two of the girls had jerked to a stop at the sound of the name. They both crossed themselves.

The Electric Kitchen was situated on Fleming Street. Ari had been told to ask for Ma Baker and had naturally assumed that was the woman's last name but when he noticed the sign of the shiny red car above the entrance to the eatery and saw the size of the proprietor, he realized it was more likely a contraction of Studebaker. The woman towed a restless ocean of fat around with her. Her eyes were all but lost in the swells of her cheeks and she was squashed into a crossover top in some kind of African print fabric over the top of which her ample bosoms oozed.

'Is a Mr Laken working today, please?' Ari asked after ordering a Coca-Cola. It came in a bottle and Ari imagined that the Mr Laken he was now seeking might well have washed this very bottle before the factory which employed him had closed down.

'No,' said Ma Baker. 'He's not the working type.'

The crowd of regulars at the counter guffawed along with her at that.

Then she seemed to feel bad about an inside joke at her customer's expense and said, 'You can talk to him in the back but what a fine piece of dandy candy like you wants with the likes of him, I ain't sure I wanna know. Best you watch that sweet tushie of yours!'

They all howled again and Ari slunk behind the counter and into the scullery she had indicated, where he could hear the sound of hissing water.

Laken wanted to know if he was some kind of truant officer. He seemed to suspect his son was dodging school.

'I'll tan his hide for him hanging around with that little nigger boy. You ain't going to amount to nothing spending your time with that sort. I keep telling him that. You here about his schooling next year?'

'I'm not from the school board,' said Ari. 'I'm not working for anyone. Besides, today's Labor Day.'

'It is?' asked Laken.

Ari wondered if there was a woman in the Laken house or if this man was trying to raise the boy alone.

'The truth is he found my friend's body on the beach the other day...'

'Yup, I tanned him for that. He shoulda been home, helping me out with the other kids.'

'Do you think he may have taken something from the body?'

Ari felt it was a mistake to accuse the boy of stealing like that but his father didn't seem disconcerted by the idea.

'He was wearing his dungarees that day. They ain't got no pockets,' he said. 'I pulled them down when I tanned him and there weren't nothing hid away neither. I'd say it was that little nigger kid. He's as sharp as a tack, that one...'

Ari thanked him and headed, as he had known he would have to, down to Bahama Village.

The town had taken on an air of expectancy, like a giant holding his breath. There was a prevalent sound of hammering and anxious activity taking place around the houses. Everybody seemed eager to conduct home improvements on this day of rest. Ari thought it was odd. As the workmen called out to one another, their voices were pulled away by some uncanny updraft that seemed to be sucking everything into the sky.

Ari had walked along this very road the night before, following Cleo. He hadn't known how dirty and frightening it was then, the darkness had soothed its edges. It looked very different now, in the harsh sunlight. He saw the house where the dog had startled him. There was no sign of it this morning. A length of chain ran out of a corrugated kennel and looped across a red-sand lawn. He spotted the rusted Coca-Cola icebox from which Cleo had taken a drink. He saw now that the place was called the Creole Café. It was the address Quozzie had given him.

Ari went up onto the porch. A boy of five or six was playing with a whittling knife on the steps – the vicious blade held inexpertly in his chubby fingers. He was carving an animal from a fallen branch – a monstrous-headed, freak-show deformity – half man, half dog. A porch swing, with half its slats missing, began a creaky swaying as Ari passed it, though the wind was quite absent.

The child looked up at him. This coffee-coloured boy had the same slightly oriental eyes he had seen on the one who'd found the body. They were probably brothers.

'Ain't nobody home,' said the boy. 'They ain't back from their visit yet.'

Ari continued up the stairs to the store's entrance. Inside, the shop was dark after the garish daylight. Ari saw empty shelves and a cash register – no doubt empty, too.

'Help you?' a man said. His voice was deep and hollow. Ari saw a face looking out from behind a beaded curtain leading to a back room. 'No Cola today!' he stated emphatically. 'We all out.'

His voice undulated like the swish of a grass skirt. He wore black sunglasses. Was he blind, Ari wondered?

'Not even for Cleo?' Ari asked.

Ari thought about Cleo and his insides went hot and soft. He was living something which would have made his heart race if he had seen it at the movies. Life seemed so exotic now, so full of potential. He would have a bride who was the envy of every other student at his university. He would take Cleo to the country club dances and they would spot her at once. She was toned and tanned, which, though unfashionable among modern women, was secretly desired by men as thrillingly feral.

The man looked at him and made a decision.

'Come on in here you wanna talk about dat girl,' he said and Ari followed him back. He felt cold and fearful as the beaded curtain swished shut behind him. Nobody knew he was here. Only the dog which must have smelled him passing by again could be sure he had travelled this way.

The back room was smaller than the one he had first entered. Ari had the distinct impression that this room was the centre of the real business of the place; the front room, the store, was only a ruse. It was so dimly lit that Ari couldn't quite make out the items on the shelves. The shelves themselves were painted white and stood out starkly from the dark walls to which they were attached. He was alone with the man who sat down in a deeply cushioned wicker throne opposite a small school chair in which Ari seated himself. There was a grass blind rolled down over a small window that had been painted red. That window supplied the room with its only light. It glowed red and the man's shiny silver suit was drenched in scarlet. His nails were as long as a woman's and they shone as if coated in clean polish.

'You mention a name before,' the man sang seductively.

'Cleo,' Ari said guilelessly. 'I'm a friend of hers.'

The man lit a pungent cigarette and puffed out purple smoke. Red and purple strands of it swirled in vortices around Ari's face.

'That her name? That girl's a cracker,' said the man. 'You got fists big enough for that there handful of a girl?' he said and he chuckled.

'I'm worried about her,' Ari was emboldened by fear. 'I think that Mr Taft is a bad man.'

Judas Jones clicked his tongue warningly and wagged his index finger 'no' at Ari. The cigarette it held flared brightly from its pointed tip. The air was very hot in the small room; outside noise did not penetrate here. Ari expected a car or a child's bicycle to go by on the sidewalk – which must be no more than three feet from where they sat – but the eerie quiet persisted.

'You wrong there, boy,' said Judas. 'You worrying about entirely the wrong man.'

Ari wasn't sure what the man was trying to tell him. The smoke seemed to make things hard to hold onto.

'Do you mean the sheriff? Is he the worry?'

The man in the wet, red suit smiled. A gold tooth flashed from the back of his jaw.

'How do you know all this?'

'I know no thing. I only tell what I feel with my own fingers.'

He held up his hands and Ari saw that his slick, ebony skin covered digits long enough to reach back and scratch his own elbows. They were almost identical to Ari's own hands in their slim refinement. There was something odd about them, though. They swayed like snakes in the purple smoke of the scarlet room. Ari's eyes followed them, not wanting to look away and see what the shelves might hold. The items were so close and he sensed glass jars and strings of hanging peppers and a smell of garlic and reptile skin. He watched the man's fingers. He knew that if he snuck up on this man while he was asleep and ever so gently lifted up the glasses, the man's lids would open to reveal no eyes beneath them at all, just pits, blackly red, sinking down into the back of his head.

'I know this man since he come here. He just running away from the war, is all. He not bringing any problems but that girl, she's bringing plenty problems to this town.'

'She needs to be helped. I want to get her away from here.'

'She want your help, you reckon?' asked the man. 'You sit here in this most private back room of my house. You come alone and unafraid. My dog leave you be. You come with reason, I think. But that makes no never-mind now. There's a big storm wind coming. Storm wind to blow everything clean and white.'

The man laughed – a sound like dry leaves crunching under a boot on a lonely path. The smoke had sunk into Ari's skin. The moisture of his eyes had absorbed it. It had snaked its way into his veins and swam along them with slippery speed. The cold, hot, red, purple room revolved lollingly.

'I love her,' said Ari.

'Love a silly thing. Anyway, that not the right girl at all for you.'

'I love her,' said Ari again. Was he drugged? His tongue felt thick and fuzzy, his vision swam. 'There'll never be another woman for me.'

'You right there,' said Judas and he sounded almost sad, then the leaves blew through his throat again. 'She buy a spell from me yesterday night,' he said. 'A spell on you. She buy your soul from me for ten dollars and I put it in a bottle for her.'

Ari remembered the small bottle Cleo had been carrying. He shivered. He had never felt closer to a slithering thing than he did at that moment. Like a man about to step over a rock who hears the dry scrape of scale on stone as the fat warm snake slips away into the scrub. Judas's hand came up and he tapped his chest with a roll of his fingers. His nails clicked together like bones in a jar.

'How do you do that?' asked Ari.

'No telling,' said the man. 'I take some of your hair from your comb...'

'At the hotel?'

The man nodded.

'I got people at the hotel.'

Ari thought immediately of Quozzie then he thought of the Cuban girls washing his sheets and pillowcases. There were any number of people who might have access to the intimacy of his skin and hair and nail clippings. He wanted to run. He had never imagined a place like this, so torn free from civilization. The smoke seemed to have dulled his disbelief in voodoo magic and he felt terror squeeze his heart. His eyes rolled in his head and he saw that the smoke had formed oily circles near the ceiling now – parting then coming together in ever-increasing spirals.

He remembered why he had come here in the first place.

'Mr Jones, did your son take anything from my friend's body?'

He thought the direct approach was best here. The man seemed to know everything anyway.

'Things from a murdered man make powerful gris-gris,' he said. 'My son knows to snatch a little something.'

He sounded almost proud.

'Did he take a piece of paper?'

'You want to buy some of that magic?' asked the man. 'That's expensive.'

'I have money,' said Ari.

He took his billfold from his pocket. Gently, the man took the whole roll and handed him back the empty clip. Ari didn't object. He just slipped the clip into his pocket.

The man stood up from his wicker throne and took a pouch from one of the shelves. It was made of a soft hide and closed with a drawstring. Ari took it with reverence. He wasn't sure if he had what he wanted. He only knew he had to escape the smoky room.

'Please, young boy,' the voice sounded wounded, 'I not steer you wayward.'

Ari was on his feet. The edges of the room were so dark and shadowed with things that had spines and quills and slitted eyes like the slats on black iron grates.

'You want the truth, you go see the lady on Amelia and Green... Dat particular titbit I give for free. This time, you go free.'

Ari knocked his chair over as he tried to leave. He stumbled over its leg and fell on all fours. Under any normal circumstances, he would have apologized several times and righted the furniture before making his departure but the windy leaves of laughter came out of the man's throat and he felt the need to run.

Ari's fall had brought his face closer to the shelves and, though the white boards tricked his eyes into focusing on them, he took in one item amid the feast of others. It was a clear glass bottle that had once held rum or gin. He saw it so sharply that he could make out where the ragged label hadn't been properly removed. The image of a ship's sail remained. It was an old Cutty Sark bottle and in it floated the alien-eyed, frog-legged form of a human foetus. The tiny creature's blue eyes were open imploringly on Ari as it bobbed forlornly on some unknowable tide of bottles.

Ari's mind revolted at the way it was being kept, but a voice in his mind kept shrieking: '*How did it get in there? Ari, how by the love of God did it get in there?*'

He was up, freeing his leg from the chair, and out through the beaded curtain in a flash. A motorcycle roared past on the street outside, throwing up marl dust. The smoke didn't follow him into the empty shop or out onto the porch, nor did the laughter.

The little boy looked up from his whittling and said, 'I told you nobody home from visiting yet!' with the irritation of a child whose truthful proclamations have been ignored.

Ari was on more respectable streets several blocks away before the most curious thing about the man came back to him. He was trying to push the memory away but until this fact was acknowledged, he knew he would never be able to forget. It was something to do with the man's hands –

those inexplicable fingers so like his own. He thought about the way those fingers had tossed ash from the cigarette and how they had tapped against the man's chest. There was only one way they could move like that and be that long. Ari saw them again in his mind's eye and knew something to be true: the man had an extra joint to all his fingers. Where a normal hand might bend once at the knuckles of the palm then twice more, the man in the wet, red suit had digits that bent four times and worse than that, each joint had bent backwards, too – curling in sickening ways that nature could never have intended.

24

Ari needed to find a secluded place where he could examine the pouch more closely. He wanted privacy since he was unsure what it might contain. He did not want to go back to the Colonial Hotel nor did he feel like taking the pouch into a public place like a café or bar. He found a banyan tree on the corner of Whitehead Street, walked around its enormous girth as far as he could go and sat down in a grassy patch among the roots. He was almost in the yard of an abandoned house, right up against the garden fence that shambled along like a drunk for several feet then passed out in a patch of nettles. He was facing away from the street now, invisible to any passers-by. It was surprisingly comfortable, cradled by the old tree. His eyes were shaded from the sun and he could hear the intermittent whine of cicadas disturbed in their sleep.

Ari tried to peek inside the pouch without opening it fully but eventually decided to bravely tip its contents out onto the grass. A black cockroach fell out of the bag and scuttled along Ari's leg. Startled, he cried out and brushed it frantically away. It scurried into the brush. It had tumbled out with half a dozen other items: a carved stone, a bone, a black feather probably from a cockerel, the desiccated body of a tree frog and something that looked like a ragged fingernail – not a clipping but a whole nail pulled out from the cuticle. There was some green moss, too. Ari tried not to imagine this being harvested from gravestones in the dead of night. He decided not to examine any of the items too intensely. The least organic and the least frightening of the small pile was a sheet of purple paper that had been twisted into a strand and then tied in a loose knot. Ari opened it carefully, trying not to damage it further. The bottom left-hand corner was torn away. Ari could see that this was where the piece he had found under Oddman's body fitted. He now held the remainder of that sheet in his hand. It was a list of some sort and it had been hastily scrawled. Ari read the items carefully.

Always with the woman, a real mother's boy
Smart and quiet, though – you get the feeling he's
* always watching you*
Hung up on his father who bought it in the war
A virgin for sure

Beneath these notes were the last few letters of the words that were missing from Ari's own piece of the puzzle. He put them together in his mind and saw the conundrum solved.

Likes airplanes
Loves redheads

Ari knew, with a deep internal tremor, that the page was about him. For some reason, Oddman had made a list of things about Ari – sporadic, hurtful observations – and he had written them down. He had got it right, too. The list was a devastating simplification of the key issues in his life. Was this his sum total? It seemed paltry. But who was Oddman going to give these details to? What was their relevance? Surely he had not written them out for his own perusal. Ari wondered whether, if he hurried, he could catch up with his mother and Underwood on Long Dead Key. Or would they already be on their way back by now. He knew he didn't care about the flight log any more. If his mother purchased a fake, she could afford it and would probably never know the truth anyway. Mr Underwood would skulk off to impress other widows at other grand hotels with other hare-brained schemes. Ari only wanted to get Cleo away now. She was all that mattered. Anyway, he didn't know what he would say if he went to the Taft house. He didn't know how Cleo felt after their lovemaking of the night before.

Some of the things Judas Jones had said

returned to perplex him. Ari felt he ought to know more about Cleo and there was only one person on the island who seemed to have had any dealings with her in the past. By Cleo's own admission, Alice had been one of the women who had taken against Silas's first trollop when she first arrived. Alice might have information which Ari could use to get Cleo safely away from Taft, the black marketeer, the liar and – Ari was now almost certain of it – the killer.

Ari alone knew that Taft's log was a fake. Oddman must have seen it and exposed it as such the day before Hella and Ari arrived. Before he could get that information to his partner Brown, however, Taft had taken his chance and silently slit the man's throat before he could ruin the deal and cost Taft considerable money. Even de la Croix had hinted that Taft had been involved in documents during the war. Ari thought it safest now to let his mother buy the fake, pay for it and get them the hell away from this island before Taft decided other lives had to be sacrificed.

Ari thought again about Judas Jones. He had mentioned that Ari should speak with a woman on the corner of Amelia and Green Street. The more he thought about it, the more he felt sure Judas had meant Alice.

Ari had still not cleaned himself up from the night before. He had the uncomfortable sense in the midday sun that he was starting to smell. His suit was completely rumpled and even though he had loosened his tie and unbuttoned his collar to allow himself a more casual appearance, he felt sure he looked very much the worse for wear.

Ari didn't want to break his new-found momentum. He would go back to the hotel after he had seen Alice. He was suddenly starving and stopped to buy a green turtle steak and potato chips for lunch but remembered he had almost no money. He went into the ice cream store with the change in his pocket and ordered a bag of *marquitas* – plantains sliced as thinly as potato chips and deep fried – and then, on an impulse, an ice cream. They had flavours he had never heard of: sugar apple and lychee. Eventually he decided on vanilla and walked slowly through the heat to Alice's place.

As he approached her house, Ari saw Alice coming out from her garage carrying a hammer. She made her way across the yard to her house. She had a few flimsy timber boards tucked under her left arm. Whatever this woodwork entailed, it must be urgent; she was scurrying.

'Your friend's not here, I'm afraid, Mr Ari,' she said politely. 'He's gone out somewhere. He told me this morning not to expect him back for the whole day.'

Alice clunked one of the boards awkwardly across her kitchen window and held it there rather unsuccessfully with one hand while she tried to hammer a nail in place with the other.

'What's all this about? Let me help, Alice.'

'I can manage,' she said tensely, clearly not managing.

'Alice,' Ari said quietly.

She looked over her shoulder at him, nails sprouting from her lips like a bizarre row of cigarettes.

314

'Please may I help?'

Alice handed him the boards and the nails, wiping each one carefully first on her apron. Now that he was occupied with work on her behalf, Ari felt sure she would not find it as easy to send him away when he started asking questions.

'I was hoping to talk to you, actually,' said Ari. 'I've met a young lady ... I think you may know her.'

'Ooo,' said Alice. 'Just a moment, this sounds like serious talk. Let me get some lemonade.'

She went into the kitchen and came back with a pitcher and two mismatched glasses. Ari was sure one had been stolen from the Electric Kitchen; he had recognized the same pattern in Pieter Laken's hand just that morning.

'What are the boards for?' asked Ari.

'Storm's coming,' Alice said blandly.

'You need shuttering for a storm?'

'It's more like a hurricane,' she said. 'Yes, we need shuttering.' Then she added, 'I'll make a bed on the floor in the parlour for Mr Brown. It won't be safe up above the garage if this thing hits head-on like they say.'

'He'll most likely be off before it arrives. We may all be going tomorrow.'

'Oh, it'll hit tomorrow morning or afternoon at the latest,' said Alice. 'Make no mistake about that.'

'Really?' said Ari.

He hoped his mother would be back well before the swells began to get dangerous.

Ari hammered up a few boards.

'Now tell me how I know your young lady.'

'Her name's Cleo,' said Ari.

'I don't know anyone called Cleo,' said Alice. She sounded disappointed. 'Cleo who?'

Ari realized he didn't know Cleo's last name. She surely wouldn't have taken on 'Taft' if he was just her guardian.

'I don't know her last name. She lives with Mr Taft out on Long Dead Key.'

'Do you mean Cherry?' asked Alice. Her voice had fallen into a flat tone of irritation. 'She's no young lady.'

'No, I mean Cleo Taft, Silas Taft's ward,' Ari baulked at his use of the euphemism. 'I know you tried to help her once when she first arrived and I wondered if you might tell me what you know about her.'

'That strumpet you're talking about calls herself Cherry Morello,' said Alice. 'I ask you! And this town needs rescuing from her, not the other way around.'

'It's not the same girl,' said Ari. He was sure they were talking at cross purposes. Even so, his heart started thumping irregularly. He focused on the boards, on getting each one straight, on hammering each nail head-on. He tried not to believe it; he tried not to cry. Ari thought about the name Cherry Morello. It was bawdy and plainly an alias rather than a given name. He could never introduce her as that in New York. It sounded like a bordello singer's name. He thought about morello cherries; as far as he knew, they were sour and only good for cheap dessert sauces.

'She came in thirty-one, or thereabouts, just before Christmas. He brought her off the train

316

and she was as thin as a slip but pretty. She had all these gorgeous long brown curls but you could see she was mature for her age, if you understand me...'

Now Ari knew Alice had the wrong girl in mind. There was no way Cleo's hair could be mistaken for brown. The woman went on with her story.

'...She was only half a girl. We were understandably concerned. She would come into the library for books and Mrs Jasper, the librarian, would try and talk to her to see what the story was. Mrs Jasper asked her if she was happy with Mr Taft and she said right back at her: "As happy as with any man!" That disturbed Mrs Jasper because it was such a knowing thing for a little girl to say and she spoke to me about it and I spoke to deputy de la Croix.

'There wasn't much we could do but whenever we had tea at one of the town ladies' houses, there was always a new story. She had been seen dressed up like a cheap tart in Sloppy Joe's. She'd rubbed herself up against somebody's husband behind the bleaches at the boxing. The town was in quite a state. We tried to get the convent sisters involved and they went out with Oscar and offered her schooling and a place to stay until she reached the age of consent but she wouldn't have it – too used to the crystal chandeliers and the fancy food by then, I expect. Still, most of them just left it at that. The child knew her own mind and every month she was older and closer to being legal to make her own decisions and it all sort of fizzled out. Most of the ladies said, "Leave

317

her to herself, then, and see if she's not in the family way by the time she's fifteen," but I'll say this for him, he's avoided that particular fiasco.'

'Taft,' said Ari, hardly able to rustle up the breath to form the word.

'Yes, he's smitten with her. Lets her call herself Cherry or Cleo or whatever it is she told you her name was. Most round here say she's poison now but I'd still have sympathy for her, if she'd only come round. I think he uses her...'

'For himself?' asked Ari.

'In any way he can to make sure he gets what he wants.'

Ari still thought she was mixing Cleo up with another girl and then he realized it. Taft was in the habit of bringing young girls down to his house. Remote from the eyes of the law, he could use them as he wished on his far-flung Key. Whatever had happened to this Cherry girl who seemed a bad sort, Cleo had been next in line. When Cherry had become fed up with the quiet life on Long Dead Key and the older man, she had taken off and Cleo had been her substitute. She had been so vague about how long she had lived with him, Ari felt sure it might have been barely a year, maybe even less. There was still time to prevent her turning into the kind of hardened manipulator Cherry Morello had become.

He wondered suddenly if Cherry had grown tired and left or whether Taft had tired of her and her illicit behaviour and got rid of her. There were plenty of places to bury a body on the islands, there were sharks that cleaned up the oceans like lethal silver submarines... He was suddenly very afraid for Cleo. Had Taft discovered that she had swum out to meet him? Did he suspect their lovemaking on the beach? Ari was cold all over in his lightweight suit. Cleo was being used in the worst possible way. Taft would discard her at the slightest whim and not even de la Croix would ever get wind of it. Ari might still be able to save her; he would make a bargain with his mother.

He kept hammering the boards as he thought, even though Alice's story had petered out. The silence and the brutal hammering seemed to force her into speech once more.

'Might still be some hope for her, I expect. Somebody ought to help her get away. If whoever takes her on knows what they're getting themselves into. You'd have to be clever about it, though. That Mr Taft seems quite a formidable fellow from what I hear. Folks say he's a gent but they say that about the devil, don't they?'

'The devil is a gentleman,' said Ari.

He pounded a nail into the last board. You had to be clever to escape; you had to do what was necessary in desperate circumstances. He thought about the sound of hammering he had heard from inside Glassen's farmhouse before his mother had flown out the door, free. He felt he understood that better now.

25

Before he left her, Ari asked Alice where Oscar de la Croix lived and she gave him directions to a room above a bar on Duval Street. She wasn't sure what the bar was called but there was a tatty flag with a skull and crossbones hanging out front. Ari would have to make one last stop before he cleaned himself up and prepared for the night ahead. His head was reeling with plans, strategies, ideas, conversations he might need to have, allies he might need to embrace.

Ari saw the Jolly Roger after a few minutes' searching. It was not on Duval Street but rather down a side alley with no name and a pile of garbage cans at its entrance. Rotting banana leaves had been laid on the floor to cover the flow of mud caused by a dripping cistern pipe. Ari went up a flight of steel stairs that would have been condemned even for use as a fire escape in New York. There were whole platforms missing and how podgy Oscar managed the gulfs, Ari couldn't imagine. The door was once yellow and was now the colour of turned cream.

He knocked on it and Oscar opened up. He was wearing a blue work shirt of some rough calico and a pair of knee-length canvas short trousers that showed off his bulging calves, each as round and meaty as a ham. He seemed surprised at Ari's appearance and quite flummoxed. If Ari wasn't mistaken, the man looked guilty.

'Alice told me where to come,' Ari confessed.

'I didn't know she knew where I lived. She's never been here.'

'You ever seen her place?'

'Just one time. Nice garden.'

A red blush like sunburn had crept up Oscar's neck. Maybe it was razor rash. He was freshly shaved. He smelled of some cheap, spicy after-shave a salesman had probably flogged him from a sample case on his doorstep. Ari felt dirtier and less presentable than ever before.

'I just saw her. She's putting up storm boards. Do you think it's coming?'

'Ain't you heard the radio?' Oscar gestured to a bedside table where a brand new wireless sat. It was burnished wood with chrome knobs and buttons. Oscar seemed to suddenly realize he'd made a mistake and he took a pillow from the chair he was about to sit down on and tossed it, as if casually, to hide the face of the set.

'Is this a social call?' Oscar said, coming to the point abruptly. He seemed annoyed now but more by the fact that he'd drawn attention to the radio than by anything Ari had done. Ari gave the room a quick glance and saw a cardboard box from which the set had clearly just been unpacked.

'I need your help actually. It's nothing to do with Mr Oddman dying, I promise...'

'Good, 'cause I'm figuring considerably on that. I'm working on it. I'm still taking it most serious, I assure you.'

He had just said the same thing in three different ways. The determined repetition made Ari aware that he was probably lying.

'I know that and I hope I haven't done anything during the course of your investigation to prevent you helping me now. You know about detective work and I don't.'

This tack was working. Oscar's chest was a sail catching the wind and swelling out.

'It's about Cleo, Mr Taft's ward. Do you think it's right her living out there with him? Isn't there a welfare department that ought to investigate?'

'Sheriff Willis's been all through this a while back,' said Oscar.

'Yes, but the State of Florida must have a welfare department ... some kind of social service...'

'We got a welfare worker who shows up here twice a year and that's for the whole of Monroe County, you understand – every Key from Largo to here. Since the Crash we've had women abandoning their babies on the doorsteps of government buildings, men prostituting their kids and wives and eating the Key deer and the pelicans. We got men beat their kids so badly they go blind and deaf and retarded. We got a little boy whose fingers got fused together when his papa poured battery acid on them to stop him touching the old man's fishing nets.'

Ari went pale.

'What we don't got is a social worker interested in a spoiled little rich girl whose of age and who gets indulged and pampered too much by an Englishman crazed by the Florida. sun.'

'I see,' said Ari. There wasn't much more to say.

'You quite taken with her, is that it?'

Ari felt ill at ease speaking with a representative of the law about his private passions but Oscar's voice was kind. He seemed relieved that they were talking about this rather than about Oddman's unsolved murder.

'I love her,' said Ari.

Oscar was the second stranger he had said it to that day. It was becoming easier on his tongue and why shouldn't he say it? It was what he felt. He loved her. Oscar looked at the boy curiously. He was still a virgin, he felt sure of that. Or perhaps he wasn't any more and that was what was stirring up all this emotion. Oscar had lost his virginity to a woman pressed up against a wall behind the first Dairy Queen in New Orleans on a Tuesday night, a school night. She was much older than him, a divorcee who wore her dressing gown all day and served the cafeteria dinners cold twice a week.

'Sit down if you like,' Oscar indicated the chair for Ari. Ari sat.

'How well do you know her?'

'We only just met,' Ari admitted. 'I've spoken with Alice, your Alice from the office, and she seems to be mixing Cleo up with another girl.'

'That your girl's name? Cleo?'

Ari nodded.

'She's slim with red hair and blue eyes. She's quiet.'

'Don't sound like the Cherry Willis told me about,' said Oscar. 'She was a hellion, Alice is right about that. Willis met her and reckoned her behaviour was more mischief and flexing her attraction. She was young and beautiful and not all used up like most of the women in this town. That gets women worked up. I kept hearing about her but I can't see we ever ran into each other. I'd have her pointed out to me in the distance and people in the stores would say: "You just missed that hellcat Cherry," but she didn't ever break the law as far as I knew. I haven't heard nothing about her for well over a year now, come to think of it.'

He looked suddenly quizzical.

'You imagine she decided to move on?' asked Ari.

'I don't think so. We get the gossip from the stationmaster and that piece of skirt moving on with all her baggage would have been quite a scene. Besides, Lucian would have had to bring her into town, wouldn't he? He'd have spoke up if that had happened.'

'Could she have come in another boat?' Ari asked.

He was hoping to raise suspicion in Oscar's mind, to have the law on his side in his attempt to wrestle Cleo away from Taft.

'She could have, I guess. But why would she? If it was an amicable parting of the ways, why not use your regular boatman? And if there is another girl out there now, then she came in by boat, too, 'cause I ain't heard no gossip about a spicy young redheaded beauty stepping down off the train neither.'

'Do you think something happened to this Cherry girl?'

'Let me tell you something about Cherry...'

Oscar cleared his throat as if he was about to

give a speech in front of a class of school children. He was chosen by Sheriff Willis to go to the high school each year and speak about law enforcement at the principal's request. He always felt it had gone well until he came home and, washing his remaining hair in the kitchen sink, felt the numerous wads of spit-soaked paper in it.

'This is how Willis relayed it to me: Cherry had been in town about six months and all the churchgoing ladies, including Alice, were up in arms about her being taken advantage of. You don't know what it's like having a woman with a mission working beside you every day of the week. She buzzed in Willis's ear like a mosquito, brought in these articles snipped by that Mrs Jasper at the library about white slavers and no-good girls on killing sprees like a regular Bonnie Parker. Eventually Willis asked me to put in a call to the Eloise County sheriff's office up near Boca where everybody seemed to think she was from. I spoke to an Irving Parrish up there, local law enforcement man. He had quite a story to tell about our Miss Cherry.

'Seems he was a young man, still wearing his very first uniform, when he got a message of complaint about sanitation from a woman who owned a cheap dosshouse near the commercial railway siding where the coal trucks and whatnot come in. It was a quiet day, I guess, or the woman was hollering something fierce because Officer Parrish, the voice on the other end of the line, decides that he'll go round to sort out the problem – first month on the job and proving his civic responsibility and all.

'What does he find in one of the locked back rooms of a neighbouring derelict house but a little girl sitting beside the dead body of her mother. The ma was some semblance of cheap hooker plying her trade with the railway workers. By the smell of her, Parrish reckoned the little girl had been sitting beside that body for nigh on three days – not knowing what to do, shocked. The woman had been beat to death and she was tied with wire to an old oil heater attached to the wall. The maggots had already been at her apparently. That little girl had witnessed such unmentionable violence she didn't speak for months. Parrish tried to keep track of her over the following years, the way you sometimes do with the early ones and the specially bad ones you can't seem to lay to rest. Every now and then Parrish would put in a call, seeing as the little one had nobody else looking out for her, and he heard they'd put her in a school for the retarded on account of her being dumb mute and all. Can you imagine a little bright spark like that locked up with the loons and the crazies? She stayed there for three years until they realized she weren't stupid and put her in a cheap school and a regular orphans' home which probably weren't much better than the nut house.

'She stayed there till she was about thirteen, and a generous thirteen so I was told. Even Parrish seemed to snicker a bit when he told Willis that, so I'm guessing she was quite something by way of tail. That's the last Parrish heard of her. He ended his story to Willis by saying he'd been called out to that very home just a few months before our call on account of two of the older boys had got in a knife fight and one had sliced off the other's ear over a girl. Parrish asked to speak with the girl and hear her side of events but the matron of the home said that was the crazy thing about the incident. The girl wasn't even there any more. She had gone. Been adopted four months before and they were still slashing at each other over her. The girl's name was Cherry Morello... She must have been something.'

'You don't think it's strange somebody that noticeable hasn't been noticed lately.'

'Maybe,' said Oscar. He seemed genuinely aroused by their conversation.

'I'm gonna ask Cleo to come home with my mother and me,' said Ari, standing up. 'I just want you to know that because if Taft tries to prevent her coming, I expect you'll uphold her rights and let her make her own decision.'

'Don't you get me involved,' said Oscar. 'I'm not getting into nothing with Mr Taft unless some serious law's been broken.'

Ari looked pointedly over at where the new radio was half covered by the carefully tossed cushion.

'That looks new,' said Ari. 'It's very nice.'

'It is new,' said Oscar defiantly. 'I bought it in town today from one of them Jew stores.'

'Must have cost you plenty.'

'I got money,' said Oscar. 'I live frugal.'

'It's just that yesterday you were crying vengeance and justice over Oddman's death and today you seem happy to sit home and enjoy the radio.'

'It's a Sunday,' said Oscar by way of answer but

he didn't shout Ari down for being wrong. He didn't try and defend himself.

'Is that storm really coming?' said Ari as he started down the steel stairs.

'I guess so,' said Oscar.

26

The Casa Marina ascended against the flint-riddled sky like a *grande dame* receiving a standing ovation. It was stylish without being ostentatious. It offered luxury and understated elegance and the drinks from its bar chinked with lots of ice. The hotel had been recently refurbished and it was as glittering as it had been when the jazz was young.

A uniformed doorman directed Ari through the entrance and into the wood-panelled lobby. He followed the posies of guests past the reception desk. Ahead was an impressive sweep of ten pairs of French doors open to the encroaching night. Ari went through one pair and out onto the front lawn that ran down to a slim bit of beach and then the sea. There was a swimming pool, lit below water level, and a few daring beauties were still splashing about in it – their shapes those of black seals in the bright, white water. The waiters hustled through the bouquets of guests carrying silver trays and trying to prevent the wind from tossing their prawn and avocado cocktails into the tropical flowerbeds.

Ari looked about for his mother but he couldn't spot her.

The wind was well up now. The sea was a fizz of whitecaps and the constant gale had added a thrilling aspect to the gathering, tugging at the ladies' dresses and beads and sucking the champagne right out of their shallow glasses. They laughed breathlessly and their laughter was blown away.

Wind buffeted the tables; a microphone stand crashed over, howling and squalling its amplified shock over the whole party. That seemed to send the women into hysterics of mirth. The men's tails were blown up about them like peacock feathers.

The band had given up on sheet music and pages of it were scattered across the gardens; some floated in the pool, bereft of ink and magic. The party was boisterous and gay with that determined verve parties that are doomed tend to take on in the beginning. Sand was blowing, too. It came all the way up from the beach, stinging Ari's cheeks so that he had to turn his back to the sea.

The Charleston gave way to 'What'll I Do?' and the dancing area, a softly lit square cordoned off by velvet ropes, cleared in a minute. The crowd did not want anything melancholy tonight. Ari spotted a maître d' with a circle of packing tape in his hands. He was trying to tape up some of the windows which looked out over the sea. Management had left it too late, though, hoping the inevitable wouldn't come. They would never save all their windows. If the storm hit head-on, they might not save any of them.

Suddenly, a beach umbrella, a red one, came cartwheeling up the lawn and a miraculous passage parted for it among the guests; it travelled onwards, viciously swirling, until it crashed through a set of the French doors and came to rest in the reception hall amid a burst of applause from the partygoers.

Looking back over his shoulder, Ari saw Cleo. She and Taft were all alone on the dance floor. She was dressed in red – a dress designed for a woman in her twenties seeking a husband, not a sixteen-year-old girl. It was a dress that shone with its own luminosity – the way rubies did, the way phosphorous in the wake of boats did. It was fireworked here and there with beads and left her whole back open to the night. Cleo didn't usually wear make-up but tonight she had on a garnet-coloured lipstick that made her eyes very blue indeed. Taft looked like any other man there, made dashing by a dinner jacket, but Cleo was the jewel. Ari looked down and saw that she was barefoot. The stone veranda was still warm enough from a day of sunbathing not to chill her feet. Every little nail was painted scarlet, too – prettier than any shoes.

The dance floor was a galaxy and Cleo and Silas were the only two planets in it, orbiting dangerously close to one another. Ari knew – the way a person can know something without a doubt, in a second and irrevocably – that they were lovers.

Cleo's blue eyes hadn't spotted Ari watching her; they were all for Silas. The wind whipped Cleo's hair and Ari saw that they were not speaking to one another; they were just looking intently into one another's eyes as secret lovers did who had no need of speech. The wind had taken everyone else's attention from them and only Ari had caught them at it.

Ari had never before appreciated what a handsome man Silas Taft was. How strong he looked even with his diminutive stature. How perfectly proportioned and muscled he was beneath his formal attire. Always, below his clothes, there had lurked the wilder, more naked skin of a man raised hard. Cleo loved him. It crushed Ari. He fell apart like a house of cards. The slightest draft had flattened him.

'Come away, Ari,' said his mother's voice. Hella was at his side. 'Leave them to it,' she said. He allowed her to turn him away from the dance floor and lead him back inside the hotel. She put her hand consolingly on the back of his head. 'I did tell you,' she said. But she did not say it unkindly.

'We have to help her,' he said.

'Shhh,' said his mother and she rocked him slightly against her as she had done when he was awakened by a nightmare as a child. 'She doesn't need your help, that girl. She's taken advantage of your good nature enough as it is.'

How had his mother seen that when he had been so utterly duped?

He decided to leave his selfishness and his reeling heart for a moment and he looked at her. He could feel the tears in his eyes.

'Did you get it?' he asked. 'Mr Taft looks as if he's celebrating.'

Hella shook her head.

'Mr Underwood was willing to pay more,' she said.

Ari stopped walking. His mother would have paid anything; something was very wrong. Hella kept walking into the dining room and Ari caught up with her. Mr Underwood was sitting at a table set for three.

'Join us,' said Hella. 'Mr Underwood won fair and square.'

Ari looked at her face and it was a perfect mask but he knew there was more going on behind it.

'You purchased the flight log?' said Ari. 'Well done.'

'Glad to have it,' said Mr Underwood. 'Your mother put up quite a fight.'

'It was worth the adventure, wasn't it, Ari?' said Hella and she squeezed his hand across the table.

'Not for Mr Oddman,' said Ari and Hella's face darkened.

'That poor man!' she exclaimed. 'I wonder if the sheriff will ever discover the culprit?'

'Where's Brown?' asked Ari.

'He's gone to pack up and visit the sheriff. Clear away the paperwork, I expect. Get permission for us to leave.'

'And if it's not forthcoming? There's a storm on its way and they could close the railway line for safety reasons. We might not be able to leave.'

'Then we'll rent a boat,' said Hella. 'Or borrow Mr Taft's airplane.'

'It's Cleo's,' said Ari. 'It was a gift.'

'Nonsense,' said his mother. 'It came with a pilot. They're only leasing it for a few weeks. Did she tell you it was hers?'

'I think she did,' said Ari. 'I can't really remember.'

'Would you excuse me?' said Mr Underwood, suddenly. 'I wanted a final word with Mr Taft.'

He stood up and Hella smiled a glittering smile at him as he went away. She took a small spiteful sip from her crystal wine glass.

'What?' said Ari.

Hella just smiled and said, 'Say "pardon", Ari.'

'What?' he demanded more loudly.

He saw that her skin was glittering beneath her light, careful make-up. There was a definite and disturbing sheen there as if she were running a slight fever.

'We didn't need Mr Oddman after all,' she said enigmatically. 'It's not genuine, Ari. Mr Underwood has just purchased, at great cost, a rather good fake.'

Ari couldn't take it in for a few seconds. He leaned across the table and grabbed her hand. Red wine spilled on the linen tablecloth and she gasped at his urgency and then giggled.

'How did you know?'

'It looked wonderful ... definitely Charles Lindbergh's writing – a brilliant forgery but a thick leather cover, beautifully aged but leather ... and heavy.'

Ari picked up the mistake at once.

'Ari,' she said breathless and delighted. 'He wouldn't take a tin St Christopher from his mother because of the weight. There was no way that log had a leather cover.'

'Quite right,' said Ari. 'Well done.'

He was trying to cope with the leaden weight of

his own heart but he was happy for his mother. She beamed as if she had solved an impossible puzzle.

'You let Mr Underwood buy it.'

'Not before I drove the price sky-high. Mr Taft owes me a debt of gratitude.'

'Then ask for Cleo!' said Ari desperately. 'Help her, please. Help me.'

Hella looked shocked at his urgency.

'She'll die if she stays here! I never ask for anything.'

'Don't make a melodrama,' said Hella.

'Get her away. Say you've taken to her. Say you never had a daughter and you want to school her in New York. Buy her.'

'Ari!' said his mother shocked.

'Get her and I'll get you the real log.'

He had said it. For the first time in the eight years since he had taken the log from the cockpit of the *Spirit of St Louis*, he had uttered the truth.

'I have it,' he said. 'You're right about this one being a fake. I wasn't sure you'd recognize it as such but you did, you have.'

Hella put her glass down on the table and placed both palms flat on the linen as if only by resting them there was she preventing herself from striking him.

'How?' she said.

'We stayed that night in the farmhouse near Le Bourget. I had seen Lindbergh, touched him, greeted him and you had been left behind. I hadn't even managed to grab you a shred of fabric as a souvenir. I lay beside you half the night wondering where we would go from there, what

334

would make you happy and then I got up out of bed but you didn't wake... I was so sure you would at any second and catch me, spare me from my adventure, and I would have been relieved but you didn't – you just slept.

'I dressed, went out barefoot and oven the field to the runway. I walked across it in the moonlight, waiting every second for the police guard to see me, knowing I was only a boy and I would just be sent home and told the excitement was over. I didn't feel like a boy, though, I felt as if I was doing the most important thing I would ever do in my life. I made it to the barn without a hitch. There was a guard there. He was smoking outside; another was asleep propped against the door. I just walked in. I suppose I was very quiet. I felt invisible and powerful. I felt as if Charles Lindbergh wanted me there, was guiding me to get you the souvenir you needed to make you happy. There was a lantern and I could see the plane. I ran my hand along the side of it. It was very cold. I saw that rip in the shape of the falling woman and I touched it with my fingers for a second. Then I climbed up onto the wing, placing my feet just where I imagined his feet had been, and I sat in the cockpit. It was so cramped and cold and it smelled of sweat and engine grease and the brown reek of oil. I had to pick up the clipboard off the seat where he must have tossed it before he climbed down. I opened the log – it was a small cardboard-covered notebook, that's all – and I saw the jottings in his handwriting – in pencil, a pencil must have been lighter than a pen...'

'The fake is in pen,' said his mother. 'I didn't think of that, see? I'm not so clever as my son,' she said to herself.

Her voice was dreamy as if she had been transported by the story and was floating along on his words the way a hypnotist's patient does.

'I wanted so badly to read what he might have written but then there was a noise. I was sure it was a guard but the noises were furtive and I thought, somebody else has had the same idea: to have a few quiet minutes alone with history before it is all stuffed in a museum. The noises stopped and I held my breath. A man lunged up onto the wing and grabbed me. He wore small steel-rimmed glasses and his mouth was too full of white teeth, they all crinkled up on one another. He punched me in the chest and tried to grab the log. I had a bruise the next day; I hid it from you. I was out the other side down the wing and past the guards, running. I heard the man say one thing before I was away, he said: "*Scheisse*".'

'A German,' said Hella. 'And also a thief like my son.'

'I was terrified of that man for years. Not Glassen, mother, but that German who had punched me so I thought my heart had been bruised.'

'But you kept it from me,' said Hella. 'Why? For spite, I suppose. As some kind of terrible punishment for being a terrible mother.'

'At first I was afraid of what you might say. Of how angry you would be that I had stolen it. Then I realized how much you might like it and I was determined to give it to you, but how? After

336

all those years how could I just confess it?'

'So you set up a plan to get me to find it?'

'I was thrilled when Oddman and Brown showed up. I knew I could take the flight log to them and have them sell it to you. You would have it. I would be free of it. You would have paid them a lot of money and it would have worked out...'

'Very clever...' said Hella.

'Except they claimed to have found it from some other source before I could speak to them about faking the deal. Then I found I couldn't tell them the truth either. So I thought, let's go to the Keys. I could still implement my plan somehow. I could get the log to Taft and have him sell it to you. Oddman and Brown didn't even have to know about it. I tried to meet him at the cockfights and make the deal but Mr Underwood was there. Out of nowhere, he arrived here to bid on the fake log. I hoped you wouldn't buy it. I hoped Underwood would spend a fortune on the fake but by then Oddman had died...'

'He must have seen it,' said Hella. She came to the same realization Ari had reached. 'He saw it and knew it wasn't genuine...'

'And Taft had to kill him before he told you or Brown or Underwood and ruined the deal.'

'That's why we have to get Cleo away,' said Ari with urgency. 'He's a forger and a killer...'

Then Hella summed up Ari's direst thought in a single sentence.

'Mr Oddman died for your lie,' she said.

Ari sat opposite her. Neither of them spoke. Hella was coming to terms with the immensity of

337

his deceit. Ari was trying to feel the relief he had imagined the expiation would bring but it did not come. He did not feel absolved; the truth was not cathartic.

'Where is it now?' asked Hella.

'It's with Mr Taft, though he doesn't know it. I took it there when we went to view the house and hid it in the attic. I was going to try and meet with him yesterday, too, to tell him I knew about the forgery. I was going to tell him where to find the original and let him sell it to you but everything went wrong. I couldn't speak with him privately and I couldn't speak with you because Mr Underwood was always there. I wasn't sure why he wanted it or how far he would go to have the original. It seemed safer to let you both assume you were bidding for the real thing and retrieve the genuine article myself later.'

'That's what we'll do,' said Hella. 'We'll go out there tomorrow. Say our farewells and retrieve the real flight log.'

'I'll go alone,' said Ari. 'I want to see Cleo.'

'Where has it been all these years?' said Hella. 'You've kept it hidden from me and the maids...'

'It was in Sweden,' said Ari.

His mother looked confused.

'I had it with me in Paris. I hid it under the car seat when we left Le Bourget and I had to go down in the night when we reached Paris and break the car window to get it back. Do you remember the police asked us about it the next morning? Then when Grandfather died, it was with us in Stockholm. I carried it in the rucksack to Mariefred. It isn't very large. I put it in the candle mould in the boathouse. It was sealed there for years.'

'And if the Karlssons had decided to make candles?'

Ari shrugged.

'I didn't think about that. The mould was quite well hidden in a corner. I thought of it as a kind of gift for my father. That was where I imagined you first ... loved him.'

'Then when we went back to sort out my mother's estate, you insisted on going with Birgit to Mariefred.'

'And it was still there. I retrieved it and brought it home to give to Oddman and Brown, only ... they claimed to have found it then and I was swept along.'

'What does it say?' said Hella suddenly.

'What does what say?' asked Ari.

'You have surely read it several times over the years... What does it say, the log?'

'Nothing,' said Ari and then, seeing her distraught face, he recounted the scant items from the pages, 'He mentions the cold and hunger; compass readings and instrument readings I don't understand. He writes about fatigue, cramps, the fear of going off-course and ice on the wings. It's only a few pages...'

Hella's face was entirely blank as she nodded her head slowly, coming to terms with how mundane reality was. Ari kept going, a pat litany of the non-events of that lonely, momentous flight, 'He talks about gulls off the coast of Ireland. He mentions seeing whales...'

27

At first when he woke, Ari thought it was still night. He lay quietly for a moment, a small shape of sadness curled beneath the blankets. He had flopped down on his hotel-room bed after arriving home from the Casa Marina and slept in his clothes. Now he sat up and looked through the window. Rain splattered the window with tears. He hugged a blanket around his shoulders and looked down into the garden of the Colonial Hotel.

The lawn was a swimming pool pimpled by constant rain. The pool itself was covered in grass clippings and leaves; Quozzie would have his work cut out for him. The green foliage had turned pewter in the dark morning. It was a Pompeii garden, covered in ash and fossilized to stone, except it moved viciously, whipping its leaves and flaying the lilac blossoms from the branches of the jacaranda.

Ari let his fingers creep across the window the way they had done in the George V so many years before. He felt the wind pull the glass pane away then press it in again, playing with the give in the old putty of its frame. He sought out Charles Lindbergh and found only a far-off sense of the man; his courage would come no closer. Ari tried to conjure an image of Cleo, too, but she was also distant – across water. Ari could see workmen hammering up hurricane boards across the hotel windows. Light peeped out of the cracks between these barriers. Everybody was hunkering down for the storm that would hit with full force later that day.

Ari pulled his legs up under him and pushed his body into the corner where the bed met the two walls of the room. He rocked for a few minutes, thinking, and then he dressed. Today would be one of those days which would chart the course of the rest of his life. He was ready for it. He knocked on the door of his mother's room then went in. She was pretending to be asleep. She looked pale and listless. He felt her forehead; she was on fire.

'Stay in bed,' Ari said. 'You're not well.'

'I'm cold,' she said.

Her body shook beneath the covers. He put a blanket over her.

'I never give you anything,' she said, repeating his accusation of the night before.

'I didn't mean that,' he said.

She smiled wanly up at him. 'Go get your girl, then,' she said. 'We'll decide what to do with her when we get her home but there will be no wedding, Ari, do you hear me?'

He kissed her forehead and it burned his lips.

'If I'm to take on another responsibility then so be it. Charles will understand.'

Ari covered her with a blanket and went down to ask Señor Bolivar to send for Dr Saul. He asked to borrow a raincoat and Señor Bolivar begged him not to venture out.

'Get the doctor for my mother before he's

341

closed in by the storm,' said Ari and he went out.

The wind was ferocious. The rain was a stinging deluge of pins and needles. Ari made his way up the street to the charter boat quay. At one point, near the corner, a bicycle cycled past him without a rider. The pedals whirred manically but it was really being flung along by wind, only seeming for a few moments to be travelling under its own steam. As it fell on its side and slid along the slick street, its tin bell jangled shrilly.

The wind was a wall Ari could not walk up. He pushed against it with his hands stretched out in front of him like a blind man. He was exhausted by the time he reached the water. The boats careened on the swells, each mast keeling over in a different direction to the one on the boat beside it. Many owners had tried to sail their craft down to Havana for harbouring; others had belted them round with old tyres, hoping they would simply jostle against each other but not be swept away.

There was nobody about. Ari saw a light showing under the door of a tavern across the parking lot. He heard music coming from inside – a mournful harmonica ululated, a banjo twanged. Ari pulled his way through the wind and hammered on the door. It was locked but somebody slid back a brace-board and Ari stepped inside, almost falling over because there was suddenly no wind to battle against.

The whole bar looked over at him in amazement. They were all swathed in yellow and blue plastic overalls. They wore hats. Rough high-necked sweaters – thick as carpets – warmed them; their boots reached their thighs. Ari was a boy wearing a white suit and a gentleman's raincoat against a dark storm. They would have laughed at him if he hadn't been so pitiful.

'There's fifty dollars in it for any man who'll take his boat out,' Ari said.

There was a second's pause and then a round of guffaws and exaggerated knee-slapping.

'Anyone willing to rent me a boat, then? One hundred dollars.'

There was not so much laughing now. One hundred dollars made its recipient the richest man in the room.

'I'll do it!' Lucian said.

He stood up. He seemed to understand Ari's urgency; he fetched his coat right away and came across the silent staring room towards the door.

'I guess I know where we're headed. If we go now, we might just survive the voyage.'

How they made it the seven miles to Long Dead Key, Ari would never know. The *Alexa Lee* left the sheltering curve of the harbour entrance and the sea clutched hold of her. Whenever Ari opened his mouth to gasp for breath, seawater flew in. Waves rose up simultaneously on both sides of the boat which seemed always to be lower than the surrounding ocean. Ari was flung about the deck, his legs bruising on the bulkhead and tangling in ropes once secured and now flying free like Gorgon hair – they snapped at Ari's face and one slashed him across the cheek.

Lucian roared at the storm swell; he shook his fist delightedly each time they tipped a crest before grabbing the helm as they slipped down the other side – often more sideways than head-on – into the next watery canyon. Ari squatted down and looped his arms through an oar stave, grasping the rusty metal with blue knuckles. Lucian tracked their course by memory; he knew this allotment of sea by heart even when it was stretched and swollen out of shape. Ari thought only of the reef – as pointed as the sharks' teeth on Lucian's necklace – and horribly eager. Somewhere below, its clawed stalagmites waited, yearning for the soft underbelly of a boat.

They found Long Dead Key by its lights – the forty hurricane lanterns that ran in two rows along its jetty. Astonishingly, most of them were still lit; few yet shattered by the vacuuming pressure. Ari thought of Lindbergh, lost for a day and a half over sea. At the end of it there were the lights of Le Bourget and thousands of people – the lights of hoping and waiting – and they had drawn him in ... a runway beckoning.

Lucian tried to bring the boat alongside the jetty but swells threatened to sweep them against it. Once, twice, their hull crunched against the wood; they splintered a pylon. Lucian cursed and tried to bank the *Alexa Lee* away. Ari reached for the wooden ladder that hung down towards the water. If he fell in, it would be a long swim to the rock-riddled shore. Being swept up onto it would tear him apart but being swept out to sea would be worse still. Ari leaped for the ladder and suddenly the deck of the boat pulled away from below him and his feet just dangled, drenched by the warm waves, then the cold air, then the warm waves that rolled past his clinging body.

Ari clambered up. His suit was soaked and snagged by nails. He managed to lift a hand to Lucian but the boat was lost on the downside of a swell, only the mast remained visible – a matchstick in the chaos.

Ari looked down the length of the jetty. He shambled on against the force of the wind. Each pair of lanterns led him closer to shore but now some of them were bursting. They flew past his head, lifted from their nails by the power of the wind. They crashed into the sea which swallowed their small flames in an instant. Ari reached the dense growth at the end of the jetty and looked back. Only three lanterns still burned and these three would endure the storm. Their fixtures were the strongest, their glass the sturdiest, their flames the most determined.

The leaves battered Ari as he stumbled along the path. At last, he made the garden. The downpour had splattered the mud from the neat beds. The sundial was on its side. Ari reached the enclosing courtyard; that sun-baked square which usually held the warmth of the day in its terracotta bricks was awash with water from the overflowing fountain.

From this very site, Ari had first seen Cleo through two pairs of doors, climbing up out of a far friendlier sea. The expensive mahogany deck chairs from some fashionable steamer or cruise ship had been stacked and tied down against the wall behind the apple tree. The windows of the house were closed and taped; Silas Taft had planned his defences. He was nothing if not cautious. Ari smashed his fist on the frame of the door and in seconds it was opened and he was pulled inside.

He tumbled to the floor, carrying with him his own compact storm. Someone closed the door behind him. Ari looked up and saw that it was Brown. The man's massive torso was wrapped in a blanket, his only concession to bad weather. Ari could hear his own breathing above everything else. It hitched in and out of his lungs, catching on every pointed edge of rib. It was bizarrely peaceful in the house. The generator was still working but there was only one lamp burning to conserve fuel. It was hushed in here compared to the riot going on outside. Ari could hear each drop of rain falling from his clothes onto the marble floor – each one ticked, tocked, ticked. He was too exhausted to stand.

Brown took Ari's coat from his shoulders and threw it into the corner. Cleo and Silas sat opposite each other under the lamp, watching him. She was wearing a pair of baggy men's trousers, socks and a cream cashmere sweater with a low V-neck. A slim gold chain hung around her throat. She looked so much older than she was. Her hair was up, loosely tied with a ribbon. She and Silas were both leaning over a table on which a chessboard sat, halfway through play. Cleo had a mug in her hand; the steam that wouldn't survive for a second outside rose slowly and calmly in here.

Silas stood up and said, 'We weren't expecting you, Ari.' It was happily stated. What might even have been admiration had crept into his tone. 'You're bleeding on my terrazzo,' he added.

Ari looked down to where his hand had been pressing against his shirt and saw a perfect bloody handprint there. He realized that a vicious splinter from the pier was embedded in his palm. He pulled it out; it stung like a spider bite.

'Cleo,' said Silas formally, 'would you take Ari upstairs and give him some of my clothes? He must be cold.'

Cleo took Ari by his undamaged hand and led him up the staircase. They went into her room. The double bed was covered with a satin comforter, stitched to stay plump and soft in quilted squares. Everything was snowy and warm. Broderie anglaise cushions covered a chair stained the colour of milky tea. There were touches of pink here and there. Pink tulips were embroidered on the curtains. Her chest of drawers and armoire were hand-painted with dozens of pale, antique roses. There was a dressing table and a silk screen on which grey cranes soared above Japanese mountains like dragons' backs.

Cleo led Ari into her private washroom – apparently she didn't have to share one with Silas. Ari sat on the edge of a porcelain bathtub. Cleo brought a towel over to him – rich, Egyptian cotton with a line of lilac seagulls sewn along the edge. Everything had been lovingly created by the hands of the poor for her, each item carefully chosen to please and entice her.

Cleo went down the corridor again, leaving the door open. Ari dried his hair and began to remove his braces and shirt. He examined the room. He opened a drawer in the bathroom cabinet and revealed, a pile of ladies' underwear – silken, glamorous and too old for Cleo – beautiful brassieres and slim panties that would barely cover her. Ari ached at the memory of them together in the water. He closed the drawer and opened the door of the medicine chest. The shelves were loaded with feminine necessities. There were perfume atomizers and powder pots, a large cut-glass bottle of Joy and a box of Ogilvy Sisters soap with a lacy parasol on its lid. Inside were four yellow soaps shaped like lemons and four green ones shaped like limes. They nestled in hollows of tissue paper, arranged in chessboard patterning. They smelled like a citrus orchard in high summer – that dense, cloudy infusion of white blossoms dying.

Ari lifted out the soapbox and saw behind it a small dark glass bottle lettered in cursive. The way the bottle was angled revealed two familiar letters: 're' just as they had been ordered on the scrap of paper he had found under Oddman's body. Ari suddenly saw what they stood for: 'red'. It was a bottle of hair dye. He completed the puzzle in his head easily now: Julian Oddman had written the list out for Silas Taft – ways in which Ari could be manipulated and controlled while his mother was about her business of buying the flight log. Oddman had probably met with Taft – not about the authenticity of the log but about Ari and his mother – and they had gone through the list together. It came to Ari that if Oddman had been in on the scheme to defraud his mother then Brown had been in on it, too. And if Oddman and Brown both knew that the

348

diary was a fraud and had colluded with Taft to sell it to his mother or Underwood, what motive was there for the murder of Oddman?

Cleo came in just then. She saw him holding the bottle of hair dye and she looked genuinely saddened.

'Turns any old brunette into a natural fiery redhead,' she said in a flat dead tone. She was quoting the copy on the back of the bottle.

She laid a fresh shirt and trousers on the seat of the commode, a suit jacket in Silas's colours of biscuit and beige, even a clean pair of brown socks. Ari would have to use his own braces, though; Silas's would be too short.

'These haven't been hemmed for Silas yet,' she said, touching the trousers. 'So they might be long enough for you.'

Ari was still holding the bottle of dye and trying to understand what had happened and where the danger might lie. The men had their money. Perhaps he could just steal back his flight log and be gone from here.

'I'm great as a blonde, too,' said Cleo. 'But I'm really just a brunette.' It was the most honest thing she had ever said to him.

'Cherry Morello,' he said dully. 'Pleased to meet you.'

'Only sometimes,' she answered.

There was nothing more for either of them to say. 'I'll leave you alone,' she said. 'To change.'

Ari changed his trousers but Silas's shirt was too tight across his chest and he left it lying on the bed. He put on the man's coat and left it un-buttoned. When he had dressed, Ari looked at himself in the glass above Cleo's dressing table and saw a younger version of Silas Taft in himself. There were no startling physical similarities between them but the clothes were so distinctly those of the older man that it was impossible not to feel somehow like him. Ari was lighter in countenance, sandy-haired and boy-faced. He was taller but not slimmer; Taft was very slender but cunningly strong. His upper body was enormously powerful in the wiry, lithe way of long-distance runners. Ari felt he no longer had the strength to sprint a hundred yards.

The house was not well designed to withstand hurricanes. Ari felt that as he reached the top of the stairs and thought he felt the whole building shift. There was lots of wood, dried out and weakened by age, and an uncertain foundation. It was as dark as night now and stubby candles had been set in saucers on every second riser to make the way clear; they flicked at Ari's soles with their tongues as he passed.

Silas's one eye watched Ari descend. It twinkled and the man smiled his sharp, yellow smile. Cleo handed Ari a cup of coffee, cloud-massed with cream, and he thanked her. He had no idea what else to do in the face of this courtesy.

Outside, the full power of the hurricane had arrived. They sat, three corners of an equilateral triangle in a glass room – rows of French doors on both sides of them. Cleo had drawn the curtains but that made things worse because the source of the sounds could only be imagined. The world was undergoing a dreadful wrenching; metal cried out and wood shattered. Something long and flat

– but heavy – crashed onto the roof, bounced and fell onto the patio outside. None of them went to look what it was but Ari had a vision of the jetty, almost half a mile away, disintegrating. As each board came free, it was being fired – a dumb projectile – at the house.

Then suddenly, there was a deep movement from the very spine of the house. They all felt it. Cleo's hands gripped the sides of her chair and they endured a long silent moment waiting for the worst.

'Too bad about your mother losing out,' said Taft. 'That Mr Underwood was determined.'

'Too bad,' said Ari.

Nobody had asked him why he was there. Everybody was pretending nothing had happened.

'Now that I know she's a keen buyer, I'm sure I can source some other documents for her.'

Ari smirked; he felt the insincerity of the smile on his lips.

'I don't think so, Mr Taft.'

'She's losing interest in Mr Lindbergh?'

'My mother likes the genuine article,' said Ari.

'Ah-hah,' said Taft. 'We thought you might have figured it out.'

'We?' said Ari, wanting it confirmed.

'Mr Brown and myself,' said Taft.

'Right,' said Ari.

'When Mr Brown contacted me, their old friend, about producing a Lindbergh flight log for a … if you'll forgive me … rather gullible buyer, I didn't expect it to draw a second party from nowhere. You can't honestly be surprised, Ari. Your mother approached these men offering a

351

vast sum for an item that nobody has ever seen. That's the easiest job in the business. If she'd bought it, she'd think it was genuine and she'd be happy, secretly coveting it for years and never discovering the truth. But as it happens, she's had a lucky escape and another patsy's paid a fortune for it. I'm quite glad, Ari. Your mother is an extraordinary woman and an impressive adversary. The price she got Mr Underwood to pay!'

'She knew it was a fake as soon as she saw it,' said Ari.

He said it with pride.

'Yes, I thought she had her doubts. I could see her pushing up the price for that fool Underwood. I am most grateful to her for that.'

'So, you have your money,' said Ari.

He only wanted to be as far away from this island as possible. He wanted to distance himself at last from the treachery. And he realized with some consternation that he still wanted Cleo, Cherry, whoever she was. He had no idea how he was going to accomplish all that now. He had managed to get himself well and truly stuck.

'I suppose Oddman came down early to help you with the details of the forgery?'

'He was most concerned about you. He felt sure you had knowledge you weren't sharing and he thought it best we deal with your mother and keep you distracted.'

'Yes,' said Ari. He didn't want Taft to elaborate. 'I see that now. But clearly you didn't use Oddman's expertise or you would never have selected a heavy leather cover for your log. That's what gave you away, even to my mother. Why didn't you take Oddman's advice?' asked Ari.

'He disappeared and turned up dead before he had the chance to consult with me,' said Taft.

'Why did you kill him?' asked Ari.

Taft and Brown looked thrown for the first time; no longer in complete control of where the conversation was taking them.

'We thought you were here to tell us that, Ari,' said Taft.

28

There was a definite crumbling of mortar from the ceiling. It hissed down onto the marble floor, no piece bigger than a pebble, most of it as fine as sea salt. Some of it landed in Ari's coffee and floated above the cream before disappearing beneath the surface.

Somebody was thumping on the door outside. Taft and Brown exchanged glances. Cleo tensed. Brown opened the door to reveal the hunched figure of a man. He was so stooped that Ari thought it was Quozzie. Brown dragged the man further into the room. It was Underwood.

'How is everybody getting out here?' bellowed Taft but he changed his tune as soon as Underwood stood up and they all saw that his crouch had been concealing a gun. He had all four of them in his range and, without speaking for he was breathless with exhaustion, he motioned them to cluster together.

353

Underwood's face was contorted with rage and pain.

'This isn't real, is it?' said Underwood. He held up a book wrapped carefully in a soaked chamois. 'Is it?' he roared.

It was Ari who shook his head first.

'I knew that bitch wouldn't give it up that easily!' he said. 'The more I thought about it last night, the more I knew I had been taken. Such a simple assignment and it's been made so difficult by the interference of snooping bitches and bastard forgeries.'

It was the word 'assignment' that disturbed Ari most.

'I met that authenticator of yours by chance in town on Thursday night,' Underwood continued, 'And he told me he was just about to go out to some Key to check up on Charles Lindbergh's flight log. He said he was going to examine it thoroughly, so I knew I had to get rid of him before he actually got to read it ... in case he picked up anything sensitive in it. I offered to give him a lift out in my hired boat. Slit his throat halfway over to the Key, threw him overboard.'

So de la Croix and Sam, the one-armed fisherman, had been right about the body coming ashore from the direction of Taft's island.

'Where's the fucking real thing?' roared Underwood.

He sounded like a madman; the more he hissed and spluttered, the more pronounced his accent became until Ari was almost sure he was about to start speaking German.

'We never had the real flight log, Mr Underwood,' said Taft.

His hands were up, palms forward, almost pleading with the man to drop his gun.

'It was just a plan to get money from Mrs Gold, is all. We don't even know where you came from.' His sheepish giggle seemed ludicrous considering the circumstances. 'But when you showed up, we saw the chance to start a bidding war and up the price. There is no genuine flight log. There never was.'

Underwood made a grab for Cleo and caught her by a handful of her hair. He twisted her round to shield his body. Her face was towards them, frightened but calm, as if she knew Taft would do something to save her. If not Taft, then Brown and if not Brown then surely Ari.

'It's in the attic,' said Ari. 'I had it. I hid it there.'

He could see that Brown and Taft thought he was lying, trying to buy them some time to think and get Cleo and the gun away from the crazed Underwood but the man wasn't taking anything for granted.

'How did you have it?' he demanded.

'I took it that night Lindbergh first landed. I stole it from the cockpit.'

'You were the little farm boy who gave my colleague the slip. We thought the flight log had been stored on some French farm by an illiterate schoolboy all these years. We've been looking for it off and on for years.'

'Why do you want it?' said Cleo.

Ari was impressed with the solidity of her voice.

'Just in case...' said Underwood. 'It's politically

sensitive right now and we'd prefer to have it in our possession, is all.'

'Politically sensitive?' said Ari. 'It's a flight log. There's nothing in it. What do you mean?'

'We weren't sure if he'd understood the significance of what he'd seen but we couldn't risk it. Not now with the agreement so close to being signed. It would be disastrous for anything to be revealed now, which is exactly why we thought the seller had chosen this moment to release it. The seller knew it would blow apart the British – German naval pact. We couldn't have that. We need our navy.'

'There's nothing in it!' said Ari again.

'Tell me what he mentions,' said Underwood.

Ari struggled to recall each entry he had memorized. He started to recite them, random snippets of Lindbergh's text that might be what the deranged man was wanting: the takeoff, the first hour, feeling strong, hunger, ice on the wing, a cloud bank, lightning, instrument readings, compass headings, cramps and the need to evacuate into a bottle, the first sighting of gulls off the west coast of Ireland, the pod of whales...'

'Whales?' said Underwood.

Ari nodded; Cleo's eyes were more fearful now that Underwood seemed to have lost his reason. There was no way of anticipating the actions of a lunatic.

'Seventeen-ten hours. I've just spotted a pod of six enormous grey whales swimming in formation. A beautiful sight from this height.' Ari quoted Lindbergh's notation exactly. He knew them all by heart. He had dragged the flight log out a dozen times over the preceding few weeks and read it again and again.

'Whales!' roared Underwood and he was laughing so crazily that tears had formed in the corners of his eyes.

'Not whales, then?' said Ari.

'Not whales,' said Underwood and his laughter hitched on his lungs as it slowed. 'Submarines. German U-boats. We had saved them in secret from the grasping allies, spared them from Scapa Flow in nineteen nineteen. They've been kept at a secret base in the Arctic and we've refuelled them there, maintained them. Six beautiful, powerful U-boats we weren't supposed to have, you see. An international disaster for Germany to be allowed a navy!' he shrieked. 'Denied the means of protection like a naughty child. We cosseted them, kept them running, kept sub teams trained and then one day out of the blue in the middle of the Atlantic they're all surfaced in a routine form-ation and that fucking man flies right overhead.

'We didn't know what he saw but we couldn't risk he might mention subs. When no legitimate nation claimed them there would be an inter-national furore. An operative in France was sent immediate instructions to claim the log as soon as Lindbergh landed but some stupid kid had run off with it. We waited for months for Lind-bergh to mention the subs but he never did. Still, we wanted the log and now, in August, the German–British naval pact will be signed, allow-ing Germany to begin building up her navy, and proof that we've held secret U-boats all along will finish that. I need the log...'

'It says a pod of whales,' said Ari. 'It doesn't mention anything else.'

'Get it!' said Underwood and he placed the muzzle of the gun against Cleo's temple.

Ari started towards the kitchen where the stairs led up to the attic but a noise of such tremendous volume assailed their ears that he had to stop and cover them. Brown and Taft were closest to the curtains. They each took hold of one drop and wrenched them apart.

29

The plane Ari had thought of as Cleo's was coming up the grass. At first, it was just a red dynamo – not recognizable as a plane – but it carried with it the ropes that had once moored it to its pier and half the planks of the pier were still attached to them. The wind had picked it up from the water like a dandelion and was pinwheeling it in their direction. The plane cartwheeled up the lawn, a firework, a Catherine wheel of steel, spewing red debris as it flew. Top over bottom, it spiralled towards the house and, at the last minute, they all found the sense to leap free of the windows, back into the room, before the plane exploded through the glass doors and brought the wall and half the back of the house in with it.

The noise of the storm was extreme. It invaded the house like an enemy platoon. The wind took up the furniture like a petulant giant and slammed all of it, all at once, into the far corner.

Ari saw Cleo in the blinding maelstrom; she was bleeding from her neck and the wind was blowing the blood about, streaking her face with red warpaint. The wind tore at Ari's eyeballs but he thought he saw Brown, that great bear of a man, lifted like a puppet from the wall-less kitchen. The vortex took him up like the amazing flying man from the Saturday morning matinées and whipped him from view at thirty feet.

Cleo screamed and the wind screamed back in her face. She grabbed hold of Ari by the shirt but he could not let go of his purchase – he didn't know what exactly he had grabbed hold of – or they would both be blown away. One of his buttons popped free and then another. The third one held. It was one of his mother's double-stitched buttons; his shirt held round his body and Cleo held onto it. He thought about his mother's obscure obsession with buttons and wondered if she had had some inkling of saving a life with her petty attention to detail. Ari almost laughed in the face of the hurricane. Perhaps Hella, in her mother's way, had sensed in the small, irrelevant rules she had adopted in raising her child, the seed of somebody's salvation. Silas was lying prone; a bubble of blood blew from his lips. Ari was closest to him and Cleo flung herself down next to them, too. All three of them held hands in a knot of weight that might be enough to hold them down.

Ari turned his head to see Underwood. The man was miraculously still standing with his gun in one hand and the fake Lindbergh log in the other.

'Get down!' Ari shouted but it was useless.

One of the boards from the pier swivelled in the air like a child's paper windmill. It had a row of nails sticking out of it and it hit Underwood in the middle of the forehead. The nails punctured both his eyes and he staggered around with the board impaled to his forehead like a Halloween trick mask. The wind held him up long after he was dead, waltzing him around the room in mad circles like a marionette then dumping him in a corner when it was tired of play.

Just when Ari thought the worst was over, the earlier creaking shift they had heard consolidated itself into a tearing that pulled the wall and ceiling apart. Cleo and Ari looked at each other. They saw each other; everything else was immensely petty in those two seconds before the wind pressed its foot down onto them. It pressed down on the remnants of the plane strewn all around them, too, and on the last of the ceiling, then crashed the entire second storey down onto them and washed it all through with a giant wave from the coldest part of the sea.

The instinct given to all small, crawling creatures gripped hold of Ari. A deep, intuitive voice whispered to him to lie still. Pain bellowed in his shoulder; there was an object weighing down on him. His ears were opening again after the din of the roof fall. He could still hear the wind screeching overhead. It seemed more distant now.

The most immediate danger was the water. It washed across the remains of the terrazzo floor. Ari could taste that its origin was the sea. How close was the ocean to the house now? Perhaps only a hundred feet away, slurping its way along the lawn. The level was rising in the house. Ari felt the Atlantic in it – that frozen heart of the Sargasso where eels spawn in water like ice.

Ari was shivering with shock; the salt he tasted in his mouth was enriched with his own blood. He turned his head so he could catch his breath. In an effort that seemed to take everything from him, he pushed up. Debris – some red metal from the plane and the raw material of trees – fell off him. He tried to stand and was surprised when he could.

He sought out Cleo first. It was as dark as night in the flattened remains of the house. He could see the ragged tops of walls that had once supported the top storey. There was a plane in the house, too, a wreck. Where was that from? Who would store a wrecked plane in a house? Then he remembered the impact. Above him, Ari could see the distant beams of the attic supports and the black sky through the gaping holes in it. The whalebone staircase was on its side, having crashed through the kitchen wall. Ari moved through the wreckage; he bumped his legs; he saw hair. Cleo was floating face down and he flipped her over. Her neck wound was still bleeding but it was not too bad. She spluttered at last and her eyes slowly focused.

At once, Cleo began to feel around her, shouting above the storm surge, 'Where is he? Where is he?'

They searched feebly. Some pieces of the detritus could not be lifted – the engine of the plane was a deadweight stone in the middle of the floor – but then they found him. Silas was trapped under part of a wing that was weighted down by an immense block of marble from his expensive staircase.

Silas Taft's lungs must have been crushed. Blood flowed from his mouth and somehow the sting of the salt in that small cut on his lip was more painful than the smashed bones and taut-to-splitting skin he felt somewhere below his waist. Taft looked up and saw Cleo but he didn't have a free hand with which to reach out for her.

'Leave me,' Taft said.

'No,' Cleo answered flatly and she went to work on pulling the marble slab free. Ari started to pull along with her. Between them, they moved the slab barely an inch as the water slipped up over Silas's chin and he closed his mouth. The tide surged in again and, as they pulled and struggled, Ari knew it would be his very last chance to save the man or let him die.

'Cherry,' Taft said half underwater. 'Cherry...' he said again.

Her name became a bubble.

The water was coming up over Silas's nose and in a moment he would have no breath left. Cleo had stopped helping; she sloshed back in the water and cried. She had accepted the man's death; she would come with Ari to New York. In time, she would forgive him. She would see that he had let Silas drown to free her and give her a better life. Was that what Hella had said to herself when she had hammered Glassen into the kitchen of his farmhouse to burn? Had Hella

362

believed that Ari would forget the act or had she hoped that he would try to understand that it was something which had to be done? The act had freed them but Ari had not forgotten; he had never forgiven her for it.

In his exhaustion and his frustration and his realization, Ari began to cry. But he did not stop pulling. In the years after the event, it would be his only comfort: he would know in his heart that he had not stopped trying to save the man. The tide kept spewing in through the walls and a remarkable thing started to happen – the sea began to lift the plane's wing. The flooding of the island was raising the marble slab as if it were a twig on a slow river. The water rose and rose and, with the effortless power of the sea, it washed the weight away.

Taft gulped for air again. Blood still frothed a little at the corners of his mouth. Ari took one side of Silas's coat and Cleo grabbed the other and they dragged him to where the stone steps in the kitchen still led up into the storm. They pulled his dead weight onto the landing slab and waited there. They could go neither up nor down. They hunkered together.

In the absolute silence, in the eye of the melee, Silas Taft looked up at Ari and said, 'Do you know something? I can't feel my legs.'

30

Key West, as Ari had known it, was gone. The worst, most dilapidated buildings had lasted; the newest had been destroyed. Some were flattened like debris in a scrapyard, some blown away entirely. Rooms in which people had prayed and squabbled and copulated stood open to the sky. The queen palms had lasted, though. Their height, which should have been a disadvantage, had kept them rooted. The wind had been unable to grab hold of the whole of them. It could twist only a portion at a time; the rest had swayed free and survived.

Ari stood in a line of people that curved around the block to the Red Cross tent. In one hand, he held two plates that were part of the bundle Cleo and he had brought back into town with them. The gold leaf that swirled around the plates' edges was embarrassing here.

They had waited almost two days on Long Dead Key. A portion of the house was still standing and they had slept in the one huge bed which had not been blown away. The three of them close together, warmed by the brilliant, shiny weather the storm had left behind it. The waves had lapped against the shore in humble rhythm, though now they carried with them odd bits of flotsam – a sign that offered locks for 5c, two keys included; a baby's bottle. They gathered tins of food from the kitchen floor; the icebox was gone. The cooking range had been ripped free of its gas cylinder and lay in one of the flowerbeds. Ari had closed the valves but the gas had already fled as part of the storm clouds.

On Tuesday morning, they had found Brown's body in the topmost branches of the Spanish lime. Cleo had climbed up – Ari had broken ribs in the storm – and she had gently tugged at Brown's shoulder until he whumped to the ground like a rotten branch. They wrapped him in a sheet and eventually decided to bury his body until it could be exhumed for proper rites. Sea-gulls were circling overhead and, despite every-thing, Ari didn't want to leave his eyes to them.

Together, he and Cleo had dug Brown's grave, secured document boxes and taken care of Silas who lay quite still in his study where they were sleeping. His one good pupil did not respond to light. When Ari came into the room, he couldn't tell if the man was dead or sleeping with his eye open, or watching him.

On the second day after the storm, the Thursday, Cleo packed a bundle of items – cash, two plates and mugs, tinned food (as much as she thought would float) and they had fashioned a raft of planks from the ruined pier. They had left Silas with the torch and some water and food and they had launched the raft and started over to Key West.

Silas had insisted that one of the boatmen would come over and fetch them but nobody had arrived and he needed a doctor. The fleet might all be wrecked; Lucian dead or drowned or drunk beyond repair. Cleo did most of the kicking. Her strong legs took them the seven miles while Ari's simply dragged useless in the wake of her work.

Eventually, they had landed on Fort Jefferson beach and simply left the raft to float away with the other wreckage. Cleo had brought a pair of Silas's shoes with her. She had anticipated debris underfoot and she was right. Wearing the expensive tan and cream leather brogues, she pushed her way through the shattered glass of shop fronts, rusty-spiked planks sucked from house walls, and the remains of fallen trees – their exposed hearts as sharp as torture stakes.

The Red Cross had arrived by boat only that morning. When Cleo saw the line, she stood Ari in it, gave him the two plates from her bundle and hurried away. A line after a disaster was always good. Someone who had not witnessed the catastrophe with their own shocked eyes had arrived and enforced order. Survivors would never have managed it – something as straight and civilized as a line would seldom enter their consciousness again.

At some point during the hours Ari patiently waited, Oscar de la Croix sauntered along the line and nudged people up onto the pavement so that the cars that were still running could ferry the injured to the mobile hospital. He had poked Ari with his truncheon and Ari had stepped up onto the pavement, meek, head hung. The deputy had not recognized him. Cleo came back an hour later, desperate that she could not find a doctor. Ari put her in the line in his place and went over to see Doc Saul's surgery for himself.

It was gone. The weight of its gargoyles had made it a challenge for the storm but the hurricane had focused on it, it seemed. The gruesome faces of the stone creatures lay smashed on the road. One of the walls had been crumbled to rubble and the examining table lay in the backyard, a bizarre silver climbing-frame for children. Several corpses from the Confederate Cemetery had been unearthed by the storm and had lain in the streets but those skeletons had been the first to be cleared away. The icehouse had acted as the morgue for a day and, after that, when the smell had become unendurable, the unidentified had been moved into a mass grave.

No figure of authority seemed interested in the mystery of Julian Oddman's death now. There was no train to carry them away either. Rumours were filtering through from the northern Keys that the carriages had been blown from their tracks and the storm had swallowed the whole system, bridges and all. 'Flagler's folly' was a joke for the sharks now, something the rays and the bass could shelter in. Hundreds of veterans had died where they'd been settled as squatters on Long Key. Key Largo had been the worst hit; Key West had been lucky. Ari found that hard to believe as he stood on the threshold of the surgery.

The sunny garden was doused in grey and Ari saw the giant incinerator kiln on its side. Its formerly trapped remains freed by wind and scattered over the shrubs.

'Doc's dead,' a passer-by called out to him. 'If

you need medicine you gotta line up at the hospital tent.'

Back at the food line, Ari saw that Cleo had found Lucian and Quozzie. The sailor was still smiling his black-toothed grin; the sharks' teeth still hung on the thong around his neck. Quozzie still smiled his naïve smile, too, unsuspecting of the truth that the world despised him.

'You son of a gun! You made it through,' Lucian greeted Ari. 'I got a story fit to tell my grand-kiddies 'cause of you.'

'The *Alexa Lee* made it?'

'Sure did. I had to tie her up on the windward quay. Most of them who sheltered early got it worst. Boats piled up on top of each other.'

Cleo took out a thick brick of money from her bundle.

'I need you to get Silas,' she said as she handed the whole lot over to Lucian.

'Sure and dandy! I ain't eaten in a day, though. We're near the front now. Can't we wait?'

Cleo handed him the rest of the bundle containing the tins of food. Lucian looked inside it and whistled low. There was tinned ham and beef and even caviar which looked like tiny, black grapes.

He threw the bundle over his shoulder and he and Cleo headed off together. Ari stayed in the line. She would be back; she had only left him for a while. In a few hours, once he had located his mother, he would find Cleo again and they would make a plan to get to New York. He had to find a way to get home now that the railroad was out of commission and the one plane he knew of completely destroyed.

A kindly woman came down the line asking questions, judging who had dysentery and who would need to take up a bed. Like Ari, these kindly women had come down south unprepared for the heat. One of them stood sweating over a steaming cauldron and slopped a spoonful of rice onto one of Ari's plates. She handed him a tin which had once held Heinz tomato soup but which was now half full of a clear, chicken-smelling liquid with yellow fat floating on the top and tendrils of egg white below the surface.

Ari took his food and went down Duval Street. Everyone was eating in solitude. Their eyes roved around fiercely, not wanting any of the other dogs in the pack to come near. Ari found his banyan tree once more. The very one under which he had opened Judas Jones's pouch and read about the petty preoccupations of his life. The tree had been here three hundred years and would survive three hundred more. It had weathered hurricanes unrecorded in human history books. Ari snuggled down into its roots like one of the desperate people who lived under bridges and ate from tins. He had no manners; he had become what both he and his mother had most feared and he felt, inside, just the same.

He waited for Cleo all afternoon and all evening. Eventually, he slept in the roots of the tree, cradled and warm under a kindly sky. She did not come.

The next morning, a gentle shake woke him. black and white face peered down at him – on of the nuns from the St Mary, Star of the Se.

Convent. Ari got to his feet. He was famished. He tried to take the sister's hand like a gentleman but he was trembling badly. She took him by the top of the arm instead and marched him along. She had been out for milk from Donkey Lane and the Catholic milkman had kept her usual order waiting for her. No government agency, no FERA man, no police officer would take the last of the island's milk from God's daughters. He had been adamant about that.

The new wing of the convent had survived. The old wing had merely been washed clean by the storm. It gleamed in the sun. The gardens were ravaged, however, and already the sisters and a few men whose places of work had been ruined, and all those who were still unemployed, were digging and replanting what could be saved and burning the rest in a fire. One man in a gas mask sprayed the standing water with mosquito poison. Ari watched him for a long while.

Sister Sarah led Ari into a pristine kitchen and poured him a glass of milk. Around them, nuns swirled in monochrome, baking bread from their prudent stores of flour, boiling vats of soup. Ari drank two sips of the milk and knew it was too rich for him. He would not waste the rest of it. He handed the glass back to Sister Sarah and went outside to vomit in a drain. Afterwards, she took him in to see his mother. Hella was white and beautiful beneath the coarse sheet; her skin as fine and unblemished as the cotton.

'Malaria, we think,' said the sister.

'We've only been here a few days,' said Ari.

'It can come on sudden, especially to visitors.'

Ari touched her forehead and she was feverish against his palm.

'She's been asking for you,' said the sister. 'She calls your name all the time.'

'Does she?'

'Yes, she says "Charles! Charles!" over and over again.'

'My name's Ari,' said Ari.

'Well, she's very sick. I'm sure it's you she wants,' said the sister.

Afterwards, he began to work with the men in the garden. Sister Sarah was too busy to notice him again. He worked planting queen palms. They harboured hidden drifts of sand that sifted down into his eyes when he least expected it. They had raw edges that stripped the skin from his fingertips, numbing them. It was hard, backbreaking work. He waited for Cleo. He left messages with all the Red Cross staff; he scribbled signs to tack up on emergency notice boards.

Later that afternoon, when he was working like an automaton – a juggernaut ploughing forward unaware of pain – he heard the buzz of propellers overhead. US army planes were flying over the island in flocks. They came in low and dropped boxes attached to white parachutes. Ari watched them land. On the other side of town, a child playing hopscotch would be killed when one landed on her, crushing her skull, but that was something he would only read about many years later. One precious parcel landed in their garden, half in a poisoned puddle, and they rescued from it spam and tuna fish and powdered milk and beef stock cubes.

Ari had not thought about his home in New York or how things were there for a long time. He thought about Cleo every moment. He would give her a few days to get Silas settled in at the hospital and organize temporary accommodation for him. In the meantime, he would fit in and help out. He would be the same as everyone else. That night he slept on the floor under his mother's bed. In the night, when her sweaty hand slipped over the side and dangled lost in mid-air, he reached out and held it.

The next day, Saturday it was by then, Ari was working shirtless in the garden – his shoes caked with mud, his sunburn shaped around his braces – when Sister Sarah came out to him.

'There's a man looking for you, Ari. He wanted to leave a note in case we found you but I told him you were here.'

He followed the sister inside. Ari tried to shake the man's hand but he pulled away and looked affronted by the state of the boy before him. Ari's hands were crusted with dried blood from where the palms had wounded him. He understood instantly that this man couldn't possibly have been here when the storm came through. He was a new arrival.

'The Gold brothers are very concerned. When the Red Cross contacted us to say you were here through the storm, they retained me immediately to see you safely home.'

'My mother is very sick.'

'The sisters tell me she's well enough to travel this afternoon. She'll be on quinine for a good while and malaria's not something that's ever really cured... The Golds had me bring a boat down. It's taken me two days to find you.'

The fact that the man's voice lacked any annoyance at this, told Ari how much he had been paid. 'We'll sail you up today; you can take a train from Miami that will get you home.'

'I need a few hours,' said Ari.

The man nodded.

'I'll see to Mrs Gold,' he said and he clicked his fingers at a passing nun to get her attention and handed her a roll of bills.

They agreed on a place to meet.

It came to Ari, after an hour of searching, that perhaps he had seen Cleo for the last time. When she had left him in the food line, he had caught her looking back, her face stretched with anxiety, as Lucian walked her away. She had made a slight, comic gesture of putting a hat on her head and Ari had immediately complied and donned his own battered hat. She had smiled. Would that be his last image of her? A makeshift bandage on her neck; her hair dulled by dirt?

She had become, in a week, the focus of his life. Most men rid themselves of their virginity as soon as possible and move on. Ari had given his to Cleo and he had taken something from her at the same time, though he had not been her first. It was a valuable event divided equally between them, and Cleo was the other half of it. Ari could never take it back and give it to another. For the remainder of his life, the moment of release would evoke her face.

He hunted desolately along the docks which were still haunted by the three-legged dog and the pale crabs.

At the appointed time, Ari boarded the *Dido*. It was crewed by three men and he became useless again. His hands rested in his lap and he sat in a corner – a rich and useless boy. He would never be at the heart of things again the way he had been in Key West. He would never again be an island cupped by a reef. His mother shivered and moaned in her stretcher at his feet. He watched for Cleo until his eyes weren't sure if they were actually seeing land or merely the bumps of waves on the horizon.

31

Key West, 1944

Sometimes, Cleo went whole days without thinking about Ari. When things were especially bad, she kept him locked away to be taken out on a better day that deserved him more. She never would have guessed that day would be the last time she would see him, that duty would prevent her having him once more for her eyes to enjoy. He was a remarkable young man, she thought. When she heard about acts of dashing bravery (which would come almost daily during the war to bolster them up) in her mind she always replaced the young man described with Ari.

374

In her memory of her last sight of him, he was standing in a line. He was holding two plates, one for her and one for himself. She knew they would never give him two servings without her being there but it seemed to reassure him that she would be back.

She was only going to settle Silas in at the hospital, hand over wedges of cash in all directions to assure he was attended to. She was going to stay with Silas until she saw the morphine take him down and leave his eyelids still.

After that, she was going back to Ari with her one brave question. '*Ari*,' she was going to say. '*How will it work?*' He would have a plan. He was a meticulous planner, she imagined. And he would get them away from the ravaged place, even though he looked like a man who had forgotten to close his eyes against the blast.

In the years and decades to come, she would associate him forever – as she looked back at him standing there – with victims of the war that was yet to come. He was filthy; his clothes were ruined. His blood and hers and Silas's had melted into the silk fibres of his shirt. The suit was a collage of the devastation on Long Dead Key. His shoes had no laces. He seemed glad of the fact that he had a plate to occupy each hand or they might have shaken uncontrollably. If he was in a line, he would be fine, she thought because a line moved inexorably forward; it did not allow for going back.

She followed Lucian to his boat and he took her out to her former home to retrieve Silas. They carried him between them to the *Alexa Lee* but not before Silas had directed Cleo to secret hiding places where gold and cash were hidden away. Some of the hidey-holes had been ripped open by the hurricane; the jewellery they had held now adorned some branch of a tree or spike of the reef. Silas was demented by pain. He rambled on incoherently until Cleo wanted to slap him and tell him to shut up. Halfway back, she began to cry and could not stop.

Lucian dropped both of them on the dock and sailed his boat away so he would no longer have to take responsibility for her. After half an hour of sobbing, nobody had come to help her. Cleo got up, shook Silas's clutching hand from hers, and went off to find a medic with a stretcher. Silas had lain there for two hours, the sun baking into his eyes and creating pus-filled blisters on his lips. Cleo, too, was burned and thirsty. At last, a harried-looking young medical student came with her and together they carried Silas on a stretcher back to the hospital tent.

Passing the food line, Cleo saw that Ari was gone. He had left her and she would have to search him out later. Just as soon as she knew that Silas would survive alone, she would tell him of her decision and leave. She was excited and terrified by turns. Amid the chaos, the carefree idea of walking away was a rock of hope.

It was six o'clock before the doctor agreed to see Silas. He was unconscious but they managed to revive him.

'Doc?' he asked.

Whenever he had been sick, it had been Dr Saul who had ministered to him.

'That doctor's dead, Si. This is another one,' Cleo told him.

Silas closed his eye. The doctor asked questions and Silas was alternately obstreperous and sarcastic. After the examination, the doctor turned to Cleo and said: 'Paralysis,' then he moved on to the next cot.

A nurse had heard the diagnosis and she put an arm on Cleo's shoulder.

'Your father can stay for the night then you'll have to move him. And you'll have to find a place to sleep. We can't have healthy folk taking up space in here, sugar.'

'I don't take up any space,' said Cleo.

She crouched near Silas's cot. If he would only wake and speak with her, she would be fine. He would tell her what to do.

'You're in the way,' the nurse said snidely as she passed by her again.

Cleo sat down and then lay down on the floor, squirming into the cramped space beneath the cot. She held onto Silas's dangling hand. She slept like that for a day and a half. Under Silas's sagging weight, she remained unseen.

The next day, Silas was given a shot of morphine and Cleo was handed several glass vials of the medicine and taught how to administer it. After that, they were told to leave. The nurses promised that Silas would be assigned a wheelchair from the next shipment to arrive – maybe in a week's time. The good FERA men and women of Savannah, Georgia were already weaving the seats for the chairs as they spoke.

Cleo bought a wheelbarrow for cash from a man who had stolen it from one of the mansion gardens. She wheeled Silas along in it, gaining only a few feet at a time. She had no idea where she was taking him.

On the corner of Duval Street, she saw a hand-lettered notice in a window: 'HOWSE 2 RENT – Furnicha.' Cleo went in and took it without an inspection. She paid the man two months' rent and he pointed out the luxury of a dust-laden bed in one corner.

Cleo went into the backyard. It was a concrete square and at the far end there was a water pump that must tap into the town's only natural underground spring. She made forty trips with a glass jug out to the pump. She boiled the water in a pot over a kerosene canister. She added that hot water to a battered steel tub. When the tub was three-quarters full, and lukewarm, she tried to lift Silas. For a short man, he was muscular and heavy. She got his bottom half out of the wheel-barrow then she threw his arms off her shoulders and he was in. Water sloshed out onto the kitchen floor. The morphine must have worn off by then but Silas never flinched. Cleo found a slither of soap under a cabinet in the kitchen. It was the unrefined, green soap used for dishes and wooden floors but she washed him thoroughly with it.

She wanted so badly to be in that bath herself, to sink down into it and go under. Tears kept coming unbidden. Tomorrow, she would have Lucian take her back to the house and she would gather sheets and duck-feather pillows and fresh clothes and perfume and food and they would make a home in these two rooms. She must send a telegram to Silas's lawyer in Miami and explain it all. The money would come; in fact, the lawyer himself would probably come and help her sort things out. They would rent a nicer place and rebuild the house.

Silas looked at her from his bath. She had scrubbed him all over. She had washed his hair as best she could and, when she ran her fingers through it and scooped it back, he looked like himself again. For the first time in days, Silas was back. He took his palm and covered his bad eye. Cleo knew he hated having it exposed but his patch was gone. She took the handkerchief from his jacket and tied it around his head so that a triangle flapped down and covered the milky retina. Silas smiled. He touched her face.

'I love you, girl,' he said.

'I know,' Cleo answered.

Then he said the one thing Cleo would never have believed he would say. She had promised herself that if he were to say it, she would give him what he asked. For being her saviour, though fallible, she owed him something yet she still could not believe he had asked it of her ... and so easily.

'Don't ever leave me,' he said.

He knew the immensity of what he was asking and he asked it anyway.

'Of course not!' Cleo said. Her voice was broken. 'Never. Don't worry about that.'

She struggled to get him out of the bath. She dragged the mattress off the bed and into the kitchen. She shook the dust and mildew from the sheet and rolled Silas up into it. She could not imagine how he must be feeling. He lay on his side. His good eye rolled with the surge of the morphine she had given him but he could still see her.

Cleo undressed in front of him and slipped into his dirty water. It was delicious. There was no Ogilvy Sisters soap, nor any powder or bath oil or scented salts but it was a cosy wood-walled room with a window that ought to look out onto cypresses tinselled with snow. It was a room in which she could imagine she was on a snowy slope in Sweden. She lay in the slightly warm water and Silas's eye watched her contentedly.

A thousand times during the days that followed, she had wanted to go out and look for Ari. She had fooled herself that she would find him only to ask him to help her move furniture and make space for the wheelchair when it arrived. Her message to Silas's lawyer had been entrusted to a man going home to Miami on a private boat. His reply on arrival would take a few days. It would be a week before she could leave Silas. Despite her promise, she would stay only that week and then she would get on the train or a boat and go up to New York. She would give Silas that week to begin his recovery, she would see him settled with his money and then she could go.

She would visit every two months and she would love them both. Thoughts like these kept her going that week – they got her through. The meticulous planning and the self-deception it involved, got her through. She lived with Silas in the house with the two rooms and the concrete garden for six months while they built another home.

Cleo stood on the edge of the sea. Their new house was on the beach in Key West – though it was not that new any more. They had moved there in early 1936 and she came down every evening to grab ten minutes for herself but she hardly ever swam any more.

This was Cleo's favourite time of day – cool and sun-blushed. Cleo always wore a white swimsuit – homage to memory – and she let the ocean tease her, the waves sip at her toes.

Suddenly, tearing across the perfect sky, a squadron of Mustangs screamed through the quiet dusk. She watched them barrelling along. She thought how planes had excited Ari. She watched the planes sweep away to the north and then bank east in the direction of the war. She imagined Ari at the throttle of one. Somehow she knew he would be a flyer. She often picked one bird from any given flock in the sky and gave it his name. Long after she had lost sight of it, she imagined it going and going. He had gone outward and upward. She knew that. She wanted to know that.

Several times, letters had made their way to her from New York. The first one had come to her care of Lucian at the charter boat key. It had been addressed to Cleo Taft. The second one, also addressed to Cleo Taft had come via Quozzie. Señor Bolivar from the Colonial Hotel had delivered the third. It was addressed to Cherry Morello. Cleo felt she knew what each of the letters would say. Their theme would be summed up in a single word: 'come'. She did not open them to receive that invitation; she could not bear it. She mailed them back to the address on the reverse of each envelope. She wrote the words 'RETURN TO SENDER' across the front in red pen. On the last letter, she altered the name Cherry Morello in the address to Violet Hayes before she returned it. He did not write again.

Cleo walked into the water, feeling it slip past her knees and up around her thighs. It calmed her. It felt all-enveloping. Cleo had always wanted to be consumed utterly. It was what she had never known as a child and what she wanted as an adult – she was twenty-five years old now and had pushed childish dreams aside.

She went down past the part of her body where the water felt coldest, across her ribcage and chest and over her heart. She sank down and the sea took her in. She tasted salt on her lips as she began to stroke her way out towards the far reef. Halfway, she stopped to tread water. Her legs were strong from lifting and moving Silas's weight when once they had been strong from swimming. She felt she could stay afloat for hours. That was what she was best at.

Her hair had been cropped short and she had allowed it to return to its natural brown. It still felt odd and unfinished above her shoulders but it seemed more mature and manageable cut that way. When it had been long, it had got in the way of her nursing; it had tangled under Silas's pillows when she leaned over him. The decision to cut it was somehow also an acknowledgement that she would never see Ari again.

Not a day passed without some measure of yearning. She hated him for not trying harder. She hated herself for not taking the chance. She longed for him. The sadness was enormous. Some days letting the chance pass was entirely his fault, some days all hers.

This was their piece of the ocean; this was where they had consummated some growing feeling between them that she had not acknowledged at the time.

There was a saying she had heard the West African sailors using on the street when one of them grew nostalgic about the continent they had lost: *You cannot step into the same river twice.* For the river you attempted to come back to, to relive, had passed by. That was the nature of rivers and life. They moved on inexorably, pulled towards the sea. They were not the same when you returned to them. Perhaps you were not the same but had been moved away from your former self by currents and time.

Cleo went under the waves. She let herself drift down until she was among the weeds and the swells of sand. She opened her eyes and saw things clearly; the way she would not have believed a person could see underwater. She saw the foothills of the reef to her right; to her left the gradual rise of the shelf leading back to the beach. There was no need for air. She just wanted to stay here caught between the reef and the world. If she could just open her mouth and breathe in the sea, in a very short while it would all be over.

She thought of Ari's mouth – his soft, unused lips. She thought of Silas's directing hand firm and safe in the small of her back. She thought of his one extraordinary eye that had charmed her throughout her life. Underwater, she smiled. If he'd had the power of both eyes, what might he have done to her? Her feet reached the bottom. The sea swayed around her.

She saw the reef.

She saw the world.

She bent her knees and pushed up with all her might, striking out towards the shore.

Inside their new house, Silas waited for her. He had recently celebrated his fiftieth birthday with much fanfare and was feeling more content and centred now than ever before. He had a wheelchair of handcrafted mahogany which he rolled along the second-storey passage of his house filled with beautiful things. There was an elevator to take him to the ground floor or up to the widow's walk. They had built the place in traditional style.

In a way, the hurricane had merely presented him with new challenges. He and Cleo had left Long Dead Key to live among the townsfolk of Key West. Nobody whispered any more as they had done in the old days. He was a man in a wheelchair with a devoted daughter. That was all there was to it. He had brought her into the public eye in fabulous dresses, dripping with jewels. The men had viewed her as a prize and they had believed that one day one of them might be deemed worthy enough to have her.

Silas knew better.

Once, years before, a singular boy had come close. A bit too close for Silas's comfort, he could admit that now. Cleo barely remembered the boy, though – Silas was sure of that – but he remembered him. He thought of him quite fondly in a way. He had been a worthy adversary, that skinny boy.

Silas pushed the wheelchair out onto the expansive veranda so he could seek Cleo out. She was never away from his sight for more than a few minutes. He looked down onto the beach. That was where she usually went at this time of night.

He saw her swimming in to shore. Her body slid through the water – a lithe, golden arrow that always came back to him.

32

England, October 4th, 1944

The letter telling Ari that his mother was going to marry Isaac Gold, Benjamin's brother who had been widowed the year before, did not surprise him. The man had nursed her through her successive bouts of malaria and they had grown 'quite fond' as she put it. He read her words on a hill overlooking the hangars at Bassingbourne where his division, the 8th United States Army Air Corp, was temporarily stationed. Nothing his mother did surprised Ari any more but neither did her actions hurt him as he had once allowed them to. She was who she was. He had decided to love her. He doubted the impending wedding would in any way deter her from pursuing Charles Lindbergh. The aviator was part of who she was and, because of his mother's adoration of the man, Ari himself had developed a love of flying. He was getting better at it, too. He was about to fly his seventh mission. Seven was a charmed number. Most pilots didn't make it past their second or third assignment. The German pilots were the best, fast and accurate, but the Englishmen were great morale builders. They were always telling the 'upstart Yanks' based with them that they had already mostly won the war before the Americans had shown up with their big mouths and their money and their Mustangs. They claimed to have Jerry running scared. It didn't feel that way, though; the bluff heartiness was only a facade for perpetual inner terror.

The roof above Ari's cot in his barracks leaked and the rain seeped in. The cold, like the insidious grey-green moss, grew on everything. It lived on his socks, in the roots of his teeth, on the back of his GI spoon which had been stamped out of a sheet of metal as thin as a flexible saw-blade.

Ari had flown, though. At first, there had been nothing but fear. Every inch of pressure he dared to give the stick seemed to hurtle him faster towards certain death but once he was up and going, it got easier. When he landed, Ari came in at a bad angle, threw the Mustang down onto the runway, skidded off the end into the mud and counted himself lucky. Then he would get down out of the cockpit, force down a cold breakfast and count those coming home on his tail – fewer and fewer of them with each passing day.

Ari was up. The runway streaked away beneath his wheels. He banked out over the sea. Like a flock of metal geese, the six planes of the 8th Squadron veered south, deep over the Atlantic. They were offering air support for a US convoy approaching Southampton, brimful of fuel and food and munitions. It was cold up there. Ice began to assume its invisible grip on the wings. Even the friction of wind speeding by was not enough to melt it. It clung like lily pollen to the skin.

Below, Ari saw shapes in the water and radioed them in. He received permission to break formation and do a little scouting. There were four long, dark vessels ploughing beneath the surface in tight formation. Ari's chest clenched. Initiating a low fly-by, he looked down quickly through his side window and saw one of the shapes break the surface and spray a plume of water into the air. Whales. Real whales. Ari laughed. It sounded hysterically high and uncontrolled inside his helmet.

Ari had been flying left wing but as he accelerated to rejoin his squadron above, he saw the Messerschmitts tilt towards them out of the sun in a formation of five. He heard the fire of their guns before he could even swivel in his seat and locate them again. The bullets made a squealing sound as they punctured the fuselage; some had penetrated the engine housing. An oil line had gone – grey-brown greasy fluid splattered the windscreen and white smoke billowed up from the exhausts where the oil had sizzled into fumes.

Ari saw his squadron scatter like a pyramid of marbles hit head-on by another. They flicked out in all directions, each one tagged by a Luftwaffe shadow. Ari watched them streak across the clouds, disappear and reappear. Nobody was on his tail. That was bad; the black cloud of smoke around his plane told them that he was finished; the enemy pilots would waste no more ammunition on him.

His engine sputtered. Inside it, the pistons were sticking and scraping. The clatter went on for a few more seconds then the engine seized. The prop stopped dead. Ari had an oil-streaked view of the distant dogfight – vapour trails intertwined like cigarette smoke rings that expanded and mingled. It was almost beautiful.

He was a glider now, the stick gave him some control and he dipped his nose to maintain air-speed. The engineless plane was quiet. He thought of the models that had swung and twirled across the ceiling of Kit Brown's room above Alice's garage in Key West.

In a dreadful rollercoaster tilt, he saw his wind-screen fill up with a grey landscape of sea. He careened towards it, pulling frantically on the control column, attempting to stay level, but it was useless. He might just be lucky enough to skim across the surface of the sea if he stayed calm and perhaps a passing boat would pick him up. They had all been told these miraculous rescue stories during training but the boat would have to be nearby and friendly – the sea was ice out here.

Ari tried to pull the cockpit shield back but his descent had been too rapid – the ice which had frozen his canopy shut hadn't had time to melt. The glass refused to budge. His chute might just pull him free from the wreckage but he would hit the ocean hard. Its surface was the colour of concrete and just as unforgiving. Ari's fingers were freezing in his gloves. He pulled frantically at the cockpit catch and tried to hold onto the stick at the same time but he was already too low for deployment.

He hit the sea. The Mustang bounced once, twice, and then the prop caught a wave and flew apart, shattering through the fabrication of the wings and nose-diving the Mustang down until its tail stuck up in the air like a crucifix set adrift at sea as a memorial for lost sailors.

Slowly, he began to go down. Ari had his oxygen on. He breathed great gulps as the cock-pit filled with water. The pant-leg of his flying suit held a flashlight and a knife. If the water melted the ice in time, he might be able to open the cockpit and swim free. He found the knife and tried to cut through his shoulder harness. He succeeded in slicing into his chest instead and blood puffed into the water like squid ink.

Ari's eyes blurred with the sting of seawater. He was going down and his head was close to exploding. He thought about Hella and all the times his mother had pulled him from the street up onto the pavement as a car whizzed past or snatched his toddling feet clear of the edge of a swimming pool. It was this very day she had been seeking to prevent and she had failed.

He was so cold. He felt each place where the water now reached his skin like a fresh burn. It was foreign water, filled with life he didn't recognize. The seaweed was skinny and mean and a vile orange colour that would spell danger on an insect or a snake.

Ari was very tired; sleep would be lovely. He would close his eyes for a few minutes and then, when he had rested for a while, he would wake up and tackle the harness again. His shoulder wound had frozen shut, cauterized by cold. His head was pounding, expanding into his helmet until the pressure was unbearable. The water was dark and it was the darkness of a night unpunctured by constellations.

Suddenly, the plane settled with a bump on the sea floor. Sand rose up around the fuselage. Ari looked through the windscreen. Rainbows drifted away from the wrecked engine into the more distant water. The oil held a thousand constituent colours.

It was warming up. Now that his eyes had grown used to the darkness, the sea had become luminous, light-split. It was the Gulf of Mexico. It grew brighter and greener-bluer. Ari watched through the windscreen as the seaweed and silt settled to the floor. It was so clean now and warm and just the way it had felt when he had slid into Cleo in this very sea. He must be close to where they had made love – near that stretch of water leading off from their beach.

If she was out swimming today – and she would

be, somehow Ari knew that – then she would find him.

Soon he would see her.

And there she was. She had taken a mighty breath and come down to him. Her arms pulled her through the water and she got closer and clearer. Her brown body in its white swimsuit was penguin-slick and it was a part of the current. The windscreen was somehow gone now and her arms reached right in to him, touched him with fingertips full of gentle knowledge.

She smiled; her long hair floated around her in a red halo. With no effort at all, she freed him from his harness. He slipped out of it. In an act of faith, Ari allowed her to loosen his oxygen mask and pull it from his face. He wanted so much to speak with her – they had years to catch up on – but they would have to wait for words. Ari smiled back at her and saltwater rushed into his mouth. He didn't gag, though. He breathed it in and it slipped down his throat as easily as air. Perhaps this had always been her unique ability: she could breathe the sea.

Cleo pulled him gently and Ari paused for just a second to look back at the cockpit. It really was a very small space he was leaving behind. He decided to follow her lovely shape. He kicked and felt the strength in his legs pushing him forward. He was a light in the water. She was a light in the water ahead of him.

Ari was so happy he felt his heart burst joyfully apart inside him. He kept pushing up and forward, up and forward – that was the secret and his mother had known it, Ari realized. To keep going up and forward and to follow something that sparkled just ahead of you in the water.

It was a long way to the surface. Below him was the reef; above him the surface of the sea which was speckled with a million glinting diamonds of sunlight.

Ahead, Cleo must have reached the top but she kept swimming up, into the air above the ocean. It could not have been sunlight on the surface he had focused on. It must be something further away, beyond water, beyond air. So, they were heading for the stars now, swimming in sky.

Afterword

On the porch of his house at the base of the Swiss Alps, Charles Lindbergh sat reading the latest scientific journal imported from the United States. The war had Europe in chaos and, as an American treasure, he was allowed to fly only unofficial missions for the United States government. He missed home. He thought about his childhood days in Minnesota and their house in Hopewell. The heavy shadows of the mountains daunted him; his son's death still haunted him. Soon, he and Anne would have to force themselves to return to the place where that tragedy had occurred but that time had not yet arrived...

Lindbergh's two spaniels, Socrates and Plato, loped into sight. It was late afternoon and they were searching for an easy meal; the dogs were fed up with the glossy pheasants that usually escaped them in the fields, leaving behind a foul-tasting mouthful of feathers.

Lindbergh whistled for them and Plato wagged his way over to his master. Socrates ignored the summons and went in through the kitchen door to Anne. It was growing chill and the blanket Lindbergh had wrapped around his legs to enable him to read outside was no longer keeping him sufficiently warm. He reached out and fussed the brown spaniel. The book, which he had closed on his lap, slithered to the floor unnoticed.

393

He looked down at Plato's face. The dog's grateful eyes gazed up at him, utterly devoted. Lindbergh did not understand this adoration he had not really earned. It made him distinctly uncomfortable.

Anne came to the back door and waved a letter at him.

'Another letter for you,' she called out. 'From that Swedish woman.'

'Throw it away,' said Lindbergh. 'I wrote a courtesy reply once and she hasn't stopped corresponding since.'

Anne stepped down from the porch and walked over to him. She pulled her cardigan closer round her breasts.

'Did you know she was living just down the road from us when we lost Po...' he told her.

They were speaking about the baby again. It had started to happen quite naturally a few years before and now it was not as painful as it had once been to remember him.

'...and when he was taken, my first thought was that it might have been her. She was one of those brittle, unbalanced women. She unnerved me.'

Anne leaned over and kissed him.

'Perhaps she was lonely,' she said. 'You have to make allowances. Some people are so unhappy.'

'I like your heart,' said Charles and he stroked Anne's cheek.

'It's getting cold out here,' she said. 'You should come in and stop brooding.'

'Throw the letter away,' said Charles again. 'I don't want to encourage her silliness.'

Anne went back inside. For some reason, Charles thought about the Swedish woman's son. That boy *had been quiet and appealing. He felt a little sorry for him, growing up with that crazy mother but the woman had been very beautiful, too, he remembered. Perhaps her son had known a side of her of which he was unaware.*

Lindbergh checked his watch. It was five minutes past three on the afternoon of October 4th, 1944. It was not a special day. Lindbergh searched back to the year they lost Po but could recall nothing remarkable that may have happened on this date in the past. It was just today – an unexceptional day that would pass by unnoticed by most. Yet Lindbergh was suffused with an intense feeling that he had forgotten something, that something of import was happening at that very moment and passing him by. He pulled Plato closer for comfort, snuggled against the animal's soft fur. Lindbergh was prone to melancholy at times and he tried to dismiss the mild anxiety he was feeling. He collected his things together and made his way towards the house.

Halfway to the sanctuary, he looked out over the fullness of sky and focused on a star which was no brighter or more exceptional than the others but to which his eyes had been drawn. He took a second to acknowledge its faint light as something beautiful. Then he went into his home where his wife was waiting for him and where he could smell his late lunch on the table. Charles Lindbergh looked back at the star and thought again that he had missed out on something, that he ought to feel something profoundly meaningful ... but still he did not.

This Large Print Book for the partially sighted, who cannot read normal print, is published under the auspices of

THE ULVERSCROFT FOUNDATION

P

Music History
from the Late Roman
through the Gothic
Periods, 313–1425

Music History from the Late Roman through the Gothic Periods, 313–1425

A DOCUMENTED CHRONOLOGY

Blanche Gangwere

Music Reference Collection, Number 6

Greenwood Press
Westport, Connecticut • London, England

Library of Congress Cataloging-in-Publication Data

Gangwere, Blanche.
  Music history from the late Roman through the Gothic
Periods, 313-1425.

  (Music reference collection, ISSN 0736-7740 ; no. 6)
  Discography: p.
  Bibliography: p.
  Includes indexes.
  1. Music—To 500—Chronology. 2. Music—500-1400—
Chronology. 3. Music—15th century—Chronology.
I. Title. II. Series.
ML162.G36 1986   780'.902   85-21934
ISBN 0-313-24764-1 (lib. bdg. : alk. paper)

Library of Congress Catalog Card Number: 85-21934
ISBN: 0-313-24764-1
ISSN: 0736-7740

First published in 1986

Greenwood Press
A division of Congressional Information Service, Inc.
88 Post Road West, Westport, Connecticut 06881

Printed in the United States of America

∞

The paper used in this book complies with the
Permanent Paper Standard issued by the National
Information Standards Organization (Z39.48-1984).

10 9 8 7 6 5 4 3 2 1

Contents

Maps

Preface

This annotated chronology of western music from 313-1425
is the first of a series of outlines covering the history of
music in western civilization. Additional volumes are planned
which will cover the music of the Renaissance, Baroque,
Classical, and Romantic periods, and the Twentieth Century.
The task of documenting the history and historiography of
western music in outline form was undertaken because of the
realization that, although there are many excellent books on
music history, no single source systematically presents
concise information on theory, notation, style, composers,
instruments, and terminology, incorporating findings from
primary sources and the results of subsequent scholarly
research. Researchers seeking accurate information at present
must consult a wide array of specialized books and
periodicals, not all of which may be familiar or readily
available. In addition, considerable background knowledge may
be needed to assess these materials.

In developing the outline for this book, an attempt was
made to consult all types of sources, to cover as many facets
of importance as possible, and to present the facts in an
organized manner. Thus a vast amount of data is digested for
ready access, and further information may be obtained from the
sources noted. As a convenience to researchers, it was
decided to document each line of the outline. Abbreviations
are used to refer to the sources, which are cited in the
bibliography following the main outline and appendices. If
the larger part of a section is from one source, the
abbreviations are placed after the appropriate heading, with
only those few lines that are from other sources having
separate abbreviations. The bibliography lists these
abbreviations alphabetically without regard to whether the
sources are books, periodical articles, or music; but the
nature of the material is made clear in the citation.
Discography is listed separately as no recordings have been
referred to as source materials in the text.

In order to help the reader use this outline to the best
advantage, many musical terms are either given a short

explanation or are followed by a reference to another page of
the outline where the term is explained in full.   Technical
terms, foreign words, foreign titles, and the names of the
vocal parts of the Mass are found in "Definition and
Pronunciation" in the back matter of the volume.   Also, at the
end of each musical period considered within the time frame of
the volume, there is a list of musical terms pertaining to
that particular period, with definitions.   Each time any of
these musical terms appears in the text of that period it is
preceded by an asterisk.   Those terms that have previously
been defined in another section are preceded by the sign +.
On the last few pages of the appendix titled "Greek Music"
there is a list of Greek terms and definitions.   These have
been included in order to assist the reader in understanding
the material included in the appendix.

The present volume contains material concerning the
background, philosophy, theory, notation, style, manuscript
sources, theoretical sources, classes or forms of music,
composers, and instruments of the Late Roman through the
Gothic periods.   At the end of each section there are maps
that show pertinent empires and kingdoms, and the areas of
musical development and activity of each historical period.
Appendices have been added in order to discuss notation and
rhythm in greater depth and to divulge some different theories
concerning the material found in the text.   Supplemental
sources for further study are found at the end of each
historical period.

The present volume begins with the Edict of Milan of A.D.
313, an edict that stated a policy of toleration toward all
religions, and ends in approximately 1425.   It seemed
appropriate to begin with the Edict of Milan because it was
this edict that made it possible for the Christian Church to
develop without fear of persecution.   Therefore, during the
following centuries the liturgy of the Roman Catholic Church
was developed and the music for the liturgy was compiled.   It
was the liturgical chant of the Roman Catholic Church that
furnished the basis for the liturgical music written during
the periods covered in this book.   It is always difficult to
decide when one period of music ends and another begins but by
1425 polyphony was well developed and notation had been
established, culminating with the Ars subtilissima (most
subtle art), which consisted of extremes in notational and
rhythmic complexities and was known as the manneristic style.
Therefore, by this time a good foundation had been laid upon
which future generations would build.

In doing the research for the period 313-1425, it became
apparent that English music of the thirteenth century excelled
in techniques and theory which were either unknown or
unaccepted on the continent.   For example, the English
acceptance of the intervals of the third and the sixth as
imperfect consonances may have made it possible for them to
compose with much less melisma and for more voices (as many as
six).   Also, their fondness for the rondellus technique may

have contributed to the first "migrant" cantus firmus and perhaps to the first polyphonic cantilenae (compositions with the melody in the top voice with two accompanying voices beneath). Therefore, while it is an accepted fact that the English composers of the thirteenth century were prone to retain certain forms of music long after they were outdated on the continent, they seemed to have developed techniques that eventually had a great effect on the music of continental composers.

It is appropriate at this time to recognize those who assisted me in the research and writing of this book. Eeva Oliver, Library Assistant at the Library of the University of Missouri-Kansas City and Carol Wallace, Music Librarian at the Kansas City, Missouri, Library were very helpful in the search for the many sources I needed. Dr. LeRoy Pogomiller, Professor of Music at the Conservatory of Music, University of Missouri-Kansas City and Dr. John Obetz, Assistant Professor of Organ at the same Conservatory and Auditorium Organist at the World Headquarters of the Reorganized Church of the Latter Day Saints in Independence, Missouri, took the time to read the manuscript and offer helpful suggestions. The art work was done by Mary Collier, a map illustrator who worked many long hours drawing the maps and figures needed to illustrate the places of interest and the different types of musical notation used in the Middle Ages. Some of the Latin words, both classical and ecclesiastical, were checked for accuracy of pronunciation and definition by Lowry Anderson, Jr., Latin instructor at Grandview High School, Grandview, Missouri. I wish to express my gratitude to all of these people for their time and assistance.

*Music History
from the Late Roman
through the Gothic
Periods, 313–1425*

The Late Roman Empire
and Carolingian Age

A. BACKGROUND

1. EDICT OF MILAN (313)   DurS III, 654-655
    a) Constantinus made Christianity the
        religion of the Imperial family
    b) Adopted a policy of toleration toward
        all religions

2. COUNCIL OF NICAEA (325)   DurS IV, 7
    a) Deliberated on the relation of Christ
        to God   EB N, 410
        (1) "Identical in nature"
    b) This proved to be a very controversial
        doctrine   EB N, 411
    c) This was not the council that produced
        the "Nicene" creed   LanE, 133

3. THE FOUNDING OF CONSTANTINOPLE (326-330) HamO, 280
    a) Founded by Constantinus on the site of
        Byzantium

4. FALL OF THE ROMAN EMPIRE (fifth century)
                                             DurS IV, 41
    a) The Papacy gained power and influence LanE, 136
    b) The Benedictine Monastery was founded

                                             LanE, 136

5. CHARLEMAGNE (ca. 742-814)   EB C, 100
    a) Fostered the use of Gregorian Chant   AngG, 100

B. PHILOSOPHY

1. GREEK PHILOSOPHY (Classical Greek Age)
    a) Pythagoras (ca. 531 B.C.)   HamO, 903
        (1) Represented the chief concordant
             intervals by simple numerical
             ratios   HamO, 705
             (a) The octave, 2:1; the fifth,

```
                         3:2; the fourth, 4:3
        b)   Plato (ca. 429-347 B.C.)                    HamO, 839
             (1)   Believed that music expressed the
                   meaning of the words and as such
                   was not always edifying              HenA, 385
                   (a)   Thought that the "low Lydian",
                         "high Lydian", and "Ionian"
                         harmoniae should be banished
                         from education
                         i)   These harmoniae may have
                              been similar to the "high
                              and low Ionian" of Pratinas
                              a - Primitive and popular
                                  style
        c)   Aristotle (384-322 B.C.)                    HamO, 114
             (1)   Doctrine of imitation                  GroH, 7
                   (a)   Music imitates the passions
                         or states of the soul
                         i)   Listening to music that
                              imitates a certain passion
                              produces said passion
        d)   For a discussion of the Greek musical
             system see appendix 1

   2.   LATIN PHILOSOPHY
        a)   Music is the servant of religion            GroH, 25
        b)   Boethius, Anicius Manlius Torquatus
             Severinus (ca. 480-524)                     BakB, 171
             (1)   Accomplished Hellenist                HamO, 171
             (2)   A Roman philosopher and a mathema-
                   tician                                BakB, 171
             (3)   He regarded music as a natural
                   result of arithmetic                  GroH, 23
                   (a)   It exemplifies in sounds the
                         fundamental principles of
                         order and harmony of the
                         universe
             (4)   Author of De institutione musica      BoeD, 79
                   (a)   Written more for students
                         aspiring to philosophy than
                         for a practicing musician       BowP, 17
                   (b)   He discusses three types of music
                                                         BoeD, 84
                         i)   Musica mundana ("cosmic"
                              music)
                         ii)  Musica humana
                         111) Musica instrumentalis
                   (c)   He believed music should be
                         divided into three areas        BoeD, 86
                         i)   Performer
                         ii)  Poet by natural instinct
                         iii) Theorist
                   (d)   He shows how tones of the three
                         genera, known as the diatonic,
                         chromatic, and enharmonic, may be
                         derived from the divisions
```

```
                of the monochord           ReeMMA, 134
                i)     He uses letters of the
                       Latin alphabet to rep-
                       resent relative posi-
                       tions and not absolute
                       pitches
            (e)  In a different part of the
                 treatise he uses the letters
                 A-P to represent a series
                                            ReeMMA, 135
                i)     The letter J is omitted
                                            PagE, 310
                ii)    He does not distinguish
                       between semitones and tones
                iii)   This may represent a
                       Greater Perfect System
                       descending
            (f)  For a further discussion of
                 letter notation as discussed by
                 Boethius see appendix 2
            (g)  Latin text                 BoeDI, 175
            (h)  English translation and
                 commentary                       BowP
```

C.   THEORISTS

```
    1.  NOTKER, BALBULUS (840-912)            SeaM, 50
        a)  Liber Hymnorum
            (1)  In the Preface of this work, Notker
                 discusses the practice of adding
                 words to the *jubilus of the Alleluia
                 (a)  He states that this procedure is
                      not new
```

D.   NOTATION

```
    1.  CHEIRONOMIC NOTATION (Ninth and tenth centuries)
                                            ApeHD, 572
        a)  Uses no staff
        b)  Uses a system of *Neumes         ColL, 38
            (1)  The word *neume is derived from the
                 Greek word neuma which means signal
            (2)  Uses Latin or Greek grammatical signs
                                            ParN, 4
            (a)  *Gravis  \
            (b)  *Acutus  /
            (3)  *Neumes were unique in the beginning
                 but became varied according to the
                 regions where they were used
            (4)  The *neumes were known by the
                 names of the monasteries where they
                 were developed, see also map no. 4
            (5)  The *neumes outlined melodic motion
                                            ApeHD, 572
```

         (6)   See also appendix 3

  2.   RHYTHM
      a) Modern views on chant rhythm   ReeMMA, 141
        (1)   Theories of the Accentualists
            (a)   Believe the syllables had
                equal time value
            (b)   Think the verbal accent was the
                principal rhythmic determinant
            (c)   This theory accepted by the
                Solesmes school   RayG, 3
                i)   Except for the theory
                     of verbal accent
        (2)   Theories of the Mensuralists
            (a)   Believe notes in early manuscripts
                indicate long and short   JeaE, 47
                i)   Believe there are two to
                     eight primary beats in a
                     group (measure)   BonM, 18

  3.   SIGNS FOUND IN ANCIENT MANUSCRIPTS   RasN, 23
      a) *Episema* (-)
        (1)   A line attached to a *neume
            (a)   Attached above a *neume (⌒)
            (b)   Added to part of a *neume (⊢,⊿)
        (2)   Indicates a lengthening of the *neume
      b) Romanian letters
        (1)   Used to indicate direction of pitch,
            duration, accent, and degree of
            tempo   RasN, 24-25
            (a)   See also appendix 3
        (2)   Invention attributed to Romanus
            of St. Gall (ca.789)
      c) Messine letters   RasN, 25
        (1)   Indicate pitch and tempo
        (2)   Derived from Romanian letters
            (a)   See also appendix 3

  4.   SQUARE NOTATION (PLAINCHANT)
      a) Evolved in the twelfth century in France
                                    ApeGC, 100
        (1)   Used in the present-day chant books
            in essentially the same form
      b) For a discussion of square notation as
        used in plainchant see appendix 4

E.   LATIN CHANT

  1.   AMBROSIAN CHANT
      a) Origins   AngL, 59-62
        (1)   Named after St. Ambrose of Milan
            (374-397)
            (a)   Actually the chant and its
                 liturgy were codified in
                 times later than St. Ambrose

        (2)   Derived from Syrian and Greek
             Christian rites
   b) Sources
      (1)   Codex Sacramentorum Bergomensis
            (tenth or eleventh century)   AngG, 62
        (a) Facsimiles   MocA, V
        (b) Transcriptions   MocA, VI
   c) Modern restoration   AngL, 63-64
      (1)   Dom Guerrino Amelli (1848-1933)
        (a) Directorium Chori (1883)
      (2)   Dom Gregory Suñol
        (a) Praeconium Paschale (1934)
        (b) Antiphonale Missarum (1935)
        (c) Canti Ambrosiani per il popolo
             (1936)
        (d) Liber Vesperalis (1939)
        (e) Officium et Missa pro Defunctis
             (1939)
        (f) Directorium Chori (unfinished)
        (g) Processionale (unfinished)
   d) Musical forms   AngL, 66-68
      (1)   Psalmody (*incipit, *reciting tone,
            and cadence)
        (a) Uses a variety of cadences
            i)   Used to connect the psalm
                 with the *antiphon
      (2)   Chants
        (a) *Antiphons
        (b) *Responds
        (c) *Tracts
      (3)   Hymns   ReeMMA, 104
        (a) "Song with praise of the Lord"
        (b) Four are generally accepted as
            authentic
            i)   Aeterne rerum Conditor   HopA, 5
            ii)   Deus Creator omnium
            iii) Iam surgit hora tertia
            iv)   Veni Redemptor gentium
        (c) Texts are written in iambic
            dimeters
        (d) Consist of eight four line
            stanzas
        (e) Nothing known definitely of the
            melodies
   e) Characteristics   AngL, 69-71
      (1)   Melodies reveal an archaic style
        (a) Show originality and simplicity
      (2)   The *mode is never indicated in
            the manuscripts
      (3)   Frequent use of the interval of the
            fourth, both ascending and
            descending

2. GALLICAN CHANT (400-800)
   a) "No single musical manuscript...has been
      preserved..."   AngL, 74

    b) There is some information available
       concerning the chants of the Mass   AngL, 75
       (1) Derived from sections of Gregorian
           chant where certain Mozarabic items
           have been inserted
           (a) _Improperia_ (Reproaches)   ReeMMA, 109
           (b) _Crux fidelis_   ReeMMA, 109
           (c) _Pange lingua...certaminis_   ReeMMA, 109
    c) There was a close connection between
       Gallican and Mozarabic chant   AngL, 75

3. MOZARABIC CHANT (400-1075)
    a) The term Mozarabic designates Chris-
       tians living under Moslem rule as
       Mozarabs   HopM, 36
       (1) A better term would be Hispanic
           chant
    b) Sources of chant   AngL, 83
       (1) Scriptoria of Toledo, San Milan
           de la Cogolla, Santo Domingo de
           Silos (eighth to eleventh century)
       (2) Antiphoner of Leon Cathedral (early
           tenth century)
    c) Notation of the chant   AngL, 84
       (1) Neumatic with Eastern and Byzantine
           elements
       (2) The Mozarabic melodies are still
           not translatable   AngL, 89
           (a) Twenty-one chants from the
               Hispanic chant have been found
               "transcribed" into a later,
               and legible notation   HopM, 37
    d) Catalog of Mozarabic chant sources   BroA, 26-66
    e) Facsimiles   BroA

4. GREGORIAN CHANT
    a) Perfection of Gregorian chant   AngG, 96
       (1) St. Gregory the Great (590-604)
       (2) _Antiphonarium cento_ (melodies)
    b) Diffusion and decay   AngG, 99-102
       (1) St. Augustine and his missionaries
           introduced the Roman liturgy and
           chant to England (596)
       (2) St. Boniface introduced plainsong to
           the Germans
       (3) Pepin (d. 768) had Roman chant taught
           to French cantors
       (4) Chant spread from England and Ireland
           to St. Gall
       (5) Charlemagne spread the Roman liturgy
           and chant in Gaul and Germany
       (6) Various reasons for the decay of the
           chant
           (a) Lack of understanding
           (b) "...Lack of education of the
               singers..."

(c) Lack of knowledge of the art of
the *neumes
(d) Rhythmic complications due to
the addition of tropes and
sequences, infra, p. 14
c) Modern restoration   AngG, 103-104
(1) Dom Guéranger at Solesmes
(2) Graduale Romanum (1907)
(3) Antiphonarium Diurnum (1912, 1919)
(4) Officium Majoris Hebdomadae (1922)
(5) Antiphonale Monasticum (1934)
d) Characteristics
(1) Two types of chant   UlrH, 27
(a) Accentus (recitative like
declamation)
i)   Used for reciting of
psalms, prayers,
Epistles, Gospels,
etc. of the Mass   ApeHD, 718
ii)   Uses a system of "psalm
tones" or formulas (melodies)
UlrH, 27
a -One for each church
mode
b - Also the "Tonus
peregrinus" (a wandering
tone which does not
conform to any of the
church *modes)
iii) Syllabic with a compass of
two to six tones
(b) Concentus (melodic)
i)   Antiphons, responsories,
hymns, Mass chants, etc.
ApeHD, 7
a - Syllabic
b - Neumatic (two to four
or more notes to one
syllable)   ApeHD, 356
c - Melismatic (ten to
twenty or more notes
sung to one syllable)
ApeHD, 356
(2) Use of Ecclesiastical *modes   HopM, 68-69
(a) A medieval system of classify-
ing the Gregorian chants
i)   Extracted from existing
plainchant
ii)   Dates from the eighth
or ninth century   AngG, 111
(b) A system of eight octave-
segments of the diatonic scale
ApeGC, 133
i)   Four authentic *modes
ReeMMA, 153
a - Octave-segments

                                    starting on D, E,
                                    F, and G (<u>finales</u>)
                    ii)   Four plagal *modes   ReeMMA, 153
                           a - Octave-segments
                             starting on A, B,
                             C, and D
                           b - The <u>finales</u> are the
                             same as those for the
                             authentic *modes   ApeHD, 165
            (c)   Each octave-segment (*mode)
                   has a secondary tonal center
                                    ApeGC, 135-136
                    i)   Commonly known as the
                          dominant
                          a - Should be called
                            tenor
                    ii)   Usually falls on the
                           fifth above the <u>finalis</u>
                           in the authentic *modes
                           and on the third above
                           the <u>finalis</u> in the plagal
                           *modes
                           a - If the tenor falls
                             on the note b it
                             is replaced with
                             the note c   ApeHD, 166
                           b - In the plagal mode
                             B-b the tenor falls
                             on the note a instead
                             of on the note G
                                    ApeHD, 166
            (d)   A tonal system which makes it
                   possible to select the proper
                   psalm tone for any given *antiphon,
                   supra, p. 9   HanG, 13
            (e)   See also appendix 5

            Fig. 1. The Ecclesiastical Modes

            Mode   Final   <u>Ambitus</u>   Tenor

            Authentic   D   D-d   a
            Plagel   D   A-a   F
            Authentic   E   E-e   c
            Plagel   E   B-b   a
            Authentic   F   F-f   c
            Plagel   F   C-c   a
            Authentic   G   G-g   d
            Plagel   G   D-d   c

    e)   Form   AngG, 113
          (1)   Psalmody (*<u>incipit</u>, *<u>tuba</u>, medial
                 cadence, *<u>tuba</u>, final cadence)
                 (a)   Five classes

                    i)   Psalmody of the Office
                    ii)   *Antiphonal Psalmody of
                          the Mass
                    iii) *Psalmody of the *invitatory
                          of Matins
                          a - <u>Venite exsultemus</u>
                    iv)   Greater *responds of Matins
                    v)   *Tracts
        f) Style   AngG, 113-119
            (1) *Liturgical recitative
                 (a) Words, phrases, or sentences
                      sung on the same note
            (2) *Antiphonal style (alternating
                 choruses)
                 (a) Dates from the fourth century
                      A.D.
                 (b) The psalmody is combined with
                      the *antiphon and sung in
                      alternating style
            (3) *Tract (psalm sung by soloist)
                 (a) "...Most ancient solo melody of
                      the Mass"
            (4) *Responsorial style (soloist and
                 choir or soloist and congregation)
                 (a) Form is ABA
                 (b) The practice dates from the
                      fifth century or earlier
                 (c) Always follows a lection
                      (lesson)

F.   <u>LITURGY OF THE ROMAN CATHOLIC CHURCH</u>

     1.   FEASTS
          a) Offices (Monastic services)   HopM, 92-93
              (1) Reached the present day form
                   about the sixth century
              (2) Consist of eight Canonical Hours
                   (a) The Hours are celebrated every
                        day at regularly stated times
                                                  GroH, 37
                        i)   Matins (after midnight)
                        ii)   Lauds (daybreak)
                        iii) Prime (6:00 A.M.)
                        iv)   Terce (9:00 A.M.)
                        v)   Sext (12:00 noon)
                        vi)   Nones (3:00 P.M.)
                        vii) Vespers (sunset)
                              a - Includes the *canticle,
                                  Magnificat   GroH, 37
                        viii) Compline (before retiring)
                              a - Concludes with one of
                                  the so-called Marian
                                  *Antiphons   HopM, 96
                              b - <u>Alma Redemptoris Mater</u>
                                                  HopA, 1

```
                    1 - Chants          LibU, 1080
          ii)   The Proper of the Saints
                a - Reserved for a special
                    occasion
                    1 - Chants          LibU, 1303
          iii)  Common of the Saints
                a - Used for a group of
                    saints
                    1 - Chants          LibU, 1111
(3)   Parts                                 GroH, 40
      (a)   *Synaxis (after the synaxis the
            catechumens, or non-baptized,
            were dismissed)                HopM, 121
            i)    Introit (psalm with
                  *antiphon )             HopM, 124
            ii)   Kyrie (choir)
                  a - Musical forms are AAA-
                      AAA-AAA, AAA-BBB-AAA,
                      AAA-BBB-CCC, and ABA-
                      CDC-EFE       HopM, 133-134
            iii)  Gloria (Priest intones
                  "Gloria in excelsis Deo"
                  and the choir answers
                  "Et in terra pax")
            iv)   Collects (prayers)
            v)    Epistle
            vi)   Gradual (soloist(s) and
                  responses by the choir)
                  a - Sung at the gradus
                                          HopM, 126
            vii)  Alleluia (soloist(s) and
                  responses by the choir)
            viii) Gospel
            ix)   Credo (Priest and then
                  choir)
            x)    Sermon
      (b)   Eucharist
            i)    Offertory (sung during the
                  preparation of the bread
                  and wine)
                  a - Antiphonal chant which
                      developed responsorial
                      form and style     HopM, 124
            ii)   Prayers and *Preface
            iii)  Sanctus (choir)
            iv)   Benedictus (choir)
            v)    Canon (prayer of conse-
                  cration)
            vi)   Lord's Prayer
            vii)  Agnus Dei (choir)  HopM, 140-141
                  a - Four musical forms
                          1 - AAA
                          2 - ABA
                          3 - AAB
                          4 - ABC
            viii) Communion (choir)
```

```
                          a - After bread and wine
                          b - Antiphonal        HopM, 125
                    ix)   Post-communion (sung
                          prayers)
                    x)    Ite missa est or Bene-
                          dicamus Domino (Priest
                          and choir)
             (4)   For a detailed discussion of the
                   music of the Mass see        HopM, 123-142
        c)   Special Mass                        GroH, 41
             (1)   Requiem Mass (Mass for the Dead)
                   (a)   The Proper of this Mass does
                         not vary
                   (b)   Chants for The Office for the
                         Dead                     LibU, 1772

   2.   MODERN LITURGICAL BOOKS                   GroH. 41
        a)   Antiphonale (Office chants with music)
        b)   Graduale (Mass chants with music)
        c)   Breviarium (Office texts)
        d)   Missale (Mass texts)
        e)   Liber Usualis (selected chants from the
             Antiphonale and Graduale)             LibU

   3.   ACCRETIONS TO THE LITURGY
        a)   Tropes and sequences
             (1)   Terminology                    HanT, 128
                   (a)   Trope
                         i)    Includes the term "se-
                               quence"
                         ii)   Used in a restricted
                               sense
                               a - Refers to the words
                                   and music added to
                                   liturgical chants
                                   other than the
                                   Alleluia
                   (b)   Sequence
                         i)    A subdivision of a trope
                         ii)   Used in a restricted sense
                               a - Refers to the words
                                   and music added to
                                   the Alleluia
                   (c)   For a further discussion, infra,
                         p. 32
             (2)   Origins                        HanT, 130
                   (a)   Until about 800, tropes and
                         sequences consisted of added
                         *melisma without words
                   (b)   Tropes and sequences are
                         found in all kinds of Latin
                         chant
             (3)   Adaptation of texts            HanT, 146-148
                   (a)   Texts which are related to
                         the liturgical chant were
                         added to the *melisma
```

       (b)   Texts are syllabic
           i)   Notker of St. Gall is
                  credited with introducing
                  the practice, supra, p. 5
       (c)   Texts gradually developed into
           long poems in free style (late
           ninth through tenth century)
                                    ApeHD, 764
           i)   The form is usually
                  a, bb, cc, dd...jj, k;
                  a - Poems begin and end
                    with a single line
           ii)   Contain four to ten or
                  more double line stanzas
                  a - They are identical in
                    the number and accentua-
                    tion of syllables with-
                    in a single stanza
                  b - The stanzas vary
                    from one another
          iii)   Absence of strict poetic
                  meter may suggest Byzantine
                  origin   ApeHD, 765
  (4)   Music   ApeHD, 765
       (a)   The melodies became separate
           from the chant
       (b)   The form of the music is the
           same as that of the text
       (c)   There are different ranges and
           tonal values in the various
           sections
       (d)   Extensive use of a rising cadence

G.   INSTRUMENTS

   1.   IDIOPHONES
       a)   Concussion and percussion   MarS, 3, 16
       b)   Shakers and friction   MarS, 80, 106
       c)   **Cymbalum**   MarMI, 137
          (1)   During the late Roman period the
                term "cymbalum" referred to concave
                metal plates with turned rims
          (2)   Sometime before 1000 the meaning was
                changed
              (a)   Set of tuned bells
              (b)   Struck on the outside with
                  hammers

   2.   MEMBRANOPHONES
       a)Drums   MarS, 118

   3.   CHORDOPHONES
       a)   Zithers (simple string bearer)   MarS, 177
          (1)   Psaltery   MarS, 209
          (2)   Monochord   MarS, 197

    b) Lyres
        (1) Strings attached to a yoke
             (a) On the same plane as the
                  resonator   MarS, 358
        (2) Kithara, see also appendix 1   MarS, 363
    c) Harp (strings run perpendicular to the
        resonator)   MarMI, 229-230
        (1) Diatonic
        (2) First evidence of the existence of
             the harp in Western Civilization
             was in the ninth century

4. AEROPHONES
    a) Aulos   MarS, 654
        (1) Single and double pipe reed
             instrument, see also appendix 1
    b) Panpipes (end blown flutes in sets)   MarS, 590
    c) Organ
        (1) A wind instrument with pipework,
             wind supply system, and action
                                               MarMI, 379
        (2) Hydraulos (third century B.C.)   MarS, 600
        (3) Bellows-blown (second century B.C.)
                                               MarS, 601
        (4) L-shaped keys (third century A.D.)
                                               MarS, 234
             (a) The short foot of the L was
                  pushed by the player
             (b) The key returned by means of
                  a spring
        (5) Compass of two octaves   MarS, 235
        (6) Not used for religious services   PerO, v
        (7) With the fall of the Roman Empire
             the organ ceased to exist in Western
             Civilization until the eighth
             century   PerO, 170
             (a) Emperor Constantine Copronymos
                  of Constantinople sent an organ
                  to Pepin in 757   PerO, 206-207
                  i)   For a description of
                       the organ see   PerO, 210
    d) Bagpipes   MarMI, 30
        (1) A reed instrument with an air
             reservoir
    e) Horns   MarMI, 244
        (1) These instruments were made from
             animal horn or tusks
    f) Trumpets   MarMI, 538
        (1) Lip-vibrated instruments made of
             straight bamboo or wood

H. TERMS

    1. ACUTUS. A *neume (/) indicating a raise of the
        voice   ApeHD, 572

2.   ANTIPHON. A short text taken from the
         Scriptures or elsewhere; syllabic style
         music sung before and after a psalm or
         *canticle   ApeHD, 41

3.   ANTIPHONAL PSALMODY. Alternation of verses
         of a psalm by two choirs   GroH, 44

4,   CANTICLE. A lyrical portion of the Bible which
         is similar to psalms and hymns: sung at
         specified times; comes from the Byzantine
         church (an example is the Magnificat)
                                                GroH, 14

5.   CANTUS PLANUS. Plainsong   UlrH, 27

6.   GRAVIS. A *neume (\) indicating the lowering of
         the voice   ApeHD, 572

7.   INCIPIT. An intonation; the first words
         of a liturgical text in Gregorian chant
                                                ApeHD, 405

8.   INVITATORY. The opening chant of Matins in
         the Roman Catholic rite: consists
         of Psalm 94, Venite, exsultemus Domino
         ("O come let us sing unto the Lord") ApeHD, 425

9   JUBILUS. *Melisma sung to the final vowel
         of the Alleluia   UlrH, 47

10. LITURGICAL RECITATIVE. In Gregorian chant, the
         speechlike singing of psalms, prayers,
         Epistles, Gospels, etc.   ApeHD, 718

11. MELISMA. An expressive vocal passage sung to
         one syllable: particularly applied to
         Gregorian chant   ApeHD, 516

12. MODES, ECCLESIASTICAL. A medieval system
         of eight scales, each with its own pattern
         of tones (t) and semitones (s), see also
         appendix 5   ApeHD, 165

13. NEUMES. Notational signs of the eighth through
         fourteenth centuries which were used for
         writing down plainsong, see also appendix 3
                                                ApeHD, 571

14. PREFACE. A solemn declaration of praise which
         begins with the words "Vere dignum et
         justum est"; along with the Sanctus, an
         introduction to the Canon of the Mass
                                                ApeHD, 692

15. RECITING TONE. The main note of the recitation

of a psalm in Gregorian chant: always on the
fifth degree of the *mode; also known as
tenor, <u>repercussio,</u> and <u>tuba</u>   ApeHD, 703

16.   RESPOND. Any textual addition or modification
      sung by the congregation before and after
      each verse of a psalm sung by a soloist
                                          ApeHD, 702

17.   RESPONSORIAL PSALMODY. Alternating recitation
      of the verses of a psalm by leader and
      congregation   GroH, 12

18.   SYNAXIS. A meeting for worship and particularly
      for celebrating the Lord's Supper   OxfD, 2111

19.   TRACT. <u>Cantus tractus</u>. Melody sung without
      interruption from beginning to end; psalm
      sung by a soloist   AngG, 119

20.   <u>TUBA</u>. The main note in the recitation of a
      psalm tone: always the fifth degree of a
      *mode   ApeHD, 703

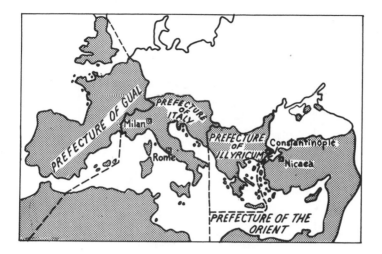

1. ROMAN EMPIRE (ca.A.D. 395)

Edict of Milan (A.D. 313)
Council of Nicaea (A.D. 325)
St. Ambrose: Bishop of Milan
    (A.D. 374-397)
(HamH, H-7)

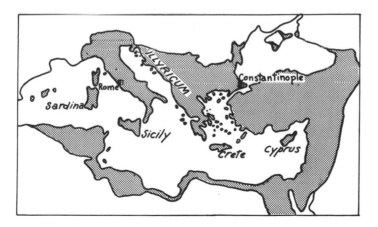

2. THE EASTERN ROMAN EMPIRE AT THE DEATH
   OF JUSTINIAN (A.D. 565)

St. Gregory the Great (ca.540-604)
    Pope from A.D. 540 to A.D. 604 (Rome)
(HamH, H-8)

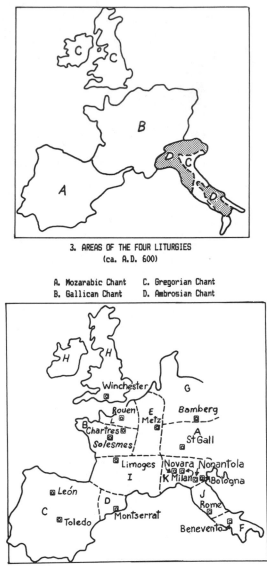

3. AREAS OF THE FOUR LITURGIES
(ca. A.D. 600)

A. Mozarabic Chant   C. Gregorian Chant
B. Gallican Chant   D. Ambrosian Chant

4. AREAS OF NEUMATIC NOTATION

A. St. Gallian (ninth century)   MocC, 11   G. German (tenth century)   KelC, 72
B. Chartrian (ca. 1000)   ApeGC, 121   H. Anglo Saxon (eleventh century)   ApeGC, 122
C. Visogothic or Mozarabic   I. Aquitanian (eleventh century)   ApeGC, 122
   (early tenth century)   BroA, 17   J. Central Italian (eleventh century)   ApeGC, 485
D. Catolonian   K. North Italian (twelfth century)   ApeGC, 266
E. Metzian (tenth century)   KelC, 77   L. French (Norman)
F. Beneventan (tenth century)   KelC, 79
   (ColH, 6)

Facsimiles of neumatic notation   MocP

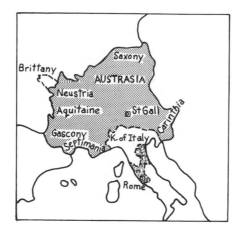

5. CAROLINGIAN KINGDOM AT THE DEATH OF CHARLEMAGNE
(A.D. 814)

Notker (Balbulus) of St. Gall (840-912)
Papal Lands
(HamH, H-9)

6. END OF CAROLINGIAN KINGDOM (A.D. 900)

Kingdoms:
   A. France
   B. Provence
   C. Burgundy
   D. Germany
   E. Italy
Hucbald of Tournai (ca. 840-930)

Supplemental Sources for the
Late Roman Empire
and Carolingian Age

BOOKS

Coussemaker, Edmond de. Histoire de l'harmonie au moyen
  âge [von] E. de Coussemaker. Paris: Reprografischer
  Nachdruck der Ausgabe, 1852; reprint ed.,
  Hildesheim: Georg Olms, 1966.

Crocker, Richard L. The Early Medieval Sequence.
  Berkley: University of California Press, [c.1977].

Farmer, Henry George. Historical Facts for the Arabian
  Musical Influence. London: Reeves, 1930; Hildesheim:
  Georg Olms, 1970.

Fellerer, Karl Gustave. The History of Catholic Church
  Music. Translated by Francis A. Brenner. Baltimore:
  Helicon Press, 1961.

Kinskey, Georg. A History of Music in Pictures. New
  York: Dutton, 1937.

Lang, Paul H., and Otto Bettmann. A Pictorial History of
  Music. New York: W. W. Norton and Co., Inc., 1960.

Mocquereau, André, Dom. Le Nombre musical Grégorien ou
  rhythmique Grégorienne. 2 vols. Rome: "n.p.", 1927.

Murray, Gregory. Gregorian Chant: According to the Manuscripts. London: L. J. Cary, [1963].

Randel, Don Michael. The Responsorial Psalm Tones for
  the Mozarabic Office. Princeton: Princeton
  University Press, 1969.

Sachs, Curt. The History of Musical Instruments. New
  York: W. W. Norton and Co., Inc., 1940

_____. Rhythm and Tempo: A Study in Music History.

New York: W. W. Norton and Co., Inc., [c.1953].

Schmidt-Görg, Joseph. *Principal Texts of the Gregorian Authors Concerning Rhythm Context*. Buffalo: Volks-freund Printing Co., "n.d.".

Smits van Waesberghe, Joseph. *Gregorian Chant and Its Place in the Catholic Liturgy*. Translated by W. A. G. Doyle-Davidson. Stockholm: Continental Book Co., 1947.

Suñol, Gregorio Maria, Dom. *Introduccio à la paléo-graphie musicale grégorienne*. Montserrat: Abadia de Montserrat, 1925; Paris: Société de Saint Jean l'Évangélists, Desclée et Cie., 1935.

_____. *Text Book of Gregorian Chant According to the Solesmes Method*. Tournai, Belgium: Société de Saint Jean l'Évangeliste, Desclée et Cie., 1930

Treitler, Leo. "On the Source of the Alleluia Melisma: A Western Tendency in Western Chant." In *Studies in Music History: Essays for Oliver Strunk*, pp. 59-72. Edited by Harold Powers. Princeton: Princeton University Press, 1968.

Wagner, Peter J. *Introduction to the Gregorian Melodies*. Translated by Agnes Orme and E. G. P. Wyatt, 2nd ed. London: Plainsong and Mediaeval Society, 1901.

Werner, Eric. *The Sacred Bridge*. London: "n.p.", 1959.

DICTIONARIES, INDICES, AND BIBLIOGRAPHIES

Bessaraboff, Nicholas. *Ancient European Musical Instruments*. Boston: "n.p.", 1941.

Bryden, John R., and David G. Hughes. *An Index of Gregorian Chant*. 2 vols. Cambridge, Mass.: Harvard University Press, 1969.

Coover, James B. "Music Theory in Translation: A bibliography." *Journal of Music Theory* 2 (1959): 70-95

De Angeles, Michael. *The Correct Pronunciation of Latin According to Roman Usage*. Edited by William Dawson Hill. [Anaheim, Cal.]: National Music Publishers, 1971.

Hughes, Andrew. *Medieval Music: The sixth liberal art*. Toronto: University of Toronto Press, 1974.

Hughes, Anselm, Dom. *Liturgical Terms for Music Students: A Dictionary*. Boston: Mclaughlin and

Reilly Co., [1951].

Kehrein, Joseph. Lateinisch Sequenzen des Mittelalters
    aus Handschriften und Drucken. Mainz: "n.p.", 1873;
    Hildesheim: Georg Olms, 1969.

Mearnes, James. Early Latin Hymnaries. Cambridge:
    "n.p.", 1913; Hildesheim: "n.p.", 1970.

Randel, Don M. An Index to the Chants of the Mozarabic
    Rite. Princeton: Princeton University Press, 1973.

ARTICLES IN PERIODICALS

Adkins, C. "The Technique of the Monochord." Acta
    Musicologica 39:1 (1967): 34-43.

Apel, Willi. "The Central Problem of Gregorian Chant."
    Journal of the American Musicological Society 9:2
    (1956): 118-127.

Avenary, H. "Formal Structure of Psalms and Canticles
    in Early Jewish and Christian Chant." Musica
    Disciplina 7 (1953): 1-13.

Bailey, Terence. "Accidental and Cursive Cadences in
    Gregorian Psalmody." Journal of the American
    Musicological Society 29:3 (1967): 463-471.

Bjork, David A. "The Kyrie Trope." Journal of the
    American Musicological Society 33:1 (1980):
    1-41.

Boe, John. "Old Beneventan Chant at Montecassino
    Benedictus." Acta Musicologica 55:1 (1983): 69-73.

_____. "A New Source for Old Beneventan Chant."
    The Santa Sophia Maundy in MS Ottoboni lat. 145."
    Acta Musicologica 52:2 (1980): 122-134.

Bonvin, Ludwig. "The 'Measure' in Gregorian Music."
    Musical Quarterly 15 (1929): 122-134.

Brockett, Clyde Waring. "Unpublished Antiphons and
    Antiphon Series Found in the Gradual of St. Yrieix."
    Musica Disciplina 26 (1972): 5-35.

Crocker, Richard L. "Pythagorean Mathematics and Music."
    Journal of Aesthetics and Art Criticism 22 (1963):
    189-198 and 325-335.

_____. "The Troping Hypothesis." Musical Quarterly
    52 (1966): 183-203.

_____. "Some Ninth Century Sequences." Journal of

the American Musicological Society 20:3 (1967):
367-402.

Cutter, Paul F. "The Question of the 'Old Roman' Chant:
a Reappraisal." Acta Musicologica 39:1 (1967): 2-20.

Evans, P. "Some Reflections on the Origin of the
Trope." Journal of the American Musicological
Society 14:2 (1961): 119-130.

Holman, Hans-Jörgen. "Melismatic Tropes in the Responsories for Matins." Journal of the American Musicological Society 16:1 (1963): 36-45

Homan, Frederic W. "Final and Internal Cadential
Patterns in Gregorian Chant." Journal of the American Musicological Society 17:1 (1964): 66-77.

MacLean, Charles. "The Principle of the Hydraulic
Organ." Sammebande der International Musik-
gesellschaft 1 (1905): 183.

McKinnon, James. "Musical Instruments in Medieval Psalm
Commentaries and Psalters." Journal of the American
Musicological Society 21:1 (1968): 3-20.

Prado, Germán. "Mozarabic Melodies." Speculum: A Journal of Medieval Studies 3 (1928): 218-254.

Schneider, W. C. "Percussion Instruments of the Middle
Ages." Percussionist 15:3 (1978): 106-117.

Steiner, Ruth. "Some Questions about the Gregorian
Offertories and Their Verses." Journal of the
American Musicological Society 19:2 (1966): 162-181.

Van Dijk, S. J. P. "Medieval Terminology and Methods of
Psalm Singing." Musica Disciplina 6 (1952): 7-26

Weakland, Rembert. "Beginning of Troping." Musical
Quarterly 44 (1958): 477-488.

MUSIC

Davison, Archibald, and Willi Apel, eds. Historical
Anthology of Music. Vol. 1: Oriental, Medieval and
Renaissance Music. Revised ed., Cambridge: Harvard
University Press, 1972.

Fellerer, Karl Gustav, gen. ed. Anthology of Music, 33
vols. Cologn: Arno Volk Verlag, [c.1960]. Vol. 18:
Gregorian Chant by Franz Tack.

Hamburg, Otto, comp. Music History in examples: From
antiquity to Johann Sebastian Bach. With the col-

laboration of Margaretha Land Wehr von Pragenan.
Translated by Susan Hellauer. Wilhelmshaven,
Locarno, Amsterdam: Heinrichshofen; New York: Peters,
1978.

Hoppin, Richard, ed. Anthology of Music. New York:
"n.p.", 1978.

Mocquereau, André, Dom, and Dom Joseph Gajard, gen. eds.
Paléographie musicale: les principaux manuscrits de
chant Grégorien, Ambrosien, Mozarabe, Galican:
publiés en facsimiles phototypiques. Ser. 1: 18
vols. "N.p.": Benedictins de Solesmes, 1889-1937,
1955-; reprint ed., Berne: Éditions Herbert Lang et
Cie Sa, 1968-.

Mocquereau, André, and Forger, Jacques, Dom, eds.
Paléographie musicale: les principaux manuscrits de
chant Grégorien, Amborsien, Mozarabe, Galican:
publiés en facsimiles phototypiques. Ser. 2:
Monumentale, vol. 1 and vol. 2. Berne: Éditions
Herbert Lang et Cie
Sa, 1968-1970.

Parrish, Carl, and John Ohl, comps. and eds. Master-
pieces of music before 1700: Anthology of Musical
Examples from Gregorian Chant to J. S. Bach. New
York: W. W. Norton and Co., Inc., [c.1951].

Schering, Arnold, ed. Geschichte der Musik in
Beispielen. Leipzig: Breitkopf and Härtel, 1931;
revised ed., Wiesbaden: Breitkopf and Härtel,
[c.1959].

Romanesque Period

A. <u>BACKGROUND</u>

    1.   FRANCE WAS DIVIDED INTO SEVEN MAIN PRINCIPALITIES
        (ca. 1000)
        a)   The seven Principalities were Aquitaine,
              Toulouse, Burgundy, Anjou, Champagne,
              Flanders, and Normandy   DurS IV, 480

    2.   FEUDALISM WAS THE WAY OF LIFE   DurS IV, 552

    3.   THE PAPACY LOST ITS POLITICAL POWER AND
        SPIRITUAL PRESTIGE (tenth century)   LanE, 230

    4.   THE ROMAN EMPIRE WAS REVIVED IN THE WEST   LanE, 176
        a)   Under Otto the Great (962)
        b)   For almost one hundred years the papacy
              was dominated by German Emperors and the
              Counts of Tusculum   LanE, 230

    5.   THE NORMANS UNDER WILLIAM THE CONQUEROR TOOK
        ENGLAND IN 1066   DurS IV, 495

    6.   THE FIRST AND SECOND CRUSADES: 1095-1099;
        1146-1148   DurS IV, 588, 594

    7.   CATHEDRAL AT CANTERBURY WAS BEGUN (1175)
                          LanE, 216

B. <u>PHILOSOPHY</u>

    1.   CHIVALRY   DurS IV, 575
        a)   Aristocratic honor and <u>noblesse obligé</u>
              of the knight
        b)   <u>Virtus</u> (manliness) restored to its Roman
              masculine sense after a thousand years of
              Christian emphasis on feminine virtues

    2.   MUCH DISCUSSION ON THE ORIGIN OF MUSIC   LanW, 86

        a)   Jubal, son of Cain, foremost contender

C.   THE BIRTH OF POLYPHONY (900-1000)

    1.   THEORISTS
        a)   Hucbald (Hugbaldus, Ubaldus, Uchubaldus)
            (ca. 840-930)   BakB, 745
            (1)   Flemish monk at St. Amand   WesN, 327
            (2)   Wrote De harmonica institutione,
                infra, p. 29
        b)   Odo de Clugny (tenth century)   BakB, 1178
            (1)   Canon and choir-singer at Tours
            (2)   Benedictine monk
            (3)   Abbot at Aurillac, Fleuri, and
                Clugny (from 927)
            (4)   May have supervised the writing of
                Enchiridion musices also known as
                Dialogus de musica, infra, p. 29

    2.   THEORETICAL TREATISES
        a)   Musica enchiriadis (ca. 900)   HugP, 278
            (1)   Discussion of musical organization
                (a)   Organum in fifths
                    i)   With the melody or vox
                        organalis on top
                (b)   Four part organum
                    i)   Vox principalis doubled
                        an octave below
                    ii) Vox organalis doubled an
                        octave above
                (c)   Organum in parallel fourths
                    i)   Using either the higher
                        or lower pair of fourths
                    ii) Recognizes the *tritone
                        but does not solve the
                        resulting problem
                (d)   "Free" organum
                    i)   Second voice may remain
                        stationary on the lowest
                        notes
            (2)   Discussion of notation (a type
                known today as Daseian notation),
                infra, p. 36   ReeF, 14
            (3)   A brief account of the contents   ReeF, 14
            (4)   English translation   AnoM
            (5)   Latin text   MusE, 194
        b)   Scholia enchiriadis (Anonymous)
            (1)   A commentary on the Musica
                enchiriadis   ReeF, 14
            (2)   Divided into three parts   ReeF, 14
                (a)   The elements of music
                (b)   More about *symphonies
                    i)   English translation   AnoS, 126
                (c)   Mathematical proportions
            (3)   Uses the letters A-G to denote

```
                    a scale                      PagE, 312
        (4)  Latin text                          HucI, 173
             (a)  See also appendix 14, no. 8
    c)  De harmonica institutione
        (1)  Written by Hucbald, supra, p. 28
        (2)  Some duplication of material found
             in earlier theoretical writings
                                                 ReeMMA, 125
        (3)  Contains the earliest unmistakable
             reference to harmonized music       HugP, 276
        (4)  Discusses a system of alphabetical
             notation                            HugP, 277
             (a)  Notes are named as ours are today
                  but the note a is of equivalent
                  pitch to our note c
        (5)  Defines consonance as ..."the
             calculated and concordant com-
             bination of two notes, which
             will only occur if two notes of
             different pitch are combined to
             form a musical unity..."            HugP, 277
        (6)  Partial summary in English             GrutH
        (7)  English translation                  BabH, 13
        (8)  Corrections and Emendations of
             the Latin text                       BabH, 45
        (9)  Latin Text                           HucD, 104
             (a)  See also appendix 14, no. 8
    d)  Enchiridion musices also known as
        Dialogus de musica (ca. 935)             OdoE, 103
        (1)  Odo de Clugny may have supervised
             the writing of this treatise
        (2)  The first source to give a complete
             series of notational letter names
             that correspond to our modern series
             (a)  Γ A B C D E F G a b c d e f g aa
                  i)   The gamma (Γ) is added
                       below the A to designate
                       G which corresponds to
                       the G on the first line
                       of the present day bass
                       staff
                  ii)  There is a distinction
                       made between b rotundum
                       and b quadratum
                       a - At only one point
                           of the gamut (b)
        (3)  English translation                 OdoE, 103
        (4)  Latin text                          OdoDM, 252
             (a)  See also appendix 14, no. 8

3.  MANUSCRIPT SOURCES OF SEQUENCES AND TROPES
                                                 HanT, 153
    a)  Paris, Bibl. Nat. lat. 1154
    b)  Munich clm. 14843
    c)  Vienna 1609
    d)  British Museum Add. 19768
```

D. THE SAINT MARTIAL PERIOD (1000-1150)
    (See also appendix 14, no. 1)

    1. THEORISTS
        a) Guido d'Arezzo   ReeF, 15
            (1) Also known as Guido Aretinus   BakB, 625
                 (a) Born ca. 990 and died 1050
            (2) Wrote treatises on musical notation
                 and vocal instruction   BakB, 624
            (3) Was educated at the Benedictine
                 abbey at Pomposa   BakB, 624
            (4) Wrote Micrologus de disciplina artis
                 musicae and Epistola...de ignoto cantu,
                 infra, p. 30
            (5) Wrote Prologus antiphonarii sui,
                 infra, p. 30   GuiP, 117
        b) Johannes (Johannes of Afflighem, John
            Cotton)   BakB, 324
            (1) No definite knowledge known as to
                 his exact identity   BabH, 87
                 (a) See also appendix 14, no. 2
            (2) Wrote De musica cum tonario (ca. 1100),
                 infra, p. 31   ReeF, 17

    2. THEORETICAL TREATISES
        a) Micrologus de disciplina artis musicae
            (1) Written by Guido d'Arezzo   ReeF, 15
            (2) Discusses organum at the fourth
                 rather than at the fifth
                 (a) "...No interval larger than a
                      fourth is permitted between
                      the vox principalis and the
                      vox organalis"
            (3) States that the use of free organum
                 is the general rule
            (4) Minor seconds are forbidden
            (5) Discusses cadences
                 (a) Oblique motion
                 (b) Contrary motion and voice crossing
            (6) English translation   BabH, 57
            (7) Latin text   GuiM
        b) Prologus antiphonarii sui
            (1) Written by Guido d'Arezzo (ca. 1025)
                                                      GuiP, 117
            (2) Discusses colored lines and the
                 four line staff
            (3) English translation   GuiP, 117
            (4) Latin text   GuiPA, 34
                 (See also appendix 14, no. 8
        c) Epistola...de ignoto cantu
            (1) Written by Guido d'Arezzo (ca. 1030)
                                                      GuiE, 121
            (2) Development of the ancient *hexachord
                 system begins in this treatise   ApeHD, 384
                 (a) Guido adds syllables to the
                      six tones C to a

```
                    i)      Ut, re, mi, fa, sol, and la
              (b)   He discusses the construction
                    of the intervals from G to e
                    and C to a
                    i)      In order to exceed the
                            compass of one *hexachord
                            two or more *hexachords
                            could be interlocked
                            a - This process was referred
                                to as mutation
              (c)   See also appendix 6
        (3)   Gives instruction on how to sing
              an unknown melody (*solmization)   GuiE, 123
              (a)   Uses the syllables ut, re, mi,
                    fa, sol, and la               ReeMMA, 150
              (b)   See also appendix 6
        (4)   Latin text                          GuiED, 43
              (a)   See also appendix 14, no. 8
        (5)   English translation                 GuiE, 121
  d)  De musica cum tonario
        (1)   Written by Johannes (ca. 1100)       ReeF, 17
              (a)   Also known as John Cotton and
                    Johannes of Afflighem          BakB, 324
        (2)   States that the crossing of voices
              is permitted in organum             ReeF, 17
        (3)   Contrary motion in the voice parts
              is preferred to parallel motion     ReeF, 17
        (4)   Latin text                            AflM
        (5)   English translation                 BabH, 101
  e)  Ad organum faciendum (Anonymous)
        (1)   Late eleventh or early twelfth
              century                             ReeF, 18
        (2)   Examples of organum with the vox
              organalis placed above the vox
              principalis
        (3)   The note b is flattened in the
              musical examples
              (a)   In earlier writing it was the
                    custom to avoid the *tritone by
                    keeping the lower voice stationary
        (4)   English translation                  HufA
        (5)   Latin text                           AofC, 229
              (a)   See also appendix 14, no. 7
        (6)   Original manuscript is in the Ambrosiana
              Library at Milan, MS 17              HugP, 285

3.  MANUSCRIPT SOURCES
  a)  Winchester Tropers (second half of the
      tenth century)                             PlaW I, 5
        (1)   Notation
              (a)   Anglo-Saxon                   PlaW I, 61
              (b)   Any attempt at reconstruction
                    of the +neumes is still
                    beyond the transcriber
                    (1977)                        PlaW I, 392
                    i)      A detailed comparison of the
```

                              textual and melodic variants
                              has helped to recover the
                              Winchester melodies for a
                              large number of the tropes
            (c)   Earliest known manuscript to
                  contain examples of *organ
                  tablature   PagE, 309
    (2)   The music of the Winchester Troper
                                                 HarM, 115-116
            (a)   More than one hundred and fifty
                  two-part settings
                  i)   ⁺Invitatory
                  ii)   ⁺Antiphons and ⁺responds
                          for the Offices
                  iii)   Troped Introits
                  iv)   Kyries and Glorias
                          a - With and without tropes
                  v)   Alleluias
                  vi)   Graduals
                  vii)   Sequences
                  viii)   ⁺Tracts
            (b)   Three stages of tropes   FreW, viii
                  i)   ⁺<u>Jubila</u> without words
                  ii)   Words added to ⁺<u>jubila</u>
                  iii)   New words and new music
            (c)   Two divisions of tropes for
                  the Mass   FreW, viii
                  i)   Tropes to the Ordinary
                          a - Kyrie, Gloria, Sanctus,
                              and Agnus Dei (the
                              greater Tropes)
                  ii)   Tropes to the Proper
                          a - Introit, Alleluia,
                              Offertory, and Communion
                              (the lesser Tropes)
                  iii)   The Alleluia tropes without
                          words and some of the
                          greater Tropes and lesser
                          Tropes without words have
                          been preserved   FreW, xi
    (3)   Terminology of the manuscript   FreW, ix-x
            (a)   <u>Sequentia</u> (sequence) is primarily
                  a musical term
                  i)   The term for the <u>jubilum</u>
                          at the end of the Alleluia
                  ii)   When Notker added words to
                          the sequence of the Alleluia
                          it became a trope as well as
                          a sequence
            (b)   Sequence-proses (lesser Tropes)
                  i)   "The term <u>prosa</u> was used in
                          France in the early Middle
                          Ages as a synonym for
                          sequence"   HarM, 67
                  ii)   In England these two terms
                          were usually kept distinct

                                             HarM, 67
                    a - A prose is in the
                        same form as a
                        sequence
                    b - Was sung at Vespers
                        on certain feasts
                        1 - At Matins on St.
                            Nicholas's day
                        2 - In processions
                                             HarM, 67
              iii) Some are clearly tropes
                                             HarM, 68
         (c) For another explanation of
              sequence and trope, supra,
              p. 14
    (4) The texts of the Winchester Troper
                                        FreW, 1-98
         (a) The texts of the tropes are
              preserved in two manuscripts
              i)   Cambridge, Corpus Christi
                    College MS 473   FreW, xxvii
                    a- The closing section
                        contains <u>organa</u>
              ii)   Oxford, Bodleian Lib.
                    MS 775   FreW, xxviii
                    a - Also contains some
                        monophonic music   HarM, 115
         (b) A synopsis of the contents of
              the two manuscripts   FreW, 60-84
    (5) Facsimiles
         (a) Early sequence melodies used
              at Winchester   FreW, Plates 1-17
         (b) Cambridge, Corpus Christi
              College MS 473   FreW, Plates 18-21
         (c) Cambridge, Corpus Christi
              College MS 473   WooE I, Plates 2-6
         (d) The Winchester Troper
                    NicE III, Plates 17, 18, and 22
         (e) The Winchester Sequentiary
                            NicE III, Plate 19
         (f) The Winchester Proser
              NicE III, Plates 20, 21, 23, 24, and 25
b) Codex Calixtinus of Santiago de Compostella
    (ca. 1150)   WagC
    (1) Uses *<u>diastematic</u> +neumes, infra,
         p. 36   ApeN, 201
    (2) Facsimiles   WagC
c) St. Martial Tropers (ca. 1150)   ApeN, 201
    (1) Uses *<u>diastematic</u> +neumes, infra
         p. 36
    (2) Manuscript sources
         (a) Paris, B.N. lat. 1139, 3719,
              3549
         (b) London, British Museum Add.
              MS 36881
    (3) Discussion and transcriptions   EvaE

4.   CLASSES OF MUSIC
      a)   Monophonic music
           (1)   Liturgical drama   SmoL, 175
                 (a)   General history
                       i)   First appeared between the
                             tenth and thirteenth
                             centuries
                             a - Most of the knowledge
                                 of the Classical stage
                                 had been lost
                       ii)   Derived form the brief
                             dialogue sung before
                             Easter Mass
                             a - Three sentences were
                                 placed before the
                                 Introit   SmoE, 1
                             b - They are known as the
                                 "Quem quaeritis" trope
                                                        SmoE, 2
                                 1 - See also appendix
                                     14, no. 3
                       iii) Music of the earlier
                             manuscripts are in the
                             style of Gregorian chant
                             a - The dramatic moments
                                 were sung by soloists
                                 in recitative style
                       iv)   Texts are usually in Latin
                             prose and verse
                       v)   Continued in various
                             countries into the sixteenth
                             century   SmoL, 177
                 (b)   Types of liturgical drama
                                                  SmoL, 177-219
                       i)   Easter Sepulcher drama
                             a - Moved from the beginning
                                 of the Easter Mass to
                                 the end of the Easter
                                 Matins   SmoE, 2
                             b - This allowed room for
                                 expansion and was the
                                 true beginning of
                                 liturgical drama   SmoE, 2
                                 1 - See also appendix
                                     14, no. 3
                             c - Dramas were always
                                 performed in a plain-
                                 song setting making
                                 them indeed music dramas
                                                        SmoE, 3
                       ii)   Peregrinus plays
                             a - Separate compositions
                             b - Tell of the journey to
                                 Emmaus
                             c - Tell of the appearance
                                 of Christ to the eleven

at Jerusalem
      d - Usually performed on
         Easter Monday evening
         at Vespers
  iii) Passion plays
      a - Extra-liturgical compo-
         sitions sung by mourners
         at the foot of the cross
  iv) Christmas plays
      a - Based on a dramatic
         trope
      b - Free dialogue and situa-
         tion
      c - Use of costumes and
         property
  v) Sundry religious plays
  vi) The Daniel plays
      a - Skilfully constructed
         dramas
      b - Probably performed at
         Matins

(2) Sequence with text   ApeHD, 765
  (a) Eleventh century
     i) Regular versification
     ii) Strict poetic meter
        (iambic, dactylic)
    iii) Sometimes actual rhyme
  (b) Twelfth century
     i) Versified hymns
     ii) Ten, twelve, or more
        stanzas
    iii) Musical treatment makes
        them sequences
      a - First half of each
         stanza has a new
         melody
      b - Second half of each
         stanza always has
         the same melody
      c - Uses *double versicle
         form: aa, bb, cc...jj

(3) Medieval song
  (a) <u>Chanson de geste</u>
     i) Liturgical type troubador
        and <u>trouvère</u> song ReeMMA, 203
     ii) Epic poem sung like a
        litany   ReeMMA, 203
      a - Lines are of equal
         length and are repeated
         over and over
    iii) The music is syllabic
                  ReeMMA, 203
     iv) Has an instrumental
        <u>cauda</u> at the end ReeMMA, 204
     v) Sung by <u>Jongleurs</u>   WesM, 222
      a - Itinerant musicians

                                                            LanW, 108
                    b - Entertainers who were
                        an outgrowth of public
                        theatrical performances
                        and other festivities
                        of antiquity   LanW, 109
                    c - Entertained at home,
                        at court, or at noisy
                        feasts of the citizen
                        class   LanW, 109
                    d - Acrobats and musicians
                                            LanW, 109
                    e - They were banned by
                        the church   LanW, 109
            (b)   English songs   ReeMMA, 241
                  i)   Narrative poems recited
                        by minstrels to the
                        accompaniment of the harp
                  ii)   English farse
                        a - Vernacular outgrowth
                            of the liturgy ReeMMA, 242
                        b - Tropes in the
                            vernacular added
                            to liturgical
                            tropes for those
                            who did not under-
                            stand Latin   ReeMMA, 192
        b)   Polyphonic music
             (1)   Organum   ReeMMA, 266-267
                   (a)   Note against note or "primitive"
                         style
                   (b)   Sustained note style
                         i)   Long notes in the tenor
                               and ⁺melisma in the
                               duplum
                         ii)   Note against note style
                               with the melismatic style
                               at the cadence only

    5.   NOTATION
          a)   Daseian notation   HugP, 278
               (1)   A clumsy system of notation
               (2)   Greek letters are cut up, reversed,
                     and placed upside-down
               (3)   Sometimes these signs are placed
                     at the beginning of a line to
                     indicate pitch   GruTH, 509
               (4)   See also appendix 7
          b)   *Diastematic notation
               (1)   "Heighted" ⁺neumes   ReeMMA, 138
                     (a)   ⁺Neumes which are placed
                           above and below an imaginary
                           horizontal line to indicate
                           the size of the interval
                     (b)   Elements of a ⁺neume are
                           detached from each other and

so placed as to indicate
the size of the intervals
ReeMMA, 138

c) The use of colored lines to indicate
pitch   HugMT, 290
(1) The use of a red line indicates
the pitch F
(2) Use of a yellow line indicates
the pitch c
d) The use of letters at the beginning of
lines   AngG, 109
(1) These letters are known as clefs
(f and c)
(2) This makes colored lines superfluous
e) The perfection of the foregoing into a
four line staff by Guido d'Arezzo   ReeMMA, 138

6. TROUBADORS AND TROUVERES   WesM, 225
a) From southern and northern France
respectively
b) Court poets and musicians
c) First and second periods
(1) End of the eleventh century and the
beginning of the twelfth century
ReeMMA, 211
(2) Notation and the performance of
the music
(a) Less than one-third of the
music is written in measured
notation   ReeMMA, 206
(b) Pitch, but not rhythm, is
indicated   ReeMMA, 206
i)   Modal rhythm may have
been applied to these
songs, infra, p. 48
ReeMMA, 207
ii) The rhythmic modes one
through three are the
most significant,
infra, p. 49   ReeMMA, 207
(c) All are ternary
(d) Used instruments for
accompaniment   WesM, 228
(3) Tonality of the music
(a) Use of church ⁺modes   WesM, 229
(b) Use of the major scale   WesM, 231
(c) Use of accidentals   WesM, 231
(4) Texts used with the music   WesM, 224
(a) Transformation of vulgar
Latin into a vernacular
i)   In the south of France
it was known as langue
d'oc
ii) In the north of France
it was known as langue
d'oïl

E. <u>INSTRUMENTS</u>

    1. CHORDOPHONES
        a) <u>Organistrum</u>   EssH, 99
            (1) Mechanical fiddle
            (2) Revolving wheels rubbed the strings
            (3) Also called Hurdy-gurdy
            (4) First mentioned by Odo de Clugny
                 in the tenth century   MarMI, 251
        b) Fiddle, <u>Vielle</u>, <u>Fiedel</u>   MarMI, 180
            (1) A medium sized bowed instrument of
                 Europe having a pegdisc
        c) <u>Rebec</u>   ReeMMA, 327
            (1) "...a lute shaped instrument played
                 with a bow"
                 (a) Three and five strings
        d) Dulcimer (introduced to Europe in the early
           twelfth century)   MarS, 223
            (1) A psaltery which was struck with
                 blade-shaped beaters or padded
                 sticks

    2. AEROPHONES
        a) Shawm   MarS, 682
            (1) A double-reed woodwind instrument
                 of conical shape and bore (introduced
                 into Europe in the twelfth century)
        b) Organ   ArnO, 2-3
            (1) Until the thirteenth century ranks
                 of pipes of the same type and quality
                 formed a large mixture
                 (a) There were no stops (means of
                     separating ranks of pipes)
            (2) Letters A-G were used to identify
                 keys (sliders) during the ninth
                 through twelfth centuries   ApeE, 209
            (3) During the thirteenth century keys
                 replaced slides
            (4) The organ was not officially
                 acknowledged by the church but was
                 tolerated   PerO, 219

F. <u>TERMS</u>

    1. <u>DIASTEMATIC</u> ⁺NEUMES. "...⁺Neumes that are
        written on a staff, either imagined or
        actually indicated by one, two, or
        finally four lines"   ApeHD, 573

    2. DOUBLE VERSICLE. A term loosely used for
        sub-divisions of long texts; two parallel
        lines   ApeHD, 899

    3. HEXACHORD. In medieval theory, a group of
        six tones that are always in a set

intervallic sequence, t-t-s-t-t (t=tone
and s=semitone). There were three
hexachords: <u>hexachordum naturale</u> beginning on c; <u>hexachordum durum</u> beginning
on g; and <u>hexachordum molle</u> beginning
on f (using b^b), see also appendix 6

                                    ApeHD, 383

4.   ORGAN TABLATURE. The various notational
       systems used to write early organ music
       (before 1600): consisted of a combination
       of notes, letters, and numbers placed
       on a staff. In Italy, France, and
       England, organ music was notated almost
       the same as today, except for minor
       variations. Only in Germany and Spain
       could keyboard notation be truly called
       "tablature"   ApeHD, 626, 829, 830

5.   SOLMIZATION. A general term for systems
       which designate the degrees of a scale
       by syllable instead of letters, see
       also appendix 6   ApeHD, 786

6.   SYMPHONY. (<u>SYMPHONIA</u>) In the Greek language
       the word means unison; during the Middle
       Ages the word meant consonance;
       the term was also applied to various
       instruments   ApeHD, 820

7.   TRITONE. An interval of an augmented fourth
       or a diminished fifth   ApeHD, 868

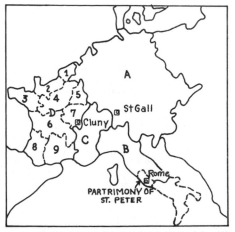

7. HOLY ROMAN EMPIRE UNDER OTTO THE GREAT (A.D. 1000)
   AND OTHER KINGDOMS OF THE SAME PERIOD

Holy Roman Empire:
   A. Kingdom of Germany
   B. Kingdom of Italy

Other Kingdoms of the Same Period:
   C. Kingdom of Burgundy
   D. Kingdom of France
      1. Co. of Flanders
      2. D. of Normandy
      3. Co. of Brittany
      4. D. of Francia (Anjou)
      5. Co. of Champagne
      6. D. of Aquitaine
      7. D. of Burgundy
      8. D. of Gascony
      9. Co. of Toulouse
(HamH, H-12)

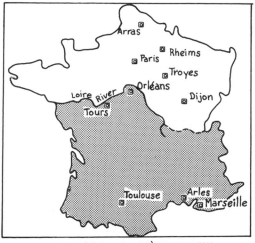

8. TROUBADORS AND TROUVÈRES (1100-1300)

A. Region of the Troubadors ☐   B. Region of the Trouvères ▨
                Troubadors and Trouvères
Adam de La Halle (Arras and Paris) Arnault Daniel de Riberac (Rheims)
Thibaut de Champagne (Troyes)   Pierre Vidal (Toulouse)
Hugues d'Orléans (Orléans)   Chretien de Troyes (Troyes)
(ColH, △)

9. EUROPE (ca. A.D. 1200)

A. The Holy Roman Empire ▨   St. Martial of Limoges
B. France   Guido d'Arezzo
C. English Possessions ▨   Johannes (Johannes of Afflighem
   (HamH, H-15)   or John Cotton)

Supplemental Sources for the Romanesque Period

BOOKS

Bailey, Terence, ed. The Fleury Play of Herod. Toronto:
Pontifical Institute of Mediaeval Studies, 1965.

Beck, Jean Baptiste. La musique des troubadors, par
Jean Beck, Paris: Renouard, 1928.

Beck, Jean Baptiste, et Madame Louise Beck, eds. Le
manuscrit du Roi. Corpus cantilenarum medii aevi:
première serié: Volume 2:2: Les chansonniers des
troubadors et trouvères. New York: Broude Brothers
Limited; University of Pennsylvania Press, [c.1938].

Briffault, Robert S. The Troubadors. Bloomington:
"n.p.", 1965.

Collins, Fletcher, Jr., trans. and ed. Medieval Church
Music-Dramas: A Repertory of Complete Plays.
Charlottesville: University Press of Virginia, 1976.

Crocker, Richard L. The Early Medieval Sequence.
Berkley: University of California Press, [c.1977].

Donovan, Richard B. Liturgical Drama in Medieval Spain.
Toronto: Pontifical Institute of Mediaeval Studies,
1958.

_____. "Two Celebrated Centers of Medieval Liturgical
Drama: Fleury and Ripoll." In The Medieval Drama
and Its Clandelian Revival. Edited by E. Catherine
Dunn, Tatiana Tolitch, and Bernard M. Peebles.
Washington: "n.p.", 1970.

Lang, Paul H., and Otto Bettmann. A Pictorial History
of Music. New York: W. W. Norton and Co., Inc.,
1960.

Luzarche, Victor, ed. Office de plaques ou de La

<u>Resurrection</u>. Tours: "n.p.", 1856.

Kinskey, Georg. <u>A History of Music in Pictures</u>. New
    York: Dutton, 1937.

Sachs, Curt. <u>The History of Musical Instruments</u>. New
    York: W. W. Norton and Co., Inc., 1940.

_____. <u>Rhythm and Tempo: A Study in Music History</u>.
    New York: W. W. Norton and Co., Inc., [c.1953].

Werf, Hendrik van der. <u>The chansons of the troubadors
    and trouvères</u>. Utrecht: Oosthoek's Uitgevers-
    maatschappij NV, 1972.

CATALOGUES, INDICES, AND BIBLIOGRAPHIES

Bessaraboff, Nicholas. <u>Ancient European Musical Instru-
    ments</u>. Boston: "n.p.", 1941.

Coover, James B. "Music theory in translation: A
    bibliography." <u>Journal of music theory</u> 2 (1959):
    70-95.

Fischer, Pieter, ed. <u>The Theory of Music from the
    Carolingian Era up to 1400. Vol. 2: Italy</u>.
    Répertoire international des sources musicales
    [International Inventory of Musical Sources],
    vol. B3:2. München-Duisburg: G. Henle Verlag,
    [c.1968].

Frank, István, comp. <u>Répertoire metrique de la poésie
    des troubadors</u>. 2 vols. Paris: "n.p.", 1953,
    1957.

Hughes, Andrew. <u>Medieval Music: The sixth liberal
    art</u>. Toronto: University of Totonto Press,
    1974.

Kehrein, Joseph, comp. <u>Lateinische Sequenzen des
    Mittelalters Handschriften und Drucken</u>. Mainz:
    "n.p.", 1873; reprint ed., Hildesheim: Georg Olms,
    1969

Reaney, Gilbert, ed. <u>Manuscripts of Polyphonic Music:
    Eleventh through Early Fourteenth Century: Volume
    I</u>. Répertoire international des sources musicales
    [International Inventory of Musical Sources], vol.
    B4:1. Müchen-Duisburg: G. Henle Verlag, [c.1968].

Smits van Waesberghe, Joseph. <u>The Theory of Music from
    the Carolingian Era up to 1400: Volume I</u>. Répertoire
    international des sources musicales [International
    Inventory of Musical Sources], vol. B3:1. München-
    Duisburg: G. Henle Verlag, [c.1961].

ARTICLES IN PERIODICALS

Avenary-Loewenstein, H.   "The Mixture Principle in the
    Medieval Organ."   Musica Disciplina 4 (1950):
    51-57.

_____.   "The Northern and Southern Idioms of Early
    European Music: A New Approach to an Old Problem."
    Acta Musicologica 49:1 (1977): 27-48.

Brockett, Clyde W.   "The Role of the Antiphon in Tenth-
    Century Liturgical Drama."   Musica Disciplina 34
    (1980): 5-29.

Crocker, Richard L.   "The Repertory of Proses at Saint
    Martial de Limoges in the Tenth Century."   Journal of
    the American Musicological Society 11 (1958):
    149-164.

Fox-Strangways, Arthur Henry.   "A Tenth Century Manual."
    Music and Letters 13 (1932): 183-193.

Fuller, Sarah.   "Theoretical Foundations of Early Organum
    Theory."   Acta Musicologica 53 (1981): 52-84.

Russell, Tilden A.   "A Poetic Key to a Pre-Guidonian
    Palm and the Echemata."   Journal of the American
    Musicological Society 34:1 (Spring, 1981): 109-
    119.

Smits van Waesberghe, Joseph.   "Guido of Arezzo and
    Musical Improvisation."   Musica Disciplina 5 (1951):
    55-63.

_____.   "The Music Notation of Guido of Arezzo."
    Musica Disciplina 5 (1951): 15-53.

Spiess, Lincoln B.   "Discant, Descant, Diaphony and
    Organum: A Problem in Definitions."   Journal of
    the American Musicological Society 8:2 (1955):
    144-147.

_____.   "The Diatonic 'Chromaticism' of the
    Enchiriadis Treatises."   Journal of the American
    Musicological Society 12:1 (1959): 1-6.

Treitler, Leo.   "The Early History of Music Writing in
    the West."   Journal of the American Musicological
    Society 35:2 (1982): 237-280.

Weakland, Rembert.   "Hucbald as musician and theorist."
    Musical Quarterly 42 (1956): 66-84.

Wright, L. M.   "Misconceptions concerning the troubadors,
    trouveres and minstrels."   Music and Letters 48
    (1967): 33-39.

MUSIC

Coussemaker, Edmund de. Drames liturgiques du moyen
     âge. Rennes: "n.p.", 1860; reprint ed., New York:
     "n.p.", 1964.

Davison, Archibald, and Willi Apel, eds. Historical
     Anthology of Music. Vol. 1: Oriental, Medieval and
     Renaissance Music. Revised ed., Cambridge: Harvard
     University Press, 1972.

Fellerer, Karl Gustave, gen. ed. Anthology of Music, 33
     vols. Cologne: Arno Volk Verlag, [c.1960]. Vol.
     9: Medieval Polyphony by Heinrich Husmann.

_____, gen. ed. Anthology of Music, 33 vols.
     Cologne: Arno Volk Verlag, [c.1960]. Vol. 2:
     Troubadors, trouvères: Minnesang and Meistergesang
     by Friedrich Gennrich. Translated by Rodney G.
     Dennis.

Greenberg, Noah, ed., and Rembert Weakland, transc. The
     Play of Daniel: A Thirteenth-century Music Drama.
     New York: Oxford University Press, 1959.

Hamburg, Otto, comp. Music history in examples: From
     antiquity to Johann Sebastian Bach. With the
     collaboration of Margaretha Landwehr von Pragenan.
     Translated by Susan Hellaner. Wilhelmshaven,
     Locarno, Amsterdam: Heinrichshofen; New York:
     Peters, 1978

Hill, Raymond Thompson, and Thomas Goddard Bergin.
     Anthology of the Provençal Troubadors, 2 vols. 2nd
     ed. New Haven: Yale University Press, 1973.

Maillard, Jean, and Jacques Chailley, eds. Anthology de
     chants de trouvères. Paris: "n.p.", 1967.

Parrish, Carl, and John Ohl, comps. and eds. Master-
     pieces of Music before 1750: Anthology of Music
     Examples from Gregorian Chant to J. S. Bach. New
     York: W. W. Norton and Co., Inc., [c.1951].

Schering, Arnold, ed. Geschichte der Musik in
     Beispielen. Leipzig: Breitkopf and Härtel, 1931.

Smoldon, William L, ed. Peregrinus, a 12th-century
     Easter Music-Drama; Planctus Mariae, a 14th-century
     Passiontide Music-Drama; Visitatio sepulchri (12c).
     London: "n.p.", "n.d.".

Taylor, Ronald J., ed. The Art of the Minnesinger. 2
     vols. Cardiff: "n.p.", 1968.

Wilkins, Nigel E., ed. Adam de La Hale: Lyric Works.

Corpus mensurabilis musicae, ser. 44. Rome:
American Institute of Musicology, 1947.

Wolf, Johannes, ed. Music of earlier times: Vocal a
instrumental examples. New York: Broude Brother.
[1955].

Early Gothic Period

A.   <u>NOTRE DAME PERIOD: FIXED RHYTHM</u> (1150-1250)

1.   BACKGROUND
     a)   The third and fourth crusades
                                         DurS IV, 598, 602
     b)   Period of Louis VI and VII   DurS IV, 688, 689
     c)   Paris established as a capitol   DurS IV, 688
          (1) New Notre Dame Cathedral started
               in 1163   DurS IV, 877
          (2) University of Paris recognized as
               outstanding by 1173   DurS IV, 920

2.   PHILOSOPHY
     a)   The dialectic process is still in the
          forefront   EB P
          (1) Particularly used for religious
               and moral problems
     b)   Metaphysical interest in the separation
          of "humanity" or "divinity" from
          particulars such as "men" or "God"
     c)   "...Church council at Paris... forbade
          the reading of Aristotle's 'metaphysics
          and natural philosophy'..."   DurS IV, 954

3.   THEORISTS
     a)   Anonymous IV
          (1) Wrote <u>De mensuris et discantu</u>
               (ca. 1270)   ReeF, 20
          (2) A discussion of Leoninus and Perotinus,
               infra, p. 61
          (3) A discussion of <u>Magnus liber organi</u>
               which is attributed to Leoninus,
               infra, p. 61
          (4) A discussion of the notation of *modes
               in *ligatures, infra, p. 50
          (5) A discussion of the principle of
               consonance, infra, p. 48   ApeS, 152
          (6) English translation   Ano IV
          (7) Latin text   AnoD, 327-365

(a)   See also appendix 14, no. 6

4.   THEORY
  a)   The rule of consonance   ApeS, 152
      (1)   In *ligatures a note is long if it
           is consonant and short if dissonant
          (a)   The penultimate note before a
               rest is always long
      (2)   Each first note is long
          (a)   If the first note is dissonant
               the tenor comes in later
      (3)   "Each final note is long and consonant"
      (4)   Two successive notes of the same pitch
           form a longa forata
          (a)   This is true whether the notes
               are consonant or not
      (5)   Currentes are preceded by a long
           note, infra, p. 51
  b)   Rhythmic *modes   UltM, 7
      (1)   The rhythmic *modes are "...the
           orderly measuring of time in long
           and short [notes];..."   WaiR, 13
          (a)   "...a succession of notes of
               differing values arranged in
               a definite pattern"   WaiR, 14
      (2)   Always in ternary meter   ApeHD, 535
          (a)   The shortest three-beat unit
               is called a "perfection"
                         ReeMMA, 277
      (3)   There are two different values
           for the longa   UltM, 7
          (a)   Originally the two-beat longa
               was known as a longa recta
               ("normal long") and the three-
               beat longa was known as ultra
               mensuram ("beyond measurement")
                         ReeMMA, 277
          (b)   Once the three-beat unit was
               called a "perfection" the
               three-beat longa was called
               longa perfecta and the two-
               beat longa was called a longa
               imperfecta   ReeMMA, 277
      (4)   There are two different values
           for the breve   ReeMMA, 278
          (a)   The one-beat breve is known
               as brevis recta
          (b)   The two-beat longa found in
               *modes three and four is
               known as a brevis altera
               i)   It is considered to
                    be a brevis
               ii)   It is altered from
                    one tempus to two
                    tempora
      (5)   Those *modes with "normal"

values are grouped as <u>modi recti</u>
ReeMMA, 278

(a)   The other modes were originally
      known as <u>modi ultra mensuram</u>
      and later as <u>modi obliqui</u>

(6)   Based on compound figures known as
      *ligatures   ReeMMA, 278
      (a)   *Ligatures were said to be
            ascending or descending
      (b)   The *ligature was said to be
            <u>cum proprietate</u> or <u>sine
            proprietate</u> depending on the
            form of the first note of the
            *ligature
            i)   See also appendix 9
      (c)   The *ligature was also known
            as <u>cum perfectione</u> or <u>sine
            perfectione</u> depending on the
            form of the last note of the
            *ligature
            i)   See also appendix 9

(7)   There are six patterns (*modes) ApeHD, 535
      (a)   They were given the names of
            the feet of ancient Greek
            poetry by Walter Odington
            (ca. 1290), infra, p. 67   ApeHD, 535
      (b)   This does not imply that the
            *modes are derived from ancient
            Greek poetic meter

Fig. 1. Ternary Patterns of the Rhythmic *Modes

No.	Greek Name	Poetic Meter	Ternary Pattern			Perfections
*1.	Trochaic	— ∪	ρ ρ			One perfection
*2.	Iambic	∪ —	ρ ρ			One perfection
+3.	Dactylic	— ∪ ∪	ρ·	x	ρ ρ	Two perfections
+4.	Anapaestic	∪ ∪ —	x ρ ρ	ρ·		Two perfections
+5.	Spondaic	— — —	ρ·	ρ·	ρ·	Three perfections
*6.	Tribrachic	∪ ∪ ∪	ρ ρ ρ			One perfection

*<u>modi recti</u> (correct mode); +<u>modi ultra mensuram</u> (modes beyond [poetic]
measure); x <u>Brevis altera</u> (UltM, 7; ReeMMA, 277-278; RasN, 38)

(8)   The choice of the *modes by the
      composers   ApeHD, 536
      (a)   The fourth *mode is seldom used
      (b)   The first, second and sixth
            *modes are used in the upper
            parts
            i)   Sometimes the third *mode
                    is used
      (c)   The third and the fifth *modes
            are used in the lower part
(9)   The <u>ordo</u> (<u>ordinis</u>)

(a) The repetition of a *mode is
     known as an <u>ordo</u>   ApeN, 222
     i)   The length of a musical
          phrase   ReeMMA, 275
     ii) The number of times a
          pattern is repeated
          before a rest   ReeMMA, 275
(b) See also appendix 9

5. NOTATION
    a) *Square notation   ApeN, 217
        (1) Introduced toward the end of the
             twelfth century
             (a) Derived from French ⁺neumes
                                             RasN, 32
             (b) Resulted from scribes using
                  Gothic script   RasN, 35
        (2) The name refers only to the external
             form   DitD, 8
             (a) It has no musical significance
        (3) Uses two systems of notes
             (a) Single notes
             (b)) *Ligatures
        (4) See also appendix 8
    b) Notation of the rhythmic *modes   HugFR, 323
        (1) Uses square notation for single
             notes and *ligatures   RasN, 37
        (2) The rhythmic *modes are indicated
             by different patterns of *ligatures
             (a) These *ligatures may have one
                  (1), two (2), three (3), or
                  four (4) notes   RasN, 39
                  i)   The pattern of Mode I is
                       3-2-2-2
                  ii) The pattern of Mode II is
                       2-2-2-3
                  iii) The pattern of Mode III is
                       1-3-3-3
                  iv) The pattern of Mode IV is
                       3-3-3-1
                  v)   The pattern of Mode V is
                       1-1-1-1 or 3¦3¦3
                       a - The vertical line
                           between the three-
                           note ligatures
                           indicates a rest
                  vi) The pattern of Mode VI is
                       4-4-4-4
             (b) Sometimes the regular patterns
                  are modified   RasN, 42
                  i)   A single note may be
                       broken into two or three
                       notes   ReeMMA, 281
                  ii) A <u>plica</u> ("fold") may be
                       inserted
                       a - "...The equivalent

                              of a liquescent
                              ⁺neume..."
                          b - A single note with a
                              tail on either side
                              1 - The tails ascend for
                                  an ascending note
                                  and descend for a
                                  descending note
                              2 - For an ascending note
                                  a single tail may be
                                  used for both single
                                  notes and *ligatures
                          c - Indicates that the
                              second note should be
                              sung lightly
                    iii) There may be repeated notes
                                              ReeMMA, 281
                          a - They are not used in a
                              ligature
                          b - They start a new
                              ligature or stand by
                              themselves
                    iv)   A conjunctura (currentes)
                          may be inserted   ReeMMA, 281
                          a - A series of rhombic
                              puncta descending in
                              scale formation   RasN, 45
                              1 - Follow a single note
                                  or a *ligature
                              2 - The puncta share the
                                  value of the previous
                                  note
                              3 - Longer values come
                                  last
           (c) See also appendix 9
     (3) The type of the *ligature is determined
          by the first and last notes of the
          *ligature   ReeMMA, 278
          (a) The first note of the *ligature
               may be cum proprietate, sine
               proprietate, or opposita
               proprietate
               i)   Indicated by the deletion
                     or addition of a tail
                     and the direction and
                     placement of the tail
          (b) The last note of the ligature
               may be cum perfectione or sine
               perfectione
               i)   Indicated by the placement
                     of the last note and also
                     by its form
          (c) See also appendix 9
     (4) There are imperfect and perfect
          modes   ReeMMA, 280
          (a) Only the perfect modes were

                              used for practical purposes
                          i)   The imperfect modes were
                                discussed by the theorists
                                but were not used by com-
                                posers
                     (b) See also appendix 9
       c) Syllabic (<u>conductus</u> style) notation   ApeN, 258
           (1) Has one continuous staff
                (a) Words are used to divide the
                     lines of the staff
                (b) This is known as *score
                     arrangement   ApeHD, 759
                (c) See also appendix 10
           (2) Each line of poetry is indicated on the
                staff by small vertical lines   GroH, 82
           (3) Has single notes in *modal rhythm
                                                  ApeN, 264
           (4) Has <u>binariae</u> and <u>ternariae</u> *ligatures
                                                  ApeN, 260
                (a) Use of the fifth *mode   ApeN, 266
           (5) Uses the <u>plica</u>, supra, p. 50   ApeN, 220
                (a) See also appendix 9
       d) Free rhythm notation (<u>organum duplum</u>),
           infra, p. 55   ApeN, 267
           (1) The rhythm of <u>organum duplum</u> represents
                a system somewhere between the free
                rhythm of plainsong and the strict
                rhythm of the rhythmic *modes
           (2) The rhythm is partly determined by
                the use of the principle of consonance
                                                  ApeS, 153
                (a) Rules concerning consonances and
                     dissonances and their relation to
                     rhythm in <u>organum duplum</u>, supra,
                     p. 48   ApeS, 152
                     i)   The laws of consonance
                           are not absolute, rather
                           they are general considera-
                           tions to be kept in mind
                           when evaluating the rhythmic
                           meaning of certain notes in
                           <u>organum duplum</u>   WaiR, 121
           (3) The rhythm is also partly determined
                by the use of the principle of
                *ligatures   ApeN, 271
                (a) The set patterns of *ligatures
                     which indicate the different
                     *modes, supra, p. 50   HugFR, 323
                (b) See also appendix 9
       e) Motet notation   ApeN, 272
           (1) "...No notational differentiation
                between the <u>longa</u> and the <u>brevis</u>"
                (a) Only one note exists for the
                     single note
           (2) The tenor of the motet is in strict
                *modal notation   ApeHD, 541

(3) The rhythm of the upper parts has
     to be accommodated to the *modal
     rhythm of the tenor
(4) This notation became necessary with
     the transition from melismatic
     notation to syllabic notation in
     the parts with text   ApeN, 271
(5) Parts are notated separately on
     one or two pages of a book   ApeHD, 759
     (a) This practice became necessary
          with the development of the
          motet
     (b) Known as part-arrangement   ApeN, xx
     (c) See also appendix 10
     (d) This practice lasted into the
          the sixteenth century
                                           ApeN, xx
f) Pre-Franconian notation (1225-1260)   ApeN, 282
    (1) The number of notational signs
         increases
         (a) Introduction of a smaller note
              value known as the semibrevis
              (♦)
              i)   It never occurs as an
                   isolated note   ApeN, 295
              ii) Two or three can be used
                   in the place of the brevis
                                           ApeHD, 579
    (2) Notational signs become less
         ambiguous   HugMAF, 380
         (a) Definite signs are used for a
              long note (⌐ , the virga of
              plainsong notation) and a
              short note (▪ , the punctum
              of plainsong notation)
    (3) All of the rhythmic *modes are used
         equally

6. STYLE
    a) Organum duplum style (also known as
        "melismatic style")   UlrH, 61
        (1) Long notes in the tenor
        (2) Many notes in the duplum
             (a) From a few notes to long
                  melismas   ApeHD, 627
    b) Discant style (also known as "note against
        note" style and "conductus style") UlrH, 61
        (1) Non-melismatic
             (a) One or only a few notes against
                  each note of the cantus-firmus
        (2) Used in clausulae, motets and
             conductus, infra, pp. 55-56   ApeHD, 236
    c) *Copula
        (1) According to Garlandia, infra, p. 66,
             "copula is midway between organum
             purum and discantus"   ApeHD, 205

        (2)   A variety of <u>discantus</u>   WaiR, 115
            (a) Must have two measured voices
        (3)   A device for dividing individual
               values of the *modal pattern into
               lesser values   WaiR, 116
            (a) Quicker note values are used
                  in the <u>copula</u> (<u>fractio modi</u>)
                                          ApeHD, 205
        (4)   It is possible that the term refers
               to the short passages that occur
               at the end of an <u>organum</u> section,
               connecting it to the next section
                                          ApeHD, 205
        (5)   Examples of *<u>copula</u>   WaiR, 117

7.   MANUSCRIPT SOURCES
    a) Wolfenbuttel I and II Ducal Lib. 677 and
        1206
        (1)   Transcriptions of 677   WaiR
            (a) <u>Magnus liber organi de gradali</u>
                 <u>et antiphonario</u> of Leoninus
        (2)   Transcriptions of 1206   AndL II
            (a) Translation of texts   AndL I
        (3)   Facsimile of 677   BaxA
        (4)   Index to the facsimile edition of 677
                                          HugI
        (5)   Facsimile of 1206   DitW
            (a) Both manuscripts contain music
                 from the <u>Magnus liber organi</u>
                 of Leoninus, infra, p. 61   CheM
    b) Florence, Bibl. Laur., plut. xxix, 1
        (1)   Facsimile   DitF
            (a) This manuscript contains music
                 from the <u>Magnus liber organi</u> of
                 Leoninus, infra, p. 61   CheM
    c) Paris Bibl. Nat. lat. 15139
        (1)   Facsimile   ThuM
    d) Madrid Bibl. Nac. 20486
        (1)   Facsimile   DitM
    e) Montpellier, Bibl. Universitaire, H. 196
        (1)   Facsimiles   RokP I
        (2)   Transcriptions   RokP, II, III
        (3)   Commentary   RokP IV
        (4)   See also appendix 14, No. 4
    f) Bamberg, Ed. IV 6
        (1)   Facsimiles   AubB, I
        (2)   Transcriptions   AubB, II
        (3)   Studies and Commentaries   AubB, III
    g) Roman de Fauvel (Paris, Bibl. Nat., fr. 146)
        (1)   Music ranging over more than a century
                up to 1316   CalM, 156
        (2)   A satirical poem on the vices   CalM, 156
        (3)   Facsimile   AubR
        (4)   Transcriptions   SchR
    h) <u>Carmina burana</u>, infra, p. 57
        (1)   Facsimile   BisC

```
        i)  Le Chansonnier Cange
            (1)  Facsimiles                          BecJ I:1
            (2)  Transcriptions                       BecJ I:2
        j)  Le Chansonnier de L'Arsenal
            (1)  Facsimiles and transcriptions            AubC

8.   CLASSES OF MUSIC
     a)  Polyphonic music
         (1)  Conductus                              ReeMMA, 307
              (a)  As many as four parts
              (b)  All parts move in more or less
                   uniform rhythm
              (c)  Latin text shared by all parts
                   i)   Normally metrical
              (d)  Forms
                   i)   Cum *cauda
                        a - Melismatic sections at
                            the beginnings and ends
                            of lines of stanzas or
                            over the penultimate
                            syllable
                   ii)  Sine *cauda
                        a - Without a *cauda
                   iii) English gymel              BukG, 78
                        a - Duplicity of harmony
                            and predilection for
                            consecutive thirds and
                            for the crossing of
                            the parts
                        b - Dated as early as the
                            end of the twelfth
                            century
                        c - Found with conductus
                        d - Written in two parts
                                                   EasH, 90
         (2)  Organum duplum                        HugFR, 343
              (a)  Consists of a slow moving
                   tenor with free melisma in
                   the duplum
                   i)   In the twelfth century this
                        type of organum was known as
                        melismatic organum and also
                        as *discant                 ApeHD, 236
                        a - By the thirteenth
                            century the term *discant
                            referred to non-melis-
                            matic music
                   ii)  The tenor is plainsong
                        and was either played
                        or sung
                        a - During this period the
                            plainsong was restricted
                            mainly to Graduals,
                            Alleluias, resposories,
                            and the "Benedicamus
                            Domino"                  ApeHD, 628
```

                                    1 - Only the solo
                                        sections were used
                                        for polyphonic
                                        development
                        iii)   Each time a note changes
                                in the tenor the notes
                                of the duplum co-ordinate
                                with it
                (b)   Gradually some sections gained
                        discernible rhythmic patterns in
                        the duplum   HugFR, 345
                        i)   These sections are called
                                clausulae or puncti   HugFR, 346
                (c)   A third voice (triplum) was added
                        making it necessary to use *modal
                        rhythm throughout   HugFR, 346
        (3)   Clausulae
                (a)   The sections of organum known as
                        clausulae gradually became
                        separate compositions   HugFR, 348
                        i)   Words were added to the
                                upper part in order to
                                help the singer learn
                                the music
                                a - Added texts are in
                                    Latin in the clausulae
                                    for the church
                                b - Words are French,
                                    Anglo-Norman, and
                                    Norman-French for
                                    the popular clausulae
                        ii)   These compositions are
                                the forerunner of the
                                motet
                                a - With the addition of
                                    words ("mots") to the
                                    duplum that part became
                                    known as the motetus
                                                    ApeHD, 541
        (4)   Motet
                (a)   Developed as a result of the
                        addition of words to the duplum
                        of the clausulae   ApeHD, 541
                (b)   Each voice has a definite
                        character   HugMAF, 353
                        i)   The tenor has long notes,
                                the motetus shorter ones,
                                and the triplum still
                                shorter ones
                        ii)   The tenor is formed
                                into ordines   HugMAF, 354
                                a - The uninterrupted
                                    repetition of a
                                    pattern (ordo)
                                b - See also appendix 9
                (c)   Texts

             i)   The tenor uses a Latin
                      liturgical text   HugMAF, 354
             ii)   The texts of the upper
                      parts are paraphrases
                      of the tenor *incipit* ApeHD, 542
                  a - These texts are not
                      always identical
                                  HugMAF, 354
                  b - Use Latin or French
                  c - Some texts are multi-
                      lingual   HugMAF, 355
   (5)   **Cantilenae**   ReeMMA, 322
      (a) Polyphonic settings of monophonic
           pieces
           i)   Dance songs with refrains
                 a - *Rondeaux*, *ballades*,
                     and *virelais*, infra,
                     p. 58
      (b) Borrowed melody is not always
           in the lowest part
           i)   Sometimes the melody is
                 in the middle voice
      (c) All voices have the same text
 b) Monophonic music
   (1)   Latin songs
      (a) Songs of the Goliards   GroH, 64
           i)   Sung by students in minor
                 ecclesiastical orders who
                 migrated from one university
                 to another
           ii)   Songs with Latin texts
                 about wine, women, and
                 satire
                 a - Popular in the eleventh
                     and twelfth centuries
                              ApeHD, 349
          iii)   The music is in staffless
                 ⁺neumes   ApeHD, 349
                 a - Written by the Goliards
                 b - Cannot be deciphered
                    1 - Some of the music
                        can be read with
                        the assistance of
                        other sources
                    2 - Facsimiles   BisC
          iv)   The Latin verse is found
                 in *Carmina burana*   ReeMMA, 200
                 a - Published in 1847
                 b - Latin verse   BisC
      (b) **Conductus**   ReeMMA, 201
           i)   Eleventh to the thirteenth
                 century
           ii)   Monophonic and melismatic
           iii)   The name means a song for
                 escorting   HanT, 172
          iv)   Sung during liturgical

composition found in
both vocal and in-
strumental litera-
ture which shows
decided difference
in structure for each
medium

2 - A favorite dance for
improvised ornamen-
tation

3 - "...Consists of four
to seven sections...
each of which is
repeated..." ApeHD, 297

4 - Earliest example of
a dance form which
approached an in-
strumental concert
piece

5 - Form is aabbcc,
etc.   ApeHD, 297

iii) Hymn   ReeMMA, 228

a - <u>Vers</u>

1 - A German term for
stanza   ApeHD, 898

2 - Melody of each
strophe is through
composed

b - <u>Chanson</u>

1 - French word for
song   ApeHD, 144

2 - Usually of a
popular nature
              ApeHD, 144

3 - Song without
refrain

4 - Two sections: One
through composed
section and one
repeated section
              ReeMMA, 229

5 - Rounded <u>chanson</u>
(aaba): opening
repeated section
is repeated at the
end   ReeMMA, 230

iv)   Litany   ReeMMA, 219-221

a - <u>Chanson de geste</u>,
supra, p. 35

b - Strophic <u>laisse</u>

1 - <u>Chanson de toile</u>

c - <u>Rotrouenge</u>

1 - Strophic <u>laisse</u>
with refrain

d - <u>Chanson avec des</u>
<u>refrains</u> (song with

                                        several refrains)
                    (c) Examples of troubador and
                         trouvère songs are found in
                         "Robin and Marion" by Adam
                         de La Halle   AdaO
                         i)   Facsimiles and tran-
                              scriptions of the music   AdaO
            (3) German <u>Minnelieder</u>
                    (a) Songs sung by Minnesingers
                         who came mostly from the
                         south: many from Austria   ReeMMA, 231
                    (b) Some are *modal   ReeMMA, 232
                         i)   The rhythmic *modes
                              cannot be consistently
                              applied   WesM, 252
                    (c) The texts cover the entire body
                         of lyric poetry of the twelfth
                         and thirteenth centuries (love,
                         religion, and politics)   WesM, 252
                         i)   Texts are in the
                              vernacular
                         ii) Contain two <u>Stollen</u> (<u>pedes</u>)
                              forming the <u>Aufgesang</u> and
                              an <u>Abgesang</u> (<u>cauda</u>)
                         iii) Narrative style poetry
                              (AAB)   ApeHD, 531
                         iv) Metrical structure less
                              rigid than the poetry of
                              the French
            (4) Italian <u>laude</u>   ReeMMA, 237
                    (a) A type of music rather than
                         a form
                    (b) Sung by fraternities of peni-
                         tents who practiced flagella-
                         tion
                    (c) Religious songs in the vernac-
                         ular   AngM, 51
                    (d) National in character
                    (e) Use of major and minor modes
                                                     ReeMMA, 238
                    (f) Use of *mensural notation
                         i)   Not *modal   AngM, 54
                    (g) Binary rhythm
                         i)   If a *ligature contains
                              an even number of notes,
                              all can be transcribed in
                              eighths   AngM, 55
                         ii) An odd number of notes
                              in a *ligature would
                              contain a triplet   AngM, 55
                    (h) Similar in form to the Spanish
                         <u>cantigas</u> and French <u>virelai</u> WesM, 267
                         i)   The form is <u>reprisa</u>, stanza,
                              and <u>reprisa</u>
            (5) Spanish <u>cantigas</u>   ReeMMA, 247
                    (a) Religious songs in the

              vernacular
- (b) *Modal notation has been applied
by some theorists
- (c) Concerned mainly with the relation of miracles performed by the
Virgin   WesM, 261
- (d) In the form of the French
<u>virelai</u> with a refrain at the
beginning and at the end of
each verse   WesM, 261

9. COMPOSERS
    a) Leoninus (twelfth century)   BakB, 940
        (1) Compiled the <u>Magnus liber organi</u>
<u>de graduali et antiphonario pro</u>
<u>servitio divino multiplicando</u>
                               BakB, 941
- (a) Settings for the Offices and
the Mass, supra, pp. 11-12   UlrH, 65
- (b) Style of music   UlrH, 65
    i)   <u>Organum duplum</u> style, supra,
       p. 53
    ii) *Discant style, supra,
       p. 53
- (c) Texture of music   UlrH, 65
    i)   Two part (<u>duplum</u> and
       tenor)
- (d) Performance of music   UlrH, 65
    i)   Unadorned plainchant
       was sung by a unison
       choir
    ii) <u>Organum</u> and *discant
       sections were sung by
       soloists
    iii) The <u>clausulae</u> could have
       been performed by
       instruments
- (e) Transcription of the music   WaiR
    b) Perotinus (active at Notre Dame during the
late twelfth and early thirteenth century)
                              ReeMMA, 299
        (1) Wrote <u>organa</u> in two, three and
four parts   BakB, 1230
- (a) "Substitute <u>clausulae</u>"   HugFR, 348
    i)   Thought to be taken
       from the <u>clausulae</u> of
       Leoninus
    ii) These <u>clausulae</u> were the
       beginning of the motet
        (2) Style of music   UlrH, 69
- (a) *Discant style, supra, p. 53
        (3) Compositional techniques   UlrH, 69
- (a) Use of <u>Stimmtausch</u> (canon technique)
- (b) Use of more than one *mode in
a single voice

B.   <u>ARS ANTIQUA</u> (1250-1300)

    1.   BACKGROUND   LanW, 141-142
        a)   The rise of towns undermined the feudal
            system and produced a middle class of
            importance
        b)   Secular music increased in importance
            (1)   Replaced the secular motet

    2.   PHILOSOPHY
        a)   Aristotelian doctrines were renewed   LanW, 138
            (1)   Translations of Arabic sources
                became known by the middle of the
                thirteenth century
            (2)   Al-Farabi
                (a)   Unity of poetry, music, and
                     dance (old Greek conception)
                     i)   See also appendix 1
        b)   <u>Musica artificialis</u>   LanW, 138-139
            (1)   "...all music humanly conceived as
                opposed to <u>mundana</u> and <u>coelestis</u>"
                (a)   Music was becoming practical
                     without symbolic speculation
                                              LanW, 141
                (b)   Christian thinkers opposed the
                     doctrine of a practical approach
                     to music

    3.   THEORISTS
        a)   Johannes de Grocheo
            (1)   Wrote <u>De musica</u> which is also known
                as <u>Theoria</u> (ca. 1300)   ReeF, 23-24
                (a)   The original does not have
                     a title
            (2)   He discusses the contemporary music
                scene in Paris
                (a)   Musical forms
                (b)   Performance practices
            (3)   Divides music into <u>simplex</u>, <u>com-</u>
                <u>posita</u> and <u>ecclesiastica</u>   LanW, 141
                (a)   A practical conception of music
                     which ushers in a new era
            (4)   Latin text with German translation   RohM
            (5)   English translation   JohD
        b)   Franco of Cologne
            (1)   Wrote <u>Ars cantus mensurabilis</u>
                (ca. 1260)   FraA, 139
                (a)   Discusses the meaning of
                     mensurable music, infra,
                     p. 65   FraA, 140
                (b)   Discusses the signs of mensurable
                   music   FraA, 142
                     i)   The <u>duplex longa</u> (▜),
                          the <u>longa</u> (▐), the
                            <u>brevis</u> (▪), and
                          the <u>semibrevis</u> (♦)

(c)   Discusses *_tempus_, perfect and
      imperfect   FraA, 142
(d)   Discusses three divisions
      of *discant   FraA, 141
      i)   Simple
      ii) Hocket, infra, p. 64
      iii) *_Copula_ (connected),
           supra, p. 53
(e)   Discusses the *modes in *discant
                               FraA, 141
(f)   Discusses the *_plica_, supra,
      p. 50
(g)   A discussion of *_plicae_ in
      composite figures   FraA, 149
(h)   Discussion of *ligatures "with
      propriety and without" (_cum
      proprietate_ and _sine proprietate_)
      i)   The term _proprietate_ is
           used only in reference
           to the beginning note
           of the *ligatures   FraA, 147
      ii) With propriety (_cum
           proprietate_) refers to
           the *ligatures in their
           orthodox form as found
           in *modal notation   HugFR, 323
      iii) Without propriety (_sine
           proprietate_) refers to
           the modified *ligatures
           of *mensural notation
                               HugFR, 323
           a - See also appendix 11
(i)   Discussion of rests, infra,
      p. 65   FraA, 149
(j)   Discussion of hocket,   FraA, 157
      infra, p. 64
(k)   Discussion of _organum_   FraA, 158
      i)   Discusses the rules of
           consonance, supra, p. 48
(l)   Latin text   FraAC, 117
      i)   See also appendix 14,
           no. 6
(m)   English translation   FraA, 139
c) Jerome of Moravia
   (1) Wrote _Tractatus de musica_   ReeF, 21-22
      (a)   Second half of the thirteenth
            century
      (b)   Makes no new contribution
      (c)   Incorporates four important
            treatises
            i)   Two by Johannes de Garlandia
                 a - _Discantus positio vulgaris_
                 b - _De musica mensurabili
                     positio_, infra, p. 66
            ii) One by Franco of Cologne
                 a - _Ars cantus mensurabilis_,

                                        supra, p. 62
                          iii)   <u>Musica mensurabilis</u> by
                                 Petrus Picardus
               (d)   Discusses musical instruments
               (e)   Discusses rules for the rhythmic
                     interpretation of plainsong
               (f)   Latin text   JerT, 1
                     i)   See also appendix 14,
                           no. 6

    4.   THEORY
         a)   Cadences   ReaF, 135
              (1)   A major sixth goes to an octave
              (2)   A minor third goes to a unison
         b)   "Successive" *counterpoint   ReaF, 135
              (1)   "The writing of contrapuntal music
                    in separate lines rather than in a
                    simultaneous process of composition"
                                                       ApeHD, 814
         c)   All parts of a contrapuntal piece had
              to be consonant with at least one other
              part, usually the tenor   ReaF, 387
              (1)   There were exceptions to this rule
                                                       ReaF, 129
                    (a)   In the case of passing tones
                          and displaced tones caused by
                          *syncopation
         d)   Consecutive fifths and octaves were
              being frowned upon   HugMAF, 387
         e)   Hocket (<u>hoquetus</u>)
              (1)   The term <u>hoquetus</u> designates both
                    a technique of *counterpoint and
                    a piece in which this technique
                    has been applied throughout   SanM, 250
                    (a)   A truncation is made over the
                          tenor in such a way that one
                          voice is always silent while
                          another sings   OdiD, 34
                    (b)   Written in all *modes   OdiD, 34
              (2)   There are different views as to the
                    origin of the hocket
                    (a)   The hocket originated in
                          improvised manipulations
                          of Gregorian melodies common
                          before the Notre Dame music
                          was composed   DalO, 3
                    (b)   The development of the hocket
                          was the result of the "spacious
                          and 'measured' rhythms" of the
                          music of Perotinus and his
                          successors in comparison of
                          that of Leoninus   SanM, 246
              (3)   The "jazzy" quality of the hockets
                    prompted ecclesiastical disapproval
                    such as the famous bull of Pope
                    John XXII (1324-1325)   SanM, 256

5. NOTATION (FRANCONIAN)   ApeN, 310-313
    a) A system of notation established ca.
        1260 by Franco of Cologne
        (1) Known as *mensural notation
             (a) Embraces a variety of systems
    b) In general there are no new signs
    c) The same rules govern the relation between
        the brevis and semibrevis as between the
        longa and the brevis
    d) The semibrevis is recognized for the
        first time as an independent note value
        (1) It occurs in any number and com-
             bination
        (2) It never occurs separately
        (3) If more than three appear they are
             arranged in pairs with alteration or
             in pairs with a final group of three
    e) Treatment of *ligatures is independent
        (1) The first note is a brevis in a liga-
             ture cum proprietate
        (2) The first note is a longa in a liga-
             ture sine proprietate
        (3) The final note is a longa in a liga-
             ture cum perfectione
        (4) The final note is a brevis in a liga-
             ture sine perfectione
        (5) The first two notes are semibreves
             in a ligature cum opposita proprietate
        (6) All middle notes are breves
        (7) The last note of a *ligature may be cum
             perfectio or sine perfectio
    f) There are six varieties of rests   ParN, 113
        (1) The double bar of modern usage
             (immeasurable)
        (2) A vertical line covering three spaces
             of a staff represents the perfect longa
        (3) A vertical line covering two spaces
             represents an imperfect longa and
             an altered brevis
        (4) A vertical line covering one space
             represents the normal brevis
        (5) A vertical line covering one-half
             space represents the major semi-
             brevis (two-thirds of a brevis)
        (6) A vertical line covering one-fourth
             space represents the minor semibrevis
             (one-third of a brevis)
    g) See also appendix 11

6. MUSICAL STYLE
    a) The triplum of Franco's motets are the
        predominant part   ReeMMA, 316
        (1) Gain in speed and rhythmic independence
        (2) Use the sixth *mode
    b) The use of one ordo after another in
        ostinato form in the tenor   ReeMMA, 317

c)   The use of a sort of <u>ordo</u> expansion in
     the tenor which creates different phrase
     lengths in the tenor from those in the
     upper parts   ReeMMA, 317
d)   Use of <u>Stimmtausch</u>   ReeMMA, 317

C.   <u>THIRTEENTH CENTURY ENGLISH MUSIC</u>

1.   BACKGROUND
     a)   The Magna Carta (1215)   LanE, 213
          (1)   A feudal document exacted by
                feudal barons from their lord
          (2)   Gave a promise of freedom and free
                elections
     b)   The arrival of the Dominicans and
          Franciscans in England (1220 and 1224
          respectively)   LanE, 213

2.   THEORISTS
     a)   Johannes de Garlandia, the elder
          (ca. 1195-1272)   BakB, 538
          (1)   Taught at Oxford and Paris   HugFR, 340
          (2)   Wrote <u>De musica mensurabili positio</u>
                (ca. 1240-1250)   ReeF, 20
                (a)   Discusses notation of the
                      rhythmic *modes in *ligatures
                (b)   Discusses the nature of consonance
                      i)   Lists three classifications
                            of concords   HugFR, 340
                            a - The unison and octave
                                are perfect concords
                            b - Major and minor thirds
                                are imperfect concords
                            c - The fifth and the fourth
                                are intermediate concords
                      ii)   Three classes of discords
                                                HugFR, 340
                            a - The semitone (minor
                                second), the ⁺tritone
                                (augmented fourth), and
                                the major seventh are
                                perfect discords
                            b - The major sixth and
                                minor seventh are
                                imperfect discords
                            c - The major second and
                                minor sixth are inter-
                                mediate discords
                (c)   Discusses <u>musica ficta</u>, infra,
                      p. 86
                (d)   Defines *<u>copula</u>, supra, p. 53
                                                WaiR, 115
                (e)   Latin text   GarD, 175
                      i)   See also appendix 14,
                            no. 6

            (f)   English translation and
                  commentary   JohG
            (g)   English translation   JohDM
    b) Odington, Walter (d. after 1330)   WesN, 462
        (1)   Benedictine monk at Evesham   BakB, 1177
        (2)   An astronomer   HarM, 115
        (3)   Went to Oxford from the Benedictine
              monastery of St. Mary's, Evesham

                                                HarM, 115
        (4)   Wrote <u>De speculatione musicae</u>
              (ca. 1300)   ReeF, 22-23
            (a)   Advocated the continental
                  rhythms and Franconian notation,
                  supra, p. 65   DitB, 40
            (b)   States that binary rhythm is
                  not new   DitB, 40
            (c)   Discusses English music before
                  the adoption of the French style,
                  notation, and rhythm
            (d)   Latin text   OdiDS, 182
                i)   See also appendix 14,
                      no. 6
            (e)   Latin text   HamW
            (f)   A discussion of <u>De speculatione</u>
                  <u>musicae</u>   HamW
            (g)   A discussion of Odington's life
                  and works   HamW

3. THEORY
    a) Major and minor thirds are considered
        imperfect concords   HugFR, 340
    b) Use of <u>musica ficta</u>, infra, p. 86   HugFR, 369
    c) Use of parallel thirds and sixths   HugFR, 351
        (1)   Two to five or more in number
        (2)   At the cadence they resolve into
              an open fifth and an octave

4. NOTATION
    a) *Square notation
        (1)   Terminology   DitD, 8
            (a)   *Square notation refers only
                  to the external form
                i)   It has no musical signif-
                      icance
            (b)   *Square notation includes both
                  *modal and *mensural notation
            (c)   See also appendix 8
        (2)   The notes   DitD, 8
            (a)   <u>Virgae cum tractu</u> alternate with
                  *rhomboids
                i)   The *rhomboids replace
                      the square form of the
                      continental <u>brevis</u>
            (b)   This English notational
                  practice drops out around
                  thirteen hundred   DitD, 11

```
(3)  Types of *square notation
     (a)  English *modal notation
          i)    The rhythmic *modes
                differed in English music
                of the thirteenth century
                from those used on the
                continent              DitB, 39
                a - Usually the third *mode
                    was binary until it
                    could be reduced to the
                    first or second *mode
                                        DitB, 40
                    1 - All English com-
                        positions of the
                        period should not
                        be transcribed
                        into binary third
                        *mode simply because
                        they have two
                        *rhomboids between
                        longae          DitAW, 10
     (b)  English *mensural notation    DitD, 8
          i)    The same as continental
                notation, supra, p. 65
          ii)   Two types
                a - Semi-*mensural notation
                    1 - Attributes *mensural
                        meanings to varia-
                        tions of the simplex
                        notes only
                b - Complete *mensural
                    notation
                    1 - Includes simplex
                        notes, *ligatures,
                        and rests
     (c)  Larga/longa notation          DitD, 6
          i)    A note with an elongated
                head is called a larga by
                the theorist J. Hanboys
                a - It may be divided
                    into two or three
                    longae
                b - The same note is called
                    a duplex longa by Robert
                    de Handlo
                    1 - May be divided into
                        two longae only
                    2 - This notation was
                        undoubtedly intro-
                        duced for the no-
                        tation of motets in
                        binary meter (the
                        normal longa/brevis
                        would have indicated
                        ternary meter exclu-
                        sively)
```

5. MUSICAL STYLE
    a) Parallel style   HugFR, 351
        (1) A succession of chords containing
             the intervals of a third and sixth
    b) Rondellus technique (called interchange),
        infra, p. 71   HugMAF, 374
    c) Use of ostinato   HugMAF, 384
    d) Independent entry of a voice   HugMAF, 385
    e) *Cantilena style (polyphonic)   SanC, 13

6. MANUSCRIPT SOURCES
    a) The Worcester fragments
        (1) Written during the thirteenth and
             early fourteenth centuries   DitD, 11
             (a) Compositions from the first
                  half of the century are in
                  note against note style
             (b) Compositions composed in the
                  first half of the fourteenth
                  century are notated according
                  to Odington's doctrine,
                  supra, p. 67
             (c) The *palimpsests are later
                  additions   DitD, 6
        (2) Preserved in three libraries   DitO, 1
             (a) Worcester, Chapter Lib. MS Add. 68
                  i)   Thirty-five items, fourteen
                       of which are harmonized
                                                    HugW, 21
                       a - The others are liturgical
                           or of a miscellaneous
                           character
                  ii) Facsimiles   DitO
                  iii) Transcriptions   DitWC
             (b) London, British Mus. Add. 25031
                  i)   Known as the "Motet
                       Book"   HugW, 22
                  ii) Facsimile   DitO
             (c) Oxford, Bodleian Lib. MS lat.
                  lit. d 20   DitWF, 12
                  i)   Contains flyleaves and
                       bindings from four dif-
                       ferent sources
                       a - Oxford, Bodleian Lib.
                           Auct. F inf. 1, 3
                           1 - Facsimiles   DitO
                       b - Oxford, Bodleian Lib.
                           862
                           1 - Facsimiles   DitO
                       c - Oxford, Bodleian Lib.
                           Hatton 30
                           1 - Facsimiles   DitO
                       d - Worcester, Chapter Lib.
                           MS Add. 68 fragments
                           1 - Facsimiles   DitO
                           2 - Nos. IX, X, XIII,

                                         XXVIII, XXXI, and
                                         XXXV
                                    3 - Formerly Oxford,
                                         Magdalene College
                                         100
                                    4 - Known as the
                                         "Worcester Psalter"
                                                        HugW, 22
                                    5 - Written for two,
                                         three, and four
                                         parts
                          (d)   These fragments were portions
                                of at least three Worcester Choir-
                                books, now lost   HugW, ix
                    (3)   A catalogue and transcription of
                          all of the music   DitWF
       b) Worcester, Cathedral Lib. Codex F.160
                                                        FreW, xxx
                    (1)   Music from the beginning and end
                          of the thirteenth century
                    (2)   Contains an Antiphonal, Pro-
                          cessional, and Gradual as used
                          at Worcester
                    (3)   Facsimiles and commentary   MocAM
       c) London, British Museum, Harley 978,
           fo. 160 (ca. 1240)   HugFR, 313
                    (1)   Probably written by William of
                          Wycombe at Leominster in Hereford-
                          shire, a cell of Reading
                    (2)   The music of this manuscript has
                          disappeared, though much of it can
                          be reconstructed from other sources
                                                        HugMAF, 355
                          (a)   The titles remain
                          (b)   One piece which has been
                                reconstructed is "Sumer is
                                icumen in"   HugMAF, 402
                                i)   The verse Perspice
                                      Christicola from an
                                      Easter day sequence
                                      has been written in
                                      red ink below the
                                      secular words which
                                      are written in black
                                      ink   HarM, 144
                                ii)   The *pes is the first
                                      five notes of Regina
                                      caeli   HarM, 144
                                iii) The technique and character
                                      are that of a sacred piece
                                                          HarM, 144
                                iv)   In the manuscript it
                                      is referred to as a
                                      rota, infra, p. 72
                                v)   Facsimile   WooE, Plate x
                                vi)   Transcription   HarM, 143

7. CLASSES OF MUSIC
    a) Monophonic music
        (1) Plainsong
            (a) "The English secular Cathedrals
                derived their liturgies... from
                Norman models"   HarM, 46
                i)   There was also some
                      continuity with earlier
                      Irish and Anglo-Saxon
                      liturgies
            (b) "The Use of Salisbury was the
                most important of the secular
                liturgies of medieval Britain"
                (Use of Sarum)   HarM, 47
                i)   There are three manuscipts
                      containing information
                      concerning the service
                      and its music
                      a - The Sarum *Customary
                          1 - Defines the persons
                            who are to conduct
                            the services
                      b - The Sarum *Ordinal
                          1 - Defines the character,
                            contents, and method
                          of the services
                      c - The Sarum *Tonale
                        1 - A handbook and
                          directory of the
                        ritual music   HarM, 100
                ii) For a detailed discussion
                    of the Sarum liturgy and its
                    chant   HarM, 58-99
                iii) Facsimiles of Sarum chant
                    a - Graduale Sarisburiense
                                    FreG
                        1 - The sequences are
                          not included
                        2 - Comments on the
                          chant
                    b - Antiphonale Sarisburiense
                                    FreA
                        1 - Music for the Divine
                          Office
                        2 - The hymns are not
                          included
                        3 - Comments about the
                          chant
    b) Polyphonic music
        (1) Rondellus
            (a) A melody consisting of three phrase
                elements (A-B-C) and then combined
                simultaneously   SteM, 263
                i)   ABC
                    BCA
                    CAB   HugMAF, 374

        (b)   Often used as a section of
               conductus   SteM, 265
        (c)   Also a name given to certain
               Latin songs written in repeat
               forms   ApeHD, 740
            i)   Forerunner of the French
                      rondeau

    (2)   Rota
        (a)   "Sumer is icumen in", supra,
               p. 70   SteM, 272
            i)   The tune is sung as a
                      round by up to four voices,
                      supported by a *pes
                      a - The *pes is in two
                          voices starting simul-
                          taneously

    (3)   Motet
        (a)   Written for three or four voices
                                  HarM, 138-139
            i)   Either two or three parts
                      have texts
            ii)   The quartus-cantus is
                      structurally an auxiliary
                      part to the tenor
        (b)   No texts in the vernacular
                                  HugMAF, 354
        (c)   Use of rondellus technique
               (interchange)   HugMAF, 375
        (d)   Skilful and artistic use of
               ostinato   HugMAF, 384

    (4)   Conductus
        (a)   Some are in simple *discant
               style, supra, p. 53   HarM, 139
        (b)   Some have an introductory
               rondellus on the first syllable
                                  HarM, 139
        (c)   Some have a rondellus beginning
               and a short cauda at the end
                                  HarM, 140
        (d)   Some end with a rondellus-
               *cauda   HarM, 140
        (e)   Sometimes the last section
               is a rota   HarM, 141

    (5)   Rondellus-motet and rondellus-
           conductus   HarM, 141
        (a)   The variety of the application
               of rondellus technique led to
               composition in forms which were
               border line between motet and
               conductus

    (6)   *Cantilena (polyphonic)   SanC, 13
        (a)   Worcester fragments nos. 82 and
               109 have commonly been referred
               to as conductus (without cauda)
            i)   They appear to carry the
                      melody in the top voice

ii)   These pieces should be
called *cantilena
(7)   English part-songs
(a)   In two parts with many parallel
thirds   HugFR, 341

D.   INSTRUMENTS
1.   AEROPHONES   MarMI, 438-439
a)   Recorders
(1)   Small wooden pipe
(2)   Six or seven finger holes
(3)   Prototypes can be found as early
as the twelfth century
b)   Organ
(1)   The number of octaves increased to
three   MarS, 235
(2)   The keyboard was developed   ReeMMA, 329
(3)   There were positive and portative
organs   GroH, 72
(a)   The portative organ was small
and could be carried   GroH, 73
i)   It may have been suspended
by a strap around the neck
of the player
ii)   There was a single rank of
pipes
iii)   The keys were played by the
right hand and the left hand
worked the bellows
(b)   The positive organ could be
carried but had to be placed on
a table to be played   GroH, 73
i)   An assistant was required
to work the bellows
c)   Shawm   MarMI, 471
(1)   Conically bored wooden tube
(a)   Used a double reed
(2)   Introduced to Europe in the twelfth
century

E.   TERMS

1.   ALTERA. The doubling of the value of the
second breve in the third and fourth
*modes of *modal notation   ApeN, 221

2.   CANTUS FIRMUS. An existing melody that
becomes the basis of a polyphonic composition through the addition of contra-
puntal voices   ApeHD, 130

3.   CAUDA, AE. In the thirteenth century,
melismatic passages in conductus without
texts   ApeHD, 138

4. CONJUNCTURA. "A symbol of *square notation
       consisting of a longa followed by two
       or more *rhombs (lozenges: the later
       semibreves) always forming a descending
       scale passage"   ApeHD, 200

5. COPULA. A combination of discantus and
       *modal organum, supra, p. 53   WaiR, 108

6. COUNTERPOINT. A term derived from puntus
       counter punctum meaning "note against
       note" or melody against melody. Until
       the fifteenth century contrapunctus
       (counterpoint) was distinguished from
       cantus fractibilis which meant several
       notes against one   ApeHD, 208

7. CUSTOMARY. A written collection of
       customs   OxfD, 442

8. DISCANT. A twelfth to fifteenth century
       term which referred to the setting of
       one voice against another; concerned
       with two voices only but other voices
       could be added;   KenW, 94
       in the twelfth century the term discant
       was also used to distinguish the style
       of composition: "note against note"
       style was known as organum and melismatic
       style was known as discant; in the
       thirteenth century the term discant
       indicated non-melismatic music in
       *modal rhythm; the term originated as
       the name for the upper voice of two part
       organum, the lower voice being known as
       the cantus   ApeHD, 236

9. LIGATURES. "Notational signs of the thir-
       teenth to sixteenth centuries that
       combine two or more notes in a single
       symbol"   ApeHD, 484

10. MENSURAL NOTATION. A system of musical notation
       that was first established by Franco of
       Cologne, infra, p. 65; concerned with
       temporal relationships between notes ApeHD, 520

11. MODAL NOTATION. A system of notation used
       mostly in the organa and clausulae of
       the Notre Dame period, so called because
       it is based on a system of rhythmic
       *modes; uses *ligatures whose value
       depends on the *mode used   ApeHD, 534

12. MODES, RHYTHMIC. A system of rhythm that is
       characterized by a consistent repetition

of certain ternary rhythmic patterns
ApeHD, 535

13. ORDINAL. A book setting forth the order
of the services of the church   OxfD, 1382

14. PALIMPSEST. A parchment which has been
written upon twice, the original
having been rubbed out   OxfD, 1418

15. PERFECTION. In *modal notation, the term
refers to the final note in a modal
pattern in modus perfectus; in *mensural
notation, the term refers to the ternary
value of the longa   ApeHD, 658

16. PES. A name for the tenor in English thirteenth century manuscripts, particularly
for the two lower parts of "Sumer is
icumen in"   ApeHD, 663

17. PLICA. "A notational sign of the thirteenth
century calling for an ornamental tone
to be inserted following the note to
which it is connected...": a longer dash
on the right side (ꟸ ꟺ); a longer dash
on the left side (ꟸ ꟺ); two dashes of
about equal length (ꟺ); two ligaturae
plicae (ꟺ ꟺ)   ApeHD, 681-682

18. PUNCTA. In the thirteenth and fourteenth
centuries the term was used to indicate
a section of music   ApeHD, 708

19. PUNCTUM, I. A ⁺neume, see appendix 3;
in the thirteenth century it became
square shaped and was known as a brevis
ApeHD, 573

20. RECTA. The term used for those notes in
*modal notation that are of normal
time value ("correct" value)   RasN, 39

21. RHOMBOID. Having the form of a rhomb, that is
four equal parts with opposite angles being
equal (two acute and two obtuse)   OxfD, 1732

22. SQUARE NOTATION. The square shape of ⁺neumes
acquired about 1200 and used for the notation of monophonic and polyphonic music:
when used in the latter they are called
*ligatures   ApeHD, 579

23. SYNCOPATION. A separating of normal groups
of notes by inserting notes of larger
value   ApeHD, 828

24.   TEMPUS, ORA. "In thirteenth century theory,
        the unit of musical time,...i.e., the
        smallest time in which a 'full sound'
        can be conveniently produced"; in the
        thirteenth century this was the brevis
                                            ApeHD, 837

25.   TONALE. A medieval "thematic catalogue"
        in which chants are listed according
        to *mode   ApeHD, 856

10. PLACES AND PEOPLE OF INTEREST (1150-1300)

Leoninus (Paris)
Perotinus (Paris)
Johannes de Garlandia (Oxford and Paris)
Anonymous IV (Paris)
Johannes de Grocheo (Paris)
Minnesingers (Austria)
Franco of Cologne (Cologne)
Jerome of Moravia (Moravia)
Walter Odington (Oxford and Evesham)

Supplemental Sources for the Early Gothic Period

BOOKS

Apel, Willi. "Imitation in the Thirteenth and Fourteenth
    Centuries." In Essays in Honor of Archibald Davison,
    pp. 25-38. Cambridge: Harvard University Department
    of Music, 1957.

Aubry, Pierre. Trouvères and troubadors: A popular
    treatise. Translated by Claude Aveling. New York:
    G. Schirmer, 1914.

Boutiere, Jean, and A. H. Schitz. Bibliographies des
    troubadors. Ohio State University Contributions in
    Languages and Literature, no. 14. Paris: "n.p.",
    1964.

Gennrich, Friedrich. Rondeaux, Virelais und Balladen aus
    dem Ende des XII JH., mit uberlieferten Melodien. 2
    vols. Dresden: "n.p.", 1920 or 1921; Gottingen:
    "n.p.", 1927.

Hoppin, Richard. "Tonal Organization in Music Before the
    Renaissance." In Paul A Pisk: Essays in His Honor,
    pp. 25-37. Edited by John Glowacki. Austin, Texas:
    University of Texas, [c.1966].

Maillard, Jean. Roi-trouvère du XIIIème siècle Charles
    d'Anjou. Musicological Studies and Documents, vol.
    18. "N.p.": American Institute of Musicology,
    1967.

Mathiassen, Finn. The Style of the Early Motet
    (c.1200-1250): An Investigation of the Old Corpus of
    the Montpellier Manuscript. Copenhagen: Dan Fog
    Musikforlag, 1966.

Mendel, Arthur. "Some Ambiguities of the Mensural
    System." In Studies in Music History: Eassays for
    Oliver Strunk, pp. 137-160. Edited by Harold

Powers. Princeton: Princeton University Press, 1968.

Munrow, David. *Instruments of the Middle Ages and Renaissance*. London: Oxford University Press, Music Department, 1976.

Reaney, Gilbert. "The Middle Ages." In *A History of Song*, pp. 37-62. Edited by Denis Stevens. 2nd ed. New York: W. W. Norton and Co., Inc., 1970.

Werf, Hendrick van der. *The chansons of the troubadors and trouvères: a study of the melodies and their relation to the poems*. Utrecht: A Oosterhoek, 1972.

Wolf, Johannes. *Geschichte der Mensural-Notation von 1250-1460*. Hildesheim: Georg Olms; Wiesbaden: Breitkopf and Härtel, 1965.

CATALOGUES, INDICES, AND BIBLIOGRAPHIES

Anderson, Gordon A. "Notre Dame and related conductus: a catalogue raisonne." *Miscellana musicologica*. *Adelaide studies in musicology* 6 (1972): 153-229.

Dittmer, Luther, ed. *Central Source of Notre Dame Polyphony: Facsimile, reconstruction, catalogue raisonne, discussion and transcriptions*. Publications of Mediaeval Musical Manuscripts, vol. 3. Brooklyn: Institute of Mediaeval Music, 1957.

Fischer, Pieter, ed. *The Theory of Music from the Carolingian Era up to 1400. Vol. 2: Italy*. Répertoire international des sources musicales [International Inventory of Musical Sources], vol. B3:2. München-Duisburg: G. Henle Verlag, [c.1968].

Linker, Robert W. *Music of the Minnesinger and early Meistersinger: A bibliography*. Chapel Hill: University of North Carolina Press, [1961].

Page, C. "A Catalogue and Bibliography of English Song from Its Beginnings to c.1300." Royal Musical Association Research Chronicle 13 (1977): 67-83.

Reaney, Gilbert, ed. *Manuscripts of Polyphonic Music: Eleventh Through Early Fourteenth Century, Vol. 1*. Répertoire International des sources musicales [International Inventory of Musical Sources], vol. B4:1. München-Duisburg: G. Henle Verlag, [c.1968].

ARTICLES IN PERIODICALS

Anderson, Gordon. "The Rhythm of the Monophonic Conductus in the Florence Manuscripts as Indicated in Parallel Sources in Mensural Notation." _Journal of the American Musicological Society_ 31:3 (1978): 480-489.

Falk, Robert. "Rondellus, Canon and Related Types before 1300." _Journal of the American Musicological Society_ 25 (1972): 38-57.

Handshin, J. "The Summer Canon and Its Background: Part I." _Musica Disciplina_ 3 (1949): 45-54.

_____. "The Summer Canon and Its Background: Part II." _Musica Disciplina_ 5 (1951): 65.

Karp, T. "Towards a Critical Edition of Notre Dame Organa Dupla." _Musical Quarterly_ 52:3 (1966): 350-367.

Levy, K. "New Material on the Early Motet in England, a Report on Princeton MS. Garrett 119." _Journal of the American Musicological Society_ 4:3 (1951): 220-239.

Ludwig, Friedrich. "Die Quellen der Motteten altesten Stiles." _Archiv fur Musikwissenschaft_ 5 (1923): 185-222, 273-315.

Obst, Wolfgang. "'Sumer is icumen in'- a Contrafactum?" _Music and Letters_ 64 (1983): 151-161

Randel, Don M. "Al Farabi and the Role of Music Theory in the Latin Middle Ages." _Journal of the American Musicological Society_ 29:2 (1976): 173-188.

Reaney, Gilbert. "Concerning the origins of the medieval lai." _Music and Letters_ 39 (1958): 343-346.

_____. "Transposition and 'Key' Signatures in Late Medieval Music." _Musica Disciplina_ 33 (1979): 27-43.

Roesner, Edward H. "The Origins of W^1." _Journal of the American Musicological Society_ 29:3 (1976): 337-380.

Sanders, Ernest H. "Duple Rhythm and Alternate Third Mode in the Thirteenth Century." _Journal of the American Musicological Society_ 15:3 (1962): 249-291.

Smith, Norman E. "From Clausula to Motet: Material for Further Studies in the Origin and Early History of the Motet." _Musica Disciplina_ 34 (1980): 29-67.

Spiess, Lincoln B. "Discant, Descant, Diaphony and Organum." _Journal of the American Musicological Society_ 8:2 (1955): 144-147.

Stewart, Michelle F.   "The Melodic Structure of Thir-
    teenth Century 'Jeux-Partis'."   Acta Musicologica
    51:1 (1979): 86-107.

Tischler, Hans.   "Ligatures, Plicae and Vertical Bars in
    Premensural Notation."   Revue belge de musicologie 11
    (1957): 83-92.

_____.   "The Structure of Notre-Dame Organa."   Acta
    Musicologica 49:1 (1977): 193-199.

_____.   "Latin Texts in the Early Motet Collections:
    Relationships and Perspectives."   Musica Dicsciplina
    31 (1977): 31-44.

Treitler, Leo.   "Regarding Meter and Rhythm in the Ars
    antiqua."   Musical Quarterly 65:4 (1979): 524-558.

Waite, W. G.   "Johannes de Garlandia, Poet and
    Musician."   Speculum: A Journal of Medieval Studies
    35 (1960): 179-195.

Yudkin, Jeremy.   "The Copula According to Johannes de
    Garlandia."   Musica Disciplina 34 (1980): 67-84.

MUSIC

Davison, Archibald, and Willi Apel.   Historical Anthology
    of Music.   Vol. 1: Oriental, Medieval and Renaissance
    Music.   Revised ed.   Cambridge: Harvard University
    Press, 1972.

Expert, Henry, ed.   Les Monuments de la Musique Française
    au temps de la Renaissance.   12 volumes.   Paris:
    Maurice Senart, 1924-1930.

Fellerer, Karl Gustave, gen. ed.   Anthology of Music.
    33 vols.   Cologne: Arno Verlag; Philadelphia:
    Theodore Presser, 1960-.   Vol. 2: Troubadors,
    trouvères, Minnesang, und Meistergesang, by Friedrich
    Gennrich.

_____, gen. ed.   Anthology of Music.   33 vols.
    Cologne: Arno Volk Verlag, 1962.   Vol. 9: Medieval
    Polyphony, by Heinrich Husmann.

Greenberg, Noah, ed., and Rembert Weakland, transc.   The
    Play of Daniel: A Thirteenth-century Music Drama.
    New York: Oxford University Press, 1959.

Hamburg, Otto, Music History in Examples: From antiquity
    to Johann Sebastian Bach.   With the collaboration of
    Margaretha Landwehr von Pragenan.   Translated by
    Susan Hellaner.   Wilhelmshaven Locarno, Amsterdam:
    Heinrichshofen; New York: Peters, 1978.

Hughes, Anselm, Dom. Early Medieval Music up to 1300.
    11 vols. London, New York: Oxford University Press,
    1954-.

Maillard, Jean, and Jacques Chailley, eds. Anthology de
    chants de trouvères. Paris: "n.p.", 1967.

Parrish, Carl, and John Ohl, comps. and eds.
    Masterpieces of Music before 1750: Anthology of
    Musical Examples from Gregorian Chant to J. S. Bach.
    New York: W. W. Norton and Co., Inc., [c.1951].

Rasch, Rudolf A. Johannes de Garlandia MS 20. New York:
    "n.p.", 1969.

Schering, Arnold, ed. Geschichte der Musik in
    Beispielen. Leipzig: Breitkopf and Hartel, 1931;
    revised ed., Wiesbaden: Breitkopf and Hartel,
    [c.1959].

Seagrave, Barbara G., and Thomas Wesley, eds. The Songs
    of the Minnesingers. Urbana and London: "n.p.",
    1966.

Smoldon, William L., ed. Peregrinus, a 12th-century
    Easter Music-Drama; Planctus Mariae, a 14th-century
    Passiontide Music-Drama; Visitatio Sepulchri (120).
    London: "n.p.", "n.d".

Stainer, John, Sir, ed. Sacred and Secular Songs:
    Together with other MS compositions in the Bodleian
    Library, Oxford, ranging from about A. D. 1185 to
    about A. D. 1505. Early Bodleian Music, vol. 1:
    Facsimiles; vol. 2: Transcriptions. Forward by E. W.
    B. Nicholson. Transcriptions by J. F. R. Stainer and
    C. Stainer. London: Novello and Co., Limited; New
    York: Novello, Ewer and CO., 1901; reprint ed.,
    Farnborough, Hants: Gregg Press Limited, 1967.

Taylor, Ronald J., ed. The Art of the Minnesinger. 2
    vols. Cardiff: "n.p.", 1968.

Wolf, Johannes, ed. Music of Earlier Times: Vocal and
    instrumental examples. New York: Broude Bros.,
    [1955].

Late Gothic Period

A. FRENCH ARS NOVA (1300-1400)

    1. BACKGROUND
        a) The collapse of the medieval order   LanW, 144
          (1)   Franco-Flemish wars
          (2)   Six decades of the Hundred Years War
          (3)   Black death
          (4)   Church and Empire lost importance
              (a)   Clement V removed the papal
                    seat to Avignon thus releasing
                    the papacy from the Germans
                    and surrendering it to France
                                    DurS IV, 815
              (b)   The Great Schism
                  i)   Urban VI became the
                      Pope in Rome (1378)   LanR, 191
                  ii)   Due to the unpopularity
                      of Urban VI, a group of
                      cardinals at Fondi elected
                      Clement VII and tried to
                      recapture Rome, but failed
                                      LanR, 191
                  iii)   In 1409, Alexander V was
                      established in Rome and
                      the two previous Popes
                      were denounced   LanR, 199

    2. PHILOSOPHY
        a) Humanism   DurS V, 77
          (1)   The study of man
              (a)   Studied the strength and
                      beauty of his body
              (b)   Discussed the joy and pain
                      of his senses and feelings
              (c)   Delved into the frail majesty
                      of his reason
          (2)   Addiction to the study of the writers
              of Greek and Roman antiquity   LanR, 268
        b) Voluntarism   LanW, 145

        (1)   The human will as a dominant factor
                in experience and constitution of
                the world

   c) St. Thomas Aquinas raised a distinction
      between theology and philosophy   LanW, 140
      (1)   He felt that the former was a divine
              science and the latter a human one

3. THEORETICAL SOURCES
   a) Johannes de Muris (ca. 1290-1351)   BakB, 1138
      (1)   Astronomer and mathematician
      (2)   Wrote <u>Notitia artis musicae</u>
           (1321)   JohN, 9
           (a) Two books
               i)   <u>Musica theorica</u>
               ii)   <u>Musica practica</u>
                   a - Later compressed into
                      <u>Compendium</u> (ca. 1322)
                                JohN, 10
           (b) Shows no knowledge of the in-
                novations of Philippe de Vitri's
                <u>Ars nova</u>
           (c) One set of rules should govern
                all relations of notes   ReeMMA, 346
           (d) English translation of <u>Musica</u>
                <u>practica</u>   JeaA, 172
                Latin text   JohN

   b) Philippe de Vitri
      (1)   Wrote <u>Ars nova</u>   ReeF, 25
           (a) Written 1322-1333   JohN, 10
           (b) First French musician to describe
                duple meter as of equal rank with
                triple meter
          (c) Discusses intervals, *gamut,
                accidentals, ⁺hexachords, and
                *mutations
          (d) Discusses <u>musica ficta</u>, infra,
                p. 86
          (e) Introduces the four *prolations
                              ReeMMA, 343
               i)   Equivalent in a way to
                     our 9/8, 3/4, 6/8, and
                     2/4   ReeF, 25
               ii)   The relation of <u>brevis</u> to
                     <u>longa</u> retains the name
                     *mode
               iii) The relation of <u>semibrevis</u>
                     to <u>brevis</u> is called *<u>tempus</u>
               iv) The relation of <u>minum</u> to
                     <u>semibrevis</u> is called
                     *prolation
               v)   For musical examples of
                     the four prolations see
                     appendix 12
          (f) An account of the use of
                colored notes   ReeMMA, 345

                  the same line length
                  and metre throughout

iv)   In this century the
        refrain is expanded
        from two lines to three,
        four, or five lines
                  ApeHD, 739

    a - The musical structure
        remained the same

v)   The form of the music
        is ABaAabAB   ApeHD, 739

    a - The refrain is
        indicated by the
        capital letters

(d) Ballade   ReaA, 14

    i)   The music has two pedes
        and a cauda (AAB)

    ii)   A less popular form is
        AABB

    iii) Text form is ababbcC
        a - Contains three
           stanzas
        b - Has decasyllabic
           lines
        c - Sometimes eight
           syllable lines with
           the fifth line having
           seven syllables

(e) Virelai   ReaA, 15

    i)   Both text and music consist
        of a refrain which alter-
        nates with three stanzas
                  ApeHD, 915

    ii)   Text form is ABccabAB
                  ReeMMA, 223

    iii) Later the text became
        restricted to one stanza
        b - Has a decasyllabic
           line

    iv)   The music form is AbbaA

(3) Secular motet   ReeMMA, 354

(a) Isorhythmic

(b) Lyrical religious and political
    texts

    i)   Different, simultaneously
        sung texts are usually
        related to each other
        a - Usually in the same
           language

    ii)   Motets in the vernacular
        use traditional Latin
        tenors   ReaA, 19

    iii) Latin motets were written
        for special occasions of
        public interest   ReaA, 19

    iv)   Some tenors are taken

    (1) Considered imperfect consonances
  b) Imperfect consonances are gaining in
    favor and importance   ReaF, 131
  c) Consecutive fifths and octaves are
    forbidden   ReaF, 131
  d) <u>Musica ficta</u> (implied accidentals)
    (1) A system devised by theorists to
      perfect the imperfect consonances
      and dissonances created by [+]sol-
      mization   HugF, 29
      (a) See also appendix 14, no. 9
      (b) In [+]solmization, the obligatory
        placing of certain syllables
        where they do not exist in
        <u>musica recta</u>   HugF, 30
        i) See also appendix 5
    (2) Two purposes   HugF, 32
      (a) To make consonances perfect
      (b) To color dissonances in order
        to make them closer to the
        consonance to which they
        resolve
    (3) General principles of agreement
                HugMAF, 370
      (a) Accidentals were not always
        written
      (b) The melody should take pre-
        dominance over the harmony
    (4) The main problem which prompted
      <u>musica ficta</u> was the [+]tritone
                HugMAF, 370
    (5) Rules of [+]counterpoint HugF, 33
      (a) The third should be minor
        before a unison
      (b) A sixth should be major when
        going to an octave
  e) New technique of isorhythm
    (1) The term isorhythm and the implied
      structural scheme were the invention
      of Friedrich Ludwig   HarMT, 100
      (a) (1872-1930)   BakB, 989
      (b) Only the terms *<u>color</u> and
        *<u>talea</u> are found in treatises
        and on manuscripts of the
        period
        i) The term *<u>color</u> most
          likely referred to the
          newly legitimized duple
          rhythm indicated by color-
          ing notes red HarMT, 109
        ii) The term *<u>color</u> also
          could have referred to
          the melodic pattern as
          the medieval term *<u>color</u>
          referred to any kind of
          pattern   ReaM, 22

   (2) A technique of rhythmic repetition
                    CalM, 164
     (a) "...division of a voice or
       voices into identically repeated
       rhythmic groups"   ReaA, 9
     (b) Thought to be the outgrowth of
       the rhythmic ⁺modes and _ordines_
                HarMT, 100
     (c) Sometimes free of ⁺modal
       rhythm   HarMT, 102
     (d) Isorhythm is found in some manu-
       scripts of the _Ars antiqua_
       period   HarMT. 100
 f) Cadences   UltM, 98
   (1) Double leading-tone cadence
     (a) Two upper voices are a half
       step below the tones-of-resolve
       i) _Musica ficta_ may be
         employed
     (b) Lower voice descends by a whole
       step
       i) Example: E, G#, c#
         goes to D, a, d
   (2) Landini cadence, infra, p. 98
     (a) Same movement as in double
       leading-tone cadence except
       the upper voice descends
       from the leading tone by
       step to the sixth degree
       and resolves upward to the
       root by a skip of a third

5. STYLE
 a) *_Cantilena_ style   GroH, 128
   (1) A solo voice with two accompanying
     instrumental parts
 b) Texture of music
   (1) Monophonic   SteM, 158
   (2) Two-part   SteM, 158
   (3) Three-part   CroH, 127
     (a) *_Discantus_ (top voice)
       i) Also known as _cantus_
                ReaA, 28
     (b) *Contratenor
       i) Sometimes a second
         cantus rather than a
         contratenor   ReaA, 28
     (c) Tenor
   (4) Four-part   CroH, 124
     (a) _Triplum_
     (b) _Cantus_
     (c) Tenor
     (d) *Contratenor
 c) Techniques
   (1) Isorhythm, supra, p. 86 GroH, 123
   (2) *Canon   ReaA, 16

```
            (3)   Hocket, supra, p. 64              GroH, 123
        d)  Characteristics
            (1)   Struggle with thirds leading to
                  harmonic thought                  GroH, 157
            (2)   *Counterpoint of rhythms          GroH, 136
            (3)   A small range moving upwards       GroH, 144
            (4)   Crossing of voices                 GroH, 136

    6.  MANUSCRIPT SOURCES
        a)  Ivrea, Bibl. del Capitolo (ca. 1360)    HopM, 369
            (1)   Represents the music of the school
                  of Avignon during the third quarter
                  of the fourteenth century          ApeFR, 1
            (2)   Facsimiles and transcriptions          StaF
            (3)   Commentary                             StaM
        b)  Paris, Bibl. Nat. nouv. acq. fr.
            6771 (Codex Reina)                      ApeFR, xii
            (1)   Compositions in the style of
                  Machaut, infra, p. 91             ApeFR, 4
            (2)   Transcriptions                        WilR


    7.  CLASSES OF MUSIC
        a)  Secular
            (1)   *Chace (caccia)                  ReeMMA, 335
                  (a)   The caccia type originated
                        in France and not in Italy
                  (b)   A hunting song in *canon
                        form
                        i)      *Canon at the unison
                                                   ApeHD, 141
                        ii)     Has no free supporting
                                tenor such as the
                                caccia             ApeHD, 141
                        iii)    Use of triple *canon
                                                   ApeHD, 141
                  (c)   Manuscripts of the *chace are
                        found in the manuscript source
                        Ivrea
            (2)   Polyphonic rondeau, ballade, and
                  virelai (chanson balladée), supra,
                  p. 58                      ReeMMA, 349-353
                  (a)   Many different variations
                  (b)   Use of *cantilena style
                  (c)   Rondeau                     ReaA, 11-12
                        i)      The form became fixed
                                by Philippe de Vitri
                        ii)     It has an eight line
                                form
                        iii)    Has a seven syllable
                                line
                                a - There is less
                                    fluctuation in line
                                    length than in the
                                    thirteenth century
                                b - Most rondeaux have
```

    i) Consisted of white notes
        outlined in black or red
        notes
    ii) There are seven different
        uses for colored notes
        a - "To indicate a shift
          in rhythm
        b - "To differentiate
          between <u>cantus planus</u>
          and <u>cantu mensurabilis</u>
        c - "To show that a melody
          was to be sung an octave
          higher
        d - "To prevent a note's
          being measured perfect
        e - "To prevent instead,
          its being measured or
          altered or imperfect...
        f - "To indicate a tri-
          partite value in
          binary rhythm
        g - "To call for diminution"
   (g) Discusses the use of *mensuration
     signs   ReaA, 7
    i) (▤) and (▤) used to
        indicate the *mode
        a - Indicates two or three
          breves to a long
    ii) (O) indicates perfect
        ⁺<u>tempus</u>
        a - Indicates three semi-
          breves to a breve
    iii) (C) indicates imperfect
        ⁺<u>tempus</u>
        a - Indicates two semibreves
          to a breve
    iv) See also appendix 11
   (h) Latin text and French translation
                  PhiA
   (i) English translation   PlaV, 204
 c) Jacques of Liège (ca. 1270-1330) BakB, 770
  (1) Wrote <u>Speculum musicae</u>   JacP, 180
   (a) Covers the entire range of the
     musical knowledge of the time
   (b) Eloquent defense of the music
     of the <u>Ars antiqua</u>
   (c) Impassioned tirade against the
     <u>Ars nova</u> and all its works
   (d) English translation of <u>Prohemium</u>
     to the <u>Seventh Book</u>   JacP, 180
   (e) Latin text   JacS

4. THEORY
 a) The intervals of the third and the sixth
  are considered consonances for the first
  time on the continent   ReaF, 130

                              from secular monophonic
                              literature   UltM, 120
        b) Sacred music
            (1)   The Mass
                   (a) Earliest settings of the
                        complete ordinary of the Mass
                                                 CalM, 170
                        i)   These settings are not
                              unified in the same
                              sense as later settings
                        ii)   Masses of Toulouse,
                              Tournai, and Barcelona
                              a - May have been composed
                                  by more than one
                                  composer
                              b - Transcriptions   SchR
                        iii) The Messe de Nostre
                              Dame by Machaut is the
                              most important Mass of
                              the period, infra, p. 92
                   (b) There is evidence that poly-
                        phonic borrowing was in use
                        in the fourteenth century   JacM, 63
                        i)   It is doubtful that this
                              practice should be given
                              the term parody
                              a - The term parody
                                  usually refers to
                                  the elaborate
                                  reworking of the
                                  polyphonic fabric
                                  of original material
                                  such as was done in
                                  the late fifteenth
                                  and sixteenth
                                  centuries
                              b - The borrowing in the
                                  fourteenth century
                                  consists of re-
                                  arranging musical
                                  sections drawn
                                  from another work

    8.   COMPOSERS
        a) Petrus de Cruce   CalM, 153
            (1)   Came from Amiens
            (2)   The first one, according to Jacob
                   of Liège, to write more than three
                   semibreves to a breve
                   (a) Written in the triplum of a
                        three part motet
                   (b) Any group of semibreves
                        taking the place of a breve
                        is marked off by a point
                        known as *punctus divisionis
            (3)   His syllabic declamation approaches

```
                the *parlando in style
        (4)     Two of his compositions are found
                in the Montpellier manuscript
b)  Philippe de Vitri (1291-1361)         ReeMMA, 336
        (1)     Wrote the treatise Ars nova,
                supra, p. 84                ReeMMA, 340
        (2)     Considered to be the one who
                introduced the technique of
                isorhythm, supra, p. 86        ReaA, 8
        (3)     Uses *diminution in his music   ReaA, 10
        (4)     Codified the rondeau form       ReaA, 11
        (5)     Wrote isorhythmic motets
                (a)  He used isorhythm in both
                     the tenor and the triplum
                                            ReeMMA, 338
                (b)  The isorhythm is free of
                     *modal rhythm          ReeMMA, 337
        (6)     Ivrea Manuscript is the main source
                of Philippe de Vitri's music
                                         ReaMP 282-283
c)  Guillaume de Machaut (ca. 1300-1377)  BakB, 1002
        (1)     Composer and poet
        (2)     Style of his music
                (a)  Uses *cantilena, ⁺discant,
                     motet, and conductus styles
                                         GroH, 123, 128
                (b)  Uses instrumental
                     interludes             GroH, 127
        (3)     Texture of his music
                (a)  Monophonic            SteM, 157
                (b)  Two-part              SteM, 157
                (c)  Three-part            GroH, 124
                     i)    *Discantus
                     ii)   Tenor
                     iii)  *Contratenor
                (d)  Four-part (Mass)          ReaM, 61
                     i)    Triplum
                     ii)   Motetus
                     iii)  *Contratenor
                     iv)   Tenor
        (4)     Techniques used in his music
                (a)  Isorhythm, supra, p. 86   GroH, 123
                (b)  Uses double leading-tone
                     and Landini cadences, supra,
                     p. 87                  GroH, 125
                (c)  Uses *canon technique  SteM, 158
        (5)     Compositions
                (a)  La Messe de Nostre Dame   CalM, 171
                     i)    Unified by a plainsong
                           canto firmo      ReaA, 22
                           a - The Kyrie borrows its
                               tenor from the Vatican
                               Mass IV          ReaM, 65
                           b - The Sanctus and Agnus
                               Dei tenors are both
                               from the Vatican Mass
```

XVII   ReaM, 65
    c - The Ite is from the
        Sanctus of Vatican
        Mass VIII   ReaM, 67
ii)   The Gloria is in <u>ballade</u>
     form   ReaA, 22
iii) The Credo is in variation
     form   ReaA, 22
iv)   The Kyrie and the last
     three movements are in
     motet style
v)   The Gloria and Credo
     are in <u>conductus</u> style
vi)   Performance of the music
    a - Uses four solo singers
    b - No instruments would
        be used except,
        perhaps, an organ
        to double the tenor
        in the motet-like
        sections
vii) Transcriptions of the music
             VanM, SchM III

(b) <u>Lais</u>
i)   Monophonic with sections
     in three part *chace   SteM, 158
ii)   ⁺Double versicle structure
             CalM, 172
    a - New music for each
        ⁺double versicle
iii) Twelve stanza form   ReaM, 30
iv)   Transcriptions of the
     music   LudML

(c) Motets
i)   Machaut composed twenty-
     three   GroH, 122
ii)   All are secular except
     for six Latin motets   ReaM, 18
    a - The secular motets
        use a liturgical tenor
        which is instrumental
             GroH, 122
iii) Have French texts   ReaM, 69
iv)   Have an <u>introitus</u>, or
     prelude, before the entry
     of the tenor or *contra-
     tenor   CalM, 173
v)   Transcriptions of the
     music   LudM

(d) <u>Ballades notées</u> (Poems with
   notes)   CalM, 174-175
i)   All but one are poly-
     phonic
ii)   Written in two, three,
     and four parts
iii) The most popular of

                Machaut's music
        iv)   Transcriptions of the music
                                         LudB
  (e) Rondeaux
        i)   Machaut composed
              twenty-one   ReaM, 39
        ii)   They seem modern due
              to the lack of triple
              *prolation   ReaM, 47
        iii) *_Cantilena_ style   ReaA, 25
        iv)   _Ma fin est mon commence-_
              ment uses "retrograde"
              motion   ReaM, 48
        v)   May have been performed
              by instruments only   ReaA, 25
        vi)   Transcriptions of the
              music   LudB
  (f) Virelai (chanson balladée)
        i)   Eight out of thirty-three
              are polyphonic   ReaM, 35
        ii)   The polyphonic _virelais_
              have a simple tenor and
              a _cantus_   ReaA, 26
              a - The tenor is textless
        iii) Use *_ouvert_ and *_clos_
              endings   ReaM, 35
        iv)   Transcriptions of the
              music   LudB
  (g) Hoquetus David   ReaM, 67
        i)   An offshoot of the thir-
              teenth century motet
        ii)   Uses the plainsong tenor
              "David" from the Alleluia
              verse _Nativitas gloriose_
              virginis
        iii) Doubtful that it was used
              in church
        iv)   Textless   ReaA, 23
        v)   Isorhythmic
        vi   Transcriptions of the
              music   SchM III
(6) His best music   ReaM, 71
  (a) _Ballades_ and _rondeaux_ of the
        Voir dit (autobiographical
        poem)
  (b) _Taut doucement_
  (c) _Rose, liz_
  (d) Last four motets
  (e) Polyphonic _lais_
(7) His unusual work is _Ma fin est mon_
     commencement   ReaM, 48
(8) Chronology of the _ballades, rondeaux,_
     and _virelai_   ReaCH
(9) Commentary on Machaut's works   LudE
(10) Transcriptions of all of ...' ut's
     music   SchM II-III

B.   ITALIAN ARS NOVA (1325-1425)   E110, 29

    1.   BACKGROUND
       a)   The last vestiges of the feudal society
          were dissolving   E11F, 31
       b)   A rising industrial and mercantile
          class   E11F, 32
       c)   A strong movement toward genuine
          democratic power   E11F, 32
       d)   Florence was the most active musical
          center   E11F, 34
       e)   By the end of the fourteenth century
          Venice became an active center of
          music   E11F, 34
       f)   The Great Schism, supra, p. 83   LanR, 191
       g)   Two great poets
          (1)   Dante (1265-1321)   EB D
             (a)   Wrote "Commedia"
               i)   In the sixteenth century
                  the epithet divinia was
                  added to the title
          (2)   Petrarch (1304-1374)   EB PE
             (a)   Born at Arezzo
             (b)   The founder of humanism
             (c)   Wrote Latin verse and prose
             (d)   Italian lyrist

    2.   THEORISTS
       a)   Marchetto da Padua
          (1)   Wrote Pomerium in arte musicae
            mensuratae (ca. 1318)   StrO, 43
             (a)   Book I
                i)   A general statement of
                  rhythm and its notation
                                    ReeF, 24
                ii)   The shape of the minima
                  (♪) could possibly be
                  credited to Marchetto
                                RieH, 188
             (b)   Book II   ReeF, 24
                i)   Discusses duple rhythm
                ii)   Discusses the difference
                  between French and Italian
                  notation
                  a - Lists eight different
                      divisionis (similar
                      to modern time signa-
                      tures   E11F, 48
                  b - See also appendix 12
             (c)   Book III   ReeF, 24
                i)   Deals with ⁺ligatures
             (d)   Latin text   MarV

    3.   NOTATION
       a)   Similar to the French notation except that
          the Italian minum never attained the divisions

of the ⁺<u>tempus</u>, supra, p. 85   CalM, 182
(1)   In the Italian notation the <u>brevis</u>
        is an unalterable value   ApeN, 370
        (a)   The <u>punctus divisionis</u> is
              used to divide the semibreves
              into groups of two, three,
              or more   EllF, 48
              i)   Each group would have
                      the value of a breve
              ii)   This practice developed
                      from Petrus de Cruce   EllF, 48
              iii)   It lasted only a short
                      time   ApeN, 385
                      a - Too confining with-
                          ·out notational means
                          for ⁺syncopation
                          over the bar line
        (b)   The <u>punctus additionis</u> is also
              used with the semibreve to
              indicate augmentation   EllF, 51
(2)   Letters are used as signatures
                                          ReeMMA, 341
        (a)   T=<u>ternaria</u>
        (b)   B=<u>binaria</u>
        (c)   P=perfection
        (d)   I=imperfection
(3)   The Italians preferred a six line
        staff   ReeMMA, 343
(4)   See also appendix 12

4.   STYLE   ReeMMA, 361
     a)   <u>Conductus</u> style
     b)   <u>Cantilena</u> style
     c)   Melismatic style

5.   MANUSCRIPT SOURCES
     a)   Robertsbridge Fragment (London, Brit.
          Mus. Add. 28550 (ca. 1320)   ApeK, iv
          (1)   One of the earliest documents
                using Italian notation   CalM, 184
          (2)   Keyboard music   CalM, 184
                (a)   Music is on one staff of five
                      lines and uses both notes and
                      letters   PlaKM, 186
                (b)   Old *German tablature   RokI, 420
          (3)   Contents   ˌ   ApeH, 24
                (a)   <u>Estampies</u>
                      i)   AA BB CC
                (b)   Three *intablatures   ApeH, 26
                      i)   Use ornamental figuration
                      ii)   Two are motets from the
                              Roman de Fauvel, supra,
                              p. 54   CalM, 184
          (4)   Facsimiles   WooE Plates xlii-xlv
          (5)   Transcriptions of the music   HugE, 89-109
          (6)   Transcriptions of the music   ApeK, 1-9

    b) Squarcialupi Codex (Florence, Biblioteca
        Medicea-Laurenziana, pal. 87)   EllF, 47
        (1)   Compiled in 1415-1419   HagI, 51
             (a) Has the appearance of having
                  been compiled as a museum
                  piece rather than a manuscript
                  for actual use   EllF, 47
             (b) May have been an attempt to
                  collect all of the works of
                  the twelve most important
                  composers of the time   EllF, 47
             (c) Was compiled either by or
                  for Antonio Squarcialupi,
                  an organist at St. Maria del
                  Fiore   EllF, 47
        (2)   Major source of the works of
              Francesco Landini   CalM, 184
        (3)   Transcriptions of the music   WolS
    c) Faenza Codex (Faenza, Bibl. Communale,
        MS 117)
        (1)   Compiled ca. 1420   CalM, 195
        (2)   Instrumental elaboration of French
              and Italian music   CarC, 7
             (a) Were most likely written for the
                  positive, organ, clavichord, or
                  spinet   PlaKM, 186
             (b) Written on two staves of six
                  lines each in *score notation
                  with barlines   PlaKM, 186
                i)   The staves are in red   CarC, 7
        (3)   Contains music of Machaut, Landini,
              Bartolino da Padova, and Antonio
              Zacara da Teramo   CarC, 7
        (4)   "...earliest known sets of organ
              Mass sections organized for per-
              formance in alternation by choir
              and organ"   PlaK, vii
        (5)   Most of the pieces are *paraphrases
              of vocal music   CarC, 7
        (6)   Some pieces are related to dance
              forms   PlaK, vii
        (7)   Contains some copies of treatises
                                      CarC, 7
        (8)   Facsimiles   CarC
        (9)   Facsimiles and transcriptions   PlaK

6.   CLASSES OF MUSIC
    a) Secular music
        (1)   Madrigal   MarF, 449
             (a) The term first appears in
                  1313
                i)   Refers to poetic forms
                ii)   Thought to have been
                     derived from the word
                     matricale meaning poem
                     in mother tongue

        (b)   Two periods
              i)   The formative period
                    (1330-1350)   MarF, 450
                    a - Two to five strophes of
                        three lines each MarF, 453
                    b - Two of the lines
                        usually rhyme
                    c - May or may not be fol-
                        lowed by a *ritornello_
                        1 - This is not a
                          refrain   MarF, 454
              ii)   The crystallized
                    period (1350-1370) MarF, 451
                    a - The form ABB, CDD, EE
                        predominates   MarF, 453
                    b - ABB is the musical
                        form   MarF, 454
                        1 - Becomes a master
                          mold for later
                          poets
        (c)   A serious, expressive art-song
                                      EllF, 52
        (d)   Closely resembles the _conductus_
            cum cauda   EllF, 54-55
              i)   Florid melismatic
                    sections at the be-
                    ginning and end of
                    each line of text
              ii)   The parts with text
                    were sung by solo
                    voices
              iii)   The parts without
                    text were performed
                    on instruments
        (e)   The predominant form is ABB,
            CDD, EE
        (f)   The musical form is ABB
        (g)   The majority of the madrigals
            are written for two parts   EllF, 55
              i)   There is a text with
                    each part
        (h)   A few were written in three
            parts   EllF, 59
  (2)   _Caccia_   ReeMMA, 365
        (a)   The upper two parts are in
            *canon
        (b)   The tenor is free
              i)   Usually instrumental EllF, 62
        (c)   Consists of one strophe and
            a _ritornello_
        (d)   Texts are about hunting,
            fishing, or market scenes   EllF, 62
  (3)   _Ballata_   ReeMMA, 366-367
        (a)   The equivalent of the French
            virelai
        (b)   Consists of two sections of

nearly equal length
- (c) Lack texts in either one or
  two parts (instrumental)
- (d) Known as a song with instrumental accompaniment
- (e) The most popular secular form
  in Italy during the fourteenth
  century   HopM, 447
- (f) The music form is ABBA   EllF, 65
- (g) The poetic form may be extended
  in order to accommodate repeti-
  tions of the music   EllF, 65
  - i) Thus the text form is
    ABCD AEFG AHIJ

- b) Sacred music   ReeMMA, 368
  - (1) Very little was composed
  - (2) Mass settings were in the style
    of the madrigal and the <u>caccia</u>

7. COMPOSERS
- a) Francesco Landini (1325-1397)   BakB, 904
  - (1) Wrote nine two-voice madrigals   HopM, 456
    - (a) Consist of eleven-syllable
      lines
    - (b) Each stanza consists of three
      lines   ReeMMA, 362
    - (c) Have a two-line *<u>ritornello</u>
  - (2) Wrote two three-voice madrigals HopM, 457
    - (a) Each stanza consists of
      three lines   ReeMMA, 362
    - (b) Set continuously in the upper
      two voices over an isorhythmic
      tenor
    - (c) Have a two-line *<u>ritornello</u>
    - (d) One of the madrigals is tritextual
      - i) A different *<u>ritornello</u>
        in each voice
  - (3) Wrote one hundred forty-one
    <u>ballate</u>   HopM, 459-460
    - (a) Three classes (two Italian
      style and one French style)
      - i) Three-part with text
        in all parts (Italian)
      - ii) Three-part with text
        in two parts (Italian)
      - iii) Three-part with text
        in one part (French)
    - (b) Ninety-one two-voice <u>ballate</u>
      HopM, 459
      - i) Eighty-two vocal duets
      - ii) Nine solo songs
  - (4) The cadence which has been
    attributed to Landini was actually
    used in France before Machaut,
    supra, p. 87   ReeMMA, 350
  - (5) Complete works in transcription   SchL

C.   ARS SUBTILISSIMA (MOST SUBTLE ART)   HopM, 472

   1.   STYLE
      a)   Extremes of notational and rhythmic
         complexity known as manneristic style
                                HopM, 472
         (1)   Use of different *mensurations
             simultaneously   HopM, 477
         (2)   Displacement ⁺syncopation   HopM, 479
         (3)   Proportional *mensurations   HopM, 481
         (4)   A combination of the Italian
             notation and the French notation
             of Philippe de Vitri   ApeHD, 580

   2.   MANUSCRIPT SOURCES
      a)   Chantilly, Musée Condé, 564 (formerly
         1047)
         (1)   Dedicatory <u>ballades</u>   ApeFR, 3
         (2)   Great complexity of notation and
             texture   ApeFR, 4
         (3)   Manneristic style   ApeFR, 10
            (a)   Extended passages in
                ⁺syncopation
         (4)   Transcriptions of the music   GunM
      b)   Modena, Bibl. Estense, a, M. 5, 24
         (formerly lat. 568)   HopM, xx
         (1)   The flowering and the fading of the
             manneristic style   HopM, 471
         (2)   A return to simplicity (called
             modern style)   ApeFR, 13
         (3)   Sixty-six percent of the music
             is French   HopM, 474
         (4)   At least thirty percent of the
             compositions are by Matteo da
             Perugia   HopM, 490
            (a)   Sacred pieces with Latin texts
                               HopM, 491
            (b)   Many French secular songs
                i)   Many are written in
                    the manneristic style
                            HopM, 491
            (c)   The majority of his pieces
               tend toward the newer more
               simple style   HopM, 491
            (d)   Transcriptions of the music   GunM

   3.   COMPOSERS
      a)   Matteo da Perugia   HopM, 490
         (1)   Lived in the early fifteenth
             century in Milan
         (2)   Wrote music mostly in the French
             style   HopM, 491
         (3)   May have led the way to a simpler
             kind of music   HopM, 492
         (4)   Music found in Modena manuscript   GruM
      b)   Johannes Ciconia (ca. 1335-1411)   HopM, 493

(1)	Most of his music is in the Italian imitative style	HopM, 497
(2)	Uses both French and Italian elements in his motets and Mass movements	HopM, 498
(3)	A forerunner of the new international style	HopM, 494

    (a)   Harsh manneristic music of France   HopM, 501

    (b)   Humanistic music of Italy

                        HopM, 501

        i)   Not humanistic in the sense of the Greek and Roman revival but music which was humanized

  (4)   Facsimiles and transcriptions of the music   FisP

  (5)   Transcriptions of the music   AdlST

D.   PERIPHERAL MUSIC

   1.   GERMANY
      a)   Geisslerlieder   ReeMMA, 239
         (1)   Consist of a four-line stanza
         (2)   Melodic pattern aabb
         (3)   Anticipates the Lutheran chorale
      b)   The Geissler   ReeMMA, 239
         (1)   Flagellants
         (2)   Celebrated penitential rites
         (3)   Rites accompanied by Lieder in the vernacular

E.   ENGLISH MUSIC IN THE FOURTEENTH CENTURY

   1.   BACKGROUND
      a)   Hundred Years War (1338)   LanE, 287
      b)   Black Death (1348-1349)   LanE, 288
      c)   English language began to be taught in the schools (1375)   LanE, 289
      d)   First complete, vernacular English Bible (ca. 1376)   LanE, 289
      e)   Chaucer, Geoffrey (ca. 1340-1400)   LanE, 290
         (1)   Chaucer, along with John Wiclif, Oxford, Cambridge, and the Court, established Midland English as the language of the people
         (2)   Wrote the "Canterbury Tales"
         (3)   Translated Boethius' Consolatio
      f)   Change in liturgical emphasis   HarE, 82
         (1)   "Tropes of the Ordinary and the Proper of the Mass gave way to settings of the ritual texts of

the Ordinary..."
- (a) This was true except for the trope of the Kyrie
- (2) The _conductus_ gave way to the *votive antiphon by the end of the century
- (3) Leadership of the monasteries gave way to cathedrals and collegiate churches and colleges

2. PHILOSOPHICAL, THEOLOGICAL, AND POLITICAL THINKING
   - a) Occam, William (ca. 1280-1349)   EB O
     - (1) Expelled from the Franciscan order in 1331
     - (2) Wrote many treatises
       - (a) He thought that the will and not intellect is the primary faculty of the soul
       - (b) He believed in the doctrine of the independence of political life from that of ecclesiastical power   EB P
       - (c) He believed in the right of citizens to choose their own rulers   EB P
   - b) Wiclif, John (ca. 1320-1384)   EA W
     - (1) Oxford don   LanE, 289
     - (2) Wrote "Civil Dominion" (Lollardy)
                                              LanE, 289
       - (a) Advocated propertyless church
         - i) Christians hold all things of God under contract to be virtuous
         - ii) Sin negates this contract and destroys title to goods and offices
       - (b) Insisted on the direct access of the individual to God
       - (c) Advocated the right of individual judgement
     - (3) Denied transubstantiation (1382)
                                              LanE, 290

3. THEORISTS
   - a) Robert de Handlo
     - (1) Wrote _Regulae cum maximis Magistri Franconis cum additionibus aliorum musicorum_   HanRM
       - (a) Probably written in England in 1326   HanR, 1
       - (b) Found in London, British Mus. Add. MS 4909   HanR, 1
       - (c) A manual for the practical musician   HanR, 1

                     i)   It consists of the
rules of ⁺mensural
notation by Franco of
Cologne, Johannes de
Garlandia, and others,
with comments and addi-
tions by Handlo   WesN, 300
- (d) English translation   HanR
- (e) Latin text   HanRM
  - i)   See also appendix 14, no. 6
- b) Willelmus   ReaO, 6-10
  - (1) Wrote <u>Breviarium regulare musicae</u> (ca.1372)
    - (a) Derived his inspiration from <u>Compendium</u> attributed to Franco
    - (b) Chapter I is missing
    - (c) Chapter II discusses the monochord division
    - (d) Chapter III discusses musical intervals, note values, and two medieval letter systems
      - i) Every note is simple or <u>fecunda</u>
        - a - A simple note is the smallest value in use (<u>semiminum</u>)
        - b - All other notes are note <u>fecunda</u> because they can be divided into parts of lesser value
      - ii) Adds a <u>largissima</u> to the system of notes
        - a - In the form of a <u>maxima</u> with a tail above and below on the right hand side
      - iii) Quotes Odington as saying the semibreve should be a rectangular shape and not lozenge shaped
      - iv) Every note except the <u>semiminum</u> may be <u>plicated</u>
        - a - This disagrees with Franco and Odington
    - (e) Latin text   ReaO
- c) Torkesey, Johannes
  - (1) Wrote <u>Declaratio trianguli et acuti</u> (late fourteenth century)   ReaO, 9
    - (a) A diagram of *mensural note values

                    (b)   Latin text   ReaO

4.   THEORY
     a) ⁺Discant
         (1)   In the fourteenth century the term
               ⁺discant was gradually changed
               to ⁎counterpoint   CroD, 10
               (a)   The term ⁺"counterpoint" was
                     first used by Johannes de
                     Garlandia in the thirteenth
                     century   BusR, 227
         (2)   Parallel perfect and imperfect
               intervals were used on an equal
               basis until the late fourteenth
               century   HarE, 89
               (a)   The third, sixth, tenth, and
                     thirteenth were considered
                     imperfect   MeeT, 58
         (3)   In the late fourteenth century the
               mean-tenor-counter technique
               appears   HarE, 97
               (a)   Consisted of a monorhythmic
                     tenor (a part written in a
                     constant note value)
               (b)   Had a composed "counter"
                     beneath the tenor
               (c)   A mean (medius) was composed
                     above the tenor
               (d)   Momentary crossing of the
                     tenor and counter parts
                     were frequent
         (4)   In the course of the fourteenth
               century ⁺discant changed from
               continuously parallel movement
               to more independence of line   HarE, 95
               (a)   Parallel triads became dis-
                     guised by voice crossing   SanC, 15
               (b)   Sometimes parallel chords
                     were disguised by ⁺syncopation
                                                   SanC, 15
               (c)   Much of the music has no
                     parallelism at all   SanC, 15
     b) Range of the music   SanC, 33
         (1)   Since the cantus-planus was often
               in the middle voice, the lower
               voice had to go very low
               (a)   This problem was solved in
                     two ways
                     i)   Use of a migrant cantus
                           firmus
                     ii)   Transposition of the
                           cantus-planus upwards
                           a fifth and sometimes
                           a fourth
                           a - The latter practice
                               is rare

5. NOTATION
    a) Most English polyphonic music of the
        fourteenth century was written in
        *score notation   SanC, 7
        (1)   Music in *score was used only for
               conducti and sequences on the continent
    b) Conservatism in notation   HarE, 83
    c) Use of the *punctus divisionis   HarE, 87
    d) Use of French *prolation   HarE, 94

6. STYLE
    a) Predilection for full sound   ReeMMA, 403
    b) Conservatism in rhythmic style   HarE, 83
    c) Parallel style   HarE, 83
        (1)   "...Use of parallel thirds and sixths
               on a parity with perfect intervals"
        (2)   Parallel style continued until the
               late fourteenth century   HarE, 89
    d) Mean-tenor-counter style   HarE, 97
    e) Rondellus-conductus-motet style   HarE, 94
        (1)   Written in rondellus technique
    f) *Cantilena style   SanC, 14
    g) Sectional structural features   SanC, 21

7. TECHNIQUES
    a) The use of a "substitute" part for the
        tenor and quartus-cantus   HarE, 84
        (1)   Makes a four part composition
               become a three part composition
        (2)   Possibly one of the earliest
               instances of a "substitute" part
    b) Rondellus technique, supra, p. 71   SanC, 9
    c) Isorhythm, supra, p. 86   HarE, 99
    d) *Paraphrases of chant phrases   SanC, 29
    e) Migration ("migrant" cantus-firmus)   SanC, 29
    f) Partial transposition of the cantus-
        firmus   SanC, 29

8. MANUSCRIPT SOURCES
    a) Oxford, New College 362 (ca. 1320)   HarA, 69
        (1)   Twelve complete pieces
               (a)   Eight motets
               (b)   Two rondellus-motets
               (c)   Two pieces in rondellus-
                      conductus style
    b) Oxford, Bodleian Lib. Hatton 81
        (ca. 1330)   HarA, 69
        (1)   One motet
        (2)   One rondellus-motet
        (3)   Two pieces in conductus style
    c) Oxford, Bodleian Lib. MS E Museo 7
        (ca. 1340)   HarA, 69
        (1)   Known as the Bury St. Edmunds
               manuscript   HarE, 93
        (2)   Four motets
        (3)   One rondellus-motet

        (4)   Three Anglo-French motets
        (5)   A discussion of two of the motets
               on St. Edmund   BukS, 17
        (6)   Transcriptions of the two motets
                                                      BukS, 29
    d) Cambridge, Gonville and Caius College
        543/512 (ca. 1336-1355)   HarA, 69
        (1)   Four motets
        (2)   Three pieces in <u>conductus</u> style
    e) Durham, Cathedral Lib. C. I. 20
        (ca. 1350-1360)   HarA, 69
        (1)   Five motets
        (2)   Five Anglo-French motets (two by
               Philippe de Vitri)

9. CLASSES OF MUSIC
    a) The monophonic carol
        (1)   "The earliest extant example of
               carol texts date from the middle
               or second half of the fourteenth
               century..."   BukPSM, 120
        (2)   It has been suggested that the
               etymon of the word "carol" is
               "Kyrie eleison"   SteMC, xiv
        (3)   Originally a dance song of
               fixed form   BukPSM, 119
               (a)   Linked to the family of
                      European lyric-forms,
                      <u>virelai</u>, and <u>ballata</u>   SteMC, xiii
               (b)   English <u>forme-fixe</u>   SteMC, xiii
        (4)   Only one carol from the four-
               teenth century has survived   BukPSM, 120
               (a)   The monophonic carol
                      "Lullay, lullay"
               (b)   Found in Cambridge Uni-
                      versity Library, Add.
                      5943
               (c)   Transcription of the carol   SteMC
        (5)   Form of the carol
               (a)   Strophic with a refrain at
                      the beginning and end and
                      between each stanza   CalM, 215
        (6)   Performance of the carol   BukPSM, 119
               (a)   The refrain, or *burden,
                      was sung and danced in a
                      round by a group of people
               (b)   A variable stanza was sung
                      by the leader or possibly
                      a few soloists
    b) Polyphonic music
        (1)   Mass movements
               (a)   Use of mean-tenor-counter
                      technique   HarE, 97
               (b)   ⁺Discant settings with two
                      parts above the tenor are
                      rare but do occur   HarE, 98

```
              (c)  Use of isorhythm              HarE, 100
              (d)  Settings of the Spiritus et
                   alme trope of the Gloria
                   without the use of the
                   plainsong                     HarE, 100
         (2)  Motet
              (a)  Use of isorhythm              HarE, 83
                   i)    Used short patterns
              (b)  Variety in the treatment of
                   the tenor                      HarE, 83
                   i)    Use of neuma (plainsong
                         melisma)                 HarE, 84
                   ii)   Use of French secular
                         songs                    HarE, 84
                   iii)  Use of a ⁺respond, an
                         ⁺antiphon, or a sequence
                                                  HarE, 84
              (c)  Use of rondellus-motet
                   technique                      HarE, 91
         (3)  Conductus                           HarE, 88-91
              (a)  Three-voice conductus in
                   interchange with a short
                   prelude for two voices
                   i)    A sequential melody
                         in *canon
              (b)  Two parts in rondellus
                   technique over a wordless
                   tenor with an independent
                   prelude
              (c)  Distinctive features
                   i)    Parallel movement
                   ii)   Use of ornamented
                         plainsong
              (d)  Use of a more developed
                   stage of rondellus
                   technique
                   i)    The vocalized
                         prelude and interlude
                         are dropped
         (4)  Hymns                               BukPSM, 114-119
              (a)  A liturgical form which
                   entered the realm of popular
                   music
              (b)  Angelus ad virginem
                   i)    A three part polyphonic
                         setting
                   ii)   Transcription of the
                         music                    BukPSM, 116
              (c)  Red Book of Ossory
                   i)    Contains cantilenae
                         a - No music
                   ii)   The popular tune that
                         was used is indicated
                         by the opening line
                         (timbres)
                   iii)  Written in carol form
```

F. PERFORMANCE PRACTICES

1. PURPOSE OF ACCOMPANIMENT IN THE MIDDLE
    AGES   BedP, 54
    a) To give rest to the singer between
        verses (organ Mass)   BedP, 57
        (1)   Known as alternatim structure   ApeH, 30
        (2)   The alternation of organ movements
               and Gregorian chant   ApeH, 30
    b) Play above or about the voice in ornamental
        style (*heterophony)

2. USE OF INSTRUMENTS
    a) Machaut mentioned that the textless
        tenors of his ballades could be played
        on a Cornemuse (single reed type) or
        on an organ   BedP, 58
    b) The average string instrument was more
        plucked than bowed and was not fit for
        "part" work   BedP, 58
    c) Trumpets and other "sweet sounding
        instruments" were allowed on occasion
        in the church service (1375)   BedP, 59

G. INSTRUMENTS

1. AEROPHONES
    a) Trumpet   Ess, 99
        (1)   Clarion
               (a) Three foot straight metal
                    tubing
               (b) Small bore
               (c) Cup mouthpiece
               (d) High pitch
               (e) Appears in folded form in the
                    fourteenth century
                    i)   It was called a trumpet
               (f) First mentioned in English
                    literature in 1325   MarMI, 109
        (2)   Buisine   MarMI, 74
               (a) A large straight trumpet
               (b) A German instrument
    b) Cornett   MarMI, 128
        (1)   The straight model was made from
               animal horn
        (2)   Curved model made from wood
        (3)   Finger holes
        (4)   Cup mouthpiece
        (5)   First mentioned ca. 1400
    c) Organ   ArnO, 3
        (1)   The use of stops to render some
               ranks silent while others were
               played may have begun in Italy
               between 1400 and 1450
        (2)   Solo stops and softer stops were

                          added
                  (3)   The pedal board was adopted in the
                         Netherlands and Germany
                  (4)   As many as three manuals
                  (5)   Fully chromatic   EssH, 100

     2.   MEMBRANOPHONES   EssH, 100
           a)   Tambourine
                  (1)   Round frame
                  (2)   Skin top and bottom
                  (3)   Jingles on the side
           b)   Tabor
                  (1)   A drum struck with sticks
                          (a)   Similar to the modern snare
                                 drum

     3.   IDIOPHONES
           a)   Triangle   MarMI, 531
                  (1)   A triangular shaped metal rod
                          (a)   Struck with a metal beater
                  (2)   First appeared in the early
                         fourteenth century
                  (3)   Early triangles were often
                         stirrup-shaped

     4.   CHORDOPHONES
           a)   The lute   ApeHD, 490
                  (1)   Stringed instrument with a body
                         and a neck
                  (2)   European lute with a central sound
                         hole most likely came by way of
                         Spain in the late fourteenth
                         century
           b)   Clavichord (also known as monochord)
                                                            MarMI, 111-113
                  (1)   An oblong wooden box
                  (2)   Originally had "fretted"
                         strings
                  (3)   Struck by metal tangents
                          (a)   Brass blades driven into
                                 the back end of the key
                  (4)   The name clavichord was first
                         used in 1404
           c)   Harpsichord (originally known as
                clavicimbalum)   MarMI, 234-235
                  (1)   Crude predecessor of the Baroque
                         form   EssH, 99
                  (2)   Strings plucked by plectrums or
                         quills
                  (3)   First mentioned in 1404

H.   TERMS

     1.   BURDEN. A refrain: used in connection with
                  the fifteenth century carol   ApeHD, 114

2.   CANON. Any kind of inscription ("rule") which
      indicates the execution of a com-
      position that is intentionally notated
      incompletely;   ApeHD, 126
      a contrapuntal device in which a melody
      in one part is imitated exactly in another
      part, or parts: usually the imitation
      begins at a short distance from the
      original voice   ApeHD, 124

3.   CANTILENA. In the fourteenth and fifteenth
      century, a term for the treble dominated
      style, such as was used for the ballades,
      virelais, and rondeaux; consisted of a
      vocal part accompanied by two instrumental
      parts   ApeHD, 130

4.   CHACE. A French composition of the early
      fourteenth century written in strict
      *canon form at the unison: usually a
      triple *canon with no supporting tenor,
      the latter usually being found in the
      Italian caccia   ApeHD, 141

5.   CLOS. A term used in dance music and vocal
      pieces of similar structure indicating
      a final cadence at the end of a repeated
      section   WeaN, 114

6.   COLOR. A special device of composition such
      as the repetition of a melodic phrase
      (isorhythm)   ApeHD, 183

7.   CONTRATENOR. A third voice part added to
      basic two voice texture of discant:
      superius and tenor; same range as the
      tenor creating crossing of voices   ApeHD, 204

8.   DIMINUTION. The presentation of a melody
      in halved values   ApeHD, 63

9.   DISCANTUS. Name for the uppermost part
      of a polyphonic piece: equals the
      second, or counter, voice   ApeHD, 237

10.   GERMAN TABLATURE, OLD. A type of notation
      which employed notes for the upper part
      and letters for the lower parts: used
      prior to 1550   ApeHD, 829

11.   GAMUT. English for scale or range   ApeHD, 341

12.   HETEROPHONY. "The principle of heterophony
      consists of a melody's being employed
      simultaneously in several voices, but in
      such a way that the melodic line of the

leading voice--which has the 'theme'--
is not duplicated in the other voices--
which play round the fundamental line
freely and vary it, without, however,
wandering so far from it that one may
say they have melodic independence"

ReeMMA, 50

13. INCIPIT. In the thirteenth and fourteenth
     centuries the term was used to indicate
     a word or two given at the beginning of
     the tenor and serving as a reference to
     the chant from which the tenor in cantus-
     firmus motets was taken   ApeHD, 405

14. INTABLATURE. A term designating a keyboard
     or lute arrangement of vocal music: used
     from the fourteenth to sixteenth century

ApeHD, 416

15. MENSURATION. The term used for the temporal
     relationships between note values of
     mensural notation, supra, p. 65   ApeHD, 520

16. MODE (MODUS). In mensural notation the
     relationship between the longa and the
     brevis   ApeHD, 537

17. MUTATION. In order to exceed the compass
     of one hexachord, two or more hexachords
     were interlocked by a process of
     transition called mutation, see also
     appendix 6   ApeHD, 384

18. OUVERT. Indicates an intermediate cadence
     at the end of a repeated section when
     performed the first time: used in
     medieval dance music and vocal music
     of similar structure   WesN, 477

19. PARAPHRASE. A free elaboration of a plain-
     song melody; original and additional notes
     blend into a new melody   ApeHD, 642

20. PARLANDO. An indication that the voice must
     approximate speech   ApeHD, 643

21. PROLATION. "In the early fourteenth century
     the term meant either all the *men-
     surations (modus, tempus, and prolatio)
     or the four combinations of tempus and
     prolatio"   ApeHD, 698

22. PUNCTUS DIVISIONIS. A point of division
     used to mark off the extent of semi-
     breve groups equalling a breve   ReeMMA, 331

23. RITORNELLO. The couplet at the end of the
        poem of the caccia and madrigal; expresses
        the thought derived from the preceding
        "description"   ApeHD, 735

24. SCORE NOTATION. All parts of the music are
        arranged one underneath the other on
        different staves; used exclusively on the
        continent before 1225 for writing down
        polyphonic music; discarded with the
        development of the motet   ApeHD, 759

25. TALEA. A repeated scheme of time values
        (isorhythm)   ApeHD, 427

26. VOTIVE ANTIPHON. A sacred composition in
        honor of some particular saint usually
        in honor of the Virgin Mary   GroH, 153

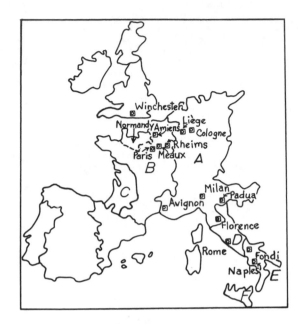

11. PLACES AND PEOPLE OF INTEREST (1300-1425)

A. Holy Roman Empire
B. Kingdom of France
C. Duchy of Aquitaine
D. Papal Lands
E. Kingdom of Naples
F. Kingdom of Sicily

Clement V: removed the Papal Seat to Rome
Urban VI: became Pope in Rome
St. Thomas Aquinas (Sicily, Naples, Cologne,
  and Paris)
Jean de Muris (Normandy)
Petrus de Cruce (Amiens)
Francesco Landini (Florence)
Matteo da Perugia (Milan)
Johannes Ciconia (Liège and Padua)

Supplemental Sources for the
Late Gothic Period

<u>BOOKS</u>

Apel, Willi. "Imitation in the Thirteenth and Fourteenth
Centuries." In <u>Essays in Honor of Archibald Davison</u>,
pp. 25-38. Cambridge: Harvard University Department
of Music, 1957.

Coussemaker, Edmond de. <u>Scriptorum de musicae medii aevi
novam seriem a Gerbertina alteram collegit nuncque
primum</u>. 4 vols. Edited by E. de Coussemaker.
Paris: "n.p.", 1864; reprint ed., Hildesheim: George
Olms, 1963.

Gennrich, Friedrich. <u>Rondeaux, Virelais und Balladen aus
dem Ende des XII, dem XIII und dem ersten den uber
Drittel des XIV Jh., mit uberlieferten Melodien</u>. 2
vols. Dresden: "n.p.", 1920 or 1921: Gottingen:
"n.p.", 1927.

Hoppin, Richard. "Tonal Organization in Music Before the
Renaissance." In <u>Paul A Pisk: Essays in His Honor</u>,
pp. 25-37. Edited by John Glowacki. Austin, Texas:
University of Texas, [c.1966].

Mendel, Arthur. "Some Ambiguities of the Mensural
System." In <u>Studies in Music History: Essays for
Oliver Strunk</u>, pp. 137-160. Edited by Harold
Powers. Princeton: Princeton University Press, 1968

Meyer-Baer, Kathi. "Music in Dante's Divina commedia."
In <u>Aspects of Medieval and renaissance Music: A
Birthday Offering to Gustave Reese</u>. Edited by Jan
LaRue. New York: W. W. Norton and Co., Inc., 1966.

Munrow, David. <u>Instruments of the Middle Ages and
Renaissance</u>. London: Oxford University Press, Music
Department, 1976.

Reaney, Gilbert. "Ars nova." In <u>Pelican History of</u>

Music, pp. 261-308. Vol. 1. Edited by A. Robertson
and Dennis Stevens. "N.p.": Penguin Books, 1960

_____. "Notes on the Harmonic Technique of Guillaume
de Machaut." In Essays in Musicology: A Birthday
Offering for Willi Apel, pp. 63-68. Edited by Hans
Tishler. Bloomington: A School of Music, Indiana
University Publication, [1968].

Smith, F. Joseph. Jacobi Leodieses "Speculum musicae":
A Commentary. 2 vols. Musicological Studies, vols.
13 and 22. Brooklyn: Institute of Mediaeval Music,
1966-1969.

Strunk, Oliver. "Church Polyphony Apropos of a New
Fragment at Grottaferrata from l'Ars nova italiana
del trecento, Secondo Convegno internazionale." In
Essays on Music in the Western World, pp. 305-313.
Compiled by Oliver Strunk. Forward by Leura
Lockwood. New York: W. W. Norton and CO., Inc.,
[1974].

Wolf, Johannes. Geschichte der Mensural-notation von
1250-1460. Hildesheim: Georg Olms; Wiesbaden:
Breitkopf and Hartel, 1965

CATALOGUES, INDICES, AND BIBLIOGRAPHIES

Fischer, Pieter, ed. The Theory of Music from the
Carolingian Era up to 1400. Volume 2: Italy.
Répertoire international des sources musicales
[International Inventory of Musical Sources], vol.
B3:2. München-Duisburg: G. Henle Verlag, [c.1968].

Hagopian, Viola L. Italian Ars nova Music: A
bibliographical guide to modern editions and
related literature. California: University of
California Press, 1943.

Reaney, Gilbert. Manuscripts of Polyphonic Music:
(c.1320-1400). Répertoire international des sources
musicales [International Inventory of Musical
Sources], vol. B4:2. München-Duisburg: G. Henle
Verlag, [c.1969].

_____, ed. Manuscripts of polyphonic music:
Eleventh Through Early Fourteenth Century:
Volume I. Répertoire international des sources
musicales [International Inventory of Musical
Sources], vol. B4:1. München-Duisburg: G. Henle
Verlag, [c.1968].

Smits van Waesberghe, Joseph, ed. The Theory of Music
form the Carolingian Era up to 1400: Volume I.
Répertoire international des sources musicales

[International Inventory of Musical Sources], vol.
B3:1. München-Duisburg: G. Henle Verlag, [c.1961].

ARTICLES IN PERIODICALS

Anderson, Gordon. "Responsory Chants in the Tenors of
Some Fourteenth Century Continental Motets." Journal
of the American Musicological Society 29:1 (1976):
119-126.

Apel, Willi. "The French Secular Music After Machaut."
Acta Musicologica 18-19 (1946-1947): 17-29.

Ellinwood, Leonard. "Francesco Landini and His Music."
Musical Quarterly 22 (1936) 4: 190-216.

Ficker, Rudolf von. "On the technique, origin and
evolution of Italian trecento music." Musical
Quarterly 47:1 (1961): 41-57.

Fischer, Kurt von. "The Manuscript Paris, Bibl. Nat.,
Nouv. Acq. Frc. 6771 (Codex Reina=PR)." Musica
Disciplina 11 (1957): 38-79.

Fuller, Sarah. "Discant and the Theory of Fifthing."
Acta Musicologica 50 (1978): 241-275

Gilles, Andre, Jean Maillard, and Gilbert Reaney.
"Philippe de Vitri-'Ars nova'." Musica Disciplina
11 (1957): 12-30.

Harlinger, Jan W. "Marchetto's Division of the Whole
Tone." Journal of the American Musicological Society
34:2 (1981): 193-217.

Kohn, Karl. "The Renotation of Polyphonic Music."
Musical Quarterly 67:1 (1981): 29-50.

Marrocco, W. Thomas. "The Ballata: A Metamorphic
Form." Acta Musicologica 31 (1959): 32-37.

_____. "The Fourteenth-Century Madrigal: Its Form
and Content." Speculum: A Journal of Medieval
Studies 26:3 (1951): 449-457.

Nadas, John. "The Structure of MS Panciatichi 26 and the
Transmission of Trecento Polyphony." Journal of the
American Musicological Society 34:3 (1981): 393-428.

Perle, G. "Integrative Devices in the Music of Machaut."
Musical Quarterly 34 (1948).

Plamanac, Dragan. "A note on the Rearrangement of Faenza
Codex 117." Journal of the American Musicological
Society 17:1 (1964): 78-81.

Reaney, Gilbert. "The 'Ars nova' of Philippe de Vitri."
    Musica Disciplina 10 (1956): 5-34.

_____. "A Postscript to Philippe de vitri's 'Ars
    nova'." Musica Disciplina 14 (1960): 29-32.

_____. "Concerning the origins of the medieval lai."
    Music and Letters 39 (1958): 343-346.

Sanders, Ernest H. "The Early Motets of Philippe de
    Vitri." Journal of the American Musicological
    Society 28:1 (1975): 24-45.

_____. "Cantilena and Discant in Fourteenth Century
    England." Musica Disciplina 19 (1965): 7-52.

MUSIC

Davison, Archibald, and Willi Apel. Historical Anthology
    of Music. Vol. 1: Oriental, Medieval and Renaissance
    Music. Revised ed. Cambridge: Harvard University
    Press, 1972.

Guillaume de Machaut. Oeuvres complètes: Guillaume de
    Machaut. Établie par S. Leguy. Paris: Le Droict
    Chemin de Musique, 1977.

_____. La Messe de Nostre Dame. Transcribed by
    Jacques Chailley. Paris: Rouart, Lerdle, 1948.

Marrocco, W. Thomas, ed. Fourteenth-Century Italian
    Caccia. Cambridge: The Mediaeval Academy of America,
    1942.

Schering, Arnold, ed. Geschichte der Musik in
    Beispielen. Leipzig: Breitkopf and Härtel, 1931;
    revised ed., Wiesbaden: Breitkopf and Härtel,
    [c.1959].

Stainer, John, Sir, ed. Sacred and Secular Songs:
    Together with other MS compositions in the Bodleian
    Library, Oxford, ranging from about A.D. 1185 to
    about A.D. 1505. Early Bodleian Music. Vol. 1:
    Facsimiles; vol. 2: Transcriptions. Forward by E.
    W. B. Nicholson. Transcriptions by J. F. R. Stainer
    and C. Stainer. London: Novello and Co., Limited;
    Farnborough, Hants: Gregg Press Limited, 1967.

Van, Guillaume de., transcriber. Les Monuments de L'Ars
    nova. Fasicule 1: Musique polyphonique de 1300 a
    1400: environ. Paris: Éditions de L'Oiseau-Lyre,
    [1938].

APPENDIX 1
Greek Music

I.   HISTORICAL MUSICAL PERIODS

A.   <u>ARCHAIC MUSIC</u> (eighth century to the fifth
      century B.C.)   ApeHD, 351

      1.   MUSIC IN HOMER'S GREECE
            a)   A sophisticated art
            b)   Epic songs sung by professional
                 bards to the accompaniment of the
                 lyre (phorminx)
            c)   Wedding songs
            d)   Dirges
            e)   Instrumental music
                 (1)   Played by shepherds on the
                       syrinx (panpipes)
                 (2)   Dance music played on the
                       lyre or aulos

      2.   THE MUSIC OF THE LYRICS   HenA, 378-379
            a)   Sprang from Ionian Greece but
                 centered in Sparta
            b)   Festival music
                 (1)   Epic songs
                 (2)   Poetic songs dedicated to
                       deities
                 (3)   The dithyramb (choric hymn)
                       (a)   (ca. sixth century B.C.)
                       (b)   Recital of the birth of
                             Dionysus
                             i)   Danced and sung to
                                   the aulos by a chorus
                                   of men and boys
                       (c)   Developed into a strophic
                             form in the early Classic
                             period
                             i)   Broke the limits of
                                   the set subjects
                 (4)   Tragedy and Comedy

(a)   May have originally
referred to Dionyaus

B.   <u>CLASSICAL MUSIC</u>   ApeHD, 351

1.   PERFECTED IN THE FIFTH CENTURY B.C.
      a)   Pindar (ca. 522-443 B.C.)   EB PI, 933-934
           (1)   Professional musician   HenA, 390
           (2)   Wrote odes in lyric forms HenA, 390
                 (a)   Hymns to deities
                 (b)   Choral, antistrophic
                       festal songs
                 (c)   Choral dithyrambs
                 (d)   Choral dance songs
                 (e)   Dirges
                       i)   Choral dances sung
                            to the music of a
                            flute
      b)   Aristophanes (ca. 448-385 B.C.)
                                         EB A, 347-348
           (1)   A citizen of Athens
           (2)   He wrote comedies for the
                 theatre
                 (a)   Satires about personalities
                       in public and private life
                 (b)   Used citizen choruses and
                       instrumentalists   HenA, 390
                       i)   No professional train-
                            ing was required
      c)   The period of Plato and Aristoxenus
           (1)   Plato (427-347 B.C.)   BakB, 1258
                 (a)   Preferred the music of
                       the early fifth century
                                             HenA, 387
                       i)   He felt that the Dorian
                            <u>harmonia</u> (idiom; tuning)
                            best represented this
                            music
                 (b)   Believed that music was
                       indivisible from the words
                       and their meanings   HenA, 385
           (2)   Aristoxenus (b. 354 B.C.)   BakB, 45
                 (a)   He preferred the music of
                       the early fifth century
                                             HenA, 387
                       i)   He thought it was
                            represented by the
                            enharmonic <u>genus</u>,
                            infra, p. 123
                       ii) It is generally be-
                            lieved that the
                            Dorian <u>harmonia</u>
                            and the enharmonic
                            <u>genus</u> were intimately
                            related   HenA, 387

    d)   The Athenian dramatists (tragic and comic)

      (1)   Used a chorus of amateur citizens accompanied by the aulos

2.   THE AULOS   MarMI, 26

    a)   A double pipe wind instrument made of wood or ivory

    b)   It used both single and double reeds

    c)   There were four fingerholes

      (1)   More holes were added at a later date

    d)   Appeared in Asia at a much earlier date

    e)   Later it was known by the Romans as a _tibia_

3.   DEVELOPMENT OF THE KITHARA   HenA, 381

    a)   Wood body

    b)   Shell shaped sound board

    c)   Oxhide stretched over the face and horns

    d)   Cross-bar with pegs

    e)   Varying number of strings (four to eleven or twelve)

4.   AEOLIAN MUSIC   HenA, 382

    a)   Aeolian _harmonia_

      (1)   An idiom and a tuning

        (a)   Pitch was relative

      (2)   Poetic forms were served by different _harmoniae_ called by ethnic names such as Dorian, Lydian, Phrygian, Ionian, etc.   ApeHD, 352

        (a)   By the end of the fifth century only the Dorian and the Phrygian terms remained

5.   THE DITHYRAMBISTS   ApeHD, 352

    a)   Later fifth century B.C. until the fall of Athens (404 B.C.)

      (1)   Broke from old poetic forms and music

      (2)   Developed instrumental improvisations which imitated nature

    b)   A period of decline

C.   MUSIC AFTER THE PELOPONNESIAN WAR (431-404 B.C.)

                                  EB PW, 611

1.   THE INVENTION OF THE HYDRAULIC ORGAN HenA, 398

2.   USE OF MASSED CHOIRS IN THE THEATRE HenA, 398

    a)   Choirs sang in octaves

3.   SOLO MUSIC ON THE KITHARA   HenA, 398

4.   AULOI PLAYED IN UNISON AND ANTIPHONALLY
                                         HenA, 398

II.   THEORY

    A. SOURCES OF THEORETICAL TREATISES

        1.   EIGHTEEN MAIN SOURCES
              a) Cover a period from the sixth
                  century B.C. to the fourth
                  century A.D.   ReeMMA, 17-19
              b) Titles and sources   ReeMMA, 17-19

    B. CONCERN WITH THE DIVISION OF MUSICAL SPACE

        1.   THE THEORY OF PYTHAGORAS OF SAMOS
              (ca. 582-500 B.C.)   BakB, 1293
              a) Bequeathed the principle of
                  expressing the division of
                  the string of the monochord by
                  ratios   HenA, 341
                  (1) Produced the theory of
                       harmonics
              b) Developed a theoretical scale,
                  conceived as a structural element
                  of the cosmos   HenA, 341
                  (1) A scale of tetrachords of
                       the perfect fourth

        2.   "HARMONISTS"   HenA, 342
              a) Immediate predecessors of Aristoxenus
                  (1) Split music into the smallest
                       intervals audible (pycnomata)

        3.   THE THEORY OF ARISTOXENUS   HenA, 343
              a) Taken from notes on his lectures
                  ca. 322 B.C.
              b) An inductive theory of music based
                  on the voice in action
              c) Divided musical space by "con-
                  sonances"
                  (1) The fourth, fifth and octave

    C. SPECIES AND TONOI

        1.   THE SPECIES WERE A PART OF THE SYSTEMS OF
              ARISTOXENUS AND PTOLEMY   WinM, 10
              a) Thought to be a systemization of
                  earlier scales   WinM, 22

(1)   <u>Spondeion</u> scale as described by
Plutarch

Fig. 1. Spondeion Scale

E F (?) a b c*
E E* F a b c
*=quarter tone; c=middle c; (WinM, 22)

(2)   The second scale is a later
version of the first scale   WinM, 22
(3)   Figure 2 shows scales as
described by Aristides   AriM, 20

Fig. 2.

Lydian: E* F a b b* c e e*
Dorian: D E E* F a b b* c e
Phrygian: D E E* F a b b* c d
Ionian: BB BB* C E G a
Mixolydian: BB BB* C D E E* F B
Syntonolydian: BB BB* C E G
*=quarter tone; c=middle c; (AriM, 20; WinM, 22)

2.   PRODUCED A COHERENT THEORETICAL STRUCTURE
WHICH BY THEORETICAL REASONING PRODUCED A
BASIC SCALE (FOURTH CENTURY B.C.)   HenA, 349

3.   "PITCH" EXISTED IN THE SENSE OF RELATIVE
POSITION   HenA, 349

4.   THE PURPOSE WAS TO NAME POINTS, BOTH
FIXED AND MOVEABLE, ON A DIAGRAMMATIC
STRUCTURE   HenA, 352

5.   THE OCTAVE-SPECIES (ARISTOXENUS)
a)   The early lyras and kitharas were
incapable of playing a <u>disdiapason</u>
                                     ReeMMA, 28
(1)   Most instruments had the
compass of an octave
b)   "The Dorian octave was the octave <u>par
excellence</u> of Greek music"   ReeMMA, 28-29
(1)   It was the "central octave" or
"characteristic octave"
c)   The other octave-scales are
thought to be redistributions
of the Dorian octave   ReeMMA, 47
d)   The octave-species were enumerated
before Aristoxenus   WinM, 11
(1)   No evidence of theorizing about
fourths and fifths   WinM, 21

(2) Modal names were attached to
them and also the term <u>harmonia</u>
WinM, 21
e) There were seven species of the octave
combined in a two-octave scale   WinM, 17
(1) An eighth species of the octave
was added at a later date
(a) Known as the hypermixolydian
(2) The two-octave scale extended
from aa to A   ReeMMA, 21
(a) This is the method of pitch
designation that has been
ascribed to Odo de Clugny
1)   The standard pitch
designation of the
middle ages from the
tenth century
f) There were three <u>genera</u> of octave-
species   ReeMMA, 28-32
(1) Figure 3 shows the diatonic
<u>genus</u> in the low tuning (e-E)

Fig. 3. The Diatonic <u>Genus</u>

```
              aa g f e d c b a G F E D C B A
Mixolydian:              t t t s t t s
Lydian:                s t t t s t t
Phrygian:            t s t t t s t
Dorian:              t t s t t t s      (c.o.)
Hypolydian:        s t t s t t t
Hypophrygian:    t s t t s t t
Hypodorian:    t t s t t s t
t=tone; s=semitone; c.o.="characteristic octave"
```


(2) Figure 4 shows the chromatic
<u>genus</u> in the low tuning (e-E)
(a) Also known as "color"   AriM, 83
(b) These <u>tonoi</u> were formed by
lowering the <u>oxypyknon</u> by a
semitone

Fig. 4. The Chromatic <u>Genus</u>

```
                o       o         o       o
              aa f#f e c#c b a F#F E C#C B A
Mixolydian:              t + s s + s s
Lydian:                s t + s s + s
Phrygian:            s s t + s s +
Dorian:              + s s t + s s      (c.o.)
Hypolydian:        s + s s t + s
Hypophrygian:    s s + s s t +
Hypodorian       + s s + s s t
+=sesquitone; o=oxypyknon; c.o.=characteristic octave
```

(3)   Figure 5 shows the enharmonic
      genus in the low tuning (e-E)
      (a)   Also known as "harmonia"

                                    AriM, 83

      (b)   These _tonoi_ were formed by
            lowering the _oxypyknon_ a
            whole tone and the _mesopyknon_
            by a quarter tone

Fig. 5.   The Enharmonic _Genus_

```
              o ∎  o ∎   o ∎  o ∎
            aa f f e c c b a F F E C C B A
Mixolydian:           t l q q l q q
Lydian:             q ∶ l q q l q
Phrygian:         q q t l q q l
Dorian:         l q q t l q q      (c.o.)
Hypolydian:     q l q q t l q
Hypophrygian: q q l q q t l
Hypodorian:   l q q l q q t
```
o=_oxypyknon_; ∎=_mesopyknon_; l=ditone; q=quarter tone

g)   Melodies were sung and played where
     it was comfortable to do so   ReeMMA, 29
     (1)   No analytical awareness of
           transposition
     (2)   Six of the octave-species were
           brought into the octave range
           of the Dorian octave
           ("characteristic octave")
     (3)   Figure 6 shows the seven
           diatonic octave-species as
           transposed to the "characteristic
           octave"

Fig. 6.   The Diatonic Octave-species Transposed

```
            aa g f e d c b a G F E D C B A
Mixolydian:         t t t$^b$s t t s
Lydian:             s$^#$t$^#$t t s$^#$t$^#$t
Phrygian:           t s$^#$t t t s$^#$t
Dorian:             t t s t t t s
Hypolydian:         s$^#$t$^#$t s$^#$t$^#$t$^#$t
Hypophrygian:       t s$^#$t t s$^#$t$^#$t
Hypodorian:         t t s t t s$^#$t
```
The flats and sharps are directly underneath the
tone to be raised or lowered (ReeMMA, 30; HenA, 354)

h)   It was impossible to obtain the
     Phrygian enharmonic in the low
     tuning (e-E)   ReeMMA, 34
     (1)   This problem may have prompted

                    the raising of the outer strings
                    of the lyra or kithara to f-F
                    (high tuning)
            (2)   The names of all of the octave-
                    species were transferred to
                    the high tuning   ReeMMA, 35-36
                    (a)   The raise of a half step
                            merged the low Mixolydian
                            with the high Lydian and
                            the low Dorian with the
                            high Hypolydian
                            i)   This produced seven
                                    tonoi in the high
                                    tuning with four *tonoi*
                                    left in the low tuning
                            ii)   This produced eleven
                                    tonoi with key-notes
                                    on every semitone from
                                    e^b down to F
                            iii)   Aristoxenus added two
                                    more *tonoi*: one on e
                                    and one on f
                            iv)   Aristides and Alypius
                                    added two more *tonoi*
                                                   ReeMMA, 37
                            v)   With the addition of
                                    these eight *tonoi* the
                                    nomenclature of the
                                    theorists changes
                                                   ReeMMA, 37
                                    a - The term Mixolydian
                                        disappears
                                    b - The terms Ionian,
                                        Aeolian and Hyper-
                                        dorian appear
                            vi)   In late Antiquity the
                                    tone-series was counted
                                    upward rather than
                                    downward   ReeMMA, 37

        6.   THE OCTAVE-SPECIES (PTOLEMY; fl. A.D.
                127-151)   EB PT, 733
                a)   He reduced the thirteen *tonoi* of
                        Aristoxenus to seven   ReeMMA, 38
                        (1)   All were in the low tuning
                                (a)   The actual practice of
                                        music did not include the
                                        enharmonic *genus*
                b)   The names of Dorian, Lydian, Phrygian
                        etc. were restored to the low tuning
                                                   ReeMMA, 38
                c)   They were an extended octave-species
                                                   ReeMMA, 40
                        (1)   Four notes were added below
                                and three notes were added
                                above   ReeMMA, 39

    d)   <u>Tonos</u> system was pitchless   ApeHD, 353
          (1)   Ptolemy presupposes that the
              <u>tonoi</u> were theoretical figures

Fig. 7. The <u>Tonoi</u> of Ptolemy

```
                    A B C D E F G a b c d e f g aa
Mixolydian:    s♭ t t t S T T S♭ T T T s t t
Lydian:        t t♯t♯s T♯T♯S T T♯T♯S t♯t♯s
Phrygian:      t t♯s t T♯S T T T♯S T t♯s t
Dorian:        t s t t S T T T S T T s t t
Hypolydian:    ♯s t♯t♯s T♯T♯T♯S T♯T♯S t♯t♯t♯
Hypophrygian:  t t♯s t T♯T♯S T T♯S T t♯t♯s
Hypodorian:    t s t t T♯S T T S T T t♯s t
```
Capital letters="characteristic octave"; the flats and sharps are
directly underneath the tone to be raised or lowered (ReeMMA, 40)

D.   THE SYSTEMS

1.   DEVISED FOR PURPOSES OF NOMENCLATURE ONLY
                                     HenA, 345
    a)   Fourth century B.C.
    b)   A melodic skeleton ("fixed notes")
        (1)   Other notes could be inserted
            (a)   The "moveable notes"

2.   THE "GREATER PERFECT SYSTEM"   HenA, 344-345
    a)   This system consisted of two pairs
        of conjunct tetrachords separated
        by a <u>diazeuxis</u>
        (1)   Each tetrachord had two
            <u>hestotes</u> and two <u>kinoumenoi</u>
            (a)   The <u>hestotes</u> were the
                skeleton notes of the
                perfect fourth
            (b)   The <u>kinoumenoi</u> were the two
                notes between the <u>hestotes</u>
                i)   Their range was clas-
                     sified by the three
                     <u>genera</u> discussed
                     previously,
                     supra, p. 122
        (2)   Other notes besides the
            <u>kinoumenoi</u> could be inserted
            into the skeleton of the
            tetrachord
            (a)   There were other varieties
                  of the <u>genera</u>   ReeMMA, 23
                i)   They consisted of dif-
                     ferent intonations
    b)   The <u>proslambanomenos</u> was placed be-
        neath the two pairs of tetrachords,
        thus forming a <u>disdiapason</u>   ReeMMA, 22
    c)   Each note of the System was called by

its name and that of its tetrachord
(1)   See figure 8, "The Greater
      Perfect System"

Fig. 8. The Greater Perfect System

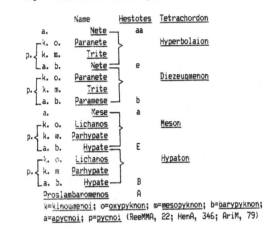

		Name	Hestotes	Tetrachordon
a.		Nete	aa	
	k. o.	Paranete		Hyperbolaion
p.	k. m.	Trite		
	a. b.	Nete	e	
	k. o.	Paranete		Diezeugmenon
p.	k. m.	Trite		
	a. b.	Paramese	b	
a.		Mese	a	
	k. o.	Lichanos		Meson
p.	k. m.	Parhypate		
	a. b.	Hypate	E	
	k. o.	Lichanos		Hypaton
p.	k. m	Parhypate		
	a. b.	Hypate	B	
		Proslambanomenos	A	

k=kinoumenoi; o=oxypyknon; m=mesopyknon; b=barypyknon;
a=apycnoi; p=pycnoi (ReeMMA, 22; HenA, 346; AriM, 79)

3.   THE "LESSER PERFECT SYSTEM"   HenA, 345
      a) The diazeuxis of the Greater Perfect
          System is dropped and the synemmenon
          is added
          (1)   Consisted of eleven notes: the
                octave from proslambanomenos to
                mese plus the tetrachord
                synemmenon   ReeMMA, 23
      b) This made modulation possible   ReeMMA, 23
          (1)   See figure 9

Fig. 9. The Lesser Perfect System

		Name	Hestotes	Tetrachordon
a.		Nete	d	
	k. o.	Paranete		Synemmenon
p.	k. m.	Trite		
	a. b.	Mese	a	
	k. o.	Lichanos		Meson
p.	k. m.	Parhypate		
	a. b.	Hypate	E	
	k. o.	Lichanos		Hypaton
p.	k. m.	Parhypate		
	a. b.	Hypate	B	
		Proslambanomenos	A	

k=kinoumenoi; o=oxypyknon; m=mesopyknon; b=barypyknon;
a=apycnoi; p=pycnoi (ReeMMA, 23; HenA, 346; AriM, 79)

III.   NOTATION

A.   EXAMPLES OF GREEK MUSIC

    1.   FRAGMENTS
        a)   There are forty-one known authentic
            fragments of Greek music dating from
            the third century B.C. to the fourth
            century A.D.   MatF, 32
        b)   For information concerning these
            fragments see the following sources:
            (1)   ReeMMA, 48-49
            (2)   MatF, 15
            (3)   WinM, 30-47
            (4)   HenA, 363-374

B.   The Symbols

    1.   GREEKS USED AN ALPHABETICAL NOTATION
                                          ReeMMA, 25
        a)   It consisted of two systems   BarP, 2
            (1)   Vocal notation
            (2)   Instrumental notation
                 (a)   This is thought to be
                     several hundred years
                     older than the vocal
                     notation   BarP, 4
                 (b)   The vocal notation is
                     thought to be a trans-
                     lation of the obsolete
                     ciphers of the instrumental
                     notation   HenA, 359
            (3)   These terms were not adopted
                 until late antiquity   HenA, 359
        b)   The two notations were not always
            rigidly separated
        c)   Consisted of Greek letters and some
            Phoenician symbols
        d)   Pitch level uncertain   BarP, 1
        e)   Given to us by the theorists,
            Aristides Quintilianus and
            Alypius   BarP, 1
            (1)   Aristides (ca. A.D. 200)   BakB, 45
            (2)   Alypius (fl. middle of the
                 fourth century A.D.)   BakB, 28
        f)   There were seventy symbols for
            the vocal notation and seventy
            for the instrumental notation   BarP, 4
            (1)   They were not all created
                 at once
        g)   Vocal notation   BarP, 4
            (1)   The Numbers forty-eight to twenty-
                 five of the vocal symbols use
                 the regular Greek alphabet   BarP, 2

(2)   Numbers forty-nine to fifty-
four may have been added to
create the Greater Perfect
System   BarP, 6
(3)   Numbers fifty-five to seventy
were most likely added after
the rest of the system had
been constructed
(4)   Numbers twenty-four to one of
the vocal symbols are inversions,
omissions or are reversed
BarP, 2
(5)   Pitch was relative   HenA, 358

Fig. 10. Vocal Symbols

No.	Staff Pitch	Hypothetical Pitch	*Quarter Step or Half Step Higher	**Half Step or Whole Step Higher
70.	gg	U′		
67-69	ff	Γ′	B′	A′
64-66	ee	Z′	E′	Δ′
61-63	dd	I′	Θ′	H′
58-60	cc	M′	Λ′	K′
55-57	bb	O′	Ξ′	N′
52-54	aa	⬤	Λ	⊥
49-51	g	U	m̂	✳
46-48	f	Γ	B	A
43-45	e	Z	E	Δ
40-42	d	I	Θ	H
37-39	c	M	Λ	K
34-36	b	O	Ξ	N
31-33	a	C	P	Π
28-30	G	Φ	Y	T
25-27	F	Ω	Ψ	X
22-24	E	⅂	R	Ⅴ
19-21	D	Ɔ	F	Ⅴ
16-18	C	—	m	И
13-15	B	W	V	Ɇ
10-12	A	Ϙ	ⅠⅠⅠ	И
7-9	GG	ℨ	Ⴆ	U
4-6	FF	ℹ	⋗	⊣
1-3	DD#	Ⴚ	Ⴒ	✳

*Depends on the genus; **depends on the genus; c=middle c
(BarP, 3; AriM, 21)

h)   Instrumental notation
(1)   Groups its letters by triads:
normal, supine and reversed
BarP, 4
(2)   Has a nucleus of fifteen
signs   HenA, 359
(a)   Some are alphabetic
but are not in order

Fig. 11. Instrumental Symbols

No.	Staff Pitch	Hypoynetical Pitch	*Quarter Step or Half Step Higher	**Half Step or Whole Step Higher
70.	gg	Z´		
67-69	ff	N´	⌐´	⌐´
64-66	ee	⊏´	u´	⊐´
61-63	dd	<´	v´	>´
58-60.	cc	⌐´	Y´	y´
55-57	bb	K´	⤮´	K´
52-54	aa	⅄	Λ	λ
49-51	g	Z	λ	⋌
46-48	f	N	⌐	⌐
43-45	e	⊏	u	⊐
40-42	d	<	v	>
37-39	c	⌐	Y	y
34-36	b	K	⤮	K
31-33	a	C	∪	⊃
28-30	G	F	⊔	⊣
25-27	F	⋏	⋖	Υ
22-24	E	Γ	L	⌐
19-21	D	⊢	⊥	⊣
16-18	C	E	⊔	Ⅎ
13-15	B	ⱨ	⅀	ᴨ
10-12	A	H	d	P
7-9	GG	⊑	ω	3
4-6	FF	⌐	⊣	T
1-3	DD#	⊂	⊕	✳

*Depends on the genus; **depends on the genus; c=middle c
(BarP, 3; AriM, 21)

IV.   GREEK TERMS

A. TERMS USED IN GREEK THEORETICAL SOURCES

1.   AIOLOS. (End of fifth century B.C.) a chromatic and quivering tuning; an idiom; also thought of in connection with the style known as Phrygian; thought of in connection with the aulos   HenA, 384

2.   BARYPYKNON. The lowest degree of the pyknon, infra, p. 134   ReeMMA, 23

3.   CHRONOS PROTOS. A unit of measurement: multiplied to produce phrases   ReeMMA, 51

4.   COLA. Instrumental interludes   AriM, 88

5.   DIAPASON. An octave   ReeMMA, 42

6.   DIAPENTE. A Greek and medieval name
            for the fifth   ApeHD, 231

7.   DIATESSARON. The tetrachord: a semi-
            tone, tone, tone   ReeMMA, 42

8.   DIAZEUXIS. A tone of disjunction   HenA, 345

9.   DIEZEUGMENON. The tetrachord of
            disjunction   GroH, 29

10.   DIESES. Derived from a verb which may
            have meant to dismiss or dissolve;
            smallest interval and dissolution
            of the voice   AriM, 81

11.   DISDIAPASON. A two-octave scale   ReeMMA, 21

12.   DISEME. A sign (—) of notation which
            lengthens the chronos protos
            to double its value (in
            modern terms an eighth note
            lengthened to the value of
            two eighth notes)   MatF, 27

13.   DITONE. An interval consisting of two
            tones   AriM, 80

14.   DORIAN. (Aeolian period: mid fifth
            century B.C.) A tuning; a
            rhythm of the voice; also known
            as Aeolian: the term Aeolian
            ceased to be used by the late
            fifth century B.C.   HenA, 383
            Stands for true rhythm and
            tuning by the voice   HenA, 384
            The scale of melodic function
            (dynamis) of the octave-
            species   ApeHD, 353

15.   DUPLE. The ratio of the octave: 2:1
                                     AriM, 80

16.   DYNAMIS. Description of the notes
            of the Greater Perfect
            System by their function HenA, 353

17.   EIDOS. A theoretical term for the
            species of the octave   HenA, 347

18.   ENHARMONIC. (Fourth century B.C.)
            Means "out of tune"; name
            of one of the three genera
                                     HenA, 388-389

19.   ENTONOS. (End of fifth century B.C.)

An idiom; a clean and
sustained tuning; typified
by the Dorian   HenA, 384

20. ETHOS.   The "ethical" character of
             the various Greek scales   ApeHD, 300

21. GENERA. Three different positions of the
             "movable notes" of the tetrachord:
             the diatonic genus consisted of
             a whole tone between the highest
             note of the tetrachord and the
             tone below; the chromatic genus
             consisted of three semitones
             between the highest tone and the
             tone below: the remaining interval
             was halved; in the enharmonic
             genus there were four semitones
             between the highest tone and
             the tone below: the remaining
             interval was halved producing
             two quarter tones   ApeHD, 352

22. GENOS.   Equaled the term genus; a tuning;
             a musical style   HenA, 347

23. HARMONIA. (Classical period: fifth century
               B.C.) A musical idiom and the
               tuning that resulted   HenA, 347
               To join together: in an
               harmonious manner   AriM, 84

24. HESTOTES. The "fixed notes" bounding
    the tetrachord   ReeMMA, 24

25. HYPATE. "Highest": refers to the
             action of the hand playing
             on the tilted kithara; one
             of the "fixed notes" of the
             tetrachords meson and hypaton
             of the Greater Perfect System
                              HenA, 344-345

26. HYPATON. "Of the highest": refers to the
              position of the strings to the
              lyre; as to position, the lowest
              tetrachord of the Greater Perfect
              System   GroH, 29
              That which was first   AriM, 78

27. HYPERBOLAION. "Of the extra" tetrachord;
                   the tetrachord of the
                   Greater Perfect System with
                   the highest position   GroH, 29

28. HYPORCHEMATA. "...Songs to be accompanied

                              by dancing..."   ReeMMA, 13

29. HYPODORIAN. One of the tonoi that pro-
                  duces the octave-species:
                  starts two and one-half
                  tones below the initial tone
                  of the Dorian tonoi   ReeMMA, 30

30. HYPOPHRYGIAN. One of the tonoi that pro-
                    duces the octave-species:
                    starts one and one-half
                    tones below the initial tone
                    of the Dorian ("character-
                    istic octave")   ReeMMA, 30

31. HYPOLYDIAN. One of the tonoi that pro-
                  duces the octave-species:
                  starts a semitone below the
                  the initial tone of the
                  Dorian ("characteristic
                  octave")   ReeMMA, 30

32. KINOUMENOI. The "movable tones" of the
                  tetrachord   ReeMMA, 24

33. LICHANOS. "Forefinger": refers to the
                action of the hand on the
                kithara; the name of the
                higher of two "movable notes"
                of the tetrachords hypaton
                and meson of the Greater
                Perfect System   HenA, 345

34. LYDIAN. One of the tonoi that produces
              the octave-species: starts two
              tones above the initial tone of
              the Dorian ("characteristic
              octave")   ReeMMA, 30

35. MELOS. Refers to the production and
             perception of rhythm, words, and
             melody   AriM, 16

36. MESE. "Middle"; the upper "fixed note"
            of the tetrachord meson of the
            Greater Perfect System   GroH, 29

37. MESON. "Of the middle"; next to the
             lowest tetrachord of the
             Greater Perfect System   GroH, 29

38. MESOPYKNON. In descending order, the
                  second degree of the pyknon
                                        ReeMMA, 23

39. MIXOLYDIAN. One of the tonoi that pro-

duces the octave-species:
starts two and one-half tones
above the initial tone of
the Dorian ("characteristic
octave")   ReeMMA, 30

40. MODES. The name for the ultimate systemi-
zation of the seven octave-species;
according to Ptolemy (second century
A.D.) modes were _tonoi_ and retained
a connection with the old names of
harmoniae   WinM, 69, 71

41. MUSICA. Had two meanings: in the broad
sense it encompassed all in-
tellectual or literary culture;
in the narrow sense it meant
music, dance and poetry   ReeMMA, 11

42. NETE. "Lowest" to the hand when playing the kithara; the name of one
of the "fixed notes" at the top
of the tetrachords _hyperbolaion_
and _diezeugmenon_ of the Greater
Perfect System   HenA, 345

43. NOMOS. "Law"; a sung strain; "law-giving"
melodic and rhythmic types: worked
over by musicians into something
more or less new   ReeMMA, 11-12

44. OXYPYKNON. In descending order, the
first degree of the _pyknon_
                            ReeMMA, 23

45. PARAMESE. "Next to middle": refers to
the action of the hand on the
tilted kithara; the lower
"fixed note" of the tetrachord
diezeugmenon of the Greater
Perfect System   GroH, 29

46. PARANETE. "Next to lowest": refers to
the action of the hand on the
tilted kithara; the name of the
higher of two "movable notes"
of the tetrachords _hyperbola-
ion_ and _diezeugmenon_ of the
Greater Perfect System   GroH, 29

47. PARHYPATE. "Next to highest": refers to
the action of the hand on the
tilted kithara; the name of the
lowest of two "movable notes"
in the tetrachords _meson_ and
hypaton of the Greater Perfect

System   GroH, 29
The prefix "par" means "beside"
                                AriM, 78

48.   PENTACHORD. Called a _diapente_; consists
                   of three tones and a semitone;
                   imperfect   AriM, 82

49.   PENTASEMA.   A sign (⊔̣) of notation that
                   lengthens the value of the
                   note or note group from a _chro-_
                   nos protos (short syllable) to
                   five times its value   MatF, 27

50.   PHRYGIAN.   One of the _tonoi_ that produces
                   the octave-species: starts one
                   tone above the initial tone of
                   the Dorian ("characteristic
                   octave")   ReeMMA, 30

51.   PROSLAMBANOMENOS.   "Added tone"; the lowest
                          tone of the Greater Per-
                          fect System   ReeMMA, 22

52.   PYCNOMATA.   Microtones along a melodic
                   register   HenA, 342

53.   PYKNON.   Consists of three degrees in
                   descending order: the _oxypyknon_,
                   the _mesopyknon_ and the _bary-_
                   pyknon   ReeMMA, 23
                   The collective interval is
                   smaller than that between the
                   top note of the _pyknon_ and the
                   top note of the tetrachord   AriM, 79

54.   SESQUIALTERAN.   The ratio of the fifth:
                       3:2   AriM, 80

55.   SESQUIOCTOVALS.   The ratio of the tone:
                        9:8   AriM, 80

56.   SESQUITERTIAN.   The ratio of the fourth:
                       4:3   AriM, 80

57.   STIGME.   Dot; A dot used to mark off the
                   first _metron_ (metre) in order to
                   define a rhythmic pattern; also
                   used to mark the long syllable
                   of the next _metron_ if the pattern
                   changes   MatF, 27

58.   SYNEMMENON. Conjunct; in the Lesser
                   Perfect System the disjunct
                   tone, _paramese_, is dropped
                   and substituted with a con-

junct tetrachord called
<u>synemmenon</u>   HenA, 345

59. SYSTEMA. Unlike species, <u>systema</u> does
             not consist of a set sequence
             of notes but deals with the
             relation of conjunction and
             disjunction between tetrachords
             (Ptolemy); a term of harmonic
             theory   HenA, 356 and 347

60. TETRACHORD. A <u>diatessaron</u> composed of
               two tones and a semitone;
               imperfect   AriM, 82

61. THESIS. Refers to the notes of the
            Greater Perfect System by the
            order of their position   HenA, 353

62. TONOS. (Noun) In the first phase it is
           a term that was used in
           relating modal octaves in the
           same pitch range as segments
           of a uniform scale at different
           degrees of pitch; in the second
           phase it is a term that means
           uniform scales with an independent
           existence as keys in the modern
           sense   WinM, 71

63. TRISEME. A sign ( )|( ) of notation that
             lengthens the note or note
             group from a <u>chronos protos</u>
             to three times its value   MatF, 27

64. TRITE. "Third": refers to the action of
           the hand on the tilted kithara;
           the lower of two "movable notes"
           in the tetrachords <u>diezeugmenon</u>
           and <u>hyperbolaion</u> of the Greater
           Perfect System   GroH, 29

65. TROPOS. Equaled the term <u>modus</u>; a
            musical style; a tuning   HenA, 347

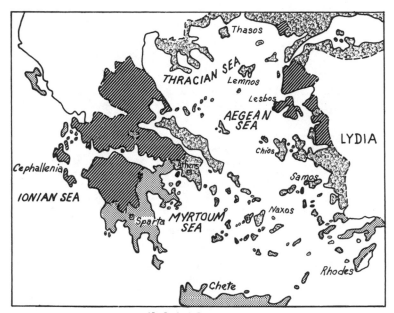

12. Ancient Greece

Aeolians
Dorians
Ionians
(HamH, H-4)

APPENDIX 2
Boethius: Letter Notation

I.   BOETHIUS, ANICIUS MANLIUS TORQUATUS SEVERINUS
    (A.D. 480-524)   BakB, 171

A.   DE INSTITUTIONE MUSICA

    1.   A TREATISE IN FIVE BOOKS   BakB, 171
         a) Source book for theory of the Middle
            Ages
            (1) Used as a textbook at Oxford
                 as late as the eighteenth
                 century   GroH, 24
            (2) Written more for a student
                 aspiring to philosophy than
                 for a practicing musician   BowP, 17
         b) Manuscript sources
            (1) Cambridge University Lib.
                 MS Ii.3.12   PagE, 310
            (2) Brit. Lib. MS Royal
                 15.B.IXf.44v   PagE, 310

    2.   A RE-ELABORATION OF GREEK HANDBOOKS
       BY NICOMACHUS OF GERASA   EB B, 779
         a) Flourished about A.D. 100   EB NI, 430
            (1) Wrote the Enchiridion
                 harmonices

    3.   A DISCUSSION OF THE NAMES OF THE
       STRINGS OF THE KITHARA   BowP, 74-82
         a) Starts with seven strings and
             ends with fifteen (these have
             the names of the notes of the
             Greater Perfect System)

    4.   A DISCUSSION CONCERNING THE DIVISION
       OF THE MONOCHORD
         a) Boethius uses Latin letters as
             symbols for the various pitches
                                    BowP, 444

(1)   They represent relative
positions   ReeMMA, 134

5.   THE SPECIES OF CONSONANCE   BowP, 267
a)   "A species is a certain position
contained within any numerical
proportion which yields a
consonance, having its _own_ form
according to any one of the
genera."
(1)   The species of the diapason
are identical to those of
Ptolemy but their numbering
is opposite   BowP,274
(2)   Boethius does not assign
names such as Dorian,
Phrygian, etc. to the
octave-species   BowP, 274
(3)   Instead he uses the letters
A B C D E F G H I K L M N O P
BowP, 445
(4)   The Latin letters are usually
thought to stand for A-aa
ReeMMA, 135

Fig. 1. The Species of Diapason
Using Letter Notation

A B C D E F G a b c d e f g aa bb

A B C D E F G H   1st species
B C D E F G H I   2nd species
C D E F G H I K   3rd species
D E F G H I K L   4th species
E F G H I K L M   5th species
F G H I K L M N   6th species
G H I K L M N O   7th species
H I K L M N O P   8th species
c=middle c; (BowP, 289)

(5)   H:P is the _hypermixolydian_
which Ptolemy added at the
top   BowP, 289
(a)   Ptolemy rejected the
eighth mode as being
identical with the
first mode
(6)   Boethius also discusses species
of the diapason, _diapente_ and
diatessaron on "fixed notes"
BowP, 272

6.   A DISCUSSION OF THE THREE _GENERA_
a)   Tones of the diatonic, chromatic, and

enharmonic genera may be derived
from divisions of the monochord

ReeMMA, 134

(1) In the diatonic genus the
     voice progresses by semitone,
     whole tone, whole tone   BowP, 84
(2) The chromatic genus is sung
     through semitone, semitone,
     and trihemitone   BowP, 84
(3) The enharmonic genus is sung
     through a diesis diesis and
     a double tone   BowP, 85
     (a) The term diesis indicates
          half of a semitone   BowP, 85
          i)   Boethius also says
               that limma or diesis
               equals a semitone: so
               called not because it
               is a real half tone but
               because it is not a
               whole tone   BowP, 161
          ii) Pythagoras refers to
               diesis (difference) and
               limma (left over) as a
               semitone   ApeHD, 710
(4) See figures 2, 3, and 4

Fig. 2. The Diatonic Genus

	Letter Notation (Boethius)	Letter Notation (Odo de Clugny)
Proslambanomenos	A	A
Hypate Hypaton	B	B
Parhypate Hypaton	C	C
Lichanos Hypaton	E	D
Hypate Meson	H	E
Paranete Meson	I	F
Lichanos Meson	M	G
Mese	O	a
Paramese	X	b
Trite Diezeugmenon	Y	c
Paranete Diezeugmenon	CC	d
Nete Diezeugmenon	DD	e
Trite Hyperboleon	FF	f
Paranete Hyperboleon	KK	g
Nete Hyperboleon	LL	aa

(BowP, 444-445; ApeHD, 467)

Fig. 2. The Diatonic Genus
         (continued)

	Letter Notation (Boethius)	Letter Notation (Odo de Clugny)
Mese		
Synemmenon	O	a
Trite		
Synemmenon	Q	b (b)
Paranete		
Synemmenon	T	c
Nete		
Synemmenon	V	d

(BowP, 444-445; ApeHD, 467)

Fig. 3. The Chromatic Genus

	Letter Notation (Boethius)	Letter Notation (Odo de Clugny)
Proslambanomenos	A	A
Hypate Hypaton	B	B
Parhypate		
Hypaton	C	C
Lichanos		
Hypaton	F	C (#)
Hypate Meson	H	E
Paranete Meson	I	F
Lichanos Meson	N	F (#)
Mese	O	a
Paramese	X	b
Trite		
Diezeugmenon	Y	c
Paranete		
Diezeugmenon	BB	c (#)
Nete		
Diezeugmenon	DD	e
Trite		
Hyperboleon	FF	f
Paranete		
Hyperboleon	HH	f (#)
Nete		
Hyperboleon	LL	aa
Mese		
Synemmenon	O	a
Trite		
Synemmenon	Q	a (#)
Paranete		
Synemmenon	S	b
Nete		
Synemmenon	V	d

(BowP, 444-445)

Fig. 4. The Enharmonic Genus

	Letter Notation (Boethius)	Letter Notation (Odo de Clugny)
Proslambanomenos	A	A
Hypate Hypaton	B	B
Parhypate Hypaton	D	*
Lichanos Hypaton	C	C
Hypate Meson	H	E
Paranete Meson	K	*
Lichanos Meson	L	F
Mese	O	a
Paramese	X	b
Trite Diezeugmenon	Z	*
Paranete Diezeugmenon	AA	c
Nete Diezeugmenon	DD	e
Trite Hyperboleon	EE	*
Paranete Hyperboleon	FF	f
Nete Hyperboleon	LL	aa
Mese Synemmenon	O	a
Trite Synemmenon	P	*
Paranete Synemmenon	R	b (b)
Nete Synemmenon	V	d

*=quarter tone ascent; (BowP, 444-445)

b) When discussing the octave-species and modes, Boethius gives two other series of letters to notate the pitches in the diatonic genus   BowP, 445
    (1) He uses A:O without the J and A:P without the J
c) Therefore no group of symbols can properly be called "Boethian"   BowP, 445

APPENDIX 3
Neumes

I.   BACKGROUND

    A. ACCENTUATION SINGS OF CLASSICAL LITERATURE

        1. IN USE BETWEEN ca. 200 B.C. AND
           ca. A.D. 200   RasN, 15
           a) Ascribed to Aristophanes of Byzantium
              (ca. 180 B.C.)   ParN, 4

        2   THERE WERE FOUR GROUPS OF DECLAMATION-
           SIGNS   RasN, 16
           a) The accentus acutus (/) and the
              accentus gravis (\)
           b) The abbreviation-signs (ˎ and ∴)
           c) The contraction-signs (~and ५)
           d) The interrogation-marks (ᴎand ⸜)

        3. THESE SIGNS BECAME THE NEUMES OF THE
           CHRISTIAN CHURCH   RasN, 15
           a) The neumatic notation of plainsong
              was fully developed between the ninth
              century and the end of the twelfth
              century A.D.
              (1) The acutus became the virga ("rod")
              (2) The gravis became the punctum
                  ("dot")

    B. NEUME WRITING   ParN, 5

        1. REMAINED STAFFLESS UNTIL APPROXIMATELY
           THE LATE TWELFTH CENTURY
           a) The virga indicated a relatively
              higher pitch
           b) The punctum indicated a relatively
               lower pitch
               (1) This practice became un-
                   necessary with the develop-

ment of the staff

2. INDICATED THE EXACT NUMBER AND GROUPING
    OF TONES   ReeMMA, 133

II. SYSTEM OF NEUMES

  A. <u>SINGLE NOTES AND LIGATURES</u>   RasN, 16

    1. THE SINGLE NOTES ARE THE <u>VIRGA</u> (/)
        WHICH MEANS "ROD" AND THE <u>PUNCTUM</u>
        (·) WHICH MEANS "DOT"
        a) They indicate upward and downward
            movement respectively

    2. THE LIGATURES (GROUP OF NOTES BOUND TO
        EACH OTHER)
        a) Consist of two or three notes
            (1) Two-note neumes   ParN, 5
                 (a) <u>Podatus</u> (·/): "foot"
                 (b) <u>Clivis</u> (/·): "bend"
            (2) Three-note neumes   ParN, 6
                 (a) <u>Scandicus</u> (⋰): "climb"
                 (b) <u>Climacus</u> (⋱): "ladder"
                 (c) <u>Torculus</u> (·/·): "twist"
                 (d) <u>Porrectus</u> (/·/): "stretch"

    3. COMPOUND NEUMES   RasN, 16
        a) These neumes consist of four or
            more notes
        b) They indicate the direction of
            melodic movement   RasN, 18
        c) Made by combining ligatures and
            single notes
        d) Names are derived by adding
            qualifying terms to the names of
            the neumes (Sangallian)   ParN, 7
            (1) <u>Podatus subbipunctis</u> (⌡·.):
                 <u>podatus</u> with "two <u>puncta</u>
                 below"
            (2) <u>Torculus resupinus</u> (⋀): a
                 <u>torculus</u> "turned back"
            (3) <u>Porrectus subbipunctis</u> (⋏·.)
                                                 RasN, 17
            (4) <u>Porrectus flexus</u> (⋒): a
                 <u>porrectus</u> "bent"
            (5) <u>Scandicus subbipunctis</u> (⋰··)
                                                 RasN. 17
            (6) <u>Scandicus flexus</u> (⌠): "bent"
                                                 RasN, 17
            (7) <u>Climacus resupinus</u> (⌐·/)   RasN, 17
            (8) <u>Climacus resupinus flexus</u> (/⌠)
                                                 RasN, 17

B. APOSTROPHIC NEUMES (Sangallian)

   1.   DERIVED FROM DECLAMATION-SIGNS

                                        RasN, 18

       a) Consist of notes of the same pitch

                                           ParN, 8

   2.   STROPHA   RasN, 18-19
       a) Also known as apostropha and
           strophicus (')
           (1) Most commonly found in groups
                of two or three
                (a) Bistropha (' ')
                      i)   Also known as
                          distropha   ReeMMA, 131
                (b) Tristropha (' ' ')
           (2) In the Solesmes tradition the
                bistropha and the tristropha
                were performed as a single
                longer note
                (a) The notes should be sung
                      separately
       b) The apostropha may have originally
           indicated a vocal nuance   ReeMMA, 131
           (1) The distropha and tristropha
                should be sung with a gentle
                vibrato and diminuendo
                (a) They should be sung
                      lightly   RasN, 18

   3.   TRIGON (∴)   RasN, 18
       a) Originally an abbreviation-sign
           (1) First two notes are the same
                pitch
                (a) Should be sung separately

   4.   BIVIRGA (//) AND TRIVIRGA (///)   RasN, 18
       a) Groups of two or three virgae
       b) At the unison
       c) Sung separately

C. ORISCUS GROUP (Sangallian)   RasN, 19-20

   1.   THESE NEUMES USE THE CONTRACTION-SIGN
       a) Oriscus ("limit")
           (1) Uses the upright forms (ʔ or
                ƨ)
           (2) Usually a single note
                (a) "...Always joined to the end
                    of a neume..."   ReeMMA, 131
                      i)   Sung in a lighter
                          manner than the notes
                        of the neume
                (b) Same pitch as the
                    preceding note

        (c)   Followed by a note of
              lower pitch
              i)   Sometimes found as the
                     second note of two
                     unison notes carrying
                     a single vowel
                     a - The note following
                       it may be higher
    (3) The oriscus is sung as a separate
        note
        (a)   The Solesmes school considers
              the two unison notes as one
              double length note
  b) Pressus ("closed")
    (1) Pressus major (⌐)
        (a)   Consists of a virga,
              oriscus, and punctum
              i)   The virga and oriscus
                     are of the same pitch
                     a - Sung separately on
                        the same syllable
    (2) Pressus minor (⌐)
        (a)   Consists of a virga and a
              punctum
              i)   The virga is in
                     unison with the
                     preceding note
        (b)   When following a clivis or
              torculus, the pressus minor
              is combined with the neume
              preceding it
    (3) May follow in apposition to a
        single note or two-note neume
                                ParN, 8
  c) Salicus ("leaper")   RasN, 19
    (1) Consists of a modified scandicus
        (a)   The second note is an
              oriscus (⌐)
    (2) Three theories concerning the
        performance of the salicus
        (a)   The accent is on the second
              note of the neume   LibU, ix
        (b)   The second note should be
              chromatically inflected
              or perhaps it is a micro-
              tone   ApeGC, 110
        (c)   The note after the oriscus
              has the accent   CarS, 102

D. QUILISMA NEUMES

  1.   QUILISMA ("ROLL")
      a) A rising inflection of the voice RasN, 20
        (1) The note before the quilisma
            is usually lower in pitch

       b) A single note (⌣ or ⌣)   RasN, 20
          (1) Usually found as part of a
               ligature
             (a) Two or three small loops
                   that are attached to a
                   <u>virga</u>
          (2) Performance
             (a) Different theories
                 i)   Ornamental tone
                            ApeGC, 114
                   a - Short trill or
                      mordent
                 ii)   Lightly sung note
                            CarS, 126

E. LIQUESCENT NEUMES

    1.   NOTATIONAL MODIFICATIONS   RasN, 21
       a) (⌐ or ⌐)   ParN, 7
       b) Indicate manner of execution and
          pitch motion   ParN, 7
          (1) Used over consonant groups   RasN, 21
             (a) Indicate a lightly sung
                   indeterminate vowel
          (2) Used when two vowels come to-
              gether   RasN, 21
             (a) No extra vowel is sung
       c) The last note of the ligature becomes
          semivocal   RasN, 22
       d) There are two classes   RasN, 22
          (1) A modification of a neume
          (2) An addition to a neume
       e) Forms   RasN, 22
          (1) If the last note is a bound
              <u>virga</u> the stroke is shortened
          (2) If the last note is a <u>punctum</u>
              a curved shape is used

III.   ROMANIAN AND MESSINE LETTERS

A. ROMANIAN LETTERS

    1.   ATTRIBUTED TO ROMANUS OF ST. GALL
       (ca. A.D. 789)   RasN, 24-25
       a) Direction of pitch
          (1) Rising
             (a) "a" for <u>altius</u> meaning
                   higher
             (b) "l" for <u>levare</u> meaning
                   rise
             (c) "s" for <u>sursum</u> meaning
                   lift up

(2) Falling
   (a) "d" for <u>deprimatur</u>
     meaning lowered
   (b) "i" for <u>iusum</u>, <u>inferius</u>
     meaning lower
(3) The same
   (a) "e" for <u>equaliter</u> meaning
     equally

b) Duration and accent
   (1) "t" for <u>trahere</u> meaning to drag
     or for <u>tenere</u> meaning to hold
   (2) "x" for <u>expectare</u> meaning
     to wait
   (3) "c" for <u>celeriter</u> meaning
     quickly

c) Modifications of pitch, duration and
   accent
   (1) "m" for <u>mediocriter</u> meaning
     moderately
   (2) "b" for <u>bene</u> meaning "well"
   (3) "v" for <u>valde</u> meaning very
     much

B. <u>MESSINE LETTERS</u>   RasN, 25

1. LETTERS INDICATING PITCH
   a) "h" for <u>humiliter</u> meaning lower
   b) "nl" for <u>ne leves</u> meaning do not rise

2. LETTERS INDICATING TEMPO
   a) "a" for <u>auge</u> meaning to lengthen
   b) "nt" for <u>ne teneas</u> meaning do not
     lengthen
   c) "at" for <u>statim</u> meaning no delay

3. LETTERS INDICATING A MODIFICATION OF PITCH
   AND TEMPO
   a) "n" for <u>naturaliter</u> meaning of
     normal value

APPENDIX 4
Plainsong Notation

I.   THE SYMBOLS OF PLAINSONG NOTATION

A. <u>NEUMES</u>

    1.   USED FROM THE NINTH TO THE THIRTEENTH
CENTURY   ApeGC, 91
        a) Used in France, Germany, Italy
and other countries
        b) In the twelfth century, a neumatic
            script consisting of small squares
            was used   ApeHD, 804
        c. For a detailed discussion of neumes,
            see Appendix 3

B. <u>SQUARE NOTATION</u>

    1.   DEFINITION
        a) Consists of notes written in a
            square shape   ApeHD, 805
            (1)   Derived from the neumes
            (2)   Used for both single notes
                and ligatures
                (a)   See also appendix 8

    2.   HISTORY OF SQUARE NOTATION IN PLAINSONG
        a) Mid-fourteenth and fifteenth
            centuries   RasN, 36
            (1)   Notation of polyphonic settings
                (a)   The chant was notated in
                    such a way as to indicate
                    the less important
                    syllables by smaller
                    note-values (the <u>punctum</u> ▪)
                (b)   In <u>alternatim</u> performance the
                    plainsong sections may have
                    been performed the same way
        b) Mid-sixteenth century   RasN, 36

(1) A quasi-mensural notation was
     used
     (a) The <u>virga</u> (ᴺ) and the
          <u>punctum</u> (▪) received
          long and short values
          i)   These were relative
                values
     (b) The rhombic <u>punctum</u> (♦)
          was used for the less
          important syllables
c) Late nineteenth century
    (1) Solesmes notation   ReeMMA, 141
         (a) In the square notation
              editions the <u>punctum</u> and
              the <u>virga</u> are used to
              represent a time unit
         (b) In the modern notation
              editions the time unit
              is represented by an
              eighth-note

3. THE SYMBOLS   HugFR, 323
    a) Basic neumes and ligatures
        (1) Single notes   RasN, 34
             (a) The <u>virga</u> (ᴺ)
             (b) The <u>punctum</u> (▪)
        (2) Two notes
             (a) Rising (♩)
                  i)   <u>Podatus</u> or <u>pes</u>
                                     ReeMMA, 130
             (b) Falling (ᴎ)
                  i)   <u>Clivis</u>   ReeMMA, 130
        (3) Three notes
             (a) Rise and fall (⁖)
                  i)   <u>Torculus</u>   ReeMMA, 130
             (b) Rise and rise (♪ or ♩)
                  i)   The <u>scandicus</u> and
                        <u>salicus</u>   ReeMMA, 130
             (c) Fall and fall (⁙)
                  i)   <u>Climacus</u>   ReeMMA, 130
             (d) Fall and rise (ᴺ)
                  i)   <u>Porrectus</u> ReeMMA, 130
        (4) Four notes
             (a) Rise, fall, fall (⁘)
                  i)   <u>Pes subbipunctis</u>
                                     ReeMMA, 130
             (b) Four rising (♩)
                  i)   <u>Virga praetripunctis</u>
                                     ApeGC, 100
             (c) Four falling (⁙)
                  i)   Conjunctura
             (d) Fall, rise, fall (⁙)
                  i)   <u>Porrectus flexus</u>
                                     ReeMMA, 130
             (e) Rise, fall, rise (ᴺ)
                  i)   <u>Torculus resupinus</u>

```
                                              ReeMMA, 130
            (f)  Fall, rise, rise ( ▶◗ )
            (g)  Fall, fall, rise ( ᛁᛟ )
                 i)    Climacus resupinus
                                              ApeGC, 100
      b)  Liquescent neumes                   ApeGC, 104
          (1)  Variations of the basic neumes
               (a)  Use a smaller head for
                    the last note
               (b)  The last note is sung in
                    a "half-voice" manner
                    i)    Used for two succes-
                          sive consonants
                    ii)   Used for vowels form-
                          ing a diphthong
          (2)  Epiphonus ( ᛟᛟ )               RasN, 34
          (3)  Cephalicus ( ⌐ᛟ )              RasN, 34
      c)  Repercussive neumes                 ApeGC, 106
          (1)  Used to indicate the immediate
               repeat of a pitch
          (2)  Distropha and bivirga (▪▪
               and ᛁᛁ )                       RasN, 34
          (3)  Tristropha and trivirga
               (▪▪▪ and ᛁᛁᛁ)                  RasN, 34
      d)  Oriscus neumes                      RasN, 34
          (1)  Salicus ( ♩ )
      e)  Quilisma neumes                      RasN, 34
          Quilisma-pes (ᛟ)

4.    SIGNS USED IN MODERN LITURGICAL CHANT
                                              SodE, 233
      a)  An asterisk indicates division of
          the choir
          (1)  This is decided by previous
               arrangement
      b)  A "v" is an abbreviation for verse
      c)  An ictus is a small vertical line
          beneath a note
          (1)  Indicates a resting place
               (a)  Usually at intervals
                    of two or three notes
      d)  Musical punctuation       ReeMMA, 132
          (1)  A bar through the fourth
               line of the four-line staff
               indicates the end of an
               incise (smallest melodic
               division)
          (2)  A bar through the second and
               third lines indicates the
               end of part of a phrase
          (3)  A bar through all four lines
               indicates the end of a phrase
          (4)  A double bar indicates the
               end of a piece
               (a)  Also means a change of
                    choirs
```

    e)   A <u>custos</u>   ReeMMA, 132

           (1)   A small note that is placed
at the end of a line

                (a)   Modified by a tail in
order to distinguish it
from the regular notes

                                            RasN, 30

                (b)   It prepares the singer for
the first note of the next
line

f)   "℟" means go back to response

g)   <u>Quilisma</u> (∿)

           (1)   Indicates that the preceding
note or group of notes should
be prolonged

           (2)   For a different theory see
"<u>Quilisma neumes</u>" in appendix 3

h)   The letters "e u o u a e" stand for
<u>Saeculorum Amen</u>

           (1)   Usually found at the end of
the <u>Gloria Patri</u>

i)   Clef signs   ReeMMA, 132

           (1)   C clef (𝄡)

                (a)   Found on the three upper
lines

           (2)   F clef (𝄢)

                (a)   Usually found on the third
line

5.   A FOUR-LINE STAFF IS USED   ReeMMA, 132

APPENDIX 5
Ecclesiastical Modes

I.   THE DEFINITION, DEVELOPMENT, AND TONALITY OF THE
     ECCLESIASTICAL MODES

   A.   DEFINITION

      1.   "...A STATIC SERIES OF TONES DEPENDENT
           UPON THE HEXACHORDS FOR STRUCTURAL
           DEFINITION..."   AllT, 63
           a) These tones are a set of interlocking
               hexachords
               (1) See appendix 6
           b) They are presented in the treatises
               without flats and sharps   AllT, 71
           c) Consist of a four-fold system of
               maneriae   ReeMMA, 153
               (1) Protus
               (2) Deuterus
               (3) Tritus
               (4) Tetrardus
           d) See figure 1

                 Fig. 1. The Hexachord Structure of the Modes

           *Protus   *Deuterus

           **Naturale   **Naturale
              D E F G a b c d   E F G a b c d e
                  **Durum   **Durum

           *Tritus   *Tetrardus

           **Naturale Naturale   Naturale
              F G a b c d e f   G a b c d e f g
                  **Durum   **Durum

           *=Name of mode; **=Name of hexachord
           (AllT, 71; ReeMMA, 153)

2.   EACH MODE HAS AN <u>AMBITUS</u> (CIRCUIT)
     OF AN OCTAVE   ApeGC, 135
     a)   Most of the Gregorian melodies
          require a <u>subtonium modi</u>
          (1)   One degree below the lowest
                note of the octave-segment
     b)   Some melodies require a tone
          above the octave
     c)   If the melodies ascend an octave,
          ninth, or tenth beyond the modal
          final and descend below the final
          by a second they are said to be
          in the <u>authenticus</u> mode   AllT, 65
     d)   If the melodies ascend to the sixth
          or seventh degree above the final
          and descend a fourth or fifth below
          the final they are said to be in
          the <u>plagius</u> mode   AllT, 65
     e)   Each octave has its own individual
          structure   ApeGC, 134
          (1)   The basic difference is the
                positioning of the semitones
                in regard to the final
                (a)   The <u>protus maneria</u> (mode)
                      has semitones at the second
                      and sixth degrees
                (b)   The <u>deuterus maneria</u> has
                      semitones at the first and
                      fifth degrees
                (c)   The <u>tritus maneria</u> has
                      semitones at the fourth
                      and seventh degrees
                (d)   The <u>tetrardus maneria</u> has
                      semitones at the third and
                      sixth degrees
                      i)   For a discussion of
                           <u>maneriae</u>, infra,
                           p. 148

3.   THERE ARE FOUR <u>FINALES</u> OR CENTRAL
          TONES   ApeGC, 133
     a)   They are D, E, F, and G

4.   EACH MODE HAS A SECONDARY TONAL
     CENTER   ApeGC, 135
     a)   Commonly known as the dominant
                                          ApeGC, 136
          (1)   Actually this term does not
                appear in any of the medieval
                descriptions of the modes
                (a)   The majority of the
                      melodies fail to show
                      a clear dominant
          (2)   It should be called tenor
                (a)   The dominant is a special
                      characteristic of such

melodies as the psalm
tones and other recitation
tones
i)   It is the pitch for the
recitation
(3) The tenor usually falls on the
fifth above the _finalis_ in the
authentic modes and on the
third above the _finalis_ in the
plagal modes   ApeHD, 166
(a) The tone b is avoided
and is replaced by c
(b) In the plagal mode B-b
the dominant (tenor)
falls on the tone a
instead of G

B.   DEVELOPMENT OF THE MODAL SYSTEM

1.   DURING THE EIGHTH CENTURY GREGORIAN CHANT
BECAME THE SUBJECT OF INVESTIGATION AND
CLASSIFICATION   ApeGC, 134
a)   Known as the "Carolingian Renaissance"
(1) The influence may have come
from Byzantium

2.   NINTH CENTURY
a)   Modal system described for the first
time by Aurelian in _Musica disciplina_
ca. A.D. 850   ApeHD, 167
b)   The modes were developed in order
to codify the existing chants   ApeHD, 167
(1) It is thought that some chants
were modified in order to make
them conform to the modes
c)   Only four _maneriae_ (four modes)
were discussed   ApeGC, 135
(1) _Protus, deuterus, tritus,_
and _tetrardus_
(a) These terms are corruptions of the Greek
words for first, second,
third, and fourth   ApeHD, 165
d)   There was no division into authentic
and plagal modes   ApeGC, 135
e)   Only the octave _ambitus_ was recognized
ApeGC, 135
(1) It was divided into a _diapente_
and a _diatessaron_

3.   TENTH CENTURY   ApeGC, 135
a)   Discussion of the modes in _Dialogus_
de musica
(1) Written by Odo de Clugny or
one of his pupils

(2)   Also known as <u>Enchiridion
      musices</u>   BakB, 1178
(3)   It shows the enlarged octave
      <u>ambitus</u>
      (a)   A ninth and a tenth
(4)   The <u>ambitus</u> was divided into
      authentic and plagal modes
b) Terminology for the numbering of
    the modes changed (Used the terms
    <u>primus tonus</u>, etc.)   ApeGC, 133

Fig. 2. The Eight Ecclesiastical Modes

Maneriae	Modus	Tonus	Finalis	Ambitus	Tenor
Protus	Authenticus	Primus tonus	D	D-d	a
	Plagius	Secundus tonus	D	A-a	F
Deuterus	Authenticus	Tertius tonus	E	E-e	c
	Plagius	Quartus tonus	E	B-b	a
Tritus	Authenticus	Quintus tonus	F	F-f	c
	Plagius	Sextus tonus	F	C-c	a
Tetrardus	Authenticus	Septimus tonus	G	G-g	d
	Plagius	Octavus tonus	G	D-d	c

c=middle c (ApeGC, 133)

4. THE MODAL SYSTEM REACHED THE HIGHEST
    POINT OF DEVELOPMENT DURING THE
    RENAISSANCE   AllT, 64
a) In the sixteenth century four new
    modes were added   AllT, 69
    (1)   The <u>nonus tonus</u>, the <u>decimus
          tonus</u>, the <u>undecimus tonus</u>,
          and the <u>duodecimus tonus</u>   ApeHD, 166

Fig. 3. The Four Added Modes

Modus	Tonus	Finalis	Ambitus	Tenor
Authenticus	Nonus tonus	a	a-aa	e
Plagius	Decimus tonus	a	E-e	c
Authenticus	Undecimus tonus	c	c-cc	g
Plagius	Duodecimus tonus	c	G-g	e

c=middle c (ApeHD, 166)

b) Another terminology for the modes
    that is used today but was seldom
    used in the Middle Ages borrows
    names from ancient Greek theory
                                            ApeHD, 166
    (1)   The names are Dorian,

Phrygian, Lydian, Mixolydian,
Aeolian, and Ionian in the
authentic modes   ApeHD, 166
  (a)   These should not be thought
      of as derivatives of the
      Greek modes   ApeHD, 167
(2)   In 1558 Zarlino, in his
<u>Institutione harmoniche</u>, placed
the Ionian beneath the Dorian
                        ApeHD, 167
(3)   In the plagal mode the names
include the prefix hypo-
(Hypoionian, Hypodorian,
etc.)   ApeHD, 166

C.   <u>TONALITY</u>

  1.   INTEGRATION OF THE MODES INTO THE
      HEXACHORDAL SYSTEM   AllT, 71
      a)   The interlocking of the hexachords
         <u>naturale</u> and <u>durum</u> formed the
         modes in their regular position
         (1)   See figure 4

Fig. 4. The Modes in Regular Position

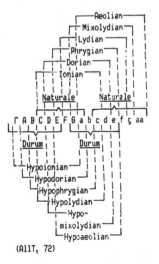

(AllT, 72)

      b)   The interlocking of the hexachords
         <u>naturale</u> and <u>molle</u> formed the
         modes in irregular position   AllT, 72
         (1)   This position included the
             Ionian, Dorian, Phrygian and

Lydian modes
(a)   See figure 5

Fig. 5. The Modes Ionian, Dorian, Phrygian,
      and Lydian in Irregular Position

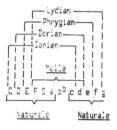

(A11, 70)

c)   The interlocking of the hexachord
     durum with a hexachord on D formed
     the Mixolydian and Aeolian modes
     in their first irregular position
     (1)   See figure 6

Fig. 6. The Modes Aeolian and Mixolydian
      in Irregular Position

(A11, 73)

II.   THEORETICAL WRITINGS ON THE ECCLESIASTICAL MODES

A.   <u>EIGHTH AND NINTH CENTURIES</u>   ApeGC, 54

     1.   ALCUIN (753-814): <u>MUSICA</u>

     2)   AURELIANUS OF RÉOMÉ (MID NINTH
          CENTURY): <u>MUSICA DISCIPLINA</u>

B.   TENTH CENTURY

   1.   ALIA MUSICA   ReeMMA, 154
      a)   A composite work
      b)   Possibly by four different
         authors

   2.   ODO DE CLUGNY (d. 942)   BakB, 1178
      a)   _Dialogus de musica_ also known
         as _Enchiridion musices_ (probably
         written under his supervision

C.   ELEVENTH CENTURY

   1.   HERMANNUS CONTRACTUS (1013-1054):
     OPUSCULA MUSICA   BakB, 700

APPENDIX 6
The System of Hexachords and Solmization

I.   HEXACHORDS

    A.   <u>THE DEVELOPMENT, STRUCTURE, AND EXTENSION OF THE HEXACHORD</u>

        1.   BACKGROUND
            a)   The system of hexachords su[erseded the Greek system of tetrachords   ApeHD, 384
                (1)   The term "hexachord" was not used until the sixteenth century
            b)   The system was presented by Guido d'Arezzo in his "Epistola ad Michaelem Monachum: de ignoto cantu", supra, p. 30   ApeHD, 384
                (1)   His purpose was to help teach choir boys to sing new chants at sight   RasN, 128
                (2)   He divided the available scale into groups of six notes   RasN, 128
                    (a)   The available scale was that which has been ascribed to Odo de Clugny   ReeMMA, 21

Fig. 1. Scale Ascribed to Odo de Clugny

Γ A B C D E F G a b♭ c d e f g aa
(ReeMMA, 149)

                    (b)   The Greek <u>gamma</u> (Γ) was used for the lowest note, G   HugMT, 292
                    (c)   The word for scale (gamut) was derived from the combination of the Greek word <u>gamma</u> and the first syllable of the solmization system (ut)
                    (d)   In the thirteenth century

                              the gamut was extended by
                              four degrees to the note
                              ee   ReeMMA, 150

2.   THE STRUCTURE OF THE HEXACHORD
      a) The six notes of the hexachord
          always contain the same structure
          of intervals   RasN, 128
          (1) A semitone with two whole
               tones on either side
      b) Guido organized the gamut into two
          basic hexachords   AllT, 16
          (1) Hexachord durum built on G
               (a) Γ A B C D E
          (2) Hexachord naturale built on C
               (a) C D E F G a
      c) Each hexachord has one note which
          is lacking in the other   AllT, 16

3.   INTERLOCKED HEXACHORDS (HEXACHORD-ORDERS)
      a) In order to cover the interval of an
          octave or the entire gamut the hexa-
          chords had to be interlocked   AllT, 16

          Fig. 2. The Durum-naturale Hexachord-order

          Γ A B C D E   (durum)
                C D E F G   (naturale)

      b) In order to go beyond the tone a
          the order of the hexachords had
          to be reversed

          Fig. 3. The Naturale-durum Hexachord-order

          C D E F G a   (naturale)
                G a b c   (durum)

      c) There is a third hexachord called
          molle which is built on F   AllT, 18
          (1) By combining it with the hexa-
               chord naturale either above or
               below, two more hexachord-orders
               are obtained
          (2) Actually there are only two
               distinct hexachord-orders
               (a) The naturale-molle and the
                    molle-naturale are transpo-
                    sitions of the durum-naturale
                    and the naturale-durum
               (b) They are used to raise or
                    lower melodies, to modulate,

and create new modes   AllT, 21

Fig. 4. The <u>Naturale-molle</u> Hexachord-order

```
C D E F G a          (naturale)
    F G a b♭ c        (molle)
```

Fig. 5. The <u>Molle-naturale</u> Hexachord-order

```
F G a b♭ c            (molle)
        c d e f      (naturale)
(AllT, 18)
```

4.   HEXACHORD-ORDERS ARE DISJUNCT AND CONJUNCT
    a)   The hexachord-order <u>naturale durum</u> has
        two disjunct tetrachords each contain-
        ing a tone, tone, semitone with a tone
        between the two tetrachords   AllT, 17
        (1)   Therefore it is a disjunct
            hexachord-order
    b)   The hexachord-order <u>Durum-naturale</u> has
        two tetrachords with a tone, tone,
        semitone but with no tone between the
        tetrachords   AllT, 17
        (1)   Therefore it is a conjunct
            hexachord-order
    c)   There is also a conjunct <u>Naturale-</u>
        <u>molle</u> and a disjunct <u>Molle-naturale</u>
                        AllT, 18

5.   TRANSPOSITIONS OF THE GAMUT
    a)   Odo de Clugny discusses the combined
        gamut in three transpositions   AllT, 19-20
        (1)   The combined gamut a second
            above (starts on the note A)
            (a)   Produces areas of oscillation
                on C-sharp and C-natural

Fig. 6. The Combined Gamut on A

Conjunct Hexachord A-D

```
A B C♯ D E F♯ G a b c♯ d e f♯ g
```

Disjunct Hexachord D-a

Conjunct Hexachord D-<u>durum</u>

```
D E F♯ G a b c d e f♯ g aa bb cc
```

Disjunct <u>durum</u>-Hexachord D
(AllT, 20)

(2)   The combined gamut a fourth
      above (starts on the note c)
      (a)   Produces areas of oscillation
            on E-natural and E-flat

Fig. 7. The Combined Gamut on C

Conjunct <u>Naturale-molle</u>

C D E F G a b^b c d e f g aa bb^b

Disjunct <u>Molle-naturale</u>

Conjunct <u>Molle</u>-heachord b^b

F G a b^b c d e^b f g aa bb^b cc dd ee^b

Disjunct hexachord b^b-<u>molle</u>
(AllT, 20)

(3)   The combined gamut a fifth
      above (starts on D)
      (a)   Produces areas of oscillation
            on F-sharp and f-natural

Fig. 8. The Combined Gamut on D

Conjunct hexachord D-<u>durum</u>

D E F$^#$ G a b c d e f$^#$ g aa bb cc

Disjunct <u>Durum</u>-hexachord D

Conjunct <u>Durum-naturale</u>

G a b c d e f g aa bb cc dd ee ff

Disjunct <u>Naturale-durum</u>
(AllT, 20)

6.   THERE ARE TWO OCTAVE DIVISIONS
      a)   The harmonic octave   AllT, 25
           (1)   A fifth followed by a fourth
                 (a)   This corresponds to the
                       disjunct hexachord-order
      b)   The arithmetic octave   AllT, 25
           (1)   A fourth followed by a fifth
                 (a)   This corresponds to the
                       conjunct hexachord-order
      c)   In the hexachord-orders the fifth
           can belong to two different fourths
                                            AllT, 26

(1)   It is the fourth that determines
      the hexachord

II.   SOLMIZATION

A.   ORIGIN AND FUNCTION

1.   "UT QUEANT LAXIS"   RasN, 128
   a)   Guido d'Arezzo named the notes of the
        hexachord by the first syllable of each
        line of the stanza "Ut queant laxis"
        (1)   It is the first stanza of the
              vesper hymn for the feast
              of St. John the Baptist
        (2)   The syllables are ut, re, mi,
              fa, sol, la
   b)   Each line of the stanza, except for
        the last one, starts one note higher
        (1)   The last line begins with the
              syllable "san" which is not one of
              the syllables used for solmization
   c)   He used these syllables to teach choir
        boys to sing new chants at sight
        (1)   This system is known as
              solmization

2.   COMPOUND NAMES ARE USED FOR INTERLOCKED
     HEXACHORDS   ApeHD, 384
   a)   These compound names were devised
        to indicate the various "functions"
        of a given tone
        (1)   The compound name includes
              the pitch name as well as its
              syllables
              (a)   Desolre indicates that the
                    tone d can appear as sol
                    or re

Fig. 9. Syllables for the durum-naturale-molle Hexachords

Γ		ut		
A		re		
B		mi		
C	C	fa	ut	(Cefaut)
D	D	sol	re	(Desolre)
E	E	la	mi	(Elami)
	F	F	fa	ut	(Fefaut)
	G	G	sol	re	(Gesolre)
	a	a	la	mi	(Alami)
	bᵇ		fa	(Befa)
	c		sol	(Cesol)
	d		la	(Dela)

3.   MODAL FLUCTUATIONS
      a) The framework of the hexachord system
          makes it unnecessary to indicate
          flats and sharps   AllT, 42
          (1) Ut-mi is always a major third
          (2) An ascending conjunct hexachord-
               order is always ut, re, mi, fa,
               re, mi, fa, sol
          (3) The ascending disjunct hexachord-
               order is always ut, re, mi, fa,
               sol, re, mi, fa
          (4) The descending conjunct hexachord-
               order is always sol, fa, la, sol,
               fa, mi, re, ut
          (5) The descending disjunct hexachord-
               order is always fa, mi, la, sol,
               fa, mi, re, ut

4.   SOLMIZATION CONTINUED INTO THE SIXTEENTH
      CENTURY   AllT,42

APPENDIX 7
Daseia *Notation*

I.   DEFINITION AND SYMBOLS

A.   <u>DEFINITION</u>

    1.   A SERIES OF TONES COVERING A RANGE OF
        EIGHTEEN NOTES   AllT, 28
        a)   Uses a series of signs based on
            the Greek aspirate (⊦)   RasN, 122
        b)   Invented by Odo de Clugny   ParN, 29
            (1)   According to Guido d'Arezzo

    2.   USES A SET OF SYMBOLS WHICH INDICATE
        A SERIES OF MODAL OSCILLATIONS   AllT, 28
        a)   The fluctuation between hexachords
            (1)   See appendices 5 and 6
        b)   These modal oscillations were used
            by medieval composers and musicians
            (1)   A composer would seldom use
                more than two modal oscillations
                at a time

B.   <u>THE SYMBOLS</u>   RasN, 122

    1.   THE SYMBOLS ARE GROUPED INTO TETRACHORDS
        a)   The second tetrachord uses the aspirate
            (⊦) for the first, second, and fourth
            notes with an "s", a reversed "c", and
            a regular "c" on top
        b)   The lowest tetrachord reverses
            the symbols
        c)   The third tetrachord inverts the
            symbols
        d)   The fourth tetrachord inverts and
            reverses the symbols
        e)   The third note of each tetrachord
            uses an alphabetic symbol
            (1)   Called accent signs   ParN, 29

(a) They indicate the upper
      note of a semitone
      interval
(b) <u>Inclinum</u> (N)
(c) <u>Iota</u> (/)
(d) <u>Versum</u> (ᒐ)
(e) <u>Iota transfixum</u> (X)

f) The illustration in the <u>Musica</u>
    <u>enchiriadis</u> shows the following
    symbols

Fig. 1. <u>Daseia</u> Symbols

Dorian mode in normal position

$$F$$

ᴦ A Bᵇ C D E F.G a b c d e f# g aa bb cc# dd ee

F=<u>finalis</u> (AllT, 28-29; RasN, 122)

Dorian transposed twice in the
<u>durum</u> direction

Dorian transposed once in the <u>durum</u>
direction or Aeolian

g) The above symbols show the areas
    of oscillation that are possible
    in the Dorian mode   AllT, 28
    (1) The B natural and B flat in
          the <u>durum</u> and <u>molle</u> area
    (2) The F natural and f sharp in
          the <u>durum</u> direction and the
          <u>naturale</u> area
    (3) The c sharp and c natural in
          the Hexachord a and the <u>durum</u>
          area
    (4) See appendices 4 and 5

2. <u>DASEIA</u> SYMBOLS WERE ALSO USED AS "CLEFS"
                                          RasN, 123

    a) The letters t and s were written
        between the <u>Daseia</u> symbols to
        indicate tones and semitones

APPENDIX 8
Square Notation

I.   DEFINITION AND DERIVATION OF SQUARE NOTATION

    A.   DEFINITION

        1.   A NOTATION WHICH USES SQUARE SHAPES
             FOR THE NOTES AND LIGATURES   ApeHD, 805
             a)   The term was introduced by F. Ludwig
                  in 1910
                  (1)   In Repertorium organorum

    B.   DERIVATION

        1.   DERIVED FROM FRENCH NEUMES   RasN, 32
             a)   Twelfth century   RasN, 33
                  (1)   Norman neumes were placed on
                        a fully developed staff
                        (a)   Used a system of notating
                              precise pitch-reference
             b)   Thirteenth century   RasN, 35
                  (1)   Neumes were written with the
                        thick and thin strokes of
                        Gothic script
                        (a)   The result was square
                              notation

II. CHARACTERISTICS OF SQUARE NOTATION

    A.   USES BOTH SINGLE NOTES AND LIGATURES   ApeN, 217

        1.   SINGLE NOTES
             a)   Theorists refer to this notation
                  as "notatio cum litera"   ApeN, 218
                  (1)   When there is a text the
                        notes are usually written

                                    separately rather than in
                                    ligature

        2.   LIGATURES (SQUARE NOTES BOUND TOGETHER)
                                                    HugFR, 322
              a)   Theorists refer to this notation
                    as "notatio sine litera"   ApeN, 218
                    (1)   When there is no text, ligatures
                           are used as much as possible
              b)   Ligatures develop into certain forms
                    and patterns in the late twelfth
                    century (modal notation)   HugFR, 322
                    (1)   Indicate a strict meter   ApeN, 218
                           (a)   The notes have no temporal
                                  significance   HugFR, 322
                           (b)   It is the pattern of the
                                  ligatures that indicates
                                  the meter   HugFR, 322
              c)   Ligatures and single notes develop
                    definite time values in the late
                    thirteenth century (mensural
                    notation)   HugMAF, 379

III.   THREE TYPES OF SQUARE NOTATION

   A.   PLAINSONG NOTATION (SEE APPENDIX 4)

   B.   MODAL NOTATION (SEE APPENDIX 9)

         1.   LATE TWELFTH THROUGH THE EARLY THIRTEENTH
               CENTURIES   ApeN, 199

   C.   BLACK MENSURAL NOTATION

         1.   FRANCONIAN NOTATION (SEE APPENDIX 11)
               a)   Last half of the thirteenth century
                                                      ApeN, 199

         2.   FRENCH MENSURAL NOTATION (SEE APPENDIX 12)
               a)   Ca. 1300-1450   ApeN, 199

         3.   ITALIAN MENSURAL NOTATION (SEE APPENDIX 13)
               a)   The middle of the fourteenth century
                                                      ApeN, 199

         4.   MIXED NOTATION
               a)   Last of the fourteenth century   ApeN, 199

         5.   MANNERED NOTATION
               a)   Late fourteenth and early fifteenth
                     centuries   ApeN, 199

APPENDIX 9
Modal Notation

I.   THE MODES AND LIGATURES OF MODAL NOTATION

A.   <u>MODES</u>

   1.   A NOTATIONAL SYSTEM THAT ORGANIZES MUSIC
        RHYTHMICALLY   RasN, 37
        a)   Embodie natural regular rhythms
                                              HugFR, 318
             (1) Dance rhythms
             (2) Rhythms founded on poetical
                  meters
             (3) The rhythm of toil
        b)   Consist of five to nine modes
             (patterns) recognized by medieval
             theorists   RasN, 38
             (1) Six are commonly accepted
                                              ApeN, 220-221
                  (a) Mode one: <u>longa-brevis</u>
                  (b) Mode two: <u>brevis-longa</u>
                       i)   The accent falls
                            on the <u>brevis</u>
                  (c) Mode three: <u>longa-brevis-
                       brevis</u>
                       i)   The <u>longa</u> has a
                            ternary value
                            and the value
                            of the second
                            <u>brevis</u> is doubled
                  (d) Mode four: <u>brevis-brevis-
                       longa</u>
                       i)   The value of the
                            second <u>brevis</u> is
                            doubled and the <u>longa</u>
                            is given a ternary
                            value
                  (e) Mode five: <u>longa-longa</u>
                       i)   Each <u>longa</u> is ternary
                  (f) Mode six: <u>brevis-brevis-</u>

                        <u>brevis</u>
              (g) The <u>longa</u> of the first
                   and second modes is
                   known as imperfect
              (h) The <u>longa</u> of the third,
                   fourth, and fifth modes
                   is known as perfect
              (i) The term <u>altera</u> is
                   applied to the altered
                   <u>brevis</u>
      c) Each mode (pattern) can be lengthened
          in order to form melodies of dif-
          ferent lengths   ApeN, 222
          (1) The repetition of a pattern
               (mode) is known as an <u>ordo</u>
               (a) Each <u>ordo</u> ends with a rest
                    i)   The duration of the
                          rest is determined
                          by the mode
                    ii)   The rest is indicated
                          by a short vertical
                          stroke known as
                          <u>divisio modi</u>   ApeN, 225

          Fig. 1. <u>Ordines</u>

          Mode I.   <u>Ordo</u> 1. L B L   r*
                     <u>Ordo</u> 2. L B L   B*L   r
                     <u>Ordo</u> 3. L B L   B*L   B L   r*
          Mode II.   <u>Ordo</u> 1. B L   B r r*
                     <u>Ordo</u> 2. B L   B L   *B r r
                     <u>Ordo</u> 3. B L   B L   *B L   B r r*
          Mode III. <u>Ordo</u> 1. L   B L *L   r r r*
                     <u>Ordo</u> 2. L   B L *L   B L *L   r r r*
                     <u>Ordo</u> 3. L   B L *L   B L *L   B L *L   r r r*
          Mode IV.   <u>Ordo</u> 1. B L   L   *B L   r r r*
                     <u>Ordo</u> 2. B L   L   *B L   L   *B L   r r r*
                     <u>Ordo</u> 3. B L   L   *B L   L   *B L   L   *B L   r r r*
          Mode V.   <u>Ordo</u> 1. L   L   *L   r r r*
                     <u>Ordo</u> 2. L   L   *L   L   *L   r r r*
                     <u>Ordo</u> 3. L   L   *L   L   *L   L   *L   r r r*
          Mode VI.   <u>Ordo</u> 1. B B B B r r*
                     <u>Ordo</u> 2. B B B B B B*B r r
                     <u>Ordo</u> 3. B B B B B B*B B B B r r*
          L=<u>longa</u>; B=<u>brevis</u>; r=rest; *=end of an <u>ordo</u> (ApeN, 222)

      d) Uses a system of ligatures   RasN, 37
          (1) The term ligature comes from
               the Latin <u>ligare</u> meaning
               "to bind"   ReeMMA, 278
          (2) Ligatures include two values
                                          ApeN, 220
               (a) The <u>longa</u> and the <u>brevis</u>
                                          ApeN, 223

        i)   There are no single
                 notational signs
                 for these values
                 a - They are always
                     combined
       ii)   They are not always
                 of the same quality
                          ReeMMA, 277
       iii)   They are derived
                 from the plainsong
                 symbols that repre-
                 sent more than one
                 tone   ReeMMA, 278

(3)   They are called ascending or
      descending   ReeMMA, 278
    (a) Depending on whether the
        second note is higher or
        lower than the first note

(4)   The first and last notes of a
      ligature determine its form
                        ReeMMA, 278
    (a) There are three forms used
        for the first note of the
        ligature
        i)   Cum proprietate
            a - An ascending
                ligature in
                which the first
                note has no tail
            b - A descending
                ligature in which
                the first note has
                a tail going down-
                ward at the left
        ii)   Sine proprietate
            a - A ligature in
                which the first
                note omits the
                tail which was
                present in plain-
                song notation
            b - A descending
                ligature in which
                a tail is added
                to the first note
                of the plainsong
                ligature
        iii) Opposita proprietate
            a - Any ligature,
                descending or
                ascending, with
                a tail ascending
                from the left
    (b) There are two forms used
        for the last note of the
        ligature

          i)   <u>Cum perfectione</u>
                a - Those ligatures
                    in which the last
                    note is placed to
                    the lower right
                    of the penultimate
                    note, or perpendic-
                    ularly above it

        ii)   <u>Sine perfectione</u>
                a - Those ligatures in
                    which the last note
                    is represented by
                    the lower end of a
                    transverse bar
                b - Those ligatures in
                    which the last note
                    is placed at the
                    upper right of the
                    penultimate note

e)   The mode is indicated by the type and
     grouping of the ligatures   ReeMMA, 279
   (1)   Patterns of imperfect modes
                          ReeMMA, 280
      (a)   These modes were discussed
           by theorists but were never
           used in a practical way
      (b)   For a discussion of these
           modes see   ReeMMA, 280
   (2)   Basic patterns of the perfect modes
      (a)   Mode I
          i)   A three-note ligature
                followed by a group of
                two-note ligatures,
                a - All <u>cum proprietate</u>
                    and <u>cum perfectione</u>
          ii)   Sometimes only three-
                note ligatures are used
      (b)   Mode II
          i)   A group of two-note liga-
                tures
                a - <u>Cum proprietate</u> and
                    <u>cum perfectione</u>
          ii)   Followed by a single
                 three-note ligature
                a - <u>Sine proprietate</u> and
                    <u>cum perfectione</u>
      (c)   Mode III
          i)   A single note followed
                 by a group of three-note
                ligatures
                a - <u>Cum proprietate</u> and
                    <u>perfectione</u>
      (d)   Mode IV
          i)   A group of three-note
                 ligatures
                a - <u>Cum proprietate</u>

and _perfectione_
  ii)   Followed by a single
          two-note ligature
          a - _Cum proprietate_ and
             sine perfectione
(e) Mode V
  i)   Three-note ligatures
         a - _Cum proprietate_ and
            perfectione
  ii)   Each three-note group
          is separated by rests
(f) Mode VI
  i)   A four-note ligature
         followed by a group of
         three-note ligatures
         a - _Cum proprietate_ and
            perfectione
  ii)   Sometimes a four-note
          ligature followed by
          a group of three-note
          ligatures
          a - _Sine proprietate_ and
            cum perfectione
  iii) Sometimes a four-note
          ligature followed by a
          group of two-note liga-
          tures
          a - _Cum proprietate_ and
            with terminal notes
            having stems on the
            right and pointing
            either up or down
  iv) Sometimes a group of
          two-note ligatures _cum
          proprietate_ and _cum
          perfectione_

Fig. 2. Ligature Patterns

Mode	Number of notes in a Ligature
Mode I:	3 2 2 2
Mode II:	2 2 2 3
Mode III:	1 3 3 3
Mode IV:	3 3 3 1 or 3 3 3 2
Mode V:	1 1 1 or 3 3 3
Mode VI:	4 3 3

(RasN, 39, 40; ApeN, 225; ReeMMA, 279)

B. __MODAL LIGATURES__   ReeMMA, 279

  1.   TWO NOTE LIGATURES
      a) _Cum proprietate_ and _cum perfectione_
        (1) Descending (♪)

(2)   Ascending (♪)
b)   <u>Sine proprietate</u>
(1)   Descending (↘)
(2)   Ascending (♯)
c)   <u>Sine perfectione</u>
(1)   Descending (⌐)
(2)   Ascending (♪)
d)   <u>Cum opposita proprietate</u>
(1)   Descending (◣)
(2)   Ascending (◤)

2.   THREE NOTE LIGATURES
a)   <u>Cum proprietate</u> and <u>cum perfectione</u>
(1)   Descending (◥) or (◤)
(2)   Ascending (♩) or (♣)
b)   <u>Sine proprietate</u>
(1)   Descending (◥), (◢),
and (◣)
(2)   Ascending (♩) or (♣)
c)   <u>Sine perfectione</u>
(1)   Descending (◠) or (♥)
(2)   Ascending (♪) or (♪)
d)   <u>Cum opposita perfectione</u>
(1)   Descending (◣) or (◣)
(2)   Ascending (♩) or (◣)

3.   MODAL LIGATURES USE A FOUR-LINE STAFF
RasN, 41
a)   A fifth line is added if the range
requires it

4.   MODAL LIGATURES CAN BE MODIFIED   RasN, 42-43
a)   <u>Fractio modi</u> ("breaking up" of the
mode)
(1)   Deviations from the regular
ligature successions within
an <u>ordo</u>   ParN, 77
(a)   Each imperfect long may
be split into three to
six notes   ReeMMA, 281
(b)   Each perfect long may be
split into three to eight
notes   ReeMMA, 281
(c)   Each breve may be split
into two or three notes
ReeMMA, 281
i)   Square notes were
added to the
ligature
ii)   The time value of the
ligature would be no
greater than that of
the ligature without
the insertions
(2)   By the use of a <u>plica</u> (fold)
(a)   Equivalent to the liquescent

neume in chant
i)   A single note having
      a tail to either side
      (⌐ ⌐)
      a - The tails go up
          for an ascending
          note and down for
          a descending note
ii)   Sometimes a single
      tail is used for an
      ascending plica
      a - Ligatures are
          sometimes plicated
          in the same way
          (♩ ♫ ♫)
iii) The pes, scandicus,
      and porrectus are
      turned to the right
      so that a tail may
      be added (♪ ♫ ♫)
(b) May indicate a changing
     note
     i)   Between notes of
           the same pitch
     ii)   Middle note of the
           interval of a third
     iii) May be used as an
           anticipation note
     iv)   May jump a third
           and then return
(c) The plica note derives
     its value from the note
     to which it is attached
                           RaaN, 44
     i)   If the main note is
           a perfect longa the
           plica takes a third
           of its value
     ii)   If the main note
           is an imperfect
           longa the plica
           takes half of its
           value
     iii) If the main note
           is a brevis recta
           the plica divides
           it into two equal
           parts
(3) Repeated notes   ReeMMA, 281
(a) These are not used in
     ligatures
     i)   The repetition of a
           note starts with a
           new ligature
           a - The ligature
               consists of the

                                        left-over notes
                                    b - More than one
                                        note is neccea-
                                        sary
                        ii)   The repetition of a
                               note can be a single
                               note
                               a - Has a stem des-
                                   cending at the
                                   right if it con-
                                   cludes the liga-
                                   ture
                               b - Otherwise it has
                                   no stem
                               c - The stem has
                                   nothing to do
                                   with duration
            b)   Extensio modi ("lengthening of the
                  mode")   RaaN, 44
                  (1)   An imperfect longa may be re-
                         placed by a perfect longa
                         (a)   When not part of a modal
                                pattern these longae are
                                notated by single notes
                                                    ParN, 78
            c)   Use of ornamental notes in the form
                  of lozenges   RaaN, 45
                  (1)   Known as currentes, ("running
                         notes") or conjunctura
                  (2)   Added after a single note in
                         the form of a virga (⁊♦♦
                         ▪♦♦)   ReeMMA, 281
                  (3)   Sometimes added after a
                         ligature
                  (4)   Always descend in scalic
                         formation
                  (5)   Share the value of the previous
                         note
                         (a)   Longer values come last
                  (6)   There may be as many as nine
                         rhombs

APPENDIX 10
Page Arrangements

I.   SCORE-ARRANGEMENT

    A.   <u>DEFINITION</u>

        1.   THE VOICES OF THE COMPOSITION ARE
            WRITTEN ONE UNDER THE OTHER   ApeN, xx
            a) Each on its own staff   RasN, 9
            b) Arranged in such a way that the
                notes appear simultaneously in vertical,
                or almost vertical, alignment

    B.   <u>BACKGROUND</u>

        1.   THE EARLIEST METHOD OF WRITING POLYPHONIC
            MUSIC   ApeN, xx
            a) From the late twelfth century to
                the beginning of the sixteenth
                century score-arrangement implied
                similar rhythm and movement of
                the voice parts   RasN, 9
                (1) The text was written only once
                    (a) Below the lowest voice
            b) In the late sixteenth century score-
                arrangement was used for didactic
                purposes   RasN, 9
                (1) For teaching or illustrating
                    points of music theory   RasN, 121
            c) In the seventeenth century score-
                arrangement was used for keyboard
                music and Italian "monody"   RasN, 9

    C.   <u>A PRINCIPLE THAT WAS APPLIED TO DIFFERENT</u>
        <u>TYPES OF NOTATION</u>   ApeN, xx

        1.   TEXT-SYLLABLES (<u>MUSICA ENCHIRIADIS</u>)
            a) Ninth century

2.   LETTER NOTATION (GUIDO D'AREZZO)
      a)   Eleventh century

3.   NEUMES (SCHOOL OF ST. MARTIAL)

4.   NOTES (SCHOOL OF NOTRE DAME)
      a)   Twelfth century

II.   PART-ARRANGEMENT

A. <u>CANTUS LATERALIS</u>   RasN, 9

    1.   MUSIC IN WHICH THE PARTS ARE WRITTEN
          "SIDE BY SIDE"
          a)   Each part treated separately on a
               different part of a page
          b)   Each part treated separately and
               covering two pages, one opposite
               the other   ApeN, xx
               (1)   Known as choir-book notation
                     (fifteenth century)   RasN, 9
                     (a)   Used by an entire choir
                           reading at a lectern

    2.   DEVELOPED IN THE SECOND QUARTER OF THE
          THIRTEENTH CENTURY   ApeN, xx
          a)   One of a number of innovations that
               accompanied the development of the
               motet
               (1)   In the earliest form of the
                     motet-layout the tenor is placed
                     across the bottom of the page or
                     pages   RasN, 9
               (2)   The two upper parts are placed
                     above the tenor   RasN, 9
               (3)   This is varied where there are
                     five or more voices   RasN, 9

    3.   THIS PRACTICE LASTED UNTIL ABOUT 1450
                                                                ApeN, xx

APPENDIX 11
Franconian Notation

I.   THE DEFINITION AND SYMBOLS OF FRANCONIAN NOTATION

A.   <u>DEFINITION</u>

    1. A NOTATION WHICH GIVES EVERY NOTE A
        STRICTLY DETERMINED VALUE   ApeHD, 520
        a) Regulated by a set of rules that
            put an end to arbitrariness and
            ambiguity   ReeMMA, 289
        b) The strictly determined value
            applies to the rests also   ReeMMA, 289

    2. A RATIONAL CODIFICATION OF SEVERAL
        SLIGHTLY DIFFERENT SYSTEMS   RasN, 47
        a) Dietricus (ca. 1275)   RasN, 46
            (1) Considered the <u>brevis</u> to be
                equal to two semibreves
                (a) The binary division of
                      modal notation
        b) Magister Lambertus (Pseudo-Aristotle)
                                  RasN, 46
            (1) Wrote about the same time as
                Dietricus
            (2) Gives the <u>brevis</u> a ternary
                division
                (a) <u>Semibrevis major</u>
                      i)   Two-thirds of a <u>tempus</u>
                (b) <u>Semibrevis minor</u>
                      i)   One-third <u>tempus</u>
         c) These innovations were known as
            "Pre-Franconian notation   ApeN, 282

    3. SURVIVED ALMOST INTACT UNTIL THE SIXTEENTH
        CENTURY   ReeMMA, 289

    4. CODIFIED BY FRANCO OF COLOGNE IN HIS
        TREATISE <u>ARS CANTUS MENSURABILIS</u>
        (ca. 1260)   ParN, 108

B.   THE SYMBOLS OF FRANCONIAN NOTATION

   1.   SINGLE NOTES AND LIGATURES
       a)   Single notes   RasN, 47
          (1)   The notes are regarded as
              ternary except for the
              duplex longa   ReeMMA, 289
          (2)   The duplex longa (▅) is equal
              to two longs in duration   RasN, 47
          (3)   The longa (▌) may be either
              perfect or imperfect   RasN, 47
             (a)   If perfect it equals
                 three tempora   ReeMMA, 289
             (b)   If imperfect it equals
                 two tempora   ReeMMA, 289
          (4)   The brevis (▪) is either
              proper (recta) or altered
              (altera)   RasN, 47
             (a)   If recta it equals one
                 tempus   ReeMMA, 289
             (b)   If altera it equals
                 two tempora   ReeMMA, 289
          (5)   The semibrevis (♦) is either
              major or minor   RasN, 47
             (a)   If minor it equals one-
                 third tempus   ReeMMA, 289
             (b)   If major it equals two-
                 thirds tempus   ReeMMA, 289
       b)   The rules which govern the single
         notes   RasN, 48-49
          (1)   "...the underlying movement
              of the music is by a series
              of perfections..."   ParN, 110
          (2)   A longa followed by a single
              brevis is thereby imperfected
              (▌▪ = ♩♩)
          (3)   A perfection may consist of
              two or three breves
              (▪▪ or ▪▪▪)
             (a)   In a pair the second brevis
                 is altered (▪▪ = ♩♩)
          (4)   With four or more breves together
              preceded by a longa the first
              brevis imperfects the longa
              (▌▪▪▪▪ = ♩ ♩|♩♩♩)
          (5)   Where a longa might be imperfected
              either by a note preceding or
              following, the note following
              takes precedence
              (▌▪▌ = ♩ ♩♩.)
          (6)   A longa followed by another longa
              is always perfect
          (7)   In order to clarify some rhythms
              which conflict with the rules
              a signum perfectionis (sign of
              perfection) is used

      (a) A short vertical line
          across one line of the
          staff
(8) A proper _brevis_ may be divided
    into two or three semibreves
                              RasN, 50
      (a) If it is divided into two
          semibreves the larger
          semibrevis comes second
          (ternary rhythm)
(9) An altered _brevis_ may be
    divided into four, five,
    or six semibreves   RasN, 50
      (a) The _signum perfectionis_
          is used to show the
          proper division
c) The ligatures
   (1) The appearance of the ligature
      is vital in determining its
      rhythmic components   UltM, 16
      (a) The _pes_ and the _clivis_ of
          plainsong notation are
          the basic ligatures used
          by Franco, see appendix
          4   RasN, 50
      (b) He assigns the same
          values to them as in
          modal notation, see
          appendix 9   RasN, 50
   (2) The terms _cum proprietate,_
      sine proprietate, and _cum_
      opposita proprietate refer
      to the first note of the
      ligature   ApeN, 312
      (a) The ligature is _cum_
          proprietate when the
          first note is a _brevis_
      (b) It is _sine proprietate_
          when the first note is
          a _longa_
          i) This is indicated
              by removing the tail
              from a descending
              ligature and adding
              a tail to the first
              note of an ascending
              ligature   RasN, 51
      (c) The ligature is _cum opposita_
          when the first two notes are
          semibreves
          i) An upward tail on a
              ligature shows it is
              cum opposita proprie-
              tate   RasN, 52
              a - Indicates that
                  the two notes

following the
tail are semi-
breves

(3)   The terms cum perfectio and
sine perfectio refer to the
last note of the ligature   ApeN, 312
   (a) The ligature is cum
perfectio when the last
note is a longa
   (b) It is sine perfectio when
the last note is a brevis
     i) Indicated by turning
the upper note of an
ascending ligature
to the right   RasN, 51
(4)   Three-note ligatures   RasN, 52
   (a) All middle notes of a
ligature are breves   ApeN, 313
   (b) All two, three, and
four-note ligatures were
called figura by Franco
     i) Only the two-note
symbols were
considered by him
to be true ligatures
a - In a multi-note
figura the first two
notes or the last two
notes are the two-
note ligatures

Fig. 1. Two-note Ligatures

	Ascending	Descending	
Cum proprietate:			=brevis
Cum perfectio:	♩ ♪ *	♫	=longa
Sine proprietate:			=longa
Cum perfectio:	(♮)♩ ♩ *	♩	=longa
Cum proprietate:			=brevis
Sine perfectio:	♪ (♦)	┈	=brevis
Sine proprietate:			=longa
Sine perfectio:	(♪)♩	➤	=brevis
Opposita			=semibrevis
proprietate:	♭ ♭	♭ ♭	=semibrevis

*=Additions made by scribes after the time of Franco;
( )=Forms which Franco mentions: states they are not correct
(RasN, 51; ApeN, 313)

2. THE PLICA
   a) The plica is less prevalent in the

notation of this period than in modal
notation   ParN, 113
b)   There are four forms   ParN, 113
     (1)   The addition of a tail to the
           right either ascending or
           descending
     (2)   The addition of a tail to the
           left either ascending or descending
c)   The value of the _plica_ depends on
     whether the _longa_ is perfect or
     imperfect   ParN, 113
     (1)   If the _longa_ is perfect the
           plica receives one-third its
           value
     (2)   If the _longa_ is imperfect the
           plica receives one-half its
           value

APPENDIX 12
French Mensural Notation

I.   THE NEW SYSTEM AS EXPOUNDED BY PHILIPPE DE VITRY
     (CA. 1320)   ApeHD, 579

   A.   THE INNOVATIONS

      1.   THE SEMIBREVIS BECOMES THE BEAT (TEMPUS)
                                                     RasN, 61
           a)   This necessitated the use of smaller
                note values
                (1)   The semibrevis minima (↑)
                (2)   The semiminim (↓)

      2.   IN THEORY DUPLE MENSURATION BECOMES
           EQUAL WITH TRIPLE MENSURATION   RasN, 61
           a)   A larger note value could be
                imperfected by remote values   ReaA, 3
                (1)   A longa could be imperfected by a
                      semibrevis or a brevis by a minima

      3.   FOUR SETS OF TIME VALUES ("degrees")
           WERE DEVISED   ParN, 143
           a)   Maximodus
                (1)   Triplex longa (◖◗) 81 minims
                      (perfect)
                (2)   Duplex longa (◗) 54 minims
                      (imperfect)
                (3)   Simplex longa (◗) 27 minims
                      ("unitary")
                      (a)   This degree was devised for
                            theoretical purposes   ParN, 144
                            i)   It is not found in
                                 the music of the Ars
                                 nova
           b)   Modus
                (1)   Longa perfectus (◗) 27 minims
                      (perfect)
                (2)   Longa imperfectus (◗) 18 minims
                      (imperfect)

       (3)   <u>Brevis</u> (∎) 9 minims
           ("unitary")
  c) <u>Tempus</u>
       (1)   <u>Brevis perfectum</u> (∎) 9 minims
           (perfect)
       (2)   <u>Brevis imperfectum</u> (∎) 6 minims
           (imperfect)
       (3)   <u>Semibrevis minor</u> (♦) 3 minims
           ("unitary")
  d) <u>Prolatio</u>
       (1)   <u>Semibrevis minor</u> (♦) 3 minims
           (perfect)
       (2)   <u>Semibrevis maior</u> (♦) 2 minims
           (imperfect)
       (3)   <u>Minima</u> (♩) 1 minim
           ("unitary")
  e) Each of these degrees has three
     divisions of notes
       (1)   Perfect, imperfect, and "unitary"
           (a)   "...the smallest of these
                in each degree becomes the
                largest of a similar set
                of relationships in the
                next degree"

4.   TIME SIGNATURES WERE DEVISED TO INDICATE
    THE METER OF THE MUSIC   ReeMMA, 344
    a) There were six time signatures
       (1)   <u>Modus perfectus</u> (⊞)
       (2)   <u>Modus imperfectus</u> (⊡)
       (3)   <u>Tempus perfectum</u> (O)
       (4)   <u>Tempus imperfectum</u> (C)
       (5)   <u>Prolatio maior</u> (⊙)
       (6)   <u>Prolatio minor</u> (₵)
           (a)   These signatures could be
                modified according to the
                need by means of combining
                two signatures
               i)   (⊙) would indicate
                    <u>tempus perfectum</u> with
                    <u>prolatio minor</u>
    b) These time signatures did not become
      an established part of French notation
      until the fifteenth century   ParN, 144

5.   THE FOUR COMBINATIONS OF <u>TEMPUS</u> AND <u>PROLATIO</u>
    CONSTITUTE THE FOUR MAIN MENSURATIONS OF
    MENSURAL NOTATION   ApeHD, 520
    a) See figure 1, p. 186

6.   THE USE OF A DOT TO INDICATE DIFFERENT
    FUNCTIONS   ReeMMA, 344
    a) <u>Punctus addictionis</u>   ParN, 145
       (1)   "...used only in imperfect mensura-
           tions..."
       (2)   Functions as the dot in modern

                         notation
              b) <u>Punctus divisionis</u>
                  (1) Equivalent of the modern bar line
                       of 3/4 meter   ApeHD, 521
                       (a) Always marks off groups of
                            three semibreves
                  (2) <u>Punctus syncopationis</u>   ParN, 145
                       (a) Also known as <u>punctus
                            demonstrationis</u>
                       (b) The splitting of a perfection
                            into two parts and then
                            placing another perfection
                            between the two parts

      6.   THE USE OF DIMINUTION AND AUGMENTATION
                                              ReeMMA, 345
            a) Diminution
                (1) Indicated by white notes with
                     the outline of the note in red
                     (a) Indicates that a part
                          should be performed in
                          the next smaller note-
                          values than those in which
                          it is written
            b) Augmentation
                (1) Indicated by a special sign or
                     number
                     (a) Indicates that the notes
                          are to be performed as if
                          written in the shapes of
                          the next larger values
                                              ReeMMA, 346

Fig. 1. The Four Prolations

	Early Signs	Later Signs	Modern Signatures	<u>Ars nova</u> Notation	Modern Notation
<u>Tempus perfectum</u> <u>Prolatio maior</u>	⊙	⊙	9/8	♦♦♦ ♦♦♦ ♦♦♦	♩. ♩. ♩.
<u>Tempus perfectum</u> <u>Prolatio minor</u>	⊖	○	3/4	♦♦ ♦♦ ♦♦	♩ ♩ ♩
<u>Tempus imperfectum</u> <u>Prolatio maior</u>	⊂	⊂	6/8	♦♦♦ ♦♦♦	♩. ♩.
<u>Tempus imperfectum</u> <u>Prolatio minor</u>	⊂	C	2/4	♦♦ ♦♦	♩ ♩

(ParN, 145; ReaA, 4)

APPENDIX 13
Italian Mensural Notation

I. NOTE-SHAPES AND NOTATIONAL DEVICES

    A. <u>BASIC FEATURES</u>

        1. THE OLD FANCONIAN LIGATURE THEORY IS
            MAINTAINED   ReeMMA, 340
            a) See appendix 11

        2. THE MOST IMPORTANT NEW FEATURE IS THE
            MEANS OF NOTATING BINARY RHYTHM   ReeMMA, 340
            a) This is also a feature of French
               mensural notation of this same
               period
               (1) See appendix 12

        3. SOMETIMES SIGNATURES ARE PLACED AT THE
            BEGINNING OF COMPOSITIONS TO INDICATE
            THE MEASURE   ReeMMA, 341
            a) T=<u>ternaria</u>
            b) B=<u>binaria</u>
            c) P=perfection
            d) I=imperfection
            e) Q=<u>quaternaria</u>
            f) O=<u>octonaria</u>
            g) S.P.=<u>senaria perfecta</u>
            h) S.I.=<u>senaria imperfecta</u>
            i) N=<u>novenaria</u>
            j) D=<u>duodenaria</u>

        4. THE <u>BREVIS</u> IS THE FUNDAMENTAL UNIT AND HAS
            AN UNALTERABLE VALUE   ApeN, 370
            a) The <u>brevis</u> always acts as the measure
                                      ParN, 167
               (1) Groups of notes of smaller
                    value are set off by dots
                    (<u>punctus divisionis</u>) into a
                    cluster whose total value is
                    that of the <u>brevis</u>

(a) There may be as many as
     twelve notes   RasN, 63
(b) If there are more or
     less notes than the
     signature indicates, the
     first semibreves receive
     their normal value and
     the last ones are shortened
     or lengthened   ReeMMA, 341
     i)   This is known as
           via naturae
(c) If lengthening is desired
     at some other part of the
     measure a descending stem
     was added to the semibreve
     affected   ReeMMA, 341
     i)   This alteration
           is known as via
           artis
     ii)   There are two forms of
           the semibrevis in via
           artis   RasN, 66
           a - The semibrevis
               minima (↑) with
               an upward tail
               indicating shortness
           b - The semibrevis
               maior (↓) with a
               downward tail
               indicating length

B.   THE SYSTEM OF PUNCTUS DIVISIONIS

     1.   THE BREVIS MAY BE DIVIDED AND SUBDIVIDED
          BY TWO OR THREE AND BY COMPOUNDS OF
          TWO OR THREE   ParN, 167
          a) Marchetto da Padua, in his Pomerium
              of 1318, discusses the meters and
              their rhythmic organization under
              the headings of tempus perfectum
              and tempus imperfectum   RasN, 63
              (1) Tempus imperfectum   RasN, 63
                   (a) There are four divisions
                        of tempus imperfectum
                        i)   "The name of each
                              division indicates
                              the maximum number
                              of minimal units
                              contained in it..."
                                         ParN, 167
                   (b) Quaternaria
                        i)   The brevis is divided
                              into two semibreves
                        ii)   Each semibrevis may
                              be subdivided into two

                              a - This produces a
                                  maximum of four
                                  semibreves in a
                                  brevis
                    iii)   If a time signature
                            is used it would be
                            the letter "Q"
                    iv)   When the normal number
                            of semibreves is
                            present (in this case
                            four) tails are added
                            above the note   EllF, 49
                            a - They become minims
                                (♪)

Fig. 1. _Tempus imperfectum_: _Quaternaria_
        (Time Signature "Q")

	Italian Notation	Modern Notation
Brevis	▪	♩
Two semibreves	◆◆	♪ ♪
*Three semibreves	◆◆◆	♫ ♪
Four semibreves	◆◆◆◆	♫ ♫
(become minims)		

*=Less semibreves than the normal number of the
divisio (4) (RasN, 64; EllF, 49)

    (c)   _Octonaria_
           i)   If smaller note-values
                  are needed than are
                  found in _Quaternaria_
                  the notes may again be
                  divided by two   RasN, 63
                  a - This produces
                      eight notes
           ii)   The time signature
                  is "O"

Fig. 2. _Tempus imperfectum_: _Octonaria_
        (Time Signature "O")

	Italian Notation	Modern Notation
Brevis	▪	♩
Two semibreves	◆◆	♩ ♩
*Three semibreves	◆◆◆	♫ ♩
Four semibreves	◆◆◆◆	♫ ♫
*Five semibreves	◆◆◆◆◆	♬♩ ♫
*Six semibreves	◆◆◆◆◆◆	♬♩ ♫
*Seven semibreves	◆◆◆◆◆◆◆	♬♬ ♬♩
Eight semibreves	◆◆◆◆◆◆◆◆	♬♬ ♬♬
(become minims)		

*=Less semibreves than the normal number of the
divisio (8) (RasN, 64; ParN, 169)

(d)   <u>Senaria imperfecta</u>   RasN, 63
      i)   The <u>brevis</u> may be
            divided into six
            parts in imperfect
            time
            a - There will be
                three subdivisions
                for each beat
            b - This is known as
                compound duple
                time   EllF, 50
      ii)   The signature is "I"
                              ParN, 167
            a - May also be S.I.
                           ReeMMA, 341

Fig. 3. <u>Tempus imperfectum</u>: <u>Senaria imperfecta</u>
        (Time Signature is "I" or "S.I.")

	Italian Notation	Modern Notation
Brevis	▪	♩.
Two semibreves	♦♦	♩. ♩.
*Three semibreves	♦♦♦	♪ ♩ ♩.
Four semibreves	♦♦♦♦	♪♪ ♩ ♪♩
*Five semibreves	♦♦♦♦♦	♫♫ ♪♩
Six semibreves	♦♦♦♦♦♦	♫♫ ♫♫
(become minims)		

*=Less semibreves than the normal number of the
<u>divisio</u> (RasN, 64; ParN, 169)

(e)   <u>Duodenaria</u>   RasN, 65
      i)   This metre is usually
            used for theoretical
            purposes only
      ii)   The maximum number
            of semibreves would
            be twelve
      iii) The time signature
            is "D"
      iv)   The metre is always
            <u>via artis</u>
      v)   The maximum number of
            semibreves may be
            written as shown in
            figure 4

Fig. 4. <u>Tempus imperfectum</u>: <u>Duodenaria</u>
        Time Signature is "D"

	Italian Notation	Modern Notation
Twelve semibreves	♦♦♦♦♦♦♦♦♦♦♦♦	♫♫♫♫ ♫♫♫♫
(become minims)		

(RasN, 64; ParN, 168)

(2) **Tempus perfectum**
   (a) There are three divi-
      sions   RasN, 65
      i)   **Senaria perfecta**
           a - The _brevis_ is di-
               vided by three
           b - Each of these
               is subdivided
               by two
           c - The maximum
               number is six
               semibreves
           d - The time signature
               is "P"
           e - May also be "S.P."
                         ReeMMA, 341

Fig. 5. Tempus perfectum: Senaria perfecta
Time Signature is "P", "S.P.", or

	Italian Notation	Modern Notation
Brevis	■	♩·
*Two semibreves	♦♦	♩ ♩
Three semibreves	♦♦♦	♩ ♩ ♩
*Four semibreves	♦♦♦♦	♫ ♩ ♩
*Five semibreves	♦♦♦♦♦	♫ ♫ ♩
Six semibreves	♦♦♦♦♦♦	♫ ♫ ♫
(become minims)		

*=Less semibreves than the normal number of the
divisio (RasN, 65; ParN, 168)

      ii)   **Duodenaria**   RasN, 65
           a - This is the type
               of _duodenaria_ that
               is usually used
           b - The maximum number
               of semibreves is
               twelve
           c - Used only in _via_
               artis
           d - The theoretical
               metrical structure
               of the maximum
               number of notes is
               shown in figure 6

Fig. 6. Tempus perfectum: Duodenaria
Time Signature is "D"

	Italian Notation	Modern Notation
Twelve semibrevis	♦♦♦♦♦♦♦♦♦♦♦♦	♬♬♬ ♬♬♬ ♬♬♬
(become minims)		

(RasN, 65; EllF, 49)

        iii) <u>Novenaria</u>   RasN, 65
           a - Subdivides each
              of the three beats
              into three
           b - Has a theoretical
              maximum of nine
              semibreves
           c - The time signature
              for <u>novenaria</u> is
              "N"   RasN, 66

Fig. 7. <u>Tempus perfectum</u>: <u>Novenaria</u>
Time Signature is "N"

	Italian Notation	Modern Notation
Nine semibreves	♦♦♦♦♦♦♦♦♦	♫♫♫ ♫♫♫ ♫♫♫
(become minims)		
(RasN, 65; E11F, 49)		

C. <u>OTHER ITALIAN NOTE-SHAPES AND NOTATIONAL DEVICES</u>

    1.   <u>SEMIMINIM</u>
        a) Has a flagged stem   RasN, 68
          (1) May indicate half of a minim
              or triplets in the time of two
              minims

    2.   THE USE OF RED AND VOID NOTES   RasN, 68
        a) The red notes came from French mensural
           notation
          (1) See appendix 12
        b) The void notes were an Italian inven-
           tion

    3.   RESTS ARE THE SAME AS THOSE OF FRENCH
       MENSURAL NOTATION   RasN, 69
        a) See appendix 12

APPENDIX 14
Supplemental Material

1. The period from 1000 to 1150 has been known as the
    St. Martial period, indicating a geographical source
    of the music of this period. According to musicol-
    ogist Sarah Fuller, the idea of a St. Martial
    "School" is a myth. According to her, there was much
    interchange and common practice among many monas-
    teries over a much larger area.   FulM, 26

2. In Leonard Ellinwood's article "John Cotton or John
    of Afflighem?" he states that Joseph Smits van
    Waesberghe is incorrect in his assumption that the
    name of the author of <u>De musica</u> could not be John
    Cotton. A manuscript found by Ellinwood shows proof
    that the name should be Johannis Cottonis (John
    Cotton).   EllJ, 650

3. Timothy McGee, in his article "The Liturgical
    Placement of the Quem quaeritis Dialogue," does not
    view the <u>Quem quaeritis</u> trope as the beginning of
    modern drama in the Western world. As a trope of the
    Easter Mass Introit it would not have been acted.
    The <u>Quem quaeritis</u> Dialogue may have been a
    dramatization from its very beginning. It is thought
    to have originated at the <u>Collecta</u> ceremony. It
    gradually acquired lines and separated itself from
    the liturgy.   McGL, 27

4. In the article "Why a New Edition of the Montpellier
    Codex" Hans Tischler states that Y. Rokseth has made
    a few errors in his book "Polyphonies du XIIIe
    siècle." In Tischler's book, "Complete Édition of
    the Earliest Motets," he states the errors and offers
    corrections.   TisC and TisW

5. Anne Swartz, in her article "A New Chronology of the
    Ballades of Machaut," states that the relevance of
    poetical studies of <u>Le Livre du voir dit</u> for
    chronological evidence of their musical settings is
    insufficient. She thinks that Machaut could have

added music specifically for the <u>voir dit</u>.   This is
in disagreement with Gilbert Reaney.   SwaN

6.   The material cited is found in Coussemaker's
      "Scriptorum de musica medii aevi."   According to
      Andrew Hughes in his book "Medieval Music: the sixth
      liberal art" this source is inaccurate and incomplete
      but an invaluable collection of medieval treatises.
      The information should be checked elsewhere.
                                                HugFA, no. 925

7.   The material cited is found in Coussemaker's "L'Art
      harmonique aux XIIe et XIIIe siècles."   Andrew Hughes
      states in his book "Medieval Music: the sixth
      liberal art" that this source should be used with
      caution.   HugFA

8.   The material cited is found in Martin Gerbert's
      "Scriptores ecclesiastici de musica sacra
      potissimum."   According to Andrew Hughes in his book
      "Medieval Music: the sixth liberal art" this source
      is inaccurate and incomplete but an invaluable source
      of information.   All information should be checked
      elsewhere.   HugFA

9.   This material used by Andrew Hughes is taken from
      the "Declaratio musice discipline" by Ugolino de
      Orvieto.

Bibliography

AdaO   Adam de La Halle. <u>Oeuvers complètes du trouvère Adam de La Halle: poésies et musique</u>. Société des sciences, des lettres, et des art de Lille. Par C. E. H. de Coussemaker. Paris: Durand and Pedone-Lauriel, 1872; reprint ed., Ridgewood, N. J.: The Gregg Press Inc., 1965.

Ad1ST   Adler, Guido, gen. ed. <u>Denkmäler der Tonkunst in Oesterreich</u>. Graz: Akademische Drukund Verlangsanstalt, 1960. Vol. 61: <u>Sieben Trienter Codices: Geistliche und Weltliche Kompositionen des XV. JHS</u>. Edited by Bearbeitet von Rudolf Ficker.

AflM   Aflligemensis, Johannes. <u>De musica cum tonario</u>. Edited by Joseph Smits van Waesberghe. Corpus scriptorum de musica, vol. 1. Rome: American Institute of Musicology, 1950.

AllT   Allaire, Gaston G. <u>The Theory of Hexachords, Solmization and the Modal System</u>. Musicological Studies and Documents, no. 24. "N.p.": American Institute of Musicology, 1972.

AndL   Anderson, Gordon, trans. <u>The Latin Compositions in Fascicules VII and VIII of the Notre Dame Manuscript Wolfenbüttel Helmstadt 1099 (1206). Part I and Part II</u>. Musicological Studies, vol. 24. Brooklyn: The Institute of Mediaeval Music, [c.1976].

AngG   Angles, Higini. "Gregorian Chant." In <u>New Oxford History of Music</u>. Vol. 2: <u>Early Medieval Music up to 1300</u>, pp. 92-127. Edited by Dom Anselm Hughes. London: Oxford University Press, 1954; revised ed., 1955; reprint ed., 1976.

AngL   _____. "Latin Chant before St. Gregory."

	In <u>New Oxford History of Music</u>. Vol. 2: <u>Early Medieval Music up to 1300</u>, pp. 58-91. Edited by Dom Anselm Hughes. London: Oxford University Press, 1954; revised ed., 1955; reprint ed., 1976.
AngM	_____. "The Musical Notation and Rhythm of the Italian Laud." In <u>Essays in Musicology: A Birthday Offering for Willi Apel</u>, pp. 51-60. Edited by Hans Tischler. Bloomington: School of Music, Indiana University, 1968.
AnoIV	Anonymous IV. <u>Concerning the Measurement of Polyphonic Song</u>. Translated and edited by Luther Dittmer. Musical theorists in translation, vol. 1. Brooklyn: The Institute of Mediaeval Music, [c.1959].
AnoD	_____. "De mensuris et discantu." In <u>Scriptorum de musica medii aevi novam seriem a Gerbertina alteram collegit nuncque primum</u>, vol. 1, pp. 327-365. Edited by E. de Coussemaker. Paris: "n.p.", 1864-1876; reprint ed., Hildesheim: Georg Olms, 1963.
AnoM	Anonymous. <u>Musica enchiriadis</u>. Translated by Leonie Rosentiel. Colorado College Music Press. Translations, vol. 7. Colorado Springs: Colorado College Music Press, 1976.
AnoS	Anonymous. "From the Scolia enchiriadis." In <u>Source Readings in Music History: from Classical Antiquity through the Romantic Era</u>, pp. 126-138. Annotated and edited by Oliver Strunk. New York: W. W. Norton and Co., Inc., [c.1950].
AofC	"Ad organum faciendum." In <u>Histoire de l'harmonie au moyen âge [von] E. de Coussemaker</u>, pp. 229-243. Edited and translated by E. de Coussemaker. Paris: Reprografischer Nachdruck der Ausgabe, 1852; reprint ed., Hildesheim: Georg Olms, 1966.
ApeE	Apel, Willi. "Early History of the Organ." <u>Speculum: A Journal of Medieval Studies</u> 23:2 (1948): 191-216
ApeFR	_____, ed. <u>French Secular Music of the Late Fourteenth Century</u>. Cambridge: Mediaeval Academy of America, 1950.
ApeGC	_____. <u>Gregorian Chant</u>. Bloomington: Indiana University Press, [1958].
ApeH	_____. <u>The History of Keyboard Music to 1700</u>. Translated and revised by Hans Tischler. Originally published as <u>Geschichte der Orgel- und Klaviermusik bis 1700</u>. Kassel: Barenreiter-Verlag, [c.1976]; revised ed., Bloomington; London: Indiana University Press,

[c.1972].

ApeHD   _____. Harvard Dictionary of Music. 2nd
                   ed., revised and enlarged. Cambridge:
                   The Belknap Press of Harvard University
                   Press, [c.1969].

ApeK   _____, ed. Keyboard music of the four-
                   teenth and fifteenth centuries. A
                   Corpus of Early Keyboard Music, ser. 1.
                   Rome: American Institute of Musicology,
                   1963-.

ApeN   _____. The Notation of Polyphonic Music.
                   5th ed., revised with commentary.
                   Cambridge: The Mediaeval Academy of
                   America, [c.1961].

ApeS   _____. "From St. Martial to Notre Dame."
                   Journal of the American Musicological
                   Society 2:3 (1949): 145-158.

AriM   Aristides Quintilianus. On Music: In Three
                   Books. Translation, with Introduction,
                   Commentary, and Annotations by Thomas J.
                   Mathiesen. New Haven and London: Yale
                   University Press, [c.1983].

ArnO   Arnold, Corliss Richard. Organ Literature:
                   A Comprehensive Survey. Metuchen, New
                   Jersey: Scarecrow Press, Inc., 1973.

AubB   Aubry, Pierre. Cent motets du XIIIe siècle:
                   publiés d'après le manuscrit Ed. IV. 6
                   de Bamberg. 3 vols. Paris: "n.p.",
                   1908; reprint ed., New York: Broude
                   Bros., 1964.

AubC   Aubry, Pierre, au Alfred Jeanroy, eds. "Le
                   chansonnier de L'Arsenal: reproduction
                   phototypique du manuscrit 5198 de la
                   Bibliotheque de L'Arsenal et tran-
                   scription du texte musical en notation
                   moderne." Zeitschrift der Inter-
                   nationalen Musikgesellschaft 11 (1910):
                   112.

AubR   _____, ed. Le Roman de Fauvel. Paris:
                   "n.p.", 1907.

BabH   Babb, Warren, trans. Hucbald, Guido, and
                   John on Music: Three Medieval Treatises.
                   Edited by Claude V. Palisca. Music
                   Theory Translation Series, vol. 3. New
                   Haven: Yale University Press, 1978.

BakB   Baker, Theodore. Baker's Biographical
                   Dictionary of Musicians. Edited and
                   revised by Nicolaus Slonimsky with 1971
                   Supplement. 5th ed. New York: G.
                   Schirmer, [c.1971].

BarP   Barbour, J. M. "The Principles of Greek
                   Notation." Journal of the American
                   Musicological Society 13 (1960):
                   1-17.

BaxA   Baxter, J. H., ed. An Old St. Andrews Music
                   Book: (cod. Helmst 628). London: H.

Milford, Oxford University Press, 1931;
reprint ed., [New York: American
Musicological Society Press, Inc.,
1973].

BecJ   Beck, John Baptiste, ed. and transc. Le
                chansonniers des troubadors et des
                trouvères. Philadelphia: The University
                of Philadelphia Press, 1927; reprint
                ed., Corpus cantilenarum medii aevi,
                ser. 1. New York: Broude Bros.,
                [1964-1970].

BedP   Bedbrook, G. S. "The Problem of Instrumental
                Combination in the Middle Ages." Revue
                belge de musicology 25:1-4 (1971):
                53-67.

BisC   Bischoff, Bernhard, ed. Carmina burana:
                Facsimile Reproduction of the Manuscript
                (Munich) Clm 4660, 4660a. Publication
                of Mediaeval Musical Manuscripts, vol.
                9. Brooklyn: The Institute of Mediaeval
                Music, 1957-.

BoeD   Boethius. "From the De institutione musica."
                In Source Readings in Music History:
                from Classical Antiquity through the
                Romantic Era, pp. 79-86. Annotated and
                edited by Oliver Strunk. New York: W.
                W. Norton and Co., Inc., [c.1950].

BoeDI   Boetii, A. M. T. S. De institutione arith-
                metica libri duo; De institutione musica
                libri quinque. Edited by Gottfried
                Friedlein. Leipzig: "n.p.", 1867;
                reprint ed., Frankfurt: "n.p.", 1966.

BonM   Bonvin, Ludwig. "The 'Measure' in Gregorian
                Music." Musical Quarterly 15 (1929):
                16-28.

BowP   Bower, Calvin Martin. Boethius' the prin-
                ciples of music: An introduction, trans-
                lation and commentary. PH.D. dis-
                sertation. George Peabody College for
                Teachers, School of Music. [Nashville,
                Tenn.], 1966.

BroA   Brockett, Clyde. Antiphona, responsories,
                and other chants of the Mozarabic rite.
                Musicological Studies, vol. 15.
                Brooklyn: The Institute of Mediaeval
                Music, 1968.

BukG   Bukofzer, Manfred. "The Gymel, the earliest
                form of English polyphony." Music and
                Letters 16 (1935): 77-84.

BukPSM   _____. "Popular and Secular Music in
                England." In New Oxford History of
                Music. Vol. 3: Ars nova and the
                Renaissance: 1300-1540, pp. 107-133.
                Edited by Dom Anselm Hughes and Gerald
                Abraham. London: Oxford University
                Press, 1960; reprint ed., 1974.

BukS   _____. "Two Fourteenth-Century Motets on
                        Saint Edmund." In Studies in Medieval
                        and Renaissance Music, pp. 17-33. New
                        York: W. W. Norton and Co., Inc.,
                        [c.1950].

BusR   Bush, Helen Evelyn. "The Recognition of
                        Chordal Formation by Early Music
                        Theorists." Musical Quarterly 32:2
                        (1946): 227-243.

CalM   Caldwell, John. Medieval Music. London:
                        Hutchinson, 1978.

CarC   Carapetyan, Armen, ed. The Codex Faenza:
                        Bibliotheca Communale, 117. Musico-
                        logical Studies and Documents, vol. 10.
                        "N.p.": American Institute of Musi-
                        cology, 1961.

CarS   Cardine, Eugene, Dom. "Semiologie gré-
                        gorienne." Études grégoriennes 11
                        (1970): 1-158.

CheM   Chew, Geoffrey. "A Magnus liber organi Frag-
                        ment at Aberdeen." Journal of the Amer-
                        ican Musicological Society 31:2 (1978):
                        326-343.

ColH   Collaer, Paul, and Albert Vander Linden.
                        Historical Atlas of Music. London;
                        Toronto; Wellington; Sydney: George G.
                        Harrap and Co., Ltd., 1968.

CouH   Coussemaker, Edmund de. Histoire de
                        l'harmonie au moyen âge [von] E. de
                        Coussemaker. Paris: Reprografischer
                        Nachdruck der Ausgabe, 1852; reprint
                        ed., Hildesheim: Georg Olms, 1966.

CroD   Crocker, R. L. "Discant, Counterpoint and
                        Harmony." Journal of the American
                        Musicological Society 15:1 (1962):
                        1-21.

CroH   _____. A History of Musical Style. New
                        York: McGraw Hill, [1966].

DalO   Dalglish, William. "The Origin of the
                        Hocket." Journal of the American
                        Musicological Society 31:1 (1978):
                        3-20.

DitAW   Dittmer, Luther. Auszug aus the Worcester
                        Music Fragments. Musicological Studies,
                        vol. 1. Brooklyn: The Institute of
                        Mediaeval Music, 1955.

DitB   _____. "Binary Rhythm, Musical Theory and
                        the Worcester Fragments." Musica Dis-
                        ciplina 7 (1953): 39-57.

DitD   _____. "The Dating and the Notation of
                        the Worcester Fragments." Musica Dis-
                        ciplina 11 (1957): 5-11.

DitF   _____, ed. Firenze, Biblioteca Mediceo-
                        Laurenziana, Pluteo 29, I. Publication
                        of Mediaeval Musical Manuscripts, vols.
                        10-11. Brooklyn: The Institute of

Mediaeval Music, 1957-.

DitM   _____, ed. Bibl. Nac. Madrid MS 20486
                          (13th c.). Publication of Mediaeval
                          Musical Manuscripts, vol. 1. Brooklyn:
                          The Institute of Mediaeval Music,
                          1957-.

DitO   _____, transc. Oxford, Bodleian Library
                          MS lat. lit. d 20; London British Museum
                          Add MS 25031; Chicago University Library
                          MS 654 app. Publication of Mediaeval
                          Musical Manuscripts, vol. 6. Brooklyn:
                          The Institute of Mediaeval Music, 1957-.

DitW   _____, ed. Wolfenbüttel MS 1099 (1206).
                          Publication of Mediaeval Musical
                          Manuscripts, vol. 2 Brooklyn: The
                          Institute of Mediaeval Music, [c.1960].

DitWC   _____, transc. Worcester, Chapter Library
                          MS Add. 68; London, Westminster Abbey
                          MS 33327; Madrid, B. N. MS 192. Publi-
                          cation of Mediaeval Musical Manuscripts,
                          vol. 5. Brooklyn: Institute of Medi-
                          aeval Music, [c.1959].

DitWF   _____. The Worcester Fragments: A cata-
                          log and transcription of all the music.
                          Musicological Studies and Documents,
                          vol. 2. Rome: American Institute of
                          Musicology, 1957.

DurS III   Durant, Will. The Story of Civilization.
                          Vol. 3: Ceasar and Christ. New York:
                          Simon and Schuster, 1950.

DurS IV   _____. The Story of Civilization. Vol.
                          4: The Age of Faith. New York: Simon
                          and Schuster, 1950.

Durs V   _____. The Story of Civilization. Vol.
                          5: The Renaissance. New York: Simon
                          and Schuster, 1950.

EA W   Encyclopedia Americana. 1971 ed., s.v.
                          "Wycliffe, John," by Frederick C. Grant.

EB A   Encyclopaedia Britannica. 1960 ed., s.v.
                          "Aristophanes," by Sir Richard Claver-
                          house Jebb.

EB B   _____. 1960 ed., s.v. "Boethius, Anicius
                          Manlius Severinus," by Lorenzo Minio-
                          Paluello.

EB C   _____. 1960 ed., s.v. "Charles the
                          Great," by Henry William Carless Davis.

EB D   _____. 1960 ed., s.v. "Dante," by Arthur
                          John Butler and E. G. Gardner.

EB N   _____. 1960 ed., s.v. "Nicaea, Council
                          of."

EB NI   _____. 1960 ed., s.v. "Nicomachus," by
                          Sir Thomas Little Heath.

EB O   _____. 1960 ed., s.v. "Occam, William,"
                          by Eligius M. Buyaert.

EB P   _____. 1960 ed., s.v. "Patristic and
                          Mediaeval Philosophy," by Lorenzo Minio-

Paluello.

EB PE   _____. 1960 ed., s.v. "Petrarch," by
               John Addington Symons and Anonymous.

EB PI   _____. 1960 ed., s.v. "Pindar," by Sir
               Richard Claverhouse Jebb.

EB PT   _____. 1960 ed., s.v. "Ptolemy," by
               Colin Alistair Ronan.

EB PW   _____. 1960 ed., s.v. "Peloponnesian
               War," by Bernard William Henderson.

EllF   Ellinwood, Leonard. "The Fourteenth Century
               in Italy." In New Oxford History of
               Music. Vol. 3: Ars nova and the
               Renaissance: 1300-1540, pp. 31-81.
               edited by Dom Anselm Hughes and Gerald
               Abraham. London: Oxford University
               Press, 1960; reprint ed., 1974.

EllJ   _____. "John Cotton or John of Affligem?"
               Music Library Association Notes 8:4
               (1951): 650-659.

EllO   _____. "Origins of the Italian Ars nova."
               American Musicological Bulletin (Dec. 29
               and 30, 1937).

EssH   Ess, D. H. van. The Heritage of Musical
               Style. New York: Holt, Rinehart and
               Winston, 1970.

EvaE   Evans, Paul. The Early Trope Repertory of
               St. Martial de Limoges. Princeton:
               Princeton University Press, 1970.

FisP   Fischer, Kurt von, gen. ed. Polyphonic Music
               of the Fourteenth Century. Vol. 24:
               The Works of Johannes Ciconia. Edited
               by Margaret and Ian Bent. Monaco:
               L'Oiseau-Lyre, 1956-.

FraA   Franco of Cologne. "Ars cantus mensur-
               abilis". In Source Readings in Music
               History: from Classical Antiquity
               through the Romantic Era, pp. 139-159.
               Annotated and edited by Oliver Strunk.
               New York: W. W. Norton and Co., Inc.,
               [c.1950].

FraAC   Franconis, Magistri. "Ars cantus mensura-
               bilis." In Scriptorum de musica medii
               aevi novam seriem a Gerbertina alteram
               collegit nuncque primum, vol. 1, pp.
               117-136. Edited by E. de Coussemaker.
               Paris: "n.p.", 1864-1876; reprint ed.,
               Hildesheim: Georg Olms, 1963.

FreA   Frere, Howard, ed. Antiphonale Saris-
               buriense. 6 vols. Plainsong and
               Mediaeval Music Society. Farnborough,
               Hants: "n.p.", [1966].

FreG   _____, ed. Graduale Sarisburiense.
               Plainsong and Mediaeval Music Society.
               London: B. Quaritch, 1894; reprint ed.,
               Farnborough, Hants: Gregg Press,
               [1966].

FreW   _____, ed. <u>The Winchester Troper</u>. New
                        York: American Musicological Society
                        Press, 1973.
FulM   Fuller, Sarah. "The Myth of 'St. Martial'
                        Polyphony: A Study of Sources." <u>Musica
                        Disciplina</u> 33 (1979): 5-27.
GarD   Garlandia, Johannes de. "De musica
                        mensurabili." In <u>Scriptorum de musica
                        medii aevi novam seriem a Gerbertina
                        alteram collegit nuncque primum</u>, vol. 1,
                        pp. 175-182. Edited by Edmond de
                        Coussemaker. Paris: "n.p.", 1864;
                        reprint ed., Hildesheim: Georg Olms,
                        1963.
GroH   Grout, Donald. <u>A History of Western Music</u>.
                        Revised ed. New York: W. W. Norton and
                        Co., Inc., [c.1973].
GruTH   Grutchfield, E. J. "Hucbald: A Millenary
                        Commemoration." <u>Musical Times</u> 51
                        (1930): 507-704.
GuiE   Guido d'Arezzo. "Epistola...de ignoto
                        cantu." In <u>Source Readings in Music
                        History: from Classical Antiquity
                        through the Romantic Era</u>, pp. 121-125.
                        Selected and annotated by Oliver Strunk.
                        New York: W. W. Norton and Co., Inc.,
                        [c. 1950].
GuiED   _____. "Epistola...de ignoto cantu." In
                        <u>Scriptores ecclesiastici de musica sacra
                        potissimum</u>, vol. 2, p. 43-50. Edited by
                        Martin Gerbert. St. Blaise: "n.p.",
                        1784; reprint ed., Hildesheim: Georg
                        Olms, 1963
GuiM   Guidonis Aretini. <u>Micrologus</u>. Edited by
                        Joseph Smits van Waesberghe. Corpus
                        scriptorum de musica, vol. 4. "N.p.":
                        American Institute of Musicology, 1955.
GuiP   Guido d'Arezzo. "Prologus antiphonarii
                        sui." In <u>Source readings in Music
                        History: from Classical Antiquity
                        through the Romantic Era</u>, pp. 117-120.
                        Selected and annotated by Oliver Strunk.
                        New York: W. W. Norton and Co., Inc.,
                        [c.1950].
GuiPA   _____. <u>Prologus in antiphonario</u>. In
                        <u>Scriptores ecclesiastici de musica sacra
                        potissimum</u>, vol. 2, p. 34-41. Edited by
                        Martin Gerbert. St. Blaise: "n.p.",
                        1784; reprint ed., Hildesheim: Georg
                        Olms, 1963.
GunM   Gunther, Ursula. <u>The Motets of the Manu-
                        script Chantilly, Musée Condi 564 (olim
                        1047) and Modena, Bibl. Estense a M.
                        5. 24 (olim lat. 568)</u>. Corpus
                        mensurabilis musicae, ser. 39. Rome:
                        American Institute of Musicology, 1965.

HagI   Hagopian, Viola L. Italian Ars nova Music:
                    A Bibliographical Guide to Modern
                    Editions and Related Literature.
                    University of California Publications in
                    Music, vol. 7. Berkley: University of
                    Claifornia Press, 1964.
HamH   Hammond's Historical Atlas. Maplewood, New
                    Jersey: Hammond Inc., [c.1960].
HamO   Hammond, N. G. L., and H. H. Scullard, eds.
                    The Oxford Classical Dictionary. 2nd
                    ed. Oxford: At the Clarendon Press,
                    1970; reprint ed. with corrections,
                    1972.
HamW   Hammond, N. G. L., ed. Walteri Odington
                    "Summa de speculatione musicae". Corpus
                    scriptorum de musicae, vol. 14. Rome:
                    American Institute of Musicology, 1970.
HanG   Hansen, Finn Egeland. The Grammar of
                    Gregorian Tonality. Translated by
                    Shirley Larsen. Studier og
                    publikationer fra Musikvidenskabeligt
                    Institut Aarhus Universitet 3. Copen-
                    hagen: Dan Fog Musikforlag, [c.1979].
HanR   Handlo, Robert de. The Rules, with maxims of
                    Master Franco. Edited by Luther
                    Dittmer. Music Theorists in Trans-
                    lation, vol. 2. Brooklyn: Institute of
                    Mediaeval Music, 1959-.
HanRM   _____. "Regulae cum maximis Magistri
                    Franconis cum additionibus aliorum musi-
                    corum complilatae." In Scriptorum de
                    musica medii aevi novam seriem a Gerber-
                    tina alteram collegit nuncque primum,
                    vol. 1, pp. 383-403. Edited by E. de
                    Coussemaker. Paris: "n.p.", 1864;
                    reprint ed., Hildesheim: Georg Olms,
                    1963.
HanT   Handshin, Jacques. "Trope, Sequence, and
                    Conductus." In New Oxford History of
                    Music. Vol. 2: Early Medieval Music
                    up to 1300, pp. 128-174. Edited by Dom
                    Anselm Hughes. London: Oxford Uni-
                    versity Press, 1954; revised ed., 1955;
                    reprint ed., 1976.
HarA   Harrison, Frank. "Ars nova in England: A
                    New Source." Musica Disciplina 21
                    (1967): 67-85.
HarE   _____. "English Church Music in the Four-
                    teenth Century." In New Oxford History
                    of Music. Vol. 3: Ars nova and the
                    Renaissance: 1300-1450, pp. 82-106.
                    Edited by Dom Anselm Hughes and Gerald
                    Abraham. London: Oxford University
                    Press, 1960; reprint ed. 1974.
HarM   _____. Music in Medieval Britain. New
                    York: Praeger, [1959].

HarMT   Harbinson, D. "Isorhythmic Technique in the
                    Early Motet." <u>Music and Letters</u> 47:2
                    (1966): 100-109.
HenA   Henderson, I. "Ancient Greek Music." In <u>New
                    Oxford History of Music</u>. Vol. 1:
                    <u>Ancient and Oriental Music</u>, pp. 336-
                    403. Edited by Egon Wellesz. London:
                    Oxford University Press, 1957.
HibE   Hibberd, L. "Estampies and Stantipes."
                    <u>Speculum: A Journal of Medieval Studies</u>
                    19 (1944): 222-249.
HopA   Hoppin, Richard, ed. <u>Anthology of Medieval
                    Music</u>. New York: W. W. Norton and Co.,
                    Inc., [c.1978].
HopM   _____. <u>Medieval Music</u>. New York: W. W.
                    Norton and Co., Inc., [1978].
HucD   Hucbaldi, Monachi. "De Harmonica institu-
                    tione." In <u>Scriptores ecclesiastici de
                    musica sacra potissimum</u>, vol. 1, pp.
                    104-152. Edited by Martin Gerbert. St.
                    Blaise: "n.p.", 1784; reprint ed.,
                    Hildesheim: Georg Olms, 1963.
HucI   _____. [Anonymous]. "Incipiunt schola
                    enchiriadis." In <u>Scriptores eccle-
                    siastici de musica sacra potissimum</u>,
                    vol. 1, pp. 173-212. Edited by Martin
                    Gerbert. St. Blaise: "n.p.", 1784;
                    reprint ed., Hildesheim: Georg Olms,
                    1963.
HufA   Huff, Jay A., ed. <u>Ad organum faciendum and
                    Item de organo</u>. Musical Theorists in
                    Translation, vol. 8. Brooklyn: Insti-
                    tute of Mediaeval Music, Ltd., "n.d.".
HugE   Hughes, H. V., ed. <u>Early English Harmony
                    from the Tenth to the Fifteenth Cen-
                    tury</u>. Vol. 2. The Plainsong and Medi-
                    aeval Music Society. London: "n.p.",
                    1913; reprint ed., New York: American
                    Musicological Socity Press, 1967.
HugF   Hughes, Andrew. <u>Manuscript Accidentals:
                    Ficta in focus 1350-1450</u>. Musicological
                    Studies and Documents, vol. 27. "N.p.":
                    American Institute of Musicology, 1972.
HugFA   _____. <u>Medieval Music: The sixth liberal
                    art</u>. Revised ed., Toronoto: University
                    of toronto Press, 1980.
HugFR   Hughes, Anselm, Dom. "Music in Fixed
                    Rhythm." In <u>New Oxford History of
                    Music</u>. Vol. 2: <u>Early Medieval Music up
                    to 1300</u>, pp. 311-352. Edited by Dom
                    Anselm Hughes. London: Oxford Uni-
                    versity Press, 1954; revised ed., 1955;
                    reprint ed., 1976.
HugI   _____. <u>Index to the Facsimile edition of
                    MS Wolfenbüttel 677</u>. Edinburgh and
                    London: "n.p.", 1939.

HugMAF   _____. "The Motet and Allied Forms." In
                              New Oxford History of Music. Vol. 2:
                              Early Medieval Music up to 1300, pp.
                              353-404. Edited by Dom Anselm Hughes.
                              London: Oxford University Press, 1954;
                              revised ed., 1955; reprint ed., 1976.
HugMT   _____. "Music in the Twelfth Century."
                              In New Oxford History of Music. Vol.
                              2: Early Medieval Music up to 1300,
                              pp. 287-310. Edited by Dom Anselm
                              Hughes. London: Oxford University
                              Press, 1954; revised ed., 1955; reprint
                              ed., 1976.
HugP   _____. "The Birth of Polyhony." In New
                              Oxford History of Music. Vol. 2: Early
                              Medieval music up to 1300, pp. 270-286.
                              Edited by Dom Anselm Hughes. London:
                              Oxford University Press, 1954; revised
                              ed., 1955; reprint ed., 1976.
HugW   _____, transc. Worcester Mediaeval Har-
                              mony of the Thirteenth and Fourteenth
                              Centuries. Preface by Sir Ivor Atkins.
                              The Plainsong and Mediaeval Music
                              Society. Nashdom Abbey, Burnham Bucks:
                              "n.p.", 1928; reprint ed., Hildesheim:
                              Georg Olms, 1977.
JacM   Jackson, Roland. "Musical Interrelations be-
                              tween Fourteenth Century Mass Move-
                              ments." Acta Musicologica 29:1 (1957):
                              54-64.
JacP   Jacob of Liège. "From the Speculum musicae:
                              Prohemium to the Seventh Book." In
                              Source Readings in Music History: from
                              Classical Antiquity through the Romantic
                              Era, pp. 180-192. Annotated and edited
                              by Oliver Strunk. New York: W. W.
                              Norton and Co., Inc., [1950].
JacS   _____. Speculum musicae. 7 vols.
                              Edited by Roger Brozard. Corpus srip-
                              torum de musica, vol. 3. Rome: Amer-
                              ican Institute of Musicology, 1955-1973.
JeaA   Jean de Muris. "From the Ars nova musicae."
                              In Source Readings in Music History:
                              from Classical Antiquity through the
                              Romantic Era, pp. 172-179. Annotated
                              and edited by Oliver Strunk. "N.p.":
                              W. W. Norton and Co., Inc., [c.1950].
JeaE   Jeannin, Jules Cécilien, Dom. Études sur le
                              rythme grégorien. "N.p.": "n.p.",
                              1926.
JerT   Jerome of Moravia. "Tractatus de musica."
                              In Scriptorum de musica medii aevi novam
                              seriem a Gerbertina alteram collegit
                              nuncque primum, vol. 1, pp. 1-136.
                              Edited by E. de Coussemaker. Paris:
                              "n.p.", 1864-1876; reprint ed., Hilde-

sheim: Georg Olms, 1963.

JohD   Johannes de Grocheo. *Concerning Music: De musica*. Translated by Albert Seay. Colorado College Music Press. Translations vol. 1. Colorado Springs: Colorado College Music Press, [c.1967].

JohDM   Johannes de Garlandia. *De Mensurabili musica. [Concerning Measured Music]*. Translated by Stanley H. Birnbaum. Colorado College Music Press. Translations, no. 9. Colorado Springs: Colorado College Music Press, 1978.

JohG   _____. "The De musica mensurabilis positio de Garlandia." Translation and commentary by C. S. Larkowski. Ph.D. diss. abst. 38:5790 A (April 1978).

JohN   Johannes de Muris. *Notitia artis musicae et Compemdium musicae practicae; Petrus de Sancto Dionysio. Tractatus de musica*. Edited by Ulrich Michels. Corpus scriptorum de musica, no. 17. "N.p.": American Institute of Musicology, 1972.

KelC   Kelly, Columba. *The Cursive Torculus Design in the Codex St. Gall 359 and Its Rhythmical Significance*. St. Meinrad, Indiana: Abbey Press, Publishing Division, [c.1964].

KenW   Kenney, S. "The Theory of Discant." In *Walter Frye and the Contenance Angloise*, chap. 5. New Haven and London: "n.p.", [c.1965].

LanE   Langer, William L., comp. and ed. *An Encyclopedia of World History: Ancient, Medieval and Modern*. 5th ed. Revised and enlarged. Boston: Houghton Mifflin Co., [c.1972].

LanR   _____, ed. *The Rise of Modern Europe*. 20 vols. New York: Harper and Row, [c.1936]. Vol. 1: *The Dawn of a New Era*, by Edward Cheyney.

LanW   Lang, Paul Henry. *Music in Western Civilization*. New York: W. W. Norton and Co., Inc., [c.1941].

LibU   *Liber usualis*. Tournai, Belgium: Desclée, [c.1953]; reprint ed. Parisus; Tournaci; Romae: Desclée et Socii, 1964.

LudB   Ludwig, Friedrich, ed. *Guillaume de Machaut: Musikalische Werke*. 4 vols. Leipzig: Breitkopf und Härtel, [c.1957]. Vol. 1: *Balladen, Rondeaux und Virelais*.

LudE   _____, ed. *Guillaume de Machaut: Musikalische Werke*. 4 vols. Leipzig: Breitkopf und Härtel, [c.1957]. Vol. 2: *Einleitung*. Edited by Heinrich Besseler.

LudM   _____, ed. Guillaume de Machaut: Musi-
                        kalische Werke. 4 vols. Leipzig:
                        Breitkopf und Härtel, [c.1957]. Vol.
                        3: Motteten.

LudML   _____, ed. Guillaume de Machaut: Musi-
                        kalische Werke. 4 vols. Leipzig:
                        Breitkopf und Härtel, [c.1957]. Vol.
                        4: Messe und Lais.

MarF   Marrocco, W. Thomas. "The Fourteenth Century
                        Madrigal: Its form and contents."
                        Speculum: A Journal of Medieval Studies
                        26 (1951): 449-457.

MarMI   Marcuse, Sibyl. Musical Instruments: A
                        Comprehensive Dictionary. New York: W.
                        W. Norton and Co., Inc., [c.1975].

MarS   _____. A Survey of Musical Instruments.
                        New York; Evanston; San Francisco;
                        London: Harper and Row, [c.1975].

MarT   Marchetto da Padua. "From the Pomerium." In
                        Source readings in Music History: from
                        Classical Antiquity through the Romantic
                        era, pp. 160-171. Annotated and edited
                        by Oliver Strunk. New York: W. W.
                        Norton and Co., Inc., [c.1950].

MarV   _____. Pomerium. Edited by Giuseppe
                        Vecchi. Corpus scriptorum de musica,
                        vol. 6. Rome: American Institute of
                        Music, 1961.

MatF   Mathiesen, Thomas J. "New Fragments of
                        Ancient Greek Music." Acta Musicologica
                        53 (1981:1): 14-32.

McGL   McGee, Timothy J. "The Liturgical Placements
                        of the Quem quaeritis Dialogue."
                        Journal of the American Musicological
                        Society 29:1 (1976): 3-29.

MeeT   Meech, Sanford, B., ed. "Three Musical
                        treatises in English from a Fifteenth-
                        Century Manuscript." Speculum: A
                        Journal of Medieval Studies 10 (1935):
                        235-269.

MocA   Mocquereau, A., Dom, gen. ed. Paléographie
                        musicale: les principaux manuscrits de
                        chant Grégorien, Ambrosien, Mozarabe,
                        Galican: publiés en facsimiles photo-
                        typiques. "N.p.": Benedictins de
                        Solesmes, 1889-1937, 1955-; reprint ed.,
                        Berne: Éditions Herbert Lang et Cie Sa,
                        1968-. Vols. 5 and 6: L'Antiphoner
                        Ambrosien: London, British Museum Add.
                        MS 34209.

MocAM   _____, gen. ed. Paléographie musicale:
                        les principaux manuscrits de chant
                        Grégorien, Ambrosien, Mozarabe, Gal-
                        ican: publiés en facsimiles photo-
                        typiques. "N.p.": Benedictins de
                        Solesmes, 1889-1937, 1955-; reprint

ed., Berne: Éditions Herbert Lang et
Cie Sa, 1968. Vol. 12: <u>Codex F. 160 de
la Bibliotheque Cathédrale de Worcester
(XIIIe siècle): Antiphonaire monas-
tique.</u>

MocC   Mocquereau, A., Dom, and Dom Jacques Froger,
                eds. <u>Paléographie musicale: les
                principaux manuscrits de chant Gré-
                gorien, Ambrosien, Mozarabe, Galican:
                publiés en facsimiles phototypiques.</u>
                Monumentale. Berne: Éditions Herbert
                Lang et Cie Sa, 1968-1970. Ser. 2,
                Vol. 2: <u>Le codex 359 de La Bibliotheque
                de Saint-Gall (IXe siècle): Cantorium.</u>

MocP   _____, gen. ed. <u>Paléographie musicales:
                les principaux manuscrits de chant
                Grégorien, Ambrosien, Mozarabe, Gal-
                ican: publiés en facsimiles photo-
                typiques.</u> Ser. 1: 18 vols. "N.p.":
                Benedictins de Solesmes, 1889-1937,
                1955-; reprint ed., Berne: Éditions
                Herbert Lang et Cie Sa, 1968-.

MusE   "Musica enchiriadis." Edited by H. Sowa.
                <u>Zeitschrift für Musikwisswnschaft</u> 17
                (1935): 194-207.

NicE   Nicholson, E. W. B. <u>Introduction to the
                Study of Some of the Oldest Latin
                Musical Manuscripts in the Bodleian
                Library, Oxford.</u> Early Bodleian Music,
                vol. 3. London: Novello and Co., Ltd.,
                1913; reprint ed., Farnborough, Hants:
                Gregg Press Ltd., 1967.

OdiD   Odington, Walter. <u>De speculatione musicae:
                Part VI.</u> Translated by J. A. Huff.
                Musicological Studies and Documents, no.
                31. Rome: American Institute of
                Musicology, 1973.

OdiDS   _____. "De speculatione musicae." In
                <u>Scriptorum de musica medii aevi novam
                seriem a Gerbertina alteram collegit
                nuncque primum,</u> vol. 1, pp. 182-250.
                Paris: "n.p.", 1864; reprint ed.,
                Hildesheim: Georg Olms, 1963.

OdoE   Odo de Cluny. "Enchiridion musices". In
                <u>Source Readings in Music History: from
                Classical Antiquity through the Romantic
                Era,</u> pp. 103-120. Selected and anno-
                tated by Oliver Strunk. New York: W.
                W. Norton and Co., Inc., [c.1950].

OdoDM   _____. "Dialogus de musica". In
                <u>Scriptores ecclesiastici de musica sacre
                potissimum,</u> vol. 1, p. 252-254. Edited
                by Martin Gerbert. St. Blaise: "n.p.",
                1784; reprint ed., Hildesheim: Georg
                Olms, 1963.

OxfD   <u>The Oxford Universal Dictionary</u>. 3rd ed.

	Revised and edited by C. T. Onions. Oxford: At the Clarendon Press, 1955.
PagE	Page, Christopher. "The Earliest English Keyboard." Early Music 7:3 (1979): 308-314.
ParN	Parrish, Carl. The Notation of Medieval Music. New York: W.W. Norton and Co., Inc., 1957.
PerO	Perrot, Jean. L'Orgue de ses origines hellenistiques a la fin du XIIIe sciècle [The Organ from Its Invention in the Hellenistic Period to the End of the Thirteenth Century]. Adapted from the French by Norma Deane. London; New York: Oxford University Press, 1971.
PhiA	Philippe de Vitriaco. Ars nova. Edited by Gilbert Reaney, Andre Gilles and Jean Maillard. Corpus scriptorum de musica, vol. 8. "N.p.": American Institute of Musicology, 1964.
PlaK	Plamenac, D., ed. Keyboard Music in the Late Middle Ages in Codex Faenza 117. [Dallas]: American Institute of Musicology, 1972.
PlaKM	_____. "Keyboard Music of the Fourteenth Century in Codex Faenza 117." Journal of the American Musicological Society 4 (1951): 179-201.
PlaV	Plantinga, Leon. "Philippe de Vitry's Ars nova: a translation." Journal of the American Musicological Society 5 (1961): 204-223.
PlaW	Planchart, Alejandro Enrique. The Repertory of Tropes at Winchester. 2 vols. [Princeton]: Princeton University Press, 1977.
RasN	Rastall, Richard. The Notation of Western Music. London: J. M. Dent and Sons, Ltd., [c.1983].
RayG	Rayburn, John. Gregorian Chant: A history of the controversy concerning its rhythm. New York: "n.p.", 1964.
ReaA	Reaney, Gilbert. "Ars nova in France." In New Oxford History of Music. Vol. 3: Ars nova and the Renaissance: 1300-1540, pp. 1-30. Edited by Dom Anselm Hughes and Gerald Abraham. London: Oxford University Press, 1960; reprint ed., 1974.
ReaC	_____. "Concerning the origins of the Rondeau, Virelai and Ballade forms." Musica Disciplina 6:4 (1952): 155-166.
ReaCH	_____. "A Chronology of the Ballades, Rondeaux and Virelais Set to Music by Guillaume de Machaut." Musica Disciplina 6:1-3 (1952): 33-38.

ReaF   _____. "Fourteenth Century Harmony and
                        the Ballades, Rondeaux and Virelais of
                        Guillaume de Machaut." Musica Dis-
                        ciplina 7 (1953): 129-146.
ReaM   _____. Guillaume de Machaut. London:
                        Oxford University Press, 1971.
ReaMP   _____, ed. Manuscripts of Polyphonic
                        Music (c.1320-1400). Répertoire
                        international des sources musicales
                        [International Inventory of Musical
                        Sources], vol. B4:2. München-Duisburg:
                        G. Henle Verlag, [c.1969].
ReaO   Reaney, Gilbert, and A. Gilles, eds. MS
                        Oxford Bodley 842, Brevarium regulare
                        musicae: MS British Museum Royal
                        12.C.VI: Tractatus de figuris sive de
                        notis: Johannes Torkesey, Declaratio
                        trianguli et scuti. Corpus scriptorum
                        de musicae, vol. 12. Rome: American
                        Institute of Musicology, 1966.
ReeF   Reese, Gustave. Fourscore Classics of Music
                        Literature: A Guide to Selected Ori-
                        ginal Sources on Theory and Other
                        Writings on Music not Available in
                        English: With Descriptive Sketches and
                        Bibliographical References. New York:
                        The Liberal Arts Press, [1957].
ReeMMA   _____. Music in the Middle Ages: With an
                        Introduction on the Music of Ancient
                        Times. New York: W. W. Norton and Co.,
                        Inc., [c.1940].
RieH   Riemann, Hugo. History of Music Theory.
                        Books I and II: Polyphonic Theory of
                        the Sixteenth Century. Translated by
                        Raymond H. Haggh. Lincoln: University
                        of Lincoln Press, 1962.
RohM   Rohloff, Ernst, ed. Musiktraktat des
                        Johannes de Grocheo. Leipzig: "n.p.",
                        1943.
RokI   Rokseth, Yvonne. "The Instrumental Music of
                        the Middle Ages and Early Sixteenth Cen-
                        tury." In New Oxford History of Music.
                        Vol. 3: Ars nova and the Renaissance:
                        1300-1540, pp. 406-465. Edited by Dom
                        Anselm Hughes and Gerald Abraham.
                        London: Oxford University Press, 1960;
                        reprint ed., 1974.
RokP   _____, ed. Polyphonies du XIIIe siècle.
                        4 vols. Paris: Éditions de L'Oiseau-
                        Lyre, 1935-1939.
SanC   Sanders, E. H. "Cantilenae and Discant in
                        Fourteenth Century England." Musica
                        Disciplina 19 (1965): 7-52.
SanM   _____. "The Medieval Hocket in Practice
                        and Theory." Musical Quarterly 60:2
                        (1974): 246-256.

SchL   Schrade, Leo, ed. _The Works of Francesco
                Landini_. Polyphonic Music of the Four-
                teenth Century, vol. 4. Monaco:
                Éditions L'Oiseau-Lyre, 1956-.

SchM   Schrade, Leo, ed. _The Works of Guillaume de
                Machaut_. Polyphonic Music of the Four-
                teenth Century, vols. 2 and 3. Monaco:
                Éditions L'Oiseau-Lyre, 1956-.

SchR   _____, ed. _The Roman de Fauvel: The Works
                of Philippe de Vitry 1291-1361; French
                Cycles of the ordinarium missae; Mass
                of Tournai, Mass of Toulouse, Mass of
                Barcelona_. Polyphonic Music of the
                Fourteenth Century, vol. 1. Monaco:
                Éditions L'Oiseau-Lyre, 1956-.

SeaM   Seay, Albert. _Music in the Medieval World_.
                Englewood Cliff, N. J.: Prentice Hall,
                [1965].

SmoE   Smoldon, William N. "The Easter Sepulchre
                Music Drama." _Music and Letters_ 27:1
                (1946): 1-17.

SmoL   _____. "Liturgical Drama." In _New
                Oxford History of Music_. Vol. 2: _Early
                Medieval Music up to 1300_, pp. 175-219.
                Edited by Dom Anselm Hughes. London:
                Oxford University Press, 1954; revised
                ed., 1955; reprint ed., 1976.

SodE   Soderlund, Gustave, comp. _Examples of
                Gregorian Chant: And Works by Orlando
                Lassus, Giovanni Pierluigi Palestrina,
                and Marc Antonio Ingegneri: For Use in
                Classes in Counterpoint_. New York:
                Appleton-Century-Crofts Inc., [c.1946].

StaF   Stäblein-Harder, Hanna, ed. _Fourteenth-cen-
                tury Mass Music in France_. Corpus
                mensurabilis musicae, ser. 29. Rome:
                American Institute of Musicology, 1962.

StaM   _____. _Fourteenth-century Mass Music in
                France: A companion_. Musicological
                Studies and Documents, ser. 29. Rome:
                American Institute of Musicology, 1951-.

SteM   Sternfeld, F. W, ed. _Music from the Middle
                Ages to the Renaissance_. A History of
                Western Music, vol. 1. London: Weide-
                feld and Nicholson, 1973.

SteMC   Stevens, J., ed. _Medieval carols_. Musica
                Britannica, vol. 4. 2nd revised ed.
                London: Stainer and Bell, 1958.

StrO   Strunk, Oliver. "On the Date of Marchetto da
                Padova." In _Essays on Music in the
                Western World_, pp. 55-61. New York: W.
                W. Norton and Co., Inc., [c.1974].

StrS   _____, comp. _Source Readings in Music
                History: from Classical Antiquity
                through the Romantic Era_. New York: W.
                W. Norton and Co., Inc., [c.1950].

SwaN   Swartz, Anne. "A New Chronology of the Bal-
                lades of Machaut." _Acta Musicologica_
                46:2 (1974): 192-207.
ThuM   Thurston, E., ed. _The Music in the St._
                Victor Manuscript: Paris, Bibl. Nat.
                MSS (lat. 15139): Polyphony of the
                Thirteenth Century. Toronto: Pon-
                tifical Institute of Mediaeval Studies,
                1959.
TisC   Tischler, Hans. _Complete Edition of the_
                Earliest Motets. "N.p.": American
                Musicological Society, "n.d.".
TisW   _____. "Why a New Edition of the Mont-
                pellier Codex?" _Acta Musicologica_ 46:1
                (1974): 58-75.
UlrH   Ulrich, Homer, and Paul Pisk. _A History of_
                Music and Musical Style. New York:
                Harcourt, Brace and World, [1963].
UltM   Ultan, L. _Music Theory: Problems and prac-_
                tices in Middle Ages and Reniassance.
                Minneapolis: University of Minesota
                Press, [c.1977].
VanM   Van, Guillaume de, ed. _Guillaume de Machaut:_
                Mass. Corpus mensurabilis musicae, ser.
                2. Rome: American Institute of Musi-
                cology, 1949.
WagC   Wagner, Peter, Hrsg. und Kommentiert. _Codex_
                Claixtinus. (Schweiz): Universitets
                Buchhandlung, 1931.
WaiR   Waite, William G. _The Rhythm of Twelfth Cen-_
                tury Polyphony. Yale Studies in the
                History of Music, vol. 2. New Haven:
                Yale University Press, 1954.
WesM   Westrup, J. A. "Medieval Song." In _New_
                Oxford History of Music. Vol. 2: _Early_
                Medieval Music up to 1300, pp. 220-269.
                Edited by Dom Anselm Hughes. London:
                Oxford University Press, 1954; revised
                ed., 1955; reprint ed., 1976.
WesN   Westrup, J. A., and Harrison, F. Ll. _The New_
                College Encyclopedia of Music. New
                York: W. W. Norton and Co., Inc.,
                [c.1960].
WilR   Wilkins, Nigel E., ed. _A Fourteenth-_
                century Repertory from the Codex Reina
                (Paris, Bibl. Nat. nouv. acq. fr.
                _6771)_. Corpus mensurabilis musicae,
                ser. 36. Rome: American Institute of
                Musicology, 1966.
WinM   Winnington-Ingram, R. P. _Mode in Ancient_
                Greek Music. Chicago, Illinois:
                Argonaut Inc., Publishers, 1968.
WolS   Wolf, Johannes, ed. _Squarcialupi Codex zu_
                Florence. Lipstadt: Fr. Kistner and
                C. F. W. Siegel and Co., 1955.
WooE   Woolrich, H. E. _Early English Harmony from_

the Tenth to the Fifteenth Century: Vol.
1.   Edited by H. V. Hughes. London:
Plainsong and Mediaeval Music Society,
1897; reprint ed., New York: American
Musicological Society Press, [1976].

Discography

Adam de La Halle. "Tant Con Je Vivrai" (Rondeau) Side 1, Band
1a. The History of Music in Sound. Vol. 3: <u>Ars
nova and the Renaissance</u>. RCA Victor LM 6016-1.
"Cappella musicale del Duomo di Milano." Die Tradition des
Gregorianischen Chorals. No. 4: <u>Ambrosianischer
Choral</u>. Luciano Miglacacca and Luigi Benedetti,
conductors. Recorded in Kirche S. Ambrogio, Milan,
1974. Archiv Produktion 2533 284.
<u>Chants Ambrosiens</u>. Performed by the Choeurs Polifonica
Ambrosiana. Directed by Mons. Guiseppe Biella.
Vox DL 343.
Ciconia, Johannes. <u>The Wandering Musicians; Flemish Composers
in Renaissance Italy</u>. Performed by the Boston
Camerata. Conducted by Joel Cohn. Turnabout TV-S
34512.
Die Tradition des Gregorianischen Chorals. No. 3:
<u>Gregorianischer Choral</u>. Coro de Monjes de la
Abadia de Santo de Silos; Ismael Fernández de la
Cuesta, conductor. Archive Produktion 2533 163.
"The French <u>Ars antiqua</u>: Music of the Middle Ages." Vol. 3:
<u>The Thirteenth Century: Compositions from the
Montpellier manuscript</u>. Experiences Anonymous 35.
<u>Gregorian chants</u>. Performed by The Dominican nuns of
Fichermont. Philips PCC-212.
<u>Gregorian Chants. Selections</u>. Performed by Choir of the
Monks of L'Abbaye St. Pierre de Solesmes.
Conducted by Dom Joseph Gajard. London 5633.
Guillaume de Machaut. <u>La Messe de Nostre Dame</u>. Performed by
the Deller Consort and Singers. Conducted by
Alfred Deller. Vanguard BG 622
_____. (a) "Ma fin est mon commencement." (b)
"'Benedictus' from 'La Messe de Nostre Dame.'" The
History of Music in Sound. Vol. 3: <u>Ars nova and
the Renaissance</u>. RCA Victor LM 6016-1.
_____. <u>Works: Selections</u>. Performed by the Early Music
Consort of London. Conducted by David Murrow.
Seraphim SIC 6092.
_____. <u>Works: Selected Secular; La Messe de Nostre Dame</u>.
Conducted by Sanford Cape. Archive ARC 3032.

"Histoire de France par le chansons." Vol. 1: Les
          Croisades. Various performers. Erato 4101.
History of Music in Sound. Vol. 2: Early Medieval Music up to
          1300. R.C.A. Victor LM 6015.
The Instruments of the Middle Ages and Renaissance: An
          Illustrated Guide to their Ranges, Timbres and
          Special Capabilities. Martin Bookspan, narrator.
          Musica Reservata of London. Vanguard VSD 71219/20.
Medieval and contemporary liturgical music. Scola cantorum of
          St. Meinrad Archabbey; Columba Kelly, director.
          Pleiades Records P 150.
Medieval and Renaissance Instruments. David Munrow. Jumbo
          album book with commentary. Angel SBZ-3810.
Medieval English Carols and Italian Dances. Performed by New
          York Pro Musica. Conducted by Noah Greenberg.
          Decca DL 9418.
"Medieval Music: sacred monophony." The Oxford Anthology of
          Music. Pro Cantione Antiqua; Edgar Fleet,
          conductor. Recorded in Charterhouse School Chapel,
          England. Peters International PLE 114.
The Medieval Sound. David Munrow. Oryx (Exp-46). Also,
          Musical Heritage Society (MHS-;454).
Music of the Gothic Era. The Early Music Consort of London.
          David Munrow. Archive 2710 0193.
Music of the Minstrels. "Le jeu de Robin et Marion," by Adam
          de La Halle; Thirteen rondeaux, Anonymous.
          Conducted by Safford Cape. Archive ARC 30032.
Music at Notre Dame, Paris, 1200. Deller Consort. Lumen.
          Archives Sonores de La Musique Sacre 5009 15010.
Perotin. Viderunt omnes fines terrae: Sederunt principes.
          Performed by Deller Consort and Singers. Conducted
          by Alfred Deller. Vanguard BG 622.
Prima Missa in Nativitate Domini Nostri Jesu Christi.
          Performed by Monks-Choir of the Benedictine Abbey.
          St. Martin, Beuron. Conducted by Pater Maurus
          Pfaff.

Definition and Pronunciation

List of Abbreviations

cl	Classical Latin
el	Ecclesiastical Latin
en.	English (also used for the English pronunciation of foreign words)
fr.	French
ger.	German
it.	Italian
l.	Latin
me	Middle English
oe	Old English
of	Old French
sp.	Spanish

Symbols of the International Phonetics Association

Sounds	Pronunciation	Symbols
ă	a in mat	a
ā	a in fate (French é)	e
à (r)	a in there, care	ε ͜e
ä	a in father	ɑː
a	a in far	ɑ
b	b in back	b
c	c in cat	k
ch	ch in chase, catch	t ʃ
d	d in dare	d
ĕ	e in fed	ε
ē	e in tee	i
f	f in fare	f
g	g in get	g
h	h in hole	h
hw	wh in where	ʍ
ĭ	i in listen	ʔ
ī	i in sigh	a ͜i
j	j in jump	d ʒ

Sounds	Pronunciation	Symbols
k	k in kite	k
l	l in lip	l
m	m in miss	m
n	n in no	n
ng	ng in sing	ŋ
ñ	n in Spanish Suñol (French gne)	ɲ
ŏ	o in not	ɑ
ō	o in toe	o
ô	o in sought	ɔ:
oi	oy in ploy	ɔi̯
ou	ew in threw	ru̯
ōō	oo in room	u:
ŏŏ	oo in book	u
p	p in pan	p
r	r in race	r
s	s in seen	s
sh	sh in share	ʃ
s	s in measure	ʒ
t	t in tall	t
th	th in thing	θ
th	th in this	ð
ŭ	u in bun	ʌ
ū	yoo in few	ju̯
û (r)	u in turn	ɔ̃
v	v in love	v
x	x in excuse	ks̯
y	y in yes	j
z	z in zip	z
	unstressed vowel	ə

Diphthongs and Other Combined Letters

Sounds	Pronunciation	Symbols
ai	ai in French quai	e
er	er in sister	ɚ
eu	eu in French peu	ø
oe	oe in French oeuf	œ
gl	gl in Italian	ɓ
ir	ir in bird	ð:
ch	ch in German ich	ç
ch	ch in Scottish lock	x
ch	ch in German ach	x
ui	ui in French nuit	u̯i̯
an	an in French Anjou	ã
on	on in French maison	ɔ̃

Unusual Single Letters

Sounds	Pronunciation	Symbols
ü	ü in German Glüch	y

Signs

Meaning	Symbols
Nasalization when over a symbol	⌐
Breath when under a symbol	o
Voice	v
Labialization (lip rounding) when under a symbol	ᴍ
Indication of synchronic articulation when under two letters	‿
Sound of preceding letter is long	:

Glossary of Terms
An apostrophe indicates stress on the following syllable

A

ABGESANG   ger.   (ap-gə̀-'zaŋ) Off; down; from: song: (<u>cauda</u>).
ACCENTUS   cl   (a-'kɛn-tʌs or tu:s) Accent.
_____   el   (at-'tʃɛn-tu:s) Accent.
ACUTE   cl   (a-'ku:-te) Sharply.
ACUTUS   cl   (a-'ku:-tʌs) Sharp, pointed.
ADDICTIO, ONIS.   cl   (ad-'dʒk-tʒɔ: or onʒs) Adjudication.
AETERNE   cl   (aį-'tɛr-nɛ) Eternal, everlasting.
_____   el   (ɛ-'tɛr-nɛ) Eternal, everlasting.
AGNUS   cl   ('ag-nʌs) The lamb as a Christian emblem.
_____   el   ('ag-ñu:s) Agnus Dei; Lamb of God; a prayer;
   the last item of the Mass before the <u>Ite missa est</u>.
ALLELUIA   el   (al-lɛ-'lu:-ja) "Praise Ye the Lord"; a part of
   the Proper of the Mass which occurs at the beginning or
   end of the Psalms.
ALTERA   cl   ('al-tɛ-ra) Of similarity, one of two.
AMBITUS   cl   ('am-bʒ-tʌs or tu:s) Going round, circuit.
ANAPAESTIC   en.   (an-ə-'pɛ-atʒk) In prosody, a metrical foot
   consisting of two short syllables followed by one long
   syllable.
ANTIPHON   en.   ('an-tʒ-fɔ:n) Plainsong settings of sacred
   words sung before or after a psalm or canticle: written
   in syllabic style.
ANTIPHONAL   el   (an-'ti-fɔ:-nal) 1. A liturgical book
   containing the chants for the Office. 2. Singing by
   alternating choruses.
ANTIPHONALE.   el   (an-ti-fɔ:-'na-lɛ) A general designation
   for books containing the texts (and later, the music
   also) of the musical items of the Roman Catholic rite.
ANTIQUA   cl   (an-'ti-kwa) Old.
ARS, TIS   cl   (ars, tʒs) Art, skill, method, theory,
   technique.
ARTIFICIALIS   it.   (a:r-ti-fi-tʃi-'a:-lis) 1. Artificial.
   2. Produced by a human rather than by nature.
ARTIFICIUM   cl   (ar-tʒ-'fʒ-kʒ-ʌm) Handcraft, skill.
AUFGESANG   ger.   (auf-gə̀-'zaŋ) On: song.

AVE   el   ('ɑ-vɛ)   Hail.

B

BALLADE   fr.   (ba-'lad)   A verse form consisting of three
    stanzas of eight or ten lines and an envoy (postscript or
    closing lines of a poem) of four or five lines. The last
    lines of the stanza and the envoy are the same.
BALLATA   it.   (bɑ:-'lɑ:-tɑ:)   Dancing song; the chief form of
    Italian fourteenth-century music: practically identical
    with the virelai; a poem consisting of a refrain and,
    normally, three stanzas that alternate with the refrain.
BENEDICAMUS   el   (bɛ-nɛ-'di-kɑ-mu:s)   Benedicamus Domino.
    (See also Domino); a salutation of the Roman liturgy used
    instead of Ite missa est in Masses lacking the Gloria; a
    blessing: sung at the end of all Offices.
BENEDICTUS   el   (bɛ-nɛ-'dik-tu:s)   Either of two canticles,
    Luke 1:68-71 and Mathew 21:9, the first word being
    Benedictus (blessed); a musical setting of either of the
    above.
BINARIA, AE   cl   (bʔ-'nɑ-rʔ-ɑ, ɑi)   Two, double.
BREVE   me   (brɛv)   Short. (See also brevis).
BREVIS   cl   ('brɛ-vʔs)   1. Short, brief. 2. In music it is
    used in regard to space; a short note introduced in the
    early thirteenth century: it became increasingly longer
    until it was the longest note to survive from the old
    notation.
BURDEN   me   ('bʒd-ən)   In music, a refrain repeated at the end
    of every stanza of a song.

C

CACCIA   en.   ('ke-ʃə)   A form of fourteenth-century Italian
    poetry and music; the text usually deals with hunting or
    fishing scenes or similar realistic subjects. The
    musical form is strict canon in two parts followed by a
    ritornello supported by a tenor line in longer note
    values.
CAELESTIS   cl   (kɑi-'lɛs-tʔs)   Coming from Heaven; belonging
    to Heaven.
_____   el   (tʃɛ-'lɛs-tis)   Coming from Heaven; belonging to
    Heaven.
CAELI   el   ('tʃɛ-li)   Heaven.
CANON   me   ('ka-nən)   1. In the Roman Catholic rite a prayer
    of consecration. 2. In music, a contrapuntal device: a
    melody is stated in one voice and imitated strictly in
    one or more other voices.
CANTICLE   me   ('kan-tʔk-l)   Used in Roman and Anglican
    liturgies; a scriptural text that is similar to a psalm
    but occurs elsewhere than in the Book of Psalms.
CANTILENA, AE   cl   (kan-tʔ-'le-nɑ, ɑi)   1. Hackneyed song.
    2. A vocal or instrumental passage in a lyric nature; a
    composition with a vocal upper part and two instrumental
    accompanying parts.

CANTO, I   cl   ('kαn-tɔ:, i)   To sing, act; predict.
CANTUS   cl   ('kαn-tʌs or tu:s)   song, melody, poetry;
    cantus planus   el   ('kαn-tu:s 'plα:-nu:s)   plainsong.
CAPITOLO   it.   (kα:-pi-'to-lo)   Chapter; matter; accord,
    agreement.
CAUDA, AE   cl   ('kaʌ-dα, aj̨)   Tail.
CELERITER   cl   (kɛ-'lɛ-r₂-tə˞)   Quickly.
CHANSON   fr.   (ʃã-'sɔ̃)   Song.
CHANSON DE GESTE   fr.   (ʃã-'sɔ̃ də dʒɛst)   An old French epic
    tale in verse: very long and divided into sections, each
    section containing a single thought.
CHANSONNIER   fr.   (ʃã-'sɔ̃nje)   Song writer, song book.
CHEIRONOMIC   en.   (kɛr-ə-'nαm-ʔk)   1. The term "chironomy"
    comes from the Greek meaning "gesticulation." 2. An
    Oratorical notation; a term for neumatic signs lacking
    clear indication of pitch: used in the ninth and tenth
    century manuscripts.
CIRCUMFLEX   en.   ('sə˞-kʌm-flɛks)   A mark used to indicate the
    combination of a rising and a falling tone.
CLAUSULA, AE   cl   ('klɑʌ-sʌ-lα, aj̨)   1. Conclusion, end. 2. A
    term used for polyphonic compositions of the twelfth and
    early thirteenth centuries that are based on a short
    fragment of Gregorian chant: usually the melisma of a
    responsorial chant. There is only a syllable or one or
    two words in the tenor to indicate the chant from which
    the tenor is borrowed.
CLOS   fr.   (klo)   Closed.
CODEX   cl   ('ko-dɛks)   Tree-trunk, ledger.
_____   el   ('kɔ:-dɛks)   A medieval manuscript in leaf form.
COELIS   el   ('tʃɛ-lis)   Heaven.
COELORUM   el   (tʃɛ-'lɔ:-ru:m)   Heavenly.
COLLECTS   el   ('kɔ:l-lɛkts)   In the Roman Catholic rite, one
    of the prayers offered by the Priest at Mass (after the
    Gloria): so called because it represents all the prayers
    of all present.
COLOR, ORIS   cl   ('kα-lor, or₂s)   1. Color, dye, beauty.
    2. In thirteenth century theory the term indicates a
    compositional device and performance, such as the
    repetition of a melodic phrase and its imitation.
COMMUNALE   cl   (kɔ:m-mu:-'nα:-lɛ)Community, state.
COMMUNION   el   (kɔ:m-'mu:-ni-ɔ:n)   The last of the five items
    of the Proper of the Mass in the Roman Catholic rite: sung
    after (originally during) the distribution of the Host.
COMPLINE   en.   ('kɔ:m-plʔn or plaj̨n)   Eighth canonical hour.
COMPOSITA   sp.   (kom-po-'si-tα:)   Composition.
CONCENTUS   cl   (kɔ:n-'kɛn-tʌs or tu:s)   Singing together,
    harmony; melody; concord.
_____   el   (kɔ:n-'tʃɛn-tu:s)   1. Singing together, harmony;
    melody, concord. 2. In music, the sung chants of the
    liturgy which have a distinctive melodic contour.
CONDUCTUS   cl   (kɔ:n-'dʌk-tʌs)   1. To bring or lead together.
    2. In music, a generic term for Latin strophic songs of
    the twelfth and thirteenth centuries. The term also
    refers to an "escorting" or "processional" song.
CONJUNCTURA   cl   (kɔ:n-'jʌn-ktʌ-rα)   1. United, connected
    with. 2. In music, a ligature of square notation

consisting of a <u>longa</u> followed by two or more rhombs:
always forms a descending scale passage.
CONTRA   cl   ('kɔːn-trɑ:)   Opposite, facing, contrary to.
COPULA   cl   ('ko-pʌ-lʌ)   1. Link, join.   2. In music, the
    short connecting passages that appear at the end of an
    <u>organa</u> section: often written in smaller note values.
CORNEMUSE   fr.   (kɔrnʌ-'myːz)   Bagpipe.
CORNETTE   fr.   (kɔr-'nɛt)   A wooden instrument with finger
    holes and a cup mouthpiece.
CREDO   el   ('krɛ-dɔ:)   A creed as the Apostles or the Nicene
    Creed. In Latin, I believe: the opening word of the
    creed; the third item of the Ordinary of the Mass.
_____   me   ('kri-do)   Same as above.
CRUX   cl   (krʌks)   Cross.
_____   el   (kruːks)   Cross.
CUM   cl   (kʌm)   With, together.
CUSTOS   cl   ('kʌs-tɔːs)   1. Guardian, goaler.   2. In music, a
    mark at the end of a staff or page to warn the player of
    the first note of the following staff or page.
CYMBALUM   cl   (kim-'bɑ-lʌm)   Cymbal, bell.

                              D

DACTYLUS, I   cl   ('dɑk-tʒ-lʌs or i)   Metrical foot consisting
    of one long and two short syllables.
DASEIA   en.   ('de-ʃiɑ)   A notation used in the ninth and tenth
    centuries in which the tones of the scale are represented
    by signs derived from the aspirate sign in ancient Greek.
    The signs indicate the tetrachord D-E-F-G. In order to
    indicate other tetrachords the signs are turned upside
    down and reversed.
DEMONSTRATIO, ONIS   cl   (de-mɔːn-'ɑtrɑ:-tʒ-ɔ:, onʒs)
    Indication.
DEO   el   ('dɛ-ɔ:)   God.
DIASTEMATIC   en.   (dɑi-ð-ɑtɛ-'ma-tʒk)   A type of early
    notation (eleventh century); "heighted" neumes; written
    on a staff that is either imagined or has one or two
    lines (finally four lines).
DIAPHONIA   en.   (dɑi-ð-'fo-niɑ)   1. Music.   2. In Latin, the
    parallel movement of voices at definite intervals from
    one another.   3. In Greek, dissonance: as opposed to
    symphony.   4. In the ninth to the twelfth centuries the
    term indicated two-part polyphony.
DISCANT   me   ('dʒs-kant)   In the twelfth to fifteenth century
    the term meant a counterpoint against the plainsong
    either composed or improvised.
DISCANTUS   l   (dʒs-'kɑn-tʌs)   1. <u>Dis</u>, against and <u>cantus</u>,
    melody.   2. In composition, the second or counter voice.
DIVISIO, ONIS   cl   (di-'vi-sʒ-ɔ:, onʒs)   Division.
DOMINO   el   ('dɔ:-mi-nɔ:)   From the Latin <u>dominus</u> meaning
    master of the house; owner; the Lord.
DORIAN   en.   ('do-ri-ðn)   The first of the church modes with a
    range of D-d with D as the final and with a tenor on the
    note a.
DUPLEX   cl   ('du:-plɛx)   Double.

DUPLUS, A, UM cl ('du:-plʌs, ɑ, ʌm) 1. Double, twice as
    much. 2. In music, it refers to the voice immediately
    above the tenor (twelfth century).
DURUS, A, UM cl ('du:-rʌs, a, ʌm) 1. Hard, rough, harsh,
    stern. 2. In music, the hexachord <u>durum</u> G-A-B-C-D-E.

                                E

ECCLESIASTICA el (ɛ-klɛ-si-'ɑs-ti-kɑ) Pertaining to the
    church.
ELEISON el (ɛ-'lɛ-i-sɔ:n) Have mercy.
EPISEMA el (ɛ-'pi-sɛ-mɑ) Found in ninth and tenth century
    manuscripts written in <u>cheironomic</u> neumes; a subsidiary
    sign in the form of a dash attached to a neume; indicates
    a prolonged note value
EPISTLE oe (i-'pɹs-tl) A selection, usually from an
    apostolic epistle, read in the communion service of the
    Greek, Roman, and Anglican churches.
ESTAMPIE fr. (ɛs-tã-'pi) 1. Stamp, punch. 2. Earliest
    example of a dance form which approached an instrumental
    piece; similar to the vocal sequence form.
EUCHARIST me ('ɛu:-kɑ-rist) A Christian sacrament in which
    bread and wine are consecrated, distributed and consumed
    in commemoration of the Passion and Death.
EXCELLENCE fr. (ɛksɛ-'lã:s) Excellence.
EXCELSIS cl (ɛks-'kɛl-sɹs) Distinguished.
_____ el (ɛk-'ʃɛl-sis) (On) High.
EXPECTARE cl (ɛks-pɛk-'tɑ:-rɛ) To look out for, wait for,
    hope for. In music, to retard.

                                F

FECUNDUS, A cl (fe-'kʌn-dʌs, ɑ) Abundant.
FICTUS, A, UM cl ('fɹk-tʌs, ɑ, ʌm) Imagined.
FIDELIS cl (fi-'de-lɹs) Faithful, loyal, sure.
_____ el (fi-'dɛ-lis) Faithful, loyal, sure.
FIEDEL ger. ('fi:-dəl) Fiddle.
FIRMO cl ('fɹr-mɔ:) To make firm or steady, to strengthen,
    to harden.
FIRMUS cl ('fɹr-mʌs) Strong, stable, constant, true.
FLEXUS cl ('flɛk-sʌs or u:s) Bend, turning.
FORME-FIXE fr. (fɔrm-'fiks) fixed form.

                                G

GALLICAN fr. (gɑl-i-'kã) Of or pertaining to Gaul.
GAMUT en. ('gam-ət) 1. The diatonic scale of musical notes.
    2. In medieval music, the first note of the musical
    scale.
GEISSLER ger. ('gaɪs-lɚ) A flagellate.
GEISSLERLIEDER ger. ('gaɪs-lɚ-li:-dɚ) Songs, airs, tunes of
    the Geissler.
GLORIA el ('glɔ:-ri-ɑ) 1. Hymn or ascription of praise to

God; a doxology. 2. A movement of the Mass following the
   Kyrie.
GOLIARD en. ('go-l?-ard) One of the class of wandering
   students; Jesters of the twelfth and thirteenth centuries
who wrote and sang Latin satirical verse.
GRADUAL en. ('gra-djual) 1. Proceeding by steps or
   degrees. 2. An antiphon that is sung at the Eucharist
   after the Epistle. 3. A liturgical book containing the
   musical items of the Mass.
GRADUALE el (gra-du:-'a-lɛ) A liturgical book containing
   the musical items of the Mass.
GRADUS cl ('gra-dʌs, u:s) Step, station, stair.
GRAVIS, E cl ('gra-vʒs, ɛ) 1. Heavy, weighty, burdensome,
   solemn, serious. 2. In music, a neume (\) indicating the
   lowering of the pitch.
GYMEL en. (gai-məl) A late medieval term for two part
   polyphony that is based on thirds, sixths, and tenths. A
   style of music used in England in the thirteenth century.

                              H

HETEROPHONY en. (hɛ-tɚ-'a-fɔ:-ni) A term used by Plato that
   has been adopted by modern musicologists to describe the
   simultaneous use of modified versions of the same melody
   by two or more performers.
HOCKET en. ('hɔ:-kɛt) See Hoquetus.
HOQUETUS el (hɔ:-'ku:-ɛ-tu:s) A peculiar device used in
   medieval polyphony of the thirteenth and fourteenth
   centuries. Consists of the rapid alternation of two
   (rarely three) voices with single notes, or short groups
   of notes, one part having a rest while the other sounds.
HYDRAULIS en. (hai-'drɔ:-lʒs) An organ invented by
   Ktesibios ca, 250 B.C. Water was used to stabilize the
   air pressure going to the pipes.

                              I

IAMBIC en. (ai-'am-bʒk) In the rhythmic modes, a pattern of
   one short note and one long note.
ICTUS cl ('ʒk-tʌs or tu:s) 1. Blow, stroke, shot; stress.
   2. In music, a resting place.
IMPERFECTUS, A, UM cl (ʒm-pɛr-'fɛk-tʌs, a, ʌm) Incomplete.
INCIPIT l. (ʒn-'sʒ-pʒt) 1. Here begins. 2. The first words
   of a liturgical text intoned by the cantor. 3. A term
   often found at the beginning of medieval manuscripts as
   reference to the chant from which the tenor is taken.
INTROIT en. ('ʒn-trɔit) An antiphon said or chanted at the
   beginning of the Eucharist.
INTROITUS cl (ʒn-'trɔ:-ʒ-tʌs or tu:s) Entrance.
_____ el (in-'trɔ:-i-tu:s) The initial chant of the
   Proper of the Mass.
INVITATORY me (ʒn-'vai-tətori) 1. A form of invitation.
   2. In the Roman Catholic rite, the opening chant of
   Matins.

ISORHYTHM en. ('aɪ-so-rɪ̣-ẟ̆ʌm) A term used to denote a
    structural principle frequently used in fourteenth
    century motets, particularly in the tenor. The
    cantus-firmus is presented in a reiterated scheme of time
    values known as talea.

J

JONGLEUR fr. (ʒɔ̃-'glœːr) Juggler, cheat, charlatan;
    acrobats and musicians.
JUBILUS el ('juː-bi-luːs) In Gregorian chant, the melisma
    sung to the final vowel of the first word, Alleluia,
    which invariably stands at the beginning of this chant.

K

KITHARA en. ('kɪ̣-θɑ-rɔ̀) Foremost instrument of ancient
    Greece; consisted of a square wooden soundbox and two
    curved arms connected by a cross-bar and a number of
    strings varying from five (eighth century B.C.) to seven
    (seventh century B.C.) to eleven or more (fifth century
    A.D.). Plucked with a plectrum.
KYRIE el ('ki-ri-ɛ) In the Roman Catholic Church, an
    ancient petition for mercy used in Eucharistic rites and
    other Offices; a part of a short litany said or chanted
    immediately after the Introit of the Mass.

L

LAI fr. (lɛ) A type of trouvère song closely related to the
    sequence. The texts are usually poems about the Virgin
    Mary or a lady. They consist of four to eight syllable
    lines divided into irregular stanzas. There is great
    variety in the meter and rhyme.
_____ en. (le) Same as above.
LAISSE fr. (lɛs) Twenty or fifty lines of a poem, such as
    the chanson de geste, with one continuous thought; a
    section of a poem.
LANGUE D'OC fr. (lɑ̃ːg d'ɔk) Old Provencal.
LANGUE D'OIL fr. (lɑ̃ːg œːj) Vernacular dialect used by the
    trouveres.
LARGUS, A, UM cl ('lɑr-gʌs, ɑ, ʌm) 1. Abundant, lavish,
    large. 2. In mensural notation the term larga is
    sometimes used for the maxima.
LAUDE of (lɑʌd) Hymns of praise and devotion written in the
    Italian language: popular in the thirteenth and
    fourteenth centuries. A monophonic song with several
    stanzas alternating with a refrain.
LAUDS me (lɑʌds) A religious service consisting of psalms,
    hymns, and canticles: immediately follows Matins; the
    second canonical hour.
LIBER cl ('lɪ̣-bɛr) Book, tree-bark.
_____ el ('li-bɛr) A book.

LIED   ger.   (lit)   A German song in the vernacular.
LIEDER   ger.   ('li-dɚ)   Songs, airs, tunes.
LIGATURE   me   ('lɪg-ə-tjr)   Notational signs of the thirteenth
     to the sixteenth centuries; a combination of two or more
     notes in a single symbol.
LINGUA   cl   ('lɪn-gʌ-ɑ)   Tongue.
_____   el   ('lin-gu:-ɑ)   Tongue.
LITURGY   en.   (lɪ-tʒ-'dʒi)   Any of the prescribed forms for
     public worship.
LONGUS, A   cl   ('lɔ:n-gʌs, ɑ)   1. Long, tall, vast, distant,
     tedious.   2. In music, one of the signs in musical
     notation established ca. 1260 by Franco of Cologne (◼).
LOZENGE   me   (lo'zinʒ)   A rhombus: all sides are equal, having
     two acute and two obtuse angles.
LYRE   me   (laɪr)   An ancient harp-like stringed instrument:
     had a hallow body and two horns bearing a cross-piece.
     Strings (usually seven) were stretched between the
     cross-piece and the body.   It was played with a plectrum.

M

MAGNIFICAT   el   (mɑ-'ɲi-fi-kɑt)   A canticle which is sung at
     the Office of Vespers.   "My soul doth magnify the Lord."
     Luke 1:46-55.
MAGNUS, A, UM   cl   ('mɑg-nʌs, ɑ, ʌm)   Large, great.
MAIOR   cl   ('mɑ-jɔ:r)   Larger, greater.
MARIAN   el   ('mɑ-ri-ɑn)   A name given to four antiphons about
     the Virgin Mary of the eleventh and twelfth centuries:
     known as Baetae Mariae Virginis.
MATINS   en.   ('mɑ-tins)   The first of the canonical hours,
     usually said at midnight.
MAXIMUS, A, UM   cl   ('mɑk-sɪ-mʌs, ɑ, ʌm)   1. Very large or
     great.   2. In music, one of the notes of mensural music
     (◼).
MEAN   me   (min)   That which is in the middle.
MEDIOCRITER   cl   (mɛ-dɪ-'ɔ:k-rɪ-tɛr)   Moderately, tolerably.
MEDIUS, A, UM   cl   ('mɛ-dɪ-ʌs, ɑ, ʌm)   Middle, neutral.
MELISMA   en.   ('mɛ-lɪs-mɑ)   An expressive vocal passage sung
     to one syllable; usually refers to Gregorian chant.
MENSURA, AE   cl   ('mɛn-su:-rɑ, aɪ)   Measurement, quantity.
MESSE   fr.   (mɛs)   Mass.
MINIM   me   ('mɪ-nɪm)   A sub-division of the semibreve; the
     shortest note value in mensural notation in the early
     fourteenth century.
MINIMUM, A   cl   ('mɪ-nɪ-mʌm, ɑ)   Very small.
MINNELIEDER   ger.   ('mɪnə-li:-dɚ)   Songs of the Minnesingers:
     texts are narrative with many being songs in praise of
     the Virgin.   The forms are derived from the ballad and
     the lai.
MINOR, US   cl   ('mɪ-nɔ:r, ʌs)   Smaller.
MINUM   cl   ('mɪ-nʌm)   Lesser.
MISSALE   el   (mis-'sɑ-lɛ)   The book containing the service
     texts for   the celebration of Mass throughout the year.
MISSAL   me   ('mɪs-səl)   See Missale.
MODUS, I   cl   ('mɔ:-dʌs, i)   Measure, quantity, limit, rhythm,

restriction, end, method, way.

MOTET en. (mo-'tɛt) A type of early polyphonic music
    written during the Middle Ages and the Renaissance:
    originated during the thirteenth century and derived its
    name from the addition of words ("mots") to the duplum.
    The tenor is usually a melismatic passage from Gregorian
    chant and is identified by an incipit. Modal rhythm is
    used. By the fourteenth century the motet became
    isorhythmic.

MOTETUS el (mɔ:-'tɛ-tu:s) The voice above the tenor,
    previously known as duplum; called motetus when words
    were added (thirteenth century).

MOZARABIC en. (mo-'zɛer-ə-bʔk) The name of the chant used
    by the Christians under Moorish rule in Spain. It is also
    known as Visigothic chant because of the influence of the
    Visigoths on the development of the chant.

MUNDANUS, A 1. (mʌn-'dɑ:-nʌs , ɑ) Earthly.

N

NATURA, AE cl (nɑ:-'tu:-rɑ, ɐi) Nature.

NATURALIS, E cl (nɑ:-tu:-'rɑ:-lʔs, ɛ) 1. By birth, natural.
    2. In music, the hexachord naturale C-D-E-F-G-a.

NEUME en. (njum) Notational sign of the eighth to the
    fourteenth centuries which was used to write down
    plainsong.

NOBLESSE fr. (nɔ-'blɛs) Nobility; noblesse obligé (nɔ-'blɛs
    ɔb-li-'ʒe) chivalry.

NONES me (no:nz) The canonical Office: originally recited
    at three in the afternoon; the ninth hour by ancient
    Roman reckoning.

NOVA cl ('nɔ:-wɑ) New, recent, fresh.

O

OBLIGÉ fr. (ɔbli-'ʒe) Obliged, compelled. See also
    noblesse.

OCTONARIA cl (ɔ:k-tɔ:-'nɑ:-rʔ-ɑ) Of eight.

OMNIA, IUM cl (ɔ:m-nʔ- ɑ, ʔʌm) All things.
_____ el ('ɔ:m-ni-u:m) All things.

OPPOSITA cl (ɔ:p-pɔ:-'sʔ-tɑ) Opposite.

ORDO, INES en. ('or-do, inz) 1. To arrange. 2. In music,
    the number of times a pattern is repeated before a rest.

ORDO, INIS cl ('ɔ:r-dɔ:, ʔnʔs) Row, rank. See also ORDO,
    ORDINES.

ORGANISTRUM cl (or-'gɑ-nʔs-trʌm) Medieval term for "hurdy-
    gurdy.

ORGANUM, I cl ('or-gɑ-nʌm, i) 1. Instrument, musical
    instrument. 2. A term for early medieval polyphony
    (ninth through the twelfth century): consists of a
    liturgical tenor and one or more contrapuntal parts.

OSTINATO it. (os-ti-'nɑ:-to) 1. Stubborn. 2. In music, a
    clearly defined phrase that is repeated over and over in
    immediate succession throughout a composition or section

of a composition.

OUVERT   fr.   (u-'vɛ:r)   1. Open. 2. A Medieval term used in
   vocal and dance pieces to indicate an intermediate cadence
   at the end of a repeated section when it is performed the
   first time.

P

PARLANDO   it.   (pɑ:r-'lɑ:n-do)   In music, an indication that
   the voice must approximate speech.
PASCHALE   of   (pas-'kal)   Pertaining to the Jewish Passover or
   to Easter.
PATRI   el   ('pɑ-tri)   Father.
PAX   cl   (pɑks)   Peace, grace, favor, tranquility.
_____   el   (pɑks)   Peace.
PEDES   cl   ('pɛ-dɛs)   See PES.
PEREGRINUS   cl   (pɛ-rɛ-'gri-nʌs)   Outlandish, strange,
   foreign, exotic.
_____   el   (pɛ-rɛ-'gri-nu:s)   Wandering.   See also tonus.
PERFECTUS, A, UM   cl   (pɛr-'fɛk-tʌs, ɑ, ʌm)   Complete,
   perfect.
PES, PEDIS   cl   (pes, 'pɛd-ʔs)   Foot
_____   en.   (piz)   1. In music, the name the English
   use for the tenor of polyphonic music of the thirteenth
   and fourteenth centuries. 2. A neume: also called
   podatus
PLANUS   cl   ('plɑ:-nʌs)   Flat, level, clear; see also
   cantus.
PLICA   en.   (plʔ-kɑ)   A notational sign (thirteenth century)
   calling for an ornamental note to be inserted following
   the note to which it is connected. The sign for the
   plica is an upward or downward dash. It may be attached
   to single notes as well as to the final note of a
   ligature.   The direction of the dash indicates the pitch
   of the added note.
PORRECTUS, A, UM   cl   (pɔ:r'rɛk-tʌs, ɑ, ʌm)   Extended.
POSITIF, VE   fr.   (posi-'tif, ti:v)   A medium sized medieval
   church organ which could be moved by two or four men:
   had one manual and two rows of flue pipes. Also a very
   small domestic instrument that was set on a table and
   played by both hands, the bellows being worked by an
   assistant.
PRAECONIUM   cl   (praj-'ko-nʔ-ʌm)   Office of herald,
   proclamation.
_____   el   (prɛ'kɔ:-ni-u:m)   Herald, proclamation.
PREFACE   me   ('prɛ-fɛs)   In the Roman Catholic Mass, a solemn
   declaration of Praise beginning with the words "Vere
   dignum et justum est."   The Sanctus follows.
PRIME   en.   (prajm)   The third of the canonical hours.
PRINCIPALIS   cl   (prʔn-kʔ-'pɑ:-lʔs)   Original, primitive,
   principal.
PRO   cl   (pro)   For.
PROLATIO, ONIS   cl   (pro-'lɑ:-tʔ-o, onʔs)   1. Postponement,
   mentioning. 2. In music, the term is used in mensural
   notation and refers to the relationship between the

semibrevis and the minima.

PROLATION   me   (pro'le-ʃɑn)   In the early fourteenth century
the term referred to all mensurations or to the four
combinations of tempus and prolatio, i.e., tempus
imperfect and prolatio imperfect; tempus perfect and
prolatio imperfect; tempus imperfect and prolatio perfect;
and tempus perfect and prolatio perfect.

PROPRIETATE   cl   (pro-prʔ-ɛ-'tɑ:tɛ)   1. Peculiarity.   2. In
music the term refers to the modifications of the initial
notes of a ligature.

PROLOGUS   cl   (prɔ:-'lɔ:-gʌs)   Prologue.

PUNCTUM, I   cl   ('pʌn-ktʌm, i)   1. A small spot.   2. In music,
a neume; also the brevis of square notation.

PUNCTUS, A   cl   ('pʌn-ktʌs, ɑ)   1. Point.   2. In music, a
sign like the dot of modern notation and having the same
meaning, but also having the function similar to the
modern bar line.

PURUS, A UM   cl   ('pu:-rʌs, ɑ, ʌm)   Pure, clean, plain.

Q

QUADRUPLUM, I   cl   ('kwɑ-drʌ-plʌm, i)   1. Fourfold amount.
2. In music of the thirteenth century, the third voice
above the tenor.

QUATERNARIA   cl   (kwɑ-tɛr-'nɑ-ri-ɑ)   four each.

QUARTUS, A, UM   cl   ('kwɑr-tʌs, ɑ, ʌm)   A fourth.

QUILISMA   el   (ku:-i-lis-mɑ)   An ornamental neume (ɰ):
indicated a rolling and rotating of the voice;

R

RECTA   cl   ('rɛk-tɑ:)   Right on; directly, correct.

RESUPINUS, A, UM   cl   (rɛ-sʌ-'pi-nʌs, ɑ, ʌm)   1. Lying on
one's back.   2. In music, part of the name of a neume
(torculus resupinus).

RONDEAU, EAUX   fr.   (rɔ͡-'do)   A short poem consisting of ten,
or in stricter sense of thirteen, lines, having only two
rhymes throughout, and with the opening lines used twice
as a refrain.

RONDELLUS, I   1.   ('rɔ:n-dɛl-lʌs)   Medieval name used for
music in triple or duple voice exchange.

ROTA   cl   ('rɔ:-tɑ)   1. Wheel.   2. In music, a medieval name
for a round.

ROTROUENGE   fr.   (rɔ:-tru:-'ɑ͡ʒ)   Strophic laisse with refrain.

S

SAECULORUM   el   (sɛ-ku:-'lɔ:-ru:m)   Ages, world without end.

SAINT   fr.   (sɛ͂)   Holy, consecrated.

SALVE   cl   ('sɑl-we)   In good health, in good condition.
_____   el   ('sɑl-vɛ)   A salutation.

SANCTUS   cl   ('sɑn-ktʌs)   Sacred, inviable; venerable; holy.
_____   el   ('sɑn-ktu:s)   Holy.

SEMI cl (′sɛ-mⱬ) Half.
SEXT me (sekst) Fifth canonical hour.
SIGNUM, I cl (′sⱬg-nʌm, ⱬ) Mark.
SIMPLEX cl (′sⱬm-plɛks) Simple, unmixed.
SINE cl (′sⱬ-nɛ) Without.
STIMMTAUSCH ger. (′stⱬm-tɔːʃ) Voice exchange.
SUB cl (sʌb) Under, beneath, near, during, towards, just
   after.
SUBTILISSIMA cl (sʌb-ti-′lⱬs-sⱬ-mɑ) Subtle.
SUMMA cl (′sʌm-mɑ) Main thing, chief point.
SUPERIOR, IUS cl (sʌ′pɛr-ⱬ-ɔːr, ⱬʌs) Higher, previous,
   former, superior.
SURSUM cl (′sʌr-sʌm) Upwards, on high.
SYMPHONIA cl (sim-′fo-nⱬ-ɑ) Harmony, symphony.
SYNAXIS en. (sⱬ-′nɑk-sⱬs) A congregation assembled for
   public worship, especially for celebrating the Lord's
   Supper.

                                T

TALEA cl (′tɑː-lɛ-ɑ) Stake, rod; graft; heavy, block.
TEMPORA cl (′tɛm-pɔː-rɑ) Times.
TEMPUS, ORIS cl (′tɛm-pʌs, ɔːrʌs) 1. Time, opportunity. 2.
   In music of the thirteenth century, the unit of musical
   time.
TENERE cl (tɛ-′nɛ-rɛ) 1. To keep. 2. In music, to hold.
TERCE en. (tɛrs) Fourth canonical hour of the Office.
TERNARIA cl (tɛr-′nɑː-rⱬ-ɑ) Of three.
TERRA, AE cl (′tɛr-rɑ, ai̯) Earth, land, ground, region
_____ el (′tɛr-rɑ) Earth.
TONUS cl (′tɔː-nʌs) 1. Sound, tone. 2. Tonus peregrinus
_____ el (′tɔː-nuːs pɛ-rɛ-′gri-nuːs) An exceptional
   psalm tone that has a different tenor for each of its two
   halves.
TRACT me (trɑkt) In Gregorian chant, an item of the Proper
   of the Mass used instead of the Alleluia for various
   Feasts during Lent, for Ember days and for the Requiem
   Mass.
TRACTUS cl (′trɑk-tʌs) Flowing, fluent, extension.
TRAHERE cl (′trɑ-hɛ-rɛ) To drag.
TRIPLEX cl (′tri-plɛx) Triple.
TRIPLUM cl (′trⱬ-plʌm) 1. Threefold, triple. 2. In music
   of the thirteenth century, the second voice above the
   tenor.
TROPE en. (trop) Accretion to the liturgy; a musical and
   textual addition to the established repertory of the
   Mass: flourished from the tenth through the twelfth
   centuries.
TROUVÈRE fr. (truː-′vɛːr) Designation for the twelfth and
   thirteenth century poet-musician active in the north of
   France.
TUBA cl (′tʌ-bɑ) Trumpet.
_____ el (′tuː-bɑ) In Gregorian psalm tones, the main
   note of the recitation: always the fifth degree of the
   mode.

V

VENI   cl   (′we-nʔ)   To come, to go; to arrive.
_____   el   (′vɛ-ni)   To come, to go; to arrive.
VERS   fr.   (vɛːr)   Poetry, line, verse.
_____   ger.   (fɛrs)   Verse.
VESPERS   me   (′vɛ-spɛrs)   The seventh canonical hour of the
    Office.
VIA   cl   (′wʒ-ɑ)   Way, manner, method, mode, right method.
VIELLE   fr.   (vi-′jɛl)   Hurdy-gurdy, a mechanically bowed
    instrument: also called organistrum; first mentioned by
    Odo de Clugny in the tenth century.   It had a
    fiddle-shaped body and three strings which were set in
    vibration by a hand-cranked wooden wheel.
VIRELAI   fr.   (viːr-′le)   A song or short lyric piece that
    consists of short lines arranged in stanzas with only
    two rhymes, the end rhyme of one stanza being the chief
    one of the next.
VIRGA, AE   cl   (′wʒr-gɑ, aị)   Twig, rod.
_____   el   (′vir-gɑ)   A neume (//): used during the ninth
    and tenth centuries.
VIRTUS   cl   (′wʒr-tʌs)   Manliness, manhood, virtue.
VOX   cl   (wɔːks)   Voice, sound, call, cry, tone.
_____   el   (vɔːks)   Voice.

Titles with Translation

A

AD ORGANUM FACIENDUM   cl   (ad ′or-gɑ-nʌm fɑ-ki-′ɛn-dʌm)
    Concerning the composition of organum.   Anonymous.
AETERNE RERUM CONDITOR   el   (ɛ-′tɛr-nɛ ′re-ruːm ′kɔːn-di-tɔːr)
    Eternal Founder of all things; an Ambrosian hymn.
ALMA REDEMPTORIS MATER   el   (′ɑl-mɑ rɛ-′dɛm-ptɔː-ris ′mɑ-tɛr)
    Kind redeeming Mother; a Marian Antiphon.
ANGELUS AD VIRGINEM   el   (′an-dʒɛ-luːs ad ′vir-dʒi-nɛm)   Angel
    to the Virgin; an English hymn.
ANTIPHONALE MISSARUM   el   (an-ti-fɔː-′nɑ-lɛ mis-′sɑ-ruːm)   A
    book for the Mass: contains the texts (later, texts and
    music) of the musical items of the Mass; a book of
    Ambrosian chant published by Dom Gregory Suñol (1935).
ANTIPHONALE MONASTICUM   el   (an-ti-fɔː-′nɑ-lɛ mɔː-′nɑs-ti-
    kuːm)   Monastic Antiphonale; a book containing the Office
    chants and their music; a book of Gregorian chant
    compiled by the monks at Solesmes (1934).
ANTIPHONALE SARISBURIENSE   el   (an-ti-fɔː-′nɑ-le sɑ-ris-
    buː-ri-′ɛn-sɛ)   Sarum Antiphonary; a plainsong manuscript
    dating from the thirteenth century containing the
    plainsong that was used at the Cathedral of Salisbury:
    known as the Sarum Use.
ANTIPHONARIUM CENTO   el   (an-ti-fɔː-′nɑ-ri-uːm ′tʃɛn-tɔː)
    Parts of the Antiphonale; a collection of Gregorian chant
    codified by St. Gregory the Great.

ANTIPHONARIUM DIURNUM   el   (ɑn-ti-fɔ:-'nɑ-ri-u:m di-'u:r-nu:m)
    Daily <u>Antiphonale</u>: compiled by the monks at Solesmes
    (1912, 1919).
ANTIPHONARIUM AMBROSIANUM   el   (ɑn-ti-fɔ:-'nɑ-ri-u:m
    am-brɔ:-si-'ɑ-nu:m)   Ambrosian <u>Antiphonale</u>.
ARS CANTUS MENSURABILIS   cl   (ars 'kɑn-tʌs or tu:s mɛn-sʌ-
    'rɑ:-bʔ-lʔs)   Art of Measured Song; a treatise written by
    Franco of Cologne.
ARS NOVA   cl   (ars 'nɔ:-wɑ)   New Art; 1. A treatise written by
    Philippe de Vitri (1322-1333).   2. Name given to a period
    of musical history (ca. 1300-1425).
AVE REGINA COELORUM   el   ('ɑ-vɛ rɛ-'dʒi-nɑ tʃɛ-'lɔ:-ru:m)
    Hail Heavenly Queen; a Marian Antiphon.

                                B

BALLADES NOTÉES   fr.   (ba-'lad nɔ-'te)   Poems with notes.
BREVIARIUM   el   (brɛ-vi-'ɑ-ri-u:m)   A breviary; a book
    containing all of the texts for the Office.
BREVIARIUM REGULARE MUSICAE   cl   (brɛ-wʔ-'ɑ-rʔ-ʌm rɛ-gʌ-'lɑ-rɛ
    'mu:-sʔ-kąi)   A Summary of the Rules of Music; a treatise
    written by Willelmus (ca. 1372).

                                C

CANTI AMBROSIANA PER IL POPOLO   it.   ('kɑ:n-ti ɑ:m-bru-zi
    'ɑ:-nɑ: pɛr il 'po-po-lo)   Ambrosian songs for the
    people: edited by Dom Gregory Suñol.
CARMINA BURANA   en.   (kar-'mi-nə bʒ⁻-'ɑ-nə)   Songs; poems;
    a thirteenth century collection of verses in medieval
    Latin, German and French; verses written by the
    Goliards.
CHANSON AVEC DÈS REFRAINS   fr.   (ʃã-'sõ a-'vɛk dɛ rə-'frɛ̃)
    Songs with refrains.
CHANSON BALLADÉE   fr.   (ʃã-'sõ ba-la-'de)   A French song; name
    used chiefly by Machaut for the <u>Virelai</u>
CHANSONNIER CANGÉ (LE)   fr.   (ʃã-'sõje kã-'ʒe)   Song-book;
    thirteenth century manuscript containing the songs of the
    troubadors and the <u>trouvères</u>.
CHANSONNIER DE L'ARSENAL   fr.   (ʃã-'sõje də larsə-'nal)
    Song-book; thirteenth century manuscript containing the
    songs of the troubadors and the <u>trouvères</u>.
CODEX CALIXTINUS   cl   ('ko-dɛks kɑ-'lik-stʔ-nʌs)   A manuscript
    volume; twelfth century codex containing two-voice <u>organa</u>
    (also <u>conductus</u>) of the School of Compostela.
CODEX SACRAMENTORUM BERGOMENSIS   el   ('kɔ:-dɛks sɑ-krɛ-mɛn-
    'tɔ:-ru:m bɛr-gɔ:-'mɛn-sis)   Manuscript in leaf form of
    sacramental music at Bergamo.
COMPENDIUM   cl   (kɔ:m-'pɛn-dʔ-ʌm)   An abridgement of a larger
    work or treatise; a concise version of <u>Musica theorica</u> and
    <u>Musica practica</u> by Johannes de Muris (ca. 1322).
CONSOLATIONE PHILOSOPHIAE   cl   (kɔ:n-so-lɑ-tʔ-'o-nɛ fʔ-lɔ:-
    sɔ:-'fʔ-ąi)   Comforting Philosophy; a book on philosophy
    written by Boethius.

D

DECLARATIO TRIANGULI ET SCUTI   cl   (de-klɑ-'rɑ-tʒ-ɔ: trʒ-
   'ɑn-gʌ-li ɛt 'sku:-ti)   Statement in Triangles and Oblong
   Shields; a treatise written by Johannes Torkesey (late
   fourteenth century).
DE HARMONICA INSTITUTIONE   cl   (de hɑr-'mɔ:-nʒ-kɑ ʒn-stʒ-tu:-
   tʒ-'o-nɛ)   About Harmonic Instruction; a treatise written
   by Hucbald.
DE INSTITUTIONE MUSICA   cl   (de ʒn-stʒ-tu:-tʒ-'o-nɛ
   'mu:-sʒ-kɑ)   About Instruction in Music; a treatise
   written by A. M. T. S. Boethius.
DE MUSICA   cl   (de 'mu:-sʒ-kɑ)   About Music; a treatise
   written by Johannes (also known as Johannes of Afflighem
   or John Cotton) ca. 1100.
DE MUSICA MENSURABILI POSITIO   cl   (de 'mu:-sʒ-kɑ mɛn-su:-'rɑ-
   bʒ-li)   About the Situation of Measured Music; a
   treatise written by Johannes de Garlandia.
DE SPECULATIONE MUSICAE   cl   (de spɛ-kʌ-lɑ:-tʒ-'o-nɛ
   'mu:-sʒ-kai̯)   About Speculation on Music; a treatise
   written by Walter Odington (ca. 1300).
DEUS CREATOR OMNIUM   el   ('dɛ-u:s krɛ-'ɑ-tɔ:r 'ɔ:m-ni-u:m)
   God, Creator of All Things; an Ambrosian hymn.
DIALOGUS DE MUSICA   cl   (dʒ-ɑ-'lɔ:-gʌs de 'mu:-sʒ-kɑ)
   Conversation about Music; a treatise written by Odo de
   Clugny.
DISCANTUS POSITIO VULGARIS   cl   (dʒs-'cɑn-tʌs pɔ:-'sʒ-tʒ-ɔ:
   vʌl-'gɑ-rʒs)   Common Situation of Discant; a treatise
   written by Johannes de Garlandia.

E

EPISTOLA...DE IGNOTO CANTU   cl   (ɛ-pʒs-'tɔ:-lɑ...de ʒg-'nɔ:-tɔ:
   'kɑn-tu:)   Letter...of unknown (hidden) song (music); a
   treatise written by Guido d'Arezzo (ca. 1030).

G

GLORIA PATRI   el   ('glɔ:-ri-ɑ 'pɑ-tri)   Glory to the Father;
   the first words of the doxology: follows the recitation
   of the psalms.
GRADUALE ROMANUM   el   (grɑ-du:-'ɑ-lɛ rɔ:-'mɑ-nu:m)   Roman
   Gradual; the liturgical book containing the musical items
   of the Mass: prepared by the monks at Solesmes in 1907.
GRADUALE SARISBURIENSE   el   (grɑ-du:-'ɑ-lɛ sɑ-ris-bu:-ri-
   'ɛn-sɛ)   Sarum Gradual; a plainsong manuscript dating
   from the thirteenth century containing the plainsong that
   was used at the Cathedral of Salisbury: known as the
   Sarum Use.

I

IAM SURGIT HORA TERTIA   el   (jɑm 'su:r-dʒit 'hɔ:-rɑ

'tɛr-tsi-ɑ)   Now Appears the Third Hour; an Ambrosian
    hymn.
IMPROPERIA   el   (im-prɔ:-'pɛ-ri-ɑ)   Reproaches; in the Roman
    Catholic liturgy, the chants for Good Friday Mass
    consisting of three passages from the Prophets.

L

LIBER HYMNORUM   el   ('li-bɛr him-'nɔ:-ru:m)   A book of hymns:
    contains the preface by Notker in which he discusses the
    adding of words to the jubilus of the Alleluia.
LIBER USUALIS   el   ('li-bɛr u:-su:-'ɑ-lis)   A book of the
    Roman Use; a book containing most of the material found
    in the four modern liturgical books: the missale, the
    breviarium, the graduale, and the antiphonale.
LIBER VESPERALIS   el   ('li-bɛr vɛs-per-'ɑ-lis)   A vesperal
    book: contains the psalms, canticles, and antiphons used
    at Vespers; a book of Ambrosian chant published by Dom
    Gregory Suñol (1935).

M

MA FIN EST MON COMMENCEMENT   fr.   (ma fɛ̃ ɛ mɔ̃ kɔ-mãs-'mã)   My
    End is My Beginning; a rondeau written by Guillaume de
    Machaut.
MAGNUS LIBER ORGANI   el   ('mɑ-ɲu:s 'li-bɛr 'ɔ:r-gɑ-ni)   Large
    Book of Organum: compiled by Leoninus.
MESSE DE NOSTRE DAME (LA)   fr.   (mɛs də nɔs-'trə dam)   Mass of
    Notre Dame; the name of a Mass written by Guillaume de
    Machaut.
MISSALE   el   (mis-'sɑ-lɛ)   A missal; a book containing all the
    Gregorian chant texts of the Mass.
MUSICA MENSURABILIS   cl   ('mu:-si-kɑ mɛn-sʌ-'rɑ:-bɹ-lɪs)
    Measured Music; a treatise written by Petrus Picardus.
MUSICA PRACTICA   el   ('mu:-sɹ-kɑ 'prɑk-ti-kɑ)   Practical
    Music; the second book of Notitia artis musicae written
    by Johannes de Muris (1321).
MUSICA THEORICA   el   ('mu:-si-kɑ tɛ-'ɔ:-ri-kɑ)   Theory of
    Music; the first book of Notitia artis musicae by
    Johannes de Muris (1321).

N

NOTITIA ARTIS MUSICAE   cl   (no-'tɹ-tɹ-ɑ 'ar-tɹs 'mu:-sɹkaj)
    Knowledge of the Art of Music; a treatise written by
    Johannes de Muris (1321).
NATIVITAS GLORIOSE VIRGINIS   el   (nɑ-'ti-vi-tɑs glɔ:-ri-'ɔ:-sɛ
    'vir-dʒi-nis)   Glorious Virgin Birth; an Alleluia verse.

O

OFFICIUM ET MISSA PRO DEFUNCTIS   el   ('ɔ:f-fi-ki-u:m ɛt

'mis-sɑ prɔ: dɛ-'fuːn-ktis) Office and Mass for the
Dead; a book of Ambrosian chant published by Dom Gregory
Suñol.
OFFICIUM MAJORIS HEBDOMADAE el (ɔːf-'fi-ki-uːm mɑ-'jɔː-ris
hɛb-'dɔː-mɑ-dɛ) Office for the ill; a Gregorian
chant-book published by the monks at Solesmes (1922).
O PETRE FLOS APOSTOLORUM el (ɔ: 'pɛ-trɛ flɔːs ɑ-pɔːs-tɔː-
'lɔː-ruːm) O Peter Prime Apostle.

P

PANGE LINGUA...CERTAMINIS el ('pɑn-dʒɛ 'lin-guː-ɑ...
tʃɛr-'tɑ-mi-nis) Sing, oh tongue; a Mozarabic
chant.
PERSPICE CHRISTICOLA el (pɛr-'spi-kɛ kris-ti-'kɔː-lɑ) All
seeing Christ; a verse from an Easter day sequence:
written in red ink below the secular words of "Sumer is
icumen in."
PRAECONIUM PASCHALE cl (prai-'ko-nʔ-ʌm) of (pas-'kal)
Proclamation or herald of Easter; one of the books
containing Gregorian chant as restored by Dom Gregory
Suñol.
PROLOGUS ANTIPHONARII SUI el (prɔː-'lɔː-guːs ɑn-ti-fɔː-'nɑ-
ri-i 'suː-i) Prologue to his Antiphonale; a treatise
written by Guido d'Arezzo (ca. 1025).

R

REGINA CAELI LACTARE el (rɛ-'dʒi-nɑ 'tʃɛ-li lɑk-'tɑ-rɛ)
Beautiful Heavenly Queen; a Marian Antiphon.
REGULAE CUM MAXIMIS MAGISTRI FRANCONIS cl ('re-gɑ-lai kʌm
'mɑ-ksʔ-mʔs 'mɑ-gʔs-trʔ frɑn-'ko-nʔs) Rules with maxims
of Master Franco; a treatise written by Robert de Handlo
(ca. 1326).

S

SALVE REGINA el ('sɑl-vɛ rɛ-'dʒi-nɑ) Welcome Queen; in the
Roman Catholic Church, an antiphon beginning with the
words Salve Regina: cited after the Divine Office from
Trinity Sunday to Advent; one of the so-called Marian
Antiphons.
SANCTORALE el (sɑn-ktɔː-'rɑ-lɛ) In the Roman rite, a
generic name for the feasts of Saints. It is subdivided
into the Proprium sanctorum ('prɔː-pri-uːm sɑn-'ktɔː-ruːm)
and Commune sanctorum ('kɔːm-muː-nɛ sɑn-'ktɔː-ruːm)
Proper of the Saints and Common of the Saints. The
latter is the feasts of the Apostles, Martyrs, and
Confessors.
SI DOLCE NON SONO it. (si 'dol-tʃɛ non 'so-no) Yes, sweet
they are not.
SPECULUM MUSICAE cl ('spɛ-kʌ-lʌm 'muː-sʔ-kai) Reflection on
Music; a treatise written by Jacques of Liège (ca. 1330).

T

TEMPORALE el (tɛm-pɔː-'ra-lɛ) Also known as <u>Proprium de tempore</u> el ('prɔː-pri-uːm dɛ tɛm-'pɔː rɛ) Proper of the Time, i.e., all Sundays and special occasions commemorating the life of Jesus.

TONALE el (tɔː-'na-lɛ) A tonary: similar to a "thematic catalog;" a medieval book containing the chants that are (or were) connected with a psalm verse sung to one of the various recitation tones; a book showing the mode of a chant.

TRACTATUS DE MUSICA cl (trak-'taː-tʌs or tuːs de 'muː-sʔ-ka) Treatise about Music: written by Jerome of Moravia.

V

VENI REDEMPTOR GENTIUM el ('vɛ-ni rɛ-'dɛm-ptɔːr 'dʒɛn'-ti-uːm) Come Redeemer of the Race; an Ambrosian hymn.

People and Places

A

ADAM DE LA HALLE fr. (ɛe-'dã: dɔ lɛe-'ɛel) Thirteenth century French dramatist, poet, and musician; a Trouvère.

AL-FARABI en. (al-fɛe-'raː-bi) (ca. 870-950) Islamic philosopher; commonly designated "The Second Teacher:" Aristotle is given priority. It was his endeavor to show that sound philosophy and true religion are variant, and not contradictory.

AMIENS fr. (a-'mjẽ) A city of northern France on the Somme river.

ANJOU fr. (ã-'ʒu) A former province of France.

AQUINAS, SAINT THOMAS en. (ɔ̃-'kwaḭ-nɔ̃s) (1225-1274) Roman Catholic theologian and philosopher; a Dominican monk; wrote <u>Summa theologiae</u>: a treatise in which he reconciled reason and religion. This work is still the basis of all Catholic theological teaching.

AQUITAINE fr. (aki-'tɛn) A region of Southern France.

ARISTOTLE en. (ɛer-ʔs-'tɑt-l) Greek philosopher; student of Plato; a botanist: used biological models as a prototype for explaining change (384-322 B.C.).

ARRAS fr. (a-'rɑːs) A city of northern France.

AVIGNON fr. (avi-'ɲɔ̃) A city in southeast France; papal seat from 1309 to 1377.

B

BARCELONA sp. (bɑːr-θe-'lo-nɑː) A port of northeast Spain; a province in Catalonia Spain.

BOETHIUS   cl   (bo-'ɛ-tɹ-ᐃs)   Roman philosopher and theologian
    of the post-classical period; compiled a treatise on
    mathematics; translated the logic of Aristotle into Latin.
BONIFACE   en.   ('bɑn-ᗡ-fes)   English missionary and
    Archbishop; a Benedictine monk; Abbot of Nursling; Bishop
    and Archbishop at Geismar; known as Apostle of Germany.
    (Saint).

C

CHAMPAGNE   fr.   (ʃᾶ-'paɲ)   A region and former province of
    northeast France.
CHANTILLY   fr.   (ʃᾶti-'ɟi)   A small town in France,
    twenty-five miles north of Paris.
CHARLEMAGNE   en.   ('ʃɑr-lᗡ-men)   First emperor of the
    Carolingian dynasty. (ca. 742-814).
CHARTRES   fr.   (ʃartr)   A city in north central France.
CHAUCER, GEOFFREY   en.   ('tʃɑʎ-sᗡ)   English poet; creator of
    English versification; translated <u>Consolatio</u> by Boethius;
    (ca. 1343-1400).
CICONIA, JOHANNES   en.   (tʃɹ-'ko-njɑ, jo-'hɑn-nɛs)   Late
    fourteenth century composer and theorist.
COLOGNE   en.   (kɑ-'lon)   A city in North Rhine-Westphalia,
    Germany.
CONSTANTINUS I   cl   (kɔ:n-'stɑn-tɹ-nᴧs)   Roman Emperor,
    surnamed "The Great" (306-337); involved in the Edict of
    Milan and the Council of Nicaea; built Constantinople and
    dedicated it as his capital.

D

DANTE   it.   ('dɑ:n-tɛ)   Italian poet; author of the Divine
    Comedy: a synthesis of medieval ideas and culture.
    (1265-1321).

F

FAENZA   it.   (fɑ:-'ɛn-dzɑ:)   1.   A town in northern Italy.   2.
    The name of an Italian musical manuscript, Faenza, Bibl.
    Communale, MS 117.   (ca. 1420).
FONDI   it.   ('fon-di)   A town in central Italy.

G

GASCOGNE   fr.   (gas-'kɔɲ)   A region and former province of
    southwest France.
GUÉRANGER, DOM   fr.   (ge-rᾶ-'ʒe, dɔm)   A monk at Solesmes.
GUIDO D'AREZZO   it.   ('gwi-do dɑ:-'rɛdz-dzo)   Famous reformer
    of musical notation and vocal instruction in the eleventh
    century.
GUILLAUME DE MACHAUT   fr.   (gi-'jo:m dᗡ mɑ'ʃo)   William of
    Machaut.   Fourteenth century composer and poet.

H

HUCBALD en. ('hʌk-bɑld) Flemish monk and musical theorist.
HUGHES D'ORLEANS fr. (yg dɔrle-'ã) A famous troubador from
   Orléans in southern France.

J

JACQUES DE LIÈGE en. (ʒɑːk də ljɛːʒ) Fourteenth century
   musical theorist.
JEAN DE MURIS fr. (ʒã də mjur-'i) Fourteenth century
   musical theorist, astronomer and mathematician.
JOHANNES AFFLIGEMENSIS cl (jo-'hɑn-nɛs ɑf-flʔ-gɛ-'mɛn-sis)
   Late twelfth to thirteenth century music theorist; also
   known as John Cotton.
JOHANNES DE GROCHEO cl (jo-'hɑn-nɛs de grɔ:-'ke-o)
   Important writer on secular music of the Middle
   Ages.
JUBAL en. ('dʒuː-bəl) A son of Cain, a musician or
   inventor of instruments. Gen. IV:21.

L

LANDINI, FRANCESCO it. (lɑːn-'di-ni, frɑːn-'tʃɛs-ko)
   Fourteenth century organist and composer.
LÉONIN fr. (le-ɔ-'nɛ́) Late twelfth century composer at
   Notre Dame, Paris; composer of organa.
LEONINUS cl (le-'ɔː-nʔ-nʌs) See Léonin.
LIÈGE fr. (ljiɛːʒ) A city in Eastern Belgium.
LIMOGES fr. (li-'mɔːʒ) A city in west central France.

M

MARCHETTO DA PADUA it. (mɑːr-'tʃɛt-tuːs dɑː pɑː-'duː-ɑː)
   Fourteenth century musical theorist.
MATTEO DA PERUGIA it. (mɑː-'tɛ-o dɑː pɛ-'ruː-dʒi-ɑː)
   Fifteenth century Italian composer.
METZ fr. (mɛs) Capital of the department of Moselle.
MODENA it. ('mo-dɛ-nɑː) A city in Italy.
MONTPELLIER fr. (mõpə-'lje) Capital of the department of
   Hérault.

N

NICAEA cl (ni'kai-ɑ) A city in Bithinia, a city in Locris,
   a city on the Hydaspes; a city in Asia Minor where the
   Council of Nicaea was held: the first ecumenical
   (world-wide) council of the Church.
NOTKER, BALBULUS cl ('nɔːt-ker, 'bɑl-bʔ-lʌs) A monk
   at the Monastery of St. Gall (ca. 840-912); one of the
   earliest and most important of the composers of
   sequences.

O

ORLÉANS fr. (ɔrle-'ã) Capital of the department of Loiret;
    former capital of the province of Orléanais.

P

PEPIN fr. (pɛ-'pɛ̃) Pepin the Short: Father of Charlemagne.
PEROTIN fr. (pɛrɔ-'tɛ̃) Celebrated composer of the twelfth
    century and of the Notre Dame School in Paris.
PEROTINUS cl (pɛ-'rɔ:-tʒ-nʌs) See Perotin.
PETRARCH, FRANCESCO DI PETRACCO it. ('pɛ-trɑ:rk, frɑ:n-
    'tʃɛs-ko di pɛ-trɑ:k-ko) Fourteenth century Italian poet
    and humanist.
PETRUS DE CRUCE en. ('pɛ-trʌs dò kru:s) Fourteenth century
    French composer; known for his use of more than three
    semibreves to a breve.
PHILIPPE DE VITRI fr. (fi-'lip dò vi-'tri) Fourteenth
    century theorist and composer.
PICARDUS, PETRUS cl (pʒ-'kɑr-dʌs, 'pɛ-trʌs) Theorist of the
    thirteenth century.
PLATO en. ('ple-to) Classical Greek philosopher: greatly
    influenced by Pythagoras; used mathematics as the
    prototype of reality.
PYTHAGORAS en. (pʒ-'θa-gò-ròs) Classical Greek philosopher.

R

RHEIMS fr. (rɛ̃:s) A city in France.

S

SANTIAGO DE COMPOSTELA sp. (sɑ:n-ti-'ɑ:-go de kɔ:m-po-
    'ste-lɑ:) A city of northwest Spain, in the province of
    Corunna.
SOLESMES fr. (sɔ-'lɛm) A Benedictine monastery established
    in 1830. In 1837 it became an abbey but was abandoned in
    1901.
SQUARCIALUPI, ANTONIO it. (skwɑ:r-tʃi-ɑ:-'lu:-pi)
    (1416-1480) An organist of Santa Maria in Florence. The
    first owner of the manuscript that bears his name.
SUÑOL, DOM GREGORY sp. ('su:-ɲol, dom 'gre-go-ri) Learned
    Spanish ecclesiastic (1979-1946): Contributed to the
    restoration of Ambrosian chant.

T

TOULOUSE fr. (tu-'lu:z) Capital of the department of Haute-
    Garonne; former capital of the province of Languedoc.
TROYES fr. (trwɑ) Capital of the department of Aube; former
    capital of Champagne.

Author and Composer Index

Subject Index

About the Author

Blanche Gangwere is a former church organist, choir director, and music teacher.